Rogue Herries

A magnificent history of a divided family which mirrors the heart and pulse of eighteenth-century England.

Here is fiction in glorious, sweeping measure, set against the wild and beautiful scenery of the Lake District, crowded with fairs, balls, weddings, duels, revels, witches, abductions, murder, strolling players and Jacobite agents.

Bestriding these events like a Colossus is proud, intolerant Francis Herries – the Dark Angel of Borrowdale – who despised his wife and sold his mistress at a public fair, yet came to love sixteen-year-old Mirabell Starr more than life itself.

'A superb work of fiction. There is not one tired, listless page'
J. B. PRIESTLEY

Hugh Walpole

Rogue Herries

Pan Books
in association with Macmillan London

For a trusted friend
and
in love of Cumberland

First published 1930 by Macmillan & Company Ltd
This edition published 1971 by Pan Books Ltd,
Cavaye Place, London SW10 9PG
in association with Macmillan London Ltd
3rd printing 1977
This book is copyright in all countries which are
signatories to the Berne Convention
ISBN 0 330 02557 0

Printed and bound in Great Britain by
Cox & Wyman Ltd, London, Reading and Fakenham

Why are we alive if not to change body into soul?

Oh, how good it was to live! I thank Thee, God,
Thou Who gavest me life!

King David, RENE MORAX

Contents

Part One
THE CUCKOO IS NOT ENCLOSED

Part Two
'FORTY-FIVE

Part Three

THE WILD MARRIAGE

Part Four

THE BRIGHT TURRETS OF ILION

Over this country, when the giant Eagle flings the shadow of his wing, the land is darkened. So compact is it that the wing covers all its extent in one pause of the flight. The sea breaks on the pale line of the shore; to the Eagle's proud glance waves run in to the foot of the hills that are like rocks planted in green water.

From Whinlatter to Black Combe the clouds are never still. The Tarns like black unwinking eyes watch their chase, and the colours are laid out in patterns on the rocks and are continually changed. The Eagle can see the shadows rise from their knees at the base of Scafell and Gable, he can see the black precipitous flanks of the Screes washed with rain and the dark purple hummocks of Borrowdale crags flash suddenly with gold.

So small is the extent of this country that the sweep of the Eagle's wing caresses all of it, but there is no ground in the world more mysterious, no land at once so bare in its nakedness and so rich in its luxury, so warm with sun and so cold in pitiless rain, so gentle and pastoral, so wild and lonely; with sea and lake and river there is always the sound of running water, and its strong people have their feet in the soil and are independent of all men.

During the flight of the Eagle two hundred years are but as a day – and the life of man, as against all odds he pushes towards immortality, is eternal . . .

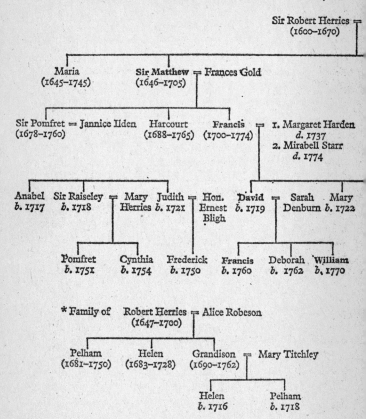

THE HERRIES

Sir Robert Herries (1600–1670)

Maria (1645–1745) — Sir Matthew (1646–1705) = Frances Gold

Sir Pomfret (1678–1760) = Jannice Ilden — Harcourt (1688–1765) — Francis (1700–1774) = 1. Margaret Harden d. 1737 / 2. Mirabell Starr d. 1774

Anabel b. 1717 — Sir Raiseley b. 1718 = Mary Herries — Judith b. 1721 = Hon. Ernest Bligh — David b. 1719 = Sarah Denburn — Mary b. 1722

Pomfret b. 1751 — Cynthia b. 1754 — Frederick b. 1750 — Francis b. 1760 — Deborah b. 1762 — William b. 1770

* Family of Robert Herries (1647–1700) = Alice Robeson

Pelham (1681–1750) — Helen (1683–1728) — Grandison (1690–1762) = Mary Titchley

Helen b. 1716 — Pelham b. 1718

FAMILY

Margaret Blaikie

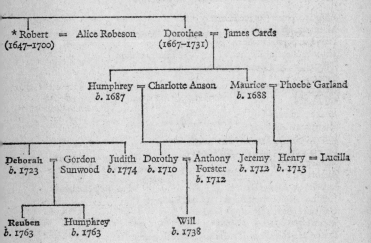

The Herries Family in *Rogue Herries*

Francis Herries (Rogue Herries)
Margaret, *his first wife*
David *m.* Sarah Denburn
Mary *m.* Raiseley Herries ⎱ *Francis's children*
Deborah *m.* Rev Gordon Sunwood ⎰
Francis
Deborah ⎱ *David's children*
William ⎰
Reuben Sunwood
Humphrey Sunwood ⎱ *Deborah's children*
Mirabell Starr, *Francis's second wife*
Sir Pomfret Herries, *Francis's brother*
Jannice, *his wife*
Anabel
Raiseley *m.* Mary Herries ⎱ *Pomfret's children*
Judith *m.* Hon Ernest Bligh (1st Lord Rockage) ⎰
Harcourt Herries, *Francis's brother*
Maria Herries, *Francis's aunt*
Robert Herries, *Francis's Uncle m.* Alice Robeson
Grandison, *his son, m.* Mary Titchley
Pelham
Helen ⎱ *Grandison's children*
Humphrey Cards, *Francis's cousin, m.* Charlotte Anson
Jeremy
Dorothy *m.* Anthony Forster ⎱ *Humphrey's children*
Will Forster, *Dorothy's son*
Maurice Cards, *Humphrey's brother, m.* Phoebe Garland
Henry, *his son, m.* Lucilla Vane

Part One

THE CUCKOO IS NOT ENCLOSED

THE INN-THE HOUSE

A LITTLE BOY, David Scott Herries, lay in a huge canopied bed, half awake and half asleep.

He must be half awake because he knew where he was – he was in the bedroom of the inn with his sisters, Mary and Deborah; they were in the bed with him, half clothed like himself, fast sleeping. Mary's plump naked arm lay against his cheek, and Deborah's body was curled into the hollow of his back and her legs were all confused with his own. He liked that because he loved, nay, worshipped, his sister Deborah.

He knew also that he was awake because, lying looking up, he could see the canopy that ran round the top of the bed. It was a dull faded green with a gold thread in it. He could see the room too, very large, with rough mottled white walls and a big open stone fireplace; there was a roaring, leaping fire – the only light in the room – and he could see very clearly the big, shining brass fire-dogs with grinning mouths like dragons and stout curly tails.

He knew, too, that he was awake, because he could see Alice Press sitting there, her clothes gathered up to her knees, warming her legs. He did not like Alice Press, but she always fascinated him, and he wondered now of what she was thinking, so motionless, her head with its red hair pushed forward, her naked neck above her silver brocade.

He knew that he was awake, because he could hear the sounds of the inn, voices calling, doors banging in the wind, steps on the stair, and even the snap-snap of horses' hoofs on the cobbles of the yard. He could hear the wind too, rushing up to the windows and shaking the panes and tearing away again, and then he shivered, pleasantly, luxuriously, because it was so warm and safe where he was and so cold and dangerous outside.

Then he shivered again because he remembered that he, with the others, must soon plunge out again into that same wind and mud and danger.

He would like to stay thus, in this warm bed, for ever and ever.

But, although he was awake enough to know all these things, he must be asleep also – asleep because, for one thing, the room would not stay still, but leapt and rollicked with the fire. All the things in it moved; the fire-dogs grinned and yawned; over a large armchair of faded red silk, oddly enough, some harness had been slung, and it lay there in coils of silver and dark brown leather, and these coils turned and stretched and slipped like snakes. Then against the wall there was a long, thin mirror in tarnished silver and, in this, Alice Press was most oddly reflected, the side of her face that was shown there being very thin and red, her hair tawny-peaked like a witch's hat; her eyebrow jumped up and down in a terrifying manner.

Only David was not afraid. He was a very fearless boy. But he thought, as he lay there and watched, how ugly she was in the mirror, and that if his father saw her thus he would not chuck her beneath the chin and so make his mother unhappy. And, although he was not afraid, he was glad nevertheless that Mary's warm arm was against his cheek and the round shape of Deborah's body against his back.

Because it might be that after all Alice Press was a witch. (He had always had his secret suspicions.) The way that she sat there now, so motionless, bending forward, was just as though she were making spells – and the silver harness blinked and the glass of the mirror trembled as the flame of the fire rose and fell again.

Then, again, it must be that he was still asleep because, although he knew that he was lying in his bed, he knew also that he was yet bumping and tossing in the coach. In that coach they had surely been for weeks and weeks, or so at least it had seemed to his tired and weary body.

At first when they had set out from Doncaster – how long ago? – he had been all pride and pleasure. It had been a fair and lovely morning – one of the last of the late summer days. The sun was shining, the birds singing, such gay bustle about the cobbled courtyard of the inn, the maids looking down from the windows, the hostlers busy about the horses, the postilions polite and eager to his father, all of them, Mother and Father Roche and Alice Press and Mary and Deborah fitting so comfortably into the soft warm inside of the coach, that had even pictures of hunting painted on the walls and little windows with gold round the edges.

Yes, it had been all gay enough then, but how miserable it had soon become! He could not now divide the days and nights from one another: moreover, he was still there in the coach, bumped up and down, thrown here and there, sleeping, waking with cramp and pins and needles, and Deborah crying and needing

comforting, and Mary cross, and his mother frightened, and
Alice Press sulky. Only Father Roche, reading in his purple book,
or looking steadily in front of him, never perturbed nor upset
nor unhappy, always grave and kind, and miles and miles away
from them all!

Then the Great North Road, which had sounded so fine and
grand when he had first heard of it, how different it was in reality!
Not fine and grand at all, but full of deep ruts and mud so fearful
that again and again the coach was hopelessly stuck in it, and
everyone had to pull and push, cursing and swearing. Once they
were almost upset. The coach went right over on its side and the
horses went down, and they were all on the top of one another.
He, David, had a bruise on his right leg, and his mother's cheek
was cut.

The farther they went the colder it became. They seemed,
almost at once, to leave summer right behind them.

Nor were the inns where they stopped fine and clean like the
Doncaster one, but cold, draughty, and the floors and walls often
crawling with spiders and other more evil things.

He seemed, lying there in the bed watching the leaping fire, to
be transferred suddenly back into one of the worst of them –
where, tired and bruised with the rough travelling, he had
stumbled into the low-ceilinged, ill-lighted, ill-smelling room,
huddled with his mother and sisters at a dirty table in a dim
corner, and there stared out into the rude, confused babble –
men, women, children, dogs, drinking, shouting and singing, the
dogs waiting, mouths agape, while the food was tossed to them,
four men playing at some game in a corner, a man with a fiddle
and a monkey dressed in a crimson jacket dancing in the middle
of the sandy floor, the heated damp of the room rising to the
ceiling and trickling in wet smeary streaks down the walls, a
smell of straw and human breath and dung and animals and
tallow – and in the middle of this his father standing, in his dark
purple riding-coat, his high hat cocked, his waistcoat of silver
thread showing between the thick lapels of his coat, his whip with
the silver head in his hand – like a god, like a king, demanding a
private room, aweing at last the fat landlord, round like a tub,
causing all that coarse roomful to feel that a great man had come
among them. There was little, tired though he was, that David
had not that night noticed, from the painting of the King over
the fireplace to a swinging gilt cage with a blue bird, and a man
who said he was from the wars and crept to their table on his
wooden stumps showing that his right hand had no fingers . . .

Yes, he remembered everything of that night (was not the man with no legs and no fingers over there now by the fire watching Alice Press, her back of stiff brocade?), because on that night a great happiness had come to him. He had slept with his father. His father and Father Roche and himself had slept in the one small, dirty room, all three on the low, dirty bed. At first it had been almost terrible because his father had been in one of his rages, cursing the place and the dirt and the cold, cursing his family, too, for persuading him to the expense and danger of a private coach, when they would all of them have been so much better on horseback.

Then, seeing his little son straight and sturdy there in his smallclothes, looking up and waiting for orders as to whether he should go naked to bed or no, with one of his sudden gestures he had caught him up and hugged him, then thrown off only his outer clothing, then taken David and wrapped him, close up against himself, in his great riding-coat – and the two of them stretched out on the bed, Father Roche bodily beside them but spiritually a world away.

How wonderful that night had been! David had slept but little of it. He had lain close against his father's heart, his hands across his father's breast, feeling the great beat of the heart and the iron ribs beneath the thin shirt, his cheek against the smooth softness of his father's neck.

That had been a great happiness, but after that night there had been only trouble. On the high ground towards Kendal they had suffered a fearful storm of wind and rain. It had seemed to them that the end of the world had come; the coach had sunk into the mud so that for hours they could not move it. They had been warned, at the last town, that they must beware of footpads, and at every sound they had started. Quite a crowd of travellers had been accompanying them for safety – farmers, pedlars and other pedestrians. The weather perhaps had saved them. All the footpads were within doors, warm and cosy beside their fires.

In Kendal they had left the coach and had ridden the remainder of their journey on horseback. David, tired though he was, had found that glorious, riding in front of his father, mounting the hills, then dropping under the faint misted morning sun down beside the miraculous waters and mountains, a land of faery such as David had never dreamt of, sheets of white and silver, the mountains of rose and amber and the trees thick with leaves of gold.

They had ridden into Keswick in the afternoon, quite a

cavalcade of them, with their possessions on pack-horses, the women and children so desperately fatigued that they could scarcely keep their seats. So, in a dream, to the inn, and the children stripped of their outer clothing and flung into the great bed, the two little girls at once dropping off into heavy slumber.

So should David have done, but instead he had lain there in this strange state of waking sleep. It was, possibly, that he was too greatly excited. For months past, in their home outside Don-caster, he had been anticipating this journey. He had not been happy in the Doncaster home. His father had been so much away, his mother so unhappy, there had been no one save his sisters with whom he could play. He had hated the stuffy little house, the rooms so small and dark, the country surrounding it so dull and uninteresting. And always there had been this un-happiness, his father angry and rebellious, his mother often in tears, Alice Press, whom he hated, supposedly looking after the children but doing nothing for them, gentlemen arriving from Doncaster, drinking, playing cards, singing and shouting all night long. His only interest had been his lesson with Father Roche, who, while teaching him Latin and Greek, would talk to him about many wonderful things, about London with its palaces and theatres and gardens that ran down to the river, and Rome where England's rightful King lived, and then of God and Heaven, and how one must live to please God – to obey Father Roche in all things and to keep secret in his heart everything that Father Roche told him.

The only other entertainment had been the times when he was with Nathaniel and Benjamin, the men-servants. Nathaniel taught him the small-sword and cudgel, and Benjamin taught him to box and to wrestle, and he had been twice with Nathaniel to a cock-fight and once to the village to see a bear baited.

Nevertheless, had it not been for his father and Deborah the days would have been heavy indeed. He was a boy of passionate affections and his whole heart was given to his father and his sister. His love for his father was worship and his love for Deborah was protection.

His father was entirely a being from another world like St Michael or St George who came in the Christmas plays. His father who was so handsome and splendid could do no wrong, although when he was drunk he was hard to understand; when he beat Benjamin until the blood ran down Benjamin's back David was sorry for the man, but yet was certain that his father was in the right.

But Deborah was of his own flesh and blood. So, too, was Mary, but he did not care for Mary. She, although she was so young, had already her own independent fashion of living and, because she was so pretty, could have her way when she pleased, which she very well knew. But Deborah was not pretty and was often afraid. Deborah believed that David could do anything, and she always came to him when she was in trouble and trusted him to help her. He could do no wrong in Deborah's eyes, and so he loved her and guarded her as well as he could from every harm.

At the thought of Deborah he turned a little and put his arm about her, which she feeling, although deep in sleep, recognized by a little dreamy murmur of pleasure.

Just then he heard the door (which was behind the canopied bed so that he could not see it) open, and an instant later it was all that he could do to withhold a cry of pleasure. For it was his father who had entered, who was now standing quite close to them, looking down upon them. David closed his eyes – not because he wanted to be deceitful, but because he knew that his father wished that he should be asleep.

Nevertheless, one look had been enough. His father was re-splendent! For days and nights now he had seen him soiled and disarrayed with the storms and struggles of that awful journey, muddied and blown and uncaring whether he were neatly kept or no. There were times when his father seemed to prefer dirt and disorder, and they were bad times too. An unkempt wig, tarnished buckles and buttons, a soiled cravat, and David had learnt to know that the disarray and rebellion were more than physical.

Only an hour ago David had seen him striding about the court-yard of the inn, mud-splashed to the thighs, raging and swearing. That had been his last thought before he had fallen into this half-slumber, that his father was still out there in the wind and rain ordering Benjamin and the rest, seeing to the horses that were to carry them the final stage of their weary journey. But now, how resplendent in the white-walled fire-leaping room! David in that one glance had seen it all.

The fine curled chestnut wig, the beautiful claret-coloured, gold-embroidered coat with the long spreading skirts, the claret-coloured breeches and grey silk stockings, the fluted grey-silk waistcoat stamped with red roses, the little sword at his side – ah! glory upon glory, was anything in the world anywhere so glorious as his father thus! No, nothing in London or Rome of which

Father Roche had told him – nothing that China or India itself could show!

His heart swelling with pride and happiness he lay there, pretending to be asleep, watching through half-closed eyes. He saw then an odd thing. He saw his father, on tip-toe, approach the fire, steal upon Alice Press, she motionless gazing into the flame, lean forward, put then his hands, deep in their splendid white ruffles, lightly about her face, closely across her eyes. She gave a little scream, but David knew that at once she was aware who this was.

Laughing, Francis Herries withdrew his hands. She looked up, smiling that strange smile of hers, half pleasure, half rebellious anger.

'Why, sir' (she was, like David, greatly surprised at his grandeur), 'what fine feathers we're wearing!'

'Hush,' he put his fingers to his lips, 'the children are sleeping.'

'I fancy so. They sound still enough. Poor babies – after such a devilish journey!' She turned again from him and stared back into the fire. 'You are dressed to meet your brother?'

'Why not to meet yourself, beautiful lady?'

He was laughing, that careless, jolly, kindly, good-to-all-the-world laugh that, as David knew, came only when he was happy. So he was happy now! David was glad.

'Myself?' She turned to him fully, showing the deep swell of her bosom beneath the brocaded vest. 'No, I think not. God! that I had not consented to come on this madcap journey.'

For answer he bent down and, still laughing, caught her head in his hands, brought his mouth to hers, kissed her on the lips, the cheeks, the eyes, then, almost violently, flung her away from him, straightening his body as he did so.

'Do you like that better? Does that make you more content with your journey?'

'No, why should it?' She shrugged her shoulders, turning back to the fire. 'Do you love me? No. Then what is a kiss?'

'Love – and love.' He laughed. 'I am no captive to it, if that's your meaning. I visit it, wish it good day, spend a pretty hour in its company – so I am never weary of it nor it of me. Love? And what do you mean by love?'

'I mean,' she answered fiercely, 'those foul, filthy, beggarly days and nights of mud and dung and stinking beds; the pains and bruises that I have known on this journey and the idiocies of your wife and the wailings of your children and the evil dirty tempers of yourself . . . And what do I receive in return for these things?'

She rose up suddenly and turned to him – a tall broad woman, with scarlet hair and a white face, who would soon be stout.

David, watching her, had never seen her like this, so alive, her big eyes with the fair, faint eyebrows staring, the big bosom under the silver brocade heaving, the big mouth in the pale face half open.

Francis Herries looked at her gently, kindly and with amusement. 'What do you get?' speaking low so that the children should not be waked. He put a hand on her shoulder, and she stood strong and sturdy without moving. David could see her full face now in the mirror and he watched absorbed because it was so awake. Always it had been yawning, the lazy eyes half closed, the cheeks heavy with indolence as she sleepily ate sugar-plums and cakes and sugar-figs.

'What do you get? . . . Something. Nothing. And what is there to get? A little hugging and fumbling, sweating and panting, and then satiety.' He looked at her even with more earnest study, as though in truth he had never seen her before, and her eyes did not fall before his. 'You elected to come – to the end of the world. No roads. Savages. A chill house with the rain always falling – and the ghosts of all your sins, my dear.'

She, with a sudden movement that surprised him, caught him round the cheek and with her white face against his ruddy brown one whispered eagerly, furiously in his ear. The fire leapt as though in sympathy with her urgency, and the figures swayed and swelled in the silver mirror.

Francis Herries withdrew from her slowly, carefully, as though he would not hurt her, no, neither her body nor her soul. But he was many, many miles away from her as he answered:

'So that's the way of it . . . To leave them in the mud and rain and find sunshine, the two of us, alone – alone.' He smiled – a beautiful smile, David, who did not understand the most of this strange conversation, thought. 'Alone with me, Alice, you'd be in despair in a half-hour. No one has been alone with me ever and not suffered the intensest weariness. I have suffered it with myself, recurring agonies of it. And you are not made to be wearied.

'Nevertheless, you will be infinitely dull. Days of rain and mud in a half-tumbled house cut off from everything but the savages. It's your own choice, my dear. And only my body to comfort you. My body without my soul, I fear. My soul has

flown. I lost it a week back. I shall find it doubtless on a tree in
Borrowdale.'

David saw that she did not understand him, that she gazed at
him with a look that he himself did not understand, a look of
rage, of love, of uncertainty, of disappointment. She was not very
clever, Alice Press. Young though he was, David already had an
instinct of that.

His father came softly to the bed and looked down on them.
David, his eyes tightly closed, could nevertheless see him, the
gold of his coat, the white silk of the lapels, the curling splendour
of the chestnut wig. It was as though his father were weaving a
spell over him – his eyes so fixedly closed that they burnt. A
spell, a spell! The crystal in the silver mirror turning, Alice Press
mounting her broomstick and riding through the dark heavy-
hung sky, and his father riding on a silver horse into the moon
and stars . . . A spell! A spell!

'Wake up! wake up!'

It was Alice Press's soft white hand shaking his shoulder. He
opened his eyes. His father was gone as though he had never
been. They were to be up and have their clothes on and see their
good uncle and aunt – Uncle Pomfret and Aunt Jannice.

The two little girls, like little round fluffy owls bewildered by
their sleep, dazed with the strange light of the leaping fire,
fastened their own clothes. Mary was eight years of age, and
Deborah seven, and they had been taught from a long time to do
for themselves. They had been wearing their winter dresses these
last days, and Mary's had dark fur edging the green velvet and
Deborah's grey fur upon crimson. David was dressed in a short
yellow jacket and long tight breeches, buff-colour, reaching
down to his ankles. He tied Deborah's ribbons and points and
fastened her shoes. She was very frightened. She was scarcely
as yet awake. She did not know what this great room was nor
where they were now going. She was terrified of her Uncle
Pomfret and Aunt Jannice. She was weary, utterly weary after
the days of the journey. She wanted her mother. She, like David,
hated Alice Press. She was like a little downy bird, her head
covered with soft flaxen curls. She stood there biting her lips so
that she would not cry. Had David not been there she *must* have
cried. But she stood near him looking up into his face. Where
David was no harm could come.

It was now time for them to go down, but they had to delay
because Mary must have her horn-book to carry with her. It was
a fine one, and its back was of gilded and embossed leather,

crimson with silver wire. David knew at once why Mary must
have it. It was to show off before Aunt Jannice that she might
notice how exceptional a child Mary was.

They searched here and there. Mary had had it with her before
she fell asleep. Alice Press swore and threatened. It was of no
use. Mary had a marvellous obstinacy when the purpose was
concerned with herself. The horn-book was found beneath one
of the fire-dogs, and Mary walked out, holding it virtuously by
the handle, her head up as though she were leading a procession.

They went down the wooden staircase, which was from
Elizabeth's time, very beautiful and broad, the newels thick and
strong, the handrails framed into the newels, the balustrade
beautifully arcaded, a lovely symmetry of delicacy and strength.
In the hall below it was very dark, save in the doorway that
looked out into the street where the light of the afternoon still
gleamed in pale shadow against black cloud. Great gusts of the
gale blew into the hall, at the end of which was a huge stone fireplace with a roaring fire. On broad tables candelabra held many
candles that also blew in the wind.

Across the shining floor servants, drawers, maids, men from
the kitchen were constantly passing into the wild light and out of
it again. Uncertain though the light was, it was enough for David
to see his father, standing very stiff and upright, his mother also,
and a lady and gentleman who must, David knew, be his uncle
and aunt.

The children were brought up to their parents. Mary at once
went to her mother, caught her mother's hand, and so stayed,
looking very pretty. David kissed his aunt's hand, bowed to his
uncle, then stood straight and stiff beside his father. His uncle
Pomfret was a big, broad, stout man with a very red face, large
wide-open eyes and a little snub nose. He was dressed in rough
country clothes, his long boots were splashed with mud. He
smelt strongly of wind, rain, liquor and the stables. He seemed
good-natured and friendly, laughed much and struck his leg
often with a riding-whip. Aunt Jannice was thin and tall, with a
peaked face and a big brown wart in the middle of her cheek.
She wore a broad hat and had a curly brown wig which sat oddly
about her yellow leathern face. She was very composed, dignified
and superior. She contrasted strangely with David's mother,
who was always so stout and red and flustered and was given to
breaking into odd little hummings of tunes from simple nervousness.

David knew that there was nothing that irritated his father so much as this habit of hers. But David's attention was fixed upon his father. He wished desperately – although he did not know why he wished – that his father had not dressed so grandly. Only half an hour before he had been so proud of his father's grandeur, now he was ashamed of it.

He was sure that Uncle Pomfret and Aunt Jannice were laughing at his father for being in such grand clothes. Not that his father would care, but he, David, cared for him. Uncle Pomfret was much older than his father (he was indeed twenty-two years older; he was the eldest, as Francis Herries was the youngest, he fifty-two years of age and Francis only thirty). He looked as though he might be David's grandfather.

There was indeed no physical resemblance between the two brothers. David discovered also another thing – that they were all striving to persuade his father of something, and his father was very obstinate. He knew how his father looked when he was obstinate, he smiled and was haughty and said little. So it was now.

They were trying to persuade him to stay in his brother's house at least tonight and not to go on in the wind and wet and darkness into Borrowdale. But his father only smiled. He had planned to be in the house tonight and be in the house he would, and the others should be there too.

David saw that his mother was very near to tears, her round mottled face all puckered, and she bit continually at her lace handkerchief. She was desperately weary, poor woman, and afraid and very unhappy.

'Why, blast you and damn you, brother,' said Uncle Pomfret very heartily. 'You must stay with us tonight or prove yourself most unbrotherly. We had always expected it so— Had we not, Janny? There's no road over to Herries. You are going among the savages there, brother. I can swear you were dismayed enough at seeing this griddling little inn after your great Doncaster houses, but this is Paradise to what you're going to. Don't say I didn't warn you now. Damn me for a curmudgeon, brother, if I bottomed you into doing it – but tonight you shall stay with us. There's your lady sunk with weariness, and the babes too, damn me if they're not.'

He shouted all this as though across a windy common, and all that Francis Herries said to it was:

'Herries sees us all tonight, and we'll take our luck with the road.'

'You'll be the rest of this day on horseback,' his brother

assured him. 'There's not a cart in Borrowdale, brother, nor a road to carry one. It's all horseback round here. Damn it, you're in Chiney in Borrowdale, but never say I didn't warn you. You wanted cheap living and you've got it. Naked bottom and bare soil! that's life in Borrowdale.'

David had never heard so rough and coarse and hearty a voice, and it seemed to him strange that this big red man should be his father's brother. He jumped, too, from the sharp contrast when a moment later his aunt spoke:

'Come now, Francis. Have some softness for the family. The children can scarce stand with their weariness. Margaret, persuade him. There is room enough with us for so long as you please to remain.'

Her voice was cold and thin like the steady trickle of a determined pump. When she spoke, she stared in front of her, looking neither to right nor left, as though she were reciting a set piece.

David's mother, thus appealed to, very nervously and not looking at her husband, answered:

'Indeed, it's very kindly of you, Jannice. We are weary and 'tis late. Tomorrow would be time enough.'

'There, brother!' Sir Pomfret broke in with a roar, 'have you no tender parts? Your wife and the children at least shall stay with us. You shall ride alone if you are resolved – you and the priest,' he added, suddenly dropping his voice.

'There – that's sufficient,' Francis Herries answered sharply. 'My wife will be thankful enough when she's there and settled. In an hour's time the horses will be moving and ourselves on them. Thank you for your goodwill, brother. And now for a meal. It is ready and waiting.'

It was now late for dining. To the children, indeed, it would, before this tremendous journey of theirs, have seemed an incredible hour, for their dinner had been at three of the afternoon ever since they could remember, but now all their customs and habits were in ruin, and they accepted, poor things, blindly and without a murmur, what came to them.

They were, however, all three, too tired to have an appetite. In the little private room they were crowded about the small table. David to his distress was next to his uncle, who roared and rattled and laughed as he helped the food, so that it was like being seated next an earthquake.

There was a good baked pie of a leg of mutton, and roasted chickens with pease and bacon, and a fine fruit tart that would, at another time, have made David's mouth water. There was

much wine, too, and of this Uncle Pomfret began to drink very
heartily indeed, and shouted to the others to do the same. The
noisier he became the more upright and magnificent was Aunt
Jannice.

Very fine, especially, was she when she rose to wash her spoon
in a bowl of water behind the table, so that, having just used it
for pease and bacon, it should not now be soiled for the fruit
tart. David's mother, who had never seen anyone do this before,
could not hide her staring wonder.

David, in spite of his weariness which made everything
around him like a dream, fancied that his aunt was storing all
things up in her mind, so that for many weeks she would be able
to retail to her genteel friends all the strange things that this
wild family had done. He did not love her the better for fancying
this.

But he was in so dreamy a state that he could be sure of
nothing. He, in his half-dream, saw – and he knew that his
mother saw this too – that his father was drinking in a defiance of
his stout red-faced brother. He knew what his father was like
when he was drunken, and he hated his uncle that he should
tempt him. Throughout this journey his father had been very
fine, drinking nothing, aware perhaps of the charge there was
upon him. And in any case he drank little when Father Roche
was there.

But in everything that he did, while his brother was present,
there was defiance. There had been defiance in his grand clothes,
defiance in his refusing to stay in Keswick, defiance now in every
gesture. David, because he adored his father, knew all this with a
wisdom beyond his years. Meanwhile, in this dreamy state, it
was all that he could do with his wits to defend himself against
his uncle, who was pushing pieces of meat and of pie on to his
plate and even holding his head back and poking food into his
mouth. But once when he was about to force some wine down
his throat Francis Herries called out quietly:

'Nay, brother, leave the boy alone. He shall have wine when
he wishes for it. It shan't be thrust on him.' Pomfret broke out
into a flurry of magnificent and filthy oaths. He then thrust
David in the ribs and cried at him: 'Why, damn thee, boy, dost
thou not follow thy father? He's a lecherous foul-dealing knave
enough, I'll be bound – no Herries, an he ain't. Drink thy uncle's
health, boy, and be damned to thy father!'

'Pomfret!' said Aunt Jannice. It was enough. The uncle was
cowed like a dog under a whip and took some sugar-plums from

a plate and swallowed them, three at a time, like a confused child. David looked across to his father. It seemed to him then, as it was to seem to him increasingly in the coming days, that they were younger and elder brother, not father and son. And, indeed, there was only the difference of nineteen years between them.

In his dreamy state it seemed to him that he and his father were circled round with light together, they two, and that his father's crimson and gold shone, and the room burnt against its panelling with a strange and sombre glow.

But his next thought was for Deborah. With every attention that his uncle had permitted him he had watched her and had seen that she was very unhappy. Poor child, with weariness and fear of her relations and her seated distance from David, she was nearly distraught. She did not understand what had happened to her, but it was something terrible. She understood that more terrible things were shortly to occur. David, watching her, could at last endure it no longer; her frightened eyes, the way that her head bobbed and nodded and then bobbed again, her fashion of pretending to eat and not eating, hurt him as though it were himself.

While his uncle was busy with a long and excited account of his country sports and pastimes, with vociferous curses on the French and praise of the Hanoverian succession, he stepped from his chair and went to her side, bending forward and whispering to her.

But, alas, this kind attention was too much for her; she broke into sobs, not loudly but with a soft titter-witter like a wounded bird.

Uncle Pomfret broke off his account of what he would do to a French Papist an he caught him, to tumble into a bellow of laughter.

'Why, pox on it, here's a little master . . . comforting your sister . . . Why, damn it, boy, but I like your heart. There's a good one for the ladies. He knows a thing or two, I warrant. But come hither, little Deb. Come to thy old uncle. He'll buy thee a baby, one of your china sorts with pink cheeks, none of your stuffed rags. Come to thy uncle, Deb, and he'll comfort thee.'

'David.' It was his father's voice. 'Leave Deborah. Come to me.' He went up to his father, fearless, but not knowing whether a caress or a blow was to be his fate. Then he looked into his father's eyes and saw that they were soft and humorous and knew that all was well.

'Go, find Benjamin. We must shortly be starting.' Then, turning to his brother, 'She has babies enough, Pomfret; she is weary, and there's a bed at Herries waiting for her.'

He did not hear his uncle's retort, which was something fine and free about beds and ladies and general courtship. He was glad to be away, he didn't care if he never saw his uncle or aunt again; he hated them and Keswick and the inn. But coming into the bustle of the kitchen where serving-men and maids were shouting and pushing, where dogs were waiting for chance pieces of food, and a man with a feather in his broad hat was seated on the corner of a table playing a fiddle, the stir and adventure of it all heartened him and he was glad that he was alive and pushing, shoving forward into this grand new world. The kitchen smelt of everything in the world – meat and drink and the heat of the great fire. He looked around him and found Benjamin seated in a corner near the fire, his arm round a girl. She was feeding him with pieces of meat off his plate.

'Benjamin,' he said, ordering him as though he were a hundred years his master, 'my father says that it's time for the horses.'

Many of them heard him and turned laughing, and a big woman with an enormous bosom would have made him come to her, and a brawler wanted him to drink, but he fixed his eyes on the stout Benjamin, who put his plate down, gave the girl a kiss, and came without a word. So much power had Francis Herries over his servants.

Benjamin was plump and rosy; he should have been a fine figure of a man, but he could eat all day without ceasing. This was one of the reasons that he was beaten by his master, but he bore his master no grudge. Everything that came his way he took, and over the bad he shrugged his shoulders and over the good he laughed and grunted.

First of all he loved himself, then food, then women (all kinds, young, old, ugly and fair – there was not the ugliest woman in the country who was too ugly for him, and with his round, rosy cheeks, merry eyes, broad shoulders and stout legs he could do what he would), then cock-fighting, dog-fighting, football, bear-baiting, rat-hunting, witch-hunting, all kinds of sport (he was himself not a bad sportsman with the staff and cudgel, and boxing and running and swimming), then every kind of a horse, then young David, for whom he cared, perhaps, more than for any other single human being, but not for him very deeply, only lazily and with easy good-nature. He was from the South, and had, as yet, no good word for this northern country.

He grumbled as they made their way into the dusky yard. 'Pox on it,' he said, 'I'll pepper my own legs with shot, but I thought his honour would give us another hour's quiet and plenty. What's he want riding on tonight for? There's but few like the master for a restless spirit . . . I'd match that white dog in the kitchen there,' he went on irrelevantly, 'for a hundred guineas against the grey bitch the master had in Doncaster. There's a dog. You could see he never blinked a bird in his life. And you needn't tell master I was kissing Jenny neither! They all say their name's Jenny—'

'I shall not tell him,' said David proudly.

'How many miles is it from this Borrowdale to Keswick?' asked Benjamin.

'Around seven, I fancy,' said David.

Benjamin nodded his head but said nothing. 'It's a little inn as you might say, this,' he remarked. 'Small beside the south-country inns. Not much business in this little town. Kendal's the way the business runs. Not but there won't be some sport in Borrowdale. I may be a poor man and not bred for writing and accounts, but I know a dog when I see one.'

David missed many more of his remarks. For one thing Benjamin was always talking, not like the other man Nathaniel, who was a little spare fellow, very silent and grim, and anyone who was often with Nathaniel must accustom himself to think his own thoughts while Benjamin chattered. Besides this, David again was in his dream state. As he stood in the yard listening to the horses striking the cobbles, hearing the curses of the hostlers, smelling the hay and straw, catching the sharp cold of the breeze about his face, he seemed to move, not on his own feet, but through the air, alighting here and there and then up again, softly, breezily like the wind.

Thus dreaming he found himself standing with the others at the inn door. Father Roche was there, and Alice Press, his father, mother, uncle, aunt, and his sisters – all dreamy and wavering together. A crowd had collected to watch their departure. A great wind was hurrying through the sky above the black gables and chimneys, carrying soft grey clouds with it, and between the clouds once and again a burning star stared and vanished. The horses were stamping and pulling at the heads. Everything was ready for this last ride.

In the doorway stood the stout host of the inn, bowing as Francis Herries very grandly thanked him for his courtesy. Uncle Pomfret laughed and shouted. Then, as it seemed, a moment later one of life's great happinesses had occurred, for David was sitting a horse in front of his father. He had expected that he would be in front of Nathaniel, because all the way from Kendal he had been with his father, and surely such luck would not come to him twice. But here he was pressed against his father's body, and he could feel the movement of his thighs and above his head the throb of his heart, and in his face the wind was beating like a whip.

They were off, trotting over the cobbles, the horse slipping now and then in the mud or refuse, his father stiffening as he pulled at the reins, and at their side seen dimly his mother, pillion behind Father Roche with Mary in her lap, Alice Press with Deborah pillion behind Benjamin, the rest duskily in the rear.

The little town was very still; a light glimmered here and there through a shutter, a watchman going from his warm room, perhaps, to his night-duty passed them swinging his lamp, a chair in which a lady highly muffled could just be seen went swiftly with its bearers round the corner. They turned out of the square to the left, and the clatter that they made as they swept round the corner drew some heads to the window and an aproned man with a candle in his hand to the doorway. Then as they began to clear the town another thing occurred. David was aware that certain figures were running at their side and a man on a little nag was keeping pace with them. The same thing had happened to them on their way to Kendal, when a number of farmers and others had gone with their coach. That had been because of footpads, and now this must be for the same reason.

That made his heart beat faster. They were passing out of the guarded town and were running into dangerous country, dangerous country that, although he did not know it, was to be his country for many a year. He had perhaps some sense of it there under the biting wind, for he shivered a little and drew closer to his father.

They pulled up a little hill and were aware now at once of the open country, for the road beneath them was treacherous. The horses began to walk, and even so they slipped and stumbled in the mud. In the centre the path (it was little more than a path) was hard and well-trodden but on either side a quagmire. There was a faint silver misty light in the sky, but this shifted and trembled with the driving clouds. On the left of them there were thick trees, but on the right the landscape sloped to the mere, and

in front of them were black shadows that waited like watchers for
their coming, and these, David knew, were the mountains. He
was aware then of a further thing, that his father was drunk. Not
bestially drunk. Not ferociously drunk. Happily drunk. His
body closed a little about his son as he sang softly the children's
game:

> 'Lady Queen Anne who sits in her stand,
> And a pair of green gloves upon her hand,
> As white as a lily, as fair as a swan,
> The fairest lady in a'.the land.
> Come smell my lily, come smell my rose,
> Which of my maidens do you choose?
> I choose you one, and I choose you all,
> And I pray, Miss Jenny, yield up the ball.
> The ball is mine and none of yours.
> Go to the woods and gather flowers;
> Cats and kittens hide within;
> But all young ladies walk out and in.'

David knew the words very well, because, although this was a
girls' game, he had played it to please his sisters. His father repeated again:

'And I pray, Miss Jenny, yield up the ball – And I pray, Miss
Jenny, yield up the ball.'

Why had he chosen the name Jenny? Was not that the name
by which Benjamin had called the kitchenmaid? Did they, as
Benjamin had said, always cry Jenny for a name? His father
swayed slightly as he sang, but the horse seemed to understand.
In any case they were going slow enough. No harm could come.
A little man trotting at their side called up to them:

'I have a fiddle with me, your honour, and will play to you by
your fire.'

And Francis Herries answered him happily: 'I'll swear you
have a fiddle and know how to play on it too.' Then he began to
talk very pleasantly to his young son. The path now was bending down until it almost touched the mere, and David could hear
the little waves, driven by the wind, slapping the shore and
rippling away again into space.

All his life he was to remember that moment; the clap of the
horses' hoofs on the path, the slap and ripple of the water, the
little panting breaths of the man running beside them,
the warmth and intimacy of his father's body, the dark woods

above them, the black hills in front of them, the fiercely moving sky, and the gentle good-humoured voice in his ear.

'And so, David, we are passing into the perilous country where the savages live, where there is only hay to eat and dirty water to drink, where it rains for a hundred days. Dost thou think there will be bears there, David, my son?'

'I don't know, Father. I hope so,' said David.

'Bears of one family or another there will be, and snakes in the grass and peacocks on the garden wall. Is it not as though we were escaping? Escaping from what, think you?'

'We are not escaping,' answered David proudly. His voice came in little jolts. They were now on harder ground and were moving more swiftly. 'You would never run away.'

'No, would I not? Art thou so sure, little son? I have run from the lions in my time and then again I have braved them. But this is the most perilous adventure of all. We will not come from this save with our naked skins; and if I am hard pressed will you always stay by me, David?'

'Always,' said David, nodding his head. 'I could never be frightened an you were there.'

'Couldst thou not, couldst thou not, my son? Although the she-devil with the silver hams and the glassy tongue came to down us both?'

'I'm afeared of no woman,' David answered, but the trees now were gathering about him very darkly, and it was cold. In spite of himself he shivered a little.

His father laughed, bent forward and touched ever so lightly with his lips the boy's neck.

'So we are together, side by side, whatever the peril – for ever?'

David straightened his back. 'Yes, sir,' he answered proudly.

''Twas a maid in the inn said her name was Jenny when I kissed her,' his father said, 'though she's no maid any more. Not by my doing, I had no time to test her virtue. Eh, little son?'

David understood this only vaguely. 'I don't like women,' he said.

'Not your sister Deborah?' His father laughed softly, deeply, as though he were thinking of other things.

'I love Deborah,' David answered.

'And your Aunt Jannice?'

But David did not reply. He could not. He was fast asleep, leaning back against his father's breast.

He woke again with a start to see that all the horses were at a standstill and were gathered about a small stone bridge. At that same moment, as though it had been arranged, a round moon, cherry-coloured, broke out from shadowy banks of cloud.

She stared down at them, and at once, as it seemed in his sleepy half-wakened state to David, the clouds fled away; she sailed gloriously in the sky of shining light scattered with stars. The world around them was like a world seen through glass, pale and unreal, with the trees and hills of ebony sharpness. A hamlet was clustered beyond the bridge and the river, which was running full and throwing up, under the moon, little white waves alive and dancing.

After a consultation they moved on upwards over a little hill with hills on their left side and the flooded gleaming river on their right. It was all very quiet and still. The storm had altogether died away. No one spoke, and the only sound was the hoofs of the horses, now soft, now sharp. The scene was now to David, who had only all his life seen flat and shallow country, incredibly wonderful.

They were passing through a gateway of high rock into a little valley, still as a man's hand and bleached under the moon, but guarded by a ring of mountains that seemed to David gigantic. The moonlight made them larger and marked the shadows and lines of rock like bands of jagged iron. In colour they were black against the soft lighted sky and the myriads of silver stars. A little wind, not sharp and cold as it had been before, but gentle and mild, whispered across the valley.

As they advanced, the only live things in all the world, it seemed that in a moment someone must break the strange moonlit silence with a cry: 'Ahoy! ahoy! who comes to meet us?'

But not even an owl hooted from the listening trees. After a while one mountain detached himself from the skies, coming towards them – large, sprawling, very dark and solid, with a ragged edge. To the left of this mountain there was a straight thin ledge like a tight-rope, and on the right a very beautiful cluster of hills, in shape like the grouped petals of an opening flower.

Then quite suddenly they stopped. 'That is the house on the left of us,' someone said. It was the first voice for half an hour, and the hills seemed to repeat: 'Yes, that is the house.' The horses trotted over soft, rather boggy, grass, up a little hill, through a thick group of trees, and at once they were all outside a rough stone wall that guarded a ragged, grass-grown courtyard. David looked at the house and was sadly disappointed. Under the black hills it seemed so very small, and in the white moonlight so cold and desolate. It appeared to be two houses: on the right it was high, with a gabled roof and thin latticed windows; then it dropped suddenly to a low rough-seeming building with shaggy farm byres at its hinder end. He noticed, especially, the windows of the higher house, because there were two little attic windows like eyebrows, and he could see, because the moonlight made everything so clear, that the door of this house had handsome carving. But the other building was low and shabby and forsaken.

While they waited at the gate three dogs came out furiously barking, and directly they were followed by a broad thick-set man, walking clumsily, who hurried down to meet them.

Then a light was in the doorway, but still the house watched, cold, desolate, under the moon, with no greeting for them.

'So – we are home,' he heard his father murmur.

Then he felt himself picked up in his father's strong arms, lifted, then carried across the courtyard.

His father set him down, and he ran over the threshold of the doorway. The hall where he stood was flooded with moonlight, and opposite him were two shining suits of armour. People were moving and talking behind him, but he did not hear them.

He was first in the house. As he stood there in the moonlight he, who had been asleep so long, was suddenly awake.

And he made his compact with the house.

THE MOUNTAIN

CHARLES FRANCIS HERRIES woke when the light of the fine new day was throwing silver shadows across the misty fields. Pushing back the creaking diamond-paned window, standing there in his purple bed-gown he looked down on the courtyard, the thick clustered yews that guarded, as though with fingers on their lips, the house, the ragged stone wall, then, beyond, the river, the thatched roofs of the nearest yeoman's farm, the fields and the dark sombre hills.

He drew a deep breath, flung off the bed-gown and stood there naked. He did not feel the cold, nor the sharp crisped air; he was at that time impervious to all physical pain and discomfort, a magnificent creature in all bodily force and feeling. He stared out, then looked back into the little, thin, low-ceilinged room. It was furnished scarcely at all – only a narrow truckle-bed on which he and his son had been sleeping – David, his flushed cheek against his arm, still lay there soaked in sleep – a big carved chest with the date 1652 roughly cut upon it, a mirror on the chest, and against the farther wall some old green tapestry (very faded) that flapped and rustled now in the breeze from the open window. There was one high-backed and clumsy chair, and into this his clothes had been carelessly flung. David's little things, carefully folded, were on the top of the chest.

He felt his body, punching it here and there, pinching it, kicking out a leg, stretching an arm. He might have been proud that he was so handsome and in such splendid health – such marvellous health indeed, considering the life that for ten years now he had led. But he was scornful of that as he was of everything else. What good had his beauty, health, strength brought him? Not so much good as that silver moon setting now in a pale rosy sky beyond the latticed window.

He stood there, the breeze blowing on his bare back and thighs, looking down on his little son. Here, too, he was scornful. His young son loved him, but would he love him as the years passed and he grew to realize his father? Would there not develop in him that same withdrawal that seemed to come to every human creature after a short contact with him – yes, even to so poor a thing as Alice Press, who was already beginning to look at him with that strange, surmising glance? David at present trusted and adored him, and in the centre of Herries's universal scorn, scorn of himself, of all human beings, of the round world and all that moved in it, there stayed this pleasure and pride that his young son so thought of him. That he could neither deny nor reject. But for how long was it to remain? Would he take any steps to retain it? He knew himself too well to fancy that he would.

He turned again to look out of the window on to the scene that was to be his now, he was determined, for evermore. Whatever came of this step that he had taken, whatever misery, ruin, disgrace, he would hold by it. It was final. Only thirty years of age, he yet seemed to see far, far into the future, and something told him that at the very last these dark hills would encircle him.

The hill that chiefly his window faced seemed especially to tell him this. The houses of this time in this country were not built that their tenants might look out on beautiful views, but rather for safety and shelter, tucked tight in under the hill, guarded by heavy yews.

Beyond the fields, in far distance, this humped, lumpish hill, Glaramara, sprawled in the early morning light. Herries knew well its name. For so long as he could remember he had known precisely how this house must stand, and all its history. In 1565, the year following the founding of the Company of Mines Royal, Sir Francis Herries, his great-great-grandfather, had come from his house Seddon, north of Carlisle, in part charge of the 'Almaynes', the foreign miners, and built him a little house here, called it Herries, and, at last, liking it and the country, had lived in it altogether, giving up Seddon to his younger brother.

In all his young days at Seddon, Francis had heard of Herries, the strange house in the strange country, shut in under the mountains behind rocky barriers, cut off from all the world. His grandfather, Robert Herries, had tried for a while to live in it, but it had been too isolated for him. That, too, his father Matthew had found, and had moved back to Seddon, and after this the old house had been held by a yeoman, Satterthwaite, farm-buildings had been added to it, and much of the older house had been allowed to fall into ruin.

When Francis's elder brother, Pomfret, had made a fortune in speculation (this largely by chance, because Pomfret was no brilliant financier) he had built him his house in Keswick, caring nothing for Herries, which, although so near to him, seemed yet at the very world's end.

Satterthwaite, a clever yeoman above the abilities of his fellows, had done well for himself, and built a farm-house over towards Threlkeld. It was then, after some years of desolate neglect, that Herries had been suggested to Francis by his brother, and, driven both by his romantic love for the notion of it and by his own desperate circumstances, he had accepted with an eagerness that had amazed the unimaginative Pomfret. Yes, an eagerness that was amazing even to himself. What was it that had driven him? That part of him that loved to be alone, that loved to brood and dream and enfold about him, ever closer and closer, his melancholy and dark superstition and defiant hatred of the world. That part of him, too, that felt, as neither Pomfret nor Harcourt, his brothers, felt, his passionate pride in his family. Why that pride? God only knew. There was no reason for it. The Herries men had never done great deeds nor supplied to the world famous figures. For hundreds of years they had been drunken, robbing Border freebooters; only, in Elizabeth's time, his great-great-grandfather, Francis, having some good fortune at the Court, had pushed up a little the family fortunes.

That Francis had been a hard-headed fellow, a flatterer, a time-server, a sycophant, but not ungenerous if he got his way, and no fool at any time. Elizabeth had a fancy for him, would have kept him with her, and was none so well pleased when, quite eagerly, he accepted the opportunity of surveying the foreign miners who were sent to Keswick.

Something hurried him thither, that odd strain that was for ever cropping up in every Herries generation, the strain of the dreamer, the romanticist, the sigher for what was not, the rebel against facts; and in that old Elizabethan Herries this romantic dreaming went ill enough with hardness, his pushing ambitions, his desire for wealth.

Between the two stools of temperament he fell to the ground, as many another Herries had done before him. This land in Borrowdale caught his fancy; he stayed on and on there, losing at length his interest in the mines, mooning, a dirty unlaced old man, behind the rocks that bounded that valley, keeping company with the yeomen, pursuing their daughters, drinking, riding, dicing – dying at last in his old tumble-down house, a little soiled rat of a man with ale dribbling at his ragged beard.

That was great-great-grandfather Herries. The place had done something to him, and Francis Herries, gazing now out of his window, thought it an odd fancy that this same sprawling hill, Glaramara, had looked across into that old man's eyes, seeing them grow ever more bleary, more dim, more obstinately sodden.

And so it might be with him! He had come even as that old man had come, in the vigour of his prime and strength, and he had in him those same things – that longing for what was not, dream of Paradise round the corner, belief in a life that could never be. And in him also, riding him full strength, were lechery and drunkenness, lasciviousness and cruelty.

As he stood there, idly gazing, he had a passionate family feeling. Not for individuals. He hated Pomfret, despised Harcourt, cared nothing for his cousins, the children of his uncle Robert, who lived London way, nor for his other two cousins, Humphrey and Maurice Cards and their children, Dorothy, Jeremy, and Henry. Humphrey Cards, a man a good deal the elder of Francis, lived now at Seddon and was said to be a tight-lipped Quaker. Francis had never seen the Cards brothers; they inhabited London when he, as a boy, lived at Seddon, but Pomfret knew them and despised them both.

No, there was not one of the family for whom Francis cared a rap, neither agricultural Pomfret and his yellow-faced wife, nor

bachelor Harcourt, there on the edge of that dirty sea-coast at
Ravenglass, nor the purse-proud Kensington children of Uncle
Robert with their family coach and fine Queen Anne house and
garden, nor Humphrey at Seddon, nor ship-owning Maurice
(his eyes, they said, so deeply stuck into his business that he
could see nothing else) down at Portsmouth – not for a single one
of them had he a warm feeling or a kindly thought – they were
all rogues and fools together – and yet here he was, new-come to
this tumbled old ruin, gazing out on a couple of shabby hills and
some grass-greasy fields, and his heart was swelling at
the thought of Herries and of the Herries men and women
before them, the Scotch and English blood that had gone to the
making of them, the English soil that had seen the breeding of
them.

He felt suddenly the cold, and with a shiver pulled to the
window and took on his bed-gown again.

There was a pump in the yard behind the house – he could
hear the handle going; he would go and soak his head under it.
He pulled on a pair of breeches, thrust his feet into some slippers,
and then softly, lest he should wake his son, stole out.

The morning was deepening now, but the small heavily
paned windows let in little light.

The part of the old house that remained had not been ill
designed, the rooms lofty and the staircase wide enough for two
to go abreast, still something of a wonder in Queen Anne's day
and exceedingly unaccustomed in Elizabeth's.

This old house was of two floors, a most unusual thing in that
country, the court-room, the dining-hall, the withdrawing-room
leading one from the other. Out of the court-room a stair led to a
loft that held the three bedrooms, two very small (in one of them
he had slept last night with David, in the other Alice Press with
the two little girls), and the other larger, containing a grand bed,
and in this his wife was still sleeping; Father Roche had a small
room below.

On the ground floor there was the entrance-hall and the
kitchen, and on to the kitchen abutted the farm-buildings rented
by Satterthwaite. These were a diminutive example of the yeoman's dwelling. This building was slated, the ridge made of what
were known as 'wrestlers', slates notched so as to interlock. The
rest was primitive enough, the upper floor open to the oaken beams,
an oak partition portioning off the sleeping-place for master and
mistress.

Below was the house-place, the parlour and the kitchen. A

man and his wife called Wilson had been caring for the house ever since the Herries family had forsaken it.

Coming down the rickety stair from the loft in the dim light, Francis Herries could see at once that their care had been neither vigilant nor arduous.

He stood in the dining-hall and looked about him. In that dim air without a sound in the world it seemed forlorn and desolate enough.

At the withdrawing-room end there was a raised dais, and at the court-room end, opposite the dais, some high oak screens, intricately carved.

Along one wall hung a fine spread of tapestry, fresh and living still, worked in colours of red, brown, amber, dark purple, its subject a hunting-scene, so handsomely wrought that all the wall seemed alive with straining hounds and noble horses, huntsmen winding their horns, and for their background dark hills and clustering trees.

This was a fine piece, and Herries, looking at it, wondered that it should be so well preserved. For the rest the hall was furnished barely – one long oak table, some stiff-backed chairs, a carved chest, and a portrait hanging above the dais.

It was this portrait that drew now Herries's attention. In the dim light it seemed marvellously alive. He did not question but that it was the portrait of old great-great-grandfather Herries himself. It had been undoubtedly painted after his coming to Herries, possibly by some wandering artist who had strayed into these wilds or by some London friend passing through Kendal on his way to Scotland – whoever had executed it, he was, in that wavering light, alive and dominating. An old man, his face wrinkled and seamed, his head poked forward out of some dark furs, his eyes dimmed, half closed, and one thin hand stretching forward out of the picture, as though to seize some prize or arrest some attention.

What Francis Herries felt, looking at it, was that there was here an odd resemblance to himself. Was it in the eyes? How could that be when his own were so bright and eager? Or the mouth? But this mouth was puffed and seemed as you looked at it to tremble. Or the skinny neck between the furs? Or the grasping hand? He looked at it, nodded his head as though the sight of it had decided some problem for him, and passed on down the stairs, through the shabby little entrance-hall into the open.

Behind the house he found an old-fashioned pump, and

leaning against the wall, scratching his head and yawning, was Benjamin.

By the side of the pump was a wooden bucket. He signed to Benjamin to come and help him, stripped (this was the blind side of the house, and in any case he did not care who might see him). Benjamin splashed him. The water was ice-cold. He pulled on his breeches again, bid Benjamin rub his chest and back. He was in a splendid glow.

Over the low wall he could see the lights of the sky clustering about Glaramara's shoulders. Long swaths of yellow lay across the pale ivory, and the edge of the hills rippled with fire. A bird sang, a little uncertainly, from the yews, and in the fresh stillness other birds could be heard beating their way through the shining air.

Benjamin, his mouth open, stared at his master, waiting for orders.

'Strip, you devil,' Francis Herries said, laughing. 'You are sodden with sleep.' Benjamin stripped at once, and his plump, stout body began to shiver and quake as the cold air caught his flesh. Francis laughed, then filled the bucket and splashed the water over the man, who did not, however, flinch, but stood there, shaking, but at attention.

'I will repay your courtesy,' Francis said, and seizing him, rubbed his naked body with a ferocious vigour. Then, giving him a kick with his soft slippers, cuffed him on the cheek and bid him put on his clothes.

'How does this place seem to you, Benjamin?'

Benjamin, pulling up his breeches, answered:

'We shall come to a handsome knowledge of one another's customs, hidden here from the world – but 'tis a good place for horses.'

Francis Herries looked about him. 'I haven't seen so clear a water nor smelt so fresh an air for years. But you can leave me when you will. I'll have no man stay who's a grumbler.'

'If I would leave you, master,' Benjamin answered with that odd, half-sulky, half-humorous speech that was so especially his, 'I'd have left you long ago. There's been often reason enough.'

'Why do you stay then?' asked Herries.

Benjamin, rubbing his wet head, answered: 'I can't tell. There's no reason for why I do things.' He paused, then added: 'Where you are, master, there's food and dogs and horses. Day come, day go, life is the same anywhere in the world, I fancy.'

'And when I beat you?'

'All men are beaten,' answered Benjamin, shuffling inside his clothes. 'I'd sooner be beaten by you than another.' He added, looking about him at the hills as though he were seeing them for the first time – 'The fellow in the house tells me there's fine bull-baiting, wrestling and other games round these parts. Life's not over for us yet, master,' and, as he shuffled off with his fat walloping walk he grinned at Herries, showing himself half servant, half friend; half hireling, to be kicked, beaten, abused; half equal, knowing secrets and sharing confidences that must breed equal contact.

As he turned to go back into the house Herries saw, looking at him from the corner of the housewall, an old, bent, infinitely aged woman. She had long, white, ragged hair, and a thin, yellow face. She stood without moving, looking at him.

'Who's that?' he asked Benjamin.

'The house-man's mother.'

The old woman raised her hand as though to feel the wind, then disappeared.

He went into the house to see his wife. The bedroom was dark. He pulled back the curtains and then stood by the window looking across at her. That was a fine bed in which she was lying, the curtains of faded crimson velvet, the woodwork splendidly carved. Crimson velvet, torn and shabby, was tacked also on to some of the panelling of the walls. There was a portrait of a young lady in a green dress and a white ruff over the fireplace.

His wife was yet sleeping. He came to the bed and stood there watching. There was something pathetic in poor Margaret Herries as she lay there, happy for a while at least in dreamless slumber. All the anxieties, woes and bewildered distresses that attacked, so increasingly, her waking life were for the moment stilled.

She looked a fool as she slept. She was a fool, she would always be one, but there was something gentle, kindly, appealing in her stout characterless features. And it might be that there was more character there than anyone, herself most certainly, at this time knew.

Maybe Herries, as he looked at her, felt something of this. Drawing his purple gown closely around him, he gazed at her, lost in his own disappointed ironical thoughts.

Why in folly's name had he ever married her? They had been young enough, he eighteen, she seventeen. They had been idiots enough, he vain beyond all vanity, she adoring beyond all conceivable adoration; she had been pretty, innocent and wealthy.

Her father, Ephraim Harden, a very successful City merchant, had died a year before their meeting, her mother being already long-time dead. She was an only child and sent to an aunt in Carlisle on a holiday. They had met at a Carlisle ball, he handsome, without a penny, loathing the dull life at Seddon, where he hung on because he had no means wherewith to live in any other more lively place.

Seddon was still his brother Pomfret's at that time, and Francis and his brother Harcourt were permitted to remain there on a kind of tolerating sufferance. How he had hated that place with its dull grey walls, its poverty and greasy indolence. You might say that this place, Herries, to which he had now come was dull and grey enough, but, from the first moment seen on that moonlit night, he had thrilled to it. It had touched, and he knew this absolutely, some deep fundamental chord in him.

But Seddon and brother Harcourt! Harcourt with his thin, shanky frame, peering eyes and most exasperating cough, his passionate absorption in his books, so that he was only happy when they were piled high around him, sending up their dusty thick smell on every side of him. Harcourt who, in his twenties, had been a gay spark in London, an acquaintance of Swift and Addison and Steele, who had helped in the exposure of the great Psalmanazar, been present at the trial of John Tutchin, and even spent an evening with the infamous Mrs Manley of the *New Atalantis*!

But as Harcourt had grown, his zeal for letters had grown with him; he had abandoned the town, buried himself in Seddon with his books, and then, at Francis's marriage, taken himself to the sea-coast, near Ravenglass, where he lived, a contented hermit.

It had not been altogether Francis's desire for money that had driven him into marriage with Margaret Harden. His motives were never unmixed in anything that he did, always there was nobility with his greed, tenderness with his cruelty, humour with his pessimism. He cared for her prettiness and innocence. He might have had her without the marriage ceremony, her body and her money too, she adoring him so that from the first moment she could deny him nothing, and he did not.

Nor was it only his weariness with Seddon. From the first he had realized that it was likely that Margaret Harden would weary him more than ever Seddon had done. He had felt a tenderness (which he might now allow was principally a weak sentiment) for this lonely orphaned girl, tied, until some man should carry her away, to the strings of a dumpy, frowzy aunt whose only interest was in cards and the scandals of the country town.

He had been stung to the venture also by the sharp pleasures of rivalry. The neighbouring squires, the sparks of the little town, even some of the graver, more aged officers of the garrison, had seen in Miss Harden's pretty face and splendid fortune an exciting prize. But from the first moment of Francis Herries's appearance there had been no chance for any other. He had been for her, poor silly fool, the god of all her dreams and maiden longings.

Yes, she had been cheated as vilely as he – nay, in the issue of it, much more vilely. She was no judge of men, poor thing, and had thought him as noble in character as he was handsome in person. The aunt, tired swiftly of the burden of this innocent girl for whom cards were too intricate a pleasure, and scandal too distressing a pastime, was delighted to have her off her hands.

Herries had, indeed, considered the thing at some surprising length for a boy so young, but even at that age he had no illusions about himself, knew himself very well for what he was. But he wanted the money, her face pleased him, he had a certain kindness for her, and so the thing had been.

Looking down at her now he could not believe that, so short a while back, she had been that pretty, slender girl. Marriage had at least agreed so far with her that, in the very first year, she had begun to thicken. The three children that had come to her (the only happiness the poor lady had known) had not assisted her beauty; you could not believe that now she was but twenty-nine years of age.

And he would swear that all their quarrels and distress had not been his fault alone. She had never tried at all to grow to his taste and wishes; she had developed in nothing during the twelve years of their life together. She had no curiosity, no inquisitiveness, no sensitiveness, no humour – only sentiment, a liking for good food, a weak indulgence of the children and an infinite capacity for tears. Unfortunately all his ill-temper, his infidelities, his squandering of her fortune had not caused her to love him less; rather she adored him more today than when she had married him. Even this last insult, of carrying Alice Press to this place with them, had not stirred her resentment.

It was that above all that irked him. Although he had tried again and again to kill it, he had deep shame at his treatment of her – a shame that never drove him to better behaviour, but that for ever irritated and vexed him. Had she abused him, sworn at him, there would have been some reason for him to despise himself less, but this submission to his unkindness made him, when he was conscious of it, hate her for his reproach of himself.

Not one of his mistresses had ever been anything to him, and Alice Press the least of all. He had taken them in a kind of impatient scorn of their eagerness. What did it matter, one thing more or less, since all had gone so ill?

She was stirring. She raised her arm, let it fall again, sighed in her half-sleep, sighed again and woke. Seeing him, she gave a little cry. He must have looked wild enough standing there in the half-light, his shaven head with its short, bristling hairs, his chest showing bare through the lapels of the bed-gown.

'Francis!' she said, and smiled that trusting, half-deprecating, appealing smile that he so thoroughly detested.

'It is a fair morning,' he answered, 'and time you were about.'

'I know.' She raised herself, putting her hand modestly over her breasts. 'I was dreaming. I dreamt that my Aunt Hattie was here again and her dog Pompey, and that she was giving it chocolate.'

'Thank God,' he answered grimly, 'that the reality is more gracious. You are at Herries, and the cesspool below this window is in full odour, and there is a witch in the house.'

'A witch?' she cried, alarmed. She was crammed with superstitions, old wives' tales of warlocks and broomsticks, prophecies and magic spells.

'A witch. I saw her but now alight on her broomstick, scratch a flea from her ear and whisper with her familiar hedgehog.'

Margaret Herries smiled that nervous smile with which she always greeted his pleasantries, not knowing whether he were in jest or earnest; whichever way her conclusion went she was always wrong.

Now she thought that he was jesting and tittered. Also she was but half awake and could not see his face clearly in the half-light. He came nearer to the bed and bent over her. He was moved by one of those sudden and to himself most exasperating impulses of compassion.

'You had best stay where you are,' he said. 'The last week has been exhausting enough for a hide-bound alligator.' He smiled, sat down on the high bed's edge and touched her hand.

'Lie here, and the woman shall bring you some food.'

Margaret was awake enough now. Any kindness from this

adored husband set her heart wildly beating, her cheeks flushing, her tongue dry in her mouth.

'If you think it wise—' she stammered. She had a desperate impulse to press his hand, even to put her arm up, pull his head towards her and embrace him, but she knew by bitter experience how dangerous those actions would be. Her hand lay pulsing in his.

'Margaret,' he said, 'if you find that I have done you wrong to bring you here, if you cannot endure the remoteness of the place and the savagery of the inhabitants, you must go for intervals of every year to some town. York is not so far – even Scotland. There is Carlisle . . .' He broke off, remembering certain old scenes in Carlisle.

'And you shall take the children with you. Only you shall not keep David too long. I have done wrong to bring you to this forsaken country.'

The flush yet on her cheeks, she answered:

'Whilst you care to have me here, Francis, I care to stay.'

It was the most aggravating thing that she could have said. It called up in its train a thousand stupidities, placidities, nervousnesses, follies that had, in their time, driven him crazy with irritation. Never a mind of her own, always this maddening acquiescence and sentimental fear of him.

He drew his hand away.

'The rocks that hem us in are not more implacable than your amiability, my dear. I remember that your aunt, prophesying (how truly!) our wedded bliss, said that you had a nature, mild, trustful and clinging. With what knowledge of human character she spoke! Cards and the frailties of her neighbours yielded her human wisdom. Then you shall not go – you shall stay and love and cherish your husband, caring nothing for the odour of the cesspool, the machinations of the household witch, the rustic brutalities of the neighbouring yeomen! I will see that some food comes to you.'

He got up from the bed with that abrupt, impatient movement that she knew so well. She recognized, poor lady, that she had already lost her momentary advantage, how she could not tell.

She looked at him, loving his every feature, then said:

'Yes, Francis, I thank you.'

She was an exasperating woman. As he went from her room he felt that he did not care how unhappy she might be in this desolation to which she had come. She might make friends with the pigs for all that he cared, and good luck to her. And she was but twenty-nine and growing fatter with every hour! Was ever man so cursed?

And yet once again, as, later in the day, he rode out on his black horse, Mameluke, he was affected by his compassion. He had escaped them all; he had not stayed for the meal which now that it was past three o'clock would soon be on the table. He must be alone and facing his own strange thoughts.

At first, as Mameluke trotted quietly along the rough path, he did not notice the country round him. He saw for a while nothing but himself and he saw himself in a mirror, his features caricatured by the distorting glass, his body lengthened to a hideous leanness, his forehead peaked to a white cone-shaped dome. Well, thus he was – and thus. This sudden quiet, this hush of the fields and sharp, refreshing coldness of the air seemed to bring the issue of the situation before him in sharper form than it had taken for many months.

The issue was this – that unlike all the men and women that he knew, the squires and boon-companions of Doncaster, the women, loose and otherwise – alone of them all he longed for something that he could not touch. He had a vision, a vision that took, when he was with Father Roche, a religious shape, when he was with Alice Press a fleshly, with little David a pride in family, with the beauty of landscape and fine stuffs and rare pieces a poetic, but all these only forms and vestures of a vision that was none of them, but of which thing all were. And with this vision there was the actuality of his life – his life wasteful, idle, cruel, sensual, selfish, vain. He did not, as he rode now on Mameluke, turn his head away from a single aspect of it.

He had once dreamed a dream. It was some five years back at the end of a race-meeting in Doncaster. He had stayed in an inn in the town for the night. Drinking heavily, he was yet not drunk as were his companions. He had shared a room with one of them, pulled his boots off him, flung him down on his bed, where he lay loathsomely snoring. Himself he had gone to the window, pushed it open and stared out on a splendid night flaming with stars.

And there, it had seemed, propped forward on a little chair, his head almost through the window (so that he might easily have tumbled on to the cobbles below), he had fallen asleep. Had he slept or no? How many times since then he had asked himself that question! In any case, through his dream he had seemed to hear the sounds of the night. The slow, lazy call of the watchman, the love duet of cats, the rumbling of a country cart on distant cobbles, the snores of his neighbour, these had been behind and through his dream.

His eyes open, he would have sworn, staring into the stars he had beheld a vision. He was in a region of vast, peaked, icy mountains. Their fierce and lonely purity, as silver-pointed they broke the dark sky, caused him to cry out with wonder. The sky was dark; the mountains glittering white, they ringed round a small mere or tarn, black as steel in shadow.

There was absolute silence in this world. Then as he looked he saw a great white horse, glorious beyond any ever beheld by man, come, tossing his great white mane, to the edge of the mere. He hesitated, lifting his noble head as though listening, then plunged in. He swam superbly, tossing his mane, and Francis could see silver drops glistening in the icy air. He swam to the farther edge; and then Francis was seized with an agonizing terror lest he should not be able to climb, out of the mere, up the icy sides of the cliff that ran sheer into the water. That moment of suspense was fearful and compounded of a great love for the splendid horse, a great tenderness, a great reverence and an anguish of apprehension.

Then, tossing his mane once more, the beautiful horse mounted out of the mere, strode superbly across the ice and vanished. Then, again, there was great loneliness.

Waking from this dream and staring back at the little room, stuffy and smelling of drink, the floor tumbled with clothes, his thick, open-mouthed, red-faced companion, he knew an instant of acute, terrible disappointment. For a moment he thought that he would throw himself out, end everything, so as to kill the disappointment; and perhaps it would have been as well had he done so, because, since then, that disappointment had been always with him.

The more that he had hated the noise and filth and confusion of his life in Doncaster, the more he had plunged into it. Now, as he slowly passed along the darkening path that was leading him gradually into the shadow of the hills, he saw one incident after another of the Doncaster life, stretching out their hands to him as though they were figures that kept pace with him. The foolish duel with young Soltery, a quarrel about nothing when they were both drunk, Soltery who was terrified, and then more terrified yet that he should seem terrified. He saw young Soltery's eyes now, as they faced one another in the early morning light on the fields outside Doncaster, eyes of a frightened, bewildered child – and he had shot away one of young Soltery's ears, so that he would be disfigured for life.

Or fat Maitchison the surgeon with his brilliance, his obscenity, his odd beliefs in magic and other humbug – that foolish night in Maitchison's rooms when they had defied the Devil, smashed the mirror, stripped Maitchison's mistress naked and painted her yellow. He could see now the room, furniture overturned, the glass of the big mirror scattered over the floor, and fat Maitchison with gusts of drunken laughter painting the naked back of the swearing girl . . . And the sudden opening of the door, the breeze blowing in from the street, the candles going out, and someone crying that bats were hanging on the ceiling . . .

Yes, the races, the cock-fights, the bull- and bear-baiting, the debauchery and smells and noise – a roaring in his ears, a stink at his nostrils, and always in his heart this longing for the icy peaks of his dream, the black tarn, the splendid horse with the snow-white mane.

He was young, and should do something with his talents. That he was talented he knew. They all told him so. He had infinite courage, splendid physique, an interest and curiosity in many things. What should it be? Which way should he go? And meanwhile the years slipped by, and now, obeying some mad, mysterious impulse, he had cut himself right off, hidden himself among the savages.

Was he to laze here, slouching about, making familiars of the yeomen, riding with them, chaffing their wives, perhaps seducing their daughters?

For what had he come here? He only knew that already the place was working into his veins – the silence, the air with an off-scent of ice in it, the hills that were perhaps only little hills and yet had so strong a power – witchcraft hills, hiding in their corners and wrinkles magic and spells. As he rode on, the outside world was beginning to slip ever farther and farther away from him. His was the only figure in the landscape; the whole country, as the afternoon shadows lengthened, seemed naked. Above the clustered group of mountains at the end of the valley a little minaret of pale grey clouds was forming, one cloud stealing upon another as though with some quiet purpose; a purple shadow fell over these hills as though a cloak had been suddenly dropped over them.

He saw on his right then a group of buildings. His empty world was in a moment peopled with life. Near him at the fork of the road was a small crowd gathered about a pedlar who had slung his box off his neck and rested it on a flat stone. Herries drew nearer and, sitting his horse, watched quietly.

The scene that had been a moment before wild and haunted was now absolutely domestic. Three healthy, red-faced girls stood there, their arms about one another's necks, laughing and giggling, one stout yeoman, some farm boys, and a little man, tow-coloured like a wisp of hay, who, by his drab dress, should be one of those itinerant parsons and schoolmen who went from house to house in country districts, taking odd services of a Sunday and teaching the children.

The pedlar was a tall, thin scarecrow of a man, having on his head a peaked faded purple hat, and round his neck some of the coloured ribbons that he was for selling. By his speech, which was cultivated, he was no native, and, indeed, with his sharp nose and bright eyes he seemed a rascal of unusual intelligence.

The little scene was charming in its peace and security. Some cattle were being brought across the long field, two dogs at their heels; a voice calling in rising and falling cadence sounded, as it seemed, from the hills, and in the foreground there was the sharp humorous note of the pedlar, the laughter of the girls and young men and, once and again, the deep Cumbrian accents of the yeoman.

At first they had not noticed Herries, but when one of the girls, looking up, gave a cry of surprise, they were not disturbed, and after a glance went on with their private affairs, governed by a certain dignity and independence of their own.

The pedlar, however, was aware of him although he continued his patter. He had 'Fine thread satins both striped and plain, Persia nets, anterines, silks for scarves and hoods, shalloons, druggets, and some Scotch plaids.' On his tray there were some pieces of fine bone lace, Chinese boxes, necklaces, gold rings set with vermilions, several gold buttons, and red watch bottles ribbed with gold – or he said it was gold. And some books. Chapbooks and calendars, *Poor Robin*, *The Ladies' Diary*, some old sheets of the *London Gazette*, and some bound volumes of Plays. These things of fashion looked strange in the open fields before the little country group, who fingered and laughed and fingered again. The jewellery, indeed, had a false air, but the ribbons and lace were pretty, and above, Herries must fancy, the purses of the locals. Herries noticed, too, that the pedlar did not seem too intent upon his sales or purchases, and that his sharp eyes went everywhere, and especially to Herries and his horse.

He thought to himself that this would not be the last time that he would see that pedlar.

The shadows of the hills now covered the valley; the light flashed palely above Glaramara and then fell. Herries turned his horse towards home. As he moved away the little tow-haired parson detached himself from the others and approached him.

His long parson's coat was green with age, shabby and stained, and his breeches were tied about the knees with string, his bony fingers purple with cold, his nose red; but he had about him a very evident dignity. He bowed, but not subserviently.

'It has been a fine afternoon,' he said, keeping pace with Mameluke's gentle step.

Herries, impressionable ever to the moment's atmosphere, his spirit touched now by some quiet and happiness, answered, as he could when he so pleased, with charm and courtesy.

'The day falls quickly in these valleys.'

'And the light is for ever changing,' the little clergyman answered with pleased eagerness. 'You are newly arrived here, sir?'

'But yesterday.'

'I know everyone in this neighbourhood – man, woman and child. You are the gentleman who has come to Herries by Rosthwaite?'

'I am,' answered Herries.

'There has been much interest in your coming, sir. It will be the wish of everyone that you will find it pleasant here, and stay with us.'

'Do you also belong here?' asked Herries.

'I do the Lord's will and go whither He sends me. For some years now I have taught the children of these villages, assisted at services, done what the Lord has bidden me.'

'You are not a native of Cumberland then?'

'No, sir, I am from the South. I was born in Bideford in Devon. For many years I was chaplain to the Earl of Petersham.'

'Why, then, have you come here? It must seem a severe exile to you.'

'The Lord spoke to me in a dream and ordered me to go North. I was to walk forward until I saw a naked man tied to a tree, and in that place to abide and do His will.'

'Where saw you your naked man?'

'After many months, begging and preaching my way through the country, I came at last to the village of Grange on a summer evening. And above the river where the bridge is, I saw a man naked and bound with ropes to a tree. The men of the village were throwing stones at him: he was near death. He had been caught robbing a yeoman of the place of two hens. I urged them to release him, the Lord prevailed, and afterwards I lodged in his house. I lodge there yet.'

'And what, then, do you teach the children?' asked Herries, entertained by this simplicity.

'The Lord's Word, the Catechism, and, when they wish it, Greek and Latin.'

'You have no family?'

'My wife is with God.'

The dark was falling more swiftly now, and it was difficult to see the path. Herries jumped off his horse and walked beside the clergyman.

'What is your name?' he asked him.

'Robert Finch.'

'How shall I like this place? It is cut off from the world.'

There was a sudden odd note of scorn in the little man's voice as he answered:

'It *is* the world, sir. Here within these hills, in this space of ground is all the world. I thought while I was with my lord Petersham that the world was there, but in every village through which I have passed since then I have found the complete world – all anger and vanity and covetousness and lust, yes, and all charity and goodness and sweetness of soul. But most of all, here in this valley, I have found the whole world. Lives are lived here completely without any thought of the countries more distant. The mountains close us in. You will find everything here, sir. God and the Devil both walk on these fields.'

'And if I believe neither in God nor the Devil?'

'You are a young man for such confident disbelief. God was speaking to me now, and has told me that you will find everything that you need for the growth of your soul here in this valley. You have come to your own place, sir. You are young and strong, but the day will come when you will remember my words.'

Herries looked back down the path. In the dusk he could see it point like a pale, crooked finger straight at the heavy black hump of Glaramara that was dark against lighter dark. Again he felt ice in the air and shivered.

'They are little hills by your foreign sort,' he said, 'and yet they impress.'

The small voice beside him answered:

'They are the loveliest hills in all God's world.' Then it continued, taking another tone, very mild and a little anxious: 'You have children, sir?'

'Three,' answered Herries.

'If you were in need—' he hesitated. 'My Greek and Latin are good, and I have authority with children. If I could serve you—'

Herries laughed.

'I must warn you,' he said, 'there is a priest in the house.'

There was a pause while the wind, rising, began to blow fiercely, swaying the branches and turning the dead leaves about their feet.

The voice began again: 'He instructs your children?'

'A little.'

'Your own religion?—'

'Nay, I am no Catholic. I have told you I have no religion. How think you, Mr Finch? In this drunken, debauched world what is your God engaged upon? He is busy elsewhere improving some other planet.'

'Christ died upon the Cross suffering a worse bewilderment.'

Herries laughed again.

'Well, you shall try your luck upon them. But we are a wild house, Mr Finch, and may, in this desolate country, become yet wilder.'

They had come to the gate that led to Herries. They paused. To Francis's surprise the little man laid his hand on his arm.

'You are young, sir. I have ten years' advantage of you. I fancy your wildness does not frighten me.'

'On thy head be it then,' Herries cried, as he led Mameluke up the path. The way here was very rough, and he began to curse as he hit the loose stones, plunged into mud, fearing that his horse might stumble and damage his knees. His mood was changing with the swiftness that belonged to his moods. Oddly enough his mind had turned to Father Roche. The little clergyman had reminded him. Why was he burdened with this priest and the risks and penalties connected with his presence? It was true that just now there was a lull in the Catholic agitation, but it might burst out again at any instant. Herries did not doubt but that Roche was busied in a thousand intrigues both political and religious, and they were intrigues with which he had no sort of sympathy. Jacobitism made no appeal to him – he hated the French influence behind it. He wanted no king for England who would be ruled by French money and ambition. Moreover, he took in any case but little interest in politics, and had no romantic feeling for that world. Nor had the Catholic religion attraction for him; he despised what seemed to him its mummery, the child's play, as he saw it, of its tinkling bells and scented air. But Roche's influence over him was strong and subtle. Ever since his first meeting with the man some five years before, it had persisted. And for what reason? Roche was stern, unsympathetic to all Herries's pleasures, showed no warmth of feeling to Herries (no warmth of feeling to anyone, indeed, save little David), used Herries's house quite openly for his own private purposes, had carried on in Doncaster, as Herries well knew, a network of plans and plots with an odd audacity and defiance. When he spoke intimately with Herries it was to rebuke him. And yet Herries would endure from him things that from another he would most furiously resent. Where lay Roche's power? In the continued suggestion that he held somewhere a solution for Herries's sickness of soul? Not in any dogma lay that solution, but in something deeper, something far more profound . . .

But (and here the house with its lighted windows loomed suddenly up before him as though it had been pushed up through the rough ground) was the priest to remain? Why? He and Alice Press should both be sent packing. One must start fair in this new place – and for a moment before he pushed back the heavy door he had a picture before his eyes of the country group in the fading afternoon light, the coloured scene, the quiet and the animals and the purple-shaded hills. Here in this good land there should be no place for the priest and the woman . . . Here in this good land – and a moment later he was caught into one of his dark, bestial, frantic rages.

He had left his horse outside the door and, calling Benjamin, pressed up the staircase to the little tapestried dining-hall. A high, thick-clustered candelabrum was burning on the table, all the candles blowing in the winds that came from the floor-cracks, the slits in wall, roof and window.

At the table his wife was seated crying. Alice Press, very gay in a crimson gown, was turning scornfully away from her, even as he entered. The three children were playing together by the oak chest. Over all the room there was a frantic disorder. Some of the boxes, brought by the pack-horses the night before, were there, and scattered about were suits, gowns, china, stuffs, linen, children's toys.

A strange thick scent of burning wax, damp straw and odours from the neighbouring cesspool lay heavy about the candle-shine.

He had ordered that the boxes were not to be touched until the morrow, when he could supervise the opening of them.

By whom had he been disobeyed? Both women began to chatter, his wife wailing, Alice Press loud and shrill and defiant. The little girls began to cry. At that moment Benjamin, a foolish smile on his chubby face, appeared at the stairhead.

Francis Herries caught him by the neck, then, raising the riding-whip that was still in his hand, cried:

'What said I to these boxes? Hast thou no wit, thou lubber-pated bastard?'

Benjamin shouted something; everyone began to call aloud at once. The room, the house, the world was filled with shouting and stink and a raging anger.

To come thus, from an afternoon so quiet and promising, to this vileness! Anger boiled in his heart, choking him. He had Benjamin's coat off his back, struck the bare flesh again and again, lashed him about the head, the legs, the thighs, and when suddenly the man hung his head and began to droop in his arms he let fall his whip and began to beat him with his hands, letting him at last drop, a huddled, half-naked heap.

The man had fainted. Raising Benjamin's head, Herries was suddenly remembering how that morning in the fresh air by the pump he had rubbed in friendliness the man's body while the birds wheeled through the sky.

A sickness caught him at the heart. He told David to run for some water, but before the boy had returned the man was reviving. He was lying back, his head on his master's knee. He looked up, then, flicking his eyelids, said:

'It was not by my word, master, that the boxes were opened.'

Clumsily he rose to his feet; he caught his coat to his bare chest—

'I'll be rubbing the horse down,' he said, and stumbled down the staircase.

FAMILY

POMFRET HERRIES lived at this time in one of the most beautiful houses in Keswick. It was beautiful, not by his own taste or fancy, but because he wished to have a better house than any one of his neighbours.

This has always been a habit with certain of the Herries. Desiring this, he chose for architect that strange, saturnine hermit, old John Westaway, known in Keswick for a madman and the best architect in the North, a desperate traveller who knew Italy as you might know Skiddaw, who had been invited again and again to London, but preferred to live in his little house above the river, seeing no one, liking no one, buried in his books and art treasures. All over the North Westaway's fame ran. He was an old man now, had been, it was said, in his youth the friend and intimate of Chesterman and Van der Vaart and Vanbrugh, a curmudgeon, a surly bachelor, in league, some whispered, with the Devil himself, pottering about that house, with its pictures and statuary, and his dark Italian servant – a devil, but the finest architect, it might be, in England.

He had made Pomfret pay for his fancy, and when it was done Pomfret had grumbled so that you might hear him from John o' Groat's to Land's End – but it was a beautiful house. People came from Kendal and Carlisle and Penrith to look at it, so that at the last Pomfret and his wife had grown proud of it and spoke of it as entirely their doing.

In fine proportion, its roof covered with red tiles, the wrought ironwork across its front showing like lace against the stone, the house was oblong without gables. The windows were for their period most modern. They were sash windows, a great rarity, and they were beautifully spaced. The doorway had fluted columns and over it there was a charming and delicate fanlight.

The house was outside the town near to Crosthwaite Church, and the gardens ran down to the weeds and rushes of the lake-end. The garden held lime trees and the lawn was bordered with tubs of orange and bay trees. There was a little terrace and a rosy wall of red brick, and beyond the formal garden a meadow, the lake and the rising hills. To the right some greenhouses, a flower garden and a kitchen garden.

Inside, the house was wide, spacious and full of light. First a pillared hall, on the right the parlour, on the left a fine, wide staircase opening into a splendid saloon. Beyond the parlour a large bedroom leading to a greenhouse. On the upper floor other bedrooms.

Pomfret's chief pride was the saloon, the decoration of which Westaway had designed and executed – the subject was Paris awarding the apple. Lady Herries had been disturbed by the naked goddesses until it was seen that no one else minded.

In this fine house Pomfret inhabited only one room, a dusky

apartment crowded with guns, stuffed animals and fishing-rods. Here he drank merrily with his friends.

Lady Herries's home was the parlour, where she read her medicine books, scolded the maids, suffered in a bitter silence that ancient lady, Pomfret's aunt, fed a screaming macaw, and gave her neighbours tea and chocolate. The three children had their own room far away at the top of the house.

There was a great array of domestics, from Mrs Bellamy the housekeeper to little Peter the black boy, who had been purchased in London, shivered in the cold, and stole everything that he, with safety, might.

Mrs Bellamy was of the family of Mrs Slipslop, and made all the mischief both in the house and in the neighbourhood that time and talents permitted her.

They could scarcely be called a united family, for they were never together. Pomfret diced, drank, rode, hunted with his masculine friends, who liked his company because he was stupid enough for them to rob him at will. Jannice, his wife, bullied him when she was with him, forgot him when she was not. She loved him only when he was ill, and this was often enough, for his intemperate habits and his swinish feeding caused him constant attacks of biliousness and vertigo. There was nothing that Jannice Herries loved like a medical treatise; her familiar and, after Mrs Bellamy, most constant companion was old Dr Ellis, who would discuss with her by the hour the whole works of that excellent practical physician, Dr Thomas Sydenham!

She experimented on her staff, her family and any neighbours who would permit her. Little Peter, who was sick every other day from stealing confitures from the store-room, was her most unhappy patient. And yet, of course, this is not all that can be said about Pomfret and his lady. At heart they were kindly and well-dispositioned. Only they had no imagination, and had been covered with a thin skin of wealth that, like a rash upon their souls, discomforted them, made them uneasy, suspicious, unhappily proud.

Pomfret loved his children, but did not know how to approach them. He cuffed them and spoiled them and cuffed them again. He was generous-natured and desired that his friends should be happy, but he suspected that they laughed at him, and so was pompous and grand when he wished to be easy and familiar.

His money he had made, as he well knew, from his obedience to the advice of a London friend, Hartwell, who, at a certain moment, had directed his affairs.

Although his companions robbed him he had wisdom sufficient to leave his affairs in Hartwell's hands. He pretended to a knowledge of commerce and exchange; it was, as he knew in his heart, a bare pretence. He did nothing well, rode badly, shot badly, fished badly. He knew moments of great unhappiness.

Jannice Herries was also without imagination. She was acrimonious and bitter, but she knew that this was not her real life. Somewhere real feeling was hidden, but day succeeded day and nothing was done. She knew that she was unpopular among the ladies of Keswick, but she swallowed every compliment that Mrs Bellamy gave her, and at the end was more lonely than before.

After her interest in medicine her most active passion was her hatred for Pomfret's Aunt Maria, that very ancient lady, who, born in 1645 and for a time in the fashionable world, was now a hideous remnant of a dead and musty past. She longed for this old lady to die, and would have poisoned her ere this, but alone of the household Aunt Maria refused all of her niece's drugs. She was now eighty-five years of age.

Finally with both Pomfret and his lady there remained a constant uneasiness about their wealth. It had come so oddly, without any true justification. It might go as oddly again. They had witnessed in the last twenty years a series of financial panics. Now with the abominable French ready for any villainy, all this new-fangled independence of servants and labourers, who knew what the next event might be? The Catholics were listening at every window. Why, here was Francis Herries coming to live in the neighbourhood and bringing with him quite openly a rascally priest. Although Walpole and the Whigs were in, who knew how strong was their power?

Jannice Herries's favourite remark to Mrs Bellamy was: 'Things are not as they were.'

To which Mrs Bellamy with a shudder would reply: 'No, my lady. If I know my own mind there was never a truer word spoken.'

'And what will you do, Bellamy, if your master is ruined?'

'Heaven strike me dead if I ever desert you, my lady! Marry come up, don't I know a virtuous place when I see one?'

But Bellamy had been lining her pocket for many a year, and being Mrs Bellamy only by courtesy had her eye on a handsome victualler in Kendal, whose hearth and home she proposed to encompass and govern on the first signs of distress in the Herries country.

The three children, Anabel, Raiseley and Judith, lived in their

own world. They, like their father, were Herries of the unimaginative, matter-of-fact breed. They took things as they came, and
each, in his or her own fashion, worked quietly and obstinately
for personal profit. Anabel was good-natured, plump and easy.
Raiseley was clever. It would not be true of him to say that he was
without imagination, but it was imagination of an educational
kind.

He was studious, priggish, aloof and cold, rarely roused to
anger but unforgetful of the slightest injury. He had the wise,
calculating side of the Herries blood; he was studious, honest to
chilliness, and despised both his father and his mother. Judith
would be beautiful; she was dark and slender and already
cherished her beauty as her most important asset.

These three were all typical Herries on the stony side of the
family character. They saw everything in front of their noses and
nothing beyond. They did not mind in the least their social isolation. They might condemn one another, but united at once in
condemnation of all other children.

They were waiting now in their high, chilly room for the visit
that their cousin in Borrowdale was to pay them. Only the little
boy, they understood, was coming with his father and mother.
They had already gathered from the conversation of their elders
that Uncle Francis was a disgrace.

Of the three of them at this time it may be said that Raiseley
and Judith held out no hope of later humanity; for Anabel,
because of her good-nature and a certain carelessness that went
with it, there were possibilities.

On this afternoon the three children were in their chill room
quietly busy. Judith was seated motionless in a high chair, a collar
round her neck, a board tied to her back. This was for her figure.
She was watching the grandfather clock in the corner. Five
minutes of her daily half-hour remained. This half-hour was
valued greatly by her, because she knew that this discipline was
for the benefit of her beauty. She was only nine years of age, but
had already a grave and considered air. Anabel, who was
thirteen, was curled up in the window-seat looking at the pictures
of some chap-books, *Babes in the Wood, Bluebeard, Little Tom
Thumb*. But she was not reading. She knew the old stories by
heart. She was wondering what her little cousin would be like.

She, unlike her brother and sister, was sometimes lonely. She
confessed it to no one, but she loved parties and fun. Maybe this
little boy would be agreeable.

Raiseley was yawning over his Virgil. Mr Montgomery, who

came every day to teach him Latin and Greek, had but just now gone.

'Jam pater Aeneas . . .' murmured Raiseley, and fingered a little box in which he had a cocoon concealed. He hid this from his parents and Mr Montgomery, because they would disapprove if they knew. But soon the cocoon would be liberated. No one told him any of the things that he wanted to know about animals, about the stars. Now, when he thought of these things, a new expression came into his eyes. He was suddenly alive with a questioning, investigating alertness. His cold, pale, pointed features gained an interesting sharpness. The book fell from his hand. There were many things that he would know one day; they should not stop him pursuing his knowledge. Mr Montgomery with his sing-song voice, his perpetual cold at the nose, his eagerness to please, how Raiseley despised him!

He would like to see Mr Montgomery whipped as little Peter was whipped, or standing as the man they had seen one day in the pillory in the market, his face smeared with the mud and the yellow of the eggs that people had thrown at him. And, as he thought of these things, his face achieved an added sharpness, coldly, intellectually speculative— 'Jam pater Aeneas . . .'

He looked at the little pile of books beside him – *A Guide to the English Tongue*, by Thomas Dyche, schoolmaster in London; *Paul's Scholars' Copy-Book*, by John Raynor; *The Use of the Globes*.

He did not look at them resentfully. He would extract from them everything that they had to give him.

'Judith,' he said, 'I should know more than Mr Montgomery knows in a year or two. I would think it fine to see him in the pillory as a week back we saw that man.'

Judith, motionless, her eyes on the clock, answered: 'We are to go downstairs when our uncle and aunt come. I am to wear the grey-blue.'

Anabel, from the window, said: 'I like David for a boy's name.'

'I heard them say,' went on Raiseley, 'that Uncle Francis is always drunken and beats Aunt Margaret.'

'But he is very handsome,' said Judith. 'He was wearing such fine clothes the other day that Father was shabby beside him.'

'Fine clothes,' said Raiseley scornfully, 'and they living in mud and dirt up to their elbows! They say that Borrowdale is full of witches and giants – wolves too. I would like mightily to see a wolf. I shall ask Uncle Francis to take me.'

The clock struck the half-hour. Judith very carefully separated herself from her board and collar. At that same moment the door opened. They were told that it was time for them to dress.

David and his mother had indeed already arrived.

Poor Margaret Herries had been for weeks dreading this visit. It was now a month since they had come to Herries, and the weather had been so terrible that the ride to Keswick had been impossible. It had rained and rained; not as it rained in Doncaster, with gusts and flurries and pauses and whispering, but in a drenching flood, falling from the grey, lowering sky like sheets of steel.

And the mountains had crept closer and closer, and the cold stolen into the very webbing of the sheets, the torn tapestries beating against the wall, and the mice boldly running for comfort to the peat fire. A horrible month it had been, but with all the courage at her command she had faced the rain, the isolation, her loathing for Alice Press, gathered her children round her as she might and made what she could out of the situation.

Oddly enough she had not been unhappy. Francis had been ever close at hand. He did not go off for nights at a time as he had done at Doncaster. That might come later – but at present it was as though the place cast a spell upon him. He pottered about the house, rode out to Stye Head, walked up Glaramara and the neighbouring hills, wandered along the lake by Manesty and Cat Bells, made himself known to some of the neighbouring yeomen, was silent often enough, drunken at times, angry once and again, but on the whole more her companion than he had been since their first marriage year.

And so there had increased in her heart her ever-constant loyalty to him. What she had suffered watching the degradation of his reputation during these past years no one would ever know. She would never tell. Here it was as though he had begun a new life. Stories long commonplace round Doncaster would here not be known. He would start again, and she would do everything in her power to assist him. Only his brother's family could spoil this fair beginning; she had seen and heard enough already to feel that Pomfret and his wife were Francis's detractors and would from the first take care to be dissociated from any scandal.

She was as fiercely prepared to fight her brother- and sister-in-law as any lioness in defence of her cubs, but her trouble was that she was not a lioness. She was a coward; while she was riding pillion behind her husband and her son, she was aware that at the first sight of Jannice in her own domain she would lose courage, she would tremble, she would show faint-heartedness. Francis had things that he must do in Keswick. He would come later to his brother's house to fetch her. She must face Pomfret and Jannice alone.

So she stood, David at her side, in the little hall with its rounded pillars, its stone floor in black and white squares, its fine picture of an Italian scene, with dim greys and purple for colour, hanging on the right of the staircase.

They were ushered into the parlour. It was lit with candles, and David had never seen such a room. But before he could examine the room he must be startled by the persons in it, by his Aunt Jannice, who was dressed superbly in a high wig mounted over a cushion and decorated with roses and daisies, her hoop spread about her, the outer skirt of crimson velvet and the front of her dress white and silver. On one brown cheek she wore a black patch. She was grander than any lady that he had ever seen; no one who came to their house in Doncaster had dressed like that. Young though he was, he realized that her thin, meagre figure and brown complexion ill suited such finery.

But his childish attention was soon drawn from his aunt to the terrific figure who sat in a high chair under the window. This was his Great-Aunt Maria.

He would never have believed, had he not seen it with his own eyes, that any person could be so old and yet live. Her wig of a bright brown colour was arranged in a fashion of fifty years ago, falling about her strange mask of a powdered, painted face in long curled ringlets. Over one eye was a black patch. Her green bodice was peaked, and her full, open sleeves were caught together with jewelled clasps. Her wide skirt was of purple satin. Her fingers, so thin that they were like the ivory sticks of a fan, were loaded with jewels.

On her lap was a small King Charles spaniel.

She appeared a painted image. Except for her one visible eye nothing in her face moved. David was a polite little boy, but again and again he had to stare. Here was a portent, a revelation in his young life.

The little black boy was standing behind Lady Herries's chair, and as soon as greetings had been exchanged they all sat down. The little black boy handed chocolate; a bright purple macaw in a gilt cage by the window screamed.

For a little while there was a terrible silence. The room was very hot; there was a large log fire. The sky beyond the window was bright with a silver glow.

When the talk had started David could look more easily about him.

He was indeed enchanted with the softness and beauty of everything. Beyond the wide window he could see the trim hedges, the paved path, the fountain with a strange stone bird, long-necked and violent-beaked, rising out of it, and beyond the fountain the line of trees guarding the waters of the lake.

Within the room there were countless objects that he longed to examine more closely, a screen worked in gold thread, a silver casket, a clock with the sun, moon and stars on its face. But more than these, the terrible old woman with her strange ringlets, her painted face, the cascades of her bright purple dress, the sharp-pointed fingers weighted with flashing jewellery . . .

'Indeed,' his aunt was saying, 'I wonder at Mr Flammery. 'Tis a poor child that doesn't know its own father, and there's a multitude of his own poor children must be in a fine confusion.'

This puzzled David, who, looking first at his aunt and then at his flustered mother sweating in the face with the heat of the room and the agitation of this her first so important visit, wondered how it could be that any child should not know its own father. He of a certainty knew his well enough.

'Yes, indeed,' his aunt continued, looking, as he was even now old enough to discern, with an odd mixture of curiosity and contempt at his mother. 'You must be well aware, Margaret, of the world into which you have come. In winter I doubt that you'll be able to move a step. You live in the heart of savages, and when the lake is too wild for passage and the roads all of a muck to your armpits the civilized world will be as distant from you as the Indies.'

'I don't doubt,' said Margaret, flushing and perspiring the more, for she knew that it was at her own abandoned Francis that these remarks were made, 'but that the days will pass. There's sufficient to do about the house to take a month of winters . . .'

David then was aware that his great-aunt's eye had turned in his direction. He was fixed by it as a rabbit by the eye of a snake . . . It was as though he, sitting on the edge of his chair, and this very ancient lady, both of them motionless, were holding some strange secret communication. Then he was aware of something further – that his great-aunt was about to speak.

In an odd, cracked but exceedingly piercing tone she said: 'God save His Gracious Majesty.'

The worst had happened. The old woman was silent often enough for days together, and this was well, because she was a burning fanatical Jacobite. The terrors into which her dangerous political opinions had again and again plunged Pomfret and his wife were both ludicrous and tragic. Sometimes for weeks she kept to her room, and on every occasion that saw her enter that sanctuary everyone about her breathed the hope that it would be for the last time, but her powers of revival were incredible, and down once more she would come to sit and watch and await her awful moment.

She had been born on the 14th of June, 1645, the day of the battle of Naseby, but her great days had been during the last years of Queen Anne, when she had known Godolphin and Marlborough and been received by Lady Masham, having her feet planted in both camps.

But she had been nevertheless, heart and soul, Jacobite, and, it was said, played some part in the intrigues of those last dramatic months. The Elector of Hanover had been for her the Devil himself, and when his cause had been definitely won she had retired from London, professed openly her Jacobite sentiments and chattered and prayed for the coming of the Day.

No one had much regarded her; she had lived in a small house in Winchester, until, her brain softening, Pomfret, driven by one of the kindest and gentlest impulses of his life, had given her shelter and protection.

How many thousands of times since then he had longed for her decease was a secret between himself and his Maker.

Now with terror and dismay Jannice Herries heard her speak. Here was their skeleton clattering straight out from the cupboard and before that fool Margaret Herries. But Margaret was too deeply buried in the warmth of her confusion to pay much regard. Only the little boy felt the power of those few cracked words; something spoke in his heart, some strange sympathy that he suddenly felt, to which he quite blindly and unknowingly responded. He was to remember at a later time this queer muffled moment.

The situation was immediately saved for Jannice Herries by the entrance of her children. The children had beautiful manners. Mrs Bellamy in black silk, her hands folded across her stomach, stood behind them – the boy bowed, the little girls curtsied. Anabel's eyes smiled at David. He was quick enough at once to perceive that the other girl was thinking of her own looks. She was like his own sister Mary in that.

And then the eyes of the two boys met, and they knew one another at once for foes. David had as friendly a heart as any

boy in the kingdom, but he realized an enemy when he saw one.
One straight look at Raiseley's cold reserve and proud consequence and something within him said: 'I hate my cousin.' Just
as the cracked voice of the old woman speaking to him five
minutes before out of an ancient past was to return to him with
significance in years to come, so that first glance exchanged with
Raiseley was to influence the Herries family fortunes for many
future generations.

Looking at Anabel, David thought to himself: 'That's a
friendly girl.' He was uncomfortable among these grown-up
persons, and hoped that it would be suggested that he should go
with his cousins to see the garden or their toys. He would like
finely to inspect more closely that fountain of the beaked bird or
to hunt among the reeds at the water's edge.

But no suggestion was made. He too was standing now, his
hands stiffly at his side as his father had taught him. The room
grew ever hotter and hotter, and with every moment he felt more
indignantly Raiseley's scornful eyes upon him.

Margaret Herries must talk to her nephew and nieces. She was
never at her ease with children.

'Fine children,' she said nervously to her sister-in-law, 'and
seemingly in grand health.'

The word 'health' was the trumpet to sound the charge to
Jannice Herries, who answered proudly: 'Fine and sound they
are, sister. Six months last sennight Judith here was sorely
threatened with the Falling Sickness – hast thou heard of the
Antepileptic Crow, sister?'

'I fear not,' said Margaret timidly.

''Tis a perfect cure for the Falling Sickness. Judith was cured
by the crow. Deplume and eviscerate a large crow, casting away
its Feet and Bill; put into its Belly the Heart, Liver, Lungs,
Bladder of the Gall, with Galangal and Aniseeds; bake it in a
new Earthen Vessel well shut or closed in an Oven with Household Bread; after it is cooled, separate the Flesh from the Sides
or Bones, and repeat this Operation of baking the second or third
time, but taking great care that it may not be burnt, then reduce
it into a fine powder.' She recited this in a high sing-song as
though it were poetry, her eyes almost closed. Opening them she
saw that Margaret was gazing at her with great humility and
reverence. Maybe the woman was not such a fool after all. She
would make, it might happen, something of a companion. A
kindliness stole about Jannice Herries's heart. It would be something to have a friendly creature near her whom she could

patronize and gratify and instruct. The days in truth were lonely enough . . .

'You must come and see us at Herries,' Margaret went on to the children.

'Yes, ma'am,' Raiseley answered, gravely bowing. 'It is said that there are wolves in Borrowdale. I would gladly see a wolf.'

Margaret smiled timidly. 'David shall show you the wolves. He has been already in the mountains. Have you not, David?'

Judith, who, since the Falling Sickness had passed as a topic, felt perhaps that she was not receiving sufficient attention, smiled her prettiest smile, so that her aunt, thinking how beautiful a child she was, said, speaking directly to her:

'My little girls, Mary and Deborah, will wish to show you their toys and babies.'

'Yes, ma'am,' said Judith in her softest, gentlest voice, so that her aunt looking at her loved her.

Once more they were interrupted, and this time it was the two men of the family. David waited for his father's entrance. First there was Uncle Pomfret, red-faced, noisy, with his: 'Well, then – here's all the family! Haste away! Haste away!' and then a sudden look of almost childish discomfort and unease. Quietly behind him David's father, kindly today and, for David, so handsome in his dark suit and lace ruffles that all the colour in the room went out before him, dimmed to abasement.

Yes, his father was in good humour today, coming forward and kissing the old lady's hand, saluting his sister-in-law's brown cheek, turning then to the children, pinching the cheeks of the girls, tapping Raiseley on his shoulder . . . How proud of him David was and how ardently longing for the moment to come when he would catch that glance and, perhaps, that smile. But for a while he did not. His father paid him no attention. The parlour was overcrowded with figures and the sound of Uncle Pomfret's demonstrations. Now he was being jolly with his children: 'You will be the death of your poor father . . . I promised your mother to give up half the afternoon to your entertainment, and wasn't I to show you the best pack of dogs in England? But no, Mr Montgomery don't allow. Pox on Mr Montgomery – and here's your uncle and little cousin come to visit us – yes, and your aunt too . . . Pleased to see you, sister . . . and there's no Mr Montgomery to stop a family welcome, odrabbit it! I am determined upon your being good children now and welcoming your little cousin . . . a fine boy, brother Francis. He shall come a-hunting. Canst ride, boy?'

'Yes, Uncle,' said David, 'a little.'

'That's more than thy cousin Raiseley can do then. Put him on a horse and he's like the Witch of Endor on a broomstick . . . Wilt thou learn to ride then, Raiseley, to please thy father?'

This public mockery was anguish to Raiseley, nor did he fail to ledger it in the account against his young cousin. But his pale face did not alter; no shadow of a change was upon it. Looking his father in the face, he answered steadily:

'I will learn, sir, an you wish it.'

'An I wish it!' His father broke into a roar of laughter – 'Hark to that now! An I wish it! Have I wished, then, to have a milksop for a son? 'Tis all your Montgomerys and their Latin grammars that have spoilt thee, boy – Here,' catching David suddenly by his breeches and raising him in the air, 'here's the spit of a tree! Here's a lad knows a dog when he sees 'un, that I'll wager! Wilt come with thy uncle hunting, David?'

But he waited not for an answer. He was aware that his wife thought him foolish and noisy. He turned confusedly to chatter to his sister-in-law.

It was then that David had a word with his father. They were standing a little back from the others. 'David, you are to go now. Your mother will ride home with me. You will find Father Roche to the left along the road. He is waiting now at the turn to Crosthwaite Church. You will ride back with him.'

At once David obeyed. He turned, bowed to his great-aunt, kissed his aunt's hand, heard above his head the excuses for his departure, smiled at his girl cousins, exchanged one look with Raiseley and was gone.

How proud he was to be treated thus – as though he were already a man!

He pushed open the heavy house-door, stepped through the courtyard, between the high gates and into the dusky road. It was almost dark; shadows lay about the broad path and little winds ran whispering about his feet.

A great sense of adventure possessed him. Behind him was the lighted town, near him the warm house with its fires and talking company, and outside the house the garden with the bird fountain and all its ordered discipline running to the wild edge of the lake with the clustered reeds. Young though he was, he yet felt the humanity and safety of this world crowded with all its persons so diverse as the ancient lady and little Peter and Cousin Raiseley, his enemy. All this within firelit walls, but, outside, the long road running, as though on a secret purpose, below the mountain that seemed to him huge in the night air, Skiddaw; by now he knew its name. But here, also, there was a church, and men might ride with ease, and at short distance all the traffic of the town. But away from it the road ran on, curving at the lake's end, running up the hill, then above the lake's side until at last it reached that little bridge and the high rocks behind it that were the barrier of his own dark country. There was danger, there, romance and adventure. Cousin Raiseley had said that there were wolves there. He did not know how that might be, but a month's living there had shown him how strange and removed a world it was, and already it was beginning to pull at his boy's heart, so that he was ready to defend it and feel that he was citizen of it. Yes, he would know every tree, every rock, every corner of it before long; he would push his way into every one of the mysteries . . .

He had been walking swiftly down the road, a little afraid, although he would not have owned it to anyone, of the sound of his own footsteps, when he saw at the parting of the two ways a horse and a figure standing beside it.

The figure came to meet him, and at first he did not recognize it, because Father Roche was dressed as an ordinary gentleman in plain riding-clothes.

'Father Roche,' he whispered. He had not intended to whisper, but the silence and loneliness of the road commanded him.

He was taken up and in another moment was seated in the front of the saddle. They started off.

'Not Father Roche any more,' the figure behind him murmured. 'Mr Roche . . . the times move, and we must move with them.'

His voice had tonight more than ever before the power to move David. He was himself already excited and stirred, and, as they moved over Derwent Hill, through the village of Portinscale and then up over Swinside Hill, with every step they seemed to be moving into some mysterious country, and it was Father Roche's power and spirit that was leading them. Was he then no longer a priest? Could you at one moment be a priest and then, at the next moment, not? Was it at his father's orders that he had ceased to be a priest? But for the moment he was too deeply excited by his own experiences. 'Uncle Pomfret's house is very grand. It is grander than ours at Doncaster. There is a garden with a fountain that is a bird's head, and a clock with the sun and moon on its face. My great-aunt Maria is a very old lady – she looks a hundred years. She has long hair falling about her face. My cousins were present, and my cousin Raiseley is very grave as though he thought well of himself . . .' He paused, then added: 'We will fight one day. And I shall win.' His little back straightened and his short legs tightened about the horse's neck. 'Uncle Pomfret always speaks at the top of his voice. He lifted me by my breeches and said that I should go hunting with him. Will my father permit me, think you?'

'Yes, David, when you are older.'

David sighed. 'It is always when I am older. My cousin Raiseley asked whether there were wolves in Borrowdale. He said that he wished to see one, but I doubt it. I think he does not care for dogs and horses and wild animals.'

They were going more slowly now, climbing the hill. It was bitterly cold, even a little snow was falling, and a few stars were like points of ice in the sky. They were climbing to high ground. There were three paths on this farther side of the lake, but as Father Roche had been warned in Keswick only one was passable for a horse and that the highest.

'My Great-Aunt Maria,' David went on, drawing a little back on Father Roche for greater warmth, 'said once "God save His Gracious Majesty". Aunt Jannice was vexed, so that I knew that it could not be the King in London. It is forbidden, is it not, to speak of the other King in Rome?'

Father Roche drew the boy closer to him. The time had come, then, to speak. The boy was now of a sufficient age. For years now he had been waiting for this moment, and he was well pleased that it should be at this instant, cold and sharp under the winter night sky, with the world so silent on every side of them. It had been the lesson of his life that he should have no human passions, and he had learnt it well, but in spite of all his lessons human feeling had grown in his heart for this boy and this boy's father. There were many other plans and schemes in his life that went far beyond his momentary relations with the Herries family. He stayed with them only because it suited his larger purposes to do so, but growing up in his heart in these last years had been the longing to turn this boy on to his own paths. During these weeks since coming to Borrowdale David seemed to have grown in mind and perception. He was already wise in some things beyond his years.

'David, will you listen a little as we ride? I have wished for some time past to speak to you. You are of an age enough now to understand.'

David nodded his head proudly. The only sound in all the world was the clap-clap of the horse's hoofs on the frozen ground.

Father Roche went on: 'There was a King in England once who was a martyr. Wicked men in the malice of their hearts slew him, and so interfered with one of God's most holy laws – the Divine Right that He hath given to those whom He has appointed as His rulers on this earth. This martyr, King Charles of blessed memory, was, perhaps more than any other man on this earth, near in his sufferings to our Saviour Himself. When Christ suffered there was darkness over all the land, and so when King Charles was under trial there were mighty wonders in the sky. You have read of the centurion who was assured that He was the Son of God, and his servant was healed; so with the Blessed Martyr, one of his guards was driven by conviction of sin to repentance. Did they not part our Sovereign's garments among them? Even so have they taken his houses, his possessions, his very garments from our master . . . And in his life, in his gentleness, his courtesy, his love of his fellowmen, did King Charles approach most closely that blessed prototype.'

Father Roche paused. The road ran now over Cat Bells and Brandelhow; from its bend the land dropped straight to the lake, which could be seen now like a dark mirror of jet below hills that were faintly silver. The horse's breath rose in front of them in clouds of steam; facing them was the hump, black as ebony, of the Castle Crag, and, more gently grey, the hills behind it. For young David, to whom this view was to become one of life's eternal symbols, he was to hear always, when he beheld it, the beautiful, melodious voice of the priest and to see again the scattered steely points of the stars in the velvet sky.

'His was an unrenounced right of sovereignty. None could take it from him. He had been placed there by God, and man had no voice in that choice and circumstance. He was murdered and betrayed by the sons of the Devil . . .'

A thrill of sympathy touched David's heart. Oh, had he been there, he would have died for that King!

'Even as Christ did, so could he work miracles. Have you ever heard how, being taken by his captors through the town of Winchester, an innkeeper of that city, who was grievously ill and suffocating, flung himself on his knees before His Majesty, crying "God save the King!", and the King said: "Friend, God grant thee thy desire," and the tumours and sores disappeared, and the man was made whole? And the kerchiefs dipped in the King's blood after his death had also this miraculous property.

'His son had also this virtue, and, it is said, touched one hundred thousand persons to cure them . . . Since this family appointed by God to rule over England have been in exile God's face has been turned away from us. Nothing is so sure and certain in this world as that our beloved country shall not again prosper until our rightful King returns to us. Do you understand what I have been saying to you, David?'

'Yes, sir,' answered David in an awed voice.

They clattered through the little village of Grange. Some woman came to a lighted door to watch them pass. Under the stone bridge the river, flooded with the recent rains, rushed to the lake. They turned into their valley under the dark rocks. 'The time may come, David, when every true man will be challenged. Under which King, God's or man's? What will thy answer be, boy?'

'Under God's King, sir,' answered David.

'Keep silence about what I have said even to your father, but talk to me when you have a mind. Wonder at nothing that you may see me do. I shall come and be gone again, but wherever I may be I shall know that I can trust thee . . .'

'Yes, sir.'

'You will not be afraid if a day should come . . .'

'No, sir. Only my father . . .' It was not for him then to know how little in later harsh fact this picture of God's King would affect him.

'Your father is my friend. He knows me.'

'Yes, sir . . . Will he, too, be ready when the day comes?' Roche hesitated—

'Every true man who loves his God and his country will be ready.'

'Yes, sir,' answered David again, suddenly sleepy and very cold. Loyalties? He now had many. To his father, to Deborah, to this King in Rome. Life was beginning to be filled with great adventure. There was his father in his dark suit with the silver cuffs, there was the old lady a thousand years old, Cousin Raiseley, whom he would one day fight, his uncle who would take him out hunting, the King in Rome who made people well by touching them, Father Roche who was now no more a priest, his mother whom he loved and Mrs Press whom he hated, and the old woman in Herries who was a witch, and the hill with the caves, and the more distant hills, where one day he would make great discoveries.

They turned to the house, black and cold under the scattered stars. But it was home, and there would be fire and something to eat, and then falling asleep in the room where his father would afterwards come . . . and then the King in Rome . . .

He was shivering with cold when Father Roche lifted him down from the horse and carried him in.

THE DEVIL

DAVID LOOKED up at the woman whom he so thoroughly detested, with fearless eyes.

'I went out because I wanted.'

'Yes, and the muck and all you've got into,' she answered crossly. 'But it isn't for me to say, I've no authority. And the horses not returned yet from Keswick, and the hills darkening the whole place. I hate this house – from the first instant I set foot in it I've hated it. A nice, pretty kind of life for one who's young enough and handsome enough for a frolic or two.'

She swung the silver chain that lay about her neck and touched the crimson velvet of her sleeves.

'And you fast with the priest all the morning,' she continued, her sharp eyes darting about the shadowy room. 'What is it he must speak so long about with a child like you?'

'He teaches me Latin,' David answered quietly.

'Yes, and many another lesson, I'll swear,' she answered.

He could see that her ears were ever straining for a sound.

'Ugh!' she shivered, 'the rain's coming down again, and all the old tapestries flapping against the wall. It wasn't so in Doncaster, I can promise you, before your father engaged me.'

'No,' said David, hating her.

'No, indeed. There was music there and dancing and the Fair at midsummer and the Plays at Yule. But here . . .'

She broke off. She thought that she had caught the clap of the horses' hoofs on the ragged stones of the little court. She sprang to the darkening window, then turned impatiently back, caught the flickering taper and held it to the leaded pane. Once again she was disappointed. There were no horses there – only the tap of some branches against the wall and the seeping drip of the rain.

'Why did you come here?' asked David.

She struck her hand violently on the table – 'Why? why? why?' she answered passionately. 'You are a child. How should you know? And yet—' She came over to him, caught him by the shoulders and stared into his eyes. 'You hate me, do you not? Young though you are, you know enough for that. You all hate me here and wish me gone. And most of all that priest – who has persuaded him against me.'

'He is not a priest now,' answered David. 'He is only Mr Roche now.'

'No priest? Yes, that is fine talk. Once a priest always a priest. And where has he gone this afternoon, riding away to Keswick? Where is it that he goes for nights together?'

'I don't know,' answered David.

'I'll tell you more,' she continued. 'He can be in prison any day. There are the laws against the Catholics, and he serving Mass in that upper room. Have I no ears nor eyes? So he shall be in prison if he returns and I have my way.'

She stopped again to listen. The house was intensely silent. The two little girls were with their mother in her room. There could be heard even through the rain and the wind the noise of falling water, the swollen stream tumbling down the side of the hill at the house's back. She stood thinking, then came closer again to David. He moved as though he would shrink from her, then firmly stood his ground.

'David, do you not think you could speak to him, to your father? When nobody else is by – he listens to you. I have noticed that when no other can speak to him he can be patient with you. Ask him if he will not ride out with me for an hour – I would tell him certain things. For weeks now I have not been alone with him, and I shall go mad . . . this desire . . . this longing . . .'

She broke off as though the words choked her, putting one hand to her throat and with the other gripping the boy's arm. David saw that she was in great suffering, and could have been sorry for her had he not hated her so. He remembered that night at the Keswick inn when his father had come in and kissed her. He hated that she should touch him, but he did not move.

'You must speak to him yourself,' he answered. 'My father, these past weeks, has had business in Keswick and in the country here.'

'Business in Keswick!' she answered scornfully, pushing him from her so that he almost fell. 'Fine business! Such as he had in Doncaster. Riding into Keswick to play at cards and look at the women, stumbling about in these mucky country paths to find a girl with bright eyes . . .'

David cried: 'You shall not speak against my father. When he wishes to talk with you he will tell you. Yes, it is true that we all hate you here and wish you gone. My mother cries because of you. You struck Deborah when she had done no wrong. You should return to Doncaster, where there are games and music . . .'

He was trembling with rage and with a desire that in some way he might persuade her to go. Oh, if only she would go away. . .

But already she had forgotten him. Her ears again had caught a sound, and this time she was not deceived.

The clatter of hoofs was on the stones of the court, and at the same instant Margaret Herries, the two little girls beside her, appeared, holding a light, at the stair's head.

'Is he come? Is he come?' she cried eagerly, and then started down the rickety stairway, moving heavily and awkwardly, the children close behind her.

The hall, that had been only a moment before so dark and drear with the faint light and old Herries sneering from the wall, was now all alive.

Francis Herries in his deep riding-coat, Wilson following him with candles, entered, and his wife and the children ran to him. Alice Press stayed in the dusk. They could see at once that he was in a good mood. He laughed as he saw them, caught Deborah and David to him, bent forward and kissed his wife.

'Yes, something to eat and drink. I'm parched and famished. The rain blew against us like the plague. I thought Mameluke would have fallen twice, and it was such thick darkness along Cat Bells that it was God's miracle we were not in the lake.' He pulled Deborah's hair. 'Thou knowest there's something here for thee and for Mary too – the other pocket for David . . .' Laughing and shouting with excitement, they felt in the pockets and pulled out the bundles. For Deborah there was a 'baby' with bright flaxen hair and a dress of green silk, for Mary a toy tea-set, cups and saucers decorated with pink roses, and for David battledore and shuttlecock.

With every moment the room grew more lively. A big log fire was leaping in the open fireplace. Wilson and his daughter were setting the table; Benjamin had come in (Nathaniel had left them at Martinmas), a bottle of wine in either hand, his round face smiling with the pleasantry of the familiar servant who knows that tonight he has nothing to fear from his master's temper. Only Alice Press stood back against the wall, without moving, her hand against her heart.

Francis Herries, his riding-coat flung into a chair, stood before the fire, his legs spread, warming his back.

'Dear brother Pomfret is to visit us tomorrow,' he said. 'He will condescend to take the journey. Keswick was a pool of muck; you couldn't stir for the mud. And so, Deb, you love your baby?'

Deborah was sitting on a stool at her mother's feet, hugging her doll. She was in an ecstasy of happiness, rocking the doll in her arms, then straightening it to smooth its stiff hair, her eyes shining, looking at her brother every once and again to see that he was sharing in her pleasure.

Francis Herries, looking out at them all, hummed in a half-whisper the children's song:

> 'Lady Queen Anne who sits in her stand,
> And a pair of green gloves upon her hand,
> As white as a lily, as fair as a swan,
> The fairest lady in a' the land.'

Tonight he was well content. The mood was upon him when everything seemed fair. It was good thus to come home to his own, to find the candles shining and his own things about him, and his children, whom he loved, longing for him. The devil of restlessness was not with him. That afternoon in Keswick he had won three fine bets at the cock-fighting. He had drunk just enough to make the world glow. Even Margaret, his wife, could seem, close to him, neither so stout nor so foolish . . . Ah, if they would let him alone, his little pack of demons, he could make a fine thing of this life yet.

His eyes, roaming, found Alice Press, motionless against the wall. His voice changed.

'Have the babies been good?' he asked her.

She came forward into the candlelight.

'Well enough,' she answered, and turning sharply, left the room.

The food came in. The others had dined long ago, but they crowded about him as he ate, and Benjamin stood behind them, smiling beneficently, as though they were all his handiwork.

While he ate and drank he told them little things about his

Keswick day – how they had been baiting a bull in the market-place and two dogs had been killed; how there had been a medicine man pulling out teeth, and he had pulled two wrong ones from an old woman, and she had demanded her money back, but he had not given it: the old woman's son had fought him and knocked his tub over; how he had had a talk with old Westaway, the architect of Uncle Pomfret's house, and what a strange old man he was and had been the world over and seen the Pope in Rome and the Czar of all the Russias, and spoke in a shrill piping voice, and trembled with anger, so they said, at the sight of a woman; how there was a little black boy for sale like the one Aunt Jannice had, and some splendid dogs, big and fierce, who would do finely for defending the house in the winter; how there had been in the market-square the day before a gathering of those strange people, the Quakers, and they had been set upon and two of them stripped naked and splashed with tar; how they told him that there was a band of robbers now in Wasdale that came down from Scafell and had murdered two shepherds in the last week; and there was a fine gathering of gentlemen for the cock-fight and he had not done so ill there . . .

Here he broke off; he knew what Margaret thought of his cock-fighting – another evening he might have teased her and been pleased to see the fear come into her eyes, but not to-night . . . He was young as David tonight. He had David on his knee, his hand fingering his hair. His wife, Margaret, was praying: 'Oh, Lord, let this last a while. Let this last a while.'

After his supper they played Blind-man's Buff. Francis Herries's eyes were bound with the handkerchief. The children ran, screaming and laughing; Margaret herself played and ran into his arms, and once again – after how many years – her husband had his arms about her, held her, kissed her cheek. It was David's turn to be blinded, and, as he stood in darkness, he could hear all the sounds – the crack and tumble of the fire and the hiss of the falling ash, the rain against the window, the breathing of the people about him; and it seemed to him that all the room was lit with red light and old great-great-grandfather Herries came down from his picture-frame and ordered him to come to him. He ran forward; an instant of awful terror came to him. But all was well; it was into Benjamin's arms that he had run, and as he felt the stout, soft body with his hands he screamed with excited relief: 'It's Benjamin! It's Benjamin!' – then Benjamin was blind man.

* * *

After breakfast the whole world is filled with light. Everything moves together. Round Herries the entire universe centres itself, spreading out to endless distances that are mysteries – China, Pera, the kingdom of Samarkand – but pouring all its waters into this one deep purple pool – purple of Glaramara, purple of the shadows and eaves and door-post, purple of the feathers in the peacock fan carried by the Princess in Deb's chap-book, purple of the darker river shadows that lie beneath the spume and froth tumbling through Grange to the lake. Through the shadows of this purple February morning, David, standing at the road-bend, Deborah beside him, saw the moving of all the people around him – Alice Press yawning at the window, his father drinking his breakfast ale; Benjamin in the little court, his hand on Mameluke; his mother hearing Mary her morning prayer; the old witch grandmother Wilson silent against the wall, her white kerchief about her chin, leaning on her stick; Wilson himself moving to the cows; then, a little more distantly, Moorcross, the home of the statesman Peel – Peel, the tallest, stoutest man David had ever seen – famous for his wrestling, with a boy of David's own age, whom David would like to know; and beyond the Peels again, all Borrowdale, with the names that were becoming part of him, Rosthwaite and Stonethwaite, Seathwaite and Seatoller, and the hills, glittering on this lovely morning, Glaramara, Scafell, the Gavel; wolves, maybe, above Stye Head, and robbers, his father had said, in Wasdale, and fairies, gnomes, devils, witches . . .

Deb's hot hand held his more tightly.

'What are you looking for, David?'

What was he looking for? He did not know. But this was to be a day of days. His happiness last evening, the games, sleeping on the small pallet beside his father's bed and then waking to so wonderful a day! After all the rain and wind, this stillness and shining glitter, small fleecy clouds like puddings or puppies plump against the shadowed softness of the blue, the branch of no tree stirring, so clear that the crowing of a cock far away towards Seatoller could plainly be heard, but, as always here, the sound of running waters, now one, now two, now fast as though an urgent message had come to hasten, now slow with a lazy drawling sound . . .

He knew that today he could have the small shaggy pony, Caesar, that his father had bought from Peel. It was a whole holiday. Mr Finch would not appear. No one would care what he did nor where he went. He would like to ask the Peel boy to go with him, but he was shy, and the Peel boy spoke so odd a language and then, of course, had his work to do . . .

At that instant, so miraculous is life, the Peel boy passed them. The Peel boy was bigger and stronger than David, very broad of the chest and thick of the leg; his eyes were blue and his hair very fair; his cheeks were rosy, and he whistled out of tune. He was whistling now, but when he saw Deborah and David he stopped. He paused and smiled.

'Good day,' said David, also smiling.

''Day,' said the boy, shuffling his feet. They grinned and said nothing.

'Have you a knife, please?' David asked.

'Aye.'

David did not need one, but when the large rough cutlass was put in his hand he chipped off the small branch of a tree.

'Thank you.' He tried again. ''Tis a fine day.'

'Aye.'

'We have holiday.'

'Aye.'

'I shall ride Caesar to the valley end.'

'Aye.'

Then the Peel boy bobbed his head and went on down the path. He turned back.

'You may have t'knife,' he said.

'Oh, no, I thank you,' said David, very greatly touched. Then seeing disappointment – 'Well – if you wish —'

He took the knife, and the Peel boy, delighted, started down the path again, whistling once more out of tune.

The day was well begun.

He walked slowly back to the house, his hand tight in Deb's. She asked: 'David, may I come with you on Caesar?'

'No,' he answered, 'I go alone.' He felt her hand give a little quiver – 'Why, you are not afeared? I shall be back by dusk.'

She nodded her head bravely. 'I shall wash my new baby.' But she had something in her mind. She noticed so much more than Mary. She was exceedingly sensitive and would always be. She would always live alone, however many people were near her, and would give herself in passionate devotion to one or two, realizing that it was the law of her life that she should give rather than receive.

Already, although she was only seven years of age, she knew of many little things in and around Herries that no one else had seen – the face of a woman, thin and sharp, carved on the oak

chest in the dining-hall; a ruby ring that old great-great-grandfather Herries wore on his finger in the picture; the way that
Alice Press had of looking scornfully at her fingernails; the
fashion that old Mrs Wilson had of walking like a blind woman,
her eyes tightly shut; the coarse crowing laugh of her grand-
daughter – and she knew everything about David: the straightness of his back when he was standing waiting for something,
how one leg would rub against the other when he began to be
eager in talking about something; his smile, when one end of his
mouth seemed to curl more than another; the roughness that a
wind would make of his hair when he wore no cap, the beautiful
coolness of his forehead when he let her put her hand on it. She
did not know that she knew these things – she had as yet no self-
consciousness.

The most common sensation for her would always be fear, and
the constant duty of her life would be building up sufficient
courage with which to meet it. Apprehension would attack her
at every turn. It was as though she had three skins less than other
folk. Even as a baby she had seen shadows in the room that no
one else had seen, heard footsteps that no one else had heard.
Things assumed significance for her beyond all fact and reason.
There had been a tree in the Doncaster garden, stout in the
trunk, thinly carved in its branches. How she had hated that
tree, what terrors undefined it had brought to her, how, in all the
other excitements of leaving Doncaster, this had been predomi-
nant – that she need never see that tree again!

And here at Herries already there were terrors. Alice Press and
old Mrs Wilson of course – these were natural alarms – but also
the pump in the yard, the two suits of armour within the house-
door that seemed to her to have faces, one white and one yellow,
and the steps of someone walking on the floor of the parlour-loft
when they were in the dining-hall.

All around her, everyone was insensitive. It was not a time
when people noticed such things. There were witches and warlocks, fairies and gnomes, but they were real and active with
persons as positive as the serving-man or the night-watchman.
She kept – as she was always to keep – everything to herself.
David alone understood something of her sensitiveness, and this
not because he shared it with her, but because he loved her so
deeply that she was like part of himself. Only when she was with
him she knew no fear. Her confidence in him was as though he
were someone divine. Where he was no fear could come, no evil
live.

This morning as they neared the house he wanted to go into the yard behind to see whether Benjamin were there. She shrank back.

'Come, Deb. Benjamin hath a new puppy Peel's man gave to him.'

She shook her head and, breaking from him, ran in by the front door. He remembered then that he must see his mother. Every morning he was with her for half an hour, and read out of the *Life of King Arthur* or the Bible for her. He read very well; he liked books when there were not horses and dogs and games like football and battledore. But today he did not want to read. It was not a day for books, and as he moved slowly into the house, he felt impatient with his mother. He shared a little with his father the intolerance of her clumsiness, her habit of tears, her absent-mindedness, and, as with all of us when we are impatient with those who love us, he wished that she did not love him quite so much.

She was so easily hurt. She was always asking him what he was doing, where he was going, with whom he had been; and although there was no reason at all why he should not tell her everything, he inclined to be secret with her because of her curiosity. Then he had seen, so many times, his sister Mary flatter and cheat her mother because of something that she had wanted, and that made him honest to the point of discourtesy. He loved her better when he was not with her; he hated Alice Press because she made his mother unhappy, but he did not mind also making her unhappy. Now, when he went in, he would be forced to tell her about what he was going to do, how he would ride Caesar to the valley's end, and fish in the stream below Stye Head and watch to see if a wolf should be prowling under Glaramara. And he did not want to tell her these things. It would spoil them a little, make them more ordinary and less adventurous.

He found her in her room, alone, the room darkened by the big canopied bed; it was a little chill.

He saw at once that today there would be no reading. His mother, dismayed and distraught, was standing in the middle of the room, her hand at her cheek, her eyes crowded with alarm.

So soon as she saw him she began: 'No, David . . . Leave me . . . This is too vile . . .' She was not near to tears: no, for once anger had mastered her. She had even a certain grandeur, pulled to her full height, massive, her gaze upon the door. Before he could wonder, someone had come in, and at once a spate of words broke about the place; the room crackled with fury.

He knew, without turning, that it was Alice Press; no need to question that shrill voice that rose in a kind of sweeping tide of temper to a scream.

'And so you mean to banter me, madam – a fine figure before your own children. Was I put here to direct them or no? It is no disparagement to a woman, I suppose, that before all your household I should be told my place and then left to find it by their easy insulting courtesy. Oh, no, indeed – I am not to be averse to every slavish duty that a gentlewoman can be put to, having been dragged from Doncaster by the heels, and then flung into this muck-heap and cesspool to keep proper company with old witches, who by rights should be stripped of every cloth on their backs and then thrown to the river to let them sink or swim! Oh, no, you say, I honour you ever more and more, but I insult you as I may, and as convenience suits me. I do not remember to have ever had the pleasure of witnessing your own rules of law and order in this house or any other. You are quiet enough until the fit moment comes to abuse me properly, and then you have words enough . . . I can't express the satisfaction, truly, that it gives me to know the meaning of your feeling towards me, and if I should go naked and be on my knees before you, that would give you satisfaction, perhaps – you who have not your own children to order, nor your husband to bed with you – yet you would teach *me* my lesson and my proper order in this house . . .'

She paused for breath. David saw her now, her pale face crimson, her hands clenched, her breast heaving.

'I will not have you,' Margaret Herries answered, 'abuse my privileges. It was not by my wish nor order that you were here. God knows I have surrendered in these years many of my proper rights, and God He also knows that I have suffered my own bitterness, and such it may be must come to every woman, but yet I am mistress in this house.'

'Mistress!' Alice Press broke in, 'and in a fine house! Mistress when there is such a master here and a house where the mice and rats are the true familiars. Mistress you may be in your own privacy, but mistress, as the veriest hireling on this place knows, in no public fashion. Mistress! Then who is master here? Know you your master and his company? Ask your master his pleasure in Keswick and the drabs that he fumbles, so that after barely a six-months' stay in this place his name is a byword! Mistress—'

'I will not,' Margaret Herries broke in. 'This is enough. I have suffered your company long enough, but now it is you or I who go – and I care not how soon!'

'Go!' Alice Press moved a step forward. 'Yes, though we had been at the same charity school and I had gone the round of neighbours asking for bread, I would not go at your bidding. No, nor do aught else at your bidding. Neither I nor anyone else in this place. You for a weak trembling fool who have neither the courage nor the discipline to bid a mouse go when you would wish it. Oh, I could tell you things, madam, that would make your eyes sore. I have waited in patience, borne your insults and laughed at your silly little pieces of pride, but now at last my silence has lasted long enough . . .'

Silence fell on the room. Francis Herries stood in the doorway, and David moved towards his mother. He came close to her, scarcely knowing that he did so, and suddenly he felt her trembling hand on his shoulder and steadied himself that he might support it.

'Well,' Herries said quietly, looking about the room, 'here is a scramble . . . the whole house shares in it.'

For once Margaret Herries was not cowed. Her hand tightening on David's shoulder, her voice trembling ever so lightly, she replied to him:

'Mrs Press has some complaint that I have ordered her unjustly before the servants. She has been impertinent . . .'

David saw, and triumphantly, that it was the other woman who was afraid. In a voice that was strangely stilled after its earlier shrillness, looking straight at Herries, forgetting, it would seem, that there was any other in the room, she answered:

'I have my place here, a place that you have appointed me. Your wife has forgotten . . .'

Herries smiled.

'Your place? No place unless you yourself fulfil it.'

It was possible that in that one quiet word she saw her sentence; she had known, it might be, that for months it had been coming to her. It might be that, beyond that again, she realized now her folly in provoking this scene, in forgetting a patience that it had been, this last year, no easy task to tutor her natural hot temper towards.

'I have fulfilled it,' she answered proudly. 'It is you who have neglected to keep me in it.'

'That may well be,' he answered lightly; 'there is so much to be done and little time to see to it all. And now I advise that you leave us . . . Wherever your place may be, it is certain that it is not in this room.'

She would, it seemed, speak; then with another glance at him, her colour now very white, she passed through the door.

He looked at his wife with a strange mixture of scorn and kindliness.

'You should know better, Meg, than to suffer her impertinence . . . but at least you shall not suffer it long.'

He went out. David felt still the pressure of his mother's hand. She did not move; then, at last, turned from him, went to the window and stood there looking out. There was nothing that he could do – only he would never speak to Alice Press again. Never! Not though his father whipped him till the blood ran. With this high resolve he left the room, and then, after a pause, the house. He hated it and everyone in it.

He found Benjamin and Benjamin found Caesar. No one prevented him; from the outside court the house within seemed dead. No sound came from it. It was strange that by merely closing a door you shut everything off – anger, fears, greed, joys. Already, at his early years, it seemed to him that one of the ways to secure happiness was to escape from people, to be by yourself in the open.

He wasn't happy as he found his way, past Moorcross, on to the main path, but he was too young and too healthy to be unhappy for long. And there was the consciousness that he was sharing now more in real grown-up life than he had done in Doncaster. But why had his father brought Alice Press with him from Doncaster? That was what he *could* not understand. It was from her that all the trouble came, she who made his mother unhappy, his father angry, Deb frightened, himself in a rage. Were she gone, they would all be tranquil again. But *why* had his father brought her? Why had he kissed her in the inn? There was something strange here that caused his heart to beat and his cheeks to redden. Children then lived from the earliest years in contact with great grossness of word and action. David almost from babyhood had been aware of the physical traffic between men and women, had at the age of seven seen a woman give birth to a child in the streets of Doncaster, but he had as yet translated none of these physical acts to mental or spiritual significance.

Life from the very first was for him far coarser and more brutal than it would be for his great-grandchildren, but for that reason, perhaps, his consciousness of it was purer and less muddled than theirs would be. In any case he drove these things very swiftly from his mind as he drew out from the Rosthwaite hamlet into the open country.

Open country, indeed, it was. At this time it was scarcely cultivated save in a few fields round Seathwaite or Rosthwaite. It lay in purple shadows with splashes of glittering sunlight, a lost land, untenanted by man, no animal anywhere visible, dominated entirely by the mountains that hemmed it in. To David's right ran the path up to Honister, where the mines were; this country was forbidden ground, for here all the rascals and outcasts of the neighbourhood would congregate to scrape among the mine refuse and then sell the scraps of plumbago to the Jews in Keswick, who would meet them at The George or The Half-Moon and then bargain with them. The stories were that titanic battles were fought above Stye Head and on Honister between rival bands of robbers, disputing their plunder, and it was true enough that many a time, walking up Honister, you would find a dead man there, by the roadside, his throat cut or a knife in his belly and often enough stripped naked.

For David, that road up to Honister was the most magical passage of all, and one day he would investigate it, robbers or no robbers, to its very heart; but today he was out to catch fish, and it was by the bridge under Stye Head that he would catch them – were he lucky! It was not a great day for fishing with this glittering sun and shining sky.

The farther he got from Herries the happier he became. Of late he had been cluttered about with people. All of them – his father, his mother, Deb, Mary, his cousins, Father Roche, the Press woman, old Mrs Wilson and her son, Peel and his boy – some of them he loved and some of them he hated, but all of them hindered his perfect freedom.

He, he was wise enough even now to realize, would always be hampered by people – you couldn't be *free* of people, nor did he want to be – but there would be moments and days when you would be free, absolutely, nakedly free, and, oh! how glorious they were!

It was such a moment now.

Caesar was no very magnificent steed, but he was a good enough pony, and quite able to grasp his own moments of freedom. As they came deeper under the hills the path was so rough and uncertain that David let him pick his own way. The group of mountains that closed the valley in were lovely in their wine-grape colour under a sky that had been a stainless blue, but that now, in the fashion of these parts, was suddenly the battlefield for two angry clouds, one shaped like a ragged wheel, the other like a battering ram. The wheel was a thin grey edged with silver and the ram was ebony. The empty valley – the little boy on the pony was the only moving thing in the whole landscape – seemed to wait apprehensively as the wheel and the ram approached one another. The sun appeared to retreat in alarm, but the wheel stretched out a wicked hand with swollen fingers and seized it – then the ram crashed down upon it.

The end of the valley was darkened although behind him, by Castle Crag, the sun was in full glory, and the world blazed like a sheet of dazzling metal. Within the shadow it was cold, and David, shouting to give himself company, kicked Caesar forward.

He came now to three houses, brooding like witches at the side of the rough path, quite deserted, it seemed, open, like many of the other cottages, to the sky.

Before the third cottage stood three men and a girl. David felt his heart beat at the sight of them. They were the wildest-looking men he had ever seen. They were copies the one of another, seemingly of the same height and the same age, the age maybe of his father, broad and strong, and all with dark rough beards. The girl was only a baby, younger than David, slight and dark like the men, but rosy-cheeked, and, as David passed them, she was laughing. One of the men stepped forward and stood in David's way.

'A fine day,' he said.

David nodded. He was frightened, but he wouldn't let anyone, not even Caesar, know it. He wished, though, that the sun would come out again.

'Where'st going?'

The man had a deep, rumbling, husky tone with a rasp in it.

'To fish at the bridge.'

'To fish at the bridge?' All the men laughed.

'Pass, little master.' The man stepped back and ironically doffed a very filthy and greasy hat. Then David, seeing the laughing eyes of the small girl fixed upon him, smiled.

She had in her hand a small switch. She ran into the path, struck Caesar's buttocks and then, as he started forward, laughed with a shrill crying tone like a bird. He looked back and saw her standing in the middle of the path against the sun.

He cared nothing for girls – Deb wasn't a girl, she was his sister – but it did seem to him exciting and adventurous that this small girl should be quite alone with these three wild men, and, apparently, happy with them. She was perhaps the daughter of one of them. It might be that they were some of the robbers who came down from Stye Head and murdered defenceless people and returned. Well, there was nothing about him for them to murder. He had a tin with worms in it, and a home-made fishing-rod and a few pence. He was safe enough.

The country now grew ever wilder and wilder. A rough, ragged stream, swollen with the rains and the snow from the tops, rushed along over a deep bed of slabs and boulders. Fragments of rock lay everywhere about him here, so that he had to dismount and lead Caesar. Above his head the two clouds had made truce and after a meeting had separated, one now in the form of a ship that, lined with silver, sailed off into the blue, the other dispersed into a flock of little ivory clouds that stayed lazily, as though playing a game, in lines and broken groups. The sun had burst out again and flooded all the land. David had already learnt that, in this country, the sky was more changeable than in any other in the world, that if you lived here your days were bound up with the sky, so that after a while it seemed to have a more active and personal history than your own. It became almost impossible to believe that its history was not connected with yours, keeping pace with you, influencing you, determining your fate. He had never considered the sky very greatly at Doncaster, but in this world, it drove itself into your very heart. The brilliant sun now struck sparks from every stone, while every splutter of the stream against a boulder flung into the air a shower of light. The whole valley glittered, while above it the mountains, streaked like a wild beast's skin with snow, were black.

He came to the bridge, let Caesar loose, clambered over the smooth wet stones to the deep, green pool under the waterfall, chose his worm and began to fish below the pool. There was shadow here from an overhanging tree and the curve of the bridge. He was exceedingly happy. He had the great gift of complete absorption in the task or play of the moment. He was never to know the divided moods, divided loyalties of his father. His character was not subtle, but steadfast, fearless, unfaltering. He did not realize for how long he fished. He moved below the bridge and then back again. He caught nothing. He never had a bite. The sun was too bright. He sat, his legs apart, his eyes intently fixed on the water. A shadow was flung. He looked up.

Leaning on the bridge, looking down at him very gravely was a pedlar with a coloured hat and a sharp bright face. He had rested his pack on the bridge's wall.

'A fine sun today,' said the pedlar.

David nodded.

'Too strong a sun for good fishing,' said the pedlar.

David sighed. 'That's true.' He scrambled up to the sward above the stones. He looked at the pack.

'Have you something for me to buy?' he asked, smiling. He had some money in his purse – money his father had given him – and it would be pleasant to buy something for Deborah.

The pedlar shook his head.

'Nothing for you.' Then he felt in a pouch at his waist. 'Do you fancy boxes? I have a little box here . . .' He fumbled, then brought out a small silver box and gave it to David. His hand was nut-brown, with long, thin, tapering fingers. It was a beautiful little box. On one side was carved a picture of girls dancing round a maypole, on the other a picture of gentlemen hunting.

David looked at it, then shook his head. ''Tis a beautiful box, but I have not money enough.'

The pedlar smiled. 'It is yours. Keep it until your marriage day.'

'Thank you,' said David, dropping it into his pocket. 'But I shall never be married.'

'You will be married,' said the pedlar, 'and have fine sons.'

'How do you know?' asked David, looking into his tin and seeing that the worms that remained were few and poor. He would not fish any more. He found bread and meat in his pocket and offered some to the pedlar, who took more than his share and ate voraciously.

'I know everything,' said the pedlar. 'I am the Devil.'

David believed him. He looked both wicked and gay as he stood there in the sunlight, and Francis Herries had always told him that the Devil was both these things.

'I am not afraid of you,' said David, laughing. 'My father has always told me not to be afraid.'

'I know your father,' said the pedlar, licking his fingers after the bread and meat and looking as though he would like also the piece that David had in his hand. 'Your father is an old friend.'

'He is the finest man in the world,' said David proudly. 'Why will you not show me the things that you have in your pack?'

'I am weary of showing them,' said the pedlar, yawning and displaying a splendid row of sharp white teeth. 'Time enough. You shall see them one fine day.'

'If you are the Devil,' said David, who was always interested in everything, 'you can tell me where there is good fishing.'

'There is good fishing everywhere,' said the pedlar, 'if you have patience. You have patience. It will carry you through the world – patience and courage, two stupid qualities but valuable.'

'Do you live round here?' David asked.

'Here or anywhere. When you have lived for ever as I have, one place or another is the same.'

'Do you never grow any older?' David asked.

'Never,' said the pedlar. 'A wearisome business. Good day. We shall often encounter one another. Keep the little box. I am not, in my intentions, always unamiable as people say.'

He shouldered his pack, started up the Stye Head and was quite suddenly lost in the sunlight.

David jogged back happily through the sunny afternoon. He took his time; he saw no human being. The sun falls behind the hills like a stone over this valley, leaving in the sky a long, wide strath of white and blue. When David reached Herries the shadows were straddling giants across the little stone court.

He found his father alone in the shadowed hall; he leant across the long table, on which a map was spread. 'He's looking grand,' David, who relished him in his plum-coloured coat, thought, 'and he has a temper.' So, like a knowing puppy, he slipped quietly past the fading fire. In the room above he heard Deborah's funny little piping voice, singing to herself or her baby. Beyond the leaded window the sky was a lovely pale green like early spring leaves and the low spread of the land was purple again as it had been in the morning. Against this gentle, pure light the room was very dark, although two candles were lit.

His father saw him.

Without looking up from the map: 'Where have you been, David?'

David told him. It might be that there would be a whipping or it might be that there would be a game – you never could tell with his father.

'Thou hast missed thine uncle, boy.'

David had nothing to say to that – as there was a pause he filled it.

'I saw the Devil by the bridge.'

His father did not answer but suddenly raised himself.

'David, come here.' David came to him.

He put his arm round his neck. 'David, I love no one but you – no one – no one in all the world. And I hate your uncle. Remember this day, for on it I surrender all wishes for a good union between your uncle and me. Silly, patronizing fool!' He looked furiously about him at the table which was clustered with a mess of things – tankards, a platter with bread on it, a riding-whip, a velvet glove with a jewelled clasp. 'I'll twist his neck for him, brother or no brother, an he comes this way again. Aye, you should have seen your uncle riding his fine horse and stepping over the muck and cobbles, he fat as an otter and red as an infant's bum. 'Tis his lady wife sent him to spy the land out – a fine stretch she'll be the wiser for his coming – a dark house, a dull woman and his debauched good-for-nothing brother . . . I'll warrant he's sad that he had me here – a fine tear on his famous reputation. And now that I'm here I'll stay. The place charms me, naked though it is. There's some ale for you, David. Drink to your good-for-nothing rump of a father, naked-bottomed in a cesspool and pleasantly forgot by the gay world.'

But David didn't drink. He felt in his pocket and brought out the little silver box.

'The Devil gave me this,' he said.

His father, his eyes angry yet good-humoured, wandered round the room then came to it.

'A pretty thing. And how did the Devil look?'

'He was a pedlar. He said he knew you.'

'Yes – there is a pedlar here I have spoken with . . .'

His mind was away, then he caught his son to him and held him close.

'My good brother's son is a damned smug; and gives him no joy – I can beat him there.'

He crooked his son's chin upwards and looked at him. David gazed back at him fearlessly.

'Remember this day,' his father said. 'We shall be alone against the world, you and I.'

CHINESE FAIR

HERRIES RETURNED, one September morning, after his walk abroad, without his coat. It had been one of his finest, the plum-coloured coat laced with silver. He walked into the house in his white sleeves, and the old witch, Mrs Wilson, leaned over the top of the stairs and smiled. She never laughed. 'You're grand without your coat,' she said. They seemed to have a kind of understanding, the two of them. He, as did all the valley, believed her to be a witch. He thought none the worse of her for it. He was happy this morning like a boy. It was a bright fresh morning, with clean white clouds leaning negligently on the hills. With the beauty and the youth and the kindly look that he had when he was happy, he was a good sight for an old witch. And she was no misanthrope. Life was too busily interesting for her to despise mankind.

'I'm going to the Fair,' he said like a boy.

She nodded her head, put out her long brown hand, and touched the white linen of his sleeve.

'You're not to give t' coat,' she said. 'It'll be remembered.'

He didn't care whether it were remembered or no. Out on the Watendlath path, looking up at a bright silver waterfall poised like a broken ladder against the green cliff, he had seen by the stones of the beck a dead man with his throat cut and a woman shivering beside him. A dead man was no extraordinary sight; this man was naked save for his shirt, and his white legs stretched stiffly as though they had been carved. The woman did not cry nor ask for alms, but she shivered in the keen September air. He did not speak to her, but obeying the impulse of the instant, took off his plum-coloured coat and threw it over her trembling shoulders. He strode back to the house. Seeing Benjamin in the yard, he leaned from the window and bade him go and fetch the woman to the house. Ten minutes later Benjamin returned to say there was no sign of woman or man.

He did not care. He was too cheerful in spirit to be bothered by a dead man or a shivering woman.

He sat in his sleeves at the window looking out on to the beautifully coloured world, Glaramara plum-coloured like his coat, and the long stretch of green valley.

He was like a schoolboy about this Fair. It was an accidental chance-by-night Fair for Keswick. It had been intended for Kendal and then for Carlisle, a motley company of entertainers and rogues and rascals travelling slowly to Scotland.

But the smallpox was savage this summer in Kendal, and so they had changed to the smaller town. In the past Keswick had had few Fairs but its own. It was too small a place. The chartered Fair on the 2nd of August for the sale of leather, and the Cattle Fairs on the first Thursday in May and on each Thursday fortnight for six weeks after; on the Saturday nearest Whitsuntide and Martinmas for hiring servants, and on the first Saturday after the 29th of October for the sale of cheese and rams.

Saturday the year through was market-day for provisions and corn.

But these Fairs were local, and business was their purpose. This present Fair was the maddest, wildest thing in Keswick's memory. It would be generations before the week of it would be forgotten. They said, too, that there was a company of Chinese people travelling with the Fair, and they wore strange clothes, such as had never been seen in that neighbourhood, and they juggled with gold balls and swallowed silver swords, and had an old man with them three hundred years of age. It was always afterwards called the Chinese Fair.

But it was not of the Fair that Herries was now thinking as he sat at the window. He was thinking of how well satisfied he was with this place. He had been here full two years, and his strange instinct that had driven him here had been right. He already loved the valley, and had even now caught some of the sense of its intimacy that led its inhabitants to cling to it with an obstinacy and stubbornness that made them a byword for the rest of the world. It was said that the men of Borrowdale were so stupid as to be scarcely human, and that they did such idiotic things, like building a wall to keep the cuckoo in their valley, that they must be half-witted – that they never stirred from their valley, that some of them had never even seen Keswick, that they spoke a strange language of their own and were like men in a dream.

Herries had heard how the people in Keswick and from Newlands and St John's and the rest mocked and gibed, but he knew now what it was that held the men of Borrowdale: although he was not yet one of them (they were greatly suspicious of newcomers), one day he would be. Something was in his blood that was in their blood: it was a doom, a judgement, the fulfilment of a prophecy.

He thought of other things too, as he sat there. He was well pleased that he had cut himself off from his brother and his brother's family. Since that day when Pomfret had ridden over to Herries he had never set foot in his brother's house. Margaret and the children had visited – he did not care whether they did or no – and when he met Pomfret in Keswick he talked with him, but he had never been within his brother's door.

He loved his pride, his fierce intolerance. He cherished it, fed it, adored it. It had been one of his fears, on coming to live in Herries, that perhaps he would find his brother a better fellow than he had thought he was, and so would be forced to see him and keep company with him because his heart drove him.

THE CUCKOO IS NOT ENCLOSED

That was why, on the first evening at the inn, he had worn his finest clothes – because that might annoy his brother, and then Pomfret would appear less pleasant than he was. And so in the event it had been. Now he cherished his scorn of his brother – it was a fine silver flower in his coat.

The thing, however, of which he was mainly thinking now was what he should do to be rid of Alice Press, for rid of her he would be. Although so reckless a man, he knew, as every imaginative Herries has always known, that you can't rid yourself of past deeds. Kill a fox, give your coat to a trembling woman, drink of the water of Sprinkling Tarn, and you are a doomed man. He was doomed because he had kissed Alice Press, doomed because he had shot off that young fool's ear in Doncaster, doomed because on entering Herries he had put the right foot before the left, doomed anyway and a thousand times a day; but to be bored, because he was young and full of life, was a worse thing than to be doomed. And he was bored by Alice Press, bored to the very hilt of his sword. He thought now that he had always been bored with her, although there had been, at the very first, a flashing moment of startling splendour. Now he was bored with everything about her, from her heavy sallow face, her long sad brooding gaze at him, her stealthy eagerness to be alone with him, down to the paste buckles on her scarlet shoes, the scarlet shoes that he had once bought for her on a Fair day in Doncaster, and that she wore now in persistent petulant reminder. Moreover, she had been insulting to Margaret, and he would have no one rude to Margaret but himself. Yes, he must be rid of her, but how?

He looked out at the great shoulder of the hill. 'How, old Glaramara? You are old enough to know. Come and tell me your plan.'

As though in answer to his question, hearing a deep breath he turned round to find Alice Press at his side.

She was very grand in black velvet, with a heavy silver chain and her scarlet shoes.

She came close to him, and the scent that she used, a scent of roses, stifled his nostrils.

'Francis,' she said, her large sombre eyes staring into his. 'You will take me to the Fair, will you not?'

'No,' he answered, smiling at her and patting her white hand. She drew her hand away from the arm of his chair.

'You promised me.'

'I break my promise.'

'You must not. I am bent to go. You have been unkind to me all these months, and I have borne you no grudge. I knew that I could wait. Today it shall be like one of our old times.'

'Old times never return,' he answered her, looking at her with an intentness that matched her own. How strange it was, this passing of love! A never-ending marvel! At one moment the merest touch of the hand is Paradise, at the next, dead flesh.

'Have you not been selfish in this,' she went on quietly, 'and blind too, perhaps? Because you are tired of loving me you think our intercourse is at an end. But no intercourse is at an end when two have loved one another as we have.'

'Loved!' he interrupted her. 'Love and love! Do you call that love? I have never known what love is. 'Tis a wonder that waits always round the corner. If ever I do know, then I will be faithful. But *our* love! My dear, you use words too lightly.'

He hit her hard there, but she gave no sign. Her eyes did not quiver.

'Of course you are faithless,' she said. 'I have always known that, but I am not quite like the other women you have kissed. I always told you I was not. You cannot rid yourself of me so easily.'

'Can I not?' He looked at her speculatively. 'I have never been false to you. I warned you not to come here. I told you what it would be. Go back to Doncaster, my dear, and find a better man.'

That 'better man' hit her the hardest of all, because, although she thought him rotten, he was yet better for her than any other man in the world. A woman's bitter fidelity is always the honestest thing she has.

'Take me with you to the Fair today,' she repeated, 'and we will see. I've made no request for months but have faithfully stayed in this house, suffered every scorn at the hands of your wife, been hated by your children, been faithful to your interests – now, today, you will take me to the Fair.'

'I will not,' he answered, smiling up at her. 'David is the only one who goes with me.'

She turned past him and stood facing him, with her back to the window, blotting out the scene as though she thought that the mountain, at which he gazed so persistently, was her enemy.

'Listen, Francis. You are a bad man but a fair one. Here is a bargain. You have spoiled my life, shamed me before everyone, wrecked all my prospects, but I will feel nothing for all this if you will give me this day, one day as we used to have it, as we had it in Doncaster that Fair day when you bought me these shoes.' He knew that she was saying to herself: 'If I can but get him from this house and away with me as he used to be, I can charm him again.'

He answered her unspoken thought. 'You cannot charm me any more, not by one day nor by twenty. It is over. All done. I never promised fidelity. I never loved you. I have never loved anyone save my son. These things are not for our asking, my dear. Nature is rough when she tosses us our moods. "This one for you," she says, "and this for you," and no tears or scarlet slippers will change her indifference. Blame no one. Life is not understood by scolding.' Then he went on very kindly. 'Alice, go back to Doncaster and forget me. There was that fellow – how was he named? Matthew Priestly – he always loved you. He loves you, I doubt not, still. Blow no more on these dead coals. Forgive my indifference. It is the fault of neither of us.'

She saw something in his face that she understood. She gave him one long look and then slowly went. An hour later he was riding with David to Keswick. He could not quite rid his mind of her. Oddly enough it was now in connexion with David that he thought of her. David, ever since that quarrel between the two women, had kept his vow. He had refused to speak to Alice Press. The woman had taken it for the most part with a cold, haughty indifference, as though she could not be disturbed by the impertinence of a child, but yesterday there had been a scene. She had demanded of Herries that he should make his son answer her. Herries had ordered him. David, with set face and an odd little frown between his brows that was his father's own, had refused. Herries would whip him for disobedience. David, his body drawn tight together, kept to his refusal. He was stripped and whipped. Herries drew blood from his young son's white back, because he loved him so dearly and was so deeply bored with Alice Press. David put on his shirt and jacket without a word.

'And now will you speak to her?' his father asked him.

'No,' said David.

Then his father kissed him and gave him some fine ointment for his back. Today it was as though this had never been. David was in perfect happiness as he rode Caesar, laughing and chattering as he did sometimes when he was excited, making Caesar gallop on the free turf of Cat Bells, coming down into Portinscale as though he were heading a charge. The boy was growing. There would soon come a time when he would judge with a man's thoughts. He was a fine boy, of a stiff, brave, honest character, full of courage and obstinate. What would he think of his father?

The Fair was on the farther lake side of Keswick, on the broad meadows that ran to the lake's edge, not far from Pomfret's grand house, and it pleased Francis to think how greatly Pomfret must dislike to have all this rapscallion world at his very door. Keswick, at this time, was a town of one fair street and a huddle of filthy hovels. In the minor streets and 'closes' the cottages, little houses and pigsties were thronged very largely with a foreign and wandering population – riff-raff of every sort who came to steal plumbago from the mines or were wandering their way northward, off the main route; these houses were crowded with foul middens and encroached on by large open cesspools, pigsties and cowsheds. The refuse stagnated and stained the air and tainted the soil. Here were women of ill-fame, hucksters, thieves, many Jews who paid high prices for the stolen lead. At once on entering the town you were in another world from the honest and independent country of the statesmen and yeomen of the valleys – these statesmen who for centuries had lived on their own land, their own masters, and owed no man anything.

In the former year, 1731, in Keswick, out of a population of some twelve hundred, nearly five hundred persons had died of smallpox, cholera and black fevers. During the summer months the channels of ordure, the cesspools, became intolerable, and in the lower parts of the town respectable citizens could scarcely breathe.

The natural inhabitants of those parts, however, showed no discomfort and made no protest.

On this fine morning the principal street was shining with its white cobble-stones and a throng of people who pressed hither and thither, giving themselves up with complete child-like abandon to the fun of the occasion. The Fair had spread from its proper surroundings out into the street, and David and his father had to push through the groups surrounding booths and cheap-jacks and fancy quacks.

But the Fair itself, when they reached it, was a glory.

So many were the booths and stalls that the waters of the lake were invisible. On every side were announcements of wonders.

'Here is the Dancing on the Ropes, after the French and Italian fashion, by a Company of the finest Performers that ever yet have been seen by the whole World. For in the same Booth will be seen the two Famous French Maidens, so much admired in all Places and Countries where they come, for their wonderful Performance on the Rope, both with and without a Pole; so far outdoing all others that have been seen of their sex, as gives a general satisfaction to all that ever yet beheld them, to which is added Vaulting on the High Rope and Tumbling on the Stage.'

And here again: 'Here is to be seen a little Fairy Woman lately come from Italy, being but Two Foot Two Inches high, the shortest that ever was seen in England, and no ways Deformed, as the other two Women are, that are carried about the streets in Boxes from House to House for some years past, this being Thirteen Inches shorter than either of them . . . Likewise a little Marmozet from Bengal that dances the Cheshire Rounds and Exercises at the word of Command. Also a strange Cock, from Hamborough, having three proper legs, and makes use of them all at one time.'

Here was a play announced in front of a booth all gay with crimson cloth and gold tinsel –

'An Excellent new Droll called *The Tempest* or *The Distressed Lovers*. With the English Hero and the Highland Princess, with the Comical Humours of the Enchanted Scotchman, or Jockey and the three Witches. Showing how a Nobleman of England was cast away upon the Indian Shore, and in his Travels found the Princess of the Country, with whom he fell in love, and after many Dangers and Perils was married to her; and his faithful Scotchman, who was saved with him, travelling through Woods, fell in among Witches, where between them is abundance of Comical Diversion. There in the Tempest is Neptune with his Tritons in his Chariot drawn with Sea-Horses, and Mairmaids singing . . .'

And then the marvellous animals: 'The true Lincolnshire Ox Nineteen Hands high and Four Yards long, from his Face to his Rump, and never was Calved nor never sucked, and two years ago was no bigger than another Ox, but since is grown to this prodigious Bigness. This noble Beast was lately shown at the University of Cambridge with great satisfaction to all that saw him . . .

'The large Buckinghamshire Hog above Ten Foot long . . . the wonderful Worcestershire Mare, Nineteen Hands high, curiously shaped, every way proportionable; and A little Black Hairy Pygmy, bred in the Deserts of Arabia, a Natural Ruff of Hair about his Face, Two Foot high, walks upright, drinks a glass of Ale or Wine, and does several other things to admiration; and the

Remark from the East Indies; and the little Whifler, admired for his extraordinary Scent.'

Although David did not know it, some of these same animals must have been of an amazing age, because the celebrated Mr Pinkeman had himself shown them in the days of Queen Anne.

For David, however, hours must pass before he could take in any detail. He did not know that already behind the colour and show there was disgust and discontent on the part of the show-men, because the takings were so small, and there was no one there but gaping country-fellows, the discontent leading in the last day of the Fair to a free fight and riot that spread, before all was over, into the heart of the town.

It all seemed to him so grand and magnificent that there had been nothing in the world like it before. Walking close at his father's side he was caught up into a world of colour and scent – the faint September blue held the flare of the fires that blazed upon roasting meat and fish, popping corn and scented sweet-meats, the thick swaying tendrils of smoke that crawled about the booths, the waving of coloured pennants, the flaunting of flags, and, under this shifting roof of colour, everything broke and mingled again, dogs nosing for food, naked children sprawling in the mud, mummers in gold and blue, women, bare-breasted, shrieking after their men, tumblers somersaulting, a monkey loosed, dragging after him a silver chain, his face weary with age and loneliness, three dwarfs in crimson hose, with huge heads, counting money, a black woman, a yellow kerchief round her head, selling silver rings, clowns, soldiers, girls dressed like angels with white wings, the booths with the drum beating and shrill trumpets blowing, men stripped to the waist, their skin pouring sweat, fighting before a shouting crowd, everywhere eating and everywhere drinking, men tumbling women and women fingering men – and through these crowds the country-men, the farmer, the dignified statesman, the gaping yokel mov-ing like strangers, suspicious, aloof, and gradually tempted by ale and women and silver, by noise and food and curiosity, tumbling into the reeking tub and so kicking and shouting and screaming like the rest as the sun went up the sky.

Yes, hours passed. Somewhere, at some time, David had a sudden curious vision of all the colour, reek and noise of the Fair parting like a drawn curtain, and there in the clear space was the lake, misted yellow under a misted sun, cool and still, the line of Cat Bells rising softly above the woods on the farther side, the water still without a ripple, very cool and sweet. Then it closed again, and the stench of roasting meat and uncleanly bodies and painted boards melting in the heat of fires and frying corn and burning wood swept over him again, bringing with it into the very heart of his nostrils the whole pageant of bright colour, purple and gold and saffron, and the odd wildness of a thousand faces, eyes staring, mouths agape, and a roar of bells and whistles, shouts and curses and cries, the neighing of horses and barking of dogs and the shrill human scream of a crimson-pated cockatoo.

He was aware then that he had lost his father. He stood for a moment dismayed. On every side figures were pushing against and around him; now someone would run past him shouting; now two singing, falling from side to side, would lurch drunkenly his way; now with a cry, as though it had come from the ground itself, there would be a rush from a whole group; and all of this dreamlike – a flash of a sword, a trembling coloured flag, a creaking board of a booth, a ringing silver bell, the scream of the crimson-pated cockatoo, the wail of the lost monkey dragging his silver chain, a man bending a woman backwards against a boarded trestle, a naked muddied baby crying for its mother, all in a dream; where the clear, tranquil, golden-misted lake was, there was reality.

But he had no fear; he would see his father again; it was fine to be independent in a noisy world and to hold your own against the Devil. So, looking around him, he saw that he was before the very booth where he had most set his heart, the booth where the Chinamen were. On the outside of the booth a Chinese curtain hung in brilliant splashes of gold and red, a temple, a grove of golden bells, soldiers in armour, a bridge of blue, and in front of the curtain a Chinaman with a yellow face and an ebony pigtail was inviting everyone to enter. A bell clanged, the Chinaman called out in a shrill voice and at the same moment the thick pushing crowd shoved forward. David was caught in it, carried off his feet; he was pressed against smelling clothes and warm, sweating flesh; he clutched, that he might not fall, at a man's waist and held to it; his fingers stuck to the damp waist-belt and his arm was driven into a soft belly. For a moment he was almost under a dozen feet, then lifted up again on the sheet of a thousand smells and so almost hurled into the inside of the booth. He did not know whether he should pay money or no, he had lost his breath and found himself enclosed within the thick arm of a huge country-fellow, black-bearded, bare at the neck; their sense of one another was instantaneous, and the black-bearded man laughed, standing him in front of him, pressing him back against his chest, his hot naked arm against David's cheek.

He could see where he was. He was high on some raised boards. Everything around him was quiet. The noise of the Fair had been shut out. On every side of him the people with staring eyes, speechless, stood waiting. A little empty stage was in front of him and above it some curtains idly flapped.

All his senses were centred on this empty stage. It became to him full of omen and suspense. What was about to happen? Who would come there? A very ancient man came with a long face of yellow parchment. He wore a long stiff garment of purple brocaded silk. He sat, quite silently and quite alone, on a little round stool. He was motionless, carved in colours against the dark shadows of the flapping tent. He looked neither to right nor left, was unaware of the sweating crowd. Perhaps he was the Chinaman who was three hundred years old. If you were three hundred years of age you would not pay attention to any crowd; you would have seen so many.

Then the curtains parted, two young men in gold trousers, stripped to the waist, their bodies glistening, came and threw into the air coloured balls. They threw up a dozen balls at once, and the balls, green, yellow, red, made whirls of colour above the head of the old man who never moved.

Then there came two short fat men with very yellow bodies; they were clad only in loincloths. Standing in a corner of the stage they began silently to wrestle.

Then six young men came in trousers of gold and jackets of silver; they had poles up which they climbed; they threw ropes to one another and with pointed red slippers on their feet walked on the ropes. Lastly a number of little yellow-faced children, also dressed in bright, shrill colours, ran silently forward, spread their legs and their arms and stood in a pyramid: the child who climbed to the top and stood balancing there with his little feet seemed only a baby with tiny black eyes and a doll's pigtail.

Now all of them – the young men with the balls, the naked wrestlers, the men balancing on the ropes, the pyramid children who suddenly melted to the floor and were turning like bright bales a hundred somersaults and cartwheels – were moving ceaselessly round the old man who sat motionless on his little stool, never flickering, you could be sure, an eyelid. Faster and faster they turned, but always without a sound, and as they moved the tightly-packed crowd moved with them: the crowd began to sway and to murmur: everyone was smiling: the black-bearded countryman who smelt of good fresh dung put his arm tight round David's neck, pressing his body to him. They were all smiling as though they were in a dream, and it must have seemed to many of them that they too were tossing balls into the air, turning somersaults, climbing poles, balancing on ropes. Their bodies must have appeared free to them and clean and strong: the ordure and the filth, the daily toil, the cruelty and sickness and pain, the darkness and rain and cold freezing nights, the life with animals and the wrestle with the hard ungrateful soil, the penury and ignorance and darkness, the loneliness of rejected lovers, the injustice of tyrannous masters, the narrow, constrained horizons, the proud brutalities of a swollen-headed upper class against whom they struggled dumbly, whom one day – and that day was not far distant – they would conquer – all these hard things fell away, the sky was bright and clear, the air fresh like crystal, all for a moment was joy and happiness in a free world where it was always day.

As for David he could see nothing but the silent old man sitting on his stool. The old man seemed to be staring directly into David's eyes. However David moved his head he could not escape that old man. He began to be frightened. He wanted to run away. The old man appeared to have a message especially for him. In another moment something terrible would happen. His father was in danger. And it spread beyond the moment – all his life he would remember that old Chinaman, and whenever he remembered him he would shiver with apprehension. Life was dangerous, and you could only know how dangerous it was when you sat quite still and listened, waiting for a sound to break.

Anyway, he must go. He must find his father.

He wriggled away from his black-bearded friend, then, dropping down from the raised boards, pushing through legs and arms, shoving with his head now this way, now that, at one instant stifled by the human stench, at another brought up against a solid body that would never move again, at last he was by the flap of the tent and tumbled into the free air, leaving behind him, it seemed, a crowd hypnotized, in a trance, a dream . . .

He was in the open air again and frantically hungry. It must be afternoon. The sun was high in the sky.

So, looking rather desolate and half lost, his father, Francis Herries, saw him. Herries was a little drunk and soon would be

more so. Somewhere in the heart of the Fair where they were
bargaining about cattle he had discovered an old woman with a
store of wine. She sat under an awning, on either side of her a
cask of wine. A strange woman, very fat, with a purple face. She
did not seem to want to sell her wine, but sat there idly. Once and
again she broke into a strange raucous song in a deep, rumbling
voice. She ladled the wine out of the casks into long, thin
glasses: the wine was a shilling a glass, Portuguese on one side of
her, Florence the other. Herries drank the Portuguese. What was
it? He neither knew nor cared. Was it White Vianna or Passada
or Barabar? Carcavellos or Ribadavia? He drank many glasses.
The old woman did not speak to him nor he to the old woman.
After that everything entertained him. He had always been very
easily amused by little things, and there was something in him
that liked the stench and the common crowd and the press of
animals human and other—

He watched for a long while two men who, drunk with gin,
tumbled about in the mud together. Close beside him was a
fellow selling medicines. The two drunkards, suddenly weary,
kissed one another and lay there in the mud head by head, looking up at the sunny sky.

The quack, long, thin and brown, like a gnarled tree-branch,
with a high black hat – 'Here's a plaister will cure old Ulcers and
Fistulas, Contusions, Tumours and any Dislocations or Hurts,
and when it has performed Fifty Cures 'twill be ne'er the worse
but still keep its Integrity.'

He moved leisurely, looking for a pretty face. Where were all
the pretty women? Here at least not one. The country girls
hanging on the arms of their lovers were each more blowzy than
the other. There seemed to be none of his own class here. What
was it that gave him a sudden sense of freedom so that he was
happy as though he had thrown off bonds?

All these strange faces interested him, wizened and twisted
and swollen; he could throw off his fine clothes, put on these
tinsel rags and go wandering with them, drinking, wenching . . .
Then looking about him he saw his small son. With a pang of
reproach, oddly sharp as he saw his air, half defiant, half frightened, he cursed himself for the rottenest parent. To leave that
child in such a place, at such a time! And yet he did not move at
once towards him, but watched him, loving him, proud of him,
sturdy and self-reliant among all the oddities, the shouting, the
flaming fires. Whatever occurred that boy would not cry out, but
would stand on his courage to the last, letting endurance father

him were no other father there. And was not that because he had
no spirit of imagination? Imagination was the devil. Let your
fancy move and there, by that booth where the boxing was, you
could see the sun roll down from the sky and sweep them all –
pimp and trollop, bully and jade, monkey and dwarf, Indian and
Chinaman – with its fiery heat, screaming into perdition. As he
one day would go. But David would not stir, not till he felt his
duty was done.

Then he moved forward and was happy to see the boy's
pleasure spring into his eyes at sight of him.

'Did you think me lost?'

'No, Father. I've been in the Chinaman's tent.'

'And what did you see there?'

'There was an old man, they say he is three hundred years old,
and young men throwing balls.'

Then he added rather wistfully:

'Father, I'm hungry.'

'Come, we'll eat then.'

They moved through the packing crowd and came to a kind of
temporary hostelry. It had a grander, larger front than the
booths, and, inside, there were long trestle tables with benches
stretched on the grass and at the far end a defended fire with a
grid. The place was very full with people eating and drinking,
and many were already drunk, singing and shouting. David and
his father found places at the end of the tent near the fire. A
stout jolly man with an apron and a white cap asked them what
they would have. There was Pudding and Roast Beef, Boiled
Beef and Ox Tripe, Pigeons, well moistened with butter, without
larding.

'Pudding and Boiled Beef,' said David. It was then that he
saw that his father had been nobly drinking. He was too
thoroughly a boy of his time to be disturbed by drunkenness, but,
during these last weeks, he had grown greatly and taken a more
manly place in the world, and in nothing more than in his
attitude to his father. His father was weak where he himself
would never be. He did not know this with any priggish sense of
virtue: it came to him simply that there were times when he
must look after his father just as there were times when he must
look after Deborah.

He was a sort of guard to them, not because he was better than
they – all his life and through everything that happened he
would always look up to them, but only because he loved them.

He was uneasy now, as looking about the tent he felt that in

some way or another this was not a place for his father to be
riotous in. The men and women around them were of mixed
kinds: there were some sober and solid yeomen and townsmen,
eating their meat with grave seriousness, with the Cumbrian air
of guarding their own; there were some rascals of the Fair's own
company, one of them in a shabby gay jacket of gold thread,
another like a pedlar in a crimson cap (he reminded David of the
Stye Head Devil who gave him the little box) with a small
gibbering monkey sitting on his shoulder. With them were two
loose women very gaudily attired, laughing and shouting. One of
the women fondled the pedlar, thrusting food into his mouth.
Near his father was a group of better-class people. They might
be townsmen from Kendal or Penrith. One was very stout with a
double chin and little mouse-eyes. He was rather drunken already
and spilt his meat on his green velvet waistcoat. Another was a
little man, thin as a spider, with a shrill feminine voice. He was
over-handsomely dressed with an elaborately curled wig, a full-
bottomed coat of bright blue, and many rings on his fingers. He
was also drunken, and said many times over that he wanted a
full-bosomed woman to go to bed with, that he might wake in
the morning and find her near to him.

Herries, as was his way when he was drunk, had become very
grand and proud. The wine that now was brought to him, added
to the wine that he had already had, increased his grand dignity.
David, who very soon had eaten all that he wanted, began to be
unhappy and to plan some way of escape out into the air again.

Glancing here and there he knew that there were a number in
the tent who had recognized his father. He had long known that
there was much curiosity about his father and his father's family,
as to why he had chosen to exile himself in Borrowdale, as to his
dangerous liking for women, as to his mingling with anyone he
met and caring nothing for the quality of his company, as to his
having a fine mistress hidden away there in Herries and his
flaunting her full in his wife's face – David knew that all these
things were said and that already a queer chancy air had grown
about the building of Herries, and that they had all become the
more suspicious to the outside world because on their first
coming they had sheltered a Roman Catholic priest (and who
knew on what errand he had vanished less than a year ago?), and
had under their roof the most famous witch in Borrowdale.

All this was in David's mind and consciousness. His determination was set on getting his father away before some open
scandal occurred, and through all the murk and smell of the

crowded tent, stinking of meat, spilt drink and unclean bodies of men, he saw the old Chinaman's eyes, that Chinaman who was three hundred years old and sat like an image.

His father was very haughty, ate and drank without speaking to anyone. He seemed like a god to his son, sitting there so grand and handsome with his thin, brown face, his clear eyes and the silver waistcoat with the ruby buttons.

The spidery man in the full wig buried his nose in his glass, and then, in his shrill high voice, bowing to Herries, said:

'A drink with you, sir.'

Herries drank.

'I am from Kendal,' the little man went on, while the very stout fellow laughed immoderately. 'I have come hither to see the pretty women, but by Jesus there are none!'

'There are several,' Herries replied, eyeing him severely.

'There are several.' The little man tittered: 'You are fortunate, sir. My name is Rosen – may I be honoured by knowing yours, sir?'

'My name,' said Herries very proudly, holding up his glass and looking at the beads of colour in the yellow wine, 'is Charles Henry Nathaniel Winchester, Duke of the Pyrenees and the district of the Amazon.'

Mr Rosen became very serious. His little brow was puckered. 'I understand you, sir – a secret, between gentlemen.'

'There are women here,' said Herries, 'but no gentlemen – all the gentlemen are at the lake's bottom feasting with the mermaids.'

'I have heard,' said Mr Rosen, who realized only the last word of Herries's sentence, 'that a mermaid was indeed seen off the northern coast of Scotland a month back. I was told by one who had read of it. I could go to bed with a mermaid,' he hiccuped, and looked gravely distressed, 'were her tail not too long. Could one choose one's mermaid?'

It was then that a terrible thing occurred. David, more and more restless, seeing that the tent was now fully crowded, that several had moved near to them and were listening, had his eye on the tent's door. Through it he could see a patch of bright sunlight, a woman dancing on a tub and many figures passing in shadow. It was clear by the door. Someone entered, a woman, Alice Press.

He stared, first thinking that he was blinded by the sunlight, then that he had mistaken some other woman of a like figure for her – there was no mistake. She was wearing the black velvet

dress of the morning. He could see the silver chain lying against
it. And she wore the scarlet shoes. She stood quite by herself
staring about her. She looked up and down the tent. Then she
saw Herries. She saw him, looked full at him, then very slowly
began to move up the tent.

David's eyes were fixed. He had become an image of apprehension and fear. He could see only the green waistcoat of the fat
man and that down it there was trickling a little stream of wine,
while his big belly rose and fell in spasms of laughter. He did not
look at his father, but he knew, quite suddenly, that his father
had seen her. He felt for a moment his father's hand touch his
shoulder, then he heard Alice Press's voice.

'I have come, you see. Will you give me something to eat?'

There was a place at Herries's other side. She took it with
great ease and composure, but David, who, because of his detestation of her, had her in his very bones, knew as though it had
been himself that she was suffering from throbbing nervousness
and a devilish fear.

Herries, his face very stern, answered her quietly.

'Yes, since you are come . . . What will you have?'

She ordered something from the smiling man with the apron,
and, attempting a perfect ease, looked about her. She must have
seen at once that no women of any quality were there, but only
drabs and Fair ladies. All stared at her. At the door-end of the
tent a thick rabble was quarrelling and laughing at its own affairs,
but at the fire-end all eyes were upon her.

She smiled swiftly at Herries, and then began to talk.

'A kind fellow from Seathwaite brought me. I watched him
passing. 'Twas dull at the house and the day bright, so I thought
that I would venture for an hour. But I am hungry and 'tis three
o'clock. 'Tis a gay Fair and of a size for a little town, as large as
the Doncaster Fair. There are things to buy, I can be sure – will
you buy me something, Francis?' She put her hand for a moment
on his arm, laughing in his face. 'Yes,' he answered slowly, 'I
will buy you something.' He did not look at her, but stared in
front of him as though he were lost in thought.

Her food was brought, and she began nervously to eat. The
heat of the tent, her fear and excitement had brought colour to
her sallow cheeks. The black dress suited her and her full half-
revealed bosom. The little spidery man in the blue coat regarded
her with all his eyes, his mouth open, the stout man also.

She continued talking:

'And will you take me to see the sights? There is a Chinaman three hundred years old and a play . . .' She broke off. She was gathering courage. ''Tis time you showed me the world again.'

Herries, for the first time since she had come, looked at her.

'I will show you the world. It would be ungracious did I not when you have come so far. First you shall eat . . .'

It was then that the little Mr Rosen of Kendal caught up his courage and spoke to her. He raised his glass.

'May I drink to you, madam? You honour us by your company.'

She smiled at him, raising her glass, but her nervous thoughts were fast on Herries.

'We are all friendly together here,' she said. 'Pleasant company. Can you tell me, sir, whether the Chinaman has truly three hundred years?'

'They say so.'

'A very Methuselah. Are you an inhabitant of Keswick?'

'My town is Kendal.' The little man's eyes were now bursting from his head at the sight of the lady's opulence and beauty.

''Tis a finer town than Keswick.'

'Larger. 'Tis not for me to say that 'tis finer. We who are citizens of it have our private conceit.' He sighed, swelled out his chest, felt for the hilt of his sword.

After a little she looked at Herries. 'I have done eating,' she said. 'Will you take me to the sights?'

Herries drank his glass, looked at it after, with a firm hand, he had placed it on the table, then turned to her gently.

'Alice,' he said, 'as you have taken this on yourself so you take the consequences. When we leave this tent we part . . . You do not return to Herries.'

His voice was quiet, but he had not wished especially to lower it. Mr Rosen and his stout friend, and indeed all at that end of the table, heard the words.

The colour in her face deepened. She put her hand to her bosom, an action of hers that David knew well.

'Come, then,' she said, half rising, 'this is too public a place . . .'

'Nay.' He put his hand on her arm, holding her down. 'You have chosen it. Before we move hence you must tell me that you understand – at the tent door we part. You go no more to Herries.'

Her rage at the public insult – her temper was always beyond her command – flushed her cheeks. She, too, had in these ten minutes been drinking to give herself control. David saw her white hand pressed with desperate force on the table until the blue veins stood out.

'Be ashamed,' she murmured. 'In this place . . .'

'Yes,' he replied. 'In this place. I want your assurance.'

'No, then,' she cried, her voice suddenly rising. 'You bought me. You shall keep me.' It was odd how, with her anger and the freedom from the drink, the commonness that was in her blood suffused, like a rising colour, all her body and spirit.

'I bought you. Yes,' he answered quietly. 'Then I can sell you again.'

Everyone around them was silent. The stout man, very drunk, rolling his head, suddenly exclaimed:

'Aye, and who would not have her, this beautiful lady – though she cost him – his – his house and – and – horses?'

But David saw that she was very afraid.

'Francis, you have been drinking. I did wrong to come – I confess it – I will do all that you wish. But not here – not in this place . . .'

But he went on steadily.

'You have said it. I have bought you, and now, our bargain being ended, I will sell you again.' He fixed Rosen with his eye: 'You, sir, how much will you give me for this lady?'

Several men murmured shame, but everyone here was very drunken: there was some laughter, and a man began to sing a song. A woman very gaudily dressed and painted had come over and, leaning her bosom on the stout man's back, eagerly watched the scene.

'You insult the lady,' little Rosen began, half rising from his seat and feeling for his sword: then something in Herries's face constrained him, and he sat down again.

'I am indeed serious,' said Herries sternly. 'This lady and I are weary of one another and would part, but she is mine and I would have compensation. You, sir,' staring into Rosen's face, 'how much will you give for her?'

Alice Press rose – 'I will pay you for this . . . in good coin . . .' She made as though to go, but he rose also, laid his hand again on her arm, then, his voice clear so that all heard, said: 'This lady is for sale – for the one who will bid the highest.'

Cries broke out – some were laughing, some swearing, most too drunken to understand the affair; the garish woman laughed loudest of all.

A man said: 'Five silver shillings.'

Rosen, fuddled but struggling, in his funny feminine voice

screamed: 'You are a filthy dog – you shall be caned for this—' Nevertheless he could not take his eyes from Alice Press. His whole body hung towards her.

Herries answered him quietly.

'Come, sir, will you give me forty shillings?'

'He'll give forty shillings . . .' some drunken voice murmured like a refrain. The garish woman cried shrilly: 'More than she's worth, the bitch.'

Something happened then to Rosen. With a frenzied gesture he plunged his hand in his pocket, flung down on the table a heap of silver coin, then leaned forward, his face almost in Herries's.

'I'll take her. I'll take her. She shall come if she's willing – I'll care for her – zounds and the devil, I will – an she's willing.'

The money struck the table, and some of the coins, like live things, danced in the air, springing to the ground. A heap, shining there, lay before Herries.

'Have her then,' he said. 'I drink to you both.'

As he did so Alice Press turned to him and struck the glass from his hand. The wine splashed in his face.

She said something to him that no one could hear. Then clearly:

'You shall never be free from this.'

She looked about her once, proudly, and David, who still hated her, nevertheless at that moment mightily admired her.

Then she turned, brushed through the men and was gone.

Mr Rosen rose and hurried after her.

Herries picked up one of the pieces of silver, looked at it intently, then placed it in the deep pocket of his coat.

Quietly, without any haste, he went out. David, his head up, his eyes shining, followed him.

THE SEA - FATHER AND SON

IT WAS on a windy April night in the year 1737 that David and his father arrived at a new understanding together. The manner of it was on this wise.

The years that had passed since the very public exit of Mrs Alice Press had suffered this and that figure to rise for a moment before their indifferent background, and then to be whirled like a tumbled leaf into windy space.

There had been the cheerful, friendly Gay, who, dying of an inflammation of the bowels in three days, had drawn this unusual sincerity from Mr Pope: 'He was the most amiable by far, his qualities were the gentlest . . . Surely if innocence and integrity can deserve happiness . . .'

It was Mr Pope's profound opinion that they could not.

On the 13th of March, 1734, one Mr William Bromley had proposed that 'leave be given to bring in a Bill for repealing the Septennial Act, and for the more frequent meeting and calling of Parliaments' – and the echoes of that appeal were one day to affect even the remotest hearthstones of Borrowdale.

Other figures, oddly contrasted, beckon for a moment on the mirror. Bolingbroke, cursing everyone save himself, takes boat for France on a windy June morning; then Louis of France, making rude gestures, fingers at nose, that he may irritate, polished sophisticate that he is, the barbarian Stanislaus; and a heavy-jowled, good-tempered cynic is fingering women in a gilded London bedroom and refusing most resolutely to be irritated by either Louis or Stanislaus. He has seen, with a smile, the packing of Bolingbroke's boxes, has sighed and smiled cynically again because Nature that leaves so many dullards lagging on the stage has taken the great Arbuthnot after only sixty-eight years of noble brilliance, has snorted with his closest friend and intimate, snuff-taking Queen Caroline, over the rude, personally insulting dispatches posted indignantly by His Gracious Majesty, the Emperor Charles the Sixth, and has turned with a grunt back to his women and bottles again, strong in this policy of masterly inactivity, this heavy-jowled, good-tempered, massive-bellied cynic Walpole.

One more, before the mirror darkens and the months hurry to a more desperate destiny – a bright-cheeked, rosy boy receiving his baptism of fire at the siege of Gaeta, aged only fourteen, Don Carlos touching the boy's arm with his long hand, and thus angering Caroline and George in their London palace so that they must send to Walpole to soothe them – that boy Charles Edward, whose happiest moment, maybe, is just this when, from that little close-walled flowered garden, he looks across, a fire of ambition at his heart, to a thin line of smoky plum-coloured hills.

In Borrowdale, at Herries, David and his father, on the morning of the 10th of April, 1737, were preparing to ride over to Ravenglass to spend several nights with brother Harcourt.

David, who was almost eighteen now, and had broadened, strengthened, darkened, so that you would not know him for the same little boy who had pretended to sleep in the four-poster at the Keswick inn, knew nothing of Gay or Arbuthnot, of *The Beggar's Opera* or the malicious devilries of Mr Pope; but he knew by now a great deal about Borrowdale.

He knew the name of every Statesman in the valley and the faces and bodies of most of the humans there. He knew the innermost, intimate history of every possible fishing locality, the name of every bird, the lair of every fox. He had seen a wolf round the Glaramara caves, he had seen a golden eagle fly in the sun above Castle Crag, he had shared (without shame or shrinking – that sensitiveness did not belong to his time) in nearly every bull-baiting, dog-fighting, cock-fighting that the valley had to offer. He had learnt something of the spinning and weaving, and there had not been a Christmas Feast, a stanging at Twelfth Night, a pace-egging at Easter, a late summer rushbearing, a Hallowe'en or a local wedding at which he had not played his part. He was as popular (although he did not know it and would not have thought of it had he known it) as his father was not.

His whole young life had become absorbed by this valley world and by the close history of his own immediate family. They had been the seven happiest years of his life. He was a boy no longer. He was on the threshold of his manhood.

This journey to Ravenglass was to show him this. He had been anticipating eagerly a visit to his uncle Harcourt ever since he had first come to Herries. Uncle Harcourt was to be different, different from anyone he had seen or known. Harcourt had lived in the great world, he cared for the Arts, he was brilliantly read, a scholar, he could answer many of the questions that, for years now, David had been longing to ask.

For, although he loved everything that had to do with the outside world, he had, too, an intellectual eagerness that was perhaps the growth from seeds that Father Roche had sown. This had not been satisfied.

Simple, gentle little Robert Finch had come and taught the three of them what he could. That had not been a great deal. From the outside world the family at Herries had been more and more shut off.

Here, in spite of his externally happy life, lay the reason for the apprehension and misgiving that were in David's heart. For himself all might be well, for his family and for those whom he loved, all, as he very thoroughly knew, was not well at all.

The clouds had begun to gather after the scandal of the Chinese Fair. That scandal had been in its effects infinitely more public than seemed at the time possible. It had, indeed, been shameful enough for himself, and its effect on him had altered the whole balance of his character. Although five years now intervened he could yet see and feel every detail of it, the close and ill-smelling tent, the leaping fire, the genial host, the garish woman with the painted face, the bright blue coat of the little shrill-voiced man, the silver coins lying on the table, the broad stout hand of Alice Press stark on the table-board – but it had been, it had seemed, a private drama for himself and his father. For months he had caught no outside word of it. All that they had known at home had been that Alice Press was gone, and for ever: that had been relief enough.

Then, even to his boy's ears, bit by bit and piece by piece the story had come to him: the Peel boy knew it, Benjamin knew it, at last, as he found, his mother and his sisters knew it. It was a story incredibly distorted. It seemed to him, when at last he met it face to face, to have no relationship to the truth. Of course he hotly defended his father – but the mischief was done. Here was the man who had sold his woman in public for 'thirty pieces of silver'. Even to that country tradition in that uncouth time the event was memorable.

It clothed his father with a kind of 'apartness' – yes, even for himself. His father had always been for him like no other man, but that had been, in his youngest years, a difference of glory. Now it was a difference of peculiarity.

His was a character that must face everything truly and honestly as it came to him, and now he must face this – that his father could do shameful things and yet feel no shame. This, oddly enough, made him love his father more than he had done before, but it was a love very different from the earlier one. Now he must guard and protect this man who moved under some kind of influence that was straight from the Devil. David, of course, believed in the Devil – did he not know him as he was in human form?

His father must be loved and guarded because he was different from other men, but no longer could he be worshipped – and this brought him nearer to David. There had been from the beginning something fraternal in their relationship. That was now strengthened.

Other changes had come upon Francis Herries in these five years. He was not the beautiful, young, elegant person that he had been on his first coming to Herries. His body had stoutened, his dress was more slovenly, his air more careless. He bore at

times – although he was worlds apart from him – an odd resemblance to his brother Pomfret. At least you could tell now
that they were brothers.

In mood he was very much as he had been, gay, charming,
sullen, angry, kindly, cruel. He did not appear to feel his apartness. He had his acquaintances in Keswick, men with whom he
rode, betted and attended the country events, also women. But
David now knew he carried his secret life within him and was
never, for an instant, unaware of its presence.

They would have been, as a family, more thoroughly isolated
than in winter they were, had it not been for David's country
popularity on the one side that made him friends with everyone
in the valley and, on the Keswick side, strangely enough, because
of David's sister Mary.

Mary was now fifteen years of age and Deborah fourteen.
Mary was handsome – she would be a true Herries woman, big-
boned, broad-breasted, carrying herself with that mixture of
arrogance and confidence and grace – that blending of hardness
and courtesy, of indifference and kindly attention, that brought
in every country, society, and age such Herries women to the
front. She was indeed hard, determined, and ambitious. Of her
true feelings for her father she had given as yet no sign, but she
must from her very earliest age have felt that he was her enemy,
her thwarting opponent in every desire and longing that was
hers. In truth, every element in him must have always been dis-
tasteful to her, his recklessness, his irony, his grossness, and,
above all, his unconsciousness of and disregard for public
opinion. For she was cautious, unaware of subtlety, grimly
virtuous and alive to every public wind that blew.

Very early, indeed, she must have surveyed the scene and
decided that not for her were the isolation of Herries, the mire of
Borrowdale, the rusticity of the country company, the coarseness
and crudity of living. She had never any eye for any beauty save
her own, her only tenderness was to herself, and she had a power
of cautious waiting on the event, an ability to spin over months
and even years the web of her own secret plans, that was both in
its strength and secrecy extraordinary.

Very soon she had begun to turn her eye to Keswick and her
cousins there. That was her future world, or rather the stepping-
stone to a larger, grander one, and, at once, she began to use it.
Very early she won the admiration of her uncle and aunt. She
was in truth the very type that they could understand and
admire.

She found, as she grew older, ways and means of reaching Keswick that only ruthless determination could have taught her. At first her father had angrily forbidden her his brother's house, but soon he had grown indifferent and lazy. He had never cared for this daughter of his. He did not mind where she went. When she was fourteen she persuaded her mother that she must have dancing-lessons and, riding her own horse, would vanish into Keswick and no one question her.

It may have been that Pomfret and his wife found a certain triumph and pleasure in thus alienating one of the children of Francis, but it is more probable that they had not enough subtlety of mind for this. They gained a certain definite pleasure in hearing the child rail against her father, as she did in quiet, measured, determined tones, but soon it was reason enough that she was there simply because she dominated all the family and had already a kind of social power and authority that neither they nor their children would ever acquire.

Of Deborah, as she grew older, no one save David ever thought. She was not a pretty child. Pale of face, very thin of body, silent. Only her brother knew her and the rare, sweet spirit that she had.

It was from her that he obtained his deeper and more subtle consciousness of the beauty of the country around him. Child though she was, she was sensitive to the minutest beauties – a brown dry tree on a moonlight night, a glittering stream, the softness that snow on the hill-tops gives to the reflective valley, the yellow bunches of leaves on the oak tree, the purple depth of the lake seen beyond a bank of primroses, the low singing of the swallows, the whiteness of frost-bleached stones, the sudden flashing out of lights after a sullen storm, a brown stream running turbulently below a white cottage – above all, the sky of whose pageantry this country seemed more than any other to offer extravagant splendours. She would watch it constantly with a deep enwrapped contemplation, and yet she did not seem a dreamer, helped with a steady unobtrusiveness in all the business of the house; but she was, like her father, although in a very different way, a spirit alone, the only citizen of her mysterious world.

She had a passion for no other human being save David. More than anyone else in the family, she was attentive to Margaret Herries, never irritated by her stupidities or exasperated by her tears; but she had no close contact with her. That was, it might be, her mother's fault. It was her husband whom Margaret

Herries loved, ceaselessly, deprecatingly, monotonously, and her daughter Mary whom she admired. She would ask Mary wistfully about Keswick and Pomfret and Jannice. She did not go to see them because she was afraid of them and because her husband would be angry if she did, but theirs was the life that she would have preferred had she had the good fortune – to be in a fine house in a lighted town with company and cards and an occasional ball – but these only if Francis shared them with her.

As he did not choose that life she preferred this isolated one so that he shared it with her. Shared was perhaps too strong a word for anything that he did with her. He told her nothing, approached her always with that same mixture of sarcastic humour and rough careless kindness: she would never understand him at all; perhaps if the moment of comprehension had ever come to her she would not have loved him any longer, so that it was well as it was.

This, however, can at least be said, that, after Alice Press's departure, she was happier than she had been before. If he had other mistresses she did not know of them, and like many another wife, after her and before, so long as she did not know she did not question.

So these years had passed, a strange, slow mist of isolation creeping up around Herries, a mist not of fact but of suggestion, an atmosphere that slowly marked off this family as different from other families, a family of another colour, as though they had been, these Herries, of foreign blood, and had come from some very distant land where odd beasts dwelt and dangerous rivers ran.

It was just about now that, for the first time, someone said in Keswick: 'He's a rogue, Herries – a fantastic rogue.'

Meanwhile, in this April month, Francis and his son David rode together to Ravenglass to stay, for several nights, with brother Harcourt. They rode over the Stye Head Pass and down into Wasdale. David rode on Caesar, and Francis on a little shaggy horse that he called Walpole because he had a belly and was cynically indifferent to any morality. The little horses picked their way very carefully up the hill with deliberate slowness.

No one hurried them. The day was grey and still with little pools of sunlight in a dark sky. The hills had snow on their tops, but in the valleys the larches were beginning to break into intense green flame. As they wound up the Pass, the hills gathered about them, not grandly and with arrogant indifference as larger hills do in other countries, but with intimacy and friendliness as though they liked human beings and were interested in their fates.

By the Stye Head Tarn it was grim and desolate. This Tarn lies, an ebony unreflecting mirror, at the foot of the Gavel – beyond it, to the left, soft green ridges run to Esk Hause and the Langdales and lonely Eskdale.

Above the green stretches there are the harsh serrated lines of Scafell Pike and the thin edge of Mickledore. It was here, however, and on this day that David had his first sharp consciousness of the Gavel, the grand and noble hill that was one day to watch him struggling for his life.

It was not to be seen at its finest here from the Tarn, for it sprawled away to the right almost without shape and form: nevertheless the spirit of it, dauntless, generous and wise, seized and held him. The sunlight, hidden elsewhere, broke above its head and caressed it; long strathes of water, blue like the cold spring streams that ran below the snowdrops, spread about its shoulders.

The whole expanse of land here is wide and strong, so that although no plan or form is visible it makes of itself a form, the Tarn, the green stretches, the grouping hills having their own visible life without any human thought or agency to assist them.

They stayed for a little while beside the black Tarn. Herries, climbing the Pass, had been very genial, speaking of anything that came into his head, of a bull-baiting in Keswick, of funny days in Doncaster and of his old long-ago life near Carlisle. When he was thus he and David were like brothers. But suddenly now beside the Tarn he became morose and gloomy. He withdrew into himself. In silence they rode down into Wasdale, along the road, past the little church to the long lake's edge. Here there was great beauty, the grey lake without a ripple and descending into it the black precipitous Screes, savage and relentless, while on the bank where they rode everything was soft with golden sand, green shelving meadow on which sheep were grazing, and the larches bursting into leaf. All the afternoon they rode in silence turning inland over rough, dull country.

It was not until they came to Santon Bridge that Francis Herries broke the silence.

'Thy Uncle Harcourt is Jacobite. He is a romantic jackanapes. Let him not talk thee over.' Then he laughed, twisting himself round on his horse to look at his stolid, thickset, square-shouldered son. 'Not much romantic notion in thy head, David.'

David to his own surprise did not answer. Perhaps it was that the scene had now of itself become romantic. They were riding through thick woods, and between the spaces of the trees the evening sky was faintly rose. A bird, singing, seemed to accompany them. But it was not only the place and the hour. David found that his father had unexpectedly touched something in him that was deep and fervid. Was this the consequence of that ride, seven years ago, with Father Roche? He could hear the melody and worship of the priest's voice now – 'Even as our Blessed Saviour, so the King . . .'

And, realizing this, he was aware that there was something in him here that his father could neither govern nor command – nay, something that his father could not touch. And yet the folly of it! What did he know about Jacobitism, its rights or wrongs? And yet he seemed in those few moments between the dark trees to have started some conflict with his father.

'Where has Father Roche been these years?' he asked.

Herries tossed his head. 'How do I know? He is a fool, a fanatic. He had fine parts but must needs waste them on a mare's nest . . .' Then he added abruptly: 'He hath been in Rome, tying the Pretender's shoe-strings.'

He went on as the evening gathered under the rosy sky. 'He had a power over me. He has had a power over many. But, believe me, if ever he returns it will be for no good. An ill-omened bird. Yes, a fanatic – better that, though, than a half-nothing like your father. David, have you ever dreamt a recurring dream?'

David shook his head, laughing.

'I am too heavy of nights to dream.'

'I believe that.' Walpole stumbled. Herries pulled at him with a curse.

'I have a dream . . .' He stopped abruptly. 'There are the lights of Ravenglass. We are almost in.' They came clattering over the cobbles of the little place and smelt the salt sea and heard the sharp questioning cry of the gulls. A fellow standing in a doorway directed them to Harcourt's house.

Although it was now dark David could see the little square white-fronted house thrust back from the street in a small, walled garden. He smelt, as they waited by the door, the sting of the sea and an aromatic scent of herbs and could see here and there the faint yellow of blowing daffodils.

A little old man, very ancient, in a white wig, knee-breeches, and with large silver buckles to his shoes, holding a candle above

his head, opened the door cautiously to them, after much un-
bolting and unbarring and rattling of chains. A moment later
Harcourt Herries was there to greet them.

They all went together round with the horses to the stables
which were at the back of the garden. The stars were coming out
and a strong wind blowing. They returned to the house, and
Harcourt, a silver candlestick held high in either hand, led them
up to their room.

In the candlelight as he stood and talked to his brother, David
could see him clearly. He was a little thin spindle-shanked man
very elegantly dressed in an old fashion. He had the high, white
forehead and the air of breeding that belonged to the Herries,
the breeding that even Pomfret could not quite lose. You could
see that he was brother to Francis, but although he was only
twelve years older, forty-nine to Francis's thirty-seven, he might
have been his brother's father.

His face was thin and drawn and covered with a network of
wrinkles; his body was so slight and delicate that as with rare
china you might expect to see through it.

Everything about him was refined, from the thin gold ring
with a green stone on his finger, to the rich rose-colour of his
skirted coat. His voice, when he spoke, was very gentle and kind,
and there was in it a note, full and harmonious, that resembled
something in Francis's voice.

He looked exceedingly fragile as he stood in the candlelight
beside his brother, whose body was beginning to thicken, and his
nephew, whose strength and health shone through his young
limbs. He had things about him that were like Francis and Father
Roche and Deborah, the three people for whom David had, in
his life, cared the most.

Harcourt left them to wash off the dirt and weariness of the
ride. The jugs and basins in the room were of old beaten silver,
and round the top of the four-poster ran a fine tapestry with
friezes in rose and old saffron.

Before they went down, Francis said to his son: 'You will find
no woman in the house. Harcourt was once in his youth crossed
in love. He cannot abide women, and will have none about him.'

Downstairs in a charming panelled parlour they had a meal
that was to David a delight. The candlelight trembled before the
dark panels.

It was late indeed for dinner, but there was fine fare – a grand
salmon, a patty of calf's brains, a piece of roast beef, a dish of
fruit with preserved flowers, spinage tarts, sweet with candied

orange and citron peel mixed with the spinage, marrow and eggs, and fresh fruit, pears and China oranges and muscadine grapes. There were French wines, Pontack and Hermitage, and later when the table was cleared and showed a pool of splendour under the candles, a bowl of Brunswick Mum, the most intoxicating liquor known to man. Neither Harcourt nor his nephew was drunk. The boy felt perhaps that for the first time, outside his own house, he was treated as a man. Harcourt was a most charming host, telling them in his gentle voice the romantic things about Ravenglass – how its name meant grey-blue river, how three rivers – the Esk, the Irt, and the Mite – joined here to make the almost landlocked harbour, how once the Romans had been here and made a camp. How in those days it was a place of importance, had its charter in the beginning of the thirteenth century, and at Muncaster Castle near by, the Penningtons would take refuge from the sea raiders, how Henry VI, fleeing there after a lost battle gave his host an enamelled bowl of green glass, 'the Luck of Muncaster', how still there was traffic in the harbour and much smuggling to and from the Isle of Man, which was but forty miles away. He said that, as he sat there in his room, he could see the Romans and the men of the Middle Ages and all the busy citizens of the place, when it was a prosperous town, come crowding about him with their long, thin faces and strange distant voices – and at that Francis, who was now drunk with the Mum, laughed at him and called him a romantic fool.

It was then that David felt again an odd wave of antagonism to his father sweep over him.

There was something moving between them, something new that had never been between them before: soon it would appear and would be defined.

He became in that first evening attached to his uncle, and it was plain enough that his uncle delighted in him; on the next morning, which was cold and windy, Francis was oddly morose and, saying very little to either of them, went off by himself. Uncle and nephew sat by the coal fire in the parlour.

Harcourt talked of the days when he was a boy in the London of Queen Anne. He had been fourteen years of age when he first went there. He had been present at the sacking of the New Court in the Sacheverell riots and had seen the huge bonfire of its furniture in Lincoln's Inn Fields; he had had nights on the *Folly*, the Thames barge opposite Whitehall, although it had already then fallen out of fashion; he described the coffee-houses as

though he were still frequenting them – Anderton's, the Bay
Tree, Button's, Child's, where you might, an you were lucky, see
learned celebrities like Dr Mead and Sir Hans Sloane; or Don
Saltero's, set up by Sir Hans Sloane's servant, where there was a
collection of curiosities such as the Queen of Sheba's cordial
bottle, Gustavus Adolphus's gloves and King Charles II's beard
which he wore in disguise in the Royal Oak.

He had been a great lover of the drama, he told David, a faint
flush of enthusiastic memory staining his wrinkled cheek.

In the Dorset Gardens Theatre, he had witnessed a performance by the lovely Mrs Tofts. This theatre was pulled down in
1709, and the world of pleasure knew it no more. In the Theatre
Royal, in Drury Lane, he had been thrilled by the performance
of the second part of *The Destruction of Jerusalem*. He would
never forget the splendour of Mrs Rogers as Berenice.

But his chief love had been the Italian Opera. He had himself
been present at the great event of its opening on the 9th of April,
1705, when Vanbrugh and Congreve had been there and Mrs
Bracegirdle had spoken the Prologue. The opera on this occasion
had been *The Triumph of Love*.

As he talked he seemed to recreate about him all the distant
and vibrating life of that old time, already so quaint and un-
modern, with the busy scenes on the river, the perils of the night
Mohawks, the chatter of the shops and coffee-houses, and great
figures like the Queen and Harley and Marlborough moving in
splendid ghostly grandeur.

But what held young David and made this talk memorable to
him for ever was the note of wistful and yet acquiescent regret in
his uncle's voice. That had been the time when life had been so
full of energy and eagerness: everything had been promised
then – love and fame and great company – now in this little
house, with the sea-coal's thin glow between the fire-dogs, the
whisper and rustle of the sea beyond the dark windows, the sense
of the little dead and abandoned town once of so busy a prosperity, the remoteness, the half-death-in-life, the eternal melancholy of the indifferent passing of time . . .

Nevertheless, Uncle Harcourt was cheerful enough. He
opened with delicate, reverent fingers his bookcases and pro-
duced his Spensers and Miltons and Ben Jonsons. His favourite
poet was Mr Pope. He had Lintot's *Miscellany* with the first
publication of 'The Rape of the Lock', and the earliest editions
of the *Iliad* as the volumes appeared from 1715 to 1720.

But most of all did he love the 'Elegy to the Memory of an

Unfortunate Lady', and, with tears in his eyes, recited, his voice quivering a little as he spoke:

> 'By foreign hands thy dying eyes were closed,
> By foreign hands thy decent limbs composed,
> By foreign hands thy humble grave adorned,
> By strangers honoured, and by strangers mourned!
> What tho' no friends in sable weeds appear,
> Grieve for an hour, perhaps, then mourn a year,
> And bear about the mockery of woe
> To midnight dances and the public show!
> What tho' no weeping Loves thy ashes grace,
> Nor polished marble emulate thy face!
> What tho' no sacred earth allow thee room,
> Nor hallowed dirge be muttered o'er thy tomb!
> Yet shall thy grave with rising flowers be drest,
> And the green turf lie lightly on thy breast:
> There shall the morn her earliest tears bestow;
> There the first roses of the year shall blow;
> While Angels with their silver wings o'ershade
> The ground, now sacred by thy reliques made.'

So long as he lived David was never to forget that scene – the little man, his wig a trifle awry, the volume in one hand, the other hand behind the heavy skirt of his coat, the gentle, melodious voice, the rain, that had now begun to fall, beating on the pane, the distant surge of the sea, the steady friendly murmur of the grandfather's clock. He was not imaginative as his father was; he was never to care very passionately for art and letters, but he made, in this morning, a new friend and acquired for ever some sense of the tragedy of the passing of time and the deep intangible beauty of old loyalties.

His uncle afterwards began to speak of his father. David at once perceived two things, one that his uncle had in his youth deeply loved his father. His older years had given him a protective maternal love of him. There was something very feminine in Uncle Harcourt's nature, and more and more as the morning passed he reminded David of Deborah. And, secondly, Harcourt was greatly distressed at his brother's appearance. He had not seen him for six years and although he said but little and asked but few questions David could see that some unexpressed alarm worked in him.

He spoke of Francis's youth, of how he had been always

different from the others, capable of the greatest things, but that some instability had always checked him. 'He hath always imagined more than he grasped, dreamed more than he could realize. There is a wild loneliness in his spirit that no one can reach.'

Then coming and putting his hand most affectionately on David's shoulder he added: 'But he hath bred his greater self in his son, who will fulfil his dearest hopes. I can see that, and it gives me great happiness.'

They were thus affectionately together when Francis Herries came in. He stayed in the doorway then came forward. 'A very pretty picture,' he said. They were both immediately conscious of anger in his voice. David drew away from his uncle, getting up and moving to the window.

'Welcome, brother,' said Harcourt. 'Be warm by the fire and tell us where you have been.'

'Nay,' Francis continued, his voice dry with sarcasm, 'I am one too many. I have a book to read – in my room.' But Harcourt came across to him, laughing, put his hand on his shoulder and drew him to the fire.

Francis was like a child. He sat by the fire, his feet stretched out, and sulked. Their evening meal was not very gay. David felt in every vein antagonism to his father. To repay his brother's courtesy with such childishness! At the age that he had, to sulk and pout like an infant! And yet behind the childishness there was something real. Jealousy? Loneliness? Discontent? Through the evening the antagonism between them grew. By the close of the meal David was miserable. This was none of the old childish quarrels that ended in a beating. And yet what was it about? Where was its growth? A ride through darkening woods, drunkenness over Mum, a flurry of rain . . .

Sitting there Harcourt raised his glass. 'The King!' He crossed the glass in the air.

Francis sprang to his feet. 'None of that humbug, brother! The boy has enough nonsense in his head.'

Harcourt flung his glass behind him. It smashed on the wall.

'I have drunk my toast in my own house,' he answered evenly.

An idiotic moonlight fluttered at the window, very feeble and wavering.

Francis walked to the door, stayed, then came back and put his hand on his brother's shoulder. 'I am become too serious. I have had a day with only ill thoughts for company.' Then, surprisingly, he turned to his son. 'Will you come out with me, David? There is a moon.'

The boy nodded, then turned, smiling, to his uncle:

'You will not be lonely for an hour?'

The little man smiled back at him.

'Mr Pope will drink a glass with me.' They all smiled at one another. Friendliness had suddenly returned.

Francis and David walked out into the little street, which was quite deserted. There were two sounds, the even whisper of the sea and some drunken fellow at a distance shouting a chorus. The moonlight was a faint, grey, glassy shadow dimming the sharp outline of the houses, but at the sea-edge it was stronger, flooding the water and giving an unreal size and shape to the distant sand-dunes that lay like lazy, grey whales on either side of the harbour.

A little boat stayed very faintly rocking at the shore's edge.

'Shall we take the boat out to the sand?' Francis asked. 'There's no one to prevent us.' They climbed in, Francis took the oars and in silence rowed over the water.

It was not excessively cold, and as they went forward the clouds shredded away, the moon came out riding in a misty, starless heaven. Round her was a ring dark red in colour.

David wondered what his father was going to do. He had some purpose. David on his side felt his own independence resolutely strengthen. Some subservience that there had always been to his father was no longer there. The boat shelved gently on to the sand and they stepped out. The sand was hard and crisp under the feet: the dune was naked save for a thick black post that stood up, like a finger in the moonlight. They walked over the dune and stood on the farther side. The sea was stronger here, coming in fiercely and drawing back with a powerful grating reluctance. They stood together looking out.

'I will not have you play with this Jacobite folly,' Francis said suddenly. 'Understand me in this. You are a child – your uncle is an old dreamer and babbles of Queen Anne.'

David straightened his shoulders. 'I have played with no Jacobite folly,' he said. 'I have only spoken of it once and that for a brief while.'

Francis felt the new tone in the boy's voice. 'You had some fine intimate confidences with your uncle,' he said scornfully. 'I should have remembered that he has a way with young men. Had I remembered I would not have brought you.'

In each of them anger was rising; their isolation, thus standing quite alone in a bare world that was all moonlight and water, increased their sense of opposition.

David said coldly: 'I am no child, Father, any longer. I must have my own judgement. My uncle is a generous host. Today you have left him all afternoon and he has not seen you for six years.'

His father turned to him passionately. 'And so the babe has grown ... By Christ, I'll sit meekly by and have my son read me a lesson. Has the hair grown above your belly yet, and how many women are with child by you?'

David stood his ground, but strange old fears, born of whippings and terrors and childish nightmares, crowded over the sand-dune and caught at his feet. 'I am on the edge of manhood and you should know it. I have been child to you long enough. If I find my uncle careworthy I have a right to care for him. It is time when I must think for myself. I love you, Father, as I love no one else alive. There is a bond between us, and, I suppose, will always be, that we can have with none other. You have often recognized it. But I am my own man. I have my own life to carry, and yield my liberty to no one—'

Francis laughed. 'Your liberty – who constrains it? You speak bravely of love, but there is also a word duty. When I say bend you shall bend. When I command you shall go. No doubt but your uncle's flattering enlarges you – but not with me ... come here.'

David came close to him. Francis caught his cheek and pinched it. 'You are mine, my fine son – strip now. Here, under this moon. I will run you naked into the sea – cold bathing for a rebellious son. That shall cool thy Jacobite notions. Strip then.'

'I will not,' David said. He was trembling from head to foot, but neither with chill nor with fear.

'You will not? ... Better for thee far to obey. Strip – naked as you were born.'

'I will not,' David said again.

Francis had in his hand a small cane with gold-stamped head. He raised it and struck David across the cheek with it. David caught it, flinging it far into the sea.

They stood staring the one at the other.

'That – never again,' David said quietly. The moonlight showed the red weal from his eye to his mouth – 'The last time ...'

Francis stayed without a word. Then he turned and walked away across the sand.

David stood there looking at the red ring around the moon, knowing that something fundamental that would affect all his life had occurred. He had the quality of common sense in melodrama; the unreality of any scene did not lead himself to unreality. This was unreal, the desolate sand, the crazy moon redringed, the mildewed sea, his father's assault, his own action – all unreal and yet at their heart a real and true fact, that he was child no longer.

He waited: he was sure that his father would return and that then, perhaps, they would be companions as they had never been before. His father did return, slowly coming across the sand, his figure thin and hard in the soft moonlight.

When he was near David went up to him, holding out his hand and smiling. 'You must know for yourself,' he said, 'that the water is too cold. And for your cane you shall have another.'

Francis caught him, gripped his shoulder, then stood close, his hand against his wounded cheek.

'You are a boy no longer. You are right in that. But I have been jealous today, suffering torture for you.

'Always I have been judged to lose anything where I put value, and to catch to me closer than a flea anything that was worthless.

'For years I have been prepared for you to go like the rest. When you were a baby I would watch and say, "Now, in a moment his eyes will change. He will know me for a rogue." And then, as one accident after another passed and still you were the same, I would say, "He is only a child. He hasn't heard. He hasn't years enough to understand." When my temper or my lust has driven me I have thought, "This will take him away the sooner," and I have almost wished for that, because my dread of losing you would be the earlier satiated. And now, today, watching your happiness with your uncle, I went out so that he should tell you everything – how as a child I did this and as a youth that, this way a rogue, that way a villain.

'I thought, "When I return he will know me for what I am, and our time together will be over. Then everything and everyone will have gone from me and I need fear no more."

'And I came in and saw his arm about your neck and hated you, loving you never so dearly as then. Never so dearly – save now.'

He broke off, then drawing David closer to him, waved his hand at the moon. 'The red ring – so it was when I ruffled my first girl, twelve years of age as I was, in a hay-loft.' Then he turned David towards him and looked at him: 'One day you will go from me – but not yet.'

David, smiling, said:

'Why should I ever leave you? I have no light sentiment about persons. You and Deborah I could never leave. You have told me,' he went on, hesitating a little, 'that I have no imagination nor fancy. I think that is true. I see what is before me and only that. But I am the easier faithful. I have noticed that those who have much fancy are but rarely steadfast. But this I know. Were I made more cleverly I would be of less enduring service to you.'

He said this with a very grave air, as though he had long been elderly.

His father answered him: 'There are only nineteen years between us, and as time goes they will lessen. Soon we shall be of an age: then you will pass me and be old before I am weaned. But remember this,' he touched the boy's arm lightly, almost withdrawing from him, 'whatever others say, I have it in me to be faithful – only as yet I have found neither cause nor person nor quality fit for that fidelity. I say this with no arrogance. I know what I am, and that is no fine thing. Nor do I say that with modesty. God may answer, if He is, for it is He that has made a man in a mouldy broken image of a divine ambition . . . But always with us Herries there have been one or two who see farther than they can reach and hope for more than they shall ever get.

'Their place is to break up that pattern formed so beautifully by such as your dear Uncle Pomfret. So the strife goes on, and will always go between the marred angels and the belly-filling citizens who have their fine houses and thank God they are not as others.

'The Herries have always been thus, and will always be, so making a fine study for your social observer.

'But I can dream of beauty, and if one day it is put in my hand . . .'

He broke off. 'What I would say,' he added, kicking the sand with his shoe, 'is that crab-apples are deceiving when they shine in moonlight, and the taste is stale.'

Then, almost passionately, he cried:

'Ah, but stay by me, David. I am going the wrong way, and what matters it? It is only another man lost. But one day I may be faithful to something, and then I would have you witness of it.'

David, who only saw the principal fact, that his father needed him, answered, as Ruth once answered:

'I will never leave you.'

His father, looking at him ironically, said:

'Your imagination saves you, Davy. That you have none, I mean. But you have made a vow here. I must have something for the loss of my gold cane.'

And then, the wind once more rising, whipping up the waves, they turned back across the sand.

CHRISTMAS FEAST

THE DECEMBER weeks that winter of 1737 were wonderful. Frost held the valley: Derwentwater Lake was frozen from end to end for thirteen days; the hills were powdered with thin patterns of snow hardening to crystal under a blue sky.

The valley was now truly enclosed. The outer world did not exist for it. The autumnal rains had been very violent, and, after them, Borrowdale barred its door.

The Herries family itself took the fashion. Even Mary deserted her Keswick cousins. As Christmas approached they were all caught into the general eagerness. In every house in the valley such a baking and brewing was going on as the Herries children had never seen in their Doncaster days. And the materials for this were all self-provided. No going into Keswick for town provisions. The valley was sufficient for itself. Down the path below Herries the Statesman Peel would be striding, his hands in huge home-made mittens, his jacket buttoned up to his chin, passing his dairymaid who, with her piggin in her hand, was hurrying to the cow-house, relishing the warmth and smell of the cows after the bitter cold that descends from the snowy hills; the boys sliding on the little pond beyond Herries in their wooden clogs, the blue sky, the snowy hills over all, the Wise Man with the pink ribbons to his moleskin hat moving up the road to Seathwaite, witches hiding, no doubt, in the Glaramara caves, the Devil warm at a farmhouse fire with his pedlar's pack, and all the wives and daughters washing, baking, churning; the puddings and pies will be enough for all Cumberland.

As Christmas approached more nearly David became uneasy and restless. It may have been that there was something ominous for him in the strange isolation of this valley. It was not that he was dull; every moment of the day seemed to be filled. He was now friend to all the valley. Whatever they might feel about his father there was no differing opinion about himself. His handsome looks and splendid body (he promised to be a giant both in breadth and height; he was already as tall as his father), his courage, openness and sincerity, the absence of all conceit and social arrogance, his simplicity, a certain animal lack of subtlety, his kindliness of heart and warmth of feeling – here promised to be a man of no ordinary colour, and everyone realized it. He had that greatest of all powers – he loved his fellows without being conscious that he loved them. Had he been a little less simple he might have seen them more justly, but in the end have judged them more untruly.

With all its simplicity, his character, as it was developing, was not uninteresting. His fearlessness, honesty and warmth of heart gave even his smallest adventures a richness of colour. He was of the race around whom legends grow: already people told stories of his strength, of how he had bent an iron bar in Peel's kitchen, beaten a shepherd from Watendlath, and whacked a Seathwaite farmer at singlestick and he champion of the valley – small stories, but he was already talked of beyond Bassenthwaite and over Buttermere and Loweswater. Borrowdale was the proudest of all the valleys and the stickiest to foreigners, but its natives already showed signs of adopting young Herries. Young Herries, but no other of the Herries family. It was possibly of this that David was subtly aware, partly this that roused his uneasiness.

It seemed to him that this valley had entrapped them. He was not sorry to be entrapped – he was happier here than he had ever been anywhere – but the sense that they were caught and held roused his fear. It was the only fear that life perhaps could give him – the fear of confinement – and now not so much for himself as for his father. He was growing now to be a man and ever since that night at Ravenglass he had been on shoulder-level with his father. His father seemed to him more alone than anyone in the world. No one in the valley was his friend. He was someone of a different nation from all of them – from his own son as well.

And the valley, because it was at this time almost savage in its isolation, hated and feared, like all savage things, what was different from itself. David loved his father now more than he had ever done, but he understood him less the older he grew, and feared for him more with every day.

He saw with his own eyes once a small child run from his

father screaming. He did not yet know that the mothers of the valley told their babies that Rogue Herries would eat them if he caught them.

Nearer to David's father than any other man in the valley was Statesman Peel. He was himself a rather isolated man, gigantic in build but silent, keeping to himself. Rendal Peel, his son, David's dearest friend, was frightened of his father and could manage no contact with him. He too was a silent boy, adoring David, following him like a dog.

So there they were this Christmas that was fated to add another legend to the Herries story. Rogue Herries who sold his woman for thirty silver pieces and Rogue Herries who was slashed in the cheek by young Osbaldistone . . . Nothing stands still. The course that the lives of Francis Herries and his son David were to take was largely fashioned that winter.

All England was at this time wrapped in superstition: the Age of Reason was only now stirring in that romantic womb – and no valley in England was more superstitious than this little one of Borrowdale. Perhaps you could not call it superstition, so active a part in daily life did they play, pixies and warlocks, gnomes and little green Johnnies, the Devil and his myriad witches. It was not far back that men of Borrowdale, seeing a red deer on the hills, had thought it a horse with horns and pursued it for a magical twist of the Devil; and the wall to keep in the cuckoo would yet have succeeded had it been but a story higher.

It was unlikely that David, a child of his time, would escape this magic. As he sat now, a week before Christmas, with Deborah before the open fire in the Herries hall and saw the snow swirl like twisting worsted beyond the leaded panes, he felt that they were both held there by a spell – the spell, it might be, of his wicked old ancestor hanging on the panelled wall.

His great shoulders and long legs sprawled beyond his chair; his fair head was thrown back; his eyes, warm in spite of their bright blueness, stared into the black beams above him. Deborah, seated at his feet, looking up at him, thought that she had never seen anyone so splendid.

'Deb, why is it that they hate Father so?'

For how long now had this question been hovering between them!

'There is a separateness about Father.' She stared into the golden cavern that hung, lit with sparks of fire, between the black logs. 'They cannot understand him nor he them.'

'Deb, do you understand him?'

'Yes, I fancy so. He dreams of what life should be and because it falls so far behind his dream he abuses it.'

David let his hand fall on her hair.

'I am no dreamer, but I can see how a man in this life may have ambitions to alter it. I am a poor oaf, Deb. I love every moment of the day. Just to feel the blood in my veins is enough for me. Such a day as yesterday with Rendal on the Gavel when, from the summit, you could look out to the sea like a green shawl and all the tops hushed with snow . . . That's enough for me, Deb. And always will be. I shall never go from here. I shall never do anything in the world . . . I cannot be unhappy like my father.' Then he added, dropping his voice: 'I am afraid for our father.'

And she whispered: 'I also.'

They had never, although their lives had been so intimate, confessed so much to one another, and in their young hearts, courageous and generous, there beat a tremendous impulse of loyalty and protection to him.

They offered their young bodies and their strong souls as shields and bucklers for his protection, whatever he might do or be. No matter how valueless his worth they were his guard and would always be.

Deborah looked up to David and clasped his hand; as they looked at one another that was what they meant. Then they both saw, leaning a little heavily against the windowledge, their mother. Her face was pallid: her hands gripped the wood. She was like a heavy ghost: she had made no sound and her eyes did not move.

'I am unwell,' she suddenly gasped. 'I have a sharp pain at my breast.'

David jumped up and ran to her. He put his arm about her and with his great strength almost carried her up the little stairs to her room. She smiled very faintly as he laid her on the bed.

'The pain is nothing,' then, closing her eyes, she murmured, 'Christ is kind . . . He moves gently . . .' She caught her son's hand. 'Don't tell your father . . . How cold it is in this valley.'

She was better again by Christmas Eve, and was up seated in the hall, watching them dance to the fiddle of old Johnny Shoestring, whose bow squeaked like a dying hen. That was the happiest evening they had yet had in Borrowdale. The hall was bright, the fire leaping, the candles burning, the floor shining. Wilson had hung three old flags that had been buried in the oak chest, one of crimson with a white cross, one of faded purple and one of green. Whose flags? From what wars? No one knew. The holly was thick with red berries that year and hung from the rafters. They could hear the bells ringing from the Chapel above the splash and crackle of the fire. Francis was a child, younger than any. They danced till they sank on the floor with weariness. Margaret Herries never moved her eyes from her husband.

Next night, Christmas night, they were invited to Statesman Peel's. It was not as it was in most parts of England where, at Christmas time, the Squire was the King of the Castle and his subjects were graciously bidden to enjoy his hospitality with a proper sense of his grand benignancy and their inferior peasantry. In Borrowdale every Statesman was master of his own house and owed allegiance to no one. Every Statesman's house was open on Christmas night to all the world, rich and poor. There were the guests, indeed, who had their special places there, but the doors were wide open to the stars and the line of friendly hills and the hard-frosted road.

Peel's kitchen this night was a place of splendour. Its warmth and colour, its happiness and hospitality, stretched to the farthest heavens. Glaramara and the Gavel looked in at the windows, the Derwent rolled its waters past the door, and every star scattered its light over the roof-tree.

There is no house like Peel's house anywhere in England any more, but, as it stood then, in its life and strength and happiness, it was thus. It was a strong place, secured with strong doors and gates, its small windows crossed with bars of iron. It held three rooms on the ground floor and two on the second storey.

The front door was covered with a low porch, the entrance from which was called the 'thresh-wood' or threshold, and on this thresh-wood crossed straws, horseshoes and so on, were laid to hinder the entrance of witches. From this there was a broad passage through the house called the 'hallan'; sacks of corn were deposited here before market-day, pigs were hung after killing, and there was a shelf over the door where sickles hung and carpentry tools were laid.

In Peel's house the hallan opened straight into the 'downhouse'. This was in his case the great common room of the family, the place of tonight's Christmas Feast. Here, in the course of the year, everything occurred, baking, brewing, washing, meals, quarrelling, courting, tale-telling. This downhouse had no second storey but was open to the rafters. In later days a second storey was often built over the downhouse. The sides of this room were smeared with clay and cow-dung. Joints of meat hung dry for winter use. From the smoky dome of the huge fireplace dropped a black sooty lee called the 'hallan drop'. Under this the women knitted or spun wool or flax, the men sometimes carding the wool, the children learning their lessons, the old men telling their tales. At the opposite end of the passage was the mill-door and beyond this another passage known as the 'heck', and this heck was terminated by a huge octagonal post. Into this post sometimes a hole was bored and in it a piece of cow-hair secured by a wooden peg for the purpose of cleaning combs, and behind the heck was a bench.

The windows were separated by stone munnions, and here were the Bible and Prayer Book, *Tom Hickathrift* and Sir William Stanley's *Garland*.

The chimney wing was spacious. Indeed, this was a really vast chamber, for it was the 'house' or dwelling-room and 'down-house' or kitchen thrown into one. Part of it therefore stood for kitchen with the great chimney and hearth; here, on the heap of wood ashes, was the 'handreth', an iron tripod on which was placed the 'girdle' for baking oat-bread. Before the fire stood a spit. The two standards, which were three feet high with seven hooks, were hinged, so that they could be folded and put away when not in use. The spit, a slender rod, was six feet in length, and on the rod were two pairs of prongs to hold the meat, and beneath it a dripping-pan. There was a handmill or 'quern', a malt mill, a spindle and a 'whorl', a spinning wheel. In the chimney wing were hung hams and sides of bacon and beef, and near the fire-window was an ingle-seat, comfortable most of the year save when the rain or snow poured down on to the hearth, as the chimney was quite unprotected and you could look up it and see the sky above you. Such was the kitchen end of the room. The floor tonight was cleared for the dancing, but at the opposite end trestle tables were ranged for the feasting. Here was also a large oak cupboard with handsomely carved doors. This held the bread, bread made of oatmeal and water. On the mantel and cupboard there were rushlight holders and brass candlesticks. In other parts of the room were big standard holders for rushlights.

All these tonight were brilliantly lit and blew in great gusts in the wind.

Francis Herries, arriving with his children, David, Mary and Deborah, found that already everything was in a whirl. Peel himself greeted them magnificently, standing his six foot four, splendid in his dark coat of native fleece and buckskin breeches, and Mrs Peel, stout, very red of face, in russet, all the little Peels (and there were very many) gathered together behind her.

Many were already dancing. It was a scene of brilliant colour with the blazing fire, the red berries of the holly glowing in every corner, old Johnny Shoestring in bright blue breeches and with silver buckles to his shoes perched on a high stool fiddling for his life, the brass gleaming, faces shining, the stamp of the shoon, the screaming of the fiddle, the clap-clap of the hands as the turns were made in the dance — and beyond the heat and the light the dark form of the valley lying in breathless stillness, its face stroked by the fall of lingering reluctant snow.

After the first greeting the Herries family stood quietly by the wall. Fragments of talk, slow cautious words like the repetition of some magic recipe, circled the light.

'Hoo ayre ye today? Hey ye hard ony news? . . .'

'Ye say reet, nowt se sartain. Gud day. Ayre ye all weel at heam? . . .'

'Aye, they said she was worth brass . . .'

'Whya, he's nobbut read about it; what can he knaw? I sud think if he minds his awn job it'll be as weel.'

Peel came and asked Francis Herries to sit by him. His elder girl took Mary and Deborah. David found Rendal.

Francis had come with some of the gaiety and happiness of the preceding night and, as always when he was happy, it seemed to shine in him. He was dressed simply tonight in a suit of grey and silver; although in these last years he had stoutened and broadened he was still handsome beyond all ordinary men. His charm, when he was charming, was so gracious and natural that it won everyone near him.

From the moment of his entering every eye had been upon him. To these people of the valley, although they had talked for months of his wickedness, cruelty, and the strange mystery that led him to isolate himself in this loneliness, he was yet at sight something miraculous and magnificent beyond belief. He was the Dark Angel of their secret dreams.

Romantic — but to himself he was not romantic. As he sat there beside Peel, he could feel the old devilish struggle beginning in him. Partly this was an evening after his heart. He cared nothing for class — all the world was his fellow. He liked to see this common happiness; he could feel in this little, hot, sweating, smelly world all the animal satisfaction that had no ill in it.

He would set them all, had he his way, eating, drinking,

fornicating, singing – the whole world singing over its surfeited belly – and mingled with this a tenderness, a kind of familiar protection so that he could love these owl faces, these humped bodies, these spindle legs for their little homely tragedies and satisfactions.

> So go we all
> Down the dark path,
> Alien, to the friendly tomb.

This sense of common luck with the veriest hind was something that had always separated him from Pomfret, Harcourt and the rest – yes, and from his own children.

Tonight he could feel it to the full as the rushlights scattered streams of light in the wind and the smell of unwashen bodies, perspiring chaps, dogs' offal, burning wood and cooking meat gathered in the air, and all the faces turning in the middle of the room, dilated with the music and the movement – dog faces, horse faces, pig faces, bird faces – but gathering an extra humanity as they felt happiness encouraging them and leading them on to confidence.

He would jump down and share this with them, the drink and the food and the tousling the girls. But he was alone. He could share nothing with anyone. His touch was enough; at the feel of it everything withdrew. Within the heart of the burning candle he was isolated; at its core it was ice. He was ringed with flame and could not get out.

He looked at Peel whom he liked, his big body set back, his broad face spread in laughter: he looked at David whom he loved, moving into the middle of the room crowded now with faces. No one was alone save himself, and he by his own mysterious fault. He was well aware by now of how suspicious they were of him.

This suspicion had blown like a subtle poison through the valley. What had he done to create it? Been drunk once or twice, kissed a girl or two, lost his temper on an occasion – nothing definite save that foolish affair with Alice Press... She had spoken truly. Since that day he had never been rid of her.

But he knew well that it was no positive deed on his part that had separated him. It was something in his spirit. They suspected that battle that was never still in himself, disgust fighting with longing, lechery with an icy purity, a driving dream with sodden reality, the devil in him that would never leave him alone, try as he would to throttle it with self-contempt, irony and the discipline of his impulses.

Sitting now beside Peel he envied that great healthy body, that steady mind, that serene soul, and even as he envied knew that this very thought was separating him, driving him into loneliness and this bitter isolation.

The door would open and the snow blow through in little impatient gusts and all the valley would pour in with it. The room was crowded now against the wall and in the corners. The ale was passing round, and voices were loud and laughter ferocious. But everyone behaved in seemly fashion: a dignity, that seemed to radiate from the grand figure and quiet hospitality of the host himself, pervaded the place. Only – as Francis Herries could feel – he could sniff it in the air – there was a kind of madness behind the dignity, something that belonged to the witches and old crippled warlocks, to the naked shapes playing under the stars above Seatoller, to the broomsticks flying dimly like thin clouds towards the moon.

Suddenly there was a cry: 'They coom. They're here.' It was the 'Play-Jigg'. This was the drama in verse played by the actors who, tonight, were passing from Statesman's house to Statesman's house.

Johnny Shoestring ceased his playing, the dancers vanished, the centre of the room was clear. Packed against the walls now were bodies and faces, legs and backs. There was whispering and tittering, but quite clearly in the immediate silence could be heard the hiss of the snow hovering down through the open chimney on to the fire.

They came forward. Francis was amused as he saw that the Master of these Ceremonies was his old friend the pedlar, David's Devil. Very roguish he was tonight in a cocked purple hat and purple tights showing his thin, spidery limbs, his face with its crooked ironic smile, and his black shining eyes.

He introduced his little company, Old Giles, a bent old man with a long chin, Pinch, a clown, a stout and jolly fellow, a husband and a wife, and young Go-to-Bed who at once in a high, shrill treble introduced himself:

> 'My father is old and decrepit,
> My mother deceased of late,
> And I am a youth that's respected,
> Possessed of a good estate.'

The old couple did a little dance of joy at this, and then Pinch the clown came forward and asked young Go-to-Bed if he wanted to increase his fortune. Of course young Go-to-Bed was eager, so Pinch introduced him to Old Giles, who said he would show him how to make money out of nothing. This young Go-to-Bed was delighted to know, so Old Giles told him that he must have his arse kicked a dozen times by friend Pinch, and then he must put his head in a bucket of water and then must sit up a night alone in a churchyard: all these things young Go-to-Bed performed to the infinite delight of the audience, especially in the churchyard when Pinch, dressed as a painful ghost, emptied a sack of flour over young Go-to-Bed and set the dogs on to him.

The 'Jigg' ended in a grand dance and in this the audience soon joined. Go-to-Bed, his face white with flour, led off with Mrs Peel, and Peel took the Old Lady, and soon all the room was turning to Johnny Shoestring's music.

Still Francis Herries did not move. He was alone on the raised seat near the fire-window. All his children were dancing; even Mary now had forgotten her superior airs and breeding and was smiling at young Curtis, son of a Newlands Statesman. The pedlar came across to Francis.

'Good day.'

'Good day,' said Francis.

'You are not dancing, sir.'

'In my own time,' said Francis.

The pedlar stood there smoothing his hands down the sides of his legs with a look of infinite satisfaction.

'It is very cold up at the valley end,' the pedlar said, 'but the moonlight warms the air. Leave this and take a walk with me.'

Herries felt an impulse to go. The thought of the cold, the black ridge of the hills, and the sky silver-thickened, the freshness, the icy air, was fiercely attractive. His dream – the splendid horse breasting the dark lake under the icy spears – seemed to penetrate the very heart of the thickly smelling, heated room. Close to him the hams and the dried beef swung ever so slightly in the great chimney. A country girl mopped her sweating brow. Beyond the fire-window he fancied that he could hear a cow, desolate in the dark field, lowing for its calf, but of course there would be no cow outside at Christmas. He was about to say that he would go when the pedlar touched his arm.

'Here are strangers,' he said, pointing with his long white finger.

Francis Herries followed his direction and saw pressed near

the door at the hallan end a man and a woman and a child. The man was rough, bony, with long black hair that tumbled on to his shoulders, the woman white-faced, crouching a little as though she feared a blow, and pressed against her dress was a very young child. It was the child that held Herries's notice. She could not have been above seven or eight years of age, her face so white that it might have been blanched by moonlight. But it was her hair that was astonishing. She was wearing a little peaked man's cap of grey with a russet feather in it and under this her hair fell almost to her tiny waist. Its colour was flame. Flame. Francis, incredulously smiling at his interest, repeated the word. Flame. As though her head were on fire. Flame smouldering, with a sudden movement of her little shoulders glancing in coloured shadow as though it were alive. It sank into darkness as fire does, then lifted into amber and rolled about her head in smoky sombre red. She pressed farther back against her mother, and the flame seemed to creep across the dress, to move, to stir, then to lie there, idly licking the dull stuff.

Between this fire the little face looked out, the face of a tired baby, weary, scornful, ironically interested and alone.

'I have never seen such hair,' Herries said, as though to himself.

'Come and burn your hand in it,' said the pedlar.

Herries got up and looked about him. The brightness of that baby's hair seemed to have dimmed and hushed the room. The candlelight was smoked, the voices, the laughter, the trampling of feet shut away behind glass. Herries followed the pedlar across the floor. As they approached the man frowned and drew his body together animal fashion. He was all animal, he smelt animal, looking out with sharp suspicious eyes from his shaggy black hair. The woman did not move, but looked up at Herries. The pedlar smiled at her: 'Hey, Jane Starr,' he said.

Then the woman spoke to Herries: he was astonished at her voice, which was soft and musical and without any real accent.

'You have forgot me, sir.'

He smiled down at the child. 'I fear that I have.'

'Once you gave me your coat,' she said softly, staring into his eyes. So that was it! The morning of the day that was to prove so eventful to him, the morning of the Chinese Fair. The tang of that walk came back to him, his happiness, the freshness, the waterfall clinging like a ladder to the rock, the dead man, the patient woman.

'You were welcome to it,' he said, looking at her for the first time. Her face was not comely. White and weary, but there was strength and courage in it.

'And this is your child?' he asked.

'My child,' the woman answered. But the man made no movement, only stared moodily into the whirling room. It was strange that her voice was so soft yet came clearly through all the racket and din of voices, music and stamping feet.

'Of what age is she?'

'Eight,' the woman answered.

Eight! – and so independent and alone in this jostling cruel world. He thirty-seven, and yet already there was some kinship between them . . .

'What is her name?'

'Mirabell,' and then after a little pause with a quick glance at the man beside her – 'Mirabell Starr.'

Mirabell Starr – so he heard for the first time the name that would never leave his consciousness again. He could be very sweet with children. He squatted on his hams, his silver sword trailing on the floor. He put out his strong hand and took her tiny one.

'Mirabell. That is a man's name, you know . . . Shall we be friends?'

Her strange grey eyes, shining with deep lights, regarded him very gravely. She sighed, then very indifferently answered:

'If my mother wishes.'

Her voice was low, sweet and distant, a little as though it were caught in the echo of a shell. He was charmed with it. Squatting a little lower he put out his arm and drew her in to him, pressing her gently between his knees. The silver thread on his sleeve rubbed her neck, but she did not draw back. Nor did she come to him of her own will.

'Where do you live, my pretty?'

'I live with my mother.'

'And where is that?'

The woman spoke.

'We are from Ennerdale, sir.'

'Ah, from Ennerdale.'

At last, drawing a little breath as though he foretold the emotion that it would give him, he put up his hand and stroked her hair: it seemed that a wave of pleasure passed through his body. Its texture was infinitely soft and lay against the back of his hand like music.

'How come you here? You should be at home on Christmas night.'

The man spoke for the first time. 'We have no settled place. I am a horse-dealer.' His voice was rough and very ungracious, but it had no tang of the North.

Herries caught the child closer. Her head was almost against his breast, and it was as though his heart leapt towards it to greet it. He felt in his pocket and found a charm, a Negro's head in gold with ruby eyes – it was a charm against the ague.

'Will you take this from me – a Christmas gift?' he asked.

For a moment, to steady herself, she laid one tiny hand on his thigh while with the other she took the little Negro. A thrill of happiness ran through him. She looked at the charm very gravely.

''Tis against the ague,' he told her. 'You will not catch it an you keep this with you.'

She looked up at her mother, then at the man.

'It is very pretty,' she said. 'I thank you.' But although her expression was that of a grown woman her fingers tightened round it as a baby's would.

He kissed her forehead, then straightened himself to his full height.

'I wish you good day,' he said, bowing to the woman very slightly, then turned and walked into the room. He turned confusedly like a man in a dream. For a while he could not see the room clearly. Strange coincidence! That this should be the woman whom carelessly that morning he had for a moment protected! What had been her history? Who was the dead man, who now this present animal, this horse-dealer, horse-thief he did not doubt? She did not look a woman who would pass lightly from man to man – but what did she at all in that company? Mirabell . . . Mirabell . . . So the child was called. Poor little misery, already bearing in her eyes the knowledge of hardship, cruelty, aloneness. What a life must she have with such a man and his company! Almost he was tempted to turn aside, go back and make some mad demand for the child's protection. A nice affair – to be mixed in such a throng! As though there were not already scandal enough. But he looked back nevertheless. There was no sign of them. They were hidden by the dancers. The Christmas Feast was at its height.

This was a scene from Breughel. The trestle tables were piled with food, pies and puddings, hams and sides of beef. The drink was for the most part ale, but there was creeping into the valley now that new destroying devil of the English countryside, the demon gin. There were signs of it here tonight – men were pressing the girls now, their faces flushed, their hands fumbling for breast and side. The women were giggling, the dogs snapping at food and legs and one another. An old man with long white hair, thin as a scarecrow, was dancing very solemnly alone in the middle of the floor, twisting his body into corkscrew shapes. At a table near the chimney a group of old people were playing at cards. But wildness was coming in, coming in from the caverns of the hill, and the high, cold spaces round Sprinkling Tarn and the lonely passes above the listening valleys. It was Christ's Day no longer. He had been turned out when the wind had changed, and all the doors and shutters of the house had rattled their shoulders at His going.

Peel himself felt perhaps that his hand was losing its hold on the scene. And perhaps he did not care. He was a man of his time, and that was a rough time, a cruel and a coarse. They had a small, wild, starving dog, strayed in from the valley, and they had tied him to the leg of a table, and were holding meat just beyond his nose, while he yelped in his agony of hunger, and his little fierce protesting eyes darted wildly about the room.

Up in the half-darkness of the hallan one of the shepherds was stripping to a whispering group of men and girls to show his tattooed body, made when he was in the Indies as a boy, marvellous, they say, a whole love-story on his legs and back. Although the night was bitter, couples twined closely together wandered out of the house up the road, kissing to the eternal murmur of the running water.

Then the house-door burst wide and a strange crew broke into the room. They came shouting, singing and very drunk. Their shoulders were powdered with snow, and their frosty breath blew in clouds about them. This was a party that had ridden over from Keswick and Portinscale and Grange, had found their way under the moon to Rosthwaite, and now, drinking at every stage, were turning back again (an they were sober enough to ride) to Keswick. Here was the Lord of Misrule and his followers, a young fellow with very flushed face, a crown awry on his crooked wig, his clothes of purple satin and gold, carried on the shoulders of four half-naked men blacked like Indians and followed by a motley baggage-heap dressed fantastically as jesters, Chinamen and clowns. There was a Hobbyhorse and old Father Neptune with his trident. They burst the doors, then paused to arrange their procession. The naked

Indians threw off their cloaks in which they had been wrapped against the cold, caught up their young Lord of Misrule and shouldered him, and so marched up the room, followed by the Jester with his bauble, a lady with a flaxen wig and very naked bosom, Neptune and a posturing, shouting throng.

The natives of the valley drew back against the wall. Here were foreigners from the town, and though their intrusion was no new thing at a Christmas time, yet it boded no good. It had ended before in a bloody riot and so might do again. Francis had been looking for his children, and finding them had bidden David take his sisters home, then, if he would, return. So he was once again alone, a great stillness in his heart in the midst of the riot, once or twice looking to see whether he could catch sight of the child and her mother: it seemed that they were gone.

Watching this new invasion he found that he recognized three at least of the company, two from Keswick. The Lord of Misrule himself was young Cuthbertson, son of a wealthy merchant; one of the black men young Fawcett, a Squire's eldest boy; and the Jester himself with his cap and bells Osbaldistone from Threap-thwaite, near Whitehaven. Young Osbaldistone was often at Keswick, and Herries had been with him at cards and cock-fighting. There was no love between them. Herries had won his money, which the young fool could ill afford to lose, and Herries had kissed a girl that Osbaldistone had also been pursuing.

At the sight of him a spasm of revolt and disgust caught his heart. He had drunk nothing: he had been moved tonight by the courteous friendliness of Peel, by the happy simplicity of the earlier part of the evening, and, at this last, by his meeting with the child. Apart and reserved as he seemed standing there alone, yet his heart had been filled with kindliness and an almost child-like desire to be friends with the world.

At the sight of this rabble he was tempted to slip away and find his bed. Had he gone, the whole course of his life would have been other. Nevertheless our lives are dictated by character, not by chance. Some foolish pride kept him. He fancied that from the corner by the fire-window the pedlar sardonically watched him. It was true that many eyes were on him, as they had been all the evening; so, because he had some conceit and felt a challenge in the air, he stayed.

Events followed then with dreamlike swiftness. Afterwards if he ever looked back to this night it seemed to him that he had from the very first been trapped. He could not have escaped; he did not pity himself for this (in all his life-history from the first page to the last there was no self-pity), but he did ask himself whether he could have avoided the event: he could not.

The procession settled itself about its Lord: drink was brought: there was much sham ceremony: subjects knelt and sentences were passed; the lady in cloth of gold with the naked bosom was proclaimed Queen. The peasants stood around, mouths agape, the little wild dog, who had been forgotten, yelped dismally, then broke his rope, crawled to a corner where he feasted ravenously. Everyone was at ease again. Dancing took the floor. Figures, fantastic, painted in orange and scarlet and purple, laughing, singing, kissing, whirled and turned; some fell upon the floor and lay there. Still in the farther corner the old people, like characters painted on the wall, played gravely their cards.

Young Osbaldistone, his cap awry, the laced waistcoat unbuttoned, pursued a girl and encountered Herries. He stopped short.

Herries gravely bowed. Osbaldistone looked. The drink cleared from his eyes. He straightened himself. He was a cold-tempered, severe lad in his natural life, debauched enough but ready at any moment to clear debauchery from his system. He stood back fumbling the hilt of his sword.

'Mr Francis Herries.'

'Mr Richard Osbaldistone.'

He yet stuttered a little. The drink was not all cleared. 'Dick to my friends,' then added softly, 'but not to you, Mr Herries.'

No one heard him. Herries frowned. He did not want a quarrel with the boy here, not tonight, Christmas night, and in Peel's house. He bowed.

'I wish you good evening,' he said and turned.

Osbaldistone touched his shoulder. Herries, turning back, was amazed at the hatred that formed and edged the other's face like a mask. To hate him like that! And for what? For nothing – a loss at cards, a girl's kiss. No – for what he himself in his very spirit was. And at the consciousness of that his heart sank and his anger grew.

'You will not wish me good evening,' Osbaldistone said. 'I will have no good evening from you. Since our meeting of last week I have been determined on a word with you. You are a cheat, Mr Herries, a liar and – it may be – a coward. For the last we will see.'

Then he raised his hand and struck Herries's cheek. Miraculously, this, too, no one saw. It gave the dreaminess of this

strange hour an added colour – the shrill, discordant music of
the violin, the thick steaming air, the great chimney with its
smoky fire, the figures confused in colour, unreal in chin and eye
and limb, the movement striving, it seemed, to make significant
pattern – and yet Herries quite alone in a frozen place with this
boy who hated him.

But no man had ever struck him and had no answer. He
frowned sternly on young Osbaldistone, who was breathing now
fiercely as though driven by some terrific emotion.

'Not here,' he said quietly. 'There is a green behind the house.
The moon is bright. I will join you there in an instant. But take
care; we must go separately. My host tonight is my friend.'

At once, again as in a dream, young Osbaldistone had disappeared. Herries looked about him. Oh! how desperately he did
not wish this to happen! It was from no fear for himself. But he
seemed to be haunted tonight by the past; something was pulling
him back into that other life that he had abandoned; something
would not let him escape.

But he must find a second. It must be, if possible, someone not
from Keswick. The less that this was known . . . He turned towards the door and saw the pedlar standing against the wall,
smiling ironically and stroking his thighs with his hands.

'You can do me a service,' Herries said. The pedlar followed
him out. The moon was full. No snow was falling.

Against the green behind the house everything was marked
as though it had been cut from black paper, the ridge of hill, the
roof-line, the thick wall of jagged stones.

Osbaldistone was waiting there and Fawcett, a stout, plump
youth, absurd with his blackened face and thick cloak heavily
furred. He came to Herries.

'For God's sake, Mr Herries, this must be avoided . . .' His
teeth were chattering.

'Too damned cold for talk,' said Osbaldistone.

They spoke in whispers.

'If Mr Osbaldistone will apologize for his insult,' said Herries.

'I will not,' said Osbaldistone.

They faced one another: every detail in the scene was clear
under the moon. It was indeed bitterly cold. The frost seemed to
creep upon the flat stones that lay about the field. Herries was
aware of the tiniest details and would remember them all his
days. A snail-track glittered in crystal on the farm wall behind
him; a little wind ran over the grass, fluttering the light snow
that lay loosely on the ground, and on the path beyond the field

he could see the moonlight shine on the ice that the cold was forming on the little pools.

They advanced. At once he knew that Osbaldistone was no swordsman – and a moment later Osbaldistone knew it too. Again the thought tapped Herries's heart: 'How he must hate me to run this crazy risk!' and again 'Why?' In another moment or two he was aware of the sword's instinct, something much more deadly and determined than his own. He could never strike another's weapon with his and not feel that separate aliveness in his blade, as though it said: 'You have called me out. You have liberated me. Now I am my own master.' And now he was very curiously aware that he must restrain this creature, use all his force and power, otherwise the boy would be hurt. But as they parried and struck and parried again a warmth of companionship with his sword swelled in his throat as though it had said to him: 'Come. We are comrades now. We march together. You wouldn't desert me when you have brought me so far.'

His pride in his accomplishment grew in him. His body grew warm, taut, eager. He forgot his opponent, felt only the moon shining above that cold field, the splendid panoply of stars exulting in his skill.

He had the boy utterly at his mercy, and, at the same moment, the boy's face swung down to him as though it had been lowered from a height. He gazed into it and saw terror there, the certain expectation of instant death.

Death. Yes, one more link in the ridiculous binding chain. This time at least he would be master of his fortune.

He lowered his blade and stepped back. An instant later Osbaldistone's sword had carved his right cheek in two, a deep riven cut from temple to chin.

His face was flooded with blood. Dropping his sword, the field whirring about his ears like a top, he sank to his knee.

He heard young Fawcett cry 'Enough . . .' and a word about honour, then the frosted stones leapt up and hit him into darkness. But before he sank he felt the pedlar's hand on his arm.

DEATH OF MARGARET HERRIES

DEBORAH FOUND her way one March afternoon through Stonethwaite Valley home.

She had been as far as the Stake Pass, turned back, stayed where the waterfall tumbles over the rocks before the Grasmere turning, looked up at the quiet hills lying against the quiet sky, then down again to the tumbling stream that spread fanwise over the white stones shining in the sun under the water.

Spring was so late here that hardly yet were there signs of it, but Deborah saw every bud and smiled at every pushing green. The spirit of spring was in the faint rain-washed blue of the sky, the purple shadow that hung intangibly about the branches and the pale primrose sunlight that fell in white patterns on rock and stone. The air was cold and snow streaked even the lowest hills.

She was a very slight and lonely child as she walked over the green turf that here in this valley was like the ancient lawns of noble families, so smooth it was and deep. She would soon be fifteen, but children in those years were almost women at fifteen. And she had had much to make her mature. Since her mother had fallen so ill this Christmas, since Mary had grown so proud and was so often with her cousins in Keswick, all the duties of the house had fallen on to Deborah. She was hurrying now for fear of what might have happened while she was away. All last night she had sat with her mother, fighting a thousand terrors, her mother's strange ceaseless talk, the house that was never still, the calling of the owls, but worst of all the anticipated presence of old Mrs Wilson the witch. Since her mother was ill Mrs Wilson had been for ever appearing, now here, now there. She spoke little, but at first had offered again and again her remedies. Deborah could hear her now in her odd, croaking voice pressing her herbs, her spells, her incantations. Deb had from the very first been terrified by the old woman, but against her will she had been forced to realize that there was something pathetic and something kind in the old wrinkled face, the little eyes almost hidden by the brown lids, but now anxious and beseeching like an animal's. The old snuff-nosed, wrinkled-faced Doctor Absom, their only resource, once a fine doctor in Carlisle but reduced by liquor to a peddling house-to-house livelihood, had soon stopped her solicitings. He had threatened her in so many words with the gaol for a witch. She had not spoken again after that, but she was always, night and day, hovering there. It seemed, so her son said, that she had formed some affection for Margaret Herries. He said, almost apologetically, that he had never known her take to anyone before as she took to Mistress Herries; and Deborah, walking now in her cold green valley, seemed still to be haunted by her presence, and, against her fear, something forced her to wonder whether after all Mrs Wilson's magic might not be of more value than the old doctor's dirty ministrations, he never sober, stinking of snuff, and with bleeding ever his principal remedy.

Poor Margaret! She had been bled enough. There was no more blood left in her. She was dying. Nothing could save her.

The stroke that had slashed her husband's face had struck her down. He had made nothing of it. His face was bound. He had called it a scratch, but from the first instant she had seen deeper than this, had known that here was something predestined.

Child though she was, Deborah had marvellously understood her mother's longing. She was perhaps the only living soul in the world to understand what her mother's love for her father was, how for years she had been praying the God in whom she believed to give her opportunity to show that love without foolishness. Now it might be that the moment had come, and she was too weak to offer it. Not that Herries gave her opportunity: he would have no pity, no tenderness, no allusion to the event. No one spoke to him of it. Everyone pretended that nothing had occurred.

But Deborah knew how her mother ached over him as though he were a child bullied at school and the agony that it was to her, far surpassing her bodily pain, that she could say nothing. She rose to great heights of character in these last days.

But for Deborah life had never yet been so threatening. How would it be when her mother was gone and she alone with her father? Again and again she tried to beat down her fear of him, but it seemed to be something in her very veins. There was David. Had there not been David she might have turned and run back, over the Stake Pass to Langdale and Grasmere, wandered the world and never returned. So long as David was there she could endure any test, but would he always be there? Anyone as wonderful as he must be caught into the outside world. They would call for, shout for him! And then . . . as the light fell and she thought of the darkening house, her father with the fresh purple scar that ran from temple to mouth, catching up one corner of his lip, of her mother's room, of Mrs Wilson, her white cap, the black stick on which she leaned, she stayed for a moment by the wall of the field and the little chapel looking back to Glaramara, her hand at her throat, her knees trembling.

The thought of David reassured her and she smiled. Where he was no harm could come.

At the turning in of the grassy court two figures made her pause

— two men on horseback. In the fading afternoon light she could not at first tell who they were, then, realizing, amazement stayed her: they were her uncle Pomfret and her cousin Raiseley.

They had but now arrived, for they got from their horses as she came to them (she was pleased indeed to see how clumsy Cousin Raiseley was as he climbed down). Uncle Pomfret greeted her with a confusion of heartiness and embarrassment, which showed that he was in no way at ease over his visit. She curtsied and he kissed her, swimming her in an odour of ale and snuff. He was becoming a mountain of flesh. His belly swung before him. Cousin Raiseley, who was pallid and thin as his father was purple and corpulent, bowed to her gravely. She hated her cousin Raiseley because David did. 'Hey, little lass . . .' (her uncle addressed her as though she were a favourite hound) 'here's your old uncle come all the way through the muck to cheer your poor mother up.' He threw a cautious look around him. 'And your father . . . is he about?' She replied quietly. She did not dislike her uncle. There was something kindly and simple about him. She thought: 'He hates coming . . . It's his good nature.'

David came out to them, and Deborah flushed with pride as she saw his splendid strength beside his pale shambly-kneed cousin. Benjamin was called to care for the horses, and they all went into the house. What deep shame Deborah felt as they climbed the stairs! She knew Raiseley would be seeing everything, sniffing the farm-smells, the dung and the cesspool, hearing the trickling of water, catching the gleam of the damp on the walls, and, as they came into the upper hall, marking down the holes in the furniture, the bareness of the rafters, the tapestry that was never still against the panelling. She hated Raiseley the more because her home was shabby.

In the hall now there were David and Mary. It was Mary, of course, who at once commanded the scene. She flung her arms around her uncle's short, thick neck and kissed his ill-shaven chin, then with a smiling demureness that was beautiful to witness offered her cheek for Raiseley to kiss, which he did with a very pleasant eagerness.

Uncle Pomfret explained with a great many oaths and confused sentences that he and their Aunt Jannice had been distressed indeed to hear of the grave illness of poor Margaret and that Aunt Jannice had sent with him some cures and recipes.

For himself, would it be possible for him to see her?

The room was dark. The evening glow penetrated the little

windows very thinly. Suddenly a figure bearing high two lighted candlesticks appeared on the staircase. It was Francis, his face quivering in the blown flame of the candles. He seemed very tall in that semi-light, in a long, purple dressing-gown, and the scar was leaping on his face.

It might be that Pomfret had not expected that: he stared, his thick legs wide planted, his chin raised. He said afterwards to his wife: ''Twas no man standing there. Someone raised from the dead. The cut lined on his cheek.'

Francis said no word, but came slowly down. Then he placed the candlesticks on the table and holding out his hand said quietly: 'How are you, brother?'

Pomfret began a tumbled and confused explanation, but in a whisper as though he were in church there; finding the whisper arduous, broke into a kind of congested roar, then sank to a whisper again.

Francis nodded his head.

'That was kindly thought . . . Margaret would wish to see you. She is awake – but she is sadly weak.'

He picked up the candles and led the way upstairs again. Pomfret, stepping with his big feet as though on eggs, followed him.

The children, left alone together, were embarrassed. Even Mary, conscious perhaps that the eyes of her brother and sister were upon her, had very little to say. At last Raiseley muttered something about going to see after the horses. He started down the stairs, and David stoutly marched after him. In the dusk, wrapped in the cold air, the two stood stiffly side by side. At last Raiseley, patronage in every word that he uttered, said:

''Tis isolated here . . . and muck at every step.'

David, anger throbbing in his throat, answered:

'It is no place for soft bodies.'

'Nor for active minds,' Raiseley answered.

'Keswick,' David said with a scornful laugh, 'is scarcely the Athens of the world.' (He thought this a fine phrase and told Deb of it afterwards.)

Raiseley sniffed. He had a maddening habit in this as though he suffered from a perpetual cold.

'I wonder, cousin,' he said, 'that you can endure the mud and rain and nothing but yokels for company. But maybe it suits you.'

'It does,' David answered. 'Better than by your looks Keswick might.'

Raiseley laughed. 'Keswick is no abiding-place. I shall be in London in a six-months.'

'Well,' said David, 'for me you can keep your London. There is air here and space, horses to ride and hills to climb. There is no finer spot in England.'

'I can understand that you would find it so,' Raiseley answered.

The poor white worm – David thought – one crack with the singlestick and he'd go over. One push with the thumb and down he'd be! He hated him with every pulse in his body, but at the heart of the hate there was a sort of wistfulness. He would be clever, Raiseley, and getting a fine education. Already he would know so many things that David would never know.

The darkness fell. Benjamin held a flare. The horses clamped with their hoofs on the grassy stones. The two boys stood without speaking, hating one another. Then the two men came out. They were very quiet. Margaret on her death-bed had brought them closer together than they had ever been or would be. Pomfret's simple heart was deeply touched.

'Poor soul,' he said. 'Poor soul . . .'

'She is a woman of great courage,' Francis said.

'Poor Margaret,' their voices echoed on the night air. Pomfret and his son climbed on to their horses.

'That was kindly of you, brother,' Francis said, and held for a moment Pomfret's hand.

'Come and visit us. There is a bed for thee,' Pomfret answered, bent down and kissed his brother's cheek. Then they rode away, their horses stumbling over the dark track.

Francis went back into the house. From these few whispered words both children had realized that their mother was indeed dying. They stood there close together in the dark courtyard, the wind that had suddenly risen whistling about their heads. Deborah began to cry. She clung to David, who put his arm around her, holding her very close. She was a little hysterical with lack of sleep, too incessant labour, fear of the future.

'Oh, David, I'm frightened. Mother will die and you will go into the world and I shall be left here with Father . . . I don't want to be left . . . I don't want to be left. 'Tis cruel, this valley, when you are alone in it, and there are spirits in the house. The house hates us. There has been no luck for us since we came to it, and I'm weary of the mice and the holes and the shabbiness that will not be cleaned . . . Oh, David, don't leave me here alone . . . Don't leave me!'

She sobbed on his breast and he comforted her. 'Deb, little Deb. There's no fear. I'll not leave you. Mother will be happier gone. She was never rightly settled here and the rain and wind destroyed her. Poor Mother. She will be warm again and comforted if there's a heaven as they say, and if there's none she'll not be aware of it. But, Deborah, you must not fear Father. He's worst with anyone who fears him.

'He will love you an you go to him bravely. He has himself a shyness of spirit. See how happy the three of us will be together – and you are the bravest of us all. The house is well enough. I'd have it a thousand times before that popinjay place of Uncle Pomfret's in Keswick.

'And I'll not leave you. I'll never leave you. You are the only woman in all the world I love, Deb, save our mother.'

Deborah smiled through her tears.

'There'll be a woman for you one day: every woman who sees you must love you.'

'Ah, but it takes two for that,' David answered laughing. 'There was a girl once up by Seathwaite hit my horse with her stick. Do you know, Deb, it was but a moment and I've never seen her since, but she had a face like a laughing rose . . . For the rest they are all alike. I warrant marriage is a false tale. I would be free, and who is free with a wife?'

Deborah sighed.

'I shall be left one day . . . 'Tis so silly, but although I'm fourteen years I'm frightened of the dark . . . The true dark when there are only owls and mice. And Mistress Wilson. David, is she truly a witch?' She dropped her voice to a low whisper.

David tightened his arm round her. 'I think she's a witch,' he whispered back. 'She never sleeps. She has a fire with blue flame. She makes dolls of wax. I've seen one with a needle through. But she cannot touch thee, Deb . . . Christ is at the back of thee, and all the holy angels.'

'Maybe,' Deborah answered, shivering against his breast, 'she is a good witch. I'm sure she means no ill to our mother. Maybe she would have cured her.'

But David shook his head. 'Better our mother die than be cured of the Devil,' he answered. Then he folded his little sister yet more closely in his arms and kissed her.

'I will swear an oath, here in this place, never to leave you, Deborah. An I marry, you come also. And if I do not marry, you shall ever keep house for me and Father. Now listen, little sister, I will swear. By Christ and His holy angels I, David Scott

Herries, will never, while breath is in my body, leave thee, Deborah Herries – unless,' he hurriedly added, 'there is hunting on the hills or travelling to see new countries – an adventure, you understand. You would not hold me from that.'

'I would not hold you from anything,' Deborah answered, standing on tip-toe to kiss him. 'I am not that sort of selfish woman. I know that you will have a grand life, David, of adventure and enterprise, and do you think I would hold you back? I love you too well.'

She was quite happy now, and, their arms around one another, they went into the house.

Francis Herries had gone to his wife's room. He sat there beside the big bed, very patient, staring into the round light of the two candles. Margaret lay, her eyes closed, breathing stertorously. There were beads of sweat on her brow, and her two hands, tightly clenched, lay on the coverlet. Little Absom had gone for a meal but would return. It might well be that Margaret would die before he came back, but it did not matter; he could do nothing.

Herries sat there without moving, looking at his wife. He had never loved Margaret: he did not love her now nor did he let sentiment chafe him, but, as he watched her, he was sorry that her life had been spent with a man whom she could not understand.

It was this lack of comprehension that affected him most deeply as he sat there. She had loved him, but had not understood him at all. He had not loved her, but had understood her only too well.

All human relationships seemed to him miserable things as he sat there – all false, all betraying. Well, for himself, it did not matter. On the Christmas night at the moment when young Osbaldistone had slashed his cheek, he had finished with human beings. As he felt the blood gush over his face he had, at that instant, stepped aside from all his fellows. He had been coming to that point through many months. Now the division was made.

In the weeks that had followed, he had nursed his cut with a quiet sense of completion. He knew that he would be marked for life and terribly, that this would be the first thought that all men would have, the first thing that they would see.

He could look back now and understand that for years he had been slowly separating himself from his fellowmen. His fault or theirs, what mattered it? Their fault because he had a dream that could not be fulfilled, or his because he was ever putting himself wrong with them by loss of temper or arrogance or other passion? So he was done with them. Even poor Margaret was leaving him. Only David remained. David he could not separate himself from, but he was sure that the hour would come when David too would go. But that would be for David to recognize.

And instead of human beings, he would embrace this valley, this soil, this house itself. He had plans that he would get some land from Peel, that he would sow corn, grow trees perhaps, have cattle. He would work with his own hands here. All day and every day during those last weeks he had, when he had not been at Margaret's side, been digging and cutting wood, mending holes, carrying water, Ben, Wilson, David, assisting, but going and coming, whereas he stayed, sweat pouring from him, his nails grimed with dirt, his face raised to Glaramara, then bent again to the ground. And it seemed to him that the soil came and built itself about his heart. He was earthed in: the smell and the tang and the grit of it were in his eyes and his nostrils. He was growing his own hair. Soon it would be long about his brows. His heavy boots were caked with mud, and when he straightened himself this fresh, sharp ache in his back called out to him with a friendly voice.

Margaret stirred. Her hands rose and fell with a little flutter as he had so often seen them do, and a rush of memory swept over him. How badly he had treated her, and how she had asked to be badly treated! What absurd ironic fate had driven them together? Why was life thus, so that you were caught of your own good intentions and held in a trap to which there was no purpose? He had meant to do her kindness and had done her nothing but ill: but was not that indeed the whole motto of his life?

He could think of so many occasions when he had returned from some ride or visit meaning so many courtesies to her, and she, in the very first word, had roused his ironic irritation. And how poor was he that, knowing her love for him and that she was stupid and could not help herself, he had not been kinder to her, more indulgent! His sins had been frightful, thrusting his mistresses under her very nose, coming back drunk to her and forcing her against her will, until in the last matter of Alice Press he had been most evil of all. For all this he must pay, and when the day came for payment he was not to squeal about injustice.

He thought then of her many, many kindnesses and of her great patience, but the thought of her patience only again exasperated him. Why had she been so patient? It would have been better had she been rash with him sometimes and called him what he was. And so, as most men do who have ill-treated their wives, he came to an odd mixture of feelings, of shame and irritation, of self-blame and wonder that women could be so persistently provoking. At least he was glad that now she suffered no pain.

She stirred and woke. She looked about her without raising her head from the pillow. Then she saw him and smiled, and then, as she had done on a thousand other occasions, checked her smile lest he should think it foolish.

'What hour is it, Francis?' she asked him in a thin, very distant voice.

'Six of the clock,' he said, bending forward and taking her hand. That pleased her and she smiled again.

'My head is very clear . . . I have had strange dreams. I would speak to David. May I?'

He nodded. That 'May I?' touched him deeply. In the first year of their marriage when she had been a young girl and first afraid of him, she had said about this or that little pleasure and excitement, 'May I?' and often enough he had answered: 'No, you may not.'

Now he nodded and went from the room to fetch his son.

He sent David in. The boy came and stood by the bed, his breadth blocking the window. Then a terrible pity and tenderness for his mother, self-reproach for himself, and a consciousness of the imminence of death wrung his heart. He dropped on his knees, put out his great brown hands and took her thin white ones. He seemed for the first time in his life now to realize her. There had always been somebody or something else standing in his view of her. He had caught from early babyhood something of his father's idea of her. Now, when it was too late, she seemed to stand before him as she really was, going on this journey all alone with no one to help her. The room was so dark that it was only by the candlelight that he saw her face, and in that flickering gleam she was not foolish any more – she had courage and dignity, and these things all her life she had never seemed to him to have before.

She put up her hand and stroked his hair. Her voice was faint and he had to lean nearer to her to catch her words. Her arm fell about his neck.

'Davy, I've not been a wise mother to you . . . I've not been a wise woman, but I have loved you with all my heart.'

'I know you have, Mother,' he answered.

'I want you to promise me . . . never to leave your father.'

'I will never leave my father.'

'It is strange,' she looked at him rather timidly, 'that love does not bring understanding. I have loved Francis so much but have never known the way to be easy with him.' She paused between the sentences, and David heard the wind tugging at the leaded panes, and in some way the little sound, as of a friendly companion, was comforting and understanding.

'It is too late now for me not to fear your father. Oh, Davy, how have I said again and again, "Now you must not mind him," but I have always minded him and the sight of him has made my heart beat and driven every word from my head. I know so well why he should be irritated with me. How should I not know, being so irritated with myself? But that is all over . . . past . . . away . . .' She stopped, lay back, closed her eyes. David placed his arm around her and held her close to him. He could feel the sweat of her body beneath the nightdress. 'I meant to make him proud of me and I have not. I meant that he should continue in love with me and he was not. I meant many things and have not wrought them, but—' and here her voice grew stronger and she seemed to wake to new life, 'I have given birth to a fine son who will be heard of in the world. Oh, I am proud of you, Davy, my darling, my darling.'

He held her closer, moved to his very soul, because in all these years she had never told him how she loved him.

'And you are strong and grand and fearless. You will be a man among men so that they look up to you and come to you. So, Davy, my darling, you must never leave your father, who is alone and will be more alone as the years go.' She raised herself a little on David's arm.

'Breed sons, my David. Great, strong-limbed men like yourself. Davy, Davy . . .' Her hand clutched his sleeve. 'I am no Herries, but I have borne a son to the Herries. Though they have mocked me, in my womb was carried the finest of them all, and from your seed, David, all the grand Herries shall come.' She sank back and the strangest elfin smile came to her lips. 'Your aunt and your uncle have bred niddering children, but two hundred years hence there shall be Herries who shall know that it was I, Margaret Herries, who gave suck to the man of them all . . . Your children, Davy . . . You must have men children to carry the Herries name further . . . further . . . further . . .' She seemed exhausted. She lay back on the pillow and he bent and stroked her forehead. 'Wrong thoughts, Davy,' she whispered, 'for a dying woman, but they have struck your father in the face and your sons must revenge . . . I have loved him so . . . even now to have his cheek against mine, his poor wounded cheek.'

'Shall I call him, Mother?' David whispered.

'Nay.' She smiled again. 'He would not know what to do or say. He was ever awkward in a scene. Like a child . . . I would have been mother to him rather than wife, but he would not allow me. Dear Francis . . . Francis, dear . . .'

Then she motioned him to raise her up. Her face was against his. She kissed him. Her lips were damp with sweat.

'Is it not odd that I who have been afraid all my life should not now be afraid? Our good Lord understandeth my awkwardness. His arms are around me . . . To die is simpler than to live . . .'

He laid her down again. Her hand closed with exceeding tightness about his.

'Dear Francis . . . Call him, Davy . . . I am dying.'

Gently he unloosed his hand, went to the door and called softly: 'Father, Father.'

Francis came in, and kneeling by the bed put his arms round her and held her as her spirit passed.

Her last words uttered against his cheek: 'Francis, dear.'

Part Two

'FORTY-FIVE

LAUGHTER OF A SPANIEL

MARIA HERRIES died on the morning of February 14th, 1745, thus missing by exactly four months the attainment of her hundredth year.

This lamentable failure afforded great grief and a sense of affronted egotism to the whole of the Herries family. Bad news flies apace, and in a surprisingly short time the event was known to, and greatly bewailed by, the children and grandchildren of Robert Herries in Kensington, the family of Maurice in Portsmouth, of Humphrey at Seddon, and the Golds (only far relations-in-law, but nevertheless of a very definite Herries consciousness) in Edinburgh.

They all united in blaming Pomfret and Jannice for this disaster, and indeed very rightly, for who was to blame if they were not? Having kept the old lady alive so long, the least for them to do was to keep her alive that little bit longer. Moreover, it was pleasant to blame Pomfret and Jannice, who had made money in a very sudden and vulgar manner, in a fashion that was not the Herries manner: Herries always inherited, or if they worked, did so slowly and cautiously and with an air of indifference.

Wealth meant little in the Herries blood: they had not at all like certain other famous English families the sense of property. They were indeed quite above and outside this sense, because to be Herries was enough and, rich or poor, you were of an equal and exceptional importance. No, the Herries pride (of which there was always God's plenty) was based on two magnificent foundations: England and Common Sense. When you said English you said Herries, and when you said Herries you said No Nonsense. In this lies any interest that there may be in a study of Herries' family history – that there was something in the Herries blood demanding that their castle of common sense should be persistently attacked, and almost always from within. Again and again these attacks occur, and with every fresh battle new history is made. 'I am a sensible man,' chanted the first Herries, striding across the naked body of his enemy, Romance or Illusion – and so ever since have his stalwart descendants chanted.

'The man's a fool.' 'The woman's an ass.' 'I can't think what he's after.' 'A madman.' 'A lunatic.' 'A dirty dog.' 'Traitor to his

country.' 'An artist.' 'A ne'er-do-well.' 'Fantasy.' 'Imagination.'
'An atheist' – such and so have ever been the words and phrases
of contempt in the mouths of following generations of Herries.

And rightly so. For just as Common Sense has always served
them soundly and well in all their history, so have Imagination,
Originality, the hopeless pursuit of the shining star, led them to
ruin and disaster, public scandal and disgrace. They have learnt
to dread and with justice the dreamer; he has ever haunted the
sleep of right-minded Herries men and women.

This Common Sense, on the other hand, has been with them
no unstudied art. They have penetrated every nook and cranny
of this temple, have studied with hundreds of years of patient
learning the shifting features of the God.

At the moment of birth young Herries know precisely the
sensible thing to do, how to watch and wait, to avoid all eccentricity, to embrace only those things and persons that are of good
report and general repute, to believe only in what they see, to
handle only what they can in reality touch, to give their blessing
to all that is normal, firmly traditional, safely found. Within the
world of common sense they are kindly, generous and open-
hearted: let them for a moment stray into that howling wilderness
of stars and mandrakes and they are ferocious and bloodthirsty:
alarm partly makes them so, the knowledge given to them by
history that they are a family especially susceptible to attacks of
the dreamer's incongruity, the rebel's immorality. They go,
therefore, armed to the teeth: divided as they sometimes are
(being yet human) among themselves, they unite instantly at the
call of one of their members: ''Ware Wolf!' They have made
England what it is: they are rightly proud of their magnificent
achievement.

But, it must be repeated, their principal interest to the
observer of them is that they have, at their heart, the poison of
their qualities and intentions. Every generation, it seems, is condemned to this warfare against its own home-born traitors, and
from this warfare comes always a stouter, more determined
resolve.

The death of Maria Herries, so lamentably previous, offered a
fine example of their common sense in action. One thing that had
never been understood by them was that Herries men must die
so soon. It was natural for the majority, who waste their days in
dreams, in pursuit of the thing that is not, in longing for what
does not exist, to wear themselves untimely away, their proper
punishment and condemnation. But for Herries, who never ran

after a vain thing nor stared at the moon, life should be indefinitely extended, and because they believed in a just God (the God of the contemporary majority) it was hard to see why His justness did not perceive exactly this.

There had been already examples in history of what a Herries could do when he tried. Old Polyphemus Herries, barnacled and lichened with tradition, who eight hundred years ago in Fife (the Herries were all Scottish then) had lived to a hundred and sixty one; old Mary Herries of the Wars of the Roses, who, defending Lancaster Castle, upset pots of boiling pitch on to the heads of invaders, she had lived to a hundred and thirty-nine, and had had fifty-eight grandchildren. Ronald Herries, friend of James I, had lived in sin and iniquity into his hundred and twentieth year – a black sheep, but honoured by the Herries because of his arrogant resolve to beat Death back to Hell, which for a hundred and twenty years at least he succeeded in doing, then drink had him and he died, his head in a butt of Canary!

Since old Ronald no one had passed the century, although Elizabeth Herries of Charles I's time had been ninety-three, and little Johnny Herries the hunchback, uncle of Maria and Matthew, had seen ninety-four.

Old Maria as she approached the century had become an object of reverence to all of them, and Pomfret and Jannice, hitherto contemned, had been more honourably considered for preserving her. Here again was something that the Herries did better than anything else – show Death that they would stand no nonsense.

There was nothing that the Herries prided themselves upon more justly than the health and excellence of their bodily vigour. They were not eccentric in this; they did not produce strong men for exhibition at a fair, or wrestlers at a pageant, but just vigorous, sound Englishmen with no nonsense about them, destined to die calmly in their beds at a ripe old age. And how often these last years had the words been murmured in Kensington, in Portsmouth, in Carlisle, in Edinburgh, at Seddon, at Hatton, at Brighthelmstone. 'The Herries live long . . . Maria Herries in Keswick neareth her hundredth year . . . Nothing ails her . . . She is bled once and again . . . She has all her teeth.'

And now she was gone and had missed her goal. A hundred in four months' time! The irony of it!

By an odd coincidence it happened that for Maria's funeral there was a remarkable Herries gathering. Movement over considerable distances was not easy, although easier than it had been, but it was not difficult, of course, for Humphrey Cards, his wife Charlotte, his daughter Dorothy, her husband Anthony Forster, and their little son Will to come over from Seddon, and Grandison, son of Robert, cousin of Pomfret and Francis, had been paying a visit in Edinburgh with Mary his wife, and Helen and Pelham his children, so they came down: and last but not, of course, least there was Henry, son of Maurice Cards, and Lucilla his wife. In this company three quite separate impulses of the Herries blood could be traced.

Humphrey Cards, hidden away at Seddon, had been suspected of turning Quaker. He had at any rate been oddly religious enough to frighten all decent-minded Herries. His daughter Dorothy, who had married one of the Northumberland Forsters, was grimly religious enough, but not, thank Providence, in any eccentrically dangerous fashion.

Dorothy Forster then (cousin to a more famous Dorothy Forster of this same time) represented the spiritual vein of the Herries body.

Her thin, pale, ramrod-straight body, her dark clothes and quiet misgivings about her other fellow-humans, made this manifest.

Robert's son, Grandison, and his children Pelham and Helen represented fashion. They lived in Kensington, and everything outside London was too odd and peculiar to be true. Grandison had never understood how a Herries could bring himself to live out of London – it was a sort of *lèse-majesté* against the blood. His eyes, protruding out of his round pale face, expressed perpetual surprise and wonder. He was tall, stout and most elegantly dressed. Clothes were of great concern to him, and food, and the order of entrance and exit. Not greatly distinguished in the village of Kensington, he was an exquisite in Keswick. Aunt Jannice thought him the most marvellous creature in all the world, and had he but allowed himself to be bled more frequently he would have been perfect.

His girl Helen was in no way remarkable, but his son Pelham promised well as the Herries rake of his generation. There must always be a Herries rake, and he must go so far and no further. He must gamble, drink, womanize to a certain degree, fight duels enough for glory and not enough for scandal, be handsome and dashing and outrageous, but always within the limits of common sense. Other Herries must be able to shake their heads over him, but admire him too, and at last when a new younger rake is maturing he, the elder, must marry a virtuous girl with wealth, settle down and breed a family.

Young Pelham, aged at this time twenty-seven, understood all this perfectly, and had in fact a certain private store of ironic amusement which bewildered at times his fat father and irritated his august mother.

This mother, a magnificent figure, both snobbish and stupid on a large scale, had been a Titchley and, as everyone knows, it is difficult for a Titchley to yield place even to a Herries. She had in fact never quite yielded. She was still just enough rebel against the Herries tradition to need watching; not that she was interesting in her rebellion – she neither thought nor spoke enough to be interesting. Only once and again she would look at a stray Herries with a dumb air of wonder as much as to say: 'In a Titchley world this creature would not be permitted.'

In her quite young days she had known Sarah Marlborough and although now she was in a Kensington set she always got Court news before anyone else.

Henry, son of Maurice, and Lucilla his wife, represented the third strain in the Herries blood. Henry, who was thirty-two years of age, was thin and spare, with eyes gravely fixed. They were fixed upon the markets and he never permitted them to rest anywhere else. For one brief moment of sensual delight he had allowed them to rest upon his wife Lucilla. Ten years ago she had been a beautiful girl. Three years following their marriage she had been attacked by the smallpox, and, quite naturally, after that business had claimed him again. They had no children; the multiplying of coins of the realm was their only increase.

Henry was able and kept his eyes open for all the mechanical improvements and developments that were now beginning to alter the country, how permanently and irretrievably even he did not suspect. He was one of the first men in England to be aware of the deep importance of John Kay's invention of the fly-shuttle in 1733, of John Lombe's discovery in Italy of those improvements in machinery that gave such an impetus to the silk trade, and, in later years, he was to recognize at once the value of Crompton's mule, of Highs's water-frame and the spinning jenny of Hargreaves.

Oddly, with all his cleverness, his attention to business and parsimonious industry, he was never to make a fortune. This too was characteristic of the Herries; they were never in their money-making destined to be middle-men because if, in their tribe, genius showed its head it was instantly suspect and exiled. Henry was no genius, but he was industrious, honest, cross-grained, conceited and quite without poetic fancy. That was well, for had this last been his he would have been unfaithful to Lucilla, who was no woman to endure patiently infidelity.

Gathered there together on some general ground, had they for an outside observer any physical characteristic in common?

Only this: that in them all there was some attribute of the horse – Pomfret the cart-horse, Dorothy Forster the funeral hack, young Pelham the dashing pony, his father the well-fed favourite of the Countess's barouche, Henry the little dark horse of the race-meeting, and so-and-so . . . these traits of chin, high cheek-bones, long forehead, brooding, patient and unimaginative eyes marking the Herries tribe, giving them their place in English life and history.

And with all this they had great qualities.

They had a great force of fidelity, so that under pain of urgent torture they would not desert their loyalties, their loyalties of creed, of family, of ethics, of social conduct. These loyalties were English, and therefore the easier because no light of imagination was ever let in upon them. Two hundred years ago they had been, to a letter, the same: two hundred years later they would not have changed to a hair's-breadth. They were loyal to their country, to their family, to their loves, to their friends, with a stolid wonder that anybody could be anything else. When those ill-smelling traitors were discovered within their own households (as with every generation they were discovered) that taunt of disloyalty was the first stone that was flung.

As to their country so also to them disloyalty meant everything that was base; abnormality, cowardice, the vilest selfishness, dirty living, obscene thinking. And the certainty of their judgements was only equalled by the swiftness.

It was tragedy for the Herries that they must live in a constantly changing world. When, as now with Maurice's son Henry, these changes were sharply perceived, the Herries strain of orthodox tradition modified the use that was made of them. Loyalty came in there.

The changes were always unfortunate, even when they were most inevitable. The old days were always the good old days for the Herries; that was why, for example, Harcourt, who on this occasion had come over from Ravenglass, was accepted by all of them as a perfect member.

For him only all that was old was worthy. It had been Mr

Pope's only fault that he was not old enough. The thought that old Maria had been born on the day of the Battle of Naseby embalmed her, even though she had so impertinently missed her hundredth birthday, with an especial fragrance.

And behind this reverence there was something very kindly and genial. The Herries men especially were warm of heart. Pomfret and Harcourt, Robert's sons, and in the younger line, Francis's David, young Pelham – there was strong generous humanity here. Only, faced with what they thought to be heresy, vain worship of false gods, treachery to Church or State, to Country and the Marriage Vows and sound fact, only then they were as fierce, as prejudiced, as bloodthirsty as any Spanish Inquisitor. And for confidence in their own eternal rightness there was no family in Britain to rival them.

Here, then, they were, two days after Maria's funeral, on an afternoon of driving rain, gathered together in Jannice's withdrawing-room: lean Henry and his pale-faced Lucilla, little dainty Harcourt, Mrs Dorothy black and austere, Pelham's mother stout and frosted, Pelham gay in a coat of orange and silver, Raiseley bitterly envious, Grandison fat and flabby, amiable Anabel and beautiful Judith – the Herries stable – one of these Herries family gatherings that any Herries chronicler is compelled in their history to confront.

Jannice, Lucilla, Grandison, his wife Mary and Helen their daughter, were busy at Ombre. The men, bored with the wet, had come in to take tea with the women. Henry was giving Pomfret a rather patronizing lecture on profit and loss (he thought Pomfret the veriest fool), Pelham was tantalizing Raiseley with London splendours and besieging the lovely Judith with all his polished arts, and on the crimson sofa the dead Maria's spaniel lay, staring with sad angry eyes at the hated company.

The room was lit with candles, but the curtains were not drawn, and beyond the windows a furious sky tore in sweeping battalions of smoky clouds from horizon to horizon. Today as so often in this country of clouds the sky imposed itself upon the farthest interior seclusion. The glittering furniture of the room, the gilt of the chairs, the jewellery of the little clocks and boxes, the crimson silk, the shining silver candlesticks, the amber of the fluttering flames of lights and fire surrendered without question to the black shapes of the sky that seemed so vast and threatening, dragging at the distant tops of the hills as though to fling them across the lake on to the houses of the town.

Everyone in the room was irritated by the storm, but no one asked for the curtains to be drawn. There had been also during these last days other irritations.

The friendly scorn felt in different degrees by them all for their host and hostess reacted upon themselves. It was exasperating to feel that a Herries, whose hospitality they had accepted, was below the proper Herries mark, and Pomfret, who was only at his ease when he was out of doors killing something, who was always too uncomfortable in his wife's presence, had flustered through these days, now roaring in a noisy and false good humour, now putting on an air of deep seriousness that his words, alas, only betrayed, now sinking into a schoolboy silence of discomfort.

Jannice too was unhappy. For many years now she had been comfortable here in her own little circle, testing neither her wit nor her beauty against broader standards. But she detested the large pompous body of Grandison's wife after the first half-hour of her arrival. For Mary Herries, Jannice had the double aggravation that she was neither a Titchley nor a worthy Herries. She had indeed, with her provincial airs, her silly cures and recipes, her little conceits and ugly appearance, everything against her. Pomfret had never cared for his wife so protectively as during these last days when 'the Titchley woman', as he called her, had mocked with every word. He longed to humiliate fat Grandison, to put him on a horse that would throw him at the first ditch, to fire a gun in his ears, to win his money at a cock-fight, even to strip the clothes off his flabby body and soak him in the lake. He would show these Kensington puppies what real life was like up here in the North Country. Even as he listened to Henry Cards's dry words, hoping that he might gather a business wheeze or two, his other ear was on the Ombre table listening to the thick voice of Mary Herries as she instructed the others in the Kensington fine shades of Ombre play.

Mary Herries indeed was indignant with every pulse in her large body at the company that she was forced to keep. The very cards that Jannice had provided seemed to her contemptible with their old-fashioned pictures of 'the Bishops in the Tower, Popish Midwife, Captain Tom, Army going over to the Prince of Orange', etc. They were Jannice's best cards, 'the best superfine Principal Ombre cards at 2s 9d a Dozen'. She had been playing with them these twenty years. If good enough for anyone in Keswick, why not for anyone in Kensington?

Mary Herries had other causes for dissatisfaction. She knew

that her son Pelham was attracted by Jannice's girl Judith. She adored her son; this was the strongest, fiercest motive of life for her. His handsomeness, cleverness, gaiety, made her the proudest woman in all England, and her pride was the more defended because it was mingled with a worshipping fear of an irony in him that she would never understand.

That by any horrible chance he should throw himself away on the girl of these country bumpkins was terrifying to her. Fool though she was she could see that Judith was a dark beauty: dressed properly and educated in Kensington she might make others than her son stare. She knew too that Pelham meant as a rule but little by his gallantries – there was already a fine list of momentary conquests behind him – but the dullness of these last days (was it for ever raining in this pernicious country?), his idleness and something arrogant and distant in Judith might lead to some desperate impetuosity. She could scarcely hold her cards as she thought of some dreadful crisis suddenly exploded before them: her husband, poor fool, would perceive nothing, and would never dream of acting until all was over.

And she had a further irritation. This was the King Charles spaniel on the crimson sofa. This, the last of dead Maria's many spaniels, was the only true mourner of that poor lady. She was missing her now with every wheezy breath that she drew. She was old, fat, the victim of many pains and tortures; life had long ago been misery to her had it not been for the touch of those strange dry fingers, the scratch of those multitudinous rings, the warmth of that thin shrivelled body, a bag of bones under the coloured shining silks. Alone she had shared her mistress's recent life, her longings, her prides, her greeds, her ignorances, her loneliness. Alone she had called out of that aged woman, so nearly deceased long before the actual moment of death, tenderness and unselfishness, the only cause in her of anxiety for another. During those long nights when Maria had lain looking up at a remorseless ceiling, seeing pageants of vanished scenes and figures, her pride her only refuge, the spaniel had breathed against her withered hand, rested its head against her dried bosom.

Together they had faced a world that seemed to them both worthless and ugly; all the old glories were over, but so long as they were together pride would sustain them both.

Now they were no longer together, and the spaniel, only aware that her mistress called her no more, ached her old heart away in angry wasted rebellion. But there was more than despair and loneliness there. There was also a spirit of impotent and sarcastic rage. She was of blood royal, descendant of a line of kings. It had always seemed to her that Jannice and Pomfret, their offspring also, were low and degenerate creatures. She hated that they should touch her, and when Raiseley or Judith teased her, her whole soul rose in affronted disgust. While Maria lived she had been protected, and in sublime confidence of her dear mistress had been able to scorn those others, but now she knew that she was open to the world . . . Pains racked her, dim fears besieged her, and with these the scorn that she knew her mistress had felt ever increased within her.

She was no Herries: her alliance had been to a single soul, not to the herd. So now as they passed around her with their strange scents and movements and sounds she hated them even as she despised them, and most bitterly of all she hated and despised the stout, crackling, silk-swishing, fan-waving, scent-distilling Mary Herries.

It may have been that in this woman beyond the others she detected false arrogances and knew that of them all it was she who would have most fiercely affronted her mistress. In any case it was upon Mary Herries that she fixed her filmed and fading eyes, concentrated her aching body, curled her upper lip, showing two sharp and yellow teeth.

Mary Herries was telling some tale of a friend: 'But a miserly temper. She is as expressive to her husband as a casket of jewels. Many's the night I've seen her lug out her old green net purse full of old jacobuses while her waiting woman in the room behind is diving into the bottom of her trunk hoping for a stray piece or two . . .' when she was aware of the spaniel's eyes.

She moved her chair ever so slightly and was aware of them the more. The spaniel was laughing at her, or maybe it was the spirit of old Maria that mocked her through the dog.

She felt suddenly an accumulation of miseries: she saw Grandison her husband as he stood in his night-shirt, his ugly naked toes spread, his bristling head bare of its wig, and in that figure, so deeply accustomed that it seemed to be part of her own, she groaned at the weariness of her life. What was all this pretence of Kensington finery, this elaborate mention of old Duchess Sarah, Sir John and the rest, when a yard away Pelham was making eyes at that hoydenish country girl, and her stomach ached beneath her tightened stays and her feet were pinched in their silver shoes, and Grandison, scratching at his wig for the thousandth time, cleared his throat over his cards preparatory to playing the wrong one? What were these Herries but second-rate country bumpkins? Henry with his spare money-calculating eyes, who yet could make no fortune, Dorothy in her thin black with her psalm-singing pieties, Pomfret stinking of drink and the miry road, his miserable Raiseley with his splay feet and mean little nose. Oh! she was sick of the lot, she had messed her life through her own silly folly, storms of rain beat the windows and the spaniel mocked her!

A point had come in the game and she flung her cards on the table. 'I play no more,' she said in her thick soft voice that was like the stirring of suet in the pan. She had been winning (a fact that until now she had quite honestly not noticed) and at once she was aware that Jannice Herries found in this the reason of her withdrawal.

Jannice had not at sixty improved in appearance. She was thinner, more sallow, more drawn and by her odd unsuited clothes more painfully quartered than ever.

'An old witch,' thought Mary Herries.

'A fat mean cook of a woman,' thought Jannice.

'Why, cousin, you are winning,' said Jannice sharply. 'You must give us our revenge.'

But Mary Herries, raising her stout body painfully, pushing back the chair, feeling freshly the agony of her pinching shoes, answered:

'That dog should be poisoned.'

Everyone felt the unseemliness. A Herries, the oldest of all the Herries, had been but two days buried. This was her dog, all that remained of her, almost you could say a Herries dog. But worse followed.

Mary, her voice quivering to an unexpected plaintiveness: 'I am sick to death of this: it rains and rains again. Maria is happily buried if it was here that she must look out of window.' Then with a toss of her head, the painted flowers in her white wig nodding their petals, she waddled from the room, her little feet protesting with sad little creaks against the weight that they must carry.

Grandison knew what this meant. She was feeling Titchley, and when she felt Titchley he was in for a terrible hour. He hastened after her. The dog still laughed, motionless like a dead dog.

But the men, Henry and Pomfret, young Pelham and Harcourt, like all Herries men when a woman made a scene, came together. Young Pelham, leaning back against the purple brocaded chair near the door, smiling, said: 'My mother has vapours often enough at this hour. She will be happy only in a land where the sun always shines. I appeal to you, sir' (smiling at Pomfret), 'this is a handsome country, but it rains unduly.'

'It would not be so handsome a country,' said Harcourt, 'did it not rain so frequently.' And he turned from them, looking out of window across the lake to the hills where a sudden flash of pale sunlight had pierced the storm, striking an arrow of gold that cleft Cat Bells in two. He loved it, every stick and stone of it! How he loved it! And as he looked, a deep homesickness for his own home at Ravenglass, his little garden, his gleaming book rows, the faint flash of the sea beyond his windows, took him.

All of them in that room caught from him some sense of English soil. The men moved together to the window and stood there side by side looking out. They were Herries in this: that however far they might be drawn from the English soil, they yet belonged to it. Even in Kensington they felt the stirrings of ancient waterways and the tuggings of prehistoric roots. Which partially explains perhaps that they were never good travellers abroad, queasy, irritable, of an arrogant critical mind; and if they must settle in a foreign land they must turn it speedily to a Scottish or English likeness.

They felt now that urgent need to break out into the open air that every Herries feels when his women are badgering him.

Pomfret's indignation at the insult to his wife was mingled with a twofold satisfaction: it was not he who for once was the clown of the occasion and, although he would never confess to this, his own dear Jannice had been found to be less than perfection. There came to him indeed at that moment, gazing out at the steel wall of rain that fell now like a vengeance from the muddy sky, a thought of what life would have been had Jannice never existed. He cast an uneasy backward glance at the spaniel, who was now wheezily sleeping. How many things dogs knew, and how greatly the more at ease he was with them than with humans! Now with a dog! . . .

And he thought again of Jannice, of how to this day, although they had been married so long, he was afraid of her, afraid of that sudden sharp tap in her voice like a knock on the window, that chilly glaze of contempt in her eye when he had been an especial fool. Yes, and his own children . . . Only Anabel was friendly and easy, and she was easy with all the world.

He was sixty-seven years of age now, a tun of a man with a floating hulk of a belly, and he was lonely as perhaps were all men of sixty-seven. Only with horses and dogs and a drinking parson and a swearing friend or two, killing, hunting those animals that he yet so dearly loved, only thus might he for a driving hour cheat himself of his loneliness. Staring out of window, not hearing anything of the voices in the room behind him, he thought suddenly of his brother Francis. Why, he could not say. He did not think of him more often than he must, partly because he was a scandal, partly because he loved him. At heart it might be that Francis was more to him than anyone else in the world: Francis, digging away in that miry patch of stinking mud in that nook-shotten valley, Francis shouted at by the peasant children, Francis, adulterer and vagabond, known to have sold his woman at a public fair, to have killed his wife with unkindness, to have driven one of his own daughters away from her home, to be sheltering under his roof the most notorious old witch in the country, Francis – 'Rogue Herries' to all the world, so that he brought with every hour disgrace on the Herries name – yet Pomfret loved him. His mind flung back to that first windy evening when Francis and his family arrived in the town, Francis so young and handsome then in all his gay clothes, and to that other time, the day that poor Margaret died, when he had ridden over to Herries and Francis had been so grave and kindly, so noble in spirit, and he, Pomfret, had kissed his brother, loving him and wishing in his own clumsy speechless way to protect him.

Oh! Francis was bad and not to be mentioned, but through the sheets of rain Pomfret had a mad, monstrous wonder of a moment whether, if he had been with him out there in rugged tumbled Herries, life might not have been richer, more valorous, better worth . . .

And so wondering, turning because he heard the door open, saw to his stricken, open-mouthed amazement his brother, Francis Herries, standing in the room.

He had not seen his brother for three years; the last time had been in a Keswick street when Francis, riding past on a huge kind of cart-horse, had patronized Pomfret and sent him home in a fuming fury.

But now how strange he looked standing there, wearing his own black shaggy hair, muddily booted to the thighs, his long brown coat faded and stained, his face brown and spare, the shape and form of it altered by the deep white scar that ran from brow to lip. His face was yet shining with raindrops, water dripped from his boots, the back of his brown hand shone with rain. Years back he had promised to be stout; now he was lean and spare, and seemed of an immense height. He had aged strangely. Pomfret had a quick vision of him that other first time at the inn when glittering in gold and crimson he had been so young and handsome. Now the soil was in the furrows of his cheeks.

To Jannice, staring from above the card-table, it was as though the Devil had sprung out of the floor. Francis was to her as the Devil. Sharing no blood with him, disliking him from the very first, her dislike was now hatred – hatred mingled with deep fear. For years he had threatened everything in which she believed, her morality, her family, her social position. Especially her social position. Every little success in Keswick was threatened with the consciousness that only a mile or two away there was this sinister figure, outlaw, adulterer, vagabond, and, because she never saw him, her sense of his evil power grew and grew with imagination. She was a woman compact of superstition. Witches and warlocks, mandrakes and goblins were as real to her as her own children. The two worlds were, with her, one. Had Francis been arrested for dealings with the Devil and been burnt at the stake she would not have thought it an injustice.

She had sworn that never again should he pass her door. He was here, and it seemed to her as she looked across the room at him that fire and brimstone smoked at his nostrils.

Harcourt was the first to speak. He was enchanted with pleasure. He came forward, holding out both hands: 'Francis, my dear brother!' That explained to the others who this was. Young Pelham, greatly interested, thought: 'So this is my dangerous and exiled relation. This is a man. Worth the lot of us here.' He was drawn naturally to the rebel in life. He had a complete intellectual appreciation of rebellion, although his love of comfort would always keep himself on the side of safety.

Francis looked about him, bowed to Jannice and Dorothy Forster, then, smiling (his smile was odd now because the scar caught his upper lip and twisted it), said:

'Forgive me. I would not have intruded, but, passing, thought that I would greet the family . . . very briefly. It can be so seldom that we are all together. Not, you know,' he continued, smiling more broadly, 'that I enjoy family gatherings, and I fear that I have not impertinence enough to invite you to Herries, unless anyone has an affection for potato-gathering. But I would not wish to be remiss in paying some reverence to my great-aunt.'

He looked at the handsome boy by the chair. 'You must be Grandison's boy?'

Francis rested for a moment his hand on his shoulder. 'You should know my son David,' he said. 'If you care for the country, a day or two at Herries . . . But I suspect that you have better things to do.'

Pomfret here blustered forward. 'Well, brother, damn it, now that thou art here . . . a drink in this damp weather . . . Why, damn it, man . . .' Then, conscious of his wife behind him, stopped abruptly.

'Nay, nay,' said Francis, smiling. 'My horse is outside and I have business. I heard you were all here. Doubtless you thought of me and wished my presence but were shy of asking me.'

He saw the spaniel, crossed to the sofa, bent down and stroked it. 'Poor bitch. You have as little place here as myself. I'll be coming to see thee one of these days, Harcourt.' Then was gone abruptly as he came.

INTO THE CAVE

FRANCIS HERRIES rode off into the rain, his mind a strange torment. To enter that house over whose threshold he had not stepped for so many years had been an impulse of the moment. He had been inside before he had known that he was going, and, brushing past the startled man-servant, he had entered that room and almost blinked, like an owl, at the unaccustomed light. It had been more than the candlelight; to himself who had been having for so long no intimate contacts save with the wind, the air, the hard grit of unyielding soil and the soft friendliness of the land after rain, these figures were like fish swimming in a strange sea. Like fish, and yet they had tugged at his heart.

He had entered the house in a childish play-acting spirit of dare-devil as though he would say 'Bo!' to a goose, but the very sight of silly Pomfret with his hanging belly and little Harcourt whose eyes had shone with pleasure at sight of him, and that handsome lad Grandison's boy, and all his Herries blood had pressed about his heart. It was to conceal this – which had been as violent as an unexpected blow in the face – that he had moved to the dog, stroked it, said those false sentimental words – the play-actor in him again. But behind the false sentiment there had been that swift ache of loneliness.

He knew it: he could confess it to himself: for all his intolerance and truculence he would have loved to stay with the men, with Pomfret, Harcourt, young Pelham, even with stiff Henry and flabby-faced Grandison, spent the night with them, laughed and drunk and changed bawdy stories with them, felt HERRIES again, felt the family blood in him and all England behind his tread and that ancient old tree-man whispering in his ears the ancient Herries password . . . and then perhaps to have taken the boy Pelham off to Herries and to have shown him David, who was a giant now and the hero of the countryside and the simplest, grandest Herries of them all. Then to have put on his decent clothes again and found a good horse once more (Mameluke buried beneath the yews behind the house) and ridden off to Seddon for a week or two, and then perhaps to stay with Grandison in Kensington . . . He! He grinned, the rain blinding him as he climbed the steep hill to Cat Bells. That was never again for him nor would he care for it did he have it. In a day he would be quarrelling with Harcourt, mocking Pomfret, laughing at Grandison, corrupting Pelham. But the Herries blood was there. He had been a fool to enter that place.

There was something further for him to consider. In Keswick that afternoon he had talked with Father Roche. He had been crossing the market-place, his head up, looking neither to right nor left, in enemy's country and knowing it, when a country fellow dressed like a carter had touched his arm. He had turned about with his accustomed haughty stare, and that voice, once so powerful over him, came back to him across all the years. He knew him immediately, the voice with its seeming musical resonance, the eyes with their strange commanding glow belonging to one man only in the world. Roche had smiled, his broad hat pulled over his brows. Francis had asked him to Herries. Roche had refused, saying that he was on his way to Carlisle. The business was urgent. Very shortly the world would hear startling things. The hour for which they had all been waiting so long had struck at last. The voice was not raised, but behind it was that old fanatical undoubting spirit, and it had for Francis its ancient power. Standing there in the market-place, the rain soaking down upon them, the old times swung back, days in Doncaster when it had seemed to him that he would follow Roche anywhere, evenings when it had appeared no odd fancy that, threading the stars, God and all His cohort of angels, the chariots of fire and the horsemen thereof, could plainly be discerned. Roche had given him an address – Walter Frith, in charge of John Stope, English Street, Carlisle. He would be found there. They had parted.

So all the old life was swinging back. You could not escape it, throw it off as you fancied, dig yourself into the very stomach of the soil – one tap on the shoulder, one glance through the dark branches of the yew and you were caught again. As Francis rode down to Grange Bridge the rain cleared. The clouds were rolling away above the Castle Crag, and a faint fair wash of crocus spread in a sea of light over the black pointed hill. On either side above Watendlath and the slow slopes beyond Grange white fleecy mists still lay low like bales of wool, but you could feel the light that burnt behind them, and the soft fields beyond the stream towards the lake were richly green.

He crossed the little bridge, turned to the right, rode between the trees beside the swift river along the track to Rosthwaite. In the village he had not seen a soul. It had been like a dead place. And well it might be. All the valley from Seathwaite to Grange had been cursed that winter. Misfortune had followed misfortune. Cattle had died, agues and fevers and plagues of pests had seemed to choose the valley for their camping-ground, and at the last smallpox had come, had raged right down the valley and only here. None over in Grasmere nor the other way in Newlands nor more than ordinary in the Keswick slums. The valley had been marked out. He knew well enough what the people were saying, that there was a curse, a spell, and he knew further that the old Wilson woman under his own roof was marked as the agent. And he knew that behind her he was himself marked out.

Yes, and he knew more than that; that, had it not been for David, weeks ago the roof would have been burned down over his head, Herries a heap of ashes and himself, perhaps, stoned to death. He did not care for their hatred, but he did not wish to die. There was something in life that was, like the beat of a drum, insistently enthralling. He had always felt it: he would never escape it: and it was as though, did he live long enough, he would discover the answer to this incredible mixture of beauty and filth, wizardry and commonplace, stagnation and unceasing activity. He did not want to die, but he did not want, either, that it should be by permission of his son that he should live.

But this was not for long. David was going: he knew it as

though David had told him. And he did not want David to go.
No, he did not ...

David was now twenty-five years of age, six feet five inches tall,
as broad as a wall, the strongest man in the county beyond
question, and many thought, with his fair blanched hair, blue
eyes and splendid carriage, the handsomest. Let that be as it
might. It did not matter. He was simple, modest, a man without
words, quite direct in thought and act and with few subtleties. He
had, for his years, scarcely stepped farther than Seascale on one
side, Penrith on the other, very rarely left his valley, made few
friends in Keswick, though all the world was friendly. His own
valley loved him and said, as Francis well knew, that Rogue
Herries had never fathered him. And yet he was clear Herries
enough, the line of his jutting chin, the high strong cheek-bones
made him plainly of the 'horse' family. He moved, tossed his
head, swung his body like some high-bred animal, held, con-
fined.

For eight years now he had helped his father in the land
around Herries, ploughing, planting, digging, all as he very well
knew, but never said, to little effect. His constant companions
were his father and Deborah; he was friend to all the valley, but
had no other close intimacy save that old childhood one with
Peel's boy, Rendal, who was now a man almost as big and strong
as David himself. Of love affair there had been as yet, it seemed,
no sign.

He was a man of few words save possibly with Deborah.
When he went to sport or meeting, to hunt or local games, and
performed some miracle of strength, he came home afterwards
without a word of it. His thoughts were certainly slow in labour:
you could almost see them move behind his smooth clear forehead. He had a long, slow laugh that began as a murmur, spread
into a long rumble, ended in a roar. He had a slow temper. He
had two faults: that he was suspicious of men and, although
courteous in manner, desperately hard to make a friend of. And
he never forgot nor forgave an injury. When, that is, he had
proved it to be one. He paid no attention to gossip, drank as
men drink, but kept the effects of it to himself. He showed no
resentment at the cruelties, foulnesses, obscenities of his time.
He was a man of his time. He did not trade with women because
he did not as yet apparently care very greatly for women's
company save Deborah's. He was tongue-tied with women
and impatient of their ways. He did not care very much for
any company and preferred best to be away on the hills

alone. He was very Herries in some things: in his passion for England – he had all the Herries's ignorant contempt for and dislike of foreigners; in his interest in the family – he would ask his father many questions about Herries history and relationship; in his inability to see anything that was not in front of his nose.

It was his father who was the rebel, not he. Unless he were passionately roused – a very rare thing – there was something lazy and comfort-loving in his great size and strength. He seemed to be never physically tired, but he liked to lie back staring into fire or sky, seeing nothing, perhaps thinking nothing, letting light and warmth soak into him.

But what were his thoughts of his father? How many times, in the instant of digging or planting, hoeing or carrying, walking or riding, Francis had looked up at the sky, at the long hump of Glaramara, or, from Grange, at the opening flower of Skiddaw, and asked himself that question. David was infinitely kind, ceaselessly patient. Since that night so long ago at Ravenglass no word of impatience had passed his lips, he had shown no angry movement towards his father. But they had moved, these last years, with a sort of mist between, loving one another and yet distrustful: or Francis on his side at least had held distrust. What must David feel about his father's isolation, self-adopted, ironically self-proclaimed, and about the ever thicker wall of hatred built by the world against him?

We love most, perhaps, those of whom we are a little afraid. David was the only creature in the world of whom Francis was afraid, and this was a fear only of a sudden blazing word, a glance of contempt. Then, the word spoken, the glance flung, Francis would pass into the final ostracism.

When Mary, two years earlier, had left him, Francis thought that the word would be spoken. Mary, who had grown increasingly beautiful and contemptuous, had gone without a sign one morning to her aunt in Keswick. She had sent a letter from there saying that she would not return. No other word came from her. They heard that she went afterwards to stay in Carlisle, then that she was back in Keswick, then in London. Then it was said that Francis had beaten and abused her. He smiled at that. In earlier days he had beaten David often and Deborah on occasion: on Mary he had never laid a finger.

Would David blame him for Mary? He did not. David blamed him for nothing. Was his silence criticism? Maybe not. He was always so very silent. Once, when they were together in

Langdale, Francis looking down the long green sward and then up to the Pikes, rosy in sunset, said:

'You must hate me, David.' And David, after a long silence while the birds swept above their heads home, answered:

'I have three friends. You are one – and the first.'

But what comfort, his irony urged on him, was he to find in that? David had not answered his question, only asserted his loyalty; and David's loyalty was so unsubtle that it offered no reward to one's pride.

Not that Francis's pride was in question. He was so proud that his son's approval or disapproval altered nothing. He was so proud that he would tell his son to go to the devil did he patronize him. But he did not patronize him. He stood at his side and worked with him. That was all.

So he rode into the little stone court of Herries, shouted to fat Benjamin to come for his horse, and longed, as he stumbled up the dark staircase, to see David waiting for him.

David was there. He was standing in the dark brown room upon whose surface the firelight was very faintly flickering, listening, and so intent was his attitude that Francis also stayed motionless by the door: the only sound in the room was the soft settling of the ash from the piled logs.

'What is it?' Francis asked at last. Then he heard, but so faint that it was like the scratching of mice on the wainscot, a trickling, crooning sound; someone, at a distance, behind walls, was singing, singing in a high-pitched murmur of a voice a little tune like an incantation or a prayer monotonously reiterated.

'Mrs Wilson,' David said, then coming close to his father and laying his hand on his arm: 'She sings to keep herself company. She's afraid.'

'Of whom?' asked Francis, although he knew the answer.

'They are very impatient . . . I've been telling her she should go from here.'

'Turn her from this roof . . . after these years?'

'No, no . . . Help her to the Low Countries. At the Hague there is some family she was nurse to once. They would take her. We could secure her a passage.'

'She is old,' Francis answered. He liked the warmth of his son's body close to his. He hoped that David would not move. That visit to the family had made him lonelier . . .

He put his arm across David's vast shoulders. His long brown fingers pressed a little into the smooth warmth of his son's neck.

'I think she is going mad with terror,' David said. The room too seemed a little mad: the dusk wrote letters on the wall with the firelight and then erased them again. The wind that was getting up and rattling the leaded panes drowned the little song and then by contrast raised it again. It was more dangerous in the dusky room because both men believed in witches and thought that Mrs Wilson was one.

Then Benjamin came clumping up the staircase, holding the lighted candles in their tall silver candlesticks in either hand, and Deborah came in to lay the table for some supper; there was life and movement and the little song could be heard no more.

Deborah, who was now twenty-two years of age, was little and insignificant until you noticed her eyes, which were large, soft, grey, very beautiful. Her shyness was her trouble. She could not be courageous about people. She was afraid of every person in the world save David, and especially of her father. She had had the same fear for seven years, ever since the death of her mother, that David would go and leave her with her father alone. That fear was now a torture, and no reassurance on David's part could comfort her.

Francis knew, of course, that she was afraid of him, and that exasperated him. Every time that she shrank from him his old ironic dislike of himself increased in him and she was included in that. When the supper had been cleared away and she had gone up to her room, the two men were left alone in front of the fire. The rain had returned and in violence; it slashed the panes, roared with the wind away, then fell again upon the house as though it would batter it to the ground; the fury passed and the rain softly stroked the windows, whispering indecent and chuckling secrets, then ran in a hurry as though it were pattering after someone, burst after that once more into a frenzy of rage and exasperation . . . an evil frustrated old woman, the rain that night.

Secure from it the two Herries drew close together. Suddenly they were intimate as they had not been for months. Francis put his hand on David's broad thigh, drawing his great body a little nearer to him. When he told him about his visit to the family that afternoon David was excited.

'Oh, why did you not stay?' he said. 'The awkwardness would have worn away. How did Cousin Pelham look? And Henry Cards . . . and Cousin Dorothy . . .' He sighed. 'I would that I'd been with you.'

Francis sharply withdrew his hand. 'You could go . . . Why don't you?'

David shook his head, laughing. 'What would they want with me? I've no head for their company. No, no. It was your opportunity, Father. But you frightened them.'

Francis said: 'David, I've been wishing to ask you. We've been working side by side these years. It's come to but little. Everything here must seem to you cursed, the house, the soil, the life, the loneliness. I fancy that it's in that very cursedness of the place that I find some salvation. I would have it hard and ungrateful. Here for the first time in all my days I've found response to my own temper and some aggravating comfort. But for you! Already you are doing good business in Keswick and with your friend in Liverpool. Why should you stay? There's no place in the world where you wouldn't make your way, and you should see the world, find a woman of your own breed, not bury yourself, in this windy hole for hinds and pigs . . . I'm other than you. The dirt of the soil is more to me than any man, aye, or woman either. I am stuck here, my feet in the clay, and am accustomed. But it is not your abiding-place and will never be.'

He was amazed then at how roughly, after he had ended, his heart was beating as he waited for the boy's answer. What would it be here without David? How could he endure it? But better that David should go rather than he should indulge his father by staying. Francis would take no patronage. Yes, but his heart hammered as he waited.

David was slow as always. At last he answered: 'I'm glad you've spoken at last, Father. All these months I've wondered what was in your mind. But I can't leave you. We're bound together, I fancy, different though we are. And yet . . . there *is* something I should say. Father, why should we stay by Herries? The place has never cared for us. As a boy I ran first into the house and shivered at its greeting. Everything has been wrong for you here. The people have been wrong for you, the soil stubborn; nothing that you have planted has grown: you have been with every year more alone here. Why should we stay? We owe nothing to the house. In the South together, the three of us, where it is warmer and the sun shines and people's hearts are more friendly . . . Father, let us leave here. Everything has been wrong for you here.'

'No,' his father answered in a strange, low voice, as though he were speaking to something within him. 'Everything is not wrong for me here. Here is my home, the only one I've ever known or shall know. I feel the touch of the peat, the scratch of the dried bracken, and it is my place.'

His voice had its accustomed ironic tone. 'So they've been per-suading you, David, my son? "Take your father away, David Herries. He stinks in our noses, he is warlock and dirty liver and murderer maybe. Remove his carcass or we will remove it for you." They've persuaded you, David . . . but there must be more than a word before they can move me. I am stuck fast, and there's my ghost to come after me when they've knocked my head in and scattered my entrails for dung over their fields: there's still my ghost, David.'

David got up. His voice was cold with anger when at last after a long while he spoke.

'That is unjust. No man could persuade me against you save yourself. I am no traitor. But guard yourself against irony with me. I am a fool, you know, and may understand it wrongly.'

He went out.

So that was that. Herries was alone. He got up very early next morning, washed himself at the pump and went off, walking, his head in the air, not caring a damn if he never saw his bullock of a son again. Or he said not. His heart within his heart ached, as it always did, for his son. That heart would have gone, waked the boy, embraced him. The only heart to which David responded, the only one that he understood. For David had all the simple sentimentality of his period; for him there were these actual contrasted powers, God and the horny Satan, Michael and all the angels, dragons and rescuing princes, shepherds, shepherd-esses, and the ravening wolf, the good old man by the fireside reading out of the Book to his family clustered at his knees, wedding bells and Innocence wed under roses to Purity and Strength. Yes, David believed in all these things. He saw life like that.

Francis, as he strode off into the early morning rain that sung about his ears in a feathering mist, said aloud: 'I'm done with the boy. What's the use? . . . No ground between us,' and the rain whispered in his ear: 'It's a lie! It's a lie!' Once he almost turned back. It would be very easy to run up those stairs, climb to David's room, see him sunk in sleep there, his chest bare, his knees curled up. Francis knew how he lay, his cheek on his hand, dreaming of his princesses and his shepherdesses. He had no more subtlety than that. The Herries sentimentalist. No, not conscious enough to be called anything. A sweet-breathed, mild-eyed animal, with the obstinacy of a mule, the strength of a horse, the fidelity of a dog. He should be breeding. He should be let out, like a stallion, to the women of the country to get fine sons. All this true enough did you forget his heart, which in its strength, sweetness, sympathy, durability was of another order from the animal. There was his immortality, and, likely enough, the immortality of all of us.

For there was immortality in us! The great white horse of Herries's dream striking up from the ebony lake to the icy peaks. Sentimentality, that again, thought Herries, and arrogance, planning for your little peapod of a marionette so handsome a destiny. But the very fact of the planning . . . Why this burning, eager, rebellious, longing fury between his miserable bag of bones, the thick coiled entrails, the stringy nerves, the flat-faced pancreas, that silly mechanism that one blow from a fool could tumble as a child tumbles a toy. Burning there between the bones and fat, the blood and gristle, this fierce arrogant ambition, this persistent dream, this lovely vision . . . 'All we like sheep . . .' Nay, like gods rather, lost in a strange land.

Herries often, as he dug and sweated, cursed the reluctant soil and his aching back and blistered hands, turned back and back to those same common platitudes, fresh to him because they were his own and mingled with so many strange things for which he could find no words. His brain, heart, generative organs: how to reconcile these three in a common harmony and drive them to a fine destiny, his brain that was clogged with lack of education, his heart that led him only to self-contempt, his generative powers that had known their best days, and they nothing to boast over. All keys to some event, but all out of control and discipline, all leading to silly ends.

Not intelligent enough, not kind enough, not even lecher enough. A botched machine set in a country veiled with mist . . .

He had crossed the fields, passed the little cottages of Seatoller and the yews, and started up the hill to Honister. On the left of him Hause Gill tumbling in miniature cataracts with the recent rain, on the right of him the ever-opening fells. He drew great gulps of air into his lungs. That was for him, that unenclosed fell. As soon as he reached a point where the moss ran unbroken to the sky all his troubles dropped away from him and he was a man. There was no place in the world for open country like this stretch of ground in Northern England and Scotland, for it was man's country: it was neither desert nor icy waste; it had been on terms with man for centuries and was friendly to man. The hills were not so high that they despised you; their rains and clouds and becks and heather and bracken, gold at a season, green at a

season, dun at a season, were yours; the air was fresh with kindliness, the running water sharp with friendship, and when the
mist came down it was as though the hill put an arm around you
and held you even though it killed you. For kill you it might.
There was no sentimentality here. It had its own life to lead and,
as in true friendship, kept its personality. It had its own
tempers with the universe and, when in a rolling rage, was not
like to stop and inquire whether you chanced to be about or no.
Its friendship was strong, free, unsentimental, breathing courage
and humour. And the fell ran from hill to hill, springing to the
foot, open to the sky, cold to the cheek, warm to the heart, unchanging in its fidelity. As he breasted the hill and turned back to
look across Borrowdale the sky began to break.

He stared, as though the scene were new to him, to Glaramara
and then over Armboth to the Helvellyn range. It was new to
him: never before had it held those shapes and colours nor
would it again: with every snap of the shuttle it changed.

Now across the Helvellyn line the scene was black and against
the black hung the soft white clouds. Borrowdale glittered in sun
like a painted card, flat, emerald and shining. Above his head all
the sky was in motion: beyond him over Honister tenebrous
shadows thrust upward to one long line of saffron light that lay
like a path between smoking clouds. All the fell smelt of rain and
young bracken, and two streams ran in tumult across the grass,
finding their way to the beck. The sunlight was shut off from
Borrowdale, which turned instantly dead grey like a mouse's
back; then the sun burst out as though with a shout over the low
fells that lay before the Gavel. A bird on a rock above the beck
began to sing.

He was filled with a delicious weariness. He lay down there
where he was, his full length on a thin stone above the beck, and
on that hard surface fell happily, dreamlessly, asleep.

He woke to a strange sense of constriction. He moved and
found amazingly that his arms and legs were tied with rough
rope. He raised his head and stared into the eyes of a man who
sat motionless on a rock near him. A horse grazed in the grass
close by.

Francis stared at the man: the man stared back again.

'You sleep fast,' the man said. 'I bound you and you didn't
waken.' He was a man with a thin dry face, long shaggy black
hair, a coat and breeches of some colour that had faded into a
dirty green. He looked like part of the fell. His legs were thin and
long and sharp. He was not young, fifty years of age maybe.

'Why have you bound me?' Herries asked quietly.

'You are my prisoner,' the man replied.

'My body is – for the moment,' Herries answered.

The man was, from his voice, not of the North. His tone was firm, quiet, reflective.

'You are Herries of Herries in Rosthwaite.'

'Yes. How do you know me?'

'I've seen you many times.'

'What have you against me?'

'Nothing.'

'Then why have you bound me?'

'You are my prisoner,' the man answered again.

'Yes; but why?'

'I have a curiosity to ask you some questions. Would you come peacefully with me?'

'Whither?'

'By Honister.'

'Yes,' said Herries.

'You swear it?'

'Yes.'

'Then I will untie you.'

He came forward and, quite gently, with some care, undid the bonds.

Herries sat up and felt his arms and legs where the rope had been, but he had been bound only a moment or so: it was the binding that had waked him. Then he rose and stretched himself. The man also got up. He was of great height and very thin with a long nose. His face was pitted with smallpox marks.

They started to walk together forward to Honister, the man leading the horse. The air was deliciously fresh and the sky filled now with little dancing white clouds.

'What is your interest in me?' Francis asked at last. They were on the higher ground, about to turn the corner, and before he turned he looked back and saw, picked up by the sun, on the low ground before Armboth a little wood of silver birch. The sun hung over the little wood in a brooding lighted mist and the thin silver trunks stood up proudly, burnished. Herries, because of what happened afterwards, was never to forget them.

This fellow was a man of not many words, but at last he said, long after Francis's question:

'Can you recall, once, many years gone, you gave your coat to a woman by the road?'

'Yes,' said Herries, his heart beating.

'And once later on a Christmas night you talked with her?'

'I remember,' said Herries.

'I was there, that second time,' the man said.

'There was with her,' Herries said, 'a young child.'

The man nodded. 'The woman was my sister. The child was her child and is with me yet.' He waited a while and then went on. 'I bound you because you would not have come with me else. Or I thought so. They say in the valley that you are the Devil and eat human flesh.'

Herries looked at the man smiling. 'Do you think so?'

The man looked back at Herries.

'No,' he said. 'When my sister died she said I was to give you the only thing she had. I have kept it for you.'

'But why,' asked Herries, 'must you bind me to give it me?'

The man answered: 'Our place is rough in Honister. We are in bad repute here, my brother and I, though not so bad as yourself. I thought you would fight before you came, and because of my sister I would not strike you. Are you as bad as men say?'

'I am as bad,' answered Herries, 'as other men. And as good. We are as the fancy hits us.'

The man nodded his head gravely. 'That's true. One man's life is this way, another's that. We have little choice.'

They struck up the fell to the left and climbed. The man led the horse patiently and with kindness. When they were high on the moor they could see the guards of the mines pacing on the path below.

All the fell rolled beneath them now like the sea, and the clouds rolled above them, driven by a sunny dancing wind. On the brow of the hill the man took Herries's arm, led him over boulders, dipped down the shelving turf, then pushed up again on the hinder shoulder of Honister.

Then, loosening his grip, he vanished. Herries stood alone, hearing no sound but the wind and running water. He could see, icily blue, the thin end of Buttermere Lake far below. He heard a whistle and saw the black head of the man just below him. He went down.

He saw then the grey opening of a cave in the hill, fenced with dead bracken and furze. He followed the man in. At first he could see nothing, but could smell cooking food, an odd sweet scent of flowers and a musty animal tang. The man had his hand on his arm and very gently, as though he were speaking to a child, said: 'Sit you there. You can sleep if you will. The straw's dry.' Francis turned back, shifting the bracken a little; and the sun flickered on to him, dancing before his eyes.

But he did not wish to look about him. He was oddly uncurious and infinitely weary. Why this weariness? It was as though the kind black-haired man had laid a spell upon him. So he slept, long and almost dreamlessly. The nearest to a dream was that he was led again through the incidents of the morning, following the lean man over ever-darkening fell, then was pushed from a height and heard, as he raised himself from a hard cold ground, a voice say to him: 'Into the cave! Into the cave! You have been outside too long.'

With that he woke, wide-eyed, oddly happy, extremely hungry. He sat up and looked about him. The sun streamed in from the fell. He could see all the cave, which was not indeed quite a cave, but rather the opening of some deserted entrance to a long-neglected mine. In the black cavern beyond him there was a fire and on the fire a round black pot. A girl sat on the ground watching the pot.

At once he knew her. Her hair, which fell all about her face and almost to her waist, told him – there was no colour like that anywhere else in the world; but something thin, poised, intent, alert, independent, in her attitude also told him: his eyes saw once again that figure never in all these years lost sight of, the tiny child, crowned with its flaming hair, pressed back against its mother's skirts. Instinctively, he put his hand up to his cheek and felt his scar.

He had found her again. He had the oddest sense of having reached the end of some quest, a sense of rest, of fulfilment, of motionless certainty.

'Well?' he said quietly.

'Well?' she answered, without turning or taking her eyes from the fire. 'So you've waked?'

'I've waked.'

'I never saw a man sleep so sound.' Then after bending forward and stirring the fire she added, but still not looking at him: 'So you've come at last.'

'At last?'

'Yes. I knew that you would come one day.' Her voice, he noticed, had the very same sweet, remote tone that all those years ago it had had. Seven years, and they were as though they were yesterday.

He got up and stretched himself. His clothes were stuck with bracken. He came across to the fire, looking at her hair that was dark in the cave like the sombre shadows in flame when the smoke is thick. Even now she did not look up.

'Well, I have waited for you too,' he said.

At that she turned and looked up at him, and as his eyes met hers he knew two things: that he loved her and that he had never before, in all his ventures, known at all what love was. He knew, instantly afterwards, a third thing: that he meant nothing at all to her and that she would be glad when he went. He knew that by the way that she looked beyond him to the mouth of the cave, a little impatiently, her mind on the fire and also on some possible escape for her.

She was a child, under eighteen. He was over forty. This folly . . .

But he could not take his eyes from her. They were locked there, and all his body moved in its inner spirit towards her so that already, although his hand had not touched hers, his arms were round her, his head, so heavy with fruitless work and anger and impatience, resting on her child's breasts.

'How did you know,' he said at last, his voice husky, 'that I would come one day?'

'Oh,' she answered, 'Mother would speak of you, and my uncle, and I would see you in the woods, Borrowdale-way. I begged once of your son by Stonethwaite. He gave me a silver shilling. He is the finest man I have ever seen. He has the grandest body. But I could never love him. He is too thick. But I have seen too much love.'

'You are only a child,' Herries said, 'and cannot know.' The force within him was too strong. Had it meant death in the next moment he could not have prevented himself. He put out his hand and touched her hair. But it did not mean for her anything at all. She did not move her head but allowed him to stroke it as he would.

He felt that, and his hand came back to him. Then she got up from the fire, straightening herself. Her body was very thin and still a child's body, but lovely to him in its slender line, the long legs and high carriage of the head and the lovely bosom, breathing on the very edge of maturity.

'My uncle is out watching,' she said. 'The guards are active today. They killed two men last night. Some day soon they will find this place and then we must move on again.'

'What does your uncle do?'

'My two uncles. Oh, they do what they can. Steal from the

mines and sell to the Jews in Keswick, or they poach, or my uncle George fights in the Fairs . . . whatever comes. But they are hoping for news soon from France. Then we will go to Carlisle or Scotland maybe.'

'From France?'

She smiled. 'They never tell me anything. Why should I care? It is all the same to me. One day they will be killed, and I shall sell myself to some wealthy man.'

'You would do that?'

'And why not? I must have food. To feed my body, I give my body. What is my body? It is not myself. That I keep for my own.'

'If your uncles are killed, you must come to me. I will take care of you.'

She looked at him, smiling. 'You are very ugly, and they say in Borrowdale that you are very wicked. I don't care if you are wicked – but how rich are you?'

'I am very poor.'

'Then why should I come to you if I don't love you?'

'Because I would care for you and work for you and protect you.'

'Maybe I should lie with your son. Would you still protect me?'

He turned his eyes away from her.

'Yes; even then.'

She put her hand lightly on his shoulder.

'No; if I ever came to you I would be honest. My mother always said a woman must be honest or she is nothing. Men can be as dishonest as they please. That is the difference between men and women.' She smiled at him like a small child, enchantingly. 'I would be honest if I came – but I will never come.'

Her two uncles crossed the light. They were in excellent spirits, amused by some joke they had had with one of the guards. One of them, Anthony, had rabbits and a hare.

They all sat round and ate. The food was excellent: savoury meat cooked in the pot, tasting of herbs and sun and all the rich juices in the world. There was good wine too. The two men – Anthony was round and fat, with a broad chest and short thick neck: he was coloured dark brown and had sharp suspicious eyes like a ferret's – curled up and went to sleep.

All through the sunny afternoon, while the clouds raced past the cave's entrance driven by the wind, Herries sat where he was, silent, watching the girl. She sat quite near to him, sewing at some garment and then afterwards lying back on the hay, the sun on her cheek, and falling easily, comfortably asleep.

He sat there thinking of nothing, nothing at all. He did not want to move. The air was cold although the sun shone, but he was hot with a kind of fever; once and again he trembled. Once he leaned forward and touched her cheek with his hand. He withdrew abruptly as though he had, by so doing, pledged himself to some awful danger. But he did not think at all, neither of his past nor of his future, nor of himself in any way. He simply knew that his fate had come and that whatever way he turned now he could not escape it.

He did not want to escape it. He, forty-five years, she sixteen. This child who cared nothing for him and perhaps never would care. A child of vagabonds. That did not matter. He was himself a vagabond. They were both outcasts. He sat staring there like a drunken man or an idiot. There was utter silence in the cave; only the wind, rushing by outside, sometimes cried out like a struck harp not quite in tune.

When the shadows began to lengthen and the sky beyond the cave was a pale washed blue with no clouds in it, the men stirred and woke together. George looked gravely at Herries as though he were going to lecture him. Then he got up, found an old green box behind the fire, fumbled in it and brought to Herries a simple rough silver chain with a little crucifix of black wood on its end.

'This was what she left for you,' he said.

Herries expected that he would say more. He had spoken in the morning of questions that he would ask. But he said no more, only stood there as though dismissing him.

Herries took the chain. He did not want to go. He wanted with a desire stronger than any that he had ever known to stay, but the two men stood there waiting for him to go.

The girl had waked, stretched her arms, then walked to the cave opening: the evening wind blew her hair so that it seemed to be fire blowing about her head and against the grey stuff of her dress.

'Hadn't you questions that you would ask me?' he said.

'No,' said the lean man.

'I don't understand why you brought me here.'

'To give you that.'

'Well, then, tell me your names.'

'I am George Endicott. He is Anthony Endicott.'

'And the girl?'

'The girl's name is Mirabell Starr.'

'Maybe we shall meet in another place.'

'Maybe.'

'In Carlisle, perhaps?'

'Maybe.'

Anthony, the fat one, turned back into the cave as though the matter were closed. George held his hand out.

'I bound you because I was afraid you wouldn't come.'

Herries exchanged a handgrasp.

'That's no harm. I shall keep the chain. My thanks for the meal. At Herries there's a meal for you.'

Then he went out of the cave. He held out his hand to the girl.

Lowering his voice, staring into her eyes, he said: 'You have promised to come to me if you are all alone.'

She answered like her uncle.

'Maybe,' she said. She let him hold her hand, and for a moment, in the wind that was now very strong blowing from the sea, his body pressed against hers.

'I will be good to you,' he said.

'So they all say,' she answered, 'until they've got what they wanted.'

'I shall never get what I want,' he answered. He longed to kiss her pale thin cheek, but the indifference in her eyes humiliated him. So he turned, bending his head a little, and went up the fell, not looking back.

WITCH

MRS WILSON stood, as was her habit, at the foot of the stairs, listening and looking up. No one was moving in the house. It was after midday. She knew that Herries was digging at the back of the house, that his son was away for that day in Keswick, that his daughter was in Rosthwaite and Benjamin the servant at the stable: she was therefore quite alone in the house.

She stood there endeavouring to make up her mind to what was for her a great venture. She was planning to go to Grange. She had not been out of that house for six months: she had not been in the village of Rosthwaite for a year. This enterprise of hers needed immense resolution and courage. Although, since

early morning, she had been summoning her will to this expedi-
tion, she was not yet completely resolved on it.

Old Tom Mounsey, deaf and dumb, had contrived to send her
word that his wife Old Hannah Mounsey was dying and wished
to see her before she went. Hannah Mounsey, once Hannah Armstrong, a gay and beautiful young thing, was Katherine Wilson's
oldest friend. She was now, like Katherine, so old that she didn't
know how old she was. And she was dying. She was the first
human who had asked to see Katherine Wilson for more than
twenty years.

The old woman had been strangely stirred by the summons.
She was so old that the days of her youth were as yesterday.
They were very vivid and alive to her. She saw Hannah still with
red cheeks, bright flaxen hair, and a blue gown. She heard
Hannah laugh as she hid with Katherine in Statesman Armstrong's barn, while young Johnny Turnbull had searched for
her to fumble and kiss her. Young Johnny Turnbull had been
hanged in Carlisle for stealing a sheep. As everyone knew, it was
not he who stole the sheep but Daniel Waugh.

She was very old, but she could make the journey. Her legs
could still carry her. It would take her two hours or more to
walk to Grange, but she could do it. It was not her legs that
frightened her. Something else.

She was frightened of the outside world, and with reason. The
outside world hated her. They hated her as much as they were
afraid of her.

They said she was a witch. Was she a witch? She did not know.
They said that the troubles of the last year were her doing. Were
they? She did not know. Sometimes she thought that they were
and felt an odd impulse of power. Was it true that by crooking
her finger or nodding her head she could kill sheep, scatter the
palsy, burn hay-ricks, poison food? It might be so. She did not
know.

It was not of course true that she could fly on a broomstick or
that she had danced naked with the Devil in Glaramara caves.

But she *had* danced naked in the woods one moonlit night.
That was a great many years ago. Many, many years. She
had had a child by Joe Butterfield because of that dancing. The
child had been happily still-born, and Joe Butterfield had been
gored to death by his own bull many years back . . . He had
been a fine big young fellow, with a tattoo of a mermaid on his
chest.

She could not remember many things, and many things she

remembered in every detail. But all that she wished now was to be let alone: all the passions save fear had died right down in her. Her love of fun and gaiety, her recklessness, her vicious tempers, her courage, her loyalty to those whom she loved, her passion for her son who, after living in this house with her so long, had left her, all these fires had sunk to grey ashes. The only thing remaining to her was fear.

The first time that she had been really afraid was one day shortly before the coming of these Herries, when, walking out on the path to Seathwaite, some boys had thrown stones and shouted 'Witch!' after her. Long before this she had been suspected of witchcraft, she and Mary Roberts and Ellen Wade and Alice Leyland. Alice Leyland had been much older than the others. It may be that Alice had been a witch. She had made an image of Gabriel Caine and burnt it at a slow fire, and he had died within three days.

She had, too, her famous love-philtre, and Katherine herself had mixed this in her own man's drink, a year after their marriage, when he was going with the Hoggarty girl in Keswick. It had not, however, caused him to leave the Hoggarty girl, not until she had had the smallpox and grown ugly.

The old woman sat down at the foot of the stairs. Did she dare to venture into Grange? She sniffed danger in the very air, but that might be her fancy. Much of it might be her fancy. She had stayed alone in this house until she scarcely knew what she believed. But, from the very beginning, there had been something about her that set her apart from the others. She had been a pretty girl: they had all said so. She had cared for men no more and no less than the others, but the difference had been that men were not enough: no, love was not enough, nor courting, nor childbirth, nor any of the dreary, dull, day-by-day life in that dreary, dull valley.

She must have excitement, but then, after that, it was not excitement that she wanted, not excitement only. She was curious, inquisitive. She wanted to see *into* things, and when she had seen Alice Leyland and the others dance naked across the grass under the moon and then vanish into the black wood she had been curious to see what they did there. So she, too, had danced naked into the wood, and all that had happened had been Joe Butterfield's baby.

Had it not been for that odd sense of power that sometimes came to her she would have left it alone.

But there had been hours when she felt that she held all the

valley in her hand to do with as she would. She felt that sometimes even now. What was that accompanying her, lifting her up,
taking her to the very verge of some discovery? Was it only her
fancy? In later years she had yielded to the temptation to see in
the eyes of others that look of fear, of terror . . .

When they came to her, as they used to do, to ask her to heal
their cattle, to help them with a lover, to injure an enemy, she
had always told them to go away again, that she knew no spells,
no charms, had no powers.

But they did not believe her, and she did not believe herself.
Had she no power? Why was it then that she would rise in the
night and walk to the window and see the shadows under the
moon come flocking to her call, and had she not killed Janet
Forsse by looking at her after Janet had called her a witch outside Rosthwaite Chapel? Had not Janet gone home, lain down on
her bed and died? That had done her much harm, that death of
Janet. They had feared and hated her from that moment. She
had felt the power rise in her breast, fill her breast, well into her
eyes. But was that truth or falsehood? Janet had eaten meat from
a poisoned pot and so died . . .

All her life she had wished others well. Only when they in-
sulted her she must turn and defend herself. And in these last
years, from loneliness, desolation, unhappiness, she had scarcely
known what she did. She had made wax figures, watched from
the window, spoken sometimes with shadows. Why not with
shadows when no one else would speak with her?

Everything had been worse with her since the coming of
Herries. From the first day she had hated the father and loved
the son. The father had something in common with her. Although she was an untaught woman, and he was a grand gentleman, yet they shared something. He had looked at her and she at
him. It might be that he was the Devil. Some thought so in the
village. It might be. He looked like the Devil once and again.
Perhaps he could answer the questions that she never dared to
ask. She was afraid of him, and she hated him. She had always
loved his son David since, as a little boy, he had run first into the
house. All that was simple and good and maternal in her responded to him. He had always been kind to her, talked to her,
asked her how she did, and now that he was the finest, grandest
man in the valley she was proud of him, as though he had been
her work. When his mother had died she had wanted to protect
and care for him. He had not needed her – he needed no one –
but she prayed for him night and morning.

That had been until the last year, but in the last year fear had grown in her breast, swallowing up everything else in her.

The thing that she feared most now was to dream, because in her dreams she was quite unprotected. So soon as she slept she was outside the house in the naked road, or the house was without walls, or she was on the mountainside. Then while she waited alone in this awful space she could hear them coming, hundreds of them; the present and past came together – Alice Leyland, Joe Butterfield, Turnbull, Hannah Armstrong, and with them many strangers. But they all looked alike. They had terrible faces, and that look in the eyes of lust and hatred, curiosity and pleasure. Years ago, when a young woman, she had seen a boy stoned to death in Keswick market. They said that he had burnt a rick. That look then had been in their faces. It had been perhaps also in her own.

In her dream they came always nearer and nearer, quite silent, and she had no strength to escape them. Then one had called 'Witch!'

She would awake trembling and the sweat would run down into her eyes; then she would sigh with relief at the respite, and would get up and touch the familiar things, the clock, the settle, the pots and pans, to reassure herself.

When her son had left her he had said nothing, but had looked at her once before he went, and the look in his eyes had held fear, just as her own eyes held fear. She had not tried to keep him. Only after he had gone she sat and remembered all the things he had done as a child and especially when he had sucked at her breast and she had crooned songs to him.

And now should she go in to Grange? It might be that it would break the spell, it might be that she would meet folk who would be kind to her, and, seeing Hannah again, she would recover her courage.

She moved slowly back into the empty kitchen. She was still strong. Her bodily health had been always amazing; she had never known a day's sickness, and that, too, had made her sometimes wonder whether she were not under the Devil's especial protection.

She stirred about the kitchen, raising her head, sniffing the air, her brown face was a network of wrinkles, her hair was snow-white, her eyes dimmed in vision. She moved on her legs easily and with freedom.

Suddenly she knew that she was going into Grange: it was as

though someone had bent over and whispered in her ear. The great grey cat, with one eye green and one brown, her only friend in the world, had come and rubbed itself against her legs. It was he, perhaps, who persuaded her.

Every witch must have a cat. She had seen Alice Leyland once take a glove that she had soaked in blood and water and rub it on her cat's belly, murmuring some spell . . . What were the words? She had known them all once. Words, words, words . . . words from where? They had come to her once, without her own desire: there had been the day when she had seen Statesman Peel's man rubbing between the horns of his oxen the grease from the Paschal Candle, eyeing her as he did so. Yes, then, against her own will, not at all by her agency, the words had come to her lips. He had seen her lips move and had told them in the village.

But her cat. She bent down and stroked it, letting her old dried fingers press into the fur, liking to feel the cat's response as it bent its back a little, stiffening, stretching its legs, its eyes closing with pleasure. She had thought often that her cat knew more than she did. Watching sometimes at night from the high window she had seen it slip off across the fields, moving with quiet secret purpose, just as Alice Leyland had once moved. The cat and Alice Leyland knew things that she would never know.

She went to the cupboard and found her cloak and high-crowned, old-fashioned hat. She found her crooked, gnarled stick. She started out.

When she came into the path beyond the courtyard her heart beat so furiously that she must stop: it leapt with wild angry stabs as though it were telling her not to go. For a whole year she had not been beyond the courtyard. She was encouraged by the stillness of the world about her, not a sound save the running water that was never silent, and the scrape, from behind the house, of Herries's spade as it struck the hard soil. She was always scornful of Herries's labour; the soil here was like stone or mire, harsh, ungrateful, contemptuous: it hated Herries as she did. A little pleasure stirred her heart as she thought of Herries's labour and the small reward he had for it.

She walked down the path, moving with marvellous strength for an old woman. She thought that she heard the cat following, and she turned to forbid it, but there was nothing there.

It was a grey, overhanging, autumn day with no wind: the light on walls and trees trembled once and again as though thunder was coming, but the leaves that still lingered, brown and shrivelled, on the trees, never shivered.

She walked as she had lived, in a half-dream. Sometimes it seemed to her that figures were walking with her, sometimes that she was alone. When she reached the river she muttered a little with pleasure, as though she were blessing it. Perhaps she was. This river, the Derwent, had been part of her from birth. Her parents' cottage had bordered it: her first instinct as an infant had been to find it, and now, because for so long she had not seen it, she greeted it again as an old friend. There had been a time in her life when, if she did not see it every day, she was miserable. From Seathwaite to the lake she had known every inch of it, its deeps and shallows, its moods of anger, rebellion, calm, blue content, shrill chatter, acquiescence, curiosity; its colours, brown like ale, blue like glass, grey like smoke, white like cloud; she had bathed in it, fished in it, sat beside it. Often, shut up in that house, she had listened to it, especially when it was in flood; then it was happiest, most violent. It was the only thing in the world now that she could trust: it would never harm her. It did not care whether she were witch or no.

As she passed beside it now, happy in a dim confused way at recovering it again, she seemed to speak to it, telling it how sorry she was that it was shrunken, that its stones and boulders must be exposed, and its voice have fallen to a murmur. Never mind. The rains were coming again. Patience, patience . . . And as she looked her husband rose out of it, his brown tangled beard wet, his eyelashes dripping water, his breast, thick with soaking hair, exposed, his flanks too shining with damp fine yellow hair, his toes crooked about the stones of the river-bed; his bare arm rose up as he brushed his hair from his eyes as he used to do. He called out something to her, and his voice had just the old husky growling note, but she could not hear what he said.

She walked on, resolutely, her stick striking the path, her head in its high black hat, and very far away, beyond Grasmere maybe, the thunder dimly rumbled. She gathered confidence as she went: a silly old woman she had been to stay in that dark house letting fear gather upon her. She would not wonder now but it was that devil Herries that had put those thoughts into her head. It was himself that the people hated, and she had taken his contempt for her own. Just because, forsooth, some boys had thrown stones after her and a labourer cast a word at her, she had hidden away and missed her proper company. It would be good to see Hannah once more. Hannah was dying, they said, but she

would be able enough to remind her of the old days when they
had both been young and happy together. One kindly look from
Hannah's eyes would be a fine thing, and she would walk all the
way back to Herries again and show the village that she was no
witch, but an old woman who liked company and chatter and
friendly faces in candlelight.

As she walked, strength seemed to increase in her. She had no
ache nor pain in all her body. She was still good for life. Death
had not got her yet. She breathed the air, even though it were
close and packed with thunder, and as the hill grew steeper by the
Bowder Stone, she set her knees to it and braced her back and
climbed bravely to the turning of the road. Then, at the sight of
the Grange cottages across the river, again her courage failed her.
She was passing Cumma Catta Wood, a place that she had
always feared because, when she was a girl, young Broadley had
drowned himself in the pool there below the wood. It was a
pretty place, a little hill thick with trees hanging over a broad
pool, where the river gathered itself together for a while and
stayed tranquilly reflecting the sky. But they said that young
Broadley haunted it, and that, in ancient days, there had been
pagan sacrifices there. You could see the two projecting stones
where the sacrifices had been.

The old woman moved on. She paused before she crossed the
bridge that raised itself up like a cat's back over the divided
strands of the river. The Grange cottages, huddled on the other
side, seemed to be waiting, watching for her.

Their faces were white, shining in the grey shadows of the
thundery air.

She crossed the bridge, wondering that she saw no human
being: she must herself, to those who, behind dark window-
panes, watched her, have seemed a curious figure alone in that
still grey landscape, in her high hat and black cloak, tapping with
her stick.

She knew Hannah's cottage, a little grey dwelling twisted like
a crumpled ear over the river. She knocked with her stick on the
door. There was no answer, and she had never felt the world so
breathlessly still. The rattle of her stick on the door had been so
sharp that she would not knock again. She pushed the door back
and went in. The interior was very dark and smelt of damp hay.
Some hens ran squawking from under her feet into the open. Her
eyes were dim and the light was dusk, but she soon saw that the
very old man, Hannah's husband, was sitting in a chair by a
black, empty grate and that a large stout woman was bending

over him, making signs with her hands. But he did not look: he stared, without any movement, in front of him.

The woman looked up and saw Mrs Wilson. She stared then with a start of recognition, turned as though she would motion to the old man, then turned again, and, with a muttered explanation, almost hurled her stout body out of the cottage. Mrs Wilson could hear her feet hastening over the cobbled path; once more there was breathless waiting silence . . .

The old man could not hear her, could not speak to her. She was as old as he, but he looked infinitely older. He was a little man like a grey nut, and on his head he was wearing a bright-red nightcap. It was of no use to waste time with him, so she fumbled her way up the twisted wooden staircase. Halfway up she paused: she was suddenly very tired. Her legs were aching and she was a hundred years old. The door of the room at the stair-head was open and she went in. A large four-poster bed with faded red hangings occupied most of the room, placed a little unevenly on the crooked wooden floor. Hannah Mounsey was stretched out on the bed in her grave-clothes, her long, thin face, with the closed eyes, looking spiteful, because the mouth had fallen in and the sharp brown chin stuck forward aggressively.

So Hannah was dead, an old grey bag of bones under the long white clothes. This was young Hannah with the flaxen hair and blue gown. There was a faint odour in the room, and a mouse scuttered across the floor. Beyond the dim, diamond-paned window you could hear the Derwent carelessly running.

Death was nothing odd to Mrs Wilson, yet peering half blindly over the bed she shivered. She would not be greeted by Hannah, then; her journey had been fruitless. Suddenly she felt a deep sorrow for herself. Hannah was gone, the only one who in all these years had sent for her. Nobody now wanted her at all. To pass from this dead house to the dead house Herries was all the same. And yet she had the capacity still to love someone, to take trouble for someone or something. She was not dead, as Hannah Mounsey was, and she had a sudden vision of herself coming out on a sunshiny morning, sitting outside her cottage, other neighbours gathering round, all of them chatting, laughing together.

Then something made her prick up her ears: she did not know what it was, but it was something that caused her altogether to forget the dead woman on the bed. Fear leapt into her body. Her legs were trembling, so that she caught the post of the bed. She had a sense of being trapped, and yet when she listened again there was no sound, only the careless running of the river. Nevertheless, she knew that there was reason for her fear. She looked about the room, at the looking-glass, the wooden box painted with red hearts, a chair with a thin curved back. She listened, her head bent forward, her hat a little crooked. There was a sound behind the soundlessness; the still air was full of it, and the odour of musty decay in the room grew with every second stronger. She must get out, get away, get to Herries.

Although her legs that had been so strong were now trembling like slackening cord, she found her way down the wooden staircase. Nothing was changed in the room below. The old man in the red nightcap still sat there without moving, staring in front of him.

She pulled back the door, peered out on to the ragged garden, and beyond it the grey smooth running water, and beyond that the field rising to Cumma Catta Wood. Then, although no sound reached her, she turned and stared, across the cobbled path, into a group of faces.

Men and women, close together as though for protection, were gathered at the end of the cobbled path. They stood, huddled together, not speaking, staring at her. Although she could not see well and was so deeply frightened that it was as though her heart were beating in her eyes, yet certain faces were very distinct to her. One belonged to a large stout man in a brown wig and green coat and breeches. His face was red as a tomato and his eyes wide and staring. There was the smooth white face of a young woman; a face with a black beard; there was a young girl's face, very fresh and rosy, with a mole on one cheek.

She looked back behind her; there was no way out there, only a thick rough-stone wall. They could easily stop her if she ran in front of the river.

She walked forward towards them, leaning on her stick because her knees trembled so badly, and at her movement a hoarse whisper broke the thick air: 'T'witch . . . t'witch . . . t'witch.' She stopped, rubbing at her eyes with her hand. The people stood and she stood; then, not knowing what she was doing now, she turned back towards the cottage door.

Her movement released them. A second later two had her, one, the big red-faced man, dragging at her arm, the other a little man with a hump who caught her with twisting hands round the waist.

She heard someone cry: 'A trial! A trial!' She tumbled on to her knees, not for supplication but because, her legs shaking as they did and the man dragging her, she had no strength. She looked now a ridiculous old woman, her hat knocked sideways, her head bent, one thin arm up as though she were shielding herself. But having gone so far with her they paused. The two men stood away from her. The rabble – for it was now a great crowd, some having run and told the others what was toward – broke into every kind of babel, some shouting one thing, others another.

Meanwhile she stayed there murmuring: 'Oh, Christ save me! Oh, Lord Christ save me! Oh, Christ save me!' but her thoughts were like wild terrified birds flying from one place to another, so that she was thinking of her knee that was cut by the sharp stone, of Hannah lying dead, and of a great weariness that had seized her, turning all her body to water. But mostly she was afraid of the large red-faced man. Then, in the pause, life coming a little back to her, she looked up and searched some of the faces to see whether there was kindness in any of them. With a horror that was the most terrible confirmation of all her earlier fears, she realized that all these faces had that look that so often, alone in Herries, she had anticipated: the look of lust and hatred, curiosity and pleasure. And they all seemed strangers to her.

As was perhaps to be expected, it was a woman who took the next step. A long, thin, elderly woman whose head wagged on her neck as though it were loosely tied there.

Crying out something in a shrill, high voice like a bird's, she rushed forward and, bending down, struck the old woman on the cheek. It was as though that had been a signal. The crowd tumbled across the path, loosed, it seemed, by a word of command. A funny babble of sound came from them, not human, not animal: 'Swim her!' 'Swim her!' 'Sink or swim!' A little girl danced delightedly round and round, like a leaf spinning, crying: 'T'witch! . . . T'witch! . . . T'witch!'

Inside the cottage, the widower of Hannah Mounsey sat staring in front of him, hearing nothing, seeing Hannah as a young, laughing, fresh-faced girl. He moved his hand a little, enclosing with his arm her waist.

They dragged Mrs Wilson along the path, bumping her head on the stones, pulling her by her feet and her hands. They tumbled her out on to the green sward between the bridge and the river.

Then again they stood back from her. She crouched there, her head hanging forward. Her hat was gone, her white hair was loose about her face, her gown was torn, exposing her withered brown breasts; she clasped her arms together over these. Tears trickled down her cheeks.

There was a desperate impulse in her now to say something, but she could not speak. Her terror urged her that if she could only make them listen she would persuade them that she was no witch, but only a harmless old woman who had never done any harm.

But she could not speak: fear constricted her throat, and her tongue moistened her dry, dead lips. Her other thought was that soon they would hit her again. She bent her head over her arms to shelter herself from the blows.

The crowd now had no individual consciousness. Some cried that they must take her to the little house at the back of the village and that she must be tried there all in proper order and decently. But these were the minority. The others must see her swim; then they'd know whether she were witch or no. Then there was a moment's strange silence. Every voice fell. For an instant the only sounds were the very distant rumbling thunder, the running river and the old woman's crying, a whimper like a child's.

Three women ran forward. They bent down over her; shouting they tore her clothes from her. They threw her clothes over their heads into the crowd. They tore her flesh as they dragged her things away. One stood up, tugging at her white hair, and so she pulled the thin, bony body up, raising it to its knees.

Someone threw a stone. It struck the body between the breasts.

Then the stout, red-faced man, shouting as though he were proclaiming some great news, called for order. Everything must be done properly. No one should say that they were out of justice. He strode forward, laughing. He caught the body in his arms, then dropped it again as he felt in his breeches pocket, from there brought faded green cord. He took the body again and roughly, as though he would tear one limb from the other, took the right foot and fastened it to the left hand, the left foot and fastened it to the right hand. So trussed, she lay motionless. Then suddenly raising her face, which now streamed with blood, she sent forth two screeches, wild, piercing, sounding far over the crowd out into the village, down the road. Then her head fell again.

Triumphantly he raised her in his arms, holding her, her head against her knees, as a woman might an infant. He danced her for a moment in his arms. Then he ran forward, the crowd shouting, yelling, laughing, and up the bridge some children ran that

they might see better, singing and dancing: 'T'witch . . . t'witch
. . . t'witch.'

He lifted his stout arms and flung her out, high into air. The
little white body gleamed for a moment, then fell, like a stone,
into the water.

Herries straightened his aching body and leaned on his spade.
He had been clearing a patch of hard, stiff ground. Later there
should be an orchard here: he saw it in his eye, the strong,
gnarled trunks, the blossom, the apples hanging in shining
clusters, the sun blinking through the leaves.

He spat on his hands and bent again to the spade. Around him
nothing had grown well save a strange ruffian-like grass that had
sharp-pointed blades like jagged knives. Some stunted blooms,
some ragged naked vegetables. It was the wrong place, the wind
caught it too fiercely, there was not sun enough, the soil was too
resolutely stubborn. Meanwhile, to the house many things
should be done. Windows were broken, pipes had fallen; one
corner towards the hill had tumbled right in, and stones lay in a
careless heap.

Nevertheless, the house looked stout and obstinate, its colour
was of a pale gentle ivory, stained here and there with orange
and pink, stains of rain and wind. Its feet were dug resolutely
in the ground. It was alone but not lonely, defiant but not complaining.

Herries, raising himself again, turning to look at it, loved it.

He saw fat Benjamin, sweat pouring from him, hurry towards
him.

'They are drowning Mrs Wilson, by Grange Bridge, for a
witch.'

He turned and listened as though he expected to hear something. Only a faint rumble of thunder over Grasmere way. He
said nothing to Benjamin, but dragging on his old faded long-
skirted coat, strode into the yard. Benjamin, silent as himself,
brought out his horse.

At once, without a word to one another, they rode off along
the rough track to Grange. Then, after a little, Benjamin, in the
husky voice which ale, weather and stoutness of body had pro-
duced in him, explained that he had been riding back through
Portinscale. Passing Grange he had heard that the old witch
Wilson was in Mounsey's cottage, saying spells over his dead
woman, and that they were going to have her out and 'swim'
her. He had hastened on to his master.

Herries had long been expecting this. He did not doubt but that Mrs Wilson was a witch. He had a horror of her for that. He was glad that now she would be out of his house. He felt no pity, no sense of a hunted thing, of a crowd lust-baiting. Such feelings were not of his time, class or education.

Had he been a magistrate and she been brought before him with evidence of her dirty dealings, he would have condemned her without hesitation and watched her sentence without a shudder. But here he also was involved. His pride drove him to protect his house. They would touch one of his servants? He would see to it. He hated them as he rode, the whole dirty foul rabble of them.

Then as he went something else moved in him. Since his day in the Honister cave a new element had stirred, a kind of softness, a glow of unanalysed, almost unrealized kindliness. He had not wanted it. He would scorn it if he dragged it into daylight.

But he did not drag it. It stayed within him like a secret fire that burnt stealthily without his feeding it. Every little thing was happier to him now than it had been.

His gaze softened, even now as he stared through the trees at the river, pounded up the hill, saw the humped bridge and the crowd at the water's edge.

He leapt off his horse and came down to them. He spoke to no one. As he came to the stream he saw an old white bundle of flesh with hair that streamed behind it rise, eddy in a little pool, sink again.

He plunged in, waded up to his thighs. The crowd said no word. The body rose again right at his hand. He plunged his arms in and caught it, dragging it to his breast. The head wagged against his coat.

He turned, standing and looking at them all for a moment, then breasted his way back to the bank. On dry ground he felt his hands chill against the bare flesh, so he laid the sodden body delicately on the ground, took off his faded coat, wrapped it round, then, holding the little corpse like a child against his shirt, strode up the hill, all the people silently withdrawing from him.

He mounted his horse and rode away.

THE ROCKING WOOD

As THEY rode through the rocking wood, the wind tearing at their heels, Herries talked to David.

It was the wild stormy afternoon of Friday, November 8th, 1745. It had been Herries's suggestion that they should be riding to Carlisle. For months now he had been longing for this.

In the *Scots Magazine* for July, at the barber's in Keswick, David had read:

'There have lately been several rumours of some designs upon Scotland or Ireland by the Pretender's eldest son.' Then, a month later, at that same barber's, it was said that there had been a landing in Scotland.

Now this very morning Keswick was frantically buzzing. The rebels were in Jedburgh. At any moment they would be South...

Francis Herries had shown no interest. His mind was elsewhere. David even was surprised at his own indifference. His principal thought was of Father Roche. After all these years his chance had come! After all these years! David was a child again riding under Cat Bells, his body tight between Roche's thighs, and that beautiful, persuasive voice in his ears: 'Even as our Lord suffered...' But he was practical now, was David, a grave and serious man with a liking for the steady security of the reigning dynasty. He had been prospering lately. He had bought land near Cockermouth. He had an interest in two vessels trading from Liverpool. There was a farm at the back-end of Skiddaw that he might buy if things went well. He had no hunger for rebellions...

But the romantic soul still breathed close to his heart. The memory of Roche could stir it, some woman one day, but most of all, now and ever, his love for his father, this strange man, removed in temperament, thought, passion so far from him, so mysterious and alone. Of late so silent, but united to him as no other human being was united.

Therefore when, quite suddenly, in the dark hall at Herries last evening, his father had said: 'Shall we ride tomorrow to Carlisle?' David had at once agreed. No more than that. No reason given. In all these years at Herries David had been only once to Carlisle, his father twice. But it seemed that now, riding alone together, they might come to some fresh intimacy. It must come from Herries. David was a man of few words and deep shyness in close relations. There was something, too, in the isolation of Herries that drove speech deep down. They talked less and less in Herries.

They were silent out of Keswick until they rode into the woods below Skiddaw. A terrific wind was surging among the trees; all the wood was rocking, and light mists spun and shifted over the two humps of the mountain-top that were powdered with snow thin like smoke. Beyond the wood Bassenthwaite Water was whipped into curls of white and angry spray.

Herries began to speak, his thought that had followed its own secret course ever since they left Herries breaking into spoken word: '. . . When I came to the river's edge she was bobbing, a white bundle, in the water. I strode in and picked her out, and they stood there while I carried her off. At that moment, David, when I held her wet and sodden against my body I felt something new in me. I had been coming to that as I had been coming to many things through these years . . . She cried against my heart although she was dead. She cried something, telling me a road to go. She was a witch and foul-living. In all those years that she was with us, David, I don't doubt but that she was evil.

'But she had been alone as I also had been alone. They hated her as they hated me. Not that I care at all for their hatred, but there was a bond in our loneliness. I had always known it.' (He thought, as he went on: Why am I telling him this? He can never understand that loneliness. He will never feel this thing that I feel.) '. . . I have had to bear my difference all my life, David, as she had to bear it. By no choice and no wish. I have no faith in God. I have never had; but for those of us who are different there is a compulsion to listen that is almost a faith. Nature, I suppose, chooses once and again to separate a few from the rest. She understands them and speaks to them. But why should we who are thus separated expect human nature to understand? Human nature must protect itself. I perceive that it must be so. Human nature is narrower than Nature, less wise and less secure.

'We who are different cannot come into that general company, however we may desire it. It is our lot. Myself, I do not grumble at it. What have I ever done worse than these others, than Pomfret or Harcourt? But every dice has been loaded against me, every act removed me further . . . Nothing strange there, since it is understood. Think you that she was a witch, David?'

Through the groaning of the boughs and the rocking wind David's voice came out sturdily:

'Most certainly she was a witch, Father.'

'Yes . . . most certainly. They were cruel because they were afraid, and I was compassionate because I, too, have suffered. Do you think it has meant nothing to me that I could not be like other men? I, too, have my pride, my sense of honour, my friendliness, although it does not do to speak of these things. But with them all, my brothers, my wife, my mistresses, my children, that final intimacy has been forbidden. Only with my own kind could I be intimate, and I could not find my kind. Often I have wished to put my case' (Herries thought: I am putting my case to him now and he does not understand it at all, not a word of it), 'but my case has not been their case. I am, in some sense, it must seem to them, against Nature, but it is not against Nature but rather against human nature.

'Nevertheless, there is compensation in loneliness. I am growing to find that. There is strength in it, and a compelled wisdom. I learnt that from the witch. The evil that she knew was not so weighty as the strength that she caught from her isolation. They might stone her, but their stones would not bring her into their company nor would they stay her. Nothing can stay us, no physical death.' (He smiled to himself thinking: All these words go to the wind. He has not caught any of them.)

And David, stolid on his horse, his back broad as a wall, his head finely set, was thinking: 'He is talking to me now as man to man. He has never before done that. But this talk of feelings: I can't be with him there. What's the use of it? I love him whatever he is, different or no, but it's uncomfortable to speak openly about love . . . Easier here, though, with this wind blowing and the trees creaking. If the *Calliope* does well this voyage I could pay a price for that farm. It will mean leaving Herries. It must come to that one day. But not yet. I must take Deb with me and that would leave him alone. I can't leave him alone; and he wouldn't go from Herries. But one day if I marry, which I shall . . .'

He felt the cold rain on his face and the wind swooping down and then up again. He threw back his head, stretched his great chest, turned to his father, smiling:

'Maybe, Father,' he said, 'you force yourself to be different by thinking that you are. Folks take one for what one says one is. You have always refused them, thought poorly of them, frightened them maybe. Will you never leave Herries, Father?'

'Leave Herries?'

'Aye. Maybe I'll buy that farm at the back of Skiddaw –

Penhays ... John Tennant and I have done well lately with the *Calliope* and the *Peggy Anne*. If this Pretender doesn't upset the world ... Herries is a hard place, Father. No soil, no sun, rock and mire. They have this thought of you in the valley and will never be rid of it.

'But at Penhays you could have your own land and work it, and it would be brighter for Deb ...' He waited, then continued more shyly. 'Uncle Pomfret loves you, Father, at heart. I know he does. Aunt Jannice is sick now and has little say. My dear cousin Raiseley is in London. If we were at Penhays we would be more in the world. At Herries ...' He broke off, afraid suddenly, as he had so often before been afraid, of his father's anger. Some word would be spoken and all the good of their talk be gone, and they would ride on in offended silence. David had his own temper in his own way and it showed most easily with his father, simply because he loved him most.

But today he need not have been afraid. His father turned to him with a strangely childlike, ingenuous gaze as though he were David's junior and had been asking advice from him.

'Herries is a bitter place for you and Deborah. I've always known it. But for me there is none other nor ever can be. I'm held there and it's for ever. But you will go, of course, when the right time comes. And, for that, I may not be alone. It may be that, one day, I shall marry again.'

The rocking wind, as though driven by that word to a frenzy of derision, cracked in his ear: 'Marry again! He'll marry again! Crack! Crack! Crack! He'll marry again!' David brushed the rain from his eyes. Marry again! He thought that his father had done with women. For a long time now there had been no sign of any traffic with them.

'Well,' he said, 'have you seen a woman?'

'Yes ... there is someone. She is a child. She could only need me through weariness and fear of loneliness. But I am in love again. Again! I have never loved before. I am very happy in the mere thought of it.'

David had an instant of deep comprehension and of an aching affection for his father. With a swift vision of imagination, born only through love and exceedingly rare with him, he saw his father as he had been, so handsome and grand. As he was now, his face disfigured, his body gaunt and bent with digging and grubbing ... Could a woman care for him now? A sense of his father's isolation came over him as it had never done before.

Now, however, they had come out of the woods and were in

open country across which the icy rain was blowing in furious
sweeps. On a good day a great stretch of land spread grandly to
the Firth and the hills behind it, but now everything was blotted
out.

For Herries, although today he could not see, this coming into
the open was like walking out of a house and closing the door
behind him. That was why he chose this route, because he loved
it. The regular riding path was by Threlkeld. That little world of
hills and lakes was gone in an instant, folded away. On a clear
day you could look back and see Skiddaw, the Helvellyn
range, the group above Stye Head, Grasmoor and the rest lying
gently like lions above the land, their heads resting on their
paws. One step and you were in a new world, a world as romantic perhaps in spirit as that other, but not this, as beautiful but
not with this beauty. That odd sense of magic, so that with one
foot forward you lost it. He would always, on reaching this spot,
know a little shiver of fear that when he came back again that
lovely country would be gone, a mirage dreamed of by him and
by him perhaps alone. But today in his head he carried with him
the rocking wood. The trees creaked around him long after he
had left them.

The wind fell: the rain drew off: the air was colder. The thick
sky watched them maliciously and once and again sent down a
flake of snow to spatter their eyes.

They had come into new country in another sense. The
cottages and farms that they passed gave them a consciousness of
agitation. Women stood at the doors. A man called after them
some question. A horseman rode past them furiously towards
Carlisle. Unconsciously themselves they drove their horses
faster, the mud scattering up about them as they went.

'The Pretender may be in Carlisle ere this,' said David
suddenly. 'What then?'

'We'll ride back again,' said Herries.

'What do you think, Father? Has he a hope? In Keswick they
wished him back in France, to a man they did. Disturbing their
affairs. It's odd to remember it, but I thought it a fine thing as a
boy when Father Roche spoke of it. Now, because I may buy a
farm, I see other things. Is Roche in Carlisle, do you think?'

'Yes, so I fancy. When I was a boy at Seddon, in '15, thirty
years ago, there was a peacock screamed under the hedge by the
pantries. I thought him the finest, most defiant bird in the kingdom, and when they were out in '15 he was like the Old Pretender, that bird. I had a fancy about him that if their foray

failed he'd die; and, sure enough, he died. Died of spoilt pride. I've always thought rebellion a grand thing, but now I don't know . . . I love this ground and the men on it, although they'd thank me little if they knew it. If Charles Edward has his way, every field will be blood-stained. Either way my peacock dies . . . No, he can't win. He's too late. And if he wins it can be only for a moment. Hanover's a hog by my peacock, but he's made his sty of our home, and it's quieter for him to lie there. I told Roche once that the notion of beauty to a plain people like the English is too upsetting. They stand by their stomachs. They are poets only by protest.'

The scene cleared: the sky lifted and the snow fell faster. A man on a horse passed them, then drew up and waited for them.

He was a short fat man on a short fat horse, hunched forward rather absurdly, not a good rider. He had a dark-crimson coat with silver buttons: his face was round, red and anxious, rather a baby face with open wondering eyes and startled eyebrows.

'I beg your pardon, gentlemen—'

They drew up their horses.

'Are you for Carlisle?'

David said that they were.

'What news have you?'

'None.'

'Ah, things are bad.' The little man looked at them beseechingly, as much as to say: 'Be kind to me. Tell me some good news, even though it's lies. Tell me anything, only that I may calm down and regain my dignity.' It was plain enough that he was frightened of Francis Herries, who, straight on his horse, his scarred face showing pale and impervious under his broad black hat, was silent and grim enough. David, with his health and ruddiness and open smile, reassured him. He confided in him.

'You see, gentlemen, I'm riding out of my way, but I had the news at Sockbridge last night that the rebels were in Jedburgh, and that they were already moving South. My God, they may be in Carlisle at this instant, and my poor wife and Hetty . . . I said to Mr Wordsworth – Mr Richard Wordsworth, Superintendent of the Lowther Estates, I was today staying under his roof, my worthy friend; maybe you know him, gentlemen? – 'Sdeath, Mr Wordsworth, I said, it can't be that they are in Carlisle already, and our house in English Street, the very centre of the town, my wife sick of a nervous complaint these last five years, ever since William Gray, the best surgeon in the whole of Carlisle, gentlemen, cut her for the bladder. And it isn't as though Hetty had a head on her shoulders neither. The sight of a soldier makes a fool of the child, and these breechless Highlanders are beyond law, as we all know well enough. Eh, gentlemen, forgive this un-easiness, but I fancied that you'd have some good news, maybe of a defeat or a rout and the Pretender taken, or driven back to France again, where, Heaven is witness, it were better for him to have stayed.'

The words came with panting eagerness, but there was a childish simplicity and good nature behind them that won David, who was as childish, simple and good-natured as himself.

'I fear, sir,' he replied, 'we can give you little comfort. We are riding from Keswick where we had only the news that you yourself have had. We know nothing of what is happening in Carlisle.'

The little stout gentleman looked anxiously about him. 'It's cold,' he said, 'and the snow is in our faces. Would you give me the courtesy of your company? With every step we may be meeting danger. I am no coward, but I will confess that this news has quite unnerved me. It is only what I have been expect-ing these thirty years, but that it should drop on to us when I was away from home and my wife none too well . . .'

'Certainly we will keep company,' said David cheerfully. 'I think you are unduly apprehensive, sir. We should have heard, I am sure, were the Pretender already in Carlisle. I scarcely think that the Royal troops will allow him so much advantage. If one may go by the common feeling in Keswick the sense of the country is against him, and a company of raw Highlanders is hardly a match for an English army. Moreover, the farther they come from their own Highlands the less stomach they'll have for the job.'

This was the kind of comfort that the little man was needing, and in return for it, as they went forward, he gave them all his history. His name was Cumberlege, John Cumberlege of the Moor House, English Street, Carlisle, and he was a corn-dealer like his father before him. He had had three children, and two had died in infancy, one of the staggers and one of the croup. He had been twice married, and Hetty, his only child, was of the second marriage. He was of good standing in Carlisle, and numbered among his friends there the worthy Dr Waugh; young Mr Aglionby, Mayor of the City; Thomas Pattinson, Deputy-Mayor; and Colonel Durand, Commander of the City. They might see from this how safely they might trust themselves to his company. He had also much to say of his late host, Mr

Richard Wordsworth, who had but recently been appointed Receiver-General of the County of Westmorland.

Altogether, as they jogged along, he recovered in this general recital of his famous friends a good deal of his natural confidence and genial humour.

David was glad of the little man's companionship. Francis Herries had fallen into one of his grim and arrogant moods again and would vouchsafe not a word. The afternoon was early dark, and there was a spectral air over the scene.

Indeed, the uncertainty of the situation influenced David in spite of himself. Moving thus through the cold dusk over a flat and silent land one could not be sure that at any moment one might not stumble upon the whole of the Prince's army. Where were they? How had they fared? It might be that this adventurer was truly destined for some glorious success and England would fall into his hands like a fine plum? Then back the Catholics would come again and with them the French dominance, and who knows after that the sequel? At this all the Herries English rose rebellious in David's soul. He wanted no French power here nor Catholic either. It was at this moment, perhaps, little Cumberlege pressing near to him, the few chill snowflakes striking his cheek and a great silence on every side of him, that he knew once and for all what he was. Scottish ancestry or no, he was English Herries. Men and women for two hundred years afterwards were to have some consequence in their lives from this moment of conviction.

Little Cumberlege asked them where they were lodging in Carlisle.

David told him that they had no settled place.

'Then, sirs, you must come to us. To be frank with you, I shall relish your company. There's no man in the house but the boy Jeremiah, and he's a witling with a wall-eye. I only took him to pleasure his father, who did me a service in '32, the year they hanged Humpy Dillon for sheep-stealing. You're a man of your inches, sir,' he added, looking appreciatively up at David, 'and might render us a service at a dangerous pinch.'

David looked at his father, who said no word. He smiled at the eager excited little man, the skirts of whose crimson coat stuck out from his fat buttocks as though with an indignant life of their own.

'For tonight at least,' David said, 'we'll take you at your word and thank you.'

A strange world had now come up about them, for the wind

had dropped, the snow ceased to fall, and instead a fog rolled in thick grey folds across the fields. This fog was to take a great part in the alarms and fears of the coming days: many, looking back afterwards and telling their story, gave it a personal form and body as though it were a creeping devil of an especial malignancy created by the Pretender himself.

David, who was never given to vague imagination, himself felt it an oddly alive thing. It came creeping towards them, now slipping along the road on its belly, licking the horses' hoofs, then raising a white swollen arm, wreathing their necks with it, then slipping away again, mounting into a wall in front of them, closing about them, stifling them, blinding them, dropping again to a thin shallow vapour that swathed the hedges with spider-web.

For Herries, it filled his dreams. For half an hour now he had not realized where they were nor cared. He rode forward, possessed by his vision. Since the word 'Carlisle' had, carelessly perhaps, passed Mirabell's lips it had been his one thought to go there. But with that burning impulse came also the resolve not to be defeated by it, because he felt that, let him surrender to it, and he would be beaten. Some prevision of the future told him that this journey taken through the fog, into the Lord knew what, was the beginning of a pursuit for him that was far more than physical, and, being spiritual, must fail in its aim.

He stared through the fog, her body, her soul, dancing in front of him. A child who had given him no single thought, a vagabond, ruthless and heartless perhaps, intolerant certainly of any of the bonds that he would put upon her. But all his history had led him to this, his rebellions, scorns, arrogances, dreams, selfcontempts, Alice Press and the like, his wife Margaret, every woman whose tongue he had ever twisted beneath his own led him to this. He wanted nothing for himself, only to be good to her, to know that she was happy, that she had what she wanted. That she had what she wanted! Ironic, ironic desire, for it would not be himself that she longed for . . . And so he rode on.

They came upon Carlisle quite suddenly and were challenged at the gate.

Carlisle had at this time a population of some four thousand persons, the majority of these living within its walls.

The Castle Walls and Citadel had still their original force: the Castle was held by a non-resident governor and a company of invalided veterans: the city gates were shut at the firing of the evening gun. Nevertheless, its life as a centre of warfare was now

still and dead. The union of the kingdoms of Scotland and
England had silenced the Border warfare, turned guns into
knitting needles and cannon-balls into peppermint rock. Here,
perhaps, lay the root of the Prince's advantage, that any Scottish
invasion of England was by now undreamt of in Carlisle and the
town was in no way prepared for it.

On this evening the bustle at the gate was tremendous. The
Herries would most certainly not have been admitted had they
been alone, but their little friend, Mr Cumberlege, had not said
too much about his popularity in Carlisle. Especially did a large,
pompous and terribly flustered military officer appear delighted
to see him, even to the extent of embracing him. He was not, Mr
Cumberlege explained, *sotto voce*, a real and proper military
gentleman, but rather a volunteer, in his time and natural state a
wealthy bachelor with a taste for wine and a talent for the game
of bowls, moreover a relation of good Doctor Bolton, the Dean of
Carlisle. He had in his private garden a fountain with a naked
mermaid who blew water out of her tail, considered by many a
marvel.

At the moment he was thinking of neither bowls nor mermaid,
but was in a dreadful flutter of indecision.

Scouting parties had been sent out to discover, if they might,
the Rash Adventurer's (such was the title decided on by those
who wanted to land safely in the ultimate result) whereabouts.
That afternoon, so Mr Bolton told Cumberlege, Lieutenant Kil-
patrick had advanced beyond Ecclefechan and sighted a body of
rebels. A Scottish quartermaster, seeking quarters for his troops
in Ecclefechan, had been seized and was now in Carlisle Castle.
That was as much as was known for the present.

A strange contrast was to be found in Mr Bolton's manner, he
suddenly rapping out most authoritatively a military order, then
sinking his voice to a nervous, confidential murmur with John
Cumberlege, who was as apprehensive as himself. They made a
funny enough pair, their contrast in size, their bodies starting at
every sound, and once when a horseman clattered over the
cobbles suddenly clutching one another as though for protection.

They rode up English Street to Cumberlege's house, which
was a neat little Georgian building with a brass knocker on the
door showing a sea-fish swallowing a trident, and a sundial on
the lawn by the street, and a fine little gate with small dragons
on either side of it. A good light burning in a cresset over the
door blew in the wind. The street was deserted. The fog had
cleared, and the sky was full of cold and glittering stars.

'Come in. Come in, gentlemen,' said Cumberlege, looking about him before he opened his front door as though he scented a Highlander round every corner. 'It's a poor hospitality I shall offer you, taking me unexpected and my wife an invalid, but—' and here he dropped his voice still further, 'there's wine in the house. Wine too good for the Highland rabble that's coming upon us.' And then to himself, as he unfastened his door: 'Poor Bolton! Poor Bolton! I'll wager he wishes himself back safe with his mermaid.'

Half an hour later they were seated in Cumberlege's gay little dining-room, a beef pie, an apple tart and some of the finest Madeira in front of them. It was a handsome little room with dark-red wallpaper hung with scenes from Mr Gay's master-piece, 'The Beggar's Opera', and a handsome oil painting of Mr Cumberlege's grandfather in a green coat and ruffles, over the mantelpiece. A noble old gentleman with a face like a codfish and a neck so thick that it was no wonder to hear, later in the evening, that he had died of an apoplexy. Silver candlesticks, a glass bowl of oranges and figs, a fire in the hearth, the curtains warmly drawn, and best of all Cumberlege's daughter Hetty, who was as pretty a dark child as David had ever seen.

Two things were very plainly visible: one that to John Cum-berlege this daughter was the life and light of his being. He sat with one stout arm round her and fed her with figs as though she had been a child in arms, his eyes moving ever and again about her pretty face with its nose a little snub, its eyelashes beautifully dark and long, its rounded chin and soft cheeks, as though all his happiness were there.

The other evident fact was that the child had fallen in love with David at sight. She sat there shyly smiling at him, her cheeks flushed, her eyes burning with pleasure and adventure. She was in a dress of white calico sprayed with pink roses, as David was long after to remember. A pretty face was a pretty face to David. Many times of late he had thought that he must fall in love, but Keswick did not offer so many varieties. Now he wondered whether his fate were not here. It was not, but it was near enough to make his heart beat, his tongue stammer and his big body move clumsily as though, in spite of itself, it must be impelled towards her.

John Cumberlege too, perhaps, as he looked across the table at David, had his dreams. It was true that he knew nothing about these visitors of his, and the elder was alarming in his taciturnity and grim seclusion, but you could not look at the younger Herries and doubt him. Honesty was in every glance, every breath, simplicity, a courageous rectitude.

For Hetty Cumberlege this threat of the Scottish invasion was a grand and enchanting game. Was it true that the Prince was the most beautiful young man? When he came to the city would there be routs and balls as she had heard there had been in Edinburgh? For herself she didn't care what her father thought; she was all for seeing him, and it would be a wicked shame were he stopped before he got to Carlisle. But he would not be. He was already there. He had been at Ecclefechan that day. Perhaps tomorrow he would be in the city, and if there was a ball she had no dress fit to wear. But oh, she was glad her dear father was safe (this with an especial hug of her father, a blushing glance at David). Mother had been in a great way all day and hadn't had her afternoon sleep and had been bled again this evening, and she had run to the window and the door a thousand times to see whether he were not coming, and would there be firing and the windows broken and people wounded?

Why shouldn't the Prince come into the town if he wanted to? That was the feeling of most of the militia anyway, and it was only that old jackanapes Colonel Durand who was for everybody fighting. She was sure that no one wanted to kill anyone else, the idea was perfectly horrid. And as the Madeira mounted into David's head and the weariness bred of his long forty-mile ride dazzled his eyes, it seemed to him that he was already kissing those blushing cheeks and stroking ever so gently that bare and gleaming shoulder.

Francis Herries said no word beyond mere politeness. He could not. He saw the figures of little Cumberlege and his daughter, the silver candlesticks, the glittering glass about the fruit, the portrait of old Cumberlege senior, in a thin and gauzy dream. He was here in Carlisle, and every beat of blood in him urged him, weary though he was, to go out and search for her. It seemed to him that there was more than mere vague urgency in this. Opposite him where he sat was a small round mirror with a dark oak frame. Its glass was blistered and cracked with age, so that the candle-flame flickered and redoubled in it, and the colours of the room, dark crimson, white and green, were a blurred and mellowed fog. Staring in it, half-asleep maybe, the voices coming to him with a faint chirping hum, he seemed to see that child Mirabell step into the mirror, break the misted colours, turn to him that strange, cold, indifferent face, gravely surveying him, oddly and harshly inviting him.

He pushed his napkin and wine-glass from him and asked his host to excuse him while he found a little air in the street. His head was hot and he must cool it before he went to his bed. He was aware that they felt, all three of them, a certain freedom from restraint at his departure.

In the street the wind had now quite fallen and only, as though dropped by the multitudinous shining stars, thin flakes of snow fell lazily as though they were too indifferent to reach the ground. No one was about. There were few lights in the windows. The sense of suspense might have been his own imagining, but it seemed to him that behind the doors and the windows folk were listening. He could hear the hearts throbbing, could see the eyes straining, and over his head and about his body the stems and branches of the rocking wood seemed still to be beating and groaning. He had been in that wood all day. He was not clear of it yet.

As though led by a guide at his elbow he turned up a dark and narrow street that was as silent as an empty pocket. On his right there was a light blowing above the name, 'The Silver Horn'. Here as well as another place. He pushed back the heavy wooden door and stumbled on to the uneven stone floor of an inn-room filled with a rough glare of men, women, smoke, thickly smelling of dried fish, tobacco and stale drink.

He sat down at a long deal table, men, countrymen, farmers, making easy way for him, too deeply intent on their talk to consider him. A thin wasp of a serving-man brought him some ale; a heavy thumping clock, hiccuping once and again as though it had taken in the drink as steadily as its customers, tick-tocked just above his head; a parrot, whose bright-green colour he could just see swaying on a perch through the smoke, called out in a thick husky caw; and still through it all the wind and creaking of the morning's wood kept him company.

He discovered soon enough that there was only one topic and that the natural one. Where was the Pretender and where his Highlanders? Even now they might be at the walls. What would Durand do? What Pattinson the Deputy-Mayor, young Aglionby being safely away in the country somewhere? What would the Dean and Chapter do? What would the Cumberland and Westmorland Militia do? What was everyone going to do? Were they all to be blown to bits? What was Wade going to do? What was the King in London doing that he hadn't sent any reinforcements? Didn't he care what happened to old Carlisle, and if he didn't why should old Carlisle care what happened to the King?

Ah! but those Highlanders! Here fear crept through the smoke, skins went shivering, the tick-tock of the old clock took on a deeper tone. Those Highlanders . . . Hadn't you heard, then, of what they'd been doing in Edinburgh and Glasgow, of the women they'd been raping and the destruction they'd been causing? The story went tonight that back at Kelso Spital they had shot all the sheep, hanged all the farmers, drunk the warm blood of the sheep like so many cannibals. There was the tale, too, of the farm-wife at Langholm who refused to tell the rebels where her husband had hid the horses and cattle, she lying in bed with a new-born child. She refused, even though the rebel officer threatened her with cutting down the beam that supported the roof of the farmhouse. He cut away at the beam, but it stoutly withstood, and the house was spared.

And what of Carlisle? What is the good of holding out, the Castle as rotten as it is, the Gate not covered by any outworks, the Wall over the Lady's Walk very low with neither parapet nor flank to defend it, the old gateway not defended by any flank, and we having nothing to oppose seven thousand rebels save a few invalids? . . . Surely better, then, to let the Pretender come in under guarantee of decent behaviour on both sides. Hick, hick, hick, stammered the clock. It was then that, staring through the smoke into the light of the roaring fire, Herries saw Mirabell.

This gave him no sense of surprise nor question of undue coincidence. It seemed to him the most natural thing in the world that she should be sitting there, and his only sensation was one of great happiness, a happiness oddly tranquil and secure. He had at first no ambition to speak to her, only to sit there and know that she was alive and in the same room with him.

He could not, from where he was, see her very clearly. She was wearing an amber-coloured hat with a feather in it and a deep dark-red cloak with a high collar; he could see, from where he was, that the cloak was faded and old. He could not deny but that she seemed bedraggled and shabby. He could not distinguish her features, only sufficient to know that it was surely she, but indeed where else in the world was there hair of such a colour? It was piled up, burning between the tawny colour of her hat and her white neck, a fire in smoke and under creaking windy trees.

He was half-asleep, perhaps, with weariness, or the heat of the room bemused him, but after a little while it appeared that he and she were quite alone in the wood and that they rode forward silently to some unknown destination.

After a while he wished to see her more clearly, rose from where he was, pushed through the farmers and countrymen and came to another place across the room. He was sitting in a corner now, near the fire, quite close to the bright-green parrot; it was fiercely hot, but he did not feel the heat.

He was beside her now, and at once his heart was shot through by a sharp and intolerable agony. That was no exaggerated figure of speech. It was like that. He felt the pain before he realized the cause. This cause was that, beside her, his arm around her red cloak, was a young man, a fellow of little more than twenty perhaps, yet a boy with a boy's fresh colour, a boy's laugh, a boy's bright eyes. Those eyes were fixed on her and her eyes on his. That they loved one another, and to a pitch that excluded the scene and everything in it, was clear to any casual onlooker. How sharply, deeply clear to Herries, in whose ears might be echoing yet the crash of the derisive boughs. 'Crack-crack! Crack-crack! He means to be married! He means to be married!'

As he watched he saw her hand come out and take the broad brown hand of the young man. Then she smiled at him, a shy, delicate, happy child's smile that drew her, although they did not move, deep into the young man's heart.

Her note for Herries had always been her remoteness; he had never seen her intimate with nor close to anything. He had never dared to imagine how she would look when she was in love. His only hope had been that she had never known what that was, and so he had wondered whether he might not be the first to teach her. For he had taught in his day many lessons in love. Now he knew that that would never be.

When some control came back to him he studied the boy carefully. He was dressed roughly in a dark coarse coat and homespun breeches, and gaitered to the thigh for riding. His body was slim and well-formed, he carried his head high: everything about him was honest and upright, strong and smiling. He was a proper man. It was after concluding this (and his pride allowed him to flinch from no challenging comparisons) that Herries noticed a third figure. This was a thick, short, black-bearded fellow who sat behind the pair, swinging his legs from the table-end. His face was covered with a shaggy black beard and his hair lay in a black tangle over his forehead. There was black hair on the back of his hands. He was dressed soberly and cleanly, and his large, steadily open, black eyes never left the face of the girl.

Once and again he said a word to her, but when he spoke it did not rouse the girl, who smiled at the boy as though it were he who had spoken. But they were all three of them very quiet, not joining at all in the conversation around them, making a little world and history apart by themselves.

For Herries it was as though a new fresh chapter of his life had opened. When we fall in love the desire in us is so strong that we argue a like desire in the other, and stay cheated so long as we may. Well, his cheat was over, but he was in no kind of way released from her. He realized at once that he was only the more strongly bound because he would never forget now how she looked when she was in love, and would never again be able to defend himself against her with a sense of her remoteness.

Often since the day in the cave, lying on his bed, working in the field, riding solitary up Stonethwaite, standing on Esk Hause and seeing the valleys glitter and smile beneath him, he had wondered how she would look at him the first time that she knew she could trust him. For that was what he had meant to do; by great kindliness and patience to make her trust him as she had never trusted anyone before. Now he knew that that would never happen.

He saw, too, how all his actions since the day in the cave had been for her. He had never once been free of her. When he had taken the witch from the river and held her to his heart it had been this child that he had held. All the new compassion and softness that had lately been growing in him so that the sterner, more ironical part of him had been frightened at the change and tried to drive it away, all this had been from her. It had been as though he had been educating himself out of the nastiness and pride of his earlier life, so that he might be ready for her when she came to him: and now she would never come.

She would never come. The trees of the wood gathered about his head very thickly and now with silence because the wind had died. The green parrot swung from bough to bough watching him with beady eyes. Then he heard her speak, and her voice was as deeply familiar to him as though he had been in company with it all his life.

She spoke to the parrot.

'For a penny,' she said, 'I'd wring your neck, you evil bird.'

The young man, looking at her as though he would drown her in his love, answered in a voice that was roughly boyish and eager:

'I shall buy the bird for you.'

And she answered, holding his hand very tightly: 'Two is company.'

The black-bearded man behind them swung off the table and stood, thick and stocky, looking up at the parrot. He went up to it and stroked its neck. The parrot bent its head, eyeing him obliquely with a beady eye.

Herries had seen enough. He went out, into the street.

SIEGE IN FOG

HERRIES WOKE early the next morning, and under a sharp agitation of disturbance and fear. The room in which he was lying was foreign and strange to him. His eyes slowly picked up one thing after another; the faded green hangings of his bed, the uneven boarding of the floor, a print hanging against the dark panel of the wall, showing apprentices playing football in the Strand, and another with a crudely coloured presentation of Bear-Baiting. On an old chest under the window was a bowl of thick green glass, rough in texture so that the colours of the green glass seemed to shift and change.

The light from the window was dim. There was no sound anywhere.

Where then was he? With a rush as of charging horses, events, pictures, words came back to him. He sprang from his bed as though, at once, he would hasten out into the street and start about his affairs. He went to the little window and pushed it back. A thin, wet, wispy fog met him. He was in the house of Mr Cumberlege of Carlisle. He was also in the 'Silver Horn', and close to him Mirabell Starr was looking into the young man's eyes, while the green parrot rocked on its perch. And he was in the ground behind Herries, digging while Glaramara humped its back over him and the light came down in misty ladders over Stye Head, and he was rowing slowly from Lord's Island, while the water slipped in ripples of steel from hill to hill.

He passed the back of his hand across his eyes, pulling himself together. He was here in Carlisle. The Prince and his High-landers ... Mirabell ... this green bowl above whose colours the thin fog shifted ... His hand touched his bare chest and felt for the chain and the wooden cross that Mirabell's mother had left for him. He had not been without it since that day, and now, as his hand touched it, a new determination came to him: that he would find the child and talk to her and see how he might serve

her. She was not for him and now would never be, but he might
help her.

He stretched his legs and his arms, smiled; his face just then
was kindly, not sardonic, but a little old and rough, battered and
torn above his body, for his skin was fair and delicate like a
woman's.

The door creaked open, and David came in. He was in an excitement unusual for his calm temper. He was fully dressed.

'Father, what are we going to do? They say this morning the
town's under siege. There's a fine to-do, and half the city's
downstairs swearing the militia are going to give in before they
are fairly started, and the other half's in the street screaming
about the Highlanders, and there's a fog so thick you can't see
the back of your hand. Are we going to stay here? I doubt if we
can get out now if we want to.'

'Of course we stay,' said Herries, sitting on the bed's end and
swinging his bare legs.

'What did you hear last night when you were in the town?'

'Oh, naught, but that a parrot has green eyes.'

'Old Cumberlege loves me like a son this morning. He's
plucky enough for himself, but his lady and his lady's woman are
raped already by bony Highlanders in their imagination. They
can't tell whether to be sorry or glad. The girl's brave, though.
She calls me her brother.'

David grinned and put his arm around his father's bare neck.

'So we're to stay here?'

'Of course we're to stay, seeing we can't get out.'

'But who are we for? The Prince and his Highlanders?'

'For ourselves.' Herries stood up, stretching his arms. 'We're
in a green city with warlocks and witches. Take care of the witch
downstairs, David. Or love her if you wish to. A fog's the place
for true love. My stomach's empty. Is there any food in this siege,
or do we live from now on upon snails and puppies' tails? And
water. There's a tin basin here, but no water.'

'I'll fetch you some.'

David returned with a bucket of water. He watched his father
bathe. 'You're strong. Stronger than you used to be.'

'Aye, I'm strong – and damned ugly. The fog's to my advantage. Hast kissed the girl downstairs, Davy?'

'Yes, I kissed her.' David was crimson. 'She liked it.'

Herries, drawing on his hose, laughed.

'Good enough now. There'll be tears later.' They went down
the crooked stairs, arm-in-arm.

But that day went for nothing. For the most part father and son were together, walking the town, watching the country people (for it was Martinmas Hiring Day), listening to a thousand silly rumours and stories.

At three in the afternoon there was a real sensation. A party of fifty or sixty horsemen appeared on Stanwix Bank, overlooking the city. The road was crowded with country people going home. When these were cleared away the ten-gun battery of the Castle fired, but the troopers were in safety by then.

Francis was in his little room washing his face in the tin basin when the guns fired. The floor seemed to quiver; the little panes of the windows rattled; a scatter of birds flew past, and there was a woman's scream, shrill and sharp, through the house. Then silence.

He went to the window. The fog was clear and the sky silver with threads of blue above the crooked roofs. He leaned out. On a cobbled corner of the side-street (he could see only a fragment of it) a man stood, looking up. Herries had the oddest fancy, seeing dimly in that faint afternoon light, that it was the pedlar standing there, the pedlar whom he had not seen since that Christmas night of the duel ... Oddly like him, with a peaked cap, the thin straining body. He fancied that he could certify the sharp, piercing eyes. He stepped back into the room in whose dusk the green glass bowl was the only light. Of course it was not the pedlar, but the fancy held him.

He yet seemed to have the echo of the guns in his ears, and the woman's scream. What was to happen to him here? An odd burning shiver ran through him like the first warning of a fever: he knew in that second, staring into the green glass of the bowl, that one of the crises of his life was approaching. He knew it quite certainly. He did not care for his life – it was not of so precious a quality to him – but this crisis that was coming was of deep import and would change, whichever way it went, all his fortune, physical and spiritual.

He knew it, as though the guns had blown away a veil from his eyes.

He went out to see what was toward. The country people were all hastening home. There was a stir in the Square like a scare among sheep when a wolf is by. Little groups collected like flies round sugar, and yet over all the bustle and movement there was a strange hush as though no one dared to raise a voice. He heard the names pass back and forth: 'Wade', 'Durand', 'Aglionby', 'Waugh', 'Pattinson'. The pigeons came strutting at his very feet, and above the roofs the sky suddenly tossed up arms and wreaths of red and gold, proclaiming the setting sun.

He turned his steps towards the Cathedral. In the Close everything was very still. Someone stood in a side door of the Cathedral looking up at the flaming sky. It was as though everyone he saw were straining an ear for the sound of the guns again.

Someone was speaking to him. 'A fine evening, Mr Herries.'

He turned, as one turns in a dream, because he knew the voice. He passed his hand before his eyes, and in his ears the cannon dimly sounded, for it was Mirabell Starr very quietly standing there.

'I have followed you, Mr Herries – most indecently. I saw you ten minutes ago.'

She looked at him with that clear-eyed indifference so known to him. But she was pleased, perhaps. The sky sank to smoky grey, and he could scarcely see her face. The bells chimed five o'clock. But she was glad to see him, less indifferent than she had been. He caught that and cherished it. She looked a baby, wearing the same shabby red cloak. His heart throbbed. He held himself sternly at attention, his arms stiff at his sides, lest he should touch her.

'I'm bold to address you.'

She saw in his eyes that he was worshipping her, this odd, ugly, elderly, scarred man.

She was frightened, perhaps, and for the honest child that she was wanted to put everything in a clear, defined light.

'I followed you—' she caught her breath a little. 'I wanted to tell you . . . There at Honister, when we talked, I told you that I didn't believe in love. Well, now, you were kind and asked me to come to you if I needed anything, and my mother trusted you, so you must know I am very happy and I love someone, and he loves me.'

'That is good,' he said sternly. 'And it is a good man you love?'

'Yes, it is a good man.'

'He will care for you?'

'Oh, always.'

'I am happy. But you should not be here. This town will be dangerous now.'

'I have been in danger all my life,' she answered. 'Danger is nothing – for myself,' she added hastily.

Then, smiling at him so sweetly that his heart ached, she said quickly:

'I wished you to know. Goodnight,' and was gone.

He stood without moving, for how long he did not know.

There was a bitter, almost despairing, pain at his heart, such as he had never known before. He had always been too proud to despair of himself, but now, under the black shadow of the Cathedral, he really despaired. He was isolated, ostracized, hateful to all men. At once, at first sight of him, these Cumberleges had drawn back . . . That he could face, but now, all pride flung aside, all fear of weakness discarded, he felt the bitterest anguish. Because, for a moment, he had been in touch with a kind of joy, a sort of happiness that he had not known before existed. He had seen it in the distance, stretched his hand, touched its wings; it had flown. Sternly, his back against the Cathedral wall as though he were hammered on to it, he stared in front of him, his palms gripped. He had not known before that his love for her was so deep that the hooks of it were in his very entrails. He knew now, and that he would always love her so.

On the following morning, the Sunday, Francis and David were summoned to the defence of the city. The fog was this morning thicker than ever and added to the general confusion and increasing alarm. Every kind of rumour was about. No one knew where the Prince and his army might be. Some said that he was already inside the city. Some said that Wade and his forces were marching to relieve them, others that they were to be left to their fate, their children would be eaten alive, their women raped and the houses burned to the ground.

Among the most gloomy of Carlisle's citizens was Mrs Cumberlege, who continued to scream from her bed of sickness. At one moment she succeeded in staggering as far as her doorway (rumour had it that she could have staggered a great deal farther had she so wished) and crying: 'The Highlanders are here! The Highlanders are here! Help! Help! We are all to be murdered!'

This was, of course, desperately upsetting for Mr Cumberlege, who was forbidden by her to leave her defenceless in the house. At the same time he wished to do his duty as a loyal citizen and surrender himself to Colonel Durand's orders. It ended in his slipping, with Herries and David, off into the fog, and leaving her in the care of her beautiful daughter.

They went to the Castle and were enrolled for defence. Prospects were not cheerful. From the room in which they stood, crowded about with an extraordinary tumbled and disorderly mixture of old men, young men and boys, they could hear the echo of trowel and hammer on the city walls. The original garrison was but eighty old 'invalid' soldiers. The guns were so ancient that they were reputed to have been, in the jest of the drinking-bouts and tea-parties, Boadicea's. Durand had augmented them with ten small ship's guns brought from Whitehaven, and the old ruined walls were now in course of being altered that they might fit these.

Forty townsmen were in charge of the Whitehaven guns, and another eighty served the Castle artillery.

Confusion was the more confounded by the bringing from neighbouring towns and villages of small companies of militia, but their arms were of different bores, and every man made his own ball fitting the size of the piece.

All the worst trouble, Herries soon perceived, came from these same militia. Colonel Durand had proposed that the militia officers should do duty by detachment from their several companies, but this they emphatically and turbulently opposed, and drew lots, among themselves, for their posts. The result of this was that there was no order nor discipline, and men wandered where they would and were already demoralized and fatigued.

As the morning drew on, the confusion in the room where Herries was grew ever more active. Men ran about like children, crying out, fingering arms in so uncertain a manner that it was likely at any instant that one would blow another to pieces, starting up and running to the windows, chattering, crying, shouting, now boasting, now bewailing. An old countryman stood near Herries, an ancient man with a long grizzled beard who, again and again, called out: 'Who is for the Lord? Who is for the Lord?' Little Cumberlege walked to the window and back, stopping every other minute by David, whose strength and imperturbability seemed to give him an immense satisfaction. It seemed to be impossible for the present to come near Durand, who was in an inner room.

Then, about midday, the fog rolled off, and a young man with a long yellow face like a turnip came in shouting:

'They are upon us. The whole army. At the very walls.'

He had scarcely spoken when the guns were heard to fire. 'That's from Shaddon Gate,' someone cried. There was a moment of transfixion when everyone stood, not seeing what to do, where to go, waiting for they knew not what. Then two men ran in, shouting hysterically:

'We have beat them. They are retreating.' And almost at once the fog came down again, blotting everything out.

Some said now that they had retreated all together, others that it was but a blind, others that they had marched round to the other side of the city and were already creeping about the streets.

Some swore that they could hear the skirl of the Highland pipes. Even for Herries who, in such an affair, had no unsteady nerves, there was an odd thrill from the knowledge that in the brief interval of clarity the whole of the Prince's army had been seen at the very walls. It was true, then. They were in the real heart of this situation, not imagining it. Shortly there might be – nay, surely would be – massacre and bloodshed. And where would she be in this? A chance bullet? A drunken Highlander? His whole body trembled . . . The old countryman clutched his arm and peered into his face.

'Who is for the Lord? Who is for the Lord?'

It was late in the afternoon before he and David were marched off to the part of the wall that was their post. As they marched through a portion of the town it had a weird effect, because the order had gone out that there were to be lights in all the lower windows, darkness in the upper. The fog, too, hung high, so that they seemed to be stepping along a stream of uncertain watery glow, while above them was a bank of blackness. All was silent; behind the lighted windows there was no sound. Against his will every man was listening for the guns.

No one spoke. They might have been moving to some secret rendezvous. Herries had at his side a short, round, very stout, little man who groaned, panted and seemed to be bursting with some tremendous secret.

They paused at a lighted corner while their destination was settled. At once the little fat man, whose face was beetroot colour (his head trembled with a queer jerky movement), burst into the middle of excited, despairing sentences as though he were continuing a long, already uttered speech. He caught Herries's arm and held it, and this oddly pleased him. There was someone in this foggy world who did not shrink from him.

'. . . The eldest but five and a half . . . One every year, and the five of them alone in the house with their grandmother, deaf as a post, to mind them . . . I said to them that I would not be gone a half-hour, and what service can I be with a musket, serving out butter and sugar for the last twenty years? . . . But what do you think, sir? Shall we beat them off, do you think? My sister would have been in to mind them, but only two days back she was on a visit to Allonby to her brother-in-law, as indeed I told her at the time that he was but inviting her to take advantage of her. He was never a man, from his boyhood up, to do a thing and not expect anything back for it, as Margaret my sister has herself said many a time . . . and the children crying their hearts out in the dark . . .'

The light from a flare that someone carried swung in the breeze, as though a tongue were licking the cheek of the fog. In that sudden illumination Herries saw two things: that David was not with him and that quite close to him, almost in touch of him, was Mirabell's young lover.

At that knowledge he caught his breath as though he expected a blow. The boy (for he was little more) stood stiffly, his head up-staring straight into Herries's face.

He did not, of course, recognize him, but he looked at him as though he would know him. And yet he was looking beyond him. Herries saw now that he was not seeing anyone. He was swimming deep in his own thoughts, and his mouth was smiling.

The order came again to move forward. The young man was very near to him. It was as though he had been placed there in David's stead.

The little fat man stayed close at Herries's side. Whistling ejaculations came from between his lips. 'Eh, sirs! . . . Eh, sirs!' 'The pity of it! The pity!' 'The waste in this town!'

Mirabell's boy, the second coincidence. First the 'Silver Horn' and now this. He felt a dead weight upon him, as though he were caught in some trap. The conviction that had been with him in his room when he heard the first gun, came back to him, that he was moving to some deep crisis in his affairs and that all his future would depend on the way that he now acted.

Oddly, at the very first sight of him under the flare, he knew that he hated him.

Inside the wall they took their places. Someone came round and told them where they were to go, and that at a certain time they would be relieved. At once it was evident that there was no discipline. The fog had lifted again and a few faint, very small stars could be seen.

Men were moving about, talking to one another. The fat man, his hand once more on Herries's arm, was about it again. '. . . Only yesterday, being Martinmas Hiring, I engaged the girl, but when she saw the trouble in the city nothing would stay her. I offered her a double wage if she'd bide with the children. She'd be safer,

too, here than out in the country, but when they fired that cannon
it frightened her. Not a word would she hear . . .'

The young man stayed at Herries' side as though he knew
that was the place for him. Yes, he had a fine, clear, noble countenance. No fear there, no meanness. His slim body was strung
to the full height of discipline and obedience. Still on his lips
was that little, happy smile.

Herries, as though under command, spoke:

'The fog clears,' he said.

The young man turned as though he had been recalled from a
great distance.

'They must be at our very feet,' he said. 'It will be cold before
dawn.' He smiled, then he added: 'I have a friend who was with
me until ten minutes back. We wished to be together.'

Three men came past, peering. One of them stopped.

'I have found you,' he said. That thick growling voice was
guide enough for Herries. He knew that the company was now
completed. The face, with its black hair, peered close at Herries.
Herries could see him again as he stepped to the parrot, tickling
its neck with his finger.

'I had lost you,' the young man said.

'I am never lost,' he laughed deep as though in the coils of his
stomach. 'Well, sir,' he said to Herries, 'this is a play.'

Herries nodded, turned away, looked out to the grey web of
the night, its texture dotted with lights that seemed to sway and
stagger because the mist came in drives, advancing and retreating.

They took their places, quietly, the three of them together,
and stood there without moving. An immense time seemed to
pass. The cold grew very intense.

Herries thought: 'Here I am, these two with me, not by my
own choice or intention.' He felt growing up in him the old man
that he had by now, he thought, discarded. Something seemed
to him to come through the night and the fog and the cold and
place in him one evil thing after another, as you pile stuff in a
cupboard. 'And now this I'll add. And now this. Yes, and this
we must have.'

Evil things, lecheries, lusts, cruelties, meannesses, desires to
hurt, to maim, purposeless maliciousness. And he himself
seemed to look on, coldly and with external deliberation. All his
love for the child, Mirabell, was tarnished and coarsened. He
now lusted for her in exactly the way that, in his younger days,
he had lusted for many women. His hands touched her hair, her

small child's face, her little breasts, her waist, her knees, coldly, with desire but no fine passion.

His evil thoughts spread over the walls into the dark plain beyond. He saw the Prince's army encamped, and it seemed to him that he could stare into every tent. Each place was peopled with evil men, men cruel and mean and lascivious as he was. They were crawling over the country, carrying naked women on their backs, naked women whose hair was loose about their bodies and down whose faces tears were pouring. He saw a farm, the house, its windows shuttered for the night, the farm buildings stacked with provender, the animals sleeping in their places, the master in the upper room asleep, his head resting on his wife's breast.

Through the gate, a little bent man, a flare in his hand, crept. He stooped lower, setting the flare now here, now there. The flames sprang up. The byres were caught. The animals screamed. The fire ate the walls of the house with greedy avaricious gestures. White faces were at the windows. There were screams, cries, odour of burning flesh. The woman, held in her man's arms, watched the flames crawl nearer . . .

The little bent man moved about the country, doing here one evil thing, another there. Herries moved with him, his body cold, like marble, his heart burning.

All the men in the Prince's camp seemed to stir before him. They moved closer to the walls, and in all that army of eyes there was anticipatory lust and longing for suffering in others and destruction and ruin. Herries himself seemed to lead them on, saying: 'Here is a good place . . . And here are women . . . Here are houses to burn.'

A shiver of bad desire ran through him. It was as though he had been sleeping there on his feet and wakened. It might be so. Everything was very clear about him, the dark ramparts, the white faces of men.

He could have said: 'I see men crawling like lice, and that is all that they are. Poor, lowest and meanest of all created things.' He tried not to think of anything. He knew that if he went much further he would face thoughts that were lower and viler than any that he had ever known. But someone went on piling the cupboard high with these. 'Here is a new one. Here is one that I have found. And here another . . .'

He turned a little and talked to the black, short man at his side, who, like the boy, had neither moved nor spoken all this time.

'What do you think,' he asked, 'of this adventurer's chances? Will he reach London?'

With that odd growl as of an animal roused by some sense of danger, the man answered: 'I neither know nor care. He can take this place when he wishes – and all England for me.'

'Doesn't it matter to you then?'

'Why should it? There is food and drink under any king. One ruler is like another, unless oneself has the chance of ruling.'

'Are you in Carlisle by hazard?' To Herries it was as though, beneath this conversation, other words were being said and other meanings of deep import were being intended.

'I am anywhere by hazard. One place is as another to me.'

'I have seen you before,' Herries said. 'The other evening at the "Silver Horn".'

'It may be,' the man replied. 'I have been there.' He spat against the wall. 'Some of us may be dead men before morning.'

'Why do you stay here,' asked Herries, 'if you are indifferent? You lose your life, maybe, for nothing.'

'My life!' The man growled a chuckle. 'I have no life. I have only moments. I am hungry, I eat. I am thirsty, I drink. I want a woman, if I can I take her. Life stops. Well, why not – when it has never begun?'

'Then you have no fear of death?'

'No. If there's no life, there's no death. There is only the body. One fills it. One empties it. One seizes with it what one can.'

Herries said: 'Then you regret nothing that you have ever done?'

'Only what I have wanted and have not had.'

'You are fortunate, then,' Herries answered. 'You have no scruples, no regrets.'

'Regrets! No! Why? Where I am strong enough I conquer. Where I am weak I take to my heels.'

'Why, then, I ask again, are you here? In this bleak place, in danger, where nothing is to be gained.'

'Ah, perhaps something is to be gained.'

The thin, faint light was enough for them to see one another's faces, and suddenly, at the same moment, they stared, the one at the other. It was indeed a strange look. Herries, gazing into that shaggy face with the bristling, black hair, the light, fiery little eyes, the low chill brow, felt that he had seen this face before, and often. He felt, too, that the man was coldly, deliberately, and without interest in anything but his own purpose, asking him to do something. What he could not tell.

'That's a deep scar you've got,' said the man.

'Yes.'

'Did you kill the man who gave it you?'

'No,' said Herries.

'I would have done: drawn and quartered him. You see my hands?' He held them out, hideous hands, the backs thick with black hair, the fingers stumped and gnarled.

'They are strong. I could strangle an ox with them.'

Herries, moved by some curiosity, touched one. It was ice-cold and damp.

'Yes. You have strong hands.'

For the first time the young man spoke:

'He is so strong that he can lift a cart with them. Can you not, Tony?'

The man did not answer. The boy went on: 'Is it not strange, sir, standing here in this cold mist, waiting for we know not what and for no real reason?' His face was charming, as he turned it to Herries. 'I am all for a fight in the open, and when you know the cause, but this chill waiting . . . and I would be loth to die, just now.'

'The boy's in love,' said the man. 'He's thinking always of his beautiful girl. Isn't it so, Harry?'

The boy laughed.

'That is no business for this gentleman,' he said. 'Another man's love affair is dull news.'

And so they would move, these men, stirring so quietly under the wall, their eyes burning, their hearts thick at the thought that with a knock or two this town would surrender. And then what fun there would be for them! No house closed to them, the women cowering in the bed-curtains; their 'Hallo! you there . . I have you!' Dragging her out, pulling back her head, loosening her hair, tearing her clothes from her – her neck, her breasts, her eyes staring in terror, the crackle of flames, the tramping of men, the warm trembling body slack in their arms . . .

'And out on the Fell I have seen the shepherd whistling to his dog and the sheep come in a cloud, while the sun strikes the stream like mirror-glass. That's what I want and will have, when this is over.' It was the boy speaking.

The man growled at his side. 'The lad's a poet. He writes reams of it. There's books already enough in the world.'

'But this, sir, too, is wonderful. Can you not feel it to be so?

The town so dark behind us and the land so dark before. We standing on so narrow a parapet that one cannon-ball would tumble it to dust. If 'twere only myself I were thinking of . . .' He sighed and turned impulsively to Herries. 'Oh, sir, we standing as we do in this dark, strangers, need not be afraid of rashness. Have you not felt often how unsafe it is to love? The agony of another's safety . . . The pain of parting . . .' He broke off. They were all very close together, and their voices low.

Herries felt that he was alone there and that these two were but voices of his own different warring selves.

The mist was thick again and the cold very sharp. They stood instinctively the closer.

It was then, with a sudden pang as though an enemy had struck a blade into him, that he realized the intensity of his hatred for this boy. This had been approaching him for a long while, keeping pace with all his other evil thoughts, but now it had outpaced the others and crept all over his body like a fever. His hands shook. He did not trust himself to speak because his voice would shake.

This was the boy loved by Mirabell. Had he not come she would have learnt to love himself. Aye, she would. With what woman had he ever failed? No matter if he were older now and face-scarred, when he chose to put forth his charm what woman resisted him? And most certainly she, a child who, in spite of her boasts, could know so little about men, would have surrendered to him. But now her heart had been taken by a chit of a boy, beardless, simple, a baby poet. She would love him and then rue it, live with him a week and tire of it. A few years and she would be a woman, complex, tyrannous, passionate. And was this boy companion for such a woman?

But, more than conscious thought, his body was moving him towards some action. His hands about the boy's throat in that thick darkness, his hands strong as iron, one throttle, a little murmured cry. There would be no witness save the other fellow, and, with that, Herries, although no word had been spoken, was aware that it was the black-faced fellow's desire that he should do this. He was aware that the man hated the boy as he did. The fellow was very close to him, thigh pressed to thigh, and even as this knowledge came to him he felt the cold, damp, hairy back of that other hand on his.

One squeeze of the fingers about the throat . . . In the hurry and panic of this especial crisis no one would hear and no one know.

His body shook now so that, touching the thick, hard body close to him, he knew that the man felt this trembling and was aware.

The fellow said to him: 'At what hour did they say they would relieve us?'

But behind the spoken words were these others: ('We understand one another, we two. Do this and there will be no sound . . .')

He replied: 'At midnight.'

(And his answer: 'I wish for no understanding with you. What I do I do for myself.')

The man growled: 'The cold is more biting with every second.'

(And behind the words: 'Press your fingers into his windpipe. I will keep guard.')

Herries answered: 'The cold will be worse for the second watch.'

('Keep guard for yourself. I am my own guard.')

The man's cold hairy hand touched Herries's fingers.

'This town can stand no siege unless Wade relieves it.'

(And behind the words: 'It will be quickly done. Catch him by the neck. Press his head back.')

Herries said: 'Well, Wade should have been here today were he coming.'

('But it is my affair. Leave me alone to my own deed.')

The boy's voice came from what seemed an infinite distance: 'I wonder what the hour should be. I have missed the Cathedral clock.'

And from a greater distance yet some other voice: 'Eh, but it's cold . . . awful cold. There'll be snow before morning.'

Every evil act of Herries's life seemed to come to him there, all that had been unrestrained, uncontrolled, self-willed and cruel. The days in Doncaster, Margaret weeping on her bed, Alice Press at the Fair, and it was he who with his own hands had bound the naked witch . . .

He seemed to encircle Mirabell, his adored, with one arm and with the other he touched the boy's neck.

The boy turned, but Herries allowed his hand to stay against the warm skin.

('One twist of the head and you have done it. I will keep silence as though it had been myself.')

Then desperately, out of the mist, from some place that was not his own heart, some sort of a prayer issued: 'Oh, God, who dost not exist, help me now for I am in perilous trouble. Oh, God, who art not, save me from this sin.'

He touched barely the boy's neck, but he felt as though he held him in his arms, and all the hatred, all the aching lonely desire for the girl so indifferent to him, all the insistent urge to kill, was in the power behind his hands, his arms, his beating heart, his straining body.

It seemed to him that he threw him over the parapet and that nothing had been done.

The boy laughed.

'Your hand is cold,' he said.

Herries dropped his arms.

'I could wrestle with you to be warm,' he said.

'Well, let us wrestle then,' said the boy laughing.

Herries answered shuddering: 'I must go to find my son.'

He stumbled off into the dark. Figures were moving, voices murmuring. And then there was a great silence as though all the world had been stricken dumb.

He pressed up against the rampart of the wall, his forehead clamped to the cold stone. And so he stayed.

THE PRINCE

CHARLES EDWARD, with his army, entered Carlisle city on Monday, November 18th.

This was the climax of days of panic and despair. There is no need here to recover the episodes of that unhappy week, to recall once again how, after unfortunate Deputy-Mayor Pattinson had gaily sent word to London that the Prince had retreated, and been officially thanked for the news, he discovered only too quickly the error of his judgement; or how, to a growing accompaniment of terror and dismay, the citizens of that gallant town learnt that they were deserted and betrayed; or how on the 15th the Highlanders were within eighty yards of the city wall and answered the disheartened fire of the garrison with scornful jeers, 'their bonnets', one commentator remarks, 'held high aloft at the end of their trenching spades'.

After this, do what Durand might, there was pandemonium in the city. That brave man did his utmost, 'assuring them', to quote again the chronicler, 'that they need fear nothing from the rebels, that they were in a very good condition to defend themselves, and that if they would continue to behave with the same spirit and resolution they had hitherto shown, the rebels would never capture the city'.

It was the militia who brought the panic to submission. To the mess-room at the 'King's Arms' they retired, and this was their Declaration:

'The militia of the counties of Cumberland and Westmorland having come voluntarily into the city of Carlisle for the defence of the said city, and having for six days and six nights successively been upon duty in expectation of relief from His Majesty's forces, but it appearing that no such relief is to be had, and ourselves not able to do duty or hold out any longer, are determined to capitulate, and do certify that Colonel Durand, Captain Gilpin and the rest of the officers have well and faithfully done their duty.'

Durand, after reading this, made one more attempt to reason with them, but they would listen to no reason and no argument.

'The majority of the officers insisted that they were resolved to treat with the enemy for themselves.'

One last attempt was made; the townsmen, having better guts than the poor militia, refused to capitulate, determined to hold the Castle, collected provisions and munition in the Castle, but, alas, the militia 'melted away through the night, and on the morning of the 15th Durand was left with his eighty "invalids" and a capful of brave townsmen'.

On this a messenger who had been sent to the Prince returned with these words: 'That he would grant no terms to the town, nor treat about it at all unless the Castle was surrendered; likewise, if that was done, all should have honourable terms, the inhabitants should be protected in their persons and estates, and everyone be at liberty to go where they pleased.'

These terms, better than the citizens had expected, decided the matter. The Duke of Perth entered and took possession of the Castle and city. The capitulation of Carlisle was effected with the loss of one man only, and he a rebel.

On the 16th of November the Duke of Perth, on the steps of the Cross in the centre of the Market-Place, proclaimed King James III, and the Town Clerk and members of the Corporation went out to Brampton, where the Prince was, and, on bended knee, yielded him the keys of the city.

So, on the 18th of November, the Prince entered the city, and

David Herries and Hetty Cumberlege were among those who saw him enter.

That was a happy day for David. It was for him, and for many thousands of others who were there, like passing out of a night-mare. Strong of purpose, courageous and unflinching as he was, these last days had begun to test his nerves. 'If only,' he had thought (as he was to think many times again in the course of his life), 'folk would keep their mouths shut.' The thick foggy weather, the uncertainty of the future, the possibility of massacre and fire, the sense of futility from beating against all these nerves and ill-controlled passions, were beginning to frighten him.

For himself he did not care, and in his father he had absolute faith, but these trembling and crying women were another matter. Little Hetty Cumberlege was among the bravest of them, but on her, too, the wild stories and frenzied anticipations were having their effect. Had he been in love with her it would have been simpler. A sort of glory would have come from that. But although he wished to be, he could not. He could not under-stand that. She was pretty and charming, and herself as far in love with him as her childishness and inexperience allowed her to be. A word, a kiss, one passionate movement and she would have been his. But he could not make that movement.

Yet she woke him to a consciousness of women as no one before had ever done. He was twenty-six years of age and had never yet kissed a woman, save in friendliness. Now, even in these few dark troubled days, he looked at the women about and around him with new eyes. Hetty Cumberlege had done that for him. But he did not love her. He was sorry, but he did not.

The consciousness that she was ready to love him at a moment's turn embarrassed him terribly. He wished that he had Deborah there to advise him. Every look from Hetty's eyes (and she gave him a great many) made him feel ashamed. He would have liked to love her. He felt now that it would be delightful to love some-one, but that someone would not be Hetty.

He would have spoken to his father about his troubles, but his father had been removed from him in some strange absorption of his own. His father had shown a surprising gentleness and kindliness these last days, but he had been alone. And by his own wish.

So here David and Hetty were watching the Prince enter Carlisle. The crowd by the city gates was so thick that they caught only a glimpse of him. David was far taller than the

majority around him. He saw, as a flash of sun struck from the
heavy winter clouds, the fine white horse and on the horse a
youth with a gallant air, his head up, a smile of pride and
courtesy and triumph on his lips. He looked like a king. He was
happy that morning as, had they all but known it, he was never
to be happy again. The horse tossed its head, a hundred pipers
played, and the sun went in again behind the clouds.

So then they went home. There was a very lively company in
the parlour. Mrs Cumberlege had found the general excitement
too much for her retirement, and there she was laid out on the
sofa. To David she was truly an amazing sight, for her stoutness
and shortness of figure gave her, lying there with a handsome
China shawl over her knees, the appearance of a bolster. Her
face was very red and she had on top of it her best wig, powdered, curled and greased, dressed high over a large cushion and
decorated with imitation fruit and a little ship with silken sails.
Mr Cumberlege was there, two ladies, and a jolly old fellow with
a wooden leg, who announced himself as Captain Bentley. He
was apparently a stranger in the house, and could not be sufficiently polite to Mrs Cumberlege, whose stout cheeks were all
smiles and whose head nodded with pleasure so frequently that
the little ship travelled on stormy seas indeed.

The talk was, of course, all of the Prince. An amazing calm,
and even gaiety, had for the moment come upon the town. It
would not last, but, just now, no one was alarmed any longer.
The Prince was here. He was charming, handsome, and who
knew but that in a week or two he might be master of the
country? Moreover, his Highlanders were here too and were be-
having with the greatest propriety. Not a single act of riot or mischief had been reported. It was whispered indeed that a number
of ladies were sadly disappointed . . .

The white favour was becoming for women with every
moment more popular.

As to Captain Bentley, you might think that there was no
Prince and no Highland invasion. He sat on the edge of his chair,
which creaked beneath his weight and the glory of his plum-
coloured breeches and silver buckles, and forced upon Mrs Cumberlege incidents of his personal experience. He was very
honest about his drink, and proud of it too. He declared that he
could swallow a bowl of punch and two mugs of bumbo without
any difficulty whatever, and told a long tale of how, being in
Wapping, he had a fierce toothache and could find no one but a
woman to pull the rogue, which she did with so muscular an

arm that he thought she must be a man in disguise, until inquiring further he found that she was a woman indeed.

'Fie! Captain,' said Mrs Cumberlege, laughing most friendlily at him, upon which he would have bent forward to whisper in her ear had not the stink from her wig been too strong for two by no means sensitive nostrils. He had also a grand tale of how in London a month or two back he had seen a show of moving pictures. Truly marvellous. You could see a coach roll out of the town, and a gentleman in the coach saluted the company, and you could watch ships sailing upon the sea and a man come to light a lamp in the Tower. In return Mrs Cumberlege had a sister-in-law who had seen a live griffin at a Fair and he had shot fire from his mouth, which had so sadly frightened her sister-in-law that she had given birth to triplets before her due time.

There was a bowl of punch, and both Mr Cumberlege and Captain Bentley became very merry indeed, and even the three ladies found their sentences coming none so clearly.

During all the gaiety Hetty and David sat close together in the bow-window. The streets were now dark outside, but many people were about. The cobbles echoed their steps. There was laughter and singing, and everywhere you felt the sudden relief, the freedom from panic.

Romance, too, was in the air. For good or ill this young and beautiful Prince was now in their city. Everything, it seemed, was giving way before him. After all, was he not one of our own people, no foreigner? Had not that sound of 'James III' cried on the steps of the Market Cross a pleasant echo in the air?

And for Hetty Cumberlege, too, this was the most romantic hour of her life. This huge young man, who sat so close to her, so brave, so strong, so proper a man, she thought that he loved her and presently would say so. It was true that she feared his father, but he would not live always with his father. It seemed to her impossible that they could be related, so different were they. The candles burning in the room, the flickering firelight, her mother for once in a good mood: now surely it was designed that he would speak.

How marvellous a chest he had, how beautiful a neck, what glorious eyes, how direct and honest he was: she could trust herself to him for ever. A little shiver ran through her body. She hung her head. She did not dare to look at him.

And David said never a word. His was not a quick nature, but yet quick enough for him to realize, with an awful sense of horror, that she was waiting for him to speak. He could see it in her hanging head, her trembling hands. This was for him the most terrible moment of his life. He longed to move, but was frozen to his chair. He heard the merry Captain and Mr Cumberlege trolling a song from an infinite distance. What must he do? By whose fault had he tumbled into this dreadful dilemma? She was so sweet, so young, so pretty. She would be wonderful for any man to hold in his arms, to press his cheek to hers; and yet he did not want to hold her. He wanted only to escape from the room. His great clumsy body seemed to him to fill the room and to swell ever larger and larger as he stayed there.

'There are many people yet abroad,' he said.

She raised her eyes, looked at him, and dropped them again.

'Yes . . . But it is cold. I think there will be snow.'

'At Herries, where we live . . .' he began desperately.

'Yes?' she said, looking into his eyes again.

'Wintertime the snow lies on the Fell to a great depth. Many sheep are lost in it.'

'Poor things,' she said.

'Sometimes in winter they must carry a corpse over the hills from valley to valley. When the snow is deep 'tis no light matter.'

'I like the summer best,' she answered.

How he longed to say: 'Hetty, dear, I like you so, but I don't love you. I wish I did.' Instead he told her about his sister Deborah. She was not interested. Her hand stole out and nearly touched his breeches. Had she touched him he might have yielded, and all his life, and the lives of many future Herries, been other, but her hand stole back again.

'Father is greatly pleased that you are here,' she ventured.

'I am glad,' he answered.

'And Mother too.'

'I am very glad.' She meant that someone else was greatly pleased too, but she did not say so.

'We must be returning home in a day or so,' he said, his face burning. 'I have business, an interest in two vessels in Liverpool. And maybe I shall purchase a farm.'

'You are very young for so much business,' she said, and again she looked at him.

The thought came to him that this proclamation of his prosperity might be considered a foreword to a proposal, so he said hurriedly:

'It is not much. A small venture.'

If something did not happen soon he was lost. Something did

happen. His father saved him. The door opened and Francis Herries came in.

David, his heart thumping his deliverance, went to meet him. Hetty, a minute after, left the room and running up the stairs, closing her door, threw herself on her bed in a passion of tears.

Herries meanwhile had had his own strange hour. He felt, because of it, soft and gentle to all the world. That night struggle on the wall had left him first as a wounded, then as a convalescent man and, in this convalescence, he was oddly gentle.

He felt a great and persistent weariness throughout his body, and everything about him – the town, the people, the crisis – was removed behind a sort of dream-curtain. Just now this Mirabell Starr was the only real thing to him in life. She was more real by far than he was to himself.

That same afternoon he had seen and talked to her. He had been wandering through the streets, lost in his own thoughts, but getting behind them an impression of this day's events very different from the one in Cumberlege's warm parlour. There was relief, it was true, but beyond the relief a sulky stiffening, a sense of humiliation and apprehension. It was as though, with a kind of second-sight that he had, he could feel the doom that was coming to this place, could touch Cumberland's swollen cheeks and smell the hot stench of that black hole where nearly four hundred poor wretches, huddled and trampled like cattle, were, in so short a time, to pant their strangled lives away. He could see, it might be (and yet not see), brave Coppock drawn on the smart new sledge through the English Gate to execution, and gaze upon that sad procession now only two months distant, the officers with their legs tied under the bellies of their horses, the privates on foot marching like felons, two abreast, fastened by rope. If he did not see these things he felt them in the air, which was growing with every moment colder and was made bitter by a driving wind that held in its lap a steely sleet.

He had reached the farther end of English Street and was about to turn when Mirabell all but ran against him. Three times now within the week chance had brought him to her, or perhaps it was not chance. There was to be one more . . .

She was cloaked up against the wind and seemed to him infinitely young and fragile. They encountered under a lamp-flare, and she knew him at once. She smiled. He could see that she was in some fear, and that stirred him at once to a sharp passion of protection.

'Mr Herries,' she said.

'You should not be out alone,' he answered her quickly. 'Not now, towards evening, the streets as they are.'

She did not repulse him. She seemed glad of his company.

'I am going to my lodging,' she said rather breathlessly. 'In Abbey Street. Behind the Cathedral. I have a room there.'

They started along English Street. She looked back.

'You see no one following us?'

'No,' he said. 'Who should be following you?'

'No one . . . but now, the town as it is . . .'

'Take my arm. No one shall touch you while I am here.' The pride he felt as he said that! And the rush of blood to his heart as he knew the touch of her hand on his arm!

'I know who it is,' he went on. 'A short, thick, black-bearded man with a chill hand.'

'You know? Yes. Anthony Thawn. But how do you know?'

'I saw you, a week back, in the "Silver Horn". I was quite near to you. There was a green parrot and this fellow stroked its neck.'

'Yes. He is a friend of Harry's. Harry is my lover. I am greatly afraid of him, Mr Herries. I have never been afraid of anyone before, and it is not for myself now but for Harry. He pretends to be his friend, but I know that he is not. He was first a friend of my uncles. He was with us here when we first came to Carlisle. Then when my uncles went to Scotland he stayed. He would make love to me if he dared. Harry is so simple that he thinks Thawn is his friend. I have told him no, but he will not believe me. Always when I leave them alone I am afraid of some evil . . .'

She poured all this out as a little child might, confident in her hearer's interest. And indeed Herries was interested, so deeply that it seemed to be his own history to which he was listening.

'I have seen your lover. He also was at the "Silver Horn". He has a noble face.'

'Harry! Yes, he is noble! When we go from here he will marry me and we will live in London, where he has a brother. Harry is a poet. He is writing a grand poem on "Dido and Aeneas". I can't tell whether I have the names rightly. I have never had any education.'

'But could you live in London, when you have been always in the open? Seeing you on Honister I had thought you could never endure a town.'

'I could live anywhere with Harry. He also loves the country as I do, and when he has made a little money we will come back

to the mountains. He will find patrons for his poem. He says that
is often done.'

How different, Herries thought, love has made her. She is still
a child, but all the wildness and rebellion are gone. His heart
ached, but the touch of her hand on his arm consoled him.
Perhaps he could help them, these two, and in being a friend to
them find his salvation. They were both so very young.

'This fellow Thawn,' he said, 'if he troubles you I will rid you
of him.'

But she shook her head. 'That is not so easy. He is very
strong.'

'I, too, am strong,' said Herries.

'I have no fear,' she answered confidently, 'when I am with
Harry. It is when I am away from him. He trusts everyone. He
can see no harm in anyone. If he had had my life he would not be
so trusting, as I am always telling him.'

They were skirting the Cathedral. They would not have
many more minutes together.

'I told you,' Herries said, 'on Honister that I am always by
you if you need me. Will you promise me, if you are afraid, to
come to this place? It is in the very middle of the town, only five
minutes from here. If I am away I will let them know, so that
they can always find me.' He gave her the name of Cumberlege's
house. 'Do you promise?'

She looked at him, then nodded her head. 'Yes, I promise.'
She sighed, he thought, with some relief. 'Here is my lodging,'
she said.

Abbey Street was a quiet, staid place behind Tullie House. It
was a thin house with neat stone steps and a light in the upper
window.

'Thank you. I am sure that Harry is here. The light is in my
room.' Her voice had changed to a radiant happiness. She had
already, he thought, almost forgotten him. She ran up the steps
and into the house. He watched her until she was gone.

All that night he dreamt of her.

Events moved swiftly with him then. That next day, November
19th, was to be a marked day for him his life long, and for more
than one reason. He left Cumberlege's house after three of the
afternoon; by six of the evening that had occurred which gave
his life a new strain never again to be lost.

By the Market Cross he was confronted with Roche. He had
been expecting this meeting. Roche had in Keswick told him

where he would be found in Carlisle, but Herries had not sought
him out. Roche belonged to his old life, not to this one. But here
Roche was and recognizing him instantly; indeed Francis
Herries, with his proud arrogant carriage, his scar, his high
sturdy figure, was not a man easily passed.

Roche's pleasure at the meeting was moving. He was dressed
in civil clothes, but as a very grand gentleman. The grandeur
suited him well. His black coat was of silk, elaborately laced, and
at his side there was a slender gold-hilted sword. He wore a tie-
wig and a three-cornered hat of dark felt and laced. His pale,
long, aristocratic face was grave and dignified, and not jubilant as
Herries would have expected it to be.

He caught Herries's arm and walked with him as though he
would never let him go again.

'Well,' said Francis, 'your prophecies have been found true.
You must be a happy man.'

But Roche was not altogether a happy man. As they walked,
their cloaks close about them because of the bitter wind, Roche,
dropping his voice, spoke his doubts. All was not as well as it
ought to be. True enough that, with Edinburgh and Carlisle in
their hands, the Government forces apparently dismayed, they
had prospered to a marvel. But there were dissensions in the
camp.

'His Royal Highness is but a boy, and has had little experience
as yet of governing men. How could it be otherwise at his age?
But there are the Irish. They have great importance, perhaps too
great, in his councils. There is Lord George Murray. He is stiff-
necked and obstinate and hates the Catholics. He has but now
sent in his resignation because His Royal Highness had left the
Duke of Perth and Murray of Broughton to arrange the terms of
surrender without consulting Lord George. His Royal Highness
had written Lord George a very sharp letter in which he had said
that he was glad to hear of his particular attachment to the King,
but was sure he would never take anything as a proof of it but his
deference to himself. This to Lord George, who considered himself the God Almighty, was a bitter word. But they could (Roche
was forced to confess) ill afford to lose Lord George, who had a
great sense of strategy and the discipline of armies. The Lord
knew they needed discipline (here Roche sighed), and it was
hard to come by in such an ill-composed army as theirs.

'There was, too, great division of opinion as to the next steps
to be taken. It was said that the Government was sending an
army of ten thousand under Sir John Ligonier to Staffordshire.

Some were for a return to Scotland, others for remaining here to wait the rising of the North Country Jacobites. The Prince himself was for marching forward.'

Herries could see that Roche was in great perturbation of mind and longing for a confidant. He seemed to have no doubt at all as to the direction in which Herries's sympathies would lie, and was, it appeared, ready to confide to him any secret. He had aged very greatly since Herries had had any long talk with him, but that was natural enough, for a number of years had passed and he had been engaged in much perilous enterprise. But he had changed, too, in spirit. He seemed to have no longer anything of the religious zealot about him, but was completely the man of affairs, and with the discovery Herries also realized that all Roche's old influence over him had gone, his power and his charm.

He was eager to know what Herries felt to be the mood of Carlisle. Were they for the Prince? Had Herries not seen in the reception of the Prince's entry a disposition to enthusiasm? One more success and might it not be that the whole of the North would turn?

Herries said what he could and, snatching at any encouragement, Roche insisted that he should come now to see His Royal Highness and assure him of this. Even though it were only for five minutes. He was himself on his way there.

Herries had no wish to be dragged into any definite partisanship, but against this his curiosity to see the Prince was very great. So he went with him.

The Prince was lodging at the house of Mr Charles Highmore, Attorney-at-law. This was a white-fronted house on the west side of English Street, standing back some yards from the main thoroughfare.

Roche and Herries passed under an archway, sufficiently wide for a carriage drive. Above the archway was a big bay-window, and the whole house seemed spacious. There were glimpses of a fine garden at the back of it.

At the doorway and in the entrance hall there was a great bustle. A big fire burnt in the hall, officers were standing in groups, messengers coming and going. Leaning over the banisters of the wide staircase Herries saw two small children watching wide-eyed all that was going forward. Roche, begging Herries to seat himself for a moment in the hall, vanished behind a green-baize door.

Herries waited there. He realized that his presence caused

very considerable interest. One stout, thick-thighed officer, grandly dressed, warming his back at the fire, stared at him persistently. He was always afterwards, for no reason that he could define, to remember this officer with his swollen cheeks, pug nose, legs tight within their sky-blue silk breeches.

It seemed to him, although this impression may have been unwarranted, that there was some carelessness and disorder over the hall bustle, too much shouting and calling out and casual argument. Only a giant Highlander, who must have been some seven feet in height and was broad in proportion, stood motionless near the entrance. It was at him that the two children, breathless on the stairs, principally gazed.

It was cold and exceedingly draughty. The fire blew out of the open fireplace in flurries of smoke and flame. Some faded green tapestries of gods and goddesses feasting flapped on the wall. Near the baize door a group of young officers stood in whispered consultation.

He had taken this all in (and for the rest of his life it would remain with him), when he saw Roche come through the door and approach him.

'His Royal Highness,' he said, 'is most anxious to see you.'

He followed Roche through the door (pursued, as he knew, by the curious eyes of everyone in the hall) into a small, darkly wainscoted room. There was a table with a bowl of fruit, a finely carved fireplace and some high-backed chairs. On the mantelpiece was a big gold clock, very handsomely mounted, with the moon and stars portrayed and a Cupid with a small gold hammer to strike the hours.

Only two persons were in the room. One was a plump gentleman with a good-natured kindly face, who stood turned to the window that he might see better some papers held in his hand.

The other was warming himself at the fire. This was a lad in a grave handsome dress of dark purple, wearing his own hair, a diamond star at his breast. This boy's face was of a most delicate oval shape, the chin weak, the mouth rather too full. His splendour (for he did that day seem splendid) lay in his eyes of a deep eloquent brown, bold and haughty, brave and inquiring, and in the magnificent carriage of his beautifully shaped head, the carriage by natural right divine of a king and a ruler of men. His hair was of a fair brown, catching the light so that it seemed gold-tipped.

This was Prince Charles Edward.

But he was a boy, a child, an infant! Herries, in that first glance and then as, bending a knee and kissing the hand, he looked up into those eyes, was transfigured by surprise.

He had known that the Prince was but twenty-five, about the age of his own David; he had himself again and again wondered what it must be for such a boy to be in charge of so wild and tumultuous and kenspeckle an army, but in some imaginative fashion the events of these last weeks had altered his vision. The Prince, seen only through event, had grown and aged in the consequence of his successes. But now, face to face, why, beside David himself who could have taken him across his knee and with one gesture broken him, he was unbelievably a child.

And then, rising from his knee and exchanging with him look for look, Herries had a curious moment of vision.

It is an old tale that a drowning man sees in one instant the whole course of his past experience laid out as on a map. So now Herries, looking into that young man's eyes, had, in one moment of time, a vision of a world.

In Paris carts rumbled over the cobbles under a snowy sky, the French King lolled on his bed, scratching his stomach, yawning, then stretching a fat naked leg to see whether last night's drinking had dulled the use of it. A courier, waiting in the cold hall with dispatches, shivered and thought tenderly of his new mistress. At Calais the snow was beginning to fall, and along the deserted beach an old man in rags that blew in the wind wandered, searching for sea-trove. On the Dover Road a coach plunged up the hill, while within it, rolling in sleep one against another, two men and a woman dreamed of money, lechery and food.

The clouds gathered ever more thickly over Europe. In Vienna it was a blizzard, by the Hague the sea was rising and tumbling in huge swollen billows along the deserted shore. In London the Hanoverian King stumbled as he climbed the stairs, swore a German oath, wondered for the hundredth time which among his treasures he must take with him to Hanover if a sudden flight caught him. He had a violent cold and that old pain in the left side that hurt him when his nerves were out of order.

All through London that afternoon panic was spreading. No one had any thought but for himself and his. A man swung from ledge to ledge above a back court of the Strand, his pocket stuffed with rings and necklaces. He dropped eight feet, stumbled and was up, running through the falling snow, like a shadow, down to the river. In a room lit only by the firelight a lover was buttoning his smallclothes, a lady arranging her hair before a mirror. The clouds descended ever lower and lower over London. Out of a window and above the river a lady was leaning, looking out to hear whether even now she could catch the High-landers coming. On the Great North Road the coaches were running, and two miles before Doncaster three footpads were waiting, their horses shivering in the cold. Such a snowy night was good for the trade.

Up on the fells above Brough and Appleby it was desolate indeed. A shepherd, trying to shield himself from the fierce wind, searched for some lost sheep, calling to his dog, glancing up at the sky as though it had some personal and especial message for him.

In Kendal and Penrith and Keswick, men sheltering by fires, busy over their money-making, had only one topic. The Pre-tender was in Carlisle. Carlisle had fallen. First Edinburgh and now Carlisle. An old man, dying in a farmhouse by Caldbeck, wandered in his delirium and called for the girl of his heart, now forty years dead. Two women, in a rich house by Grange, quarrelling over cards in their high gilded drawing-room, paused suddenly to listen, because above the fall of the stream under the bridge they seemed to hear the tramp of soldiers . . .

What did Herries see? What did Herries hear? He only knew that before him was a child, ignorant, impetuous, brave and tragic, and that as he breathed, as his hand went to finger the lace at his throat, as he felt for the skirt of his purple coat stiff with whalebone, Europe, carrying on its wheeling surface, as on an indifferent turntable, the hearts, the souls of these little men, wheeled another turn in her history, this boy for a single bitter instant the moving force.

Tragedy! Herries could see it in every stir and flicker of the flame behind him. This boy to rule England, this boy to meet those heavy, cumbrous, cruel forces now advancing to encounter him! He could, in that second of understanding, have taken that boy in his arms, hastened with him to deep obscurity, protected him until the crisis was past.

Then the Prince spoke, and it was a king who was speaking.

'Mr Herries,' he said, smiling most charmingly, 'you are welcome. Mr Roche here says you are an old friend of his.'

'Yes, sir. It was pleasant to meet again.'

'And what do you think of the feeling in this city? Is it favourable to us?'

'I am a stranger here, sir. From the little I have seen I would say that feeling is divided. Many are waiting to feel the current of the wind.'

The Prince looked at him. Here was a man. Young though he was, he was no poor judge when his prejudices were not already stirred and his liberty not threatened. Years later, in 1771, when he was sheltering shabbily under the roof of the tailor Didelot, hunting round for a wife, the Irishman Ryan introduced him one drunken evening to a tall lean fellow, with a scarred face, a famous ragamuffin duellist. Lolling, paunchy and red-faced, on the shabby sofa, looking up at the fellow, Charles Edward remembered that other man with a scar. Where had it been? And when? In the close, hot, smelly room, thick with smoke and stinking with drink, his bemused mind went back to that other scene: Carlisle, high burning hopes, courage, pure ambitions, England open before him, and that strange, stern, ugly fellow who carried himself and spoke like a leader. The grease dropping from the slobbering candle was mixed with his own maudlin tears. That day . . . and this . . .

'Sheridan, this is Mr Herries of Keswick.'

The stout man turned from the window, smiling. They bowed and shook hands.

'What do you advise, Mr Herries; that we should go forward or stay where we are?'

The unexpected and casual directness of this startled Herries: he fancied that some lack of caution in it had startled Sir Thomas Sheridan, too, and not for the first time.

His natural honesty, as always, drove him.

'I cannot tell what information Your Highness has obtained. I am sure that time is a most important element in your favour. I am sure, too, that many who are secretly on your side are waiting for your success before they join you. If by pressing forward very rapidly you are likely to reach London within a very brief period of time, I should push forward. If your progress is likely to be slower, then I should remain in the North until more of your friends come out to you.'

'Yes, yes . . .' answered the Prince impatiently. Then it seemed that he caught Sheridan's eye, for he turned abruptly back to the fire, stared into it a moment, then wheeled round to Herries again.

'Of what sort of a place is Keswick, Mr Herries?' he asked.

'It is a small town, sir, very remote from the world.'

'Your place is in the country?'

'Seven miles from Keswick, in a valley beyond the lake.'

'You have much rain there, I have heard.'

Herries smiled. 'It is a changeable climate, sir. We have every sort of weather.'

The Prince shrugged his shoulders. '*Peste!* Every sort of *bad* weather. I know the changes; hail one fine day, sleet another, snow a third. You should try the south of France, Mr Herries. There it is all sunshine and beautiful ladies.'

Herries smiled. 'I have no doubt, sir. But I love this cold North Country. It has something magical for those who feel it.'

The Prince laughed.

'Eh, Sherry? Shall we leave this business we're on and settle down in the mountains to shoot bears and frighten the wolves? Poor Sherry! Mountains and bears are not for your stomach. For myself, I don't know. But, Mr Herries, you had better come with us. We will lead you into the sunshine.'

Herries paused, then looking the Prince between the eyes he answered: 'I am afraid the public world is no longer for me, sir. I am forty-five years of age and no very good company.'

The Prince looked back at him, honestly and quietly. They liked one another.

'*Eh bien!* Yours is no doubt the better part. We have little choice in our destinies, I believe. Fate is with us, and then, a change in the wind . . .' He shivered, made as though he would kick the fire with his foot, half turned his face.

'At least you wish me well.'

Herries said: 'I will always wish you well, sir.' He hesitated, then went on: 'I would only say that I love England with a passion. I believe that you have the same love. And, were I younger—' He broke off. 'I hope you will believe, sir, in my sympathy.'

The boy looked at him with some touching appeal in his eyes. There was fear there, some hint of dismay and confusion as though, only now, he were beginning to realize the impossibility of the task that he had at first so gaily shouldered. Herries's heart went out to him, just as it might have gone to David in trouble.

He bent the knee and kissed the hand again, bowed and left the room.

In the street again he said goodbye to Roche, promised to meet him shortly, saw him vanish into the dusk. He did not know that he was never to set eyes on him again.

A little bemused, he stood hesitating. Then, as though he could step no other way, he turned down English Street towards the Cathedral. It was not dark yet: there was a queer, green, owl-ish light through which snowflakes were falling, fragments of ghostly wool. Very few persons were now about. He crossed into Abbey Street, which was quite deserted. He stood in the shadow by the long wall of Tullie House. It was cold, but he did not feel it. There was no wind.

How absurd! He was watching, like any young moon-calf, outside his mistress's window. There was no light in the demure, thin-lipped house, where she was lodging. He could see the number – Thirty – in clear Roman numerals above the door. There was no stir of life anywhere.

But he knew the strangest satisfaction in standing there. It was as though he were protecting her, although, for all he could tell, she might be in the other end of the town. And there was also a sense that he was expiating a little the frantic temptation that he had known on the wall. That gave him, oddly enough, the only conviction of sin that he had ever known. He had done many evil things in his life and had dealt ironically with them all. But this . . . He had stepped farther then into monstrous countries than ever before. Was it only because this had touched her? Or because he was, in his old age, developing a new sense of sin? Time perhaps that he did. Or was it that sentimentalism, a senti-mentalism of the very kind that he had always most despised, was creeping over him? Or was it a sort of frustrated lust? Because he would not yet possess Mirabell he imagined a noble aim in himself? Ah, that last, God forbid! He did not want to possess her – or at least not that mainly – he wanted to care for her, be good to her, make her happy . . . And then, having used her, would he not tire of her and forget all his nobility, as he had with so many women before her? For the instant the picture of Alice Press came back to him; Alice Press when he had first seen her, when he had first had her, when he had tired of her, hated her, sold her . . .

He nodded his head to himself. Yes, this was most truly some-thing other, something quite new in him, something growing, like a plant, in his soul. If there were indeed a soul . . . If there were not, there was at least something in him that was not only animal; his great white horse plunging through the black lake, climbing the splintered hills – she was, for him, of the world of that dream.

The door of the house opened. He was almost opposite it, but the shadow, thickening as the early winter darkness crept upon the city, covered him.

Two came out. They were Mirabell and her lover. He caught her face for a moment under the light by the door, and she seemed in an ecstasy of happiness. She was pressed close to the boy, who had his arm around her. He watched them go, quietly, down the street. He was never afterwards to know what still kept him there. His business was over. She was well protected, and, as his constant irony drove him to perceive, by the only protection that she coveted. She had, he could not doubt, lost all awareness of him. Perhaps, after seeing him, she had told her lover, and together they had laughed at the thought of that ugly, elderly courtier, laughed kindly but with the selfish, indifferent confidence of blissful lovers.

He felt the cold now and drew his cloak close about him. Yes, it was cold and he was alone, and the street was very silent. He was conscious again, as he looked at the light above her door, of a sense of doom that lay over the city and over the Prince whom he had just left and, it might be, over himself. For himself he did not very much care.

But for Mirabell . . . Mirabell . . . Mirabell . . . An absurd name . . . a man's name. He looked back to that Christmas feast so long ago, the woman standing by the door, the child huddled against her skirt. It had been that woman's romantic notion to call the child Mirabell after some play perhaps. Congreve's *Way of the World*, was it? or perhaps she had heard the name spoken or seen it on a news-sheet. Mirabell . . . Mirabell . . . Yes, the mother to whom he had once given his coat must have been a romantic creature, filled, he had no doubt, with unsatisfied longings.

The door opened again. A man came out. It was Thawn.

Herries caught his black face in the light, but there was no mistaking the fellow's walk, that lurch, that slouch, that roll from heavy foot to heavy foot. He walked, too, with his head sunk between his thick shoulders as though he had no neck.

An animal, by God, a wild hairy animal, possessed by the Devil. He paused by the door. He was considering something, and his face was as evil as a face may be and yet be in some sort human. Then he lurched away, moving, in spite of his awkwardness, with great speed.

There began then a strange pursuit. Herries followed as though he had been ordered to do so. But it was like a pursuit in a dream. They seemed to move in a dead city. Herries could never remember afterwards that he passed a living being. As he moved anxiety grew in him. He had no reason, but with every step his fear increased. Thawn never looked back, nor hesitated. He seemed to know exactly his direction and purpose.

They kept to the dark side-streets, came to the Castle, skirted it and, turning a corner near the city wall, saw the girl and boy but a little in front of them.

Then it was they whom Thawn had been following.

The girl was standing folded by her lover's arms. His back was towards them.

There was a sudden alteration in Thawn's movement. He walked more swiftly, but very silently. His feet made no noise at all.

At that same instant Herries understood.

He ran, crying 'Look out! Look out! . . . Take guard!' But he was too late. The boy turned, but with that same movement Thawn struck, his black arm, the pale chill of the back of his hand, the knife shining. Herries caught these and his thick, pulsing, stertorous breath like a bear's grunt.

The boy fell without a cry, and Thawn was gone, moving like a shadow into the shadows of the dusk.

The girl flung herself down, then stared up at Herries, not seeing who he was.

Herries knelt, pulled the shirt down, felt the heart. The boy was dead. His own hands were a mess of blood.

'He's dead,' he said, touching her hair, which fell, loosened, about his hands.

'You lie,' she answered.

Then he bent his will and purpose to do all that should be done.

Part Three

THE WILD MARRIAGE

CANDLELIGHT RESPECTABILITY

On a beautiful summer afternoon, in the year 1756, David and Deborah rode into Keswick. Deborah was proud because, for the first time, she was riding her new horse, Appleseed, that David had given her. Old fat Benjamin had named him. It seemed to Deborah a very pretty name. She was excited, too, because they were riding in to a Ball and were to sleep three nights at Keswick. Although Deborah was now thirty-three years of age, a very great age indeed, she was still wildly excited by a Ball. She could not think how David could remain so calm.

But David was always calm. As she looked at him now, gigantic (he was six foot six inches in height, and broad with it) but placid, smiling to himself at some notion that was, she was quite sure (she thought to herself), to do with ships or tallow or grain, she loved him more than ever, but was a little indignant with him too. She would have liked to stick a large and sharp pin into the rough broadcloth that covered his immense, immovable back.

It was a Ball at the Assembly Rooms (the first of the season), and they were to stay for three nights with, technically, Uncle Pomfret, in reality, Cousin Raiseley and sister Mary.

In the year 1750 Cousin Raiseley had married sister Mary. Deborah who, in spite of her placidity, had some good strong feelings within her, hated her cousin Raiseley and had always disliked her sister Mary. It was, she had thought at the time, a very suitable match, only she had supposed that Mary would have made a smarter one. Heir to a baronetcy though he was, Raiseley was, after all, with his poor health and country background, no very great catch for anyone. It was true that his social value had risen a little after his sister Judith married the Honourable Ernest Bligh, who might, with good fortune, be one day Lord Monyngham, but Judith, after her marriage, disregarded her family entirely, and never again came near Keswick – no, not even when her mother died.

It was well known, too, that neither Raiseley nor Mary had been a grand success in London. That was why, perhaps, they had married one another, a fellow-feeling making them wondrous kind. So back to Keswick they had come, Raiseley to cheer the remaining years of his poor old father, who could not move for the gout, Mary to rule the household, and so much of Keswick as she could ensnare, most tyrannously.

They did not often invite Deborah to come and see them, and Deborah had determined to refuse when they did, because Mary would not see her father, would not come out to Herries, would not speak to him if she saw him in Keswick.

'If Father is not good enough for Mary I am not,' said Deborah, and then sighed because there were so many who would not speak to her father.

But now, on this occasion, her father had insisted that she should go. He had kissed her, looking at her with that queer, ironical smile that still, even after all these years, frightened her so strangely.

'Thou'dst best go, Deb. And maybe there'll be some spoiling of the Egyptians. Anyway, it will help Davy.'

So they had left him, standing in the little grass-grown court-yard with fat Benjamin and Benjamin's thin wife Marjorie (whom he had married out of Newlands some ten years ago), standing there gaunt and shabby, grand and lonely, shading his eyes against the sun, then turning back to the old house with that odd, absorbed, dreaming look as though he had already for-gotten them, almost, with that one turn of the heel, putting them out of existence.

They were climbing up out of Grange, and soon the lake came into view. It was an early autumn afternoon of crystal clarity; the lake, Skiddaw, and Saddleback behind it, were as though they were enclosed in a series of mirrors. The lake was a bowl of pale-blue glass, cracked here and there with silver splinters. Over a portion of it shadows of rose amber tumbled with a faint, rippling stillness, as though one were breathing on it to stir it. Lord's Island lay on this silver-blue like a ball of ebony ruffled at its edge by the silhouette of its trees. On the farther side the fields, bright green in the sun, rose to the slopes of Saddleback that was beginning gently to change from amber to purple, and behind the dark line of the hill the sky was almost whitewashed, with a little colour.

So, as the eye travelled upwards, it moved from dark to light, from light to dark, but always with the tranquillity of perfect harmony. The air about them, as they rode, shared this crystal purity with the scene. One pale cloud, blown open into the shape of a great white rose, travelled over their heads.

For Deborah this Lake had grown to have almost a magical splendour. Although Rosthwaite was some miles away, she walked continually to Grange, to Manesty, even to Portinscale, to sit beside it, listen to the trees whispering and the broken ripple of the tiny waves against the stones. Even physically she had some kinship with the Lake. In no way beautiful, rather broad and shapeless of figure, her pale gentle face, her hair faintly gold, her steady honest gaze, her spiritual *quietness* belonged to the coves and shallows and wooded shelters of the Lake-side. There was strength and force, too, behind her gentleness, just as the Lake had strength and force. She lived securely and proudly within her borders as the Lake lived.

As they rode she noticed all the trees, mountain-ash, holly, ivy, hawthorn, yew; and they were all transformed for her into a sort of glory. Rocks here and there by the side of the lake glittered in the sun. She thought to herself how passionately moving this world would be were she seeing it for the first time on such a day. She would surely say to herself: 'This must be a very holy place.' But now that she knew it so very well it was not less holy, and in every different mood it seemed to have a different holiness.

David broke the beautiful silence.

'We're coming to a new time, Deb, a modern world; with these new toll-roads our valley will be enclosed no longer.'

'It will be better for riding to Keswick.'

'Aye, there'll be good things doubtless, but it will be sad to see the old world go. I doubt that you will find anything grander in the world than our Statesmen – Peel and Elliot, and Curtis and Ramsay, more self-dependent, more self-sufficing, owing nothing to any man . . .'

'They have been cruel to Father,' she answered fiercely, an odd fierceness to come from her placid countenance.

'Nay, not cruel,' he answered with his customary slowness, as though he thought every word out before he uttered it. 'He's strange to them, and I don't wonder. These last eleven years – we've talked of it many a time – he's been like a man lost. Since the Rebellion, when we were in Carlisle, he's been a "fey" man. As though he were searching for something he could never mind. He loves me, I know, but he'll tell me nothing. He's as strong and hearty as he was twenty years gone – more hearty for all the walking he does – but it's of no avail to try to keep him to business. He is happier walking the Fell than any other way, he's happier silent than speaking, happier alone than with company. There was something in Carlisle, all those years ago . . .' He broke off, then turned on his horse towards her, speaking more rapidly: 'I've never told you, Deb. I've never told any man. There was a night in Carlisle – after the Prince made his entry – I was climbing into my bed: I had gone an instant to the window to see whether the snow was falling. I heard the door open and turned. Our father was in the doorway, white as a cleaned stone. He stumbled and held by the bed post. I thought he would fall and ran to catch him. He held by my shoulder. His nails dug into the flesh. I asked him what it was, whether he were sick. He nodded his head and looked as though he did not see me. He put his hand flat on my naked heart.

'"Aye, sick," he answered me, "and unhappy, Davy." Then he went out. I did not dare to follow him. I waited, listening for a sound. There was none. In the morning he was as he has been since – closed, lost and alone. They are right to fear him, Peel, Curtis, and the rest. He's a man lost.'

Deborah answered at last:

'He was never as we were, never like any other. But I love him now as I never did. I always feared him. Now I would be proud to comfort him, would he let me.'

'Aye, but he will not let you – nor anyone.'

They rode on silently for a time. Then David spoke again.

'I have a hard evening, Deb,' he said. 'I've to tell Christina that I'll not be marrying her.'

'Oh!' cried Deborah. 'I'm glad!'

'Yes.' He nodded his head. 'You never liked it, Deb. I fancy you will never care for me to marry. But it must be one day. I must have children. But it'll not be Christina who'll be their mother.'

'What's decided you?' she asked him.

'I do not love her. I have never loved her. I thought she'd be grand for a wife, in all the outward things, you understand. Mellways would be a fine house and there's broad land with it. She's kind, but wearisome. Her voice has a fearful monotony. And she doesn't love me herself. It's her dogs and her horses that have her real fancy. She's been thinking I'd be good for looking after the horses.' He chuckled in his slow, drawling way. 'And her eyes are not even,' he added.

'I'm glad, I'm glad.' Deborah almost sang it. 'I knew that you were not lovers and that she would contemn Herries and would take you away and would think me a dolt. Aye, she does that already.'

David sighed. 'But it will be uneasy telling her. I'm not grand at speeches. Love's a strange thing, Deb. You go to your bed thinking that you love a girl and you wake in the morning to know her eyes are crooked . . .' He hesitated, then went on: 'I should be marrying. I was six-and-thirty last Martinmas, and I've money enough now. But it's the children rather than the woman I dream of.'

Deborah answered: 'You're in luck, Davy, because you're a man. I'm younger, and yet I'm now an old maid. I could have loved a man, but no man has ever fancied me.'

'Tonight, maybe,' said David. 'Don't lose heart, Deb.' But he didn't say it with great conviction. It was true. Deborah had always been an old maid and would always be one. Not like her sister Mary, who had made eyes at men since she was a baby.

As they rode through Portinscale village over the stream by old Crosthwaite Church into Keswick (the shadow of Skiddaw, russet and silver-grey, sprawling above them), he fell into thought.

He had very much to think of. He was a boy no longer, a man of thirty-six. Things were approaching a crisis, and he must come to some man's decision. He could see, looking back over the last ten years, that he had been almost incredibly influenced in his actions by his father's: incredibly because his father had neither by word nor action tried to influence him, had told him indeed, again and again, that he must break away, make his own life now, leave him and even forget him.

His affairs had developed beyond all reasonable expectation during those years. The little enterprise in Liverpool that had started with a share in two small trading vessels had grown until he had his finger now in half a dozen Liverpool ventures. He had bought land in Borrowdale, beyond Keswick towards Troutbeck and at the farther end of Bassenthwaite towards Cockermouth. It was not that he had a brilliant head for commerce, but he was notably honest and upright, very sure if also slow, kindly and agreeable to deal with. He had, too, a wider and deeper sense of the social changes that were moving under his feet than had most of the men around him. He perceived that these years that followed the '45 Rebellion were opening up the North. He could not perceive that he was now living at the commencement of England's great new industrial life, but he understood something of the new inventions and sniffed more in the air. It would be fifty years yet before the world that he foresaw was in true being, but, in his own small individual way, he was part of it.

But, with this new and exciting world of affairs, his father

would have no touch; nay, would not, could not. He had been
willing, almost eager at first, to help in the little Keswick office
that David had now for his own behind the Assembly Rooms towards the Kendal road. He had a brain far abler and more brilliant
than David's, but it would not stick into these items of lading
and shipping and transport. He did not care: he could not
bother with it.

So, after a while, he slipped back to Herries, and David was
glad that he went, for not only did he confuse any issue that he
touched, but his own unpopularity with the outside world hampered the business at every step. It was not only the old evil
reputation that he already had, but the new evil reputation that
he was for ever creating. He no longer kissed the women and
gambled and drank with the men. It had been better maybe if he
had. He held aloof from all social contact; when he met a man he
looked at him with his cold ironic eyes and as often as not turned
on his heel without a word, and this, as David knew, not from
scorn, arrogance or pride – these fires had remarkably died in
him – but rather that his mind was altogether elsewhere, searching for something, dreaming of something, regretting, hoping –
at least in no mood for Liverpool trade.

So back to Herries he went. Here, too, he was odd, almost to
madness. He would have no stranger in to improve the house.
He or Benjamin or David might support a tottering wall, mend a
gaping stair, fill in a window – no strangers. Nor would he permit
David to buy more land to go with the house. There was at one
time a fair lot available that would have made Herries a fine
property, but Francis would have none of it. He dug still in his
one or two barren fields as he had always done, planted what
would not grow, dug to sterility, and was quiescent. This and his
rovings gave him a kind of restless contentment. With every year
he roved farther – looking for what? for whom? On horse or on
foot he had covered all the country from Shap to Gosforth,
from Uldale to Stanley Gill. Every stream and every hill he
knew. Here, in this soil and rocky fell, lay his passionate devotion. One of two; the other unsatisfied.

To David and Deborah his manner remained always the same,
jestingly ironic, scornfully loquacious, lovingly friendly of a
sudden, then for a day, two days, a week utterly silent, while his
eyes roved, his ears were a-cock listening for a step. It was
keeping company with a haunted man.

But where in this lay his influence? David could not say,
except that quite simply he loved him. He loved him, it seemed,

more with every year and understood him less. As Deborah had once said, where she and David left off, their father began. He was in country that they had never so much as seen a map of.

But things were reaching a crisis. David hated Herries. He had perhaps always at heart hated it since, the first of that family, he had crossed its threshold and seen those chill suits of armour receive him. He hated the house for its darkness, gloom, damp, moth-eaten, grudging spirit. He hated it because of the things that had happened there – the long-ago evil of Alice Press, his mother's death, old Mrs Wilson the witch, and all the superstition and avoidance that had grown up around his father there. He wanted to leave it to die its own death. He was convinced that if he could take his father away from there his father would become another man. This odd wearisome passion his father had for finding something that would put everything right and fair would die in another, healthier atmosphere. David loathed everything that was dark and damp, morbid and introspective, superstitious and nightmare-ish. These things, he thought, did not properly belong to his father, but had been bred in him by the place.

At his engagement to Christina Paull he had expected a settlement. They would live near by Penrith, and his father would live with them. But Christina had plainly denied that, and so had his father. His father had loathed Christina, calling her a 'tight-nostrilled bitch', but had in no way persuaded David against the marriage.

'A mare like that,' he had said, 'cannot step in between our lives together, not though you live in China.'

And David had found that true. Without saying a word, his father had in some way shown him how truly impossible Christina would be.

David had been greatly relieved to see the impossibility; but yet, did it mean that he was never to escape his father, never have his own life, nor children, nor freedom? Why did he love his father so fiercely, when he did not at all understand him and often was infuriated by him? There was some bone in him that was his father's bone. That was the only answer.

As they rode into Keswick he shook his head with a kind of despair, and Deborah, who had been riding quietly on Appleseed beside him, looked up as though she expected him to speak. But he said nothing, only sighed very deeply.

And so they came to old Uncle Pomfret's house.

Externally it had not changed very much in the last twenty-five years. When David, as a small boy, had first seen it on that memorable occasion of his visit with his mother, it had seemed a palace of a shining and a glittering splendour. Now it was a small place. The trees had grown in the garden, the fountain, once of so incredible a beauty, was now diminished and stained with rain: *sic transit gloria!*

But within Mary had made everything as fine and modern as Raiseley's stingy habits would allow her. She had two footmen, and in the saloon (which appeared now to David amazingly small) a beautiful Bury four-backed settee and some exceedingly handsome Chippendale chairs with cabriole legs.

Although, as David very well knew, she cared nothing at all for literature, she had *Sir Charles Grandison*, Thomson's epic poem, *Liberty*, and Glover's tragedy, *Boadicea*, prominently displayed on her table.

He regarded his sister critically: never having liked her, he had not denied her opulent beauty. She was yet beautiful, but was too thin and haggard, and her eyes and mouth wore a discontented and peevish expression. The Herries, because of their prominent horse-like bones, were not advantaged by thinness. Her cheeks were strongly painted, and her wig very high and decorated with pompoms.

She greeted her brother and sister with the condescension she always used, but, David thought, with a certain anxiety, as though she would, if she knew how, win them to her side. At their entrance the two infants, the boy Pomfret, aged five, and Cynthia, aged two, were in course of display to their reluctant relatives. They were plain children, the girl clear Herries, thin, pale and bony, the boy plump, with the features of his grandfather. They howled lustily, and had to be removed by their fat kindly Aunt Anabel, whose complacency seemed armoured against any vexation.

The little parlour was hot and over-filled with Herries. Grandison, his wife Mary, and Cousin Pelham were there; Uncle Harcourt, now sixty-eight years of age, frail and delicate like a piece of china; and Dorothy Forster, stiff in creaking black, as gloomy and funereal as ever.

Pelham was the grand one of the party. He was now thirty-eight years of age, still a bachelor, very elegant indeed, and kindly with it. He seemed to Deborah's country eyes the handsomest man she had ever seen, with his slim body, suit of black and silver; he was Herries at its most elegant. All the Herries breeding seemed to have concentrated in his repose of bearing, humorous knowledge of the world, languor, superior indifference. Deborah could not but wonder what it was that had brought him to so rustic a ball in so small a country place.

It was his mother who had brought him, he having gone to her, as on many another occasion, to see whether she had a plan that would relieve him of some of the more tiresome of his debts. These were the only occasions when he did go to her, her maternal solicitude and anxious care of him boring him exceedingly. But he was always courteous to her when he *was* with her, making up in manner what he omitted by his constant absence.

This time she had the excellent notion that Uncle Harcourt might be of use. Here was a source untapped, and, if Herries gossip were to be trusted, a rich source too. It stood to reason that a bachelor, living alone in a world-away seclusion like Ravenglass, with no one but himself to consider, must have a fair sum of money put by. Moreover, little Uncle Harcourt was sixty-eight, and, as things were, could not be expected to live for ever ... So Pelham had already suggested to his little uncle that he should come and stay for a while at Ravenglass, and the charm of his manner had been no whit abated by the obvious reluctance of his uncle (who was not born yesterday) to have him.

Mary Herries, stout, overbearing and ill-mannered, had tried to subdue her personality to the desperate needs of her son, and had wooed Harcourt like any sucking-dove. This had been no easy task for her, and the entry of the large handsome David, who was, she knew, Harcourt's favourite nephew, did not please her at all. She gave David the barest of greetings, and poor Deborah no greeting whatever.

Deborah indeed found her ultimate comfort with poor old Uncle Pomfret alone in his room, trophies of the chase mouldering about him, and his leg (already huge enough) swollen to twice its natural size and laid out on a chair in front of him.

Poor Uncle Pomfret, rotten now with gout, and deserted in his own house, seventy-eight years of age, and no one caring whether he lived or died! Gone were all his blustering, hunting years; gone his oaths, his country pastimes, his childish prides, his simple pleasures!

When his wife Jannice had died, he had thought, poor fool, that it was not a bad thing. She had worn him to an irritable thread with her medicines, tempers and dominance. Now, on how many a lonely afternoon he would wish her back again! His gout would have been for her the very thing that she wanted! Would she not have loved to posset him and bleed him and cosset him! Might they not have found in their mutually sick old age a mutual love and comfort?

It was true that his daughter Anabel did for him what she could, but it was Anabel's mania these days to be, of all things incongruous with her stout form and rosy cheeks, a blue-stocking.

She had corresponded with Mrs Delany and sent a long screed to Lady Mary Montagu on the smallpox, and, on a visit to London, she had attended a meeting in Mrs Elizabeth Monta-gu's famous Chinese drawing-room in Hill Street. Nothing would hold her after her return, and although she was kind to her old father when she thought of him, she forgot him for most of the time.

So there poor Uncle Pomfret was, and tears poured down his cheeks as Deborah sat beside him, stroked his puffed and swollen hands and settled his pillows. Huskily he asked her how her father did, and could not hear enough of what she had to tell him.

'Brother Francis! Brother Francis! He was closer to me than any of them. But I was afraid of your aunt, my dear . . . And Francis didn't want me, didn't want any of us . . . I mind when I went to see your poor mother afore she died – poor soul! Sitting up in bed for manners' sake when she was almost gone. Francis felt her going, although he was always too clever for her . . . Here, bend thy head a moment, little darling, and I'll whisper thee something.'

Deborah bent her head and felt his hot liquorish breath and the odd touch of his burning hand against her fresh cheek.

'When thou hast a man, don't take one too clever like thy father, for he'll dream without thee; nor stupid like thy old uncle, for he'll not dream at all. Do thou the dreaming, and he'll never leave thee.' He thought this mighty clever and lay there chuckling until the chuckle brought on the gout, and his pain was a torment to see.

On the third night was the Ball.

They did not go until nearly eleven o'clock, because they were the gentry and it was not genteel to go too early.

The Assembly Room was a small room, even by Carlisle or Kendal standards, but to Deborah it seemed like Paradise indeed.

She would have clapped her hands, had she dared, at the shining candles, the little gallery with its gilded scroll where the musicians were, the alcoves where the food was – jellies,

syllabubs, cakes, orgeat, lemonade, fruits and the rest – the
gleaming floor, the hangings of red and blue, the rows of benches
down the side all covered with persons in the most beautiful
dresses.

It was the second ball only of her life, although she was thirty-
three, and by contemporary standards an old maid. But she did
not look thirty-three that night in the new dress that David had
bought for her in Liverpool. This dress was not grand, with its
modest hoop and gentle frills and fichus, but its rose colour went
prettily with the freshness of her cheeks and bosom. Her figure
was too large and full, but this tonight gave her strength and
honesty, and she had always masked gracefully, like the well-
born lady that she was.

At first she could see little, because of her terror of the enormous Mary Herries at whose side she seemed remorselessly
attached. Mary Herries and Grandison were almost the largest
persons in the room, and looked double their natural size because
of their magnificent clothes. Mary Herries's hoop was as wide as
the globe, and her wig, in which nestled birds, flowers and fruit
of the gayest colours, towered to heaven.

Grandison in crimson and silver, as stout as he was tall, as
superb in his own estimation as he was stout, was thought by
some of the yokels peering in through the door to be the King of
England. Well, they were Herries from London, and so must
show these country bumpkins!

In a brief while, happily, they forgot Deborah, and she was
able to sit on a bench and look at the world.

The townspeople were dancing country dances; the minuets
would come later.

Deborah, who had a sharp Herries eye, saw many things: how
the townspeople grew demure with the appearance of the gentry
and plainly less happy; how little Mr Gibbon of the china shop
(whom she knew well and liked greatly) was already drunken, and
his wife in an agony of alarm; how charming Pelham was, moving about so gracefully, speaking to everyone with such kindness;
how greedy and sulky Raiseley was, going to one of the alcoves
by himself and helping himself to syllabub; how grand Mary
thought herself, moving about among the townspeople as though
she owned all of them, but always with that unhappy, discontented look in her eyes; how speedily David had caught a glimpse
of Christina Paull and moved hurriedly in another direction (and
what a darling, and how handsome and how superior to everyone
else in the room!); and what fun the country dances were (her

feet were moving to the gay tinkling little tune!), and how she did hope that someone presently would invite her to dance; and what fun balls were, and why had she not been to more of them; and how the girls clustered together and giggled and made eyes at the men (and how odd it was that she had not a girl friend in the world, nor had ever had one), and—

At this moment she was aware that someone was sitting very close to her, and this someone a man. She turned round and saw, next to her on the bench, a short, sturdy little clergyman with a chubby face.

He must, she thought, be someone's private chaplain, perhaps from the Castle at Cockermouth or one of the grand country houses. He looked a gentleman (she stole several very careful glances). Many of the clergymen known to her had been little better than the peasantry, living a life of the utmost poverty and treated accordingly. Most of the grander clergymen she had heard of never went near their parishes, and visited Bath or Harrogate.

This clergyman – his hair was tinged with grey – looked healthy, strong and a gentleman. She thought him very pleasant. And apparently he thought her so, for presently he shifted his broad shoulders and turned to her, smiling most charmingly. He apologized for not allowing her room and stood up that she might have more. She, blushing, begged that he should sit down again. But he looked very well standing there on sturdy legs, his face a fresh colour, his eyes (as she was ashamed to notice) very large and fine.

'Pray, sir, be seated,' she said, smiling in her turn.

'I fear I incommode you.'

'Why, no, sir, there is room.'

He sat down again.

'The music is excellent,' he remarked.

'For a little place, I agree,' Deborah replied, feeling a proper woman of the world.

Very soon they were talking. He told her that he was but newly come to the neighbourhood, being in charge of a Cockermouth parish. He told her that he had been chaplain to Lord and Lady Padmont in Rutlandshire, and very kind patrons they had been. She discovered, too, that he was greatly interested in Nature and especially in birds, and this was a great link between them, because she was interested in Nature too.

Then he asked her whether she would not care for a little refreshment, and they walked together to the alcove. She did not know whether she were not exceeding proper modesty in this, but after all she was thirty-three and he was a clergyman.

Then, over a syllabub, he introduced himself. His name was Gordon Sunwood, the Sunwoods of Gloucestershire. He was, he told her, thirty-eight years of age and (blushing at the confession) a bachelor.

He then added, touching (quite accidentally) the back of her hand with his, that he was a bachelor because he had not until now seen anyone who combined the qualities of a saintly spirit, a beautiful person and a merry heart. He wasn't sure, he added, whether the last were not the most important of the three. He did enjoy a joke, and had found nothing in Holy Scripture to condemn such a taste. But there: of course, were he ever so fortunate as to discover the Fair Divinity with the triple merit, it was unlikely that she, on her side, would be ready to share his modest Parsonage and slender stipend. But to *that* he must add (this he almost whispered, sinking his voice to an incredible roguishness) a certain little fortune of his own, left him by a friendly aunt, so that things were not so bad, and in case of offspring . . .

But, at this point, Deborah could only decide that he had been drinking a little. And yet, even though he had, she could not but think him charming. It was true that clergymen were little higher in the social scale than hostlers or dairymen, but Deborah was no snob and, considering that she lived in a tumbledown manor with a father ostracized by all the countryside, she had no reason to be. In any case she did not care. She liked this little man with the round bullet head and cheeks like a russet apple and thick sturdy back and warm voice and clear twinkling eyes. Nay, although she had spoken with him but ten minutes, she more than liked him already. And this was her first adventure with a man in all her thirty-three years!

David meanwhile was having an experience less agreeable than that of his sister. He noticed neither the shimmering candles nor the fiddle, fife and drum, nor the orgeat and syllabub. He had eyes only for Miss Christina Paull, and they were not, alas, eyes of love.

He wondered as, fixed into a little corner with this lady, he glanced at her, how he could ever have contemplated matrimony with her. And as with many a man before and after him, behind the immediate misery of his horrid task was a glimpse of the glories of later freedom.

Miss Paull made things more easy for him by, most rashly, laying down some laws for their future comfort. She was a very determined young woman, Amazonian in build and colour, smelling freshly and quite pleasantly of the stables and spreading her legs apart as though she were always, in her imagination, astride a horse.

What she wanted to say was that she was very sorry indeed, but that after their marriage David must leave his father behind him. She had heard rumours that he intended to move his father along with him.

David saw his advantage. Like many another who contemplates diplomatically a quarrel, he snatched at any trivial excuse for one.

'My father is not to be moved thus lightly,' he said. 'If he cares to come with me, he will come.'

Christina, with that kindly good-humoured patronage that she applied to all human beings (regretting that for their own advantage they were not horses or dogs), explained patiently that she meant no criticism of his father; she had no doubt but that he was an excellent man. Nevertheless he was not a comfortable man, not an easy man, not an ordinary man. Married persons were better without relatives in their house.

That was undeniable. David did not contradict it, but, shifting his huge body on the little gilded chair until it creaked again, he remarked that perhaps, maybe, after all it were possible . . . The words choked in his throat.

But Christina Paull knew well enough what it was that he intended to say. She was not at all sure but that he was right. She was as independent as any of her feminine descendants two hundred years later were likely to be. Her only relation was her old father, who was drinking with the stable-boys most of the day and drunk with the neighbouring Squire all the night. Nevertheless she had, since her plighting with David, heard so much of his own scandalous father that she was already half shrinking from her bargain.

She was no very sensual female; men would never mean very much to her, but David had caught her with his strength, health, amazing bodily vigour. But when she had bedded with him a month or two and the novelty of it was worn a little, what then? – there would be the father, the strange family history, witches and adulteries and general vagabondage . . . She was not so sure.

But David was quite sure. His mind was suddenly clear, his courage certain and undaunted.

He smiled at her charmingly, as though he were offering her a kingdom, and said:

'We'll not be marrying, Christina.'

She took his statement as clearly as he gave it.

'It is, perhaps, wiser.' She looked at him, and liked him better than she had ever done before.

'I think,' she said, 'I'm not a marrying female.'

In his relief David would have offered her the gold of the Indies had his hands contained the treasure.

He nodded his head. 'I also. Marriage is a hampering state.'

She laughed, then bent towards him, tapping his shoulder with her fan, like a horse in skittish mood. It was a frank age. 'There is nothing against going to bed with you, David, on a dark night,' she said.

David crimsoned to his fair hair.

'I doubt that you'd like it,' he said. 'I'm a heavy sleeper.'

So they parted most excellent friends; and, a year later, Christina married Sir Roger Bollinger, who knew more about horses, cock-fighting and the breeding of spaniels than anyone in the north of England. She had nine children, and behaved to them as a bitch does to her puppies, caring for them when they were young and tender, but, when they grew, forgetting them entirely in the odours of the stable and the ardours of the chase.

And David – but that is another story.

The minuet was over. David, watching its last delicate graces, was amazed to see that his Deborah had for her partner a little stout parson, who, strutting, preening, flaunting, bowing, was like a cock before its mate.

The dance concluded, the little parson bowed and retired after showing Deborah to a seat. There David found her. She was flushed, her bosom heaved, her eyes shone; she was prettier than he had ever seen her. He seated himself beside her.

'Why, Deb,' he said, 'what's this? A clergyman?'

She seemed scarcely to hear him, then turned to him and answered: 'He is the Reverend Gordon Sunwood. He is of a Gloucestershire family. He has now a living in Cockermouth. He has been very attentive, David.'

David took her hand between his. 'Dear Deb . . . And is he already a suitor?'

She took her hand away. 'That is unkind. He has only talked with me a little. He is interested in Nature, and has a remarkable knowledge of birds.'

David chuckled. 'Beware, then, of his bird-nesting.' Then,

boyishly happy over his freedom, he went on: 'It is done, Deb. The task is over. She is of the same mind. As I am no horse nor a rare-bred dog, she is to be yet a maid. And we are good friends over it.'

Deborah almost danced on her bench.

'Oh, Davy, I'm so glad. 'Twould never have done. She'd have made you sleep in a kennel and given you a fine bridle. Oh, Davy, I am so happy! I was never so happy before nor saw anything so beautiful as this is! Are not the lights fine? – and although I had not danced since Christmas, Mr Sunwood found me "exquisite". That is what he said! I – exquisite! But to watch the world and its follies; I swear I could sit here the night through!'

'Yes,' said David, smiling at her, 'with the bird-fancier at your side.' As he looked at her, a tender compassion over her happiness pervaded him. She who had for so many years, without grumble or complaint, borne the closed-in, stifling, melancholy life of Herries, making no friends, having no gaiety, fighting her fears and loneliness and depression without a word to anyone, there was courage and character there! And to be so deeply pleased with this little country scene and amateur gaiety! Shame on himself and his father that they could have suffered it so long!

He could have kissed her there where she sat before them all, but they were interrupted by the portentous figure of Aunt Mary Herries, who hung over them like a battleship and finally demanded his company.

But Deborah was not to be alone for long. Of all amazing things, the elegant and wonderful Pelham had sought her out and was sitting at her side.

She would have been afraid of him had she been less happy. As it was, he caught her happiness and her freshness, and to his stale thoughts, plain though in truth he thought his country cousin, there was charm and pleasure here. His heart was good, though his morality was worn.

He was at his most delightful. Timidly she asked about London and the grand world. Gaily he told her tales and anecdotes and adventures, all of a decorous kind. He told her how a friend of his, Mr Spencer, had married Miss Pointy, and come up to town in three coaches-and-six with a company of two hundred horsemen.

He gave her dreadful details of the Lisbon Earthquake. He described to her the London fashions: how gowns were pinned rather closer than before, hoops as flat as though made of pasteboard and as stiff, the shape sloping from the hips and spreading at the bottom, enormous but not so ugly as the square hoops. Heads now very variously adorned, pompoms with some accompaniment of feathers, ribbons or flowers; lappets in all sorts of sizes; long hoods worn close under the chin, the strings go round the neck and tie with bows and ends behind. Night-gowns worn without hoops. He was as gay and attentive as though she were the only lady in the world. It was true that he did not ask her to dance, but perhaps he was wearied of dancing.

Before he left her, very earnestly looking her in the eyes, he said: 'Dear Cousin Deborah, pray for me on occasion. I wish all the world well, save myself. I have the taste to be a monk, but, alas, not the character. I am going to the devil as fast as may be, but have dreams of another world.'

As he said this, he had, she thought, a strange look of her father, something ironical, regretting and doomed. She felt very, very tender towards him. But when he was gone, the most charming and distinguished person in the room, her eyes were looking, her heart was beating for her little clergyman. She could not help herself. She did not know whether it were right or wrong. She did not care.

And he returned to her. He bent towards her, sinking his voice to the most delicious of confidential whispers. He told her that he had been thinking only of the moment when he might come to her. He offered her his arm. They walked the length of the room together. He complained of the heat. She acquiesced. They passed behind the hanging curtains, pushed a door, and they were in a little yard at the back of the Assembly Rooms, under a sky sheeted with stars, a faint breeze whispering at their ear.

'You will take cold.'

He put his arm about her. She leaned against him, and could feel his heart beat against her arm.

He asked whether he might write; she murmured 'Yes'. And he bent his head and kissed her, the first kiss from a lover that she had ever received.

So the evening had gone well for Deborah.

THE WILD MARRIAGE

THEY RODE off next morning in the pouring rain. This rain was the especial and peculiar property of the district, rain that must often fall behind any chronicle of human lives here.

It was rain of a relentless, determined, soaking, penetrating kind. No other rain anywhere, at least in the British Isles (which have a prerogative of many sorts of rain), falls with so determined a fanatical obstinacy as does this rain. It is not that the sky in any deliberate mood decides to empty itself. It is rain that has but little connexion either with earth or with sky, but rather has a life of its own, stern, remorseless and kindly. It falls in sheets of steely straightness, and through it is the rhythm of the beating hammer. It is made up of opposites, impersonal and yet greatly personal, strong and gentle, ironical and understanding. The one thing that it is not is sentimental.

The newcomer is greatly alarmed by it, and says: 'Oh, Lord! Lord! how can I live under this!'; the citizen of five years' habitation is deprecating to strangers but proud in his heart; the true native swears there is no rain like it in the world and will change it for none other.

Any true chronicler of the Herries family will be forced, frequently, to speak of this rain.

David and Deborah, their horses, Absalom and Appleseed, passed through it as though it were their only wear. The whole country was blotted out by it, the lake quite invisible, the hills smothered in quilted cloud. The path, that could not yet be dignified by the name of road, was in a condition of indescribable mire and ruin. It needed a very little to make it difficult; tomorrow it would be impassable. But the horses plunged and waded their way through, while the trees bent to the deluge and the hammer beat, beat, beat in the clouded barriers of the mist.

David and Deborah were very happy, riding home. They said very little to one another, because it was difficult to talk through the rain and because each had important thoughts to investigate and arrange.

David was happy because he liked (as all true Herries like) his meeting with the other Herries. He had felt a warm companionship with his poor old Uncle Pomfret, with Uncle Grandison, with dear little Uncle Harcourt and especially with Cousin

Pelham. With all of them, different as they were, there had been a blood tie which he had recognized and they also.

Pelham had shown especial friendship and had invited him to London. David thought that he would go. It would be good for his business; he felt, too, a sympathy with this world of brocade, silver candlesticks, soft voices, delicately nurtured women. He had been a savage too long. He knew now that he was not much longer for Herries. He was happy, too, because he had escaped from Christina Paull, and escaped so politely, with neither harsh words nor hurt feelings.

And Deborah? Deborah swam through the rain in a streaming and glorious splendour. Her happiness was so great that she was truly and magnificently born again. The kiss of last evening had transformed her. She rode, her head up, her eyes alight, her mouth curved in a retrospective smile. She did not doubt but that she would marry him. He had not asked her, but he would. He was honest and good. A clergyman? Well, but she was very suited to be a clergyman's wife and the mother of a clergyman's children. At the thought of the children her heart hammered with joy to answer the hammer of the rain. How good, how generous, how well-wishing life was!

So they rode, and it was not until they were feeling their way cautiously through the mud below the Bowder Stone that Deborah was suddenly uneasy. What distressed her? She could not say. She was very sensitive to these mysterious, unreasoning impressions, and especially in this valley, which had always seemed to her to have a peculiar, magical quality of its own. She told herself at first that it was her thought of Mrs Wilson and her horrible death that still, after all these years, lingered with her. She always hated Cumma Catta Wood, with its pagan sacrifices and scent of murder. But soon, as they turned down the lane that led to Rosthwaite, she knew that it was not that.

She was increasingly apprehensive. It might be her dislike of Herries; especially it seemed to her dreary and forbidding after the social brightness of last evening. But it was not Herries alone. On the little mound that rose above the shaggy path that led to the house her father was standing. They could see him, waiting there in the rain, his cape over his head, leaning on his stick.

David said: 'Father is waiting for us. Something has occurred.'

And Deborah, as so often she had felt before at the thought of her father, knew a sickening apprehension of dismay. Some evil thing had come.

Then when she was face to face with him she knew that he was radiantly, wildly happy. She had never seen this light in his face before. It transformed him, even as she herself had been transformed last evening. At the sight of his happiness she, too, was happy again. Her apprehension left her, and when he held her and kissed her wet cheek she stayed with him, letting his arm encircle her.

He was happy and he was shy too. They had dismounted from their horses, but he kept them there. 'Wait!' he said. 'Before you go to the house . . .' He seemed like a boy, in spite of his grey hair, long about his neck, and his figure, bent a little from his persistent labours.

'There is someone . . . I must tell you . . .' He stammered a little. He put his arms about both of them, drawing them to him, and the rain fell all round them in walls of silver steel.

'There is a lady here in the house; this very day I am to marry her. Davy, Deb, be kind to her. She is strange here . . . Please me in this.' His voice was triumphant, as though he wanted all the world to hear his news.

They were bewildered; intent upon their own affairs, this sudden transition was amazing, paralysing. Marriage? Their father? Now? At once? At Herries? But whom? Was this some sudden freak, mad gesture, crazy eccentricity?

'Marriage, Father? Today? Here?' David was stammering in his turn.

'Yes – today. Here.' His father mocked him, pressing him closer to his side. 'I was in to Keswick yesterday. I have been bustling; have been with the surrogate, and have the licence. And this afternoon there will be the clergyman. Don't be angry with me, Davy, for not telling you. For eleven years now I have served my 'prenticeship, and she has come to me of her own free will. These last months it has gone hard with her. Be gentle with her.'

David was silent. What was he to say? Who was this woman? Another Alice Press? But behind his almost breathless astonishment was the thought that this new move would, whatever else it involved, help him to his own freedom. But then, as they neared the house-door, his love for his father overwhelmed every other emotion. It might be that this would be some woman who would be good to him, care for him, devote herself to his comfort.

He turned at the house-door and put his hand on his father's arm. 'If this is for your happiness, Father,' he said, 'Heaven bless her, whoever she may be.'

He had in his mind (thinking still, possibly, of Alice Press)

the image of some large opulent woman who had caught his
father's fancy. He mounted the stairs and turned into the
dining-hall, which was, even now in this morning hour, brilliantly lit by a high cluster of candles on the broad table and a
great fire in the open fireplace. Under all this splendour the
tapestries, the portrait of old Herries leapt in the air, and the
room was alive with the drumming of the rain on the panes.

A girl in some dress of flaming orange and crimson, seated on a
low stool, was crouching towards the fire, her head in her hands.

As they all came in she turned round facing them, and then,
seeing them, jumped to her feet as though to defend herself.

The three stood for a moment motionless by the stair-head
while the girl confronted them. She made indeed an astonishing
picture. For David she would always be the figure of that first
moment. But it was not for him the first moment. He recognized
her at once as the 'robber-girl' (so he used to call her) whom, in
the old long-ago days, he had met up and down the roads,
begging of him, mocking him once and again, always – to his
Herries sense of order and decency – the outlaw and vagabond.

But indeed she had changed since then. That had been a
child: this was a woman. She was of a bitter thinness, tall, and
her small white face like a mask set with fierce hostile eyes. Her
wonder, then as now, was her hair, which fell in ringlets about
her shoulders and in the firelight was, with that glow, its own
lambent flame. Her dress was fantastically over-coloured: a
bodice of bright orange with silver buttons, a hooped skirt of the
old-fashioned shape a burning crimson, and faded yellow shoes.
She was, in her small peaked face, like an angry child, but her
body was mature and her hands, long, thin and very white
against her dress, those of a grown woman.

Francis Herries went across to her. 'Mirabell,' he said (and
David wondered at the gentleness of his voice), 'this is my son,
David, and this my daughter, Deborah. They will be loyal to you
and devoted as they have been always to their father.'

David went over to her and took her chill, lifeless hand.

'We are old friends,' he said smiling, 'so it is not hard to be
new friends too. I hope you will be happy with us.'

She did not answer, but looked at him with her fierce, protesting eyes.

Deborah went and kissed her on the forehead. 'Indeed I hope
so,' she said.

The girl, at the touch of Deborah's lips on her forehead,
trembled, but still said nothing.

Herries said to his son: 'Come away, Davy. I have business with you.' He smiled back at the two girls. 'We will return, but you will be better friends without us.'

He clattered down the stairs, David following him.

Deborah, left alone with this strange hostile creature, had an impulse to turn and flee. A sort of terror seized her, as was often the way with her; but her own deep happiness, which nothing here could touch, reassured her, and there was something in that white, small face and the wide, staring eyes that moved her heart. That her father was to marry this wild girl seemed to her an incredible thing; but everything about her father was incredible to her, and had always been.

She came close to her.

'I did not hear your name,' she said. 'Mine is Deborah.'

'Mirabell.'

'Mirabell! What a pretty name!'

'No, it is a crazy name. My mother had it from a play. It is a man's name.'

Deborah did not know what to say, what question to ask, but the girl broke in fiercely:

'You may hate me as much as you will. It matters nothing.'

'But why should I hate you?' Deborah asked.

'To be here, in your house, a stranger. It is not my will. I have no will any more. I came to your father yesterday because I was hungry. Once, many years ago, he told me to come. If I had had food I would not have come. They put me in prison in Kendal for a wanton. I was three months in their filthy gaol. And then for two weeks I have been hungry. Your father has been good to me; therefore because he wishes to marry me I will marry him, and then, when he is weary of me, I will go away again.'

She spoke in a kind of fierce defence of herself, her eyes never still, roaming about the room like those of a captured animal.

Deborah was touched to pity. She put her arm round the girl and drew her down to the settle by the fire.

'Oh . . . in prison! How cruel! And hungry for two weeks!' She caught her cold hand and held it to her.

'Cruel? No. Why? I may have robbed or lain with men, asking them in the streets.'

'Well . . . If you did . . . Still it is cruel. Kendal gaol . . . I have heard of it.'

'I did not steal nor lie with men. But only because I was proud. Now I am proud no longer. Anyone can do anything with me.' Her thin body under her gay dress shivered.

'But now you must be happy,' Deborah said. 'We will make you happy, all of us.'

'No, you cannot make me happy. I can never be happy again, but I will work for your father and give him what he needs – if I can.'

'And Father has known you a long while?' Deborah said.

'Since I was eight years old. And now I am twenty-seven.'

'You must not be unhappy . . .'

But the girl drew away from her, rose up, stood looking down on her.

'Happy? Unhappy?' she said scornfully. 'That is nothing . . . It is only that when you have been hungry long enough you must have food.' She turned her back on Deborah and stood looking into the fire.

They were silent then, until Herries came back. After this he dominated the scene. In their own separate fashions they all surrendered to him. The strange girl seemed to have a driving desire to make herself of use, and, speaking to no one, moved down and up to the kitchen, taking plates from Benjamin's wife, helping with the potatoes, rubbing the silver – all with a kind of hostile fierceness.

Herries showed his wisdom by not attempting to prevent her, nor did he speak to her, but his eyes were never away from her when she was near to him. It was as though he could not believe in his luck. He had thrown off his years. He was almost a boy again. His body was straightened, the thin, pointed face with the high bones had lost its grey pallor and was flushed with colour. His head was up and his voice rang with joy.

He had been shopping in Keswick, raided the neighbouring farms, stirred Mrs Benjamin (who could cook when she liked) to make pies and puddings. Soon a great feast was laid out on the broad table under the portrait of scornful old Herries. There was a fine paste of almonds with candied cherries, plums and currants. There were two fowls, a splendid pie (for which he must have paid dear, thought David, remembering also that it was his mother's money that bought it), wheaten loaves, China oranges, walnuts and plums, candied Madeiras, citrons and muscadine grapes.

To drink, there was to be a grand bowl of punch made after Major Bird's famous recipe, Batavian arrack and good honest ale.

For whom was all this? Were there to be guests, and if so, who? No questions were asked. Everything went forward.

The little chapel was only a step away. The rain, too, had now ceased to fall, and the sky was filled with little round fleecy clouds stained with blue shadows.

Herries appeared in his grandest dress, a suit that had lain in the big oak chest for many a year, something almost of Queen Anne's reign, strangely out of fashion, its colours faded, fitting oddly with his ugly scarred face and long grey hair. He had a dove-coloured waistcoat woven with gold. His cloth coat was of cinnamon colour, his sword was silver and gold-hilted, with figures on the handle, and he carried a cane with an amber head.

A strange pair the bride and bridegroom made as they started out together down the lane, he walking very proudly, she, her arm through his, hanging her head and looking like a gipsy from a fair. Deborah and David walked behind.

At first no one saw them. Some men and women were working in one of Peel's fields, and looking over the hedge caught a sight of all this glitter and colour. Then an old woman at a cottage door had a glimpse and called out after them. Then some children playing by the great oak tree near the inn had a sight of them, and all came trooping after.

At the door of the inn there was a little wizened, hunch-backed pedlar selling his wares. He, too, came hobbling behind.

Little Rosthwaite Chapel by the village was one of the smallest in England, and passing under the porch Herries and David had to bow their heads.

The clergyman was waiting for them, and almost at once the little place was filled with the children, the pedlar, some old women. For Herries the scene was some dream long dreamt by him, now accomplished in reality. Since the moment when she had come knocking at the door of Herries and he had opened it to her (would that be for ever the most miraculous moment of his life?), his happiness had been so strong, so universal, so overwhelming that he could neither realize nor see objects outside it. There *were* no objects outside it. This joy had covered all the world like a great cloak of surpassing brilliance. The others, David and Deborah, had but just ridden off to Keswick. He had gone back into the house and set about polishing the silver on some harness. The knock had sounded through the still, withdrawn place, mingling with the eternal murmur of running water. He had seemed to know that the knock announced great news, for he had hastened down the old stairs, flung open the door. And there she had been in the little grass-grown court, at fainting-point with hunger, in her bright shabby clothes. He had caught her in his arms and carried her in. From that moment his happiness, unquestioning, undoubting, had risen like a wave all about him and drowned him. He scarcely saw the girl herself in his triumph.

She was here; she needed him, and she would stay. Would she marry him? Yes, she would marry him. At once? Yes, at once if he wished it. Would she stay with him? Yes, she would stay with him. She acquiesced in everything, while he fed her and gave her drink. He placed her in Mrs Benjamin's care, then went out for the licence, the parson, the grand food, the liquor and a chain of fine gold that he bought off a Jew in Keswick. All that night he lay alone on his naked bed, seeing only her, thinking only of her, staring into radiant bliss. How David and Deborah would take it scarcely stirred his imagination. He loved them. He hoped that they would be glad; but if they were not, the brilliance of his happiness would not waver.

So now, when he stood in the tiny chapel and took Mirabell Starr for his wedded wife, the shabby little place was ablaze with glory. He bent and kissed her cold unresisting mouth, then passed down the aisle again between the children, the hunch-backed pedlar and the old women. Outside a crowd of people had gathered. He waved his hand to them and, in a voice ringing with joy, told them that they would one and all be welcome at his house. They all followed after, whispering among themselves.

Deborah's memory may be the truest mirror to catch the scene that followed. Into the heart of her old age that scene remained as something framed off by itself, apart in colour and shape and fashion, something wild and fantastic beyond conception.

First, the quiet of the Borrowdale road and the little grey village, the peaceful sky in which all the little clouds were turning rose as the sun went down, the barking of dogs, the fields softly lit by the gentle sun, Rosthwaite Fell a kindly guardian hovering above them, ducks waddling in silly procession, an old woman sweeping her doorway – and through this placid quietness Herries and his bride in their silver and cinnamon, their orange and crimson, he marching as though he were conqueror of the world, she beside him, looking in front of her, neither to left nor right, her face a mask; then David, striding towering over the rest but shy of this pageantry; herself, Deborah, feeling the rosy sky, the pale green of the sunlit fields, the dark shadows of the hills and, as she was always to remember, the conscious-ness of her new life that the kiss of the night before, pervading everything, had given her. And, after them, the whole rabble of the village, gathering force with every step, children running to keep up, farm boys, women from the fields, old dames from the cottages, dalesmen and labourers, headed by the little round fat clergyman and the hump-backed pedlar, all of them crowding along, but, so strangely, not speaking above a whisper, wondering in excited awe what it was now that Rogue Herries would be at.

Deborah knew this well enough, and one question she was soon asking was: Would they step into the house? For many, many years Herries had been forbidden, warlock ground to them. Had not the witch, Mrs Wilson, lived there, and was it not back there that Rogue Herries had taken her after her drowning? Had he not lived there with his painted woman of the town, had not his poor wife died there? – poor soul, poor soul! Aye, it was a wicked house, evil enough, a place of spells.

But now it was as though they themselves were under a spell. They followed as though the pedlar were piping some magical tune that they could not resist. Deborah knew, too, that they had recognized, well enough, the bride. Already she was aware of the scandal that that would be, only adding to the other scandals.

It seemed that every step that her father took must only be the more fatal to his name. They had seen the girl in the roads, on the Fell, begging, dancing, stealing, one of the robbing gipsies, and now Rogue Herries had married her. And he fifty-six, who should surely now be repenting of his sins (that were so many) and making ready for the next world, where, whatever he did, his place could be no easy one.

She knew so well what they were thinking, and, when they came to the bend of the road where the lane to Herries, turning up to the right over the stream, met it, she felt the pause, the hesitation.

Herries and his bride went on, the pedlar and the clergyman went on, a second's wavering and the crowd followed too. Coming to the gate before the courtyard they waited. Herries turned, his grey head bare in the evening light; he waved, with a sort of joyful gesture, his stick with the amber head in the air. He cried:

'Here is food and drink and no grudging. Welcome, my friends, this day at least. We will drink to the bride.'

He marched on, carrying his hat in one hand, waving his stick in the other. They all followed. An odd and wild scene it was after that. The two old suits of armour had never seen the like. The dark stair was narrow. They crowded up it, pressing upon one another, still whispering, no word above a whisper.

The clergyman, sweating with the pace at which they had gone, and the pedlar were the first to follow into the dining-hall. The pedlar, as though he owned Herries and all in it (he had a crooked body and a pock-marked face and thin strands of carroty hair on his bald poll), laid his pack on the table and scattered the contents. 'A bride's gift!' he called in a funny cracked voice. 'A bride's gift! What will you have, lady? A grain gold watch-chain, cambrics, gold buttons, watch bottles . . . What will you have? A gift for the beautiful bride!'

Soon they were, most of them, in the room, peering about them, staring at the old chest, the tapestries, the portrait, the wide stone fireplace. They crowded together like animals, but many of them, although they were in the witch's house, remembered their Cumbrian manners, than which there are no finer in dignity and self-respect and courtesy the wide world over. Many of them might have fled, it could be, had it not been for David, but they knew Mr David Herries, they trusted him to see that they would come to no harm; not his fault that he was the son of the Devil, who had danced with witches and now married a gipsy. And another reason why they did not go was that they could not, for there were so many crowded on the stairs that they could move neither up nor down.

They might have been forgiven that day for thinking that Herries was of another world. He stood at the end of the table, lit by the jumping fire, the scar standing out on his face, even his clothes – in spite of their grandeur – of another age, and his voice was strange, glorified, filled with a triumphant power as though he had won a great victory, or, as an old woman said that night, 'made new contract with t'Divil'.

He filled the glasses and the cups with the brandy and the arrack and passed them round. This was fiery stuff, stronger than their accustomed ale, so it was no wonder if soon their voices were loosed.

The feasting began, only the bride, sitting at the table-end with the bridegroom, did not eat and did not speak. Herries seemed not to see her. He pressed those close to him, his children, the clergyman, the pedlar, a stout broad-shouldered dalesman with a vast black beard, a farming woman with crimson face and swelling breasts, already a little drunk, all of them near to him he pressed to eat the fowls and the pie, the fruit and the mound of beef. Soon they were eating right enough, and as the drink went round they began to pull at the food, the more drunken of them reaching across the table, cracking the nuts and catching the shells in the air, and throwing pieces of flesh to two or three hungry dogs who had crept in with them.

Then Herries rose to make a speech. He had drunk very little, but he seemed a drunken man, his hand trembling, and his eyes, always brilliant, now glittering with an eager fire.

'Friends and neighbours,' he said (and the pedlar, looking round him, echoed in his shrill cracked tones, 'Friends and neighbours'), 'I welcome you all here on this the happiest day of my life. The moon is silver in the sky' (now once again the rain was pouring down torrentially and clattering at the panes), 'and all the good dogs are baying at it. This is the valley of our hearts: in every stream there are fish of gold, and on the hills through the heather the blessed angels are picking the blackberries and singing under their wings as the rabbits run from their holes to listen to them.

'In no other valley in the world can these things be, and to-night, when the stars are blinded by the light of our happiness, the Old Man will be tramping the road, his pack under his elbow, and the stones hard to his stubborn toes. That is what happens in our wonderful valley, so drink to the Bridegroom and the Bride, whose nakedness your loving thoughts will cover and whose roof is your roof, and the snail on the wall has left his silver track for your guidance. Drink, friends and neighbours, and tumble downstairs as you may.'

No one understood a word of it, and for years after there were some who said that Rogue Herries, on his marriage night, had invoked the Devil. They had heard him with their own ears, had they not?

Then an old man, very grave and reverend, with a white beard and a nobly shaped head, stepped forward to make a speech.

'We mun thank Mr Herries,' he said. 'When I was young, we did varra weel off labscourse en stirabout fur dinner and we'll do varra weel yet. But Mr Herries has grudged neet.' He wandered off into disconnected reminiscence. 'Folks was harder lang sen ... When I was a lad wi' a bit of bluemilk cheese en breed I never ailt nowt ... In my opinion ther's nowt bangs good muck ... good muck wi' plenty o' suction in't 'll bring a crop any time. Anyways it's nobbut dry work talking without summat to sup on, and ther's plenty to sup on here ... But cuntra's turned upside-down. It'll be lang afore they see any mair times like t'oad uns ... any mair times like t'oad uns ... afore t'Rebellion ... afore t'Rebellion ...'

His voice sank into his beard; moreover, the noise now was too general for him to be heard. The arrack was having its way. There was stamping and singing, some child was crying. They were crowding more and more about the table. A glass fell and crashed. The rain slashed the windows until they rang again.

Deborah had watched the riot growing. In spite of the festivity there was a false element in it. Her father's happiness had something protesting in it, and was made the stranger by the girl's silence. David was doing what he could for friendliness, moving among them all in his quiet natural fashion, but with the heat of the great fire, the strength of the drink, the ferocity of the storm outside, a crisis seemed to be mounting over them.

It came, and with a wild suddenness. The pedlar, whose little skimmy eyes had scarcely left the face of the new Mrs Herries, had been coming ever closer to her. He seemed himself to be mad with some sort of sensual desire or arrogant conceit. At first he fingered the orange sleeve of her coat, then bent forward, put his hand under her chin, lifted her face. 'A kiss,' he said, 'from the happy bride.'

A moment later Herries's fist had crashed into his misshapen ugly face, and he tumbled backwards into the noisy crowd. Herries, pressing after him, seemed to be seized with an exultant rage. He struck right and left.

Everyone scattered to the door, and, as he pursued them, they turned pell-mell, one upon another; men, women, children were heaped to the door, were stumbling, leaping, flying down the stairs, rushing into the court, away, away through the gate, and down the lane, as though the Devil were after them.

In a leap of the fire the room had been cleared, the table, the floor messy with food, glasses overturned, only the pedlar, unconscious, flat on his back.

'You with the rest!' cried Herries, and, picking him up, threw him down the stairs, ran down the stairs after him, picked him up again, dragged him through the court, threw him over the wall into the lane, returning then, found his pack still on the table, picked it up, stuffing ribbons and chains and gold buttons back into it, ran down with it, and threw that too over the wall. The rain came soaking down upon it.

Back in the hall again he saw that Deborah and Mirabell were gone. Only David stood, tall and considering, above the ruined feast.

Herries broke out, roaring with laughter.

'Well, Davy . . . Our first hospitality.'

And David answered, picking up an orange from the table

and biting into it with his teeth: 'Well, Father, you made the
punch too mighty for them.'

By evening a quiet contentment seemed to have come to them.
No sign of the feast, no sign of the feasters. An hour before,
Herries had gone out to look for the pedlar to see whether he
were killed or no. There was no glimpse of the pedlar, nor of his
pack; only the cold muddied path, the trees sighing under the
rain.

Now they were all about the fire, Deborah sewing, David
doing his accounts at the table, Herries in the oak chair with the
big arms to it, and Mirabell quietly near to him, silent as before
but a little flush now in her face, and looking up once and again,
first at one of them, then another. The riot had, it seemed, in no
way disturbed her. She had known many like it before.

Herries's joy was quiet now and tranquil. He would look
at her, an odd smile playing about his lips, then glance away
again.

He nursed his knee, bending forward towards the fire. The old
house seemed to fit into their mood. Somewhere Benjamin could
be heard, beyond the rain, raucously singing a tune. He was
drunk a little. The room was dry and warm for once; the firelight
played about the brown figures in the tapestry and threw a
strange shadowing on the beams. Sometimes a mouse scratched
behind the panelling. Deborah was thinking of love, David of
business. It was plain of what Herries was thinking. No one
knew Mirabell's thoughts.

The evening wore on, the storm died down, and with the ces-
sation of the rain all the rivers and streams of the fields and rocks
seemed to rush into the house. The whole valley was vocal with
running water, and some little wet stars came out and blinked
between the black driving clouds.

Deborah and David went to their beds. Deborah, before going,
bent down and kissed Mirabell's forehead.

When they were gone, their doors closed, and all silent again,
Herries rose and said to her softly:

'Mirabell . . . speak to me. Say that you have trust in me.'

'Yes,' she said. 'I have trust in you.'

He stooped and picked her up. He carried her, her hair
strayed across his breast, up the stairs, along the tumbling passage to the little room where he had slept with small David on
their first night in the house.

He laid her on the bed, knelt down beside it, stroked her hair, kissed her eyes and mouth; then, very tenderly, with a gentleness of a woman, he undressed her. When she was naked he took her in his arms again, and, with one hand free, turned down the bed, and laid her in it, smoothing the pillows for her head.

Then he knelt down beside her again.

'My darling,' he said, 'when I saw you in the cave on Honister I loved you so that I knew then and for ever where my haven was. After that day I have had no other desire than that, to worship you and serve you. Many of my days have been evil, but I have had no shame of that. I let things pass me by because my eyes were set on a dream. I knew always that in some place or person or act there lay the fulfilment, so that when I came to it I would find myself. I was always searching. No man has been more lonely than I, and by my own fault. I would receive no pity, that most contemptible of the vices, and I would give none, but I could be honourable could I find a place for my honour, and I could serve if I could see an altar. And now I have found it. I have years left. I am strong. There is no task too hard for me now I have got you, and if you stay with me no unhappiness can touch me.'

She looked at him then, full in the face. Then she put her hand up and, very gently, stroked his cheek where the scar was.

'You know,' she said, almost in a whisper, 'that I loved once and when he was killed I was slain too. I am a dead woman, Francis. I was a child when I talked to you in the cave. I was a woman at that moment in Carlisle. I care for you. I feel sorry for you. But I have no love for you. I told you yesterday. I can never love anyone again, I think. And so I wish that you did not love me so much. But you have shown me more kindness than anyone has ever shown me. I will do my very best to please you. Indeed I will.'

They remained for a while, he kneeling by the bed, she stroking his cheek. Then he took off his clothes and went in with her.

He put his arms round her and held her icily cold body close to his heart. Her head was on his breast and suddenly she began to cry, without sound, but he could feel her tears wet against his arms. She cried for a long time, he consoling her and stroking her long hair.

THE VOICE

IT WAS not strange, when you think of it, that the valley should now determine that it was a witch Herries had married.

It was, after all, only what they had expected him to do. It was, after all, only what they had always expected her to be. After the wild marriage party, so grotesque in its conclusion, every sort of fantastic story was abroad. Some said that Rogue Herries had, all in a moment, shown a fiery tail between his coat-ends and that two brown crooked horns had sprung out from behind his ears. Others that the girl had flown of a sudden above the table and was carrying in her right hand a broomstick. All agreed that they had been beaten with mysterious blows from a hundred invisible arms. The pedlar, who seemed, with his hump and carroty hair, to have settled down in the valley, went about everywhere whispering, in his cracked voice, stories about Herries.

No, this was not odd, but what was strange was that, as the months passed, Mirabell won the name among them of a good witch, almost of a kind of well-wishing fairy. No one could quite say how this idea began to grow. It was not that she did anything for them; she did not, indeed, take any part in the lives of the farmers and dalesmen. It was said (and most of the stories came from Mrs Benjamin, who was a very talkative woman and had friends in Rosthwaite, Seatoller, Seathwaite, Grange, everywhere in the valley, in fact) that she was busy all day in the house, quietly going about her duties. That she was kindly to everyone, never out of temper, never proud nor haughty, never gay, but never sad either. She was not a bad witch in any case; only a poor gentle woman who had let her spells lie forgotten in their pack. Nevertheless the village children were warned not to speak to her when she went about, walking or riding, with her flaming hair and the brilliant-coloured clothes that she loved to wear.

After a time the village women began to pity her. They could not charge Herries with unkindness to her, although that they would have loved to do. It was plain enough that he worshipped her and would do anything in the world for her. He was a changed man, Mrs Benjamin declared, when she was about, although he would curse and swear and strike Benjamin with his whip or cane, as he had always done, when she was away.

The story was gradually told that Mirabell Herries had been in love with the Devil himself, who had been disguised as a beautiful young man, and then, when she saw her sin, she had fled from him and been broken-hearted ever since. This, the farmwomen said, might happen to any woman. She was not to be blamed for it.

Within the house David and Deborah became greatly attached to her. This did not say that they had any intimacy with her. She remained apart, reserved, secret, but she was in all her ways so gentle, so ungrudging in her service to all with whom she came in contact, that even the old wind-blown house itself seemed to gather a warmth and kindliness from her presence in it.

They must feel, too, their father's worship of her. Oddly they did not resent that nor charge her with taking his love from them. It was her purpose plainly that she should take nothing, but only give, and that shyly, as though she had no right to think that her gifts would be received.

There came a day, a warm dim February day, when Deborah was taken a little closer into this girl's privacy, and that perhaps because of Deborah's own confidence to her.

It was, as often happens in this country, a sudden flash of sun and warmth and promise between storms of wind and rain.

When they saw how it would be the two of them rode out under Cat Bells through little Braithwaite village, up Whinlatter, and then, finding a sheltered corner and letting their horses feed in the grass by the road, seated themselves where they could look down upon Bassenthwaite, smooth under the sun like a gold shield, and across to Skiddaw that opened like a flower of steel and silver against the windy sky.

Deborah, moved by some quick impulse, told Mirabell that she had a lover; Mirabell turned towards her with a gesture of more eager friendliness than she had ever shown to her.

'Oh, tell me about him,' she said. So Deborah, with the sedate deliberation that, even when she was in love, could never leave her, told Mirabell about the Keswick Ball, and the little clergyman and the kiss under the stars.

'And I had a letter yesterday delivered by horse from Cockermouth,' she added, blushing and looking very happy in spite of her sedateness. 'Is it not foolish to be so in love at my years? . . . But then he is not a boy,' she added, smiling with love at the picture of him in her heart. 'I fancy that we are greatly suited,' she said, feeling for the letter in her bosom.

She read the letter, while the breeze rustled over the Fell and the shadows passed like wings of gigantic birds across the slopes of the hills.

'MY DEAREST FRIEND – When I had read your letter I grumbled, for I would have had it so lengthy that it would stretch the reading of it until I might see you again. I have now read it twelve times and could, were I put to it, read it blindfolded and make no mistake in it. It was a sweet letter nevertheless, and I love you at my heart with so great a devotion that I cannot subscribe to your absence, you resting in my heart and so being never away from me.

And so you being here in my parlour, what do you think of it? Everything is smart and everything elegant. There are the short candles and the long ones, the tea-urn and the two screens with the Chinese figures upon them, of which I have told you already. And even now I have been busy on my sermon, whose text is: "Suffer the little children", and I have also a Latin inscription to compose for the tomb of Mr Harvey, the principal solicitor of Cockermouth, who passed away a sennight back, as I fancy my last letter informed you. There is also my good dog Rufus at my feet, who already loves you who are now his only mistress, and has looked at your letter with an obeisance marvellous in so dumb a beast.

Two chairs also are newly come to the parlour, purchased by me a fortnight back at the sale of poor Mrs Newbiggin's effects (of this also, I think, I have told you). They have a certain lameness at the moment, but I know how to steady them against your coming. When am I next to *expect* a letter? They are as careless at the Crown as at every other inn in the country, and the thought that a letter from you may be even now in the wrong hands is a constant anxiety for me.

You know how I love you, my dearest, and that with every hour my love increases . . .

'The rest is nothing,' said Deborah, folding it up and looking at Mirabell with a sudden anxiety. After all, how slightly she knew this woman, how different their natures and origins. Such a letter might seem to her the last foolish pettiness, and if she laughed . . .

But Mirabell did not laugh. She turned and, drawing Deborah to her, kissed her. This she had never before done of her own accord.

'You are happy,' she said. 'That is a very kind letter. No one has ever written me a letter. He would have—' She broke off, stared down with her strange elfin eyes to Bassenthwaite, that is always from a height like a lake ebbing its life away between marshy strands; then crept closer to Deborah as though she sought protection from something.

'You are all so kind to me. As no one has ever been. And I wish to return your goodness, but I am outside it. I want to be drawn into your friendliness, but my spirit is dead. My mother, after my father had been killed (he was slain by my uncle, who had always hated him), told me that when he was stabbed every other was stabbed also. She lived with dead people after that. I was so young that it meant nothing to me then, but now . . . Oh, how well I understand!'

'Had you some tragedy then?' Deborah asked. She knew, of course, that there had been tragedy here, but she had never asked any question. Her father had told her nothing.

'It has always been tragedy all my life, but never tragedy that touched me – until this last. My father was murdered, struck in the back in the dark by my uncle. My mother died on the Fell in the rain, her feet deep in mire, no one near us but the kites and the sheep. Then I was with my other uncle, wandering, thieving, hiding, escaping, in caves, on the Fell, begging in the street, beaten, always moving from one hill to another, from one road to another. I was ravished when I was twelve. I had seen four men foully murdered before I was sixteen years of age; one was all night dying, his head in my lap, his blood soaking my clothes. But nothing could touch me. I was apart, by myself!' She sprang up, as though inspired, and cried: 'Ohè! Ohè! Ohè!' and her call echoed from hill to hill, perhaps from Grasmoor down Crummock to Red Pike, from Red Pike to Langdale, from Langdale to Coniston Old Man.

'I would call and so thrust them from me. With my call I expelled them. Touch me? I was not there to be touched!' She called again and heard the echo come back. Then she crouched down once more close to Deborah, her hand on her arm.

'Your father came and found me in a cave on Honister Crag. I told him that day that I was myself, free, by myself, and it was true. But I had remembered him. He gave me that when I was a child with my mother.' (She felt in her dress and brought out the golden head with ruby eyes that he had given her at that Christmas feast.) 'He went away, but I still remembered him. He is not easy to forget. He is a Man, not half a man or a piece of one, but a whole one made in one block like a carved stone. I remembered him, but I did not care for him. I cared for no one; only the memory of my mother made me lonely sometimes, and when men wanted me then I was lonely too, because I hated men.

'Then—' (she broke off, caught her thin breasts with a sudden pathetic, driven gesture as though she must control some beating impulse) 'we came to Carlisle. My uncles were much on the Border, thieving, wrestling, carrying messages. They had been for a long time working with the Scottish rebels, you see, and were paid by them as secret agents. After the Prince landed they went to Edinburgh. I was left in Carlisle. There was a man whom they knew there, a devil, he was evil as Satan, and more evil than that; they knew what he was and what he intended to me, but they were still his friends, and for that I will never forgive them, nor speak to them, nor drink with them, neither here nor in eternity.' Her face was suddenly cold and mask-like with hatred.

Deborah had never seen that figure, the white mask-like face, so small, so carven, so cold under the red smoke-gleaming hair. But she was full of pity, and she put her arm out and drew Mirabell closer to her.

'This man said he loved me; he was hideous in his body as in his soul: squat, black, always cold to the touch. He came to my bed and I fought him. I dug my nails into his eyes, and naked as I was I forced him to creep away, under the smoky candle, his tail between his legs, dog as he was. He did not attempt me again, but he watched me; he was always there watching me, waiting until my uncles should return. He thought they would give me to him. Then Harry found me. We loved at the very first sight, as I came to the door of my house on a fine morning, he riding by. It was always a surety. He was beautiful, he was brave and noble-hearted, he was young and a grand poet, he was mine and I was his . . . And oh! Deborah, Deborah' (she began to weep, tears pouring down her cheeks, beating her hands, clenched, against her breast), 'Thawn killed him, he stabbed him in the back, he fell dead at my feet, and I dead with him! Deborah, Deborah!' (she turned, clinging, holding to Deborah's body) 'what shall I do? I am not alive. I died with him. When he fell, I fell! Oh, how shall I live again if Harry cannot come back to me? He comes. He beats at the window. When I lie beside your father I hear him crying. When I am moving about that dark house he is a light ahead of me, but I can never come to him, and he can never come to me. I want him so, but he is dead on one side of the wall, and I am on the other. What shall I do when you are so kindly to me, and your father loves me so, and I only a ghost in the middle of you? Oh, what shall I do? Oh, what shall I do?'

In all these months Deborah had never seen her display feeling. She had been kind, and had served them all, and been quiet. Now she clung to Deborah, sobbing on her breast, holding Deborah's arms, weeping as though her heart were all tears.

'Hush! Hush!' Deborah kissed her hair, her forehead, keeping her very close. 'It will pass. It will pass. We will all love you and have a home for you. You are not alone any more. We love you. We love you.'

But Mirabell raised her head, staring into the faint pale sky as though she would find some answer there. 'It will never pass,' she said. 'It is eleven years now, and it was yesterday that he died at my feet.'

She quieted as suddenly as she had cried out. The clouds came over, gathering together in fleecy, windy companies, cloud forming with cloud in ribs and ripples of gauzy vapour. Soon all the sky was a ribbed shore of pale ghostly sand. The fells grew black, and little streams that laced their forms were rents in their strong flanks. Bassenthwaite paled, as the sun withdrew, into the curve and colour of a grey shell. The wind raced over the moor and up the Fell, suddenly liberated, delighting in its freedom. It was cold and sharp with the tang in it of sheep's dung and new young bracken and coming rain.

'Let us go home,' said Mirabell. 'It is cold.'

They mounted their horses and turned down the hill. For Deborah, Mirabell's story had flung the whole life at Herries into a new, dramatic and, for her timidity and quiet mind, sinister shape. Mirabell was something now apart from all of them; she was to be pitied, cared for, comforted, but she could give none of them anything. She could not give her husband anything. She did not love him at all. Through all these months Deborah had supposed that in her own strange way Mirabell loved her father, and now it appeared that she had no love for him, but thought only of some ghostly young man who had been dead for eleven years. Well, but if she did not love her father who himself adored her so! Why, that must mean torture for her father, despair, misery. What end could it have but disaster?

This was the first moment in Deborah's life, now as their horses were picking their way through the stream that runs through Braithwaite village and starting up the winding hill to Cat Bells, that she truly loved her father without any sense of fear or dismay. She was overwhelmed with pity for him, caught after all his rough and lonely life into this great passion for someone who did not love him, and could not. 'Oh, poor Father, poor Father!' she thought. 'How he must be suffering, and under what restraint!' She remembered all his goodness and gentleness these last months, and how, when Mirabell was there, so quietly and with such courtesy he waited on her and cared for her. Deborah's heart, that was all softness and tenderness, ached for him. She cared, too, for Mirabell. It was not her fault that she had come, and she was doing all in her power. But so little was in her power! Nothing was in her that he needed, and yet she was his only need!

That evening in the house Deborah watched with a new understanding and sensibility. And Herries seemed to detect that there was some change in her. She went with him to the door of the house before going up to her bed. The wind that had risen while they looked down on Bassenthwaite was now raging through the valley. It carried in its arms a new young slender moon, and seemed to be tossing it from leafless tree to leafless tree. The trees bent with their bare arms to catch it and then tossed it in and out of the rushing clouds. There was a great noise, a noise of streams, of branches cracking, of the wind itself, and the beams and rafters of the old house.

Herries listened, loving it.

'One wind more and everything will tumble,' he said. 'You'd best go, Deborah, before the fall.'

She timidly put her hand through his arm and stood close to him.

'Father, I love Mirabell,' she said.

'I am old for a husband,' he said, seeming not to hear her. 'When I was young I ranged from door to door, and now that I have found her I am old, bent, twisted ... Deborah, will you not marry before it is too late?'

She wondered whether he had heard something. She herself had said nothing. It had not yet seemed the right time. She nearly spoke then, but she did not. While he wanted her, she must stay.

'One day, Father ...' she said, 'but not now.' And then the wind, with a great scream of happiness and freedom, drove them indoors.

The following day Herries took his wife, riding pillion, into Keswick. He was terribly proud of her. He wanted to show her to everyone; he knew what they said of her, that she had been

gipsy, tramp, thief. That was nothing. It was the truth for him
that she was glorious, extraordinarily, magnificently glorious.
She was as glorious to him now as she had been before he married
her. And she was also as mysterious. Intimacy had not made her
less mysterious. But perhaps, although he did not know it, there
had been no intimacy. Did he know that? He was a deep man
who knew many things, but often did not realize them.

She rode behind him into Keswick in a crimson dress with gold
buttons. He was in his old shabby country clothes, wearing his
own hair. When he touched her he was happy so that he could
sing, but behind his happiness he was unhappy: he had questions
that he wanted to ask her and he did not dare.

As they drew near to the town, along the path and across the
watery meadows, people were walking and riding. In the Town
Square there was a thick pressing multitude. He asked a fellow
what the matter was, and someone told him it was the Meth-
odists, and then another fellow volunteered that it was George
Whitefield, the most remarkable preacher of them all.

Herries was interested in all that he had heard of the Meth-
odists, who had now for a number of years been strengthening
their position in the country, and especially of this Whitefield,
concerning whom and his extraordinary preaching he had had,
like everyone else at this time, many reports.

He knew that this was a courageous man who was ready, for
his religion, to meet any form of contempt, abuse and danger. He
knew that he was sincere, of deep piety, of constant energy, of
selfless industry. Against these things he weighed what he had
heard of his emotionalism, theatricality and fanaticism, all
qualities to which Herries, by his own reserved and private mind,
was deeply hostile.

He had heard that Whitefield had but one desire, to save souls
for God, that often he preached fifty or sixty hours in the one
week, and that his journeys, involving as they did at that time so
much physical discomfort, were ceaseless.

He knew, too, that he was a man free of all meanness; his
bitterest adversary did not attribute to him small ambitions,
petty jealousies, sly revenges. He appeared to Herries, from
what he had heard of him, to be feminine in his hysteria, weak-
nerved, histrionic, ill-balanced, but he was, even because of these
defects, exactly suited to move great masses of people by im-
passioned appeals, passing from place to place like a torch of
fire.

When he heard that it was Whitefield who was here he decided that he must listen to him. He backed his horse out of the crowd, and, dismounting, took the horse by the bridle and Mirabell by the hand, finding some higher ground where he could watch what was going forward.

He told Mirabell of the reason for the crowd. She did not seem to be greatly concerned, but, as he had noticed before when she was in any crowd of people, to be looking about her searchingly, as though she would find someone.

He stood, his arm around her, holding her close to him. He felt as though some crisis were arriving between her and himself; this was no new feeling, but had been present with him for the last two months or more, and he knew that was because something was urging him with every day more pressingly to ask her certain questions with regard to himself. He was aware, too, that it was better that he should not ask these questions, that her answers might precipitate a crisis that would make him much unhappier than he had ever been before. But he could not help himself. With every hour he was urged further. He must know, he must know – whether now, after these months, she did not love him a little, a little, a very little . . . the first stirring of some new emotion in her . . . and at the thought of asking her and of her answer he trembled as though with cold.

Very soon he was aware of a voice coming to him very clearly over the heads of the people. He could see, only indistinctly, any figure. The crowd, of every type and order of person, was packed tightly across the Square; they seemed to press against the houses behind them, as though they would bend them back. It was an intent and silent crowd, so intent that the urgency seemed to spread to the distant line of hills, Causey and Cat Bells and Maiden Moor, beyond the roofs, so that they, too, were listening.

The figure was indistinct, someone lit with the pale February sun, a body of grace and good proportion, but it was the voice that came straight to Herries, as though it were to him alone that it was appealing. He realized then that every man and woman in that crowd felt as he did, that it was to him or her alone that the voice was speaking. At once, hostile though he was to public emotion and theatrical display, he yielded to the beauty of the voice. It was, beyond any sort of argument, by far and far the most moving and lovely voice that he had ever heard. Every word was distinct and clear, running to him with a separate and special urgency, and the words were bound into a general rhythm most melodious and musical; yes, it was like music, the perfect and rounded notes following one after another, to make, at the fitting moment, a completed harmony. So lovely was the voice that for a little while he did not listen to the words, then they were forced upon his attention with a pressing gentleness, as though someone, very gracious and kindly, were at his elbow, saying, 'You must hear this; this is for you and for you alone. It has great importance for you.'

He listened then with the utmost attention.

'It is simply as an occasional preacher that I am come to preach the Gospel to all that wish to hear me, of whatever denomination. I have nothing to do with denominations, for it is the righteousness of Jesus Christ that I am preaching, and that righteousness has no denominations. You have heard many times of the righteousness of Jesus Christ, and at every time you have been wearied or indifferent to Him or busied with affairs. It may be that this is the last time you will hear of Him and the last time that I shall preach of Him. Here into this town He has come, knowing that it is for the last time, but you do not know. The clouds have circled over your heads, the sun is about to set and, setting tonight, it will not come again. You are returning to your homes, your candles are lit, your children are at your knee, and distantly from over the hills there is the faint sound of a trumpet. The sound is distant, for the hills cover it, and your many daily businesses, the food for gossip, the food for the belly, the food for pride and vanity, these make a babel in your ears and blot out the distant call. But soon,' and here the voice rose to a high bright summoning call, 'the trumpeters have crossed the hills. The trumpeters have crossed the hills! The trumpeters have crossed the hills!'

He paused as though he were listening. It seemed that everyone else was listening too. The crowd was tense and concrete, as though its eager attention had moulded it into one man. Across the silence there struck stray sounds, the crowing of a cock, the sharp bark of a dog, the stamping of some horse's hoofs against cobbles. These emphasized the stillness. They could see the hills where the trumpeters were. They could name them – Skiddaw and Saddleback, Helvellyn and Fairfield, Langdale Pike and the Gavel, Seatallan and Haycock, and through that circle of grey listening hills they could see the trumpeters moving.

The voice took a personal colour. 'The Trumpeters come first, moving down the valleys, and after them the cohorts of the Saints in their shining armour, and after them the Priests and Prophets with judgements in their hands, and after them' – the voice sank to a whisper and through the crowd there ran a little rustle of apprehension – 'after them the Great Judge Himself.'

There was silence again. A stout country-woman near Herries began to sob.

'Who in this valley shall be ready for that awful army? Now, outside your door, there is one summoning blast. No time for preparation, for hiding the things that should not be seen. THY JUDGE IS THERE... THY JUDGE IS THERE... And He is just and He is merciful. Yes, but He is just. Think not only of the mercy; think also of the Justice...' And then, with a sudden agonizing, beseeching cry: 'Oh, my hearers, the Wrath to come, the Wrath to come!'

There was a terror and imminent fearful apprehension in that last cry that even a man like Herries, steeled against every sentimental appeal, could not resist. He started as though someone at that instant came running to him, crying out that the end of the world was upon him. He looked hastily around him, as though a wild animal or flaming fire were at his back. And on the crowd the effect of that cry was immediate and tremendous. Superstitious, ignorant, simply and often savagely moved, cut off as they had been for many centuries from all contact with a larger world, they were ready to be seized by any swift emotion, ready and eager. Here Whitefield, however, had won his hardest victory, for these North Country people were not Celts as the Cornish and Welsh were. They were neither dreamers nor fanatics. As Herries knew, five years before they had stoned the Methodist preacher almost to death, and the whole district from Kendal to Carlisle had a name of great danger for the sect.

But they would not stone Whitefield now. He himself began to be moved with the crowd; his body swayed, his arms rose and fell, his voice was torn with distress and urgency. Tears, they said afterwards, were pouring down his cheeks. He picked out men and women from the crowd. 'Oh, sir, are you indeed ready? Have you your garments packed for the journey, your horse harnessed, and your conscience clear? For Heaven and Hell, Death and Judgement are not names only for you. They are real, they are present. Eternity is a true word and Everlasting Punishment is no lie. Can you be led to the Judgement Seat before that awful crowd of Witnesses and not tremble? Your deeds are behind you. There is no hope now that they may be altered, for they are written in the book. There is the pause. You have made your plea. You are waiting for the sentence, and even as you stand here now, so it is certain that you will stand before your God.

Eternal Damnation! Damnation for ever and ever more, suffering and torment and the agony of a repentance that is out of time!'

His voice sank again to a pleading whisper, while now his utterance could be heard to be broken with sobs. 'O God, where is Thy mercy? O God, whither shall I turn?' Then, with a great cry that ran, glittering, resonant through the air: 'In Christ Jesus! In Christ Jesus only is there any hope! But even He is Just.' His voice was now of an awful solemnity: 'Sinner, I must do it. I must pronounce sentence upon you.' Again there was a terrible silence, and then, in a voice of thunder as though the very cobbles of the town must rock:

'Depart from me, ye cursed, into everlasting fire!'

The crowd began to cry out: 'O Christ, save me!' 'Christ be kind to me!' 'God have mercy upon me!' Men were pushing against one another to reach nearer to the preacher, tears fell from many eyes, and suddenly, with a great burst of sound that had in it something gloriously strong and victorious, the hymn 'Our God, our help in ages past' broke out and was carried, it must seem, far beyond the confines of the town.

The voice had ended and Herries was freed. He turned to find that Mirabell was clinging to him, her face very white, her eyes closed.

'Come. It is growing dark. We will go home.'

She nodded. He led his horse out of the crowd and then, in a little dusky side-street where there was a deep silence, he lifted her on to the horse and climbed on behind her. With his arms about her he started away. The horse went gently.

Herries thought: 'There is this Damnation then. I, too, shall be damned with the rest.' He had stirred to a consciousness, through this scene, of a general movement behind his own personal history, of some new world coming to England. Ten, five years ago those men and women would have driven White-field with stones and abuse out of the town. Now he held them, although it might be only by a kind of superstition and senti-ment. He felt that all around him there was a new consciousness, a fresh curiosity, a novel enterprise. For himself, he belonged to the old world that was passing. He had still a link with the boy who, sniffing his way through Queen Anne's London, had not been so far removed from the Rebellion, the tumbling of King Charles's head, the Plague and the Great Fire. But David and Deborah had no touch with that world at all; it was a dream, a fairy-tale to them. David's enterprises were consciously engaged, through his vessels and the things that they carried, with other worlds that were not dream-worlds of adventure and romance, as China and India and Russia had been to Francis's childhood, but definite practical places in which men walked on their legs, ate mutton for their dinner and read the news-sheets. Everything was opening up before him, and at the same time closing in about him. This very rough path on which tonight his horse was picking his way would soon be a toll-road that would carry carts and carriages. This modern world so novel, strident, ill-fitting. In the hearts of those people listening to Whitefield he had detected a new curiosity. And (here his Herries blood drove him) he disliked and distrusted this modernity. Queen Anne's age appeared to him as something infinitely quiet, cosy, picturesque and easy.

They were talking now of inventing things to make the lot of the common people easier. The common people! No one had thought of the common people when he was a boy. Why invent things only to make them restless? He thought of the old London scenes, so dim now in memory; the crowds on holiday all upon pads and hackneys, Mob's Hole where the ox, roasted whole, was eaten, the dancing to a bagpipe, the fiddlers scraping, an old trooper from the Royalist wars tootling upon a trumpet. The shopping in the New Exchange, that he had so adored as a boy, the beautiful ladies in coach or sedan chair, the ladies with their pets, marmosets and Barbary doves, scarlet nightingales and milk-white peacocks. And the Coffee Houses which to him, taken there as a boy on a London visit by Harcourt, twelve years his senior, had seemed the great paradise of glory; the Coffee Houses with the fine glass lanterns hanging without, the pretty Phyllis smiling at the bar, the young swells of a morning, whether at Searle's or Squire's or the Grecian, dressed, as Steele had it, 'in gay cap and slippers with a scarf and party-coloured gown'. The drinking, the smoking, the gaming, the singing – oh, the Life, the Life that it was! . . .

And now, now, how drab and busy this new world, with no respect from youngsters to elders, no romance, only money-making, business, and the whole world in your pocket!

It was his age. How old he was, and only now his true life beginning!

At that his arms tightened about her body, he bent forward and touched her neck with his lips. He fancied that she yielded to him a little. Did she or no? How often, in these last months, he had wondered that!

And then the temptation that had been behind him so fearfully

all day rushed to his lips. He could not stay it now. He had run
in upon his fate.

'Mirabell,' he said, 'I must ask you a question.' He felt his
heart hammering in his breast. His hands trembled.

'Yes,' she said, and then, most unexpectedly, asked him one:
'Do you think there can be a God, Francis?'

A God? A God? What did it matter whether there were a God
or no now when the only urgency in this world was, had she
come to love him a little.

'That Methodist thinks so,' he answered her lightly.

'Those poor people whom he threatened with damnation,
what right has God to judge them, having made them so?
And yet—' she looked round at him into his eyes. 'He had
a great eloquence. I saw the trumpeters coming through the
valley.'

'Mirabell,' he began again, 'I must ask you a question.'

'Yes,' she said patiently.

'Am I,' his hands tightened about the reins, 'am I so very old
to you?'

'Old! Why, no!'

'I am old. All my life is behind me and yet, loving you, it is
but beginning.'

She said nothing.

He went desperately on: 'You told me on your wedding night
that you did not love me, that you could not. I have never
questioned you again. But now it is too much for me. I can wait
no longer. Have you not, in these months, learnt a little, a very,
very little, to have love for me? Or is it, can it never—' He broke
off, so terribly agitated that he could not speak.

At last she answered, turning round again, and looking up at
him like a little child.

'I do not feel you old. I feel you so very good, better far than I
had ever thought. But love . . . are we not friends, good friends,
trusting friends? I am not made for love. Only once, and that
was a dream. But your friend . . .'

Then he broke out (although he knew very well the fool he
was, and that maybe in these words he was breaking up all the
foundation of their happiness together): 'Friend, friend, friendship! What is that for a man? I have never had a friend. I do not
want a friend. But my love for you is eating me up, tearing at my
heart. As that man today desired his God so I desire you. It must
be. I cannot live if I haven't it. Your cruelty . . . I lie with you in
my arms and you are not there. I touch you and you are gone. I

must have a little of you, a touch, a breath, a word that is yours meant for me. I am in torment, dying of thirst, of hunger . . .'

He could not make the words, he held her, letting the reins fall, as though he would drag her into his very breast. He felt her body stiffen against his.

'No,' she said, almost beneath her breath, 'I will not lie to you. I cannot. Even though you kill me I will not be dishonest. It is not my fault that I am apart. I am apart from all the world, yes, and from myself.

'Francis, I would give you everything. I have never but once wanted so to give myself, but I cannot. I cannot! Oh, I should never have come! I am wicked, I am a cheat . . . I care for you so much, I would give everything to make you happy. But love – it escaped me that night. I cannot find a way to get it back.'

He answered nothing. He rode the horse more swiftly. After a long time, fear in her heart, longing to comfort him, she spoke again:

'I would do everything. Teach me. I will learn.'

He said, between his teeth:

'I have my answer. You have so generous a heart. I will be patient.'

As they rode on (and now it was very dark) her unhappiness seemed to her more than she could bear.

SAGA OF DAVID

I

THE YOUNG SARAH

THE place has now come for David's story. These events occurred in early May 1758. David was in his thirty-ninth year in the course of them.

David did not appear a man of thirty-eight at this time. His face was very young, unlined, fresh in colour, strong in profile, with the prominent bones of all the Herries, but his forehead was as clear and smooth as a young boy's. Just at this time, because he was working considerably at the little Keswick office, he was beginning to stouten. His huge frame would gather fat very easily. But this did not diminish his strength, which was now, and would be for another fifteen years, prodigious. It was at this time that he picked up Statesman Peel in one hand and Benjamin with the other and held them, without any effort, suspended for a considerable time.

Men would come from Ennerdale and Eskdale to see him wrestle, and they said that he was, if he pleased, a terrible man with his fists. The twisted carroty-haired pedlar, Peter Dolfin, who was now for ever hanging around Rosthwaite and Grange, hated him and said that he would be hanged for murder any day that he lost his temper. But he never did lose his temper these days. There was a certain sluggishness in him at this time (except when he was occupied on his business; then he was wide awake enough). This is the story of how he lost his sluggishness.

The most remarkable thing about him, as he grew, was the sweetness of his nature. This sweetness of temperament has been a continuous strain in the Herries blood. There has been no generation lacking certain examples of it.

This is no merit to its possessor, entails no virtue, deserves no reward. It is a quality of personality extremely vexing to many who think it sentimental and untrue to life. It is not sentimental because it is a quite natural element in the character of the possessor, and the possessor is unaware that he has it. David did not find life gentle, kindly or considerate. He knew that it was fierce, callous and dangerous. It was companionship with a tiger who, with one careless scratch of the paw, produces tragedy, ruin, catastrophe, and then yawns his indifference. But although he knew life to be dangerous and quite heedless of his personal good luck, his nature drove him to choose the better parts of the men and women about him, to enjoy the happy and bright moments, to perceive beauty without having any imagination about it, to wish everyone well and to rejoice at others' good fortune. It was easy for him just now because of his superb health, but afterwards, in bouts of pain, distresses and anxieties, the loss of someone who was dearer to him than all else, this sweetness of nature did not leave him. It came, as it always comes, from something remote and deep, beyond the business of the body, a central radiance of spirit.

He was, of course, no saint. He was exasperated, sulky, unjust, as everyone is, but only for the moment. These moods never dwelt in him. They tried him and found him uncomfortable as a living-place.

During this year 1758 his sluggishness did not prevent him from restlessness. After he had freed himself from Christina the restlessness increased. He began to wish, as he had never wished before, to make love to someone. He had matured very late. In Liverpool on an occasion he had gone with a woman and, after a brief moment of physical excitement, had known that such encounters were for ever barren for him. But his restlessness was not springing only from need of the love of woman. He seemed to have, at this time, no exercise for his warm, affectionate heart. He was, and had always been, quite undemonstrative, but he must have someone to love. He had loved his father and Deborah, and, in lesser degree, Peel's son. But Rendal was dead (killed in a brawl in Penrith), Deborah's mind elsewhere, his father married again.

It was his father's marriage that mainly caused his restlessness. He had never, in his own simple and unexperimenting mind, suspected the possibility of such utter absorption in another as he perceived now was his father's case. He himself realized the attraction of Mirabell, he thought her beautiful and gentle, and strangely different from other women, but he soon saw that she did not love his father, but was doing what she did from a sense of gratitude and duty. He saw, too, that his father was hungry and thirsty for what he could not have, and that his soul was set on this eluding quest. His father had, for the time, forgotten him. And so, because he loved his father with an unanalysed persisting love, having its roots in his very earliest years, he missed increasingly his contact with him. He did not know how to recover it again; he never knew, in his relations with people, how to change anything. He could not analyse nor examine himself. He had never done such a thing in his life, but he felt, as a loving animal feels, isolated and pushed aside. He blamed no one, felt no jealousy, but was increasingly, with every week that passed, lonely. His business, although it interested and occupied him, was nothing to him compared with his relations to one or two people.

So, although he did not know it at this time, he was very lonely and would soon be very unhappy.

More and more it became clear to him that he must marry. Well, what then? Could they all live together at Herries? There was room enough, but the sense of drama, of events that happened always just out of sight, began to bewilder him as though he were beginning to be asked to look in many different directions at once. This was no place for his wife, whoever she might be. There was some money (his mother's, as he often ironically reflected), but everything was shabby, out-at-elbows. It was not that they did not wish to have everything in fine colour, but there was some movement inside the house itself; as soon as a window was mended a door was off its hinges. Everything blew against the wall and along the floor. There was a draught in every corner, and rats behind the panelling.

In the old kitchen, where Mrs Benjamin officiated, everything accumulated. Mrs Benjamin was slatternly and careless. Nobody minded.

His father's wife helped about the house as though she were a servant. Those seemed to be the times when she was happiest, when she was carrying plates, sweeping floors, polishing the brass and silver. She was oddly most at her ease with old Benjamin. It was as though they had some secret friendly understanding. As though they had come from the same place . . .

Herries would enter and find her scouring the plates. He could not endure that; he would ask her to go and dress in her finest, and then he would sit her in the high-backed chair in the dining-hall, and he would change his clothes (he had been, as usual, digging, trying to turn rock into pasture, plucking up weeds, or simply standing staring at Glaramara, watching as it turned from amber to purple, purple to jet, jet to silver), and then there they would sit, the two of them, she in gold and crimson, he in cinnamon and silver, on either side of the fire, saying nothing at all.

No, all this was too eerie for David. He didn't know what would happen soon; something, he thought, that would make them all unhappy.

And no one wanted him. When he rode in from Keswick, evening time, he would see them sitting like that in the firelight. They were two ghosts to him. Everyone now was just out of his reach. He had never been so alone in his life before.

So one day he rode over to Wasdale. He went to see about some sheep that, he had heard, were for sale, and cheap. They belonged to a man called Denburn. This man Denburn was a gentleman, they said, from London, fallen on evil days. He had a tumbledown farm at Wasdale Head called Scarf Hall, a place half gentleman's house half farm. They told him in Keswick that Denburn was a ruffian, but clever, had a library of books that he set great store by. He had a daughter too.

He had some sheep, and David wanted some for his fields by Herries, so he rode over.

It was dark when his horse (he was riding Deb's Appleseed) had picked its way to the bottom of Stye Head, and it was difficult to find his way. He found his path across Lingmell Beck, and then plunged into a black thicket of trees. Here he stumbled for a long while, hearing water tumbling all about him, and the wind roaring down the pass.

He was not a man to mind wind and tumbling water, but he was uncomfortable nevertheless. This lake-end valley, cut off from the world, was an excellent rendezvous for smugglers from the sea-coast, only a few miles away. The inn at that time, the Wasdale Inn, was a wretched place, as he well knew, both in accommodation and reputation, but it was there that he must pass the night.

As he blundered among the trees, scarcely able to see his thumb before his mouth, he felt for his knife and his pistol. He might need them before the night was through.

He came through the wood and almost stepped on to the inn. There was a light in the window; he banged on the door, which was opened by an old woman with a shawl over her head and a shabby patch over one eye. He called for someone to look after his horse, and a lad went with him to a tumbled stables at the rear.

After seeing to his horse's comfort (poor comfort, but all that he could have) he stood for a moment swallowing the mountain air, looking up at the great shoulders of the Gavel behind him and the black sprawl of Lingmell, the sharp edge of the Pike in front of him. The night was clear. Stars, as the dusk faded into night, were breaking, in their thousands, into the stuff of the sky.

Reluctantly he shouldered his way across the floor of the close-smelling inn-room. All eyes were upon him as they well might be. He was so tall that he could, standing on his toes, touch the ceiling; so broad that he seemed to be at elbows with every man there. It was a small place, dim with the smoke from the fire, smelling of food, ale, dung, human unwashed bodies. The bodies were there, a dozen men, the old woman and another. His eyes were on her instantly. She was turning to go as he came in. She was dressed for riding, and wore a large hat with a feather and a great gold buckle that glittered and flashed in the firelight.

She was a young girl of strong, sturdy build, an open laughing face, broad shoulders, big-breasted, brown-haired. She might be, David thought, of any age from seventeen to twenty. She was tall, carrying her head grandly on her shoulders. As David came in her head was half turned, she laughing at someone, striking her whip against her thigh.

She was the most natural, open creature David had ever seen. Beside her was a man of some fifty years, very tall and skeleton thin. This man was dressed quietly in grey coat and breeches with a white stock; he wore a brown tie-wig. His face was as sharp and pointed as his body was thin and long. He had very thick, dark, beetling eyebrows and his complexion was sallow, his face deeply furrowed. A very ugly man. As he talked he bent his body about as though he would snap it.

For the rest there was the host of the inn, Sol Beddowes, who was as thick, black, and dirty as a tar-barrel, some rough fellows who might be smugglers, and one or two honest dalesmen. But David's eyes were all for the girl.

He spoke to Beddowes; was, with a brusque word, told that he could have a bed, came to the fire and so was companion to the man and girl. He heard someone say 'Mr Denburn', so he spoke: 'Am I speaking to Mr Denburn?' he asked. The long sallow hatchet of a face wheeled slowly in his direction and the little eyes receded into the eyebrows.

'I am Mr Denburn.'

'My name is Herries,' said David. 'I have a piece of business with you. May I come and call on you some time tomorrow?'

The body rose, as though on its heels, and leaned towards him like a whip, then the voice, cold, chill, and filled with self-importance, answered:

'Business of moment?'

'To the advantage of both of us, I fancy,' he answered.

'I am at home tomorrow evening.' Then he added, a little more graciously (he had been examining David with great care, and appeared to find him interesting), 'but possibly you prefer to be away before evening. . . I could arrange a meeting in the morning.'

David, with a thought of the girl, answered that the evening would be a perfect appointment. He knew that the girl had been intently aware of him, and, suddenly, he looked at her, catching her gaze. She did not flinch, but looked at him squarely, then smiled.

'A dark night to come over the Pass,' she said. Her voice delighted him, rich, warm, deep. It was as though he had heard it before, many times, and recognized it, coming home to it. He was excited by the sound of it, as he had never been by a woman's greeting.

Mr Denburn went to the door. She followed him. Before she went out she looked back, smiling again, and David smiled too.

Until he slept he thought of her. Was he in love at last? He sat by the fire, looking into the flames, his legs stretched out, as he loved to sit, talking to nobody, thinking slowly and steadily.

He remembered the women he had ever made any court to. The woman in Liverpool, a woman in Seatoller, Christina, one or two more. Little approaches that had been amusing, casual, leaving his heart alone. This was different: already it was different.

It seemed to him, poor David, the newest, most unusual experience in the world. It *was* unusual possibly. Strong healthy men in that age were seldom as virgin as he at thirty-eight.

He felt about twenty, and as he thought of her with every thought he was younger. He recalled the tones of her voice again and again with a happy luxury. She was only a child in years, but the voice seemed to him to have in it wisdom, fun, and good health, three splendid things as he saw the world.

When he went to his bed in a little room over the stables he found that he must share it with a stout dalesman. At any other time there would have been trouble. Tonight he did not care. The dalesman was asleep and snoring like a pig, his hairy chest heaving under the candle. David shoved him to the wall. He only grunted and turned on his side. Then David lay down, pulling up his knees, as he had to do in most beds, and, instantly, with a happy smile on his face, he was asleep.

He did not, unfortunately, dream of the brown-haired young woman, but he found himself in the little dark wood, lost, bewildered, stung by sharp thorns, his feet in plosh and mire. Beyond and above him on Stye Head someone was waiting for him, someone in peril, and it seemed, oddly enough, that this someone was himself. Did he not reach this figure to rescue him there would be disaster, but with every effort that he made his feet stuck the faster and the thorny trees tore his face more savagely. The voice from Stye Head called to him: 'Help. Help! I can do no more!' He made a last gigantic effort for freedom, and woke to find himself clutching the hairy throat of the stout farmer, his knee planted on his chest. Even this did not wake the slumberer, who, lost in his own pleasures, murmured: 'Coom, lass, pour oot for t' lot.'

David could not sleep after that. He lay there, listening to a first lonely bird, smelling the stuffy odour of straw, blanket, dried cow-dung that the room enclosed. He lay, his arm behind his head, gazing at the grey square of the little window, wondering how now, in clear day-time, he would find her. Was it perhaps only his longing to be in love that had cheated him? Would he discover her now like the rest, ordinary pleasant womanhood,

with no magic about her? He didn't know. He wished urgently
that he could summon her there, immediately, that he might sat-
isfy that question.

At last he got up and went out. The fresh morning air caressed
his eyes, his mouth, as though it loved him. He found the beck
and washed his face and hands in it. It was icy cold. The light
crept out above the black edge of the Pike, the trees came forth
as though rising from their sleep, the hills moved grandly into
their places. The few birds and the whispering beck greeted him
with a happy, aloof indifference.

He didn't see her again until the evening.

Scarf Hall was hidden in the woods under Green How.

When David came to it the moon sailed out from above the
Screes and an owl hooted. The house swam in a pale light that
flowed about it like green water. An odd building surely; one old
tower and on either side of it bow-windowed circular rooms like
ears. The grass and bushes of an entangled nettled garden spread
almost to the old door, whose front was lined with thick iron bars,
studded with large flat-faced nails. Out of one of the upper windows a garment was hanging to dry, and it flapped humorously
in the moonlight. A big white cat came out of the shadows and
rubbed itself against David's legs, mewing.

He banged the old knocker, that was an old man's face with
nose and chin meeting, against the thick wood. His knock re-
sounded as though it would wake the heart of the Screes, but it
didn't disturb the cat that continued to mew and rub against his
boots.

After a while an old man, holding a lamp high, unbarred the
door and opened it an inch. David must have looked giant-tall in
that moonlight, for the old man nearly dropped the lamp in his
astonishment. But he had been told maybe that there would be a
visitor, so he opened the door wider, and the cat slipped into the
hall.

He was a funny old man, bent and hairy, wearing a green
apron. He had quite a little company of hairs on the end of his
nose. Without a word he led the way, David striding after.

They were seated about a table in a dining-room eating and
drinking. Because of the odd uneven shape of the tower this
room was like a box with its corners pushed in. It seemed that
the corners of the ceiling (which was an ornate one, painted with
faded pink-bottomed cherubs festooned with chains of roses)
would fall in also, for they bulged as though under a heavy weight.
The room was badly lit with two candles in silver candlesticks.

There was a spinet in one corner and a large yellow globe like a huge dried melon in another. The white cat was curled up on the broad window-seat.

About the table were Mr Denburn, Miss Denburn, an ancient lady in rusty black and a high white wig, and a broad thickset coarse-looking fellow with a round red face like a sun. In the poor light Mr Denburn was more sallow and hatchet-faced than ever. With his long protruding chin his face had the shape of a yellow-pointed shoe, and his eyebrows looked as though they were made of horsehair and fastened on with glue.

He tried to be genial this evening, but geniality was difficult for him. He bade David welcome, pushed a cold pie towards him, and filled his glass with wine. The thickset man was introduced as Captain Bann. He was drunk quietly, and, it appeared, in no good temper.

'I must offer my apologies,' David said. 'My business is with some of your sheep, Mr Denburn. I should have told you so last evening. You will be forced to have two visits from me.'

But Mr Denburn was delighted to speak of his sheep. His self-sufficiency was amazing. To hear him speak you would think that there were no sheep like his in the whole of northern England – and yet David knew that he was a poor farmer – almost no farmer at all. While he spoke he wriggled his body up and down, as though there were a perpetual itch between his shoulder-blades.

In a very patronizing tone he cursed the neighbourhood, the climate, the Hanoverian government, the war with France, and humanity quite in general. He gave David to understand that he had for long led a life in London very different from this present one; that had it not been for certain rogues and vagabonds he would now have his place at court, and that he had rendered this same cursed Hanoverian family much personal service in the '45, but that he could wish now that the Pretender had pushed on to London when he might have done, and thrown the whole London lot into the Thames.

'Aye, aye,' gurgled Captain Bann, his nose in his glass. 'Pox on the lot and into the Thames with the bastards!'

At this point Miss Denburn and the ancient lady rose to retire, and David hurried to open the door. The cat stretched itself and followed them out. At the door he bowed and Miss Denburn curtsied, smiling with the greatest friendship as she did so, and he, as she smiled, felt his body tingle all over.

Returning to the table David found that the two gentlemen were regarding his physique with great interest. Indeed Captain

Bann, who was now far gone in liquor, proposed that the two of them should strip there and then and try a fall. There should be stakes which Mr Denburn should hold. He was beginning immediately, swaying on his stout legs, having taken off his coat, to undo his stock. David, however, firmly declined the honour.

It was shortly plain enough to him that these were two very considerable scoundrels. They had an understanding which hinted at many mutual past knaveries, and Mr Denburn was the master of the other. Denburn did not drink; his eyes under the absurd eyebrows were never still. He cracked walnuts in his sharp bony fingers as though he were cracking beads.

Captain Bann was made quarrelsome with drink, and wished to provoke David to some argument. He spilled wine on the table-cloth and paddled his fingers in it, even flicking a drop or two into David's face. But David was not to be provoked. It occurred to him, however, that had Denburn been of that mind the two of them would have set upon him without any uneasiness of conscience; it was an unpleasant notion to have Denburn's long fingers at his windpipe and the Captain's brawny shoulders pressed on his stomach. That he could manage them both he did not doubt, but it was a lonely spot, lonely and most ominously silent. There was no sound at all but the tapping of a branch against the pane behind the green curtains.

So, very shortly, he made his excuses to depart. Denburn did not attempt to stop him, and they arranged for a morning visit to the sheep.

He had no further word with Miss Denburn.

Quite early, however, next morning he encountered her, and had with her what was for him a very eventful conversation. Waking again very early (this last night he had had his bed to himself) he went down to the lake and stood watching the silver ripples break from the mirror, running out of the glassy stillness as though with childlike delight into the young stiff reeds at the water's edge.

He stood there, looking down, as the light broadened over the Screes, heard steps, looked up and saw Miss Denburn. She had not seen him in the half-light, but was walking along the lake path, her head up, her body beautifully free, taking in the morning air.

He straightened himself and bowed, smiling very shyly. He had read few romances and little poetry, books gave him poor pleasure, but if he had he would have known that this was a fitting time and place for a lovers' meeting. As it was, he did not think of himself as a lover but only as David Herries, delighted at the presence of a most beautiful lady. In actual truth he did not think consciously of anything at all.

She was as little self-conscious as he. To reveal a secret, she had fallen in love with him instantly at first sight in the inn yesterday. It had seemed to her as natural as mounting a horse. She had fallen in love a number of times in her young life already. She thought falling in love exceedingly pleasant. She was by nature impetuous and fond of all natural things – eating, sleeping, hunting, fishing, chattering, loving, hating.

When she saw a handsome thing she went directly towards it. David was by far the handsomest man she had ever seen. She had thought about him incessantly since first meeting him and how she might meet him again without anyone else being by. She had come out this morning on the chance. He was the kind of man she fancied would be up early.

Had he said at once this morning: 'I love you. Marry me,' she would have answered at once: 'Yes, I will,' without a moment's proper hesitation.

All her life she had been with bad, ugly-thinking, vilely-acting men, and she would have followed a tramp to get away from them. It was the mercy of a sometimes benevolent Providence that young Sarah was not by now wedded to a tin kettle and a baked hedgehog with a rabble of ragged children at her skirts. She had no caution whatever. But, as David was shortly to learn, escaping from Mr Denburn was not so easy as it might be.

As a matter of history David did, within a surprisingly short time, tell her that he loved her. As has been already explained, he was in a state very imminent on declaring his passion to someone or other, and this was a girl most exactly after his physical desire. Whether they were, either of them, after the spiritual needs of one another was something neither gave a thought towards. By good chance for the blood-history of many later Herries they were, both of them, fine creatures. Every once and again these chancy things happen fortunately.

In any case, Sarah looking at him with the smiling eagerness with which a young puppy looks at some human who promises a walk, David naturally advanced in boldness very swiftly.

They walked beside the lake together while the sun came over the hill and worked patterns of gold into the black reflections of the precipitous Screes. Over their shoulders Middle Fell looked down upon them benevolently.

David began with becoming modesty. He explained some facts about himself and that he lived at Rosthwaite in Borrowdale.

'I know Rosthwaite,' she remarked reflectively. Then she added: 'My name is Sarah.'

He told her that he had a business with Liverpool trade, that he was buying land thereabouts, and, in fine, that things were going well with him.

'You are married, Mr Herries?' she asked him, giving him a very quick look and thinking him so handsome that she longed to pull his ears.

No, he was not. He looked at her as he said it, and blushed. Gathering boldness, he asked her whether she lived alone here with her father, and said that it must be bleak enough in the wintertime.

She startled him by the answer:

'Mr Denburn,' she said, 'is not my father.'

He was astonished indeed.

'No. He is my uncle. My parents are both dead. My father died in the year previous. My uncle is my guardian.'

David was encouraged then to hint that it had not seemed to him natural that Mr Denburn should be her father. He hinted that he did not like Mr Denburn.

'Like him indeed!' her voice rang out. 'He is detestable! I have always hated him. He was my father's brother and held a strange influence over my father. In his last years my father was, I fear, quite in my uncle's hands. I inherit some wealth – no great sum – from my dear mother. I was their only child. My uncle removed to this lonely spot that he might influence my determination. It is his desire that I should marry that pig of a Captain whom you saw besotted at the table last night.

'My resolve for my own independence irritates them vastly. I am only seeking some opportunity to return to London. But this guardianship is strict. Even now the Captain is, I wager, if he is not sleeping off his drunkenness, somewhere on the watch. If not the Captain, then my uncle. You see, Mr Herries, I am a captive.'

She said it laughing, and he greatly admired her spirit, but he fancied that behind her laughter there was an apprehension. She was not, he imagined, as happy as she seemed.

She told him that she must return. Even now it was dangerous for her to be away.

He offered then his assistance, in any sort, in any kind. And a moment later, without realizing the extravagant speed of his progress, he was telling her that he loved her, that he had loved her at the first sight in the inn, that he had never truly loved anyone before, and that he would love her, he fancied, for ever and ever.

'What!' she cried. 'You the age you are and the handsome man you are and never loved anyone before!'

'Never!' he declared, and with more truth than she could dream of. She did perhaps, young as she was, realize that there was something different in the freshness and sincerity of his declaration from the ordinary fashion of men.

Her eyes softened and her face shone with pleasure as she looked at him. She could not help herself. He was so very delightful. She gave him her hand and told him that she would meet him again that afternoon. She would walk across the fields to a farm at the foot of Lingmell with the old woman who was her duenna. She would see that the old woman did not disturb them.

They parted like two children enchanted with one another's company. He was very young for his years.

He saw Mr Denburn that morning and Mr Denburn's sheep. He bought the sheep and hated Denburn. He would in any case have hated him, but now, because he knew that Sarah was oppressed by him, it was difficult for him to keep his hands away from him.

Denburn of course noticed nothing. As with all self-appreciatory persons he was lost in his own glories. Because David said little he discovered him to be good company. His condemnations covered the whole world: no one and nothing escaped them. With his scorn there was mingled a mean anger and an avaricious greed. He would have haggled over the sheep's price for an hour but David gave him at once what he asked. He scarcely saw the sheep, he did not see Denburn at all; he saw only young Sarah with all the glories of heaven about her head and himself in bliss at her feet. He also saw himself as the inevitable father of her children. When he had left him and was back at the inn he went up to the stuffy little chamber, into which the May sun was now pouring, sat on the miserable truckle-bed and endeavoured to control his fire. But he could not. It lapped him around with a burning, shining flame. Never, in his thirty-eight years, had he approached this sensation of worship, happiness and almost agonizing wonder. He had not known that love would be like this nor that it could descend with such precipitate suddenness. He had no doubts about its issue. He would shortly marry Sarah and that was enough.

How he would marry her, snatch her from her captivity, did not yet occur to him; nor did he at present think of his father nor

Deborah nor Herries. He had never been able to think of more than one thing at a time.

And so when he met her on a sunny meadow under Lingmell he could not at first speak at all.

The ancient lady who accompanied her had been left in the farmhouse asleep. It was her virtue that, placed in a comfortable chair, her handkerchief over her face, she fell instantly asleep, like any bird with a cloth over its cage. Sarah had discovered this pleasant trait in her and profited by it.

So in that meadow, the shadows from the hill gathered about it as they walked, they confessed their love. It was not, it could not be, a very lengthy business, when two are instantly of the same mind, afraid of nothing and regardless either of the present or future.

David, when at last he found words, said: 'I told you this morning. I must repeat it. I cannot help it if you are angry. I have been thinking of you incessantly since the morning and I must tell you again that I love you.'

Sarah replied: 'I am not angry at all. I loved you the first instant in the inn.'

David said (but not meaning it): 'You should consider it. I am very old.'

And Sarah answered: 'Young men never pleased me.'

Then he kissed her, very gently, not as he intended to kiss her later on.

They were both so exquisitely happy that for a long time they could not speak at all but looked at one another, walked a little and looked at one another again.

After a while it occurred to them (the gathering shadows warned them) that the old lady would soon wake and that something must be done.

'Of course,' David said, 'you must come away with me.' He stood drinking in her loveliness. She was none of these thin willowy women that you could crack over your knee, but strong, broad-breasted, of noble carriage, health, vigour, energy, simple directness in every look and gesture. A third, watching them, might have thought them of the same family.

'Of course I must,' said Sarah and then moved, with more practical directness than he, on to the difficulties.

It seemed, at first sight, an easy matter. All, David said, that she had to do was to walk out of the house. He would have a horse at hand, and so, over the Pass and home. Indeed his first suggestion was that she should come with him immediately.

That, so eager and impetuous were they, might have been (and much trouble spared them) were it not for the old woman. Sarah would not leave her to the fury of her uncle. She must go when the old lady was not on duty. From this she would not stir.

David began now to be once more his true, slow, cautious self. This needed thinking of; there was Herries, there was his father. There were his own affairs. He hesitated less than ever as to his purpose, but everything must be soundly based at home, ready for her when she came.

He discovered then that she was being guarded as a prisoner. Although she might laugh with her young indomitable courage, he began to realize that these last months had been torture for her, and that, had he come or no, she would not in any case have endured much more of it. A more suspicious soul than David might at this point have asked himself whether she were not using him only as a means of escape. But with all his simplicity he was astute. He knew that she was in his own state of blissful bewildering love.

They could not, in fact, make any very serious decisions that afternoon. After a sentence they would stop and walk in a world together so magical and removed from argument that all plans were monstrously unreal. The most that it came to was that, early tomorrow morning, he would take his sheep home, and then shortly return to take her after the sheep.

Only it must be soon. For every reason, but chiefly because waiting seemed an incredible folly – it must be soon.

Once again he kissed her, behind the thick body of a chestnut tree (lest they should be observed), and this time it was a long embrace, with all heaven in it. That was the first true kiss of David's life.

Once, as they neared the farm, she turned to him, and there was a new seriousness in her voice. 'Do not think,' she said, 'because I have told you so quickly that I love you that it is a light word. I have been moving to this my whole life long.' She spoke as though she had already lived an eternity. And he very gravely answered: 'I will love you, dear Sarah, for ever.'

They came into the farm and found the old lady fast sleeping under a red handkerchief, and snoring lustily.

SAGA OF DAVID

II

THE FIGHT ABOVE WASDALE

ABDUCTIONS were common enough at that moment in the world's history; they roused no sort of comment unless the persons concerned were of social or financial splendour. David and Sarah were of neither. It was in fact a completely minor affair to everyone save the few persons concerned.

It was unimportant to David's father. David hinted to him that he had discovered the lady and might, if fortune favoured, bring her home. Herries was digging. He looked up, his face muddy, his eyes angry at withdrawing from their proper business.

He told David to go to hell, find anyone there he fancied, and do with her what he pleased. He was in one of his old moods, cursing the mud that splashed into his face, cursing his aching bones, but happy and tranquil in his occupation.

And David in his turn was angry in the old way. He abused his father handsomely, and going into the house felt a proper relief. He could do as he pleased: whatever way he went his father would be behind him.

In the doorway he met Mirabell. She was standing there watching a flight of birds cutting their way through the fresh spring air.

She was holding in both hands a tub filled with dirty water, her thin spare arms straining to the weight. Her face, beautifully pale like ivory under the tawny hair, was raised to the sky with a childlike pleased curiosity.

She smiled shyly at David. 'You see them best on the Fell,' she said, 'where you may follow them for a fine distance . . . The hills have taken them.'

He tried to relieve her of the tub but she wouldn't allow him. She was always shy with him, eager to please him without giving him any of herself.

But what he felt now was the amazing contrast that she made with young Sarah. On every occasion that he saw a woman now, Sarah was the more wonderful to him. This fancy of his father's – he liked her, felt kind to her, would be glad to please her, but she was a fade-away unhappy wisp, holding herself in against everybody, while Sarah!—

At the thought of her he was in such a glow of happiness that he could have picked Mirabell up in his arms and tossed her like a feather.

She, with her funny, almost witch-like perception of the moods of others, said:

'You're happy today.'

'I am,' he answered, throwing his arms up to the sky. 'I am! I am! I am!'

He was in a mood to tell her of it.

'I have found a maid – over the hill. I'm going to fetch her back, and marry her.'

To his surprise Mirabell was happy, as though good news had come to herself.

'I'm glad. Where will you live?'

'Here.'

'Yes, don't leave your father.' She put down the tub and caught his great hand in her thin bony fingers. She looked up at him, smiling. 'Is she young? And beautiful? And a fine mother for your children?'

'She is young and beautiful, and a fine mother for my children,' he repeated after her, smiling back at her. They had never come so close together before.

'Bring her here, Davy. There is room enough.'

'Oh yes,' he answered, looking up at the old house where in one corner the roof was slipping, and where a chimney cocked sarcastically with a drunken leer. 'There is room. But, Mirabell, why should we not all go from here? There is money enough for a fine place where they can take Father newly. Here they have always hated him. Persuade him, Mirabell.'

But she shook her head. 'In that I can't move him. He is stuck in the place.'

'For you he'd do anything.'

'No. That – never.'

Then she picked up the tub again, moved into the court, and over her shoulder repeated: 'Bring her here, Davy. Good luck to your hunting.'

Next morning he went back to Wasdale. He walked over. After much thinking he had decided that a horse would be a danger, that he must be as little visible as possible before the event. He was inclined at this moment to consider but lightly of the whole business

For Sarah to escape from two such elderly ruffians as Denburn and the Captain would be surely no problem. It seemed to him as he walked under a clear blue sky, singing, the very simplest thing in the world . . .

In the little valley by the beck under the Pass at the foot of Lingmell there was a deserted shepherd's hut that he had marked on the last occasion. This, he thought, would do very well to pass a night in without observation.

He reached it in the late afternoon when the light was failing. The silence was profound, broken only by the gentle running of the beck. There was a sweet air scented with water and fresh grass. He sat in the little hut on a pile of dry bracken while the colours faded and the sky whitened, thinking, happily, triumphantly, of all the joy that was coming to him. He hadn't known that love could so change the world in a second of time.

He stretched his body out, his arms behind his head, and looked up at a little hole in the turfed roof through which the sky was like a crystal cup.

His imagination had Sarah in his arms, and he whispered to her: 'My darling, my little love,' and enjoyed himself hugely.

When it was dark he went out. He met nobody until before he reached the wood of Scarf Hall. The world seemed to be entirely deserted.

When he came to the grass-grown drive he stole carefully to the rear of the tower to see whether a window were open. On the left side he found a window brilliantly lighted. The shine streamed out, illuminating a strange little garden that had once been carefully tended. There was a thick box hedge with animals cut upon it – a cock, a swan, a dog – and in the centre of the little lawn a square sundial. This was all lit with the pale shadowed light from the candles in the room.

Standing in the dark by the box hedge he could see into the room. The table, whose surface shone like a mirror, had on it a large bowl of fruit, a bottle of wine, and a board of red and yellow chessmen set out as though for play. The white cat was curled up near the yellow globe. A large silver candelabrum with many branches threw a fine dazzling radiance over the broad figure of the Captain, who was seated, alone in the room, at the table, his large red face between his hands, staring in front of him, a grand picture of drunken stupor. The room was so still that it might have been a painted scene.

After a while a breeze descended among the trees and, as though he had been roused by that (although he could not have heard it), the Captain took the bottle of wine with a shaking hand, filled a long thin glass, raised it to his mouth, drank it, and then, amazingly, climbed to his feet and shook his fist threateningly and savagely in the air, at nothing in particular.

He was the picture then of a man very angry and very foolish. His rage seemed to possess him for he suddenly, with a curve of his stout arm, swept all the chessmen off the board, raised the board itself and flung it to the ground. Then he stared about him as though he had just awakened from a dream. It was odd enough to see all this in dumb show and hear no sound.

A thin cold rain began to fall, pattering among the leaves.

The door opened, the Captain turned, and, miracle of miracles, Sarah entered. She was dressed exquisitely in a silver dress, and she carried a candle. When she saw the Captain she would retire again, but he stumbled to the door and stood with his back to it.

She blew out the candle, placed it quietly on the table and turned to him, her head raised. She said something to him; he replied, very ludicrously falling on one knee. She came to the window and at that same moment David stepped forward into the light. He stood there in an agony of apprehension lest the Captain should see him, but the Captain, drunken as he was, could not balance himself on his knee and sprawled to the floor.

Sarah laughed (and a fine splendid sight it was to see), stepped over his body and, at the moment that her hand was on the door, looked back into the garden.

She saw him. Heaven be thanked, she saw him! Her face was rosy, she put her hand for an instant to her breast, then left the room. The Captain lay there where he had fallen, his face in the chessboard.

Some window must have been slightly open, for the candles began all hurriedly to blow as though they were laughing at the Captain, and in that same new flurry of wind Sarah had joined David by the hedge.

They exchanged no word. He drew her face to his, his hands were about her neck, the rain blessing both of them.

At last, withdrawing from one another, they began to laugh in sheer joy of seeing each other again. He drew her away into the back of the little garden out of the light, then hurriedly told her his plan: 'It must be tomorrow night. I will be here in this same place. At what hour?'

She whispered back: 'At this same time. But I may not escape at once. I will come from that window . . .' Then in sheer

happiness she caressed his face with her hand, tracing his mouth,
his eyes, his nose.

'I hadn't dreamt it would be so soon. I have watched two evenings. I must pull your ears. It was the first thing in the inn I
desired.'

'You will be damp. The rain—'

'Kiss me again. Hold me tightly. If I had other clothes I would
come now . . .'

'Do you love me? Have you thought of me?'

'I love you so . . . I haven't ate a thing these two days. My
uncle . . .'

She broke off, listening. The Captain had come through the
window, lurched on to the bright square of lawn, took off his wig
and lifted his naked scalp to the rain. He stumbled towards them,
holding his wig in his hand.

'Water,' they heard him say. 'Damned refreshing . . . cool to
the head.' He rocked into the sundial which he clasped with both
arms.

They waited, scarcely breathing, while he hugged the dial.
Then they kissed again, a long embrace, suddenly not caring for
the Captain. She came out into the light, walked right past him,
through the window into the house.

He stood, scratching his head, not knowing whether he had
seen anything or no. David slipped away.

He slept the sleep of the innocent, the just and the healthy that
night in the hut and dreamt of nothing and nobody. He woke to
a cold day with a great wind that drove bellying grey clouds in
riotous hurry over the hills as though preparing for some grand
show when the clouds should be packed away. All day they rolled,
leaving the tops clear, sharp and cold beneath their smoky procession. All day David stayed in the little valley, eating the bread
and meat that he had brought with him and drinking out of the
stream. He climbed the Pass as far as Stye Head then, to warm
himself. It was but a little way down into Borrowdale. There
could be but little trouble in the affair. They would be at Herries
by early morning.

He had but one encounter; a thin wiry choleric Squire with
some hounds who, attended by two men, was going up the Pass
as he came down. The Squire wanted company and held David
by the coat while he enlarged on his affairs. Like another Squire
of his time he was all for 'lending' anyone who disagreed with
him 'a flick'. He had a long matter in his head about an estate
that joined his own, somewhere, David gathered, Eskdale way.

'Join the two and there's no larger estate in the kingdom. I had rather bate something than have the pox of a fellow advising me on my own ground.' He had an especial cursing fury at the towns and London in particular. 'I'd be a Hanoverian 'fore I'd show my arse among their smoking chimneys. Pox on all Hanoverians and Presbyterians either. Thou must come drink a bottle at my table. I'll show thee some trees and some horses also. You show your fancy very plainly. I'm ne'er mistaken in a man. Thou'rt no Hanoverian.'

He would then back with David and drink with him in the Wasdale Inn. Then, to David's consternation, suggested they should impose themselves on Scarf Hall. He knew, it seemed, Denburn. 'He's a mean varlet,' and he'd doff his clothes to give him a lick as soon as spit in his face; nevertheless there'd be wine there and they'd make a rousing night of it.

It took a quarter of an hour's good work to dissuade him from this and to push him on up the hill again, but at last, swearing at his men and his hounds, he vanished round the bend, his little wiry legs the last visible part of him.

The only merit of this adventure was that it was pleasant to realize the general unpopularity of Denburn. All humankind doubtless loathed him. David had through the afternoon some apprehension lest the testy Squire, in search of good liquor, should turn and descend again, and he watched the Pass with some anxiety. But there was no figure on the Pass. Doubtless he had gone, cursing, down into his own place in Eskdale.

The rain threatened all day but never fell. When at last darkness came, the hills were clear and later there would be a moon.

In the little garden again he performed the silliest act of his life. Looking back afterwards he never could see what drove him to it. It may have been the cold, which was bitter, or impatience to bring things to an issue, or sheer childish playfulness.

In any case the garden was chill, half an hour's waiting made him stamp his feet with restlessness, the house was dark without a visible light. He stepped over the lawn, brushing against the sundial, felt for the window of the dining-parlour, found it unlatched and was inside.

There he paused, his hand on the table-edge. He listened; there was not a sound but a hysterical clock that giggled somewhere like a schoolgirl. He opened the door, crept into the hall, a wavering candle turned the corner, and in a moment he had the old lady in his arms.

He clasped her to him as though he loved her, his broad hand over her mouth, and pulled her, lighted candle and all, back into the parlour, and closed the door very quietly behind him. The old lady was in a strange garment of faded green, her grey hair about her shoulders and on her lined wrinkled face an expression of such convulsive terror that it touched his compassion. But she did not speak, only gaped at him, her mouth open like a young bird's. He took the candle from her trembling hand and set it down on the table.

'You love Miss Denburn,' he said hurriedly. 'I know you do. Miss Denburn is in great peril and must be away with me tonight. I would not put you to any sort of inconvenience, madam, but every moment has its danger. Assist us and you shall be rewarded magnificently.'

Her mouth opened and shut. She kept plucking at her green gown that it might cover her négligé. The leaping candle made the queerest figure behind her on the wall. She said at last in the oddest voice, between a squeak and a whisper:

'There's the Captain coming down and we're all undone.'

He saw from that that she was on the right side and had probably been already warned by Sarah, but she trembled like a flower and he, he feared, might at any moment drop to the ground in a faint.

So he pushed her into a chair, poured some wine from a decanter on the table into a glass and made her drink it. She gasped and gurgled, but, it was plain, enjoyed it.

'Now, madam, you must return to Miss Denburn and tell her that I am waiting for her here. Then go to your chamber and remain there.'

He spoke sternly, but he smiled. And she, to his astonishment, smiled back at him, put her finger to her lip with an evident enjoyment of the conspiracy and, clutching her gown about her, stole softly out of the room again.

A moment later, listening in the darkness, he heard the Captain's voice. The Captain was not drunk tonight. He sounded another man, rallying the old lady with quite a deep dignity and precision.

She, David gathered, was endeavouring to escape up the stairs and he detaining her.

'No shame on your attire, Sister,' he was saying (that plainly his jocular name for her). 'You shall drink a glass with me – a handsome night-cap. The moon will be up and we will salute it through the open window.'

She replied something and then David could hear her hastening upstairs. A second later the Captain was through the door, so near to David that he could feel the hot breath on his cheek.

He was himself pressed back against the wall as flat as his great body would allow, his hand ready on his sword-hilt.

The Captain went past him and began to curse for a light. He had a fashion, it seemed, of talking to himself. 'Curses on the dark! 'Tis a house of no discipline. But I'll not drink this evening. I'll match Ned with his sobriety, blast his superior elegance. And I'll not be longer here neither; it's a job or it's no bargain, nasty skinflint.'

He moved to the window. David could see his broad bulk, in the thin light that preceded the moon, his hands in his breeches pocket, his legs straddling. He continued to talk as an angry boy might: 'I'm no such fool as he'd think me, as he'll find in his own time. The girl's well enough, but she hates me sober and loathes me drunk.

'And there's Jane at Newmarket. . . A shrew's a shrew however much gold she carries. . . And this plaguy country where it rains like Egypt's plague, and no company to make a night of it . . .' He yawned prodigiously, then, with an exclamation, found in his pocket what he wanted. He fingered the tinder-box, struck a light, turned and saw David.

In another second he would have shouted but with a leap David was across the room, had knocked the light from him and hurled him with a crash to the ground, his hand over his mouth. The noise of the crash must surely rouse the house and as, after that, they struggled, David's ears were alert for Denburn's footsteps. But there was nothing save the chattering clock that seemed suddenly to redouble its pace in a violent excitement.

That was no mean struggle. The Captain must in earlier days have been a man of his hands, and even now, weakened by lazy living and drink, his big body had energy. Had David been free it would have been a matter of a few moments, but as it was he must keep his hand over the man's mouth, which hampered him sadly. The Captain wriggled like a worm, now bottom up, then with his legs twisting like a centipede's, then with a sudden force in his belly that turned it into iron, pressing against David's arm. He had his hand in David's eye and was knuckling him lustily until, throwing his body on to the man's stomach, David had a free arm and could press the other's hand back to the floor.

Their panting breath and the roll of their bodies on the floor was the only sound.

Then the door was open and there was a light. David could not turn to see and had an awful fear it was Denburn. But it was Sarah's voice:

'Quick,' she said. 'My uncle is on the stairs.'

'The bands from the curtains,' he gasped. 'Fasten his legs.'

With admirable energy and dexterity she had them there and (as she told him later) tied them about those stout ankles with the greatest satisfaction. She was as brisk as though her life had been spent in such tasks.

'The garden-house . . . Over the lawn . . .'

They pushed the window and dragged him out. David's wide and deep kerchief was over his nose and mouth, the curtain-bands over his arms and legs. These were temporary enough and would stand little resistance, but for the moment they must do.

David's huge arms dragged him across the lawn (his head bumped the sundial), through the path by the box hedge, and, hidden in thicket, there was the garden-house. It was a small enough place, piled with straw and gardening-tools, but they bundled him in, closed the door and bolted it. Then they ran.

By the path that skirted the lake-end they stopped. She caught his hand and leaned against him, recovering her breath. They listened intently. It was strange after those moments of hot panting struggle to stand still in a world, cold, motionless, at their feet the grey rounding of the lake and about them everywhere the dim shapes of the hills. The house, the room, the heaving body of the Captain, all in China . . .

A dog barked somewhere. The reeds rustled. He held her to him as though she were part of himself.

'Now . . . how long may that garden-house bolt last?'

'Not long; the wood is rotten.'

David laughed. 'He had an immoderate taste of my fingers . . . Come. We'll do the kissing later. There's no time . . .'

They were off again, through the little gathering of houses, then the foot of the Pass.

'Soon there'll be the moon.'

Before they started to climb, in that strange milky glow, they turned towards one another and kissed. Her immediate ready courage of the last half-hour pleased him most divinely. That was the companion that he would have, a man in swiftness, eagerness of perception, a woman when the softer time demanded it.

He was proud of her mettle beyond any personal pride that he had ever known.

'You did that bravely. Oh, I love you a thousand times for it!'

She took his head in her hands, fondling it, bending it to her breast. 'I did not know that love would be thus,' she murmured. Silly stuff to both of them had they heard others whisper it, but they might be allowed it, the night before them being sterner than they knew.

Indeed so little concerned were they that they started up the Pass hand-in-hand, like two children.

She told him her adventure. The old lady had warned her, she had started down the stairs when she heard the crash of the tumble. Then there was panic for her! What to do? To go forward and risk what she might find below or to turn back and wait? The door of Denburn's room opened. It was dark on the stair and she waited, listening for his movement. He asked her from his door had she heard anything.

'Only an owl,' she had called back to him, her heart thumping. He went in again, closing his door, and once more she listened. Now everything was still save the clock. Only the white cat (that had doubtless slipped through the door when the Captain opened it) slithered up to her, rubbing against her legs. She had taken that as an omen, and so went forward. Then, most foolishly, when she saw the pair of them struggling on the floor she had wanted to laugh. The Captain's broad beam and his knuckle in David's eyes . . .

But at the thought of that she caught David's hand the tighter.

So they walked on, unconscious of anything save the splendour of being in love, of the health of their bodies. One hundred and fifty years later a descendant of theirs would be walking up this same Pass with the lady of his choice to whom he had just declared his passion. She had accepted him, but, as he kicked the rough shale from under his feet, he would be wondering, in the manner of his time, whether he had done wisely. She was pretty enough, but might she not sicken after children? Of course with birth-control methods as safe as they were . . . Her nose certainly went blue with the cold (although tomorrow was the first of May it was damned cold) and her taste in Chinese art was uncertain . . . 'Darling,' he was, a hundred and fifty years later, remarking, 'that book of Breasted's shows quite plainly . . .'

And now at this same moment David, looking back down the milky path and feeling at his sword, said most happily: ''Twould be no bad place for a fight . . . if your uncle has the stomach for it.' Only the wind, whistling by, answered them. There was no suspicion of a pursuer.

He kissed her again. He really couldn't kiss her enough; this kissing was so different from any that he had ever known.

Then the moon peered over the edge of Lingmell. She scarcely showed herself, a fingernail of pale colour, but she was rising; very soon the Pass would be flooded with light, the moon that ushered in May.

But it was not to be just yet. There drifted, in the odd fashion of inconstancy that these hills have, sudden filmy wisps of mist, the edges of the thinnest gauze, having no especial purpose, rising from nowhere, born of nothing, so thin as to be transparent with the dim preface of the moon behind them. And at the same moment a new wind began to shrill up the valley between Lingmell and the Pass.

David after many years knew this country well and something in the wind told him that these vapours would not remain transparent for long. An odd unanalysed anxiety caught him. Mist was the one thing of which he had not thought.

'Oh, look!' Sarah caught his arm and pointed to the valley. ''Tis as though a great kettle were boiling.' The vapour was coming up towards them in spirals of smoke and, you might suppose, little clouds of steam. David was not imaginative, but, in his anxiety to have this adventure safely over, he was ready to fancy some active agency down there in the valley, some enemy raising a huge fire of damp logs to send up a torrent of twisting smoke.

'We must press on,' he said. 'The Pass can be cursedly confusing in the mist.' The thin gauze skirted the Pass like a live thing and as it thickened above them, obscuring the rising moon, the world darkened again and chilled, the wind whispering at their ears.

An odd thing happened then to David. He fancied that his father was walking beside them. He could almost see the man, tall and powerful, with his long hair, his shoulders a little shrunken, his whole body moving forward with that obstinate energy that was so peculiarly his, his eyes staring into some imagined dream of space.

It was as though he said: 'There is trouble for you now, and so I am here. You have taken this girl in a single second, forgetting our bond together. But you will not be permitted to forget it. We are Herries always, and we Herries are always together against the world whether we wish it or no, and so it will always be. Our bond is for no time or termination. It endures infinitely. A weariness, perhaps, but nevertheless a law.'

Indeed David may at this moment have been thinking these things, for he was suddenly conscious of his father, and not very long ago, at Herries, his father had said something of this kind to him when he asked him why he did not marry, and added that marriage would be no escape for him because he was indubitably a Herries, and must always belong to those of his own blood rather than to anyone from outside.

It was only for a second in time that David saw his father striding there beside them, but it was a second that contained many centuries in its form.

The incident thirteen years back, in Carlisle, came to him when he had watched in the fog on the walls. He had lost his father and then, in the early morning, his father had found him. There had been an extraordinary relief in that reunion, something far beyond the immediate circumstance of the incident.

Now again, for nearly two days, he had lost his father, absorbed by his sudden love for this girl. His father had held him once more and, for that moment, it had been as though Sarah did not exist.

He had her again, catching her hand. The Pass was really steep here with a sharp edge, and the mist was now boiling up from the valley in thick rolling masses of cloud.

He stayed her to caution her, and at that same instant the tops cleared, the moon sailed out, full and faintly red-cherry coloured. Everything was illuminated, the Gavel on their left, Lingmell, Scafell, the Pike, the rough track of the Pass winding down into the valley.

They turned to look back, and there, sharply clear in the moonlight, pressing up the Pass were two figures, Denburn and the Captain.

Each saw the other and stood transfixed. David was happy.

'If only the mist holds off I can deal with them. They won't use their pistols so long as you are here. Oh, but I'm longing for a cut at your uncle—'

The distance between them was short. The two men were standing on a green promontory that stretched out of the Pass over the valley, looking to Wasdale and the sea. They were exceedingly clear in the moonlight, first like statues, then beginning with feverish energy to scramble forward up the Pass. Denburn shouted something and David, laughing, shouted back:

'Ohè! Ohè! Ohè! Cut-throat and Captain! I'll buy you both for a farthing.' He was like a boy again at the thought of a fight.

'I could meet them here,' he said reluctantly. 'At this bend.
I'd have the command of the path.'

But Sarah urged him on. Her courage, although she would
never let him know, had failed her. She didn't want him to fight,
she was sick in the stomach, she was suddenly a child of her own
really tender years. She had been brave enough in the house
because that had been a matter of escape, and her uncle had not
shared in it. But now he was almost upon them, and all the terror
and sense of malignant power with which he had always possessed
her returned to her.

Since she had been an infant in the little house, with her father
and mother, in Kensington village, she had known this. She had
caught it first, perhaps, from the terror that her father and
mother had of him.

When he had reached to her and tried to take her on his knee,
she had shivered and gone pale with apprehension. The comfits
that he had given to her had always seemed to her poisoned, the
touch of his hand the touch of a frog.

The natural buoyancy and health of her disposition had prevented this from breeding in her any permanent unhappiness.
Her terror of him was intermittent, only really present when his
physical body forced her to realize it. It was his physical
body that she realized now. Although he was only a manikin of a
figure against those moonlit hills, he was as real and powerful as
though he were there beside them. She was sure that he
would kill David! He had the evil power. There was something
in him that must be stronger than the goodness and courage in
David.

So she urged David forward, running ahead of him, and he
followed, joy in his heart that now he might at last settle with
that dirty fellow who had ill-treated his beloved Sarah, stroking
his sword-hilt as though it were the best friend he had.

They had reached the turn, climbed the boulders, came to the
point where the signpost now assists the aspiring tourist, saw the
tarn lying before them black under the moonlight.

'I will meet them here,' David said, his pistol in one hand, his
sword drawn in the other.

Sarah implored him to go on. He saw then her terror and was,
privately, disappointed in it.

'I will but make a statement or two,' he said quietly, but with
the obstinacy of a small boy. 'Your uncle must understand my
feeling for him before I take you from him. That is justice.'

Then he saw the rising ground that leads past Sprinkling Tarn

and Allen Crags to Esk Hause. 'That would be better,' and, with
her following him, he took the higher fell.

Then, without an instant's warning, the moon was blotted out
again. The mist swept up in an array of thin cloud that veiled the
hills, the fell, the tarn. Before it thickened into a wall of white
muffling vapour they saw the two figures round the corner and
start up the fell towards them.

'Now we are caught indeed,' David whispered. He stood
listening. He felt for her hand, clutching it. 'Don't move from
me,' he cautioned her. ''Tis easy to miss in this cloud. I must
listen for their step.'

But, as always in that mountain-mist, listening he heard every
imagined sound. Rocks seemed to fall from a great height, water
rose in a whirlwind from the lower ground, voices were everywhere, animals rustled at their feet, there was secret laughing, an
army of curses, the ringing of bells, and behind and around all
this a dead cold stillness like the grave.

Forgetting his own caution and thinking he heard his enemy,
he moved away from her.

Again he listened, and suddenly, quite near to him, so that it
was almost at his ear, he heard the Captain's voice: 'I'll not
move till this mist thins. It's the Devil's work . . .'

David turned and there, looming right up at him, and seemingly twice its natural size, was the Captain's body. The Captain
saw him at the same instant and immediately a shot struck the
wind. The echo of the pistol fire was volcanic, as though the
whole system of rock and fell had split with one heave.

Then they were breast to breast and, a moment after, sword to
sword. It was the strangest duel, their bodies visible one moment,
invisible the next, the swords flashing as though with life of their
own, lunging into emptiness, coming up sharply in defence
against no opponent, and for David always the agony that he did
not know where Denburn was; he might have Sarah in his arms
by this; and there was also the part that the mist itself seemed to
take in the affair, eddying around him, sweeping by with a swing
of the wind's arm, beating against him, as though with a personal
meaning.

He realized very quickly that the Captain was in a rage, and
that the anger was personal because they had trussed him and
piled him in the garden-house.

At first he muttered the dirtiest oaths: his personal vanity had
been meanly affronted: but soon his strength began to fail him.
The tussle with David earlier that night, the pressure up the Pass,

the force of his age and his evil living all swiftly told on him. He made a lunge into cold fog, staggered with the impetus, and David's sword was through his arm. With a gurgle as though he had tumbled into a tub of water, he dropped.

David turned to find that the mist had slipped off the lower slope and was hastening, like a live thing, up the hill, torn away like a theatre curtain and flinging into the moonlight all the higher ground as far as Sprinkling Tarn. He could see the edge of that water a curdled grey against banks of vapour. The clouds were everywhere thinning, and the moon shone behind them with a thin glow, giving the shadows of watery ghosts to every rock and stone. As the mist pulled away Sarah ran to him: at his feet curled unconscious was the Captain; quite near to them Denburn, his sword in his hand, watching them. Phantasmal all these figures were, in a world so shadowy and faint that with every moment and shift of the clouds it was a new world.

So David put his arm about Sarah and thought he would say a word to her uncle.

'Go home, Uncle,' he cried. ''Tis cold, and you must be abed. Sarah has said her farewells. She leaves thee the white cat. She is weary of thy company. Go home, go home. Thou art old for the fells at nightfall.'

He saw from where he was that Denburn had no pistols. He was flicking his sword back and forth. The moon was now in full splendour again, and the clouds had rolled back to veil the Gavel and crowd the Pike. The stretch of moor, the edge of the tarn, the Stye Head Tarn below them were brilliantly lit, and all the hills were ebony.

Denburn answered: 'You have killed my friend, ravished my house where you were hospitably entertained, and shall most immediately repent of it.'

The charge of broken hospitality vexed David, for it was, in a manner, true.

'I have not killed your friend,' he answered. 'You had best gather him together and go home with him or he will catch an ague. As to your hospitality I ask you now, with proper deference, have I your leave to wed your niece Sarah Denburn, whom I love and shall cherish always? I have money enough, and prospect of more. I am thirty-eight, and in admirable health. Give us your blessing and I will carry the Captain down myself.'

To this Denburn answered with some foul oaths. His voice had an odd note of surprise in it, as though he could not credit his senses that anyone should treat him with so arrant a disrespect.

'Well then,' said David, 'I will beat thee home for a dirty rascal and bragging bully. Run now, or I'll drive thee down.'

He moved forward. Denburn said nothing, but circled round towards the hills, then ran forward up towards Sprinkling Tarn.

There was something oddly comical in this long man with his waggling moonlit shadow running, but there was method in it. He found his higher ground with the Tarn behind him to the left.

'I'm afraid of no long-legged country bastard,' he cried. 'Leave the girl and go to your own place or I'll slit your ears.' Even here there was yet this odd note of astonished disappointment that he should be so inelegantly treated.

David moved up to him; he saw then that Denburn had been skilful in choosing his place. The moon, richly full, stared down at him; the shadows were baffling and at every step upwards he was under a disadvantage.

Their swords touched and it seemed to Sarah that the hills crowded nearer to watch the better. For her it was indeed the issue of her whole life.

Were David even wounded to unconsciousness she knew that she had no hope of Denburn's mercy after this affront to his pride. She crouched, watching, her hands clasped, her eyes hot and burning. She might possibly have aided him. Already she understood David well enough to realize that if she did he would never forgive her.

But Denburn was no very able swordsman. On higher ground though he was, David, whose reach was tremendous and eye certain, drove him step by step towards the Tarn. Denburn lunged, parried, lunged again with fury, overbalanced, and David had struck his sword from his hand. David himself was no very grand swordsman although he inherited an instinct of it from his father. He had wished all his days to do precisely this, in the manner of all the approved tales and poems.

With joy at his heart he followed the pattern of the romancer. His foot on Denburn's sword, he threw his own on to the turf.

'Now, Mr Denburn,' he said, 'we'll wrestle for it.'

Very certainly he meant to kill him. The man was a dirty misshapen dog who had done nothing but evil and had no right to be in this beautiful world at all. Especially had he no right to be in a world that contained young Sarah.

So he ran forward and they were locked excellently in one another's arms. Denburn was wiry and his fingers were quickly about David's neck. David too was embarrassed by his height and, whether it were his anxiety for Sarah, his climbing to higher ground, or some extra energy that he had put into his swordplay, certainly he could not find his usual easy strength.

Denburn was strong in two particulars. His fingers would not be dislodged from David's throat, his feet would not be dislodged from the ground.

Sway as they might it seemed that his feet had some magic contact with the soil. The fingers tightened and there was a firm thought in David's brain. What if after all he were to lose this? His breath began to come pantingly. The fingers dug inwards like live things with their own live purpose. It was as though his eyes were being pushed from their sockets. The moon rose like a flaming disc, hurled itself through the sky and swept back to its place again, while the black shoulders of the hills rocked and bent. His knees began to sag and the turf to run up to him like the swaying deck of a vessel. He released one arm to catch at those hands, tore at them, but they neither bent nor shook. Only pressed deeper. Denburn's head came curiously towards him, the eyes small, detached, the mouth curved and, as always, coldly self-pleased.

'O Christ!' The voice came from far away, from the very heart of the red and fiery moon.

'I am a strangled man . . .'

He reeled, and with that reel lay the fortune of his destiny. Denburn's hand was shaken. David's body rose; like a dog he shook his throat free. His giant arms crushed the other's in a great grip. He lifted him from his feet, raised him in air, turned staggering with him, and flung him into the Tarn.

The man splashed, sank, did not rise. Heaving with gusts of strangled breath David waited. The ripples died under the moon, but Denburn did not come again. The scene was as still as a glass mirror and the quiet wonderful.

Yet he waited. Then, when he saw that for a certainty Denburn would never return any more, he ran to Sarah.

HERRIES IN 1760

BEAUTY is aroused by Beauty and change answers to change. But in this valley at this time Beauty was spread in vain for natives. They had not yet learnt to find it in the eyes of the outsider. Poet Gray nine years later, peering to find Castle Crag and

Glaramara 'indescribably fearful', was to open a gate that has grown since then most uncomfortably wide.

As to change; perhaps in no corner of England had the escapades and accidents of history made less stir than here. Looking over the flat green surface sheltered so tenderly by its protecting hills, you may see the monks of Furness Abbey riding their nags on survey of their property, or Sir Wilfred Lawson of Isell protecting his German miners, or Radcliffe of Derwentwater in the Civil War turmoil dredging peasants from the Borrowdale fields to support the King and to meet in that conflict their own near neighbours who, under Lawson of Isell, fought for Parliament, stored munitions on St Herbert's Island, burnt the Radcliffe house on Lord's Island, and, riding up Borrowdale over the Stake Pass to Rydal, pleasantly sacked Rydal Hall.

And so to present memories, the old men and women of 1760 who could remember well enough the events of '15 when the Radcliffe house was still standing on Lord's Island and the last Lord Derwentwater lost his poor young head, dying by the axe as a last distinction – and so the Rebel Hunts on the hills after the '45, the terrified fugitives hiding behind the kitchen door, and Butcher Cumberland waiting in Carlisle. And now there was the new road, and more new roads after it, and soon Gray's postchaise and, later, the little boy struggling over his sums at Hawkshead School, and the eyes of the world turning in wondering patronage towards this small square of ground . . .

On this very afternoon of early November 1760, David Herries was looking out from his fields behind Herries on to a scene that no events could alter, that would for two hundred years to come wear the same quiet face. This November weather is cold and sharp, but the sun is out lying flat upon the fields; some of the sheep are away on the fells, on the lower slopes of Thornythwaite and High Knott and Watendlath, some are cropping the short turf in Stonethwaite, some hiding from the wind in the crannies and coverts of the rocks.

The valley has just learnt that on October 25th old George II fell down dead in Kensington Palace. No one has been greatly stirred by this. Only some of the women gave a thought to a young Prince, only twenty-two years of age, a Prince who is really English at last, who says in his opening speech that 'he glories in the name of Briton'.

But, for David, this news meant something. He could not see young Charles James Fox, a boy of eleven, standing in front of his father and reciting in a shrill treble and with proud gestures

lines from *Samson Agonistes*, nor John Wesley, in spite of his
fifty-five years, preaching at five in the morning and finding it a
'healthy exercise', nor Joseph Priestley, twenty-seven years of
age, nosing his nonconformist way to his principles of oxygen,
nor Samuel Johnson, an odd fifty or so, pushing his cumbrous
path through the Strand, cracking his fingers as he went – he
could not tell what the larger world might be at, nor indeed why
it should be at anything at all (he was never a philosopher), but
he did know that a crisis was arriving in his own affairs that must
be met and met with courage and wisdom, and that, behind his
own personal crisis, the solitude and isolation both of this valley
and of his own history were passing and could never return again.

What must he do? What was the right thing not only for himself but for all?

He had married Sarah Denburn in May 1758. It was now the
fourth of November 1760. From then until now, he and his wife
had resided at Herries. Last evening (and here he leant his arms
on the little rough stone wall, staring out in front of him, not feeling the cold, so lost was he in his grave anxiety and distress for
what had occurred) there had been a terrible scene. It had been,
of course, the fault of his father; it had been only the worst of a
number like it that, through this past year, had increasingly
occurred.

It came in the first place from this cursed obstinate determination of his father to remain at Herries. When on that early May
morning he had brought Sarah down to Herries it had seemed
natural enough, even inevitable that they must stay. In the first
place they had remained to face any trouble that might arise. The
Captain, who on that eventful night had found his own way back
to Wasdale, had at once, nursing his wounded arm, ridden off to
his own place, wherever that might be, without word to anyone.
David, remembering the chessmen scattered on the floor and the
futile gestures of vexation, fancied that he had not regretted
Denburn.

No one else, it seemed, had regretted him either. His body had
been found a week later by some of the smugglers who used the
Borrowdale–Ravenglass secret paths for their expeditions and
were none too anxious for much investigation. They had left the
body at the Wasdale Inn, and ridden away. That Sarah Denburn
had married David Herries was proof enough that the Herries
family knew something of the matter, but Denburn, it now
appeared, was so deeply loathed and David himself was so widely
popular, that no more questions were asked. In any case, a

murdered man or so found in the hills was no matter for much curiosity.

The only local consequence of it was that once again 'old Rogue Herries' was connected with darkness. His son had killed the father, and married the daughter (as Sarah was in the outer world supposed to be). They skipped David in their superstitions, allowing him to do as he pleased, but the Rogue had another deed to his reckoning – and, as the wives whispered over the kitchen fires, "twould most surely not be the last'.

But for David, worried just now as perhaps he had never been in his life before, there was no superstition or rumoured chatter involved; there were facts, definite and hard.

The main fact was that the stress and odd circumstance of his father's marriage had been increased and aggravated by the arrival of his own beloved Sarah in this dark, damp and tumbledown place. If David had loved her at sight in Wasdale that love was nothing at all compared with what he felt for her now after a year and half of matrimony.

She was ideally his desire. In her freshness, common sense, cheerfulness, kindness, tenderness she combined for him all the possible virtues. She had with these one fault only, and that would be no fault in any place of her own – it was that she must be putting anything to rights that she saw wrong.

It was not that she was meddlesome, but she was young – even now, after all this matrimony, but twenty-two – and where she saw dirt, incompetence, neglect, she must alter it. Not then with any officiousness or judgement of others, but she must alter it.

What she needed, as David only too clearly saw, was a place of her own. She had done what she could to Herries. She had in a way transformed it. Swept the corners, cleaned the floors, stopped the doors from creaking, ridden pillion with David to Penrith and Kendal to buy a chair, a table, and even, miraculously, a harpsichord. She aired the beds with warming-pans, mended her father-in-law's small-clothes, taught Mrs Benjamin new dishes (and Mrs Benjamin didn't thank her for it) and, through it all, was cheerful, merry, never out of temper, always busy and, it seemed, happy. Only David knew that she was not happy.

Deborah adored her (she pining, poor dear, to be married, and crying on Sarah's shoulder over it). Herries himself liked her. He found her merry and pleasant company. He didn't care how often she whisked about the house with a broom, or told Mrs

Benjamin how to keep the kitchen clean, or scrubbed the old worm-eaten floors. He liked to hear her play on the harpsichord, and often, with her, his old humorous ironic nature would return; he would have fits of his old playfulness again, and race her about the house, and hide behind doors to jump out on her. At these times he seemed to have half his sixty years, and they, the girl of twenty-two and the man of sixty, had a wonderful comradeship. Indeed, David was bitterly reflecting, were it not for Mirabell, they might be now a happy family.

Mirabell! Mirabell! Mirabell! He repeated the name, that had always seemed to him a fantastic and stupid one, aloud. He was beginning to hate her.

He hated her (he had always definite and solemn reasons for everything) because she made (wantonly, as it seemed to him) his father so unhappy, and because she, Mirabell, hated Sarah.

Sarah did not hate Mirabell; on the contrary she liked her, was sorry for her, would have made a friend of her had it been possible. It was true that she did not understand her, but who could understand this melancholy, dreamy, unnatural woman who, although she was now thirty-one years of age, was yet a child in so many things?

His exasperation with her began before he had realized her attitude to Sarah. Why could she not give his father more of what he desired? Even though she did not love him could she not pretend it? Women were good at pretending. Even though she had once had a lover must she mourn him for ever? To watch his father's unceasing tender care of her, to feel his unresting devotion, and to discover at the end of it his unhappiness – this was exasperating enough.

But when she began to avoid Sarah, not to speak to her could she help it, to leave a room when Sarah entered it, his exasperation grew to something deeper. It seemed (David was not good at these states of mind) that Mirabell's dislike had its origin in a resentment that Sarah took to herself the management of the house. She fancied, poor silly child, that it had been her affair. On a day she burst out before them all; this was the only thing she could do, the only service she could render, and now this service had been taken from her. Why, she was mad in this! What had she ever done before Sarah came but carry plates hither and thither, rub the furniture, make the beds? She had had no talent for managing the house at all. How could she, she who had been a gipsy, a liver in caves, a companion of rogues, smugglers?

It was marvellous enough that she had the decency, the

decorous manners that she had; how could she hope to be a
house-woman in the fashion of Sarah who was gentle-born?

And there was more than this. She must always fancy that
Sarah was mocking her, noting her country habits, laughing at
words that she used, and the rest. Sarah never mocked her; she
could not do anything so unkind. It was true that Sarah felt
her difference from the rest of them, but she did not show
Mirabell that she felt it.

Still the hostility grew, and with that hostility the girl's unhappiness, and with that unhappiness his father's strange out-
bursts of rage. They were roused always in the same way, and
directed always against Mirabell. He seemed to rush from serving
her and loving her directly into a tempest of passion when, before
them all, he would abuse her, order her out of the room, surrender to a fit of dreadful violence. Then, after a while, a sort of
horror would come into his eyes, as though he had done an awful
thing, he would sit silent among them, then leave them and go to
her.

When he abused her like this she answered nothing, only her
pale face grew paler, and she would hang her head and go. She
never disobeyed him, never answered back to him, was indeed
submissive to everyone. It was perhaps this very submissiveness
that exasperated David, not being himself a submissive man.

Well, it could not continue. Sarah could endure little more of
it. If his father would not leave Herries then he and Sarah must
leave it. On the other side there was the promise made to his dead
mother and made to himself that he would never leave his father.

But against this there was now the strongest reason of all:
Sarah was with child. Such a scene as last night's was impossible
for her in her condition. The crisis had arrived. There was a fine
house, half manor, half farm, to be bought in Uldale, behind
Skiddaw. Just the place for him in which to start his family. But
to leave his father . . . What must he do? What must he do?

He turned at a sound and saw Sarah coming across the field to
him. He was exceedingly pleased to see her. She would understand precisely the point that he had reached.

She came to him, and put her hand on his broad shoulder. She
didn't speak. Clasping her with his arm he drew her closer.

'Dearest, it is cold for thee. We will go in.'

She laid her head on his shoulder.

'I am weary, Davy. Mirabell has tears in every word that she
speaks, and your father does not speak at all, and there is a pool
of water under the stair.'

He stayed thinking; then, looking down into her face, he said, as though he had at last reached the conclusion of long doubt: 'Yes, we must go.'

She waited, then said: 'It has been wrong here for me from the beginning. Why? I have no immoderate vanity, but I had not intended officiousness. Davy, *am* I so officious? How can I know? Deborah says not. . . In all those ill years after my mother's death what I did for my father was necessary. Anything to protect him against . . .' (She stopped. Inured to any sort of beastliness though she was, that death on the fell still haunted her.) 'But I was a child. I grew to be a woman that night you took me away. And being of a sudden a woman I must justify myself – for myself, you see, and for you whom I loved. Have I interfered too greatly in this last year? But what could I do? The discomfort, the disorder, the uncomeliness—' She caught him closer to her with her arm about his neck. 'And why should Mirabell grudge it? I would not take her place. I have not, I could not – but to stay still and watch the dirt grow. 'Tis ill enough in a morning when your father, black and half naked in his old robe stained with drink, takes his ale . . . I would not have you like that, not though you reach a hundred, but I have said nothing, all these months, not a word. But last night – that rage and Mirabell lying speechless at his feet! Oh no, Davy, it's not to be endured. 'Tis not wholesome nor natural . . .'

'It shall not be endured, dear one,' he said, kissing her. 'I have been in the wrong to persist in this. It is settled. We will go to Uldale for a time at least. I must tell my father.'

But Sarah was an understanding and tender-hearted woman. She realized something of the long history that lay, far back, between those two.

'But you cannot leave him. We must think out a plan. To be at Uldale part, and here part, or for him to come—' She broke off, wrinkling her brow. In her heart at that moment she felt that she could not endure Herries another instant! How she loathed it, with its old musty furniture, its draughts and dripping water and constant disorder and rats and owls! The thought of a good, clean house at Uldale, a house of her own and David's that their children should be born in! Away from these strange underground disturbances that she could not understand any more truly than David. That brought her to her next word:

'Davy, your father and Mirabell are in another world from you and me, from Deborah too. We see things plainly as they are, and always will. A road is a road to us, and a house a house. But

Mirabell and your father see nothing as it is. I cannot sit still like a puss in the corner to wonder which way the wind is blowing. For me, give me a fireside and you, a square screen to keep off the draught, a work-basket, and I can do well enough; but for them they see neither screen nor work-basket. But always something beyond the window that they have not, or once had or would have, or will have if they wait long enough.

'We must be doing something, they must only be thinking. Your father is sixty, and has been here these thirty years doing exactly nothing.'

'Yes,' said David, 'because facts are not sufficient for him. He could have done well with them if he would; you may call it an epidemical distemper, a madness, but he bears his condition with grand fortitude. He could not change it. He must have more than facts, and find something that will be a key for him to all existence.'

'''Tis well,' said Sarah dryly, 'that he has money sufficient to keep him, even though it is your mother's, and a roof over his head, even though it is full of holes.' Then her heart reproaching her, she went on: 'Nay, I care for him greatly and would for Mirabell too if she would let me. 'Tis their unhappiness that distresses me. If I could bring them together I would never say a word for our going. But our being here separates them the more. They are of another world than ours. They are poets, maybe, and see everything fantastically. We' – she laughed, and pressing her cheek against his, very lightly bit his ear – 'we, Davy, are the farmers of this world, and are for ever taking our eggs to market.'

'And poor Deb,' he added. 'She cries her eyes out to be with *her* farmer *and* to have a child by him. 'Twill be too late an she does not hasten.'

Sarah looked back at the house, her strong broad body pulsing with health, her cheeks glowing with the cold. 'That he can remain here and love it so! What he sees here or feels! If she would but love him as he loves her, then his dream would be fulfilled, I suppose, and he understand the universe . . . As he loves her! But no two love alike. Do we love alike, Davy?'

'I love thee the more.'

'Nay, no man loves a woman the more. You love me but you love also your Liverpool trade, and the fields here, and the sheep, and a cock-fight in Keswick and chatter with the Keswick men . . . Heigh-ho! We women – a poor circumstance to be a woman and a poor end, were it not for the children,' she added more softly. 'What's a man beside a child?'

They turned to go back and saw Herries coming towards them.

When he was near he had the face of a naughty child conscious of guilt. He wore a plum-coloured coat with silver buttons, and at his side a little sword with a chased silver hilt. He had dressed up and shaven properly. Thus, his head high and with that look of a child caught out in his odd angular face, high-boned, crooked with its scar, lined, stern and gentle, scornful and friendly, thus David, knowing that the moment had come at last when he must leave him, loved him. Sarah too wanted, as she saw him come so proudly and yet so submissively, to comfort him, the thing in all the world, as she knew, that he would most resent.

'Well,' he said angrily to David. 'You will kill her of ague in this wind. Bring her in.'

He looked out over the landscape, over the scrubby, stony ground, thick with bush and tree, here cleared for cultivation, there wild again. That was what he loved, that wildness! He looked on to Rosthwaite Fell and Glaramara behind it, greeting them.

'Softly,' said David, laughing. 'Sarah has tolerable strength. She does not faint at sight like the town ladies.'

He turned to them and looked at her with his old ironic smile. He bowed to her gravely. 'Madam, my daughter-in-law, I am an old gentleman reaching dotage and beg to be excused for most unhandsome meddling.' He took her hand in his and went on most gently. 'My dear, forgive me. I forget sometimes my place. But soon you will be gone, and free; then you will look back and pardon me because you have a loving heart.'

'Be gone!' she cried. 'Why, in what condition? . . .'

He shook his head, smiling, at both of them.

'Why, you know, I'm no such fool. I lost my temper painfully last night, my dears, and now you have been saying: "Poor old man, it is too terrible," and David has said "You cannot endure it, my love," and Sarah has said "Nay, my dear, you must stay with your father," but meanwhile there is a fine property at Uldale, and there is a child coming who must have a clean place to be born in, and – there are other things.' His face was suddenly stern. He looked out to Rosthwaite Fell as though to find comfort there. 'Davy has spoken of his promise to stay by his father, and Sarah has told him that he must not break it, and both of them are thinking how a way can be found.' He put a hand on David's shoulder. 'Is it not thus?' he asked.

It had been so exactly thus that they could neither of them answer him. He nodded.

'Yes, and so the property must be bought at Uldale, and I will trot over on my nag for a glass of ale and then – most contentedly trot back again.'

It was done. There was nothing to be said. In the hearts of all three of them they knew that it was the inevitable necessity. No one had spoken of Mirabell, but she was there, the final cause.

So David rode over to Uldale and in a short while was the owner of the manor farm and the land about it.

This was a modern house that had been standing only some ten years or so, charming in spirit and colour, built for comfort rather than display. Above it ran the moor free and unfettered to the skyline, and from that moor you could see behind you the Solway Firth and the Scottish hills, before you across the valley to Skiddaw and Saddleback, and then, curving to the right, the whole range from Helvellyn through the Pike and the Gavel to Robinson and Grasmoor.

Under this glory the house nestled, catching the sun, sheltered from wind and rain.

As David looked upon it, its walls faced with red brick that was already mellowing, the sash windows of happy proportions, the roof with its strong cornice, the dormer windows, the trim garden, the farm-buildings, the little orchard, a great pride and happiness filled his heart.

He seemed to know, as though someone had whispered to him, that this was to be the home of his children and his children's children, and that he was beginning here a history that must have eventful consequences far beyond his own small consciousness.

All the world here seemed open and free. Near to Cockermouth, Keswick, Carlisle and Penrith, he was in the main world and was a man of that world. As he rode back to Herries he felt as though he were plunging into the dark bowels of the earth.

Weeks of restraint and discomfort followed. Sarah felt a desperate guilt. Mirabell seemed to show by attempting a shy, awkward friendliness that she was herself to blame, and poor Deborah, when she knew that she was to be forsaken, could not disguise her terror.

Nevertheless, in her heart, when she heard that David was going, she felt certain of her own coming freedom . . .

On the last night that they were together David and Herries sat up late by the fire. They did not speak much. David tried at last to say something.

'Father, it isn't a real parting. There'll be always a room for you and for Mirabell too. 'Tis no distance. It will be a pleasant change for you. And I will come here whenever you need me.'

Herries grinned. 'We are fastened together for life, Davy, but I don't care for having you by. That's the truth. I'm set on another plan from yours. Thou art a fine healthy lump of flesh and wilt breed children like a rabbit, fine children, I don't doubt, with no maggots in their heads. I've always had a maggot and it's made me lonely. By desire, mind you. I prefer it. I love you against my will, Davy, for you are everything that I would not be. To make money, build a house, have land, breed children, honour the King, pay your taxes, leave your mark on the country though it may be but the impression of your bottom on your counting-house chair, I can see 'tis an ambition as good as another. Myself I've stuck in the mud here for thirty years, been given a contemptible name, done nothing whatever save see the house drop over my head, married a wench from the road who doesn't love me, although she'd wish to, poor lass, out of a churchy kind of gratitude. . . 'Tis as useless a life as a man can find and as pitiful, but I've had moments, Davy, that you will never know, and 'tis by the height of your divining moments that life must be judged. I love this woman that I have got here as you and Sarah will never love, in the entrails, Davy, down among the guts, my boy. And I'll have her yet, struggle as she may, and when I have her I'll know what the stars are for and why the moon's a silver treachery and what God has in His anointed beard . . . And they'll not drag me from this house till the rats are gnawing at my toes and there's lice in my ears. For this is my home, this spot, this ground, this miry waste, and here I'll die – and the third day I'll rise again. I love thee, Davy, but thou art the damnedest fool of a good fellow that was ever made between sheets. So goodnight to thee, my little son.'

After which he yawned loudly, stretched his arms, scratched his thigh and stamped up to his bed.

After this it was Deborah's tragedy. Poor Deb, a woman now of thirty-seven, an age at this time when, still unmarried, you were an old maid and as good as buried. She looked her age too, for she was broad and massive-bosomed, with sturdy arms and haunches, and a wide good-natured double-chinned face. She looked well in a mob cap, aproned and in pattens.

Nevertheless her little clergyman loved with a devoted unfaltering patience. He did not mind how broad she grew – he was no slim beauty himself. He would wait for ever if need be. He told her so again and again in his letters which were filled with love and little snatches of news and pieces about his health and his food.

'Little Love –' (he always addressed her thus, nor saw any humour in it) 'I had a fine visit yesterday to Sir Whickham Partridge's seat at Highloft. The gardens are very fine, of uneven ground diversified with valleys and hills. There is also a monstrous fine dairy with churns of butter, prints and skimming dishes all of the handsomest kind. We had fine weather and a most pleasant journey... I have had three Baptisms in the last four days, but one infant hath died of the croup since and is now safe in the arms of Christ Jesus, which is all the better for the family in that there are nine of them already and the man, a good honest fellow, making little at his business – he is a cordwainer... Little Love, you say nothing in your last letter about our marriage, for which I pray night and morning. I wait on your circumstances, which are, I know, uneasy of settlement. But my sister is ready to receive you here whenever the proper time comes.'

Or again:

'I rejoice at the good account you give of your health, Little Love. You have so cheerful and happy a disposition that you are able to endure the discomforts of your watery valley... The bed in the guest-chamber has gone weak in one leg, and my sister Mary slept there the last two nights and found it unevenly balanced in the morning... Thou knowest how dearly I love thee, Little Love, and wait only thy signal for all to be in readiness here...'

Yes, he could wait for ever, but she could not. Four years gone and nothing done. Four years gone and not a word said to her father. Whether he guessed or no she could not say. He was a strangely perceptive man and, when he wished, a strangely silent one.

After Mirabell came, for a while Deborah conquered her fear of him. He was softer, gentler, and seemed himself to care for her more openly. Then she might have spoken to him about her little clergyman. She had no reason to suppose that he would be angry. Why should he be? He had never shown any dislike of her marrying, or that he wanted to keep her with him for ever. But he would laugh. He would look at her in that terrible ironical way and, with a word or two, drive her into the very centre of the shyest reserve.

But what of that? He cared for her in his own fashion. He would not be unkind to her, he would even give her his own sort of ironic blessing. But here the accumulated effect of her years with him, of her old frights and old loneliness, her sense of his strangeness, above all, her terror of some sudden outburst of rage, held her back. Again and again she would tell him; again and again she postponed the occasion.

Then after David brought home Sarah it seemed certain that she would go. There was no need for her now that Sarah was here, but then, as the new situation developed so uncomfortably for them all, as Mirabell retired unhappily more and more into herself, Deborah stayed because she seemed to be the only link between Mirabell and Sarah. They liked her, both of them, although Mirabell said very little. But she, out of her own reserves and deep shynesses and perception of tiny things, understood Mirabell's wild, unhappy heart better than any of them, and Mirabell knew it.

But, when Sarah and David departed, her mind was made up. She would wait no longer. Stay in this house alone with the two of them she could not. They did not need her. She could do nothing for them; it was between Mirabell and Sarah that she had been able to help, never between Mirabell and her father.

Another thing also drove her to her decision – the knowledge that Sarah was going to have a child. That was the one ever-present, ever-dominant idea, the children that she would have.

She thought of it, dreamt of it, whispered the names that she would give them (to herself). But she was thirty-seven; soon it might be too late.

So a week after David and Sarah had gone she wrote a little letter:

MY DEAR LOVE – I can wait no longer nor suffer you to wait neither. On Tuesday next I shall be in Keswick at four of the clock standing at the corner by the Assembly Rooms. – Shortly to be your True and Loving Wife,

DEBORAH HERRIES.

I have not told my Father and shall bring only a small Basket fearing to upset him with my News.

When the letter was dispatched by the carrier, her happiness flooded over her in a radiant shower. Why had she not done this before? She could not tell. A spell seemed to be broken. Surely then it would be easy to tell her father. 'Father, dear, next Tuesday I am going to Cockermouth to be wed with a clergyman.' But she could not say it even now. She knew how he would take it.

'Wed with a clergyman? Bedded with a parson?' and then his eyes, loving her but despising her too, then his shrug of the shoulder as he went out to his digging, or his tramp over the fells, or his riding to some distant valley. She also said nothing to Mirabell lest she should afterwards be charged with deceitfully keeping a secret. But on the last evening she went over to her and kissed her.

'Dear Mirabell, remember I am for ever your friend.'

The girl (for she seemed still a child with her slender body, little breasts, small rounded head) looked at her from under her pile of fiery hair and said, smiling:

'Why, Deborah, are you going on a journey?'

'Maybe,' whispered Deborah, nodding her head. Mirabell suddenly clung to her, resting her little head between Deborah's big breasts.

'Come back again one day. And if you travel think of me who would like to travel too.'

'Aye,' Deborah said, 'I will come back.' They kissed then, very lovingly.

When she kissed her father goodnight that evening he was abstracted, reading a play of Shakespeare's, *Antony and Cleopatra*, and calling it nonsense one minute and miraculous marvel the next, so he nodded goodnight, scarcely seeing her.

Next morning she rode into Keswick on Appleseed. Herries was out in the fields, cutting scrub away, and did not see her go. She left on the dining-table a letter:

DEAR FATHER – I have gone to Cockermouth to be wed to a clergyman, Mr Gordon Sunwood. I have known him these four years but did not tell you, not to weary you with it. He is a Good Man, I am sure. I shall write to you at Cockermouth and then we will come to visit you if you wish us. – Your loving Daughter,

DEBORAH.

Herries did not return until evening. He saw the note on the table and read it. He read it again and then again. He smiled, then he laughed, then he threw back his head, roaring.

Then he called loudly for Mirabell. When she came he shouted:

'We are alone. We are alone. We are alone!'

He strode to her, caught her up, held her high, then kissed her over and over. His old wild joy of his wedding day seemed to have returned.

'Poor Deb! She is wed to a parson, to a stummicky, bottomy, garlic-smelling parson. I love my daughters, I cherish them, I give them all I have, but now they are gone and I have done my duty, my duty, my full and fitting duty. They are gone and we are alone, my Sweet, my beloved, my darling wife . . . You and I, and there is no one to care for you but I, and no one to watch when we kiss nor when we quarrel . . . I love my Deborah, but I like her better away sitting on the fat knees of her rummidgy parson, breeding young parsons to fill the pulpits with their precious tidings . . .' He set her down on a chair, knelt before her, his head bent into her lap. 'Mirabell, there is no one in the whole green world but ourselves.'

When at last he was quiet she said anxiously: 'Is Deborah gone then?'

'Aye, Deborah is gone to wed with a parson.'

'Ah, that was what she meant when she kissed me last evening.' She shivered a little, but he could not see her; then, straightening her thin body against the chair, she said:

'And now if there is no one else you must be served by me.'

'Nay, nay,' he said. 'I shall be server, and you shall be the queen, for you are my love whom I adore. And shall ever adore through this death and the next after it and after that, to eternity again.'

But she, as though she had not heard him, and were following her own thought said: 'The Trumpeters coming through the valley . . . I know that they must come.'

That evening he would not allow her to do anything, made her sit in the high chair at the end of the table, served her with food and drink, and at last when he had his own, sat on a stool at her feet. 'Deborah is a good woman,' he said once, 'and will make her parson happy,' and that was the only allusion he gave her.

Mirabell seemed to feel his happiness and respond to it. They sat together by the fire and she told him of her adventures with

her uncles, and times that she could remember in London, and
she let him hold her hand and stroke it, and when he kissed her
she returned his kiss.

He rose and went upstairs and came again with a small cedar-
wood box. He poured the contents on to her lap. They lay glittering there. There was a gold Moco stone chain set in gold, a neck-
lace with pearls and vermilions, a gold watch, a rumphlet of diamonds set in silver and gilt, a large rose diamond set in silver and
fastened to a bodkin, a gold ring with seven diamonds in the form
of a rose, and a diamond cross.

She cried out at sight of them, a child now in her pleasure. He
told her that they had been his mother's and that he had kept
them for a fitting time to give them to her. He did not tell her that
he had been storing them for the day when at last she would,
freely, of herself, tell him that she loved him. She had not yet told
him, but now that they were alone again, with everyone out of
the way, soon, soon she would tell him.

He knelt before her and hung them all on her until she glittered
and glistened in the firelight, all the stones winking and shining
under the flame of her hair. Her fingers were loaded with them,
and her neck and bosom, and she wore the diamond cross in her
hair.

Then, very friendly together, they sat at the table while he
gave her her writing lesson. At this, and at reading, she was very
slow and stupid. It seemed that she *could* not learn. But tonight
she was docile, and did her utmost to please him, sitting there in
her old gown and covered with jewels.

She went to sleep quietly that night in his arms. He slept also.
Later he woke to find that in her sleep she had got out from him,
and was standing at the window in her nightdress, beating at the
panes and crying:

'Harry, Harry! Take me out! I can't get out! Harry, Harry, I
can't get out!'

He could hear her sobbing. He lay very still. Later she came
into bed again, and he stayed very quietly, longing to touch her
and to comfort her, but doing nothing. So he lay for many hours
beside her in great trouble.

THE LOVER

HERRIES and Mirabell were alone in the house.

Except for Benjamin and his slatternly greedy wife there was no human being near them. Herries watched Mirabell as a cat watches a bird, and he watched out of love and terror lest at any moment she should escape.

Now most truly he was paying for all the infidelities of his long life. He knew in the depths of the bitterest truth what the anguish of unrequited love was. He was sixty-two years of age and had never yet known such burning desire of the flesh, burning because it was eternally unsatisfied. Night after night he might lie with Mirabell and do with her what he would, and night after night, when she slept, he would get up from bed and walk the house like a frantic ghost because she did not love him.

But this agony bit far deeper than any unsatisfied desire of the flesh could do. He was ready to surrender any physical connexion for ever and ever if only she would love him a very little, and she was ready to give him everything she had out of kindness.

And so they came terribly to fear one another. She was afraid of his rages, his silences, his miseries and his absences. She was so fond of him that when he was away she longed for him to return so that she might be kind to him, and then, when he was there, she longed for him to be away again because she found that she could not give him the love that he desired.

Although she was now thirty-three years of age she was still very much of a child, and she was hoping that suddenly one morning she would find that she loved him. She was so fond of him that she could not understand why that fondness was not love. But it was not. Her heart never beat the harder when he was coming. Her face never flushed when he looked at her with passionate desire; at such times there was terror in her heart and she would wonder whether this night perhaps she would find that she could not surrender her body to him any more, and must tell him so.

That would be fearful, that night when it came. They both trembled at the idea of it. She thought that perhaps after she had shuddered apart from him, he would get up and go out and kill himself. She knew that he was aware of her reluctance, and that he loathed himself for pressing her. Sometimes when he had not, but had only kissed her and turned over to sleep, she almost loved him, put her hand up to caress his cheek and then put it down again lest he should take it as a sign that at last she really loved him.

But, although she guessed so much, she did not guess the half of his real torture; how before every step that he took towards her he hesitated lest she should make some movement, exclamation, sign that showed how she shrank from him.

She was troubled, too, by an increasing stifling sense of imprisonment. It was not only that now he watched her every step. It was also the personality of the house that she had always hated from the first. It watched her even as its master did. There were things in it that were spies, she was sure: the portrait of the old Herries in the dining-hall, the two suits of armour, the drunken tumbling chimneys. She could hear the suits of armour clanking after her at night, and she would stay in her room, the door ajar, listening to them as they whispered about her.

She hated it that always there was the same view from the windows and the yard. All her life long she had wandered, and now, wherever she looked, she must always see those two horrid hills, Rosthwaite Fell and Chapel Fell. The very hills that were Herries's passion were her loathing, and she hated most of all the way that he would talk about them as though they were persons and his very dear friends. They *were* persons and her very dear enemies.

But worst of all for her – and this thing, as the months passed, became an obsession – was her consciousness of all the little stone walls running up the sides of the hills. All her life long these stone walls had been the dearest things in the world to her. When she was an infant and could not walk, they would put her, wrapped in a shawl, under one of these walls out of the wind. As she stayed there, she could see the wall running, like a live thing, first across the turf straight like a taut string, then suddenly turning and leaping upwards until it was lost at the high bend of the hill. Over all this landscape she saw these little walls running, gay, free, vigorous, and when she walked – the wind blowing her hair – pressing up the side of the hill, the wall went with her, keeping her company. Now she was tied to this house. From the back of the yard she fancied that she could see a thin black line on Rosthwaite Fell; this was the wall and it would run to the ridge, then straight with only the sky over it, then it would dip again, catching its breath in the little valley before it mounted up again. Tears would fill her eyes as she gazed, and an impatience that made her heart beat angrily.

'He is kind to me, he loves me, but what would it hurt him if I were gone a week? I would return.' But would she? She could not honestly answer that. She was honest above all else. With all her faults of childishness, temper, rebellion, ignorant boasting, she was immaculately honest. It was because she knew that if she once went away she might never return that she never begged him that he might let her go.

Another thing her honesty showed her to her great distress and pain. She was beginning to forget Harry. This was the cruellest thing of all, because she had nothing with which to replace him. In all her bitterest distress at the agony of having lost him, there was a kind of bitter happiness because her love for him, although he was gone, was so wonderful. A thousand times a day she would recall everything that he had said and done, how he had looked here, how he had smiled there, what his eyes had done when he told her that he loved her. They had not had so very long a time together, so that the collection of her memories must be conned over and over. But the years had passed, and the conning had become almost mechanical; her honesty drove her to discover this and then drove her further, to realize that days and even weeks went by and she did not think of him at all.

She was indeed a strange mixture of childishness and maturity, of anger and submission, of knowledge and ignorance. Her best parts were her kindliness and honesty and a kind of instinctive poetry she had, and her industry. She always wanted to be at work on something, but unfortunately she had no gift for housework or keeping a place clean, or remembering what she must do. Untidiness seemed to follow her; things were broken, forgotten, disordered wherever she was. Nor would she learn. Her stubbornness was terrible. In these two years, Herries had taught her neither to read nor write. She would begin a lesson with him in all docility. He, for so restless and scornful a man, was marvellously patient with her. The lessons would start, both of them in great amiability, then her stupidity would irritate him, she see that he was checking it, and so she would burst into tears and run to her room.

What she liked best was when they sat in front of the fire, she on a cushion at his feet resting her head on his knees and he telling her stories. Then there was a great peace between them; he would forget his passion for her and be only her friend, and she would feel so kindly to him that she thought that in another moment she would love him.

They mingled strangely little with the outside world. Deborah lived, serenely happy, with her little clergyman in Cockermouth. She had only one grief – that as yet she had no children and soon she would be too old. But a Wise Woman had told her that she would have two sons, and Wise Women knew. David rode over often from Uldale although he was so busy a man. He was always urging his father and Mirabell to go and visit them, and Deborah too sent pressing invitations. But Mirabell would not go any more. She was frightened of Sarah, so efficient, businesslike, normal and happy. She thought that Sarah despised her, and so in her heart perhaps Sarah did.

But no. Sarah was of too generous a nature to despise her. She could not understand her. Mirabell with her odd looks, baby face, bright-coloured untidy clothes, sudden silence, odd sayings, was incredible to her. She did not understand her at all, and remembered that she was only a gipsy. Sarah was not a snob, but it was a time when the middle classes thought of the peasants as of another world from themselves, like dogs or cats or horses. Then Mirabell could not bear to see the neatness and grandeur of Uldale. It was not really very grand, but it seemed so to Mirabell with its solid walls and fine fires and trim garden, clocks and pictures and comfortable beds. There the rain did not drip through the roof, nor were the meals thrown anyhow on to the table, nor did the beds stay unmade all the day long. After a day's visit to Uldale she came back to Herries resolved to set everything into marvellous order. The next morning she was up in the dark busy and eager. But nothing would go her way; after she had swept, the dust was still there, the mud seemed to walk of itself into the house and lie about the stairs, the mice would come on to the table and nibble at the bread. And Herries did not care; he did not mind in what disorder he was living. He would curse Benjamin and his wife in a splendid rage, and then forget it all again. He was always dreaming, of the weather, the country, the clouds, the running water, and of herself.

So, this winter of 1762, things went from bad to worse.

A week before Christmas there was a great frost. A frost that holds is, in this district, rare; but round Christmas there is much cold spicy weather, the air nutmeg-scented, the waters running down all the hills with a tinkle of ice in their chuckles, the trees are red, amber to rose, and the sky grey, dove-winged, often very clear and shot with stars.

Mirabell was having a reading lesson in a house as still as the dead. A great fire leapt in the stone fireplace and the light of it clambered about her jewels and her orange-coloured dress. She had a silver shawl over her hair to see what it looked like, and when she should have attended to her lesson she was moving her head against the old round cracked mirror that hung by the window to see how it shone. It was not vanity that moved her, but childishness and restlessness; this last because out in that grey frost-held world she knew that the little walls were running up the iron-clad hills to the grey snow-gathering sky. On such a late winter's afternoon she would be running ahead of her uncles over the turf, through the keen icy wind, to reach the edge of the Tarn. Here the water would lie black under a thin crinkle of silver ice, and the first cold stars would come out, and perhaps the slip of a frozen moon . . .

Herries, his patience constrained with difficulty, was reading out of Swift's *Polite Conversation*. He chose this work because the English was good and the words were mostly of one syllable. Also it entertained Mirabell because of the pictures of, as it seemed to her, ridiculous polite society.

It was Herries's plan to read a piece very slowly and with great patience. Then Mirabell was to read it after him. This did not please her. She liked him to read straight on. What did it matter whether she herself should learn to read or no? He was always there to read to her.

Herries read:

'MISS. Lord, Mr Neverout, you are as pert as a Pear monger this morning.

NEVEROUT. Indeed, Miss, you are very handsome.

MISS. Poh, I know that already; tell me news.

(*Somebody knocks at the Door. Footman comes in.*)

FOOTMAN (*to Col.*). An please your Honour, there's a Man below wants to speak to you.

COL. Ladies, your pardon for a Minute.

(*Col goes out.*)

LADY SMART. Miss, I sent yesterday to know how you did, but you were gone abroad early.

MISS. Why, indeed, Madam, I was hunched up in a Hackney Coach with Three County Acquaintance, who called upon me to take the Air as far as Highgate.

LADY SMART. And had you a pleasant Airing?

MISS. No, Madam; it rained all the Time; I was jolted to Death, and the Road was so bad, that I screamed every Moment and called to the Coachman, "Pray, Friend, don't spill us."'

Herries paused. Mirabell was seated beside him, her head screwed round to the mirror.

'You don't attend,' he said sharply.

She looked back quickly to the book like a frightened child. 'I do indeed,' she said hurriedly. 'What a childish Miss, to scream every moment because the coach jolted her! I could make her scream if I had her here.'

'Come,' said Herries sternly. 'Now you shall read.' He did not wish to be stern. His hand was very near her flaming hair that was now ungathered and fell about her shoulders under the silver shawl and over the orange satin gown. It needed all his strength not to stroke it. His hand would move up and then down again while his heart thumped beneath his waistcoat. He must not touch her. All hope in an ordered lesson would be over if he did. She would sit on the floor in front of the fire and demand a story – a woman, thirty-three years of age. At least she did not look a day more than twenty. So, to check himself, he was stern.

'Cease glancing at that mirror,' he said, 'and read this for me.'

She began, very slowly:

'Miss. Lord! Mr Nev-er-out, you are as p e r t as a Pea—'

She stopped.

'What is this long word?'

'Pear,' he answered.

'Pear.'

'Monger.'

She looked at it and shook her head. 'I have never seen such a word before.'

'No, doubtless. But how will you ever learn to read if you see only the same words every time?'

'Why should I learn to read?' she asked. 'Why do you force me? There are many ladies can't read. Besides I am not a lady, and will never be one. There are other things I can do, but not this.'

'You are thirty-three years of age.'

She jumped up.

'And older, older, older! I'm just as young as I was when I was five. I knew everything then and nothing. It is the same now.'

It was true. As he looked at her he saw her both as woman and child and loved her as both.

'Yes, that is true,' he said sadly. 'I am neither old enough nor young enough for you.'

'Oh, don't let us talk of ourselves!' She turned away to the mirror again. Then she softened, coming back with a smile. 'Oh, Francis, take me as I am! I cannot change with your wishing it nor you with mine. We must make what we can with what we've got.' Then she threw the silver shawl on to the table.

'I will go and do some sweeping,' she said. She was interrupted by a noise at the door. It was Benjamin, who said that there were some children there to sing carols. Then there was a strange light in Herries's eye, a curious smile at his scarred mouth. It was many years that the children had not come near his house to sing carols. Proudly he had always said that he did not care whether they came or no. But he did care. It seemed like a good omen that they should come to his old house at last.

So he ordered Benjamin to have them up, and soon in they trooped, some seven or eight boys and a short stout man in a red coat and with a double chin and a big belly.

They stood all together over by the fire, close, as though they were a little frightened. They had doubtless heard things about the house and its owner. But the sight of Mirabell reassured them. She was enchanted with them. She loved children, being a child herself, and now she clapped her hands, and went and stroked their cheeks and asked them their names, speaking in broad Cumberland just as they did.

Then she stood near Herries: his arm was about her, and so they listened to the music. All their years afterwards they remembered this scene and especially one carol. The stout fellow had a little viola on which he played very sweetly. The boys, at a sign from him, all lifted up their heads together like young birds and began to sing.

They sang 'The Three Kings' and 'The Cherry Tree' and others, but it was this one, 'The Angel Gabriel', that Mirabell never afterwards forgot. The simple sweet tune greatly touched her, and later she learnt the words and remembered them, she who could never get anything that Francis taught her by heart. It was, she would afterwards think, the last scene of her childhood – yes, her childhood, although now she was thirty-three, and the background had always exquisite beauty in her memory – the grey frosted world outside hard like iron, and inside the room everything melting in the coloured firelight, the flickering ceiling, the crimson logs, the faces of the children, and Herries

himself, grave and kind and generous-hearted, as she liked best
to see him.

So the children sang 'The Angel Gabriel':

> The Angel Gabriel from God
> Was sent to Galilee,
> Unto a Virgin fair and free
> Whose name was called Mary:
> And when the Angel thither came,
> He fell down on his knee,
> And looking up in the Virgin's face,
> He said 'All Hail, Mary!'
>
> Then sing we all both great and small,
>   Noël, Noël, Noël;
> We may rejoice to hear the voice
>   Of the Angel Gabriel.
>
> Mary anon looked him upon,
> And said, 'Sir, what are ye?
> I marvel much at these tidings
> Which thou hast brought to me.
> Married I am unto an old man
> As the lot fell unto me;
> Therefore, I pray, depart away,
> For I stand in doubt of thee.'
>
> Then sing we all, both great and small,
>   Noël, Noël, Noël;
> We may rejoice to hear the voice
>   Of the Angel Gabriel.
>
> 'Mary,' he said, 'be not afraid,
> But do believe in me.
> The power of the Holy Ghost
> Shall overshadow thee;
> Thou shalt conceive without any grief,
> As the Lord told unto me;
> God's own dear Son from Heaven shall come,
> And shall be born of thee.'
>
> Then sing we all, both great and small,
>   Noël, Noël, Noël;
> We may rejoice to hear the voice
>   Of the Angel Gabriel.

This came to pass as God's will was,
Even as the Angel told.
About midnight an Angel bright
Came to the Shepherds' fold,
And told them then both where and when
Born was the child, our Lord,
And all along this was their song,
'All glory be given to God.'

Then sing we all, both great and small,
    Noël, Noël, Noël;
We may rejoice to hear the voice
    Of the Angel Gabriel.

Good people all, both great and small,
The which do hear my voice,
With one accord let's praise the Lord,
And in our hearts rejoice;
Like sister and brother, let's love one another,
Whilst we our lives do spend,
Whilst we have space let's pray for grace,
And so let my Carol end.

Then sing we all, both great and small,
    Noël, Noël, Noël;
We may rejoice to hear the voice
    Of the Angel Gabriel.

When they had ended Herries could not do enough for them.
That strange mood of excited gaiety that sometimes swept over
him was on him now. He sent old Benjamin to the kitchen for
cakes and sweetmeats; he would stuff the children till they were
sick. He took the smallest, who would not be older than six or
seven, on to his knee, and a great softness of feeling pervaded
him when he saw that the child did not shrink but played with
his heavy gold chain and told him his name, Richard Watson.
Was the legend finished then? Was he no longer Ogre or Rogue?
Oh, this was surely a good omen for him, and now everything
would be right with Mirabell too. Before they were in bed she
would tell him that at last she loved him . . .

The boys had lost all their shyness, and were moving about the
room, filling their mouths with cake, and examining everything.
He gave the fat man richly from his purse, and clapped him on

the shoulder. He carried little Richard on his shoulder down the stairs when they were all going. He saw them from the door with their lighted lanterns go across the frosty court. He saluted the myriads of stars so bright above the black line of the hills with a wave of his arm before he came back into the house.

He stood in the doorway of the room smiling at her, and she smiled back at him. She was sitting at the fire humming to herself the 'Angel Gabriel' tune.

> 'Like sister and brother, let's love one another,
>   Whilst we our lives do spend.'

He went to her at once, made her sit on a cushion at his feet, and, following on the triumphant current of his mood, drawing her head back against his knee, burst into a wild flow of talk:

'It is the first time all these winters that the children have been here. They've gone to every house but this one. Why should I care whether they have come or no? But I have cared, and now that you are here I have wanted everyone to be friendly. Yes, for the first time in my life I've wanted friendship . . .'

He drew her closer to him, and she felt his hands hot and trembling against her cheek.

'Don't be angry with me. Don't turn me away. You must shrink because my hands are old, old and dry, but there's no age in my heart. I *was* old when I came here first, proud and young. I thought I could do just what I liked then – with anyone or anything. But I've learnt wisdom. Time has taught me. I haven't done what I liked with anything. Even the soil – I haven't even a fine potato out of it. And the trees have all gone crookedly against me, and the wind has blown the hills sideways. But I toiled on, because I knew that there was an answer somewhere to my question if I refused to be beat.

'What's my question been? I don't know myself. That's the odd thing. I don't know either the question or the answer. I puzzle my head sometimes till it breaks. Yes, breaks. Splits like a fig. Then I think the answer will be in there. It must be. That's the thing that spins round and round and asks all the questions. But if it has the questions then it must have the answers too. These questions. Why is the sky grey today, my dear, and being grey, with a touch of rose to it, why does my heart thump? Why cannot I leave this place, this tumbled heap of stones, but must hang on always staring at a humped hill and a pocketful of rank grass? Yes, split your brain and dig in the mess with your fingers for the answer.

'Nay, it's not in the brain but in the wind behind the brain and the soft sly voice behind the wind. Ah, that voice! I tell you, Mirabell, there are times when I've almost heard it. I've stood on Honister, where I found you, my darling; I've stood there listening, and He's been almost in my hand. A sly dog, conceited of His power, with all the beauty that He's got and all the strength to frighten us. And at the last, maybe lazily, out of idleness, He drops a present into our lap, a golden rose, a string of glass beads.

'I say damnation to His power. I care not a rabbit for it, but 'tis the mystery plagues me, Mirabell, the oddity, grotesque like a map of China, bits here and there, offal and star-dust together. That's why I stare and stare, looking at a hill or a tree or a lump of this rotten soil, for the secret may be in any place, and by a hair's-breadth of laziness we may have missed it.

'The Herries have always been like that, one mystery-monger and the rest good sober citizens. David's the sober sort. There have to be both in the world. But David finds nothing odd. It is all as it should be. But for me, until I found you, there's been no answer.

'Now, if you loved me, there'd be an answer to every question. I am your lover, Mirabell. I'm not an old man past sixty, but young and strong, always your lover. Can you love me a little, Mirabell? I have been patient all this time with you here. Is it coming to you a little? I am so hungry for it. I think I must not be without it much longer. Mirabell, Mirabell. Love me a little, a very little . . . I want you so.'

His voice ended in an almost breathless whisper and she held herself taut so that he should not feel the shiver that was running through her body.

At first while he talked she had been hypnotized by his voice, but had not listened to his words. It was comfortable here by the fire; she liked him when he was kind and friendly. She always loved his voice when he was telling her a story or talking about his ideas. She found his ideas incomprehensible. She did not understand one of them. The things that he said were completely unreal to her. This mystery that there was in life, she could not see any of it. Her own life was clear enough. She had been beaten and ill-treated and must fight for herself, then she had loved a man, as many a poor girl had done before her, and he had been murdered most foully, and after that this man had been kind to her and given her a home. She could not love him; that was not her fault; she was generous, she would give him anything, but that was something that you could not give unless it happened so. There was no mystery here.

He was always talking of staring at stones and trees. When he came to this her mind slipped away and she would think of other things – of the little walls running away under the frosty air, of old Mrs Benjamin who was a slattern, of Sarah's fine household gifts (odd how often she thought of Sarah!), and tonight of those children singing their carols. How fresh their voices had been, how fresh and how sweet!

But when he came to his love-making, fear snatched her back to attention. Oh, how she hated it, that now so familiar change from friendliness to love! She was like an animal caught, all her senses alert for any chance of escape.

Everything was changed. The tone of his voice, the touch of his hand; she could feel all his body trembling behind his fingers. Not a simple lustful desire to possess her – that she could have understood and to that she would have submitted – but this thing, far more deadly, this praying, pleading passion that she should love him. How could she when she did not? Oh, how could she? . . . There was danger here, dreadful danger both to herself and to him. Yes, she held herself taut lest that inner revulsion should escape her and rouse his fury. It was, she understood, fury and rage and disgust with himself rather than with her, but that did not make it less awful.

'I love you, Mirabell, dear, dear Mirabell . . . Give me a little in return . . . Love me ever so little.'

Stiff against him, her head up, staring into the fire, she answered:

'We are so happy thus, Francis. Let us stay tranquilly . . .'

'Tranquil!' He caught her closer. 'A fine word to use, but I have never been tranquil. I have not been worthy of any tranquillity.'

She understood that. This man was in reality the shyest and most modest she had ever known. She did not comprehend men who were fighters with themselves. Every man in her life had taken himself for what he was and thought no more about it. But this man was different. She did dimly perceive that everything in his history – rebellion, outrage, ostracism, irony, sense of beauty – had come from his own restless dissatisfaction, and that if she saw his soul naked it would be a soul on its knees. But she did not want to see his soul bare. Any close terms with him meant violence and the demand for something that she hadn't to give.

Moreover on an occasion like this her fear was so great that such wits as she had were away.

'Let us read again,' she said, trying to smile at him. 'I will be cleverer this time.'

He put his hand to her neck and held her head up to him.

'Understand this. I am out of breath now. I can endure no more. You must love me. You can if you will. You have love in you. You could give it to that other man. And have I not done more for you than he could ever do, more in every way? Has a man ever loved you as I love you? I want nothing . . . Love me and I will never ask you a favour. Love me and I will sleep in another bed. Love me and I will work for you like a dog. We shall leave this place that has always fretted you. We shall go where you will and I will never even kiss your hand. I will not touch you, Mirabell, if you can love me a little. My heart is starved . . . after these years . . . I have no more power to resist.'

He was at her feet, kneeling. All his pride was gone, all his power over himself. His scarred face lifted to hers, if she had been able to see it, was beautiful.

But she could not see it; she was so frightened that she could see nothing. This was the worst that he had ever been. With a little cry she tried to rise. He caught at her dress. He held her round her knees.

'Say that you love me even though you do not. I will cheat myself.'

But she could not. Her lips moved but no words came. He caught her, pressing his face to her bosom. Then he felt her tremble. That flung him into madness. He had been always afraid of this and had been on his guard. Now he guarded himself no longer.

'I will beat you into it. Can you stand outside me and I not compel you to come in? Have I waited so long for naught? Have I no strength?' He caught her and strained her to him. He covered her face, half averted, with kisses. He dragged her head back by the hair and kissed her neck, tore her gown open, burying his face in her breasts, murmuring: 'An you will not come to me, I'll make you . . . I shall conquer your stubbornness, do you see? You are inside me, at my heart . . . shall never escape . . . I carry you with me.'

Her fear was so frantic that she managed to break away from him and crying out: 'Oh, never, never any more!' ran, half naked, across the floor and up the wooden stairs. She heard him stumbling after her, crossed the dark passage, found her room, bolted the door with its wooden bolt and then crouched against the wall, listening. She thought that he meant to kill her, but it was not the fear of death that frightened her, but something far deeper, a mingled terror and sorrow for him was part of it.

He came to the door and battered on it, shouting: 'Come out, then ... I will end it for us both ... Come out that I may finish it.'

He paused, and the silence in the house was terrible; not only in the house but in all the frost-bound, star-shadowed world outside. There was moonlight in her room, splashed against the wall. Her eyes devoured the door.

He battered again, then flung all his weight. The whole house rang to his blows, the door that was very old cracked. He kicked and it fell.

From the doorway he saw her crouched against the wall. He waited, his breast heaving.

She did not speak, she could not. So they stared at one another.

His madness left him. The moonlight seemed to lap it up. He knew that he had done something for which he would never forgive himself.

He turned and with hanging head went away.

MIRABELL IN FLIGHT

THERE is a work of particular interest to members of the Herries family – Letters in England, 1757–1805 – edited by Dorothea Leyland (Satters and Bonnin, 1876).

This is a book worthy of more general reading. Miss Leyland tells us how, after the purchase by her father of Rockington Hall in Shropshire (the home of the Durward Herries from 1830 to 1854), she discovered in an old oak chest a red leather box stuffed with old letters. They were hard to decipher, yellow and torn, but after some difficulty and the exercise of much patience they were all transcribed.

They included letters preserved and formed into little packets neatly tied with red ribbon by that solemn and serious Mary Titchley, wife of Grandison Herries and mother of the gay Pelham; of all of whom we have already caught glimpses.

They were not of necessity letters written entirely to or by members of the Titchley and Herries families, although these formed the larger portion of them. This, one may suppose, was why Miss Leyland decided against giving the collection a family name. The volume excited very much less attention than it deserved. There was not at the time of its publication the interest in eighteenth-century minutiae that there is today. It has been long out of print. In any detailed chronicle of the Herries family during the years included by it, it must be of great value.

There is one letter – dated April 4th, 1763 – which is pertinent here. It is written to Pelham Herries (at this time a bachelor of forty-five years of age living in King Street, St James's) by his cousin Frances Titchley, a single lady of middle years who was at the time making a tour of Scotland and the North of England with her brother Reginald and his wife.

After certain details that do not here concern us (the full letter can be found on page 331, in the volume above referred to) it proceeds as follows:

. . . I was about to close my letter without communicating to you my most interesting Adventure, most interesting at least to Yourself who, if you will remember, begged me to ascertain any News of your Cousin whether in Keswick or the Barbarous Wilds of Borrowdale.

In my own solitary Person I had not the courage to invade the Fortress of dear Raiseley and dearer Mary. You know how they are thought of by the Family as a Pair of Unconscionable Ogres from whose Hospitality no Cakes and Ale are to be hoped for, but only the Chilly Fingers of Uneasy and Insincere Politeness. In short, dear Pelham, neither Reginald nor Coelia would accompany me on a Call and I would not go alone, so although we were three whole days in Keswick and expecting momentarily the most Inconvenient of Meetings we escaped without a sight of them.

Blame me if you will, dearest Pelham, but remember that you have not yourself been over Punctilious in your Obedience to Inexorable Duty.

You know that I can always see more faults in my own Performances than I love to think on, but at least You shall not be entirely Disappointed in me; I have something yet to offer you.

You know that Reginald has, from his Cradle, a love of the Horrible and that no Terror is so Great but that he must tickle his Palate with it. We have seen, as I have told you in my other letters, Sights of Superb Splendour and the Grandest Magnificence in Scotland. For my part I felt that I had seen enough

and even my Love for You was not Spur sufficient to drive me
into the (so rightly named) Jaws of Borrowdale to catch maybe a
glance of the ferocious Herries who inhabits there. But you
know how 'tis the nature of the Common People to hate all
Novelties and the nature of Reginald to be drawn by them, so
when the Boots at the Keswick Hotel assured us that there was
Nothing in Borrowdale to be seen but Horrid Crags and Violent Waterfalls this decided Reginald immediately. He was
ready indeed to go alone, and Coelia, when she heard that the
only Transport was on Horseback, decided violently against
going but, a little thro' Charity to myself and a great deal thro'
Charity to You because I was aware of your Eager Curiosity to
hear something of your strange Francis for whom you bear,
you always tell me, so odd an Affection, I agreed to accompany
Reginald and to share with him whatever Perils and Dangers
there might be.

Strong Temptations rise within my heart to make of this a
story as fearfully absurd as any thing in the History of Miss
Betsy Thoughtless, but I will spare your Sensitive Feelings
and I am sure you will consider my Behaviour has been very
handsome. In short we set out on the fairest of Young Spring
Days and discovered the most lovely of England's uninhabited
though Cultivated Vallies. I say Uninhabited but am not quite
Literal. Houses and Farms there are scattered here and there
in a wilderness of Scrub under the Frowning Eyebrows of
horrid Crags and Precipices. Whatever you wish to offer up to
your Idol, Taste (and you know that I have ever applauded
your taste in the Arts, extravagant tho' some of your Relations
have found it) as We saw it under a brilliant Sun with fresh
Green glittering from a recent Shower I was not altogether resolved against coming to live in these Regions for the remainder of my Days and indeed might seriously so consider it were
it not for the too close Juxtaposition of dear Raiseley and Mary.
But now to my Story. Our Guide, who both in his Corpulency
and abruptness of Speech reminded me strongly of Uncle Roger
(whose Partiality for green corn partridges and ill success at the
Oxfordshire Poll you will certainly remember) showed us the
Beauties and Curiosities of the district as we passed them, the
Ingenuity of the Bowder Stone, the Beauties of the River Derwent, a wood above the river where not so long back they
drowned a Witch, but I will not detain you with these, knowing, dearest Pelham, your Unmitigated Impatience with anything that has not to do with a graceful Ankle or a Pack of

Cards, and so proceeding over the Wildest Country, all Horrid Boulders and Little Trees growing in grotesque profusion, we approached at length the village of Rosthwaite. You have heard me say that I am a Philosopher only in the fields, and never in the Fields but when the sun shines, so should I have been most surely a Philosopher now, but I confess to a most unphilosophical Tremor when the Guide says, as quietly as you please, 'And that is the House of Herries,' pointing with his stick to a strange Building on a rising Hillock so near to us that only a rivulet and a rustic Bridge divided us.

The Afternoon was gathering in and the Shadows fast falling across the Valley. There was a Purple Light over all the scene and the Mountains had assembled in front of Us as though to close us in with their Black and Jagged Sides. It was a fearful Scene, dear Pelham, and I am thankful indeed that I had Reginald with me Who being destitute of all Imagination suffers no Distress from Nature at her darkest nor the forebodings of Man's untimely End. How Strange, how Abandoned, how Desolate this House of Francis Herries! I have seen you draw a Gothick Hog-sty for a customary Freeholder in Northamptonshire but this would be entirely beyond your Pencil.

From where our horses stayed We could see the deserted grass-grown courtyard, Walls from which the bricks were already falling, windows so Dark that they must be always foreign to the Sun, and the Garden behind a tangle of Weed and Stone. The House must be in part Elizabethan or of an earlier date and it had, in this Shadow that crept about the silent Valley, so unhappy an Air that I have never seen a House speak so eloquently. And now see what follows! We had been watching in silence for some five minutes when of a sudden a Woman comes into the Doorway.

She stands for a moment in Hesitation then crosses the Courtyard and turns down the Path towards us. We had, as You might imagine, a Perfect View of her and I ask you to imagine how Romantick a Picture with this tumbling dark House behind her and the Black Hills on every side and no Sound in the World. As she came towards Us I saw that she was beautiful or so Unusual as to be named a Beauty. She passed us by silently as a Ghost might. She wore nothing over her Head, and her Hair was the Reddest in Hue I ever saw. Over her shoulders she had a Orange Shawl.

Her Face was small and white like a Child's but by her Person I should say she was near thirty Years. Lost in her

Thoughts she gave us no Notice. Then, when She was scarcely past us a man came from the same door, walks to the Lane, sees her in front of him and also draws near to us. This was of course your admired Francis.

He also passed Us without the merest Glance, slowly as though He would not accompany the Figure in front of him but yet would keep Her in His Eye.

You have seen Him, Pelham, and so I need not waste Paper in describing Him to you, but how Striking and how Strange is his appearance. His Clothes are Shabby and stained with mire. He had a Black Hat and a Coat with wide old-fashioned skirts of rusty Brown, he was gaitered to the Knee.

But his Face – scarred on one Cheek from brow to lip – his Eyes of a most tender and Romantick Cast, grave and yet kindly, his Body so straight (save for the slightest stoop of the Shoulder) that although You tell me He is over Sixty it is yet difficult of Belief. There seemed a sort of Desperation in his eye although You, knowing my Romantick Disposition, will attribute this Embroidery to my excess of Sentiment.

He passed Us and followed the Lady but, as I have told You, not to be up with her but rather to keep Her in his Watch. We saw her turn into the shadow of the darkening Road. He slowly behind her and so the two of them out of our Sight.

Forgive, dearest Pelham, the Length of this Epistle but I had resolved that I must give you the fullest details of this Occurrence although Reginald pshaws me and assures me that We have seen nothing at all but a husband and wife on their Daily Walk. For myself there is something more Romantickal and I will confess to you that I have altogether fallen in Love with your Francis and would perhaps try my Fate with Him were he not so obviously already Captured.

My Health is much after the old fashion; yours, I hope however, is quite recovered . . .

There is nothing further in this letter that calls for attention. The other view of Francis and Mirabell during this month is Deborah's. For a long time past Deborah and her husband had been demanding a visit. Francis had never come near to them since Deb's marriage.

One afternoon towards the end of April, Francis and his wife (riding pillion) appeared outside the little, squat, rosy-faced rectory. The Reverend Gordon Sunwood was cleaning out the pigsty. Deborah was baking a cake. She arrived at the doorway, her face rosy from the heat of the fire, her hands thick in dough.

She was pleased and frightened at the same time. They looked so strange sitting silently on a large black horse as though they had been conjured out of the ground.

It was altogether the strangest visit. There seemed no actual reason for it. Neither seemed glad to be there. But, by the second day, Deborah seeing that something was terribly amiss between the two of them, her warm heart was deeply touched and she tried to draw close to them. No easy matter. They were like foreigners who are uncertain of the language spoken around them. They looked foreign, too, sitting in Deborah's amazingly neat and bright parlour with its shining brass, its handsome pictures of King George and his Queen, its Chippendale chairs.

But altogether it was the prettiest of little rooms, hung round with India paper, with Chelsea china, and a pagoda, and a looking-glass in a frame of Chinese paling.

This room was Deborah's pride, and how happy she was, sewing by the fire, listening to the steps on the cobbles, and interrupted once and again by the fat, cheerful countenance and round plump person of Mr Sunwood, who would look in to tell her about the new litter of pigs or how the hens were laying or the text he had chosen for his next sermon or how Mrs Jameson, the lawyer's wife, was faring in her childbirth.

Deborah had all she wanted in the world, for now she knew that she was to have a child. (She was delivered of boy twins on the morning of October 3rd, 1763.)

Socially, too, the Sunwoods were very popular. It must be remembered that Deborah had never all her life long known what social popularity was. There had been always over them the atmosphere of her father's sin and social impossibility. She had also been in Doncaster too young to know what society was, and at Herries there was no society.

She yielded herself, therefore, now to all the friendliness and neighbourliness with a full will, and happy were her days. But all her life came back to her full flood in the presence of her father; yes, right back to her infancy when they arrived at Keswick on that stormy afternoon and Alice Press sat beside the fire.

Old shadows, old terrors. She was not afraid of him now quite as she had been; married life had given her independence. Besides, he was strangely kind and gentle. He seemed to have lost all his authority, acquiesced in anything that was suggested; he charmed Deborah the most by his exceeding courtesy to his wife, rising to offer her any attention, always with his eye on her.

But they talked scarcely at all together, only smiled occasionally, and then as though they were strangers.

Deborah did her best to come to close terms with Mirabell and, until the final evening, altogether failed. She took her over the little house, showing proudly all her treasures. Especially the bedstead in which Mr Sunwood and his lady enjoyed their marital comforts. This was a mahogany bedstead with fluted posts and dark crimson hangings. Other glories of the house were a walnut-tree writing-table, three India-back walnut-tree chairs with stuff silk damask seats, a pier-glass in a black and gold frame, blue and white china, and a Turkey carpet.

It may be wondered what contrasts Mirabell made in her heart between this and Herries. Poor woman! A house like this, cosy, warm, clean, bright with frilly things, and an air everywhere of love and safety, had never been, all her life, in her way. Would she have cared for it or would it have driven her wild? If it had been this that she wanted, and she had urged Francis Herries sufficiently towards it, there is little doubt but that he would have tried to get it for her. She did not belong to this comfort.

With every hour Deborah felt the distance between them growing. Physically they were of separate worlds, Deborah plump, with cap and apron, keys at her girdle, with her bright happy face, placid too and yet sensitive with that perception, kept by her from childhood, of small unexpressed things.

It was this perception that made her bond with Mirabell, that separated her from Sarah and David and gave her kinship with her father, although she feared him. She was in that way nearer to her father than to her own husband. She watched Mirabell. She saw her stand near the mirror in the parlour, half reflected in it. Her face was elfish, both tragic and impatient. Under its great burden of hair it was poignant in its loneliness. And at last Deborah, unable to endure the woman's silent suffering any longer, caught her in her arms and held her there.

'Tell me, my dear, what is it? What is wrong? Why are you unhappy?'

Mirabell did not try to escape as Deborah had thought that she would. She stayed there looking down.

'We are both unhappy,' she said at last, 'because I cannot give him what he would have, and he has done something for which he will never forgive himself.'

Deborah drew her to a chair. She felt close, close to her. She suddenly seemed to understand her as she never had before, understand the good honest heart, her wild nature uneasy at captivity, her gratitude for his kindness to her, her misery because she could not love him. These things were all told to her as though Mirabell had spoken.

She did speak; she looked up into Deborah's face, seemed to find comfort in those quiet eyes.

'It is all my own sin, all because I came to him for shelter that first time when I was hungry.' She began to speak passionately as Deborah had seen her do once before above Bassenthwaite Water.

'I could not know then; I was a child in so many ways. I knew that he loved me, but not that for so long, with so much refusal, he would still love me. His love is terrible; it is like a pain in his heart and in mine. If I cared nothing for him it would be easy. I would have told him and left him. But how can I not care for him when for so long he has been so good to me, and for so long asked nothing in return? Now at last he does ask something. He cannot help himself . . . And then there is more. I am imprisoned in that house. I am a woman now, not a child, and it seems that I am a woman accursed because I cannot rest anywhere. I think that when Harry was killed I was struck a blow here at my heart. I can feel it, a pain that nothing can heal. After all, I am of no family and of no place. I am not in my own world with him. If I loved him, then nothing would matter, but because I cannot . . .'

She broke off, threw up her head. 'I have a great scorn of women who go about bewailing everything. We had a woman once who was like that; she was mistress of one of my uncles. "Oh," she was always saying, "he has struck me," or "He neglects me," and therefore he did strike her, no blame to him. I would wail about nothing of myself, but to see him so wretched when I care for him . . .' She broke off again, then turned eagerly to Deborah. 'Oh, you don't know, Deborah, how good he can be! He is quite changed now. Of course he is older, but it is not only age. There is a new gentleness – can you not see it?'

'Yes,' said Deborah, 'but it is because he is unhappy.'

'I know, I know!' Mirabell caught Deborah's arm. 'I cannot endure that quietness, not for much longer. If we could speak together – but, after Christmas last, he will say nothing concerning the two of us. There was an angry scene. He beat down the door of my room. I thought he would kill me. I would not have cared had he, but the fit passed and since then he has had a shame that has no cause. What is that – beating the door down? He himself has done many things worse – and to me what have they not done? Beaten me and kicked me, and many worse things. I would not have minded if he had beaten me, but it was of a sudden to withdraw, as though he had done some shameful thing.'

'That is because he loves you,' said Deborah.

Then Mirabell said, dropping her voice very low:

'It cannot go on like this. It must have a turn. It were better for him that I were not there.' And then, with the oddest smile, looking close at Deborah again: 'And perhaps I am not there. No woman at all. The real woman is somewhere else and loves him. I feel that I have no soul, that I must go out to find one.'

At that Mr Sunwood came in and they had supper.

Deborah had one word with her father. After supper he went to the door with her to see the rich red spring moon. He stood there, feeling through all his body the peace of the little town. The cobbled path, the white houses shining in the moonlight, the rooms behind them with their warmth, no sound, and the moon riding through the serene sky. But he turned to her:

'I will not accept this world of ghosts,' he said. 'He has laid it thus, so and so. "And now you take it," says He. "This is good enough for you." But it is not good enough. It is a botch, a mess, a frustration, and man is frustrated in the middle of it. But for every man, one twist and it would be right enough. "Jog this for me a turn to the left," says Man, "and I shall have comfort." "Not I," says God. "Jog it yourself if you can."' He laughed and tweaked Deborah's ear very gently. 'Thou art happy, Deb?'

'Very, Father,' she answered.

'Aye, so I see. And I like your parson, even though he likes not me.'

'Oh, but he does,' said Deborah indignantly.

'Nay,' said Herries laughing. 'I am an old serpent in his nest. I can see him wondering, as we sit at table, "Now, how doth my adored Deborah come from that thief's loins?" But 'tis my seed, Deb, that you are, never shame thy mother else.' He sighed, shrugging his long shoulders. 'Poor sainted Margaret! Old days. Think you that she is behind that moon now, Deb, watching us?'

'Where Heaven may be,' said Deborah.

'Aye, where Heaven may be – a plaguy caterwauling place.'

Taking all her courage she said: 'How sweet Mirabell is, Father; and she cares for you most deeply.'

He looked at her as though he had not heard, then, very low, staring at the moon and speaking into the air:

'She has no right to care. I have treated her very evilly;

everything in me turns to evil.' Then, shrugging his shoulders again: 'Come in. Do you know that I am sixty years old and more? Every part of me from nose to belly, from belly to knee-joint, is aware of it. Only I, I myself, will not recognize it.'

They went inside, and next morning the two rode back to Herries.

As they rode Mirabell knew that he had some fresh plan in his head. She heard him laugh softly to himself, saw him turn to look back at her, then toss his head as though he were proud of making his mind up. And she was intensely miserable. She had never before known such misery. When Harry had been killed, that had been unhappiness of another sort – deep, biting agony with grandeur in it; this was unhappiness that came from failure. Somehow in these years, with all the chances that she had had, she should have made a better job of it. Had Deborah's parson felt passion for her but she no passion in return, would she not have made the best of it, have satisfied him in some way, have 'taken him in' for his own good as so many women must do with their men?

Ah, but Deborah's parson and her Herries, what different men they were! There was no one like her Herries (here she felt a queer sort of pride) for oddity, suddenly stepping inside himself where you could not get him. And herself and Deborah! Here, too, there was a bed-rock difference. Deborah was a lady and she, Mirabell, was not. She did not know what she was – something for nothing, an absurd misfit belonging to no place, no person. And here such a bitter sense of desolation came to her that it was all she could do to hold back her tears.

It would never do that he should see her weeping, so she turned away blinking at the thin sunshine radiant with promise. Derwentwater lay below them. The air seemed to be filled with the sound of waterfalls, and in contrast to this delicious murmur the lake was softly still. One boat floated upon it, the hills were most delicately reflected in purple shapes, a looking-glass world. Lord's Island was a cloud of green. Everything was freshly green – the copses, the hawthorns. Birds were singing everywhere – bullfinches, robins, thrushes – and on all sides the gentle fields sloped lazily up to the rocks and spurs of the hills that would soon have a shadow of green smoke on them from a hint of the new bracken.

Such peace must seem unreal when life is at impossible odds, but for Mirabell this free and open nature had always been the only true certain thing that she knew. She did not analyse it, she could not have described it, because it was part of her, and, just as she was at a loss about her own moods and nature if she were asked for any definition, so she was at a loss here. But the lake, that had slipped so beautifully down between the hills and now lay in perfect peace, rose up to her and for a moment drew her into its own tranquil reassurance.

For some days after their return Francis Herries kept his plan, whatever it was, to himself; then at last one evening he told her.

Herries was at its best in the spring and the early summer. Daffodils blew about its walls, birds were everywhere nesting, the old rooms seemed to take the sunlight more readily, the windows could be flung open; the place lost its musty smell of ancient cobweb and leaking wainscot. Herries himself worked all day on the ground, and now at last, after all these years, it seemed to be responding and yielding to his long care of it. People, too, seemed to be losing some of their long avoidance. Women would greet him at their doors as he passed, men exchange ' Good day' with him, and sometimes children would hang about the courtyard, stroke the dog and watch Benjamin groom the two horses.

They were standing by the wall at the house's back looking at the light fading over Rosthwaite Fell, when he turned abruptly to her and said:

' Soon we shall be leaving this.'

For a moment she did not understand what he said. He repeated it, looking at her shyly, but watching her to see the surprise of pleasure flash into her eyes.

' Leave Herries?'

' Yes . . . Since our visit to Deborah I have been thinking. This is no place for you. You have always hated it. We will find a bright trim house like hers, with modern walls and India paper on them, no dripping water, no disorder . . . a proper parlour for you to sit in.'

' Leave Herries? . . . But you love every stone of it.'

' Yes. But you do not. I can do you that service.'

She was terrified. A mature, profound understanding came to her at this moment. There was some crisis at this time when she became a woman. It may have been this. She saw in a flash of intuitive comprehension that this was his last throw. If she had learnt anything about him during these years with him, it was that Herries was everything to him, that it had a power over him, as some places have over some men, deeper than thought, deeper than reason.

She saw in his eyes, in their light dancing attack on her, that he was saying: 'Now – now – you must love me. I have found a way at last. I am giving up everything, the only thing I've ever really cared for. *This* must win you.' And she knew, as she looked about her, at the darkening fells, the stony fields, the house that seemed to grin malignantly at her, with what loathing she regarded it, with what poignancy she felt the pathos of his abnegation, with what wretched certainty she knew the hopelessness of his desire.

A panic seized her. She felt as though she could run to the house and beat on it with her hands until they bled.

'You must not. You shall not. Do you not realize that I have no power to change this, that no giving up of anything can alter it? Oh, I am wretched indeed to have come, wretcheder to stay, cheating you, cheating myself, when I care for you so. If I did not care it would be easy. But I do not love you. I shall never love you. Nothing can change it.'

'This can change it,' he said. 'We will go from here where you will. It is this house and its discomfort that has chilled you. I was a fool not to have seen it before. I know my way.'

She bowed her head. There was only one thing for her to do.

In the four days that followed, she must have gone, again and again, over every aspect of it. By leaving him might she not liberate him? What was her presence to him save a goad, a torture? She was by now obsessed with this sense that she had, from the beginning, only harried him, and that now the harm that she did was touching insanity. Leaving Herries, what could there be for him but continual remorse and regret with no compensation?

Possibly she had never cared for him so tenderly and so regretfully as now. Those last days of April when the sun shone and the water glittered on the rocks, and green burnt like fire, they moved apart, he, it seemed, resolved that he had won her by this last surrender to her, but suffering, it may be fancied, a brutal hurt with every glance that the house gave him. She saw that he dug no longer, nor planted, nor went out to the hills.

During those last nights he never touched her, and she, lying awake at his side, hated with shivers of revulsion this passion that seemed so necessary to men that they must die if they could not have it.

Oddly, the more deeply she cared for him, the more now she detested the thought of his physically possessing her. She wanted no man ever to touch her again.

On the last night of April, a starless, moonless night, about two of the morning, she rose from his side, crept to the other room where some clothes were, wrote on a piece of paper, left it where he should see it, and fled. By seven o'clock she was on the coach for Kendal.

That night by an odd chance he slept heavily, having been much awake other nights. When he woke and saw that she was not with him in bed, he went to the passage and called her.

It was May Day; the light over the house was dim. All the way down the stairs he called her. On the table where he had so often tried to give her lessons was a piece of paper, and very childishly written:

It is beste to goe. You will have Piece better without me.
                                        MIRABELL.

He stood, holding the paper towards the window, reading it over and over, rocking on his feet.

The sun, surmounting the hill, pierced the window, but he saw nothing.

ULDALE

I

FOUNDING OF A FAMILY

MEANWHILE David and Sarah had made a fine start of family life at Uldale. They had two children – Francis, born in 1760; and Deborah, born in 1762. They were both grand healthy children.

David, indeed, was at last in his full and proper element. You could see this in the happy confident gaze that he threw over his wife, his children, his square house with its rosy brick set so comfortably in its little walled-in garden, his little farm, his servants, his farm hands, and even over the high and swelling downs stretching towards Scotland and the sea – all, in a sort of fashion, his, because he loved them with a personal love and was proud of them with a personal pride.

This was what he had always been intended to be – patriarchal founder of an English family with his great stature, huge limbs, splendid carriage.

As he strode about the soil, his flaxen head up, his chest spread, his eyes shining with health and vigour and happiness, he was already the patriarch gathering these men and women, these beasts of the field and birds of the air under his protecting shelter.

He was now forty-three years of age, and had much worldly wisdom hidden in his round solid-looking head. He was beginning to make very real profits through his Liverpool trade, and, had he wished, could have become a wealthy man. He had the talents, the persistence, the courage. But here the real Herries strain came out in him, also the touch of softness of sentiment that belonged to the little boy who had adored to ride in front of his father, who had hated Alice Press and been thrilled by the dreams of Father Roche. The Herries strain in him made him weary of money-getting, just as it began to be important.

Herries did not care for property; they were too proud to think it worthwhile to amass it. They cared so much for family, for their own standing, their own importance in England, that no vulgar amassing of wealth could do anything but damage their self-approval. But then again their family pride was so unselfconscious, so completely taken for granted, that they never thought of it, talked of it or defended it. The English have always had this quality of confident security, and this makes them remote from the rest of the world and will always isolate them whether their island continues to be an island or no. It accounts for their universal unpopularity, for their insular stubbornness, their hypocrisy and their profound calm in a crisis. It accounts also for a generous warmth of heart hidden under an absurd armour of frigid suspicion of strangers. It accounts for their poetry, their lack of imagination, their peculiar humour, their irritating conceit and ignorance in foreign countries, and a certain naïve youthfulness which is both absurd and attractive.

Any history of any English family must be concerned with this confident security and the shocks that it receives from time to time. These shocks never ultimately affect it; the history of any English family therefore is, basically, comedy rather than tragedy; comedy decorated with incongruous things like spring flowers, teapots, the Battle of Trafalgar, London fogs, beer and country vicarages. This confident security is the true reason of our magnificent sequence of great poets. Poetry is roused by sheer rebellious indignation, so vilely exasperating is it to anyone with imagination.

David, however, thought in these days little of poetry. He was so busied from early morning (he was up at five-thirty every day) until evening, that life flashed like a meteor before his eyes and was gone.

In actual fact the times were propitious for him. There was possibly no period in the history of the village labourer so black, degraded and hopeless as that between the years 1760 and 1832. Let there follow some items important in the Herries family chronicle. The agricultural labourer at this time earned fourteen pence a day or eight shillings a week, and his wife, were she lucky, might earn sixpence a day. Here are some of the things that the labourer must provide for his family: candles, 3*d*; bread or flour, 1*s* 8*d*; yeast and salt, 4*d*; soap, starch, 2½*d*; tea, sugar, butter, 1*s*; thread, worsted, 3*d*. The weekly total would be some 8*s* 4½*d* or £21 15*s* 6*d* per annum, his earnings being £20 16*s*:

In addition to the weekly expenses, there were clothing, rent, fuel, amounting to some £8, and leaving the happy villager with a yearly deficiency of nearly £9. He could buy neither milk nor cheese. He could not brew small beer save for some especial occasion. So difficult was it to obtain soap for washing that they burned green fern and kneaded it into balls. A quarter of wheat cost in 1787 forty-eight shillings, and that amount was trebled later.

Everywhere and in every way the labourer was oppressed by the farmer. Landlords and farmers were, at this time, advocating enclosures everywhere. The common field system was utterly wasteful; far better to throw all the fields into large farms.

David found that here in all the country that stretched between Uldale and Carlisle matters were very different from the independence and security of the Statesmen in Borrowdale and Newlands. There a labourer could rise by thrift and diligence until he should be in some sort his own master. In all the country districts about Uldale, by enclosure the labourer was losing his right of cutting fuel on the common, his piece of land, his pig and cow. Privilege of gleaning after harvest, whereby poor families often obtained enough corn to last them through the winter, was also now withdrawn.

Signs of the new world were also to be found in the arrival of the middleman; the farmer sold his corn to the miller, the miller to the mealman, the mealman to the shopkeeper, the shopkeeper to the poor.

In short, the halcyon time for the poor man at work on English fields was over, never, alas, to return.

David was fortunate in that his farm was small and his means were large. His heart was warm and kindly, his character patient, his intelligence shrewd. It was not long before his name began to be known for wise charity and true understanding; it would not be long before 'Squire Herries' was his designation.

His whole heart and soul rose to his new position. He was founding a family, not a new family, but a new branch of the finest family in the world, the Herries of England. Here, from every possible motive, both his spiritual and physical energies were engaged. At the heart of it were his wife and children. Here both his love and his pride knew no bounds. Beyond them were all the Herries (with one very important exception).

After he had been at Uldale a year or so, he wrote to various relations informing them that here he was, and that they were welcome to a bed and a sup any time they passed that way.

In dueness of time he heard from Cousin Pelham, a very gay and frivolous epistle, saying that Uldale was the very place for flight when the bailiffs should become too pressing; a stiff angular letter from Dorothy Forster, complaining of the weather and her rheumatism; a grand document from London from his cousin Judith (now the Hon Mrs Ernest Bligh), informing him that her social duties were so onerous that she was sadly afraid that she could spare no time for the bleak North (where, she knew well from her unhappy youth, it always rained); a delightful letter from dear Uncle Harcourt (now seventy-five years of age), wishing his nephew every prosperity, but intimating that gout had him by the leg and David must come to Ravenglass to see him rather than he to Uldale. There were others: Will Forster, now twenty-five years of age, who wrote from Alnwick to inquire about the hunting; an aunt of Pelham's, an ancient Titchley, who, drinking the waters at Bath, begged him to subscribe to her Home for Indigent Sedan Chairmen; and young Morgan Gold of Edinburgh, who wrote to ask David to be a subscriber and patron to his forthcoming epic, *The Tower of Babel*.

In one way and another David felt his bag had not been a bad one. This was his first step towards bringing the family together, making it a real force and power in the progress and happiness of England.

It was England that he always ultimately saw; England expressed in the downs, streams and hills of his own surrounding country; England in the names so immediately close to him – Skiddaw Forest, Bassenthwaite Common, Great Calva, Bowscale Fell, Blackhazel Beck, Mungrisdale, Scarness, Jenkin Hill; England in the little streets of Keswick; England spreading and dipping and rising again, through town and country, from county to county, until on every side it claims the sea.

His patriotism was like the patriotism of most men, founded on a stone, a flower, the sound of a stream, a clod of earth, the rustle of a tree, but it spread from these things until it embraced the earth, the moon and stars at one reach, and dug pits in his soul at the other.

All fine enough, but there was one festering strand in his ambition which was not so fine. That was his hatred of and scorn for his dear cousin and brother-in-law, Raiseley Herries.

Raiseley, who was forty-five years of age now, had never been a very fine physical specimen, and now, from idleness, a bad constitution and much early coddling, had developed into as complete a valetudinarian as his mother had ever been. In his youth he had had brains of a rather scientific sort, but for lack of encouragement and because of a bad education they had run to seed. He had not had all the best chances. His health had always been bad: *that* was not entirely imagination. His marriage had been unfortunate. Mary, David's sister, had never cared for him, had indeed never cared for anyone but herself, nor did her two children, Pomfret, aged twelve, and Cynthia, aged nine, care for him either. His appearance was distressing, his long thin face yellow like a turnip, frequently coloured with the ravages of dyspepsia, his lanky body gaudily and untidily clothed, always on his features the malcontentedness of a thoroughly disappointed man. He added to these unamiable qualities an overweening pride in his position and a hasty but cowardly temper.

His quarrel with David had begun at a very early age, from that day, in fact, when David had paid his first Keswick call with his mother so many years ago. For long Raiseley had had the best of it. David, living in disgraceful obscurity with a father who was the scandal of all the world, was no very possible rival. It was true that Raiseley had married David's sister, but this was because Mary had turned her back on her family and disowned them all. Afterwards matters had not been improved by the fact that whenever Mary wished to scorn or abuse her sickly husband (and these occasions were not rare as the intimacies of marriage strengthened) she found an easy weapon in the size and ability of her brother (whom, nevertheless, herself she termed for many years 'clodhopper'). It was not, however, until David came to Uldale that the feud was really proclaimed.

At first when they had heard of David's purchase of the place, both Raiseley and Mary had laughed scornfully. Their position

in Keswick was nothing very fine (they were not even contemptu-
ously popular as old Pomfret had been before them), but they
nevertheless represented the only kind of Herries of which Keswick socially had any cognizance. It was not so much that English
society in the middle of the eighteenth century was snobbish, as
that the members of it simply felt that those who were not members of it were not human. It was easy enough. A man who was
not a gentleman was hanged for stealing a sheep or whipped at
the public stocks until the blood ran, or a child would be imprisoned in a gaol too filthy for rats for stealing a loaf of bread, or a
woman who was not a lady would suffer the grossest of public
indignities for no reason other than that she answered her mistress impertinently.

There was no question but that any Herries was a gentleman;
unfortunately Francis Herries had declassed himself completely,
and must be therefore doubly disowned. How ridiculous then of
his son to expect, because he bought a small property in the
neighbourhood, that he would be received or accepted! It was
true that Rogue Herries's daughter had been accepted, but that was
because she had disowned her monstrous father at the earliest
possible moment, and then had been washed, as it were, pure in
London's chastening waters before returning to Keswick. David
not only approved of his monster of a father, but openly declared
his devotion to him, and was seen with him as often as possible,
yes, even though the man, after selling his mistress in public and
murdering his first wife, had married a common gipsy off the
fells.

Oddly enough, none of these things seemed to stand in
David's path. After all, he was not new to Keswick; he had done
business there since he was a boy; everyone knew his rectitude,
his courage, his humour. He was a proper man; he could carry an
ox on one shoulder; stripped, he could fight any man in the North
Country. Had he not carried off his wife single-handed from the
villain of a father and a posse of attendant villains? True, he had
killed the man, there under Esk Hause. The thing was already an
epic, and ballads had been written about it.

This was the Keswick view, and soon neighbouring squires
were calling at Uldale, and David was hunting, fishing, shooting
with them, and it began to be noised abroad that some of the jolli-
est evenings to be enjoyed in Cumberland were to be found at the
Fell House, Uldale.

It was then that the bitterness of his hatred for his brother-in-
law was felt to the full by Raiseley Herries. His view of life was

in any case a bitter one. Ill-health made him bitter, a conviction
of wasted brains and opportunities, disappointment both in his
wife and his children, hurt vanity, wounded conceit – these all
made him bitter.

David's scorn and contempt for Raiseley was a bad, unworthy
element in his warm, generous, noble nature, as Sarah well knew
and deplored.

'It isn't worthy of you,' she would say after he had boasted to
her of some small triumph, 'and one day it will come back badly
to you. Our children will suffer for it, if not ourselves.'

'Not they!' said David laughing, throwing his babies up into
the air and catching them. ''Tis an old feud, Sarah, my love, and
it began with his laughing at my father when we were infants
together. With his wheezly, flammering body, I could break him
over my head.'

And so in pride and scorn and derision he rode himself over to
invite the two of them to his first grand festivity, this May Day,
1763. Sitting his horse outside their door, a magnificent sight for
all to see, he gave his messages to young Pomfret, a stout, sturdy
boy, who carried his head proudly so that David took to him at
sight.

It was plain that young Pomfret had been trained to disapproval of his uncle, but he could not drag his eyes from the horse.

'Wilt have a ride?' asked David, laughing.

But young Pomfret shook his head and ran into the house.

Sarah also shook her head when David returned and laughingly
told her of it.

'Why should we breed our children to this? What affair is it of
theirs that you and Raiseley Herries have a spite?'

She was nursing her own baby, Deborah, not yet a year old, as
she spoke. She looked down, smiling, her eyes bright with love.
'We have had feuds enough in our lives – my uncle and your
father; now there must be peace. This is not like you, Davy; it
is not your generosity.'

'I feel no generosity,' he answered sharply. 'My sister left us
and stayed in Keswick to mock us. Raiseley has been our enemy
since he was weaned.'

But Sarah shook her head. 'Then it is the more reason the
thing ceased. It has lasted long enough. See that you are not
proud, Davy, in your new place. Of all things pride is the worst.'

He bent over the mother and child, himself a child at that instant. 'I have reasons for my pride. Two good reasons.' Then,
kissing her, his great hand cupping her chin: 'And how can I not

be proud when I love you so? Having such a wife, what is a man worth an he is not stiff with pride?'

So Mary and Raiseley Herries did not come to the May Day Feast at the Fell House. But all the rest of the world came.

It was a grand May Day, soft and warm. David had the downs above his house for his games – for the Archery, the Football, the Wrestling and the Dancing. Upright on the downs, its head proudly lifted to heaven, was the Maypole, its hanging streamers lazily lifting like live things in the breeze. He stood with Sarah on the lawn in the brick-walled garden to receive his guests. He wore a plain suit of mulberry trimmed with silver. His fair hair (he was beginning, as were many others, to wear – save on very state occasions – his own hair) shone in the sun. His rosy face – strong, clear-eyed, broad-browed – beamed happiness. Sarah stood beside him in a pretty grey dress, the hoop sprayed with roses, a fine white wig with cherry ribbons, and she wore silver shoes. She looked as healthy, confident, happy as he.

Around them, too, everything was happy: the pigeons cooed, cows softly lowed, birds sang in the elm tree, young Francis was sturdy enough in his three years to stand beside his mother holding tightly to her with one hand and with the other cracking his whip.

David and Sarah insisted on receiving all alike; today there were to be no class distinctions. David had sent invitations to all his old friends in Borrowdale, and many of them had ridden over – Peels and Satterthwaites and Mounseys and Bells. Sarah, although truly she was no snob, could not but be gratified to see how the gentry and their wives were appearing – Mr Bonstead from Keswick, Squire Osmaston and his lady from near Troutbeck, Squire Worcester and his lady from the other side of Threlkeld, the Peaches and Sandons and Ullathorpes from Keswick, the Brownriggs all the way from Patterdale, the Newsomes of Newlands, the Robertsons of St John's in the Vale, the Kendals from the other side of Bassenthwaite.

Soon Sarah found that she was compelled to observe social distinctions, so she led Mrs Osmaston and Mrs Worcester and old Miss Mary Peach and the Misses Gwendolyn and Frances Brownrigg out to the seats that had been arranged on the down with an awning to protect them from the wind. The farmers and their wives and children gathered in their own groups, and splendid Statesmen like Richard Bell, towering with his white head and six foot five above all the others, and George Satterthwaite, like a bull for thickness and strength, walked on the springing turf as though they owned the world and were rightly proud of it.

Yes, this was perhaps the happiest day of his life for David. It had come to this: that he had now his true independent place in the world, his place, his wife and children, this turf on which he was treading, this English turf under English hills, watered with English streams – these things were his and he owed them to no man alive. Men of all kinds, from old Osmaston, who was a sort of king of Cumberland at this time, from Richard Bell, as noble-hearted as he was ironically cautious and loyally steadfast, to old Ducken the ploughman, who was now moving towards the Maypole, a string of children at his heels, these men and their womenfolk had greeted him, welcomed him, received him into their world.

And he thought as he stood there, his legs spread, his head up, his face flushed with happiness, of himself as a small boy at Herries listening to Alice Press as she screamed at his mother; of the Chinese Fair and the ancient Chinaman with the old, old face; of that awful scene in the tent when his father sold Alice Press; of how he stood in the courtyard sparring with Raiseley while his mother was dying upstairs; of old Mrs Wilson the witch; of the ride to Carlisle; of that awful moment when his father, looking a dead man, had come into his room in Carlisle; of the day when Mirabell had met them in Herries – a thousand other scenes were called up by his memory. He knew now that, in spite of his devotion and loyalty to his father, that strange mist of disgrace and isolation had always been hanging over him, although he was too proud to acknowledge it.

Now at last, at last he was clear of it!

All this while his eye was on the road beneath him to see whether his father and Mirabell would appear. He had, of course, sent word to them – a special letter on horseback – that they must most certainly come. He wanted them to come; it would not be a real complete day for him if his father were not there, but with that, if he were honest with himself, there was a feeling too that they would be strange, his father and Mirabell, in this company. They were always strange, his father with his arrogant look that went so oddly with his scarred face, his silence, his sudden ironical statements, his wandering eye so that his mind seemed to be always elsewhere, and Mirabell like a play-actress with her gaudy clothes and ill-easiness in proper and normal company. He wanted them to come, but he dreaded a little what the result of their coming might be.

Now everything is in movement. The coloured ribbons of the Maypole flash in constant change against the blue of the sky and the green of the turf. The girls pass like notes of music sounding in regular rhythm against the air.

On a grassy mound above the road an old man with two chins and a frizzy white wig stands fiddling, and he has an attendant piper. Birds fly across the sun, bells sound, clouds lighter than smoke, with the soft colour of swan's down, collect and hover and disperse.

Beyond the Maypole there are benches, a barrel of ale, apples soaked in sugar and thick flat cakes crammed with raisins, damp in the middle. Men and women cluster here; there is wrestling, kissing and hugging and drinking, and, beyond them, as the sun slides down the sky, the sloping black side of Skiddaw catches the light: it is as though it rolled its coat off and spread there, basking, while the clouds are shadowed across the shining surface. And David stands, his head up, breathing the air, catching the light, feeling that the whole world is his, joy in his heart.

A farmer passes. He turns, laughing, rolling his thick back towards the Maypole.

'T'dancing is grand,' he says. Osmaston's huge body draws near, seeming to darken the sun with its bulk. He happens very gravely to talk politics with young Herries. 'Now Grenville . . . And these American Colonies? . . .' They are just beginning, in other places beside Uldale, to seem impertinent.

Sarah's task was harder today than her husband's. About her were seated, their hoops spreading wide around them, the Misses Gwendolyn and Frances Brownrigg and the great Mrs Osmaston. Mrs Osmaston was a tremendous lady, with her high white wig, her enormous white bosom half naked to the sun, her round white arms. With all this massive flesh her features were small and tightly pinched together. But out of her little mouth a tremendous voice proceeded, deep and bass like a man's, and with this voice she had been accustomed for forty years to give commands to all around her, save only her husband whom she resolutely obeyed. She was like a great white whale lying there in the sun. She had never been out of Cumberland in her life, and had all the knowledge of and confident scorn for the rest of the world that such determined staying-at-home produces. She had been, both in the '15 and the '45, an ardent Jacobite, and could never say enough about the Hanoverian dynasty. Many of her oaths and similes were of an excellent coarseness, and she alluded to all the natural processes of man with much freedom and gusto.

When in good humour, as she was today, she would slap her friends on the back or pinch their arms or yield them even more familiar gestures. She often made the oddest noises, and was, in honest fact, none too cleanly in her person, so, as her own devoted husband said, ''twas best to sit to windward of her'. Better than all else, she loved to discuss the love affairs of her neighbours and friends, and had, as she said, 'a nose for copulation like the nose of a dog for a hare'. She liked Sarah and told her so. Seated there, her great knees wide-planted inside her hoop, her fat arms akimbo, she told one bawdy story after another and was ably abetted by the Misses Brownrigg, who, being supposedly virgins, had their eyes eternally at the keyholes of all their neighbours' bedrooms.

Sarah, a woman of her time, was amused by the bawdy stories when she could keep her ear to them, but she must watch first one side, then another, to see that all went well, that nobody was offended, that everyone, even to the smallest child of the least important labourer, was happy. But everyone was happy. Happiness was everywhere.

Now it was time for the great Football game. Everyone streamed towards the upper down where the game was to be. The goals were distant nearly half a mile the one from the other. There were few rules, if any; all cunning and trickery were at advantage, but brute force was the greatest power of all. There were fifty players a side to start with, although before the game ended there were nearly a hundred a side. It was a match between the Uldale men and the Keswick men, wide latitude allowed for district partisanship.

It was a superb sight to see the hundred men – farmers, labourers, townsmen, woodsmen, sailors from the coast, dalesmen, shepherds – stripped to their smallclothes, rush together with great shouts of joy and triumph. The ball rose into the air and at once the battle began, clumps of men binding together, arms locked, rushing head down to meet other bands with a great crash of neck and shoulder.

Soon the giants on either side were to be seen. Willie Peel of Mungrisdale with his two sons, a mountain of a man, his sons as big as he, the three rushing forward, the ball at their feet, lesser men clinging to their sides and buttocks, leaping at their necks, trying to trip them at the feet, while to meet them came John Ringstraw and his brother George from Threlkeld, men like bullocks, crimson of face, thick of neck, with backs like walls. Willie Peel meeting John Ringstraw, for a while all lesser men drew back and watched them hurl themselves the one at the other, arms interlocked, backs straining, legs planted for a throw, while the air was beaten with the shouting and all the dogs barked and the shadows lovingly stroked the sides of Skiddaw. Then Willie's belt was burst and his smallclothes were flapping about his ankles; nothing mattered that to him, and he played for the rest of the game half naked, but the ball now had passed to a wily little devil, Jock Mounsey from Grange in Borrowdale, who was away across the downs with the thing at his feet, half a hundred men after him.

All the downs now rolled like a sea towards the sun and the hills. Little waves of dark shadows broke the pale primrose glow. Skiddaw and Blencathra grew dark, and seemed to billow with gestures of lazy self-indulgent satisfaction out towards the tender colours of the May Day sky.

And against this fair scene the battle rose and fell. Little Mounsey was for a while detached, a small figure springing along like a deer, controlling the ball as though it were tied to his shoe-strings, but then the two Grimshaws, stocky shepherds from Troutbeck, had caught him up. One of them tripped him and he fell, but before the ball had turned back to the goal at Skiddaw end half a hundred men had arrived and thrown themselves upon it.

Here now was a *mêlée* in the grand old style, no quarter asked and no quarter given. Over the ball in a wriggling, writhing heap twenty men were lying, and over these another thirty were striving, while behind them were the outguards, arriving from every part of the field, and, if they could not reach the central scrimmage, wrestling and boxing on their own. So that now there was a grand and noble sight, this central mass of heaving men, detached groups of fighters, and the spectators shouting, roaring, the dogs barking as though they were mad. The fine ladies themselves cursed and swore in their interest, and it was all that her husband could do to prevent Mrs Osmaston from rushing on to the field of play and lending assistance.

All is fair in love and war, and no chronicler would dare to catalogue some of the things that were done in that scrimmage; shirts were torn from many a back, once and again a head would rise, as though seeking for the stars, and stare vacantly skywards, blood pouring, eyes blackened, and once and again, a figure for an instant stood completely stark and so faced the world in utter nakedness, like some primeval hero before clothes were.

Then, alive with its own devilry, the ball suddenly emerged

and sped forward, pursued by Willie Peel and one of his sons. Willie, his long hair flying, naked to the waist, his shaggy chest broad as a wall, his eyes on fire, crying his war-cry 'Peel! Peel! Hey Peel!' was well away, the ball at his feet. Staggering that so huge a man should run so swiftly and keep the ball at his toe with so astounding an accuracy, but now he was away from them all, the field streaming at his feet, and in his size, strength and beauty he joined partnership with the strength and beauty of the scene, the grand type of all Cumbrian strength, sureness of purpose, largeness of grasp, as good as anything the world has seen, and as lasting.

The only man in his way was Jock Elliot of Crosthwaite, and he was a kind of ogre of a man, almost deformed, so short of stature, so thick, so shaggy, with such long swinging arms.

With a great grin, his little eyes burning under his black bristling eyebrows, he advanced to meet Willie Peel. Peel tried to 'slip' him, but, heavy though Elliot was, he was agile too, and was in front of him. Their bodies met with a shock that would have slain two ordinary men and could have been heard, you would swear, away in the streets of Keswick itself.

The two men drew a breath and closed. A moment later Peel had Elliot in his arms, held him as though he loved him dearer than any woman, and actually raised him from the ground. Elliot's head was up. He seemed to be staring at the heavens as though imploring the gods to do him this last great service, then, his short legs about Peel's thighs, he brought him crashing to the ground, himself on top. That seemed to end their struggle. They lay, full length, one on the other, softly heaving, while the world roared its approval and, gently, quietly, rosy clouds drifted like miniature galleons towards the west.

But the ball was out again. Three men had it and were racing towards the Uldale goal. All Uldale drew its breath; soon most of the remaining audience, save the very aged, were rushing into the field to join the game.

David too. He had been all this time like a dog straining at the leash. Now stripping off his mulberry coat and flowered vest, he rushed into the fray. Peel's two sons were with him. Together they raced the field, and David as he ran, felt that this was truly the grandest moment of his life, with the wind brushing his cheeks, the mountains crowding to meet him, the turf strong and resilient beneath his feet.

He touched the ball; it passed to young Isaac Peel, then over to Rumney Peel, back to himself again. He could feel the field

streaming behind him. Two men were in their way. David
feinted; the ball obeyed him like a living thing, and now the three
of them, sharing for an instant a comradeship that was as true and
strong as though long companionship had made it, were away,
away with only the hills to meet them.

Skiddaw smiled; Blencathra clapped his hands; all the rosy
clouds sang together; and to the roar of the approving world, the
ball slipped between the posts.

Glorious never-to-be-forgotten moment – and David, turning,
throwing his arms high for victory, saw, quite near to him, above
the road, waiting beside his horse, the figure of his father.

He moved towards him, joyfully greeting him. Then he
paused. Something very terrible had occurred. He felt it come,
through the lovely evening air, darkening the sky, dimming the
sounds of the games, removing him to a circle of silence wherein
he stood alone with his father. Afterwards he remembered that
he had thought: 'Why, he's old . . . and a terrible thing has come
to him.'

In Herries's voice when he greeted him, however, there was no
tremor, and his hand, in its long black glove, was hard and firm.
His clothes were dark, his face was pale, drawn, as it often was,
a little crookedly. Whence did David have his sense of some disaster?

Herries said, very quietly, but holding his son's hand:

'Davy, has she been here?'

'She? . . . But who?'

'My wife.'

'Mirabell? No. Is she not with you?'

'She left me early this morning, and I must find her.' The
hand in David's gave a slight quiver.

'Why did she leave you?'

'I cannot say. But I must find her.'

David put his hand on the other's shoulder and felt an odd
pride that it should be so hard and strong. All this while he had
been looking into his father's face, and now, beneath the customary ironical gaze and twisted mouth, he felt such a force of controlled agony that he dropped his eyes. He had never yet loved
his father so deeply as now, when he realized that he was unable
to help him.

'She cannot have gone far,' he said urgently, longing to do or
say something to assuage that unhappiness. ''Twas a momentary
pique or resentment. She had secret moods unlike other
women—'

But Herries stopped him, raising his hand and gripping his son's shoulder so fiercely that David winced. He wore only his shirt.

'No, it was no pique,' Herries said quietly. 'I had told her that we would leave Herries because I fancied that she would be happier so. She thought it would kill me to leave Herries, so, for my comfort, she went away. I must find her that she may understand.'

He turned, stroking his horse's neck.

'Father, I will come with you. I will sleep with you tonight, and tomorrow—'

Herries shook his head, smiling.

'Nay, this is my affair. You are a good son, Davy. I shall find her. Nothing in heaven or hell shall stay me.'

He mounted his horse.

'Return to your guests. Farewell.'

He started down the white road and, before he turned the corner, looked back once and waved his hand.

HERRIES STARTS HIS SEARCH

VERY early the next morning, Herries, after bidding farewell to Benjamin, his servant and friend, started out on his search.

Part Four

THE BRIGHT TURRETS OF ILION

RETURN OF A WANDERER

ON a sharp clear autumn afternoon of the year 1768, Mr Simeon Harness, pastor, schoolmaster, and general man-of-all-work in the districts of Rosthwaite, Watendlath and Seatoller, climbed to the top of the Brund Fell and looked appreciatively about him. With so little a climb he had reached an elevation of great splendour. He was a short, pursy man, normally scant of breath, but for the last five years he had walked these tops on his daily occupations, and so friendly and kindly had they come to seem to him that he did not realize any arduousness in surmounting them.

His own home – two rooms of a farmhouse – was in the hamlet of Watendlath, the smoke from whose chimneys he could see now lazily curling beneath him.

He had indeed a fine view. On these tops you could walk for miles and scarcely be compelled to descend. Beloved names came to meet him as he looked. Towards Derwentwater, Brown Dodd and Ashness Fell and High Seat; towards Thirlmere, Armboth and Watendlath Fell; towards the Langdales, Coldbarrow and Ullscarf and High White Stones. The ranges lay all about him in shapes more human than those of his friends, moulded and formed, now sharply with rocks and steeples and slanting cliffs of shining colour, then gently in sheets of flaming bracken lifting to smooth arms and shoulders embossed like shields of metal. Wild profusion, and yet perfect symmetry and order. One colour faded to another, purple cliff above orange sea, deeps of violet under shadow of rose, and a great and perfect stillness everywhere.

When he turned and looked across the valley to Stye Head he saw, falling over the Gavel and Scafell, ladders of sunlit mist that were indeed to his devout soul like steps to heaven. It did not seem strange to him that, on a sudden call, one should climb these ladders and so, to the sound of trumpets, pass into that other glorious company.

He sighed. He did not wish to pass over. He supposed that there was still much work to do, but there were times when his scattered flock seemed to be past all stirring, when, if he looked back, he had achieved exactly nothing at all, when the pain in his side, which had been his constant companion ever since, three

years before, some drunken revellers had in the friendliest of
spirits thrown him off a hayrick, was sharper than he could silently
endure, when his own sins, his ingratitude to God, his liking for
ale, the greed of his stomach, and the sudden sharp temptation
of a handsome woman, mounted crimson-high – on such occasions, in spite of all fortitude, he sighed for the ladders of God.

He had a round bare face like a baby's, wore a small tie-wig
and a coat and breeches of rusty black, and carried in his hand a
worn copy of Mr Chapman's translation of the *Iliad*, which
appeared to him to be, after the Bible, the finest book in the
world.

It was his intention, although the afternoon was chill, to sit on
the ground, with his beloved hills all around him, and read. He
knew that in a short time the peace of the scene would steal about
him and quieten his distresses. This magical charm had never
failed him. He sat down, facing the silver ladders, and opened his
book, gathering the skirts of his coat about him for greater
warmth and smiling amiably at the three or four sheep who were
tranquilly grazing near him.

He began to read:

> Fires round about them shined,
> As when about the silver moon, when air is free from wind,
> And stars shine clear, to whose sweet beams, high prospects, and
>   the brows
> Of all steep hills and pinnacles, thrust up themselves for shows,
> And even the lowly valleys joy to glitter in their sight,
> When the unmeasured firmament bursts to disclose her light,
> And all the signs in heaven are seen that glad the shepherd's
>   heart;
> So many fires disclosed their beams, made by the Trojan part,
> Before the face of Ilion, and her bright turrets showed.
> A thousand courts of guard kept fires, and every guard allowed
> Fifty stout men, by whom their horse ate oats and hard white
>   corn,
> And all did wishfully expect the silver-thronéd morn.

He repeated the phrases aloud that the hills might also enjoy
them.

'The lowly valleys joy to glitter in their sight.' The 'bright
turrets' of Ilion. The 'hard white corn'. 'The silver-thronéd
morn.'

He was himself something of a poet and had once written an

'Elegy to Sophia Countess of Balebury', his one-time patroness. It had, of course, never been published, but he showed it once and again to an intimate.

All very well to be a poet, but when you had but thirty pounds a year, a pain in your side and a sadly lascivious nature, where was the time for poetry? He was concerned too for the country. The fate of the American Colonies was dwelling just now heavily on his conscience, although no others of his friends seemed to be concerned with it. Grenville's Stamp Act of three years before had appeared to him an injustice unworthy of his country's greatness; but on the other hand he had only now, in a belated newssheet, been reading of the episode of the sloop *Liberty* in Boston and the abominable riots that followed the seizure of the cargo. Hard, hard the ways of this world; so easy would men only love one another, but that very thing how difficult, as he could see in his own case, because try as he might he could not love Willie Richards, the farmer in whose house he lodged, as he truly should.

So he sighed and envied the sheep, then smartly abused himself for an ungrateful wretch whom God had placed in this marvellous world, hemming him in with ladders of silver and gold, extending to him with every new day the signs of His grace and favour, while even the pain in his side was troublesome but a little and nothing at all compared with what many poor folk had to suffer. He could not, however, return tranquilly to his Homer. He was sitting on a natural platform of turf, and now he rose and walked back and forth, two hands clasped behind his back, his eyes drinking in the constant change of scene as the light and shadow ran beneath the sun, his mind biting on its troubles, its successes (as when last Sunday forenoon he had preached in Keswick market-place to some hundred souls), its fears and surrenders.

He had just thought that his stomach was queasy and it was time he made his way down to Watendlath for a meal, when, looking in the direction of the Pikes, he perceived someone approaching. This was a man moving with a remarkably easy and resolute stride, and, as he came nearer, Mr Harness saw that he carried on his back a bundle and in his hand a very stout staff.

The stranger (for Mr Harness could see at once that it was no one familiar to him) appeared to hesitate as to his choice of descent; then, seeing the little clergyman, he came to meet him.

Now, close at hand, he was clearly remarkable for his height, his strong leanness, his white hair (he wore his own hair, which was cropped to his neck), and for the unusual character of his features. His eyes were large and brilliant, his countenance haughty and reserved but marked by a deep scar which ran from the forehead to the upper lip.

So soon as he saw the scar Mr Harness knew who it must be. This was Herries of Herries in Rosthwaite, the extraordinary man who had gone mad after his wife, a common gipsy woman, left him. That at least was the gossip of the valley. Although Mr Harness had been for five years at Watendlath and Herries had been on several occasions during that period at his home, Mr Harness had not yet seen him.

Opinion locally differed as to whether the man were mad or no. Some said that he had been always crazy since he first came there; others that he was not mad at all but cursed by God; others that he was not wicked even, but only a poor soul with whom everything had gone wrong. And a few said that he was a good man and generous and very wise. It was true at least that after his wife left him opinion became gentler towards him, and the old term 'Rogue Herries' had a note of kindliness in it; but it was still said everywhere that once he had had league with the Devil, had lived with a witch in his house and, when they drowned her, carried her home and buried her in his garden.

So, for all these opinions, Mr Harness was greatly interested to meet with him.

'Good day,' he said smiling.

Herries took off his broad black hat and wiped his forehead.

'It is warm walking,' he said, looking at Mr Harness with a very kindly expression in his dark eyes. His hat off, there was something indeed very remarkable in his appearance, for his hair was of a most beautiful snowy whiteness that seemed to catch the afternoon light. His face too was brown and spare with health.

'Have you come far, sir?' asked Mr Harness.

'From Furness.'

'That is a long distance. By Langdale is shorter.'

The other laughed. 'I am sixty-eight years of age, but have no sense of it.'

'Sixty-eight!' said Mr Harness in admiration. 'You are accustomed to walking, sir?'

'I never knew what true health was before I adopted it.' Then he added very simply, 'My name is Herries and I am going to my house in Rosthwaite. Perhaps you are yourself going that way?'

'My name is Harness,' answered the other. ''Tis odd that we
have not met before.'

'I have heard of you, sir,' said Herries. 'We will go together,
then.'

As they turned he went on: 'I have been all day alone and shall
be glad of a little company. 'Tis odd how you may walk these
hills for a week and meet no human soul. There was a time when
I preferred my own company to any man's, but now it may be
that I know my own self too well.' Then, after a moment's pause,
he added very quietly, 'I have been for a long time in search of
my wife who left me in a misunderstanding five years ago.'

'I have heard something of it,' said Mr Harness, gravely.

Herries nodded his head. 'I speak of it to everyone I meet, for
it may by chance happen that they have heard of her.'

Mr Harness was very sympathetic. He liked this man.

'It is scarcely likely,' he said, 'that she will have remained all
these years in the district.'

Herries nodded. 'Nay, it is not likely. But the North Country
was her only home. Though she has gone south for a while she
will return. Of that I am certain.' Then, very cheerfully: 'But
these are personal matters; I know did you have news of her from
anyone you would inform me. I am hoping that she may be at
my house, waiting for me. I have considerable hope. It is three
months since I was here, and as this is the only spot of the whole
earth for me it is a great happiness to return.'

'Have you been far, sir?' asked Harness.

'I have been for the first time for many years in London.'

'And pray tell me, sir,' said Mr Harness, eagerly, 'how did you
find the Town? I have, alas, never been there, and must trust to
the descriptions of others.'

'I found it grievously altered,' said Herries. 'There is scarce
any of the old Town left. They are pulling down here and destroying there until it is pitiful to realize that in a year or two the character of the Town will be gone. 'Tis this craze for modernity. I
assure you, sir, there is such a rush and tumble in these days that
one must hesitate to cross the street for the fierceness of the
traffic.

'But what appears to me the most lamentable is that the Town
is losing its character, and might be as modern as the town of
New York for its new buildings, the vulgarity of the people, the
craze for wealth, and the rest. But indeed, sir, I am an old country
cousin, and 'tis a shock to my system to comprehend that Queen
Anne is truly dead.'

'You spoke of the town of New York,' said Mr Harness. 'Pray tell me, did you hear much talk of our American Colonies?'

'Scarce a word. America is too remote for men to worry over.'

Mr Harness sighed. 'I fear there is a great injustice there. We shall worry before all is done.' He went on more tentatively: 'And you heard no news of your wife in London?'

'No, sir, I did not. I had one evening, however, an odd adventure.'

'Pray let me hear it, sir,' said Mr Harness.

'I was minded one evening to go to the theatre. They were playing the *Othello* of William Shakespeare. Before the first act was over I was conscious that there was a fellow near to me who was aware of my nearness to him. I looked again and again, but could see only his back. After a while he turned, and I perceived that he bore an odd resemblance to a fellow many years ago in these parts, a pedlar, a vagrant who, by accident rather than any design, had played some part in incidents of my former life here.

'I am a man of no superstitious feeling. This world is interpenetrated, we cannot but doubt, with many others, but it is our business to deal with this one and leave the rest to a future time. But it has ever been my misfortune to be dreaming when I should be most practical, and to see my way cloudily when I should be most exact.

'The lights were blowing, there was a wind stirring in the theatre, and I had a strange conviction that in another moment or so I was to die. I don't know, sir, how it may be with you, but life has so tormented me with its riddle that to die without any answer to it has always seemed to me an exasperating indignity.

'The theatre grew dark to me, the wind blew about my ears, the candles leaping before my eyes, and the fellow of whom I have spoken appeared to come close to me and whisper with malicious amusement in my ear. The theatre was crowded to my eyes with dancing figures grotesquely attired, and in the centre of them I seemed to see my wife begging me to come to her.

'In the increasing uproar of wind and light and many men shouting, I fought my way towards her, this fellow at my side striving to prevent me. With the utmost difficulty, and after much roughness, I reached her, and, at the touch of her hand and the consciousness of the great joy that we both were feeling, everything seemed to be made clear to me. I wondered that for so long it should have been so perplexing. The intensity of that joy made my past life of no account . . . We fell together, our hands clasped, between a crowd of whirling figures, the candles dancing before our eyes. Such a mutual death was greater than anything that life had been. It was in all the experience of a moment, but so vivid that it was impossible to deny its positive occurrence. Nevertheless I had not vacated my seat, nor missed, I fancy, any detail of the play. When, in my clear mind, I looked for this fellow again he was not there.'

'It was a dream,' said Mr Harness gravely. 'God has many fashions of making Himself clear to us.'

'Well, well,' Herries answered briskly, with a smile. 'It may be so. But I doubt the benevolence of your God. He is plaguily roundabout in His plans for serving us, nor have I found life so sweet that I am minded to thank Him so heartily for what He has done for me.

'It may be,' said Mr Harness, 'that sweetness is not its purpose, but rather a very varied experience for the growth of our poor wisdom. The beauties of Nature and the unexpected nobility of man under severe trial are sufficient justification for living, to my mind.'

Herries answered quietly: 'An God will give me my wife again, I will ask Him for no further justification.'

They were reaching now the foot of the Fell and approaching the road. It was plain that with every step Herries's pleasure at returning to his home was increasing. They turned left towards Rosthwaite, and walked very happily together along the path that ran down above the river bed. It was a beautiful evening of great quietness; the air smelt sweetly, and the sky was rosy above the hills.

Mr Harness, thoroughly at ease with his companion, talked freely on his affairs, how the pain in his side troubled him, and how his appetite was shamefully strong, and he had been drunk ten days back, and sung, he was afraid, a number of lascivious songs. But the Devil was always round the corner with a remarkable knowledge of each individual's weakness. They parted in great friendliness, and Herries went on up to his house.

At the entrance to the little court he hesitated. Dusk was coming rapidly now, and he could see only dimly the stone wall, and beyond it the huddled dark mass of the house, its line ragged against the sky. A little wind had come with the evening, and was whistling and whining over the ground, a tune so familiar to him in its thin desolation, mingled as it was with the rhythm of running water and the chill of oncoming night, that it was like the hand-grip of a friend. But it was not the wind to which he was now listening. How often, during these last years, he had waited thus on his return!

Sometimes he had been absent only a week, sometimes months, and once, directly after her flight, nearly a year had passed. Always the same. Listening, his hand on the gate that was swinging now on its hinges, because he must postpone a little longer the moment when he would put it to the test whether she were waiting for him or no. One day it would be – of that he had no doubt – but how soon? How soon? Could he endure this time the blow of the disappointment? He set back his shoulders, looked up to the last yellow strands that struck like whips across the darkening sky, then went forward with a firm tread.

The door was open. He could see the familiar things, the old armour, the yellow-faced clock like a moon against the shadow, and he could hear the sounds, the clock's voice, a banging door monotonously complaining, and the stir that there was always about the old house, rats in the wainscot, maybe, and the dust of the years sifting from ceiling to floor.

She was not here. He knew it instantly. Never mind; she would come – if not now, another time. Tomorrow, soon, it could not be long delayed. So he went slowly up the old creaking stairs, stood in the dark hall, and then shouted for Benjamin. He was suddenly very weary, dropped his bundle and stick on the floor, and sank into the armchair by the fireplace.

Soon he heard Benjamin come clambering up the stairs. A moment after, Benjamin was in the doorway, holding two lighted candles, his face wreathed in smiles.

'Master! Master! You're back!'

He set the candles on the table, and came over with his old familiar rolling gait like a shapeless porpoise. His face was round like the moon, he had three chins now, and a belly that hung over his stout legs like a pillow, but he was not soft. His hair was short and erect on his head, his eyes wore their old expression of sound surprise, and on his nose there was the same old brown wart. The same! Of course he was the same! It was as though Herries had taken him with him on his travels. He came to his master, and his master greeted him with his old gesture, pulling him towards him, pinching his cheek, then driving him away again with a smack and a gentle kick.

'Well, old ass, old noddle, with us again . . . with us again . . . The world over, and thy round face always behind the candles – Satan be thanked for it!'

Benjamin went on his knees and pulled off his boots, looking

up once and again into Herries's face with a pleasure that was
none the less precious for being simple. Herries rested his hand
on the broad back. So she had not come, she was not here. One
more delay – how many yet would he endure?

He drove it from him.

'Food, fire, drink, Benjamin. There has been no one here?'

'Master David, master. Miss Deborah once. Statesman
Peel . . .'

'Aye; more of that in a moment. Has Mrs Benjamin a fowl or
can slaughter one? Has she a pie? I could eat thy own chaps, thou
monstrous swine.'

The man sat back on his haunches.

'My wife is gone, master.'

'Gone!' Herries sat back astonished. 'What! A-whoring!'

'No, poor woman. She's dead.'

'Dead! Dead! Why? how? when?'

''Twas Midsummer Night. She'd had a pain in her belly. I'd
cursed her for a whining woman, and told her I'd take a whip to
her, always moaning about her belly as though she'd a child there
and was eight months gone. But it was real enough. She wasted
day after day to the thinness of a hickory stick. She wouldn't eat,
she who could swallow a leg of mutton and a beef pie quicker
than any woman. And she was gentle – terribly gentle and for-
giving. I cursed her for that too, but she could do nothing with
it. "My temper's gone down with my belly," poor soul, she'd say.
Mother Dawlish of Stonethwaite physicked her. There's no one
finer. She has herbs from Solomon's time, they say. But 'twas no
use. Comes Midsummer Night, as fine and warm an evening as
you could search for, but she was mortal cold and would lie in
my arms, a thing she'd not wished for these many years. She had
never been a loving-tempered woman, and would always be in a
tantrum if I wanted to press her a bit. But now she was there,
with my arms round her and a mighty pain in her belly, poor
thing, and as fine and warm a night of stars and moonshine as
you'd wish for. She was wandering at the last, wanting a green
nettle to tickle Tom Prommice that she'd had a mind to be married to before I plagued her. Aye, all she wanted was a green
nettle and I had none for her, and so she passed, with the moon
coming in at the window, there in my arms.'

'Why, poor old Benjamin!' Herries drew him closer, enclosing
his neck with his hand. 'You are alone – and I also. And since
then, there has been no one with you in the house?'

'No one, master, and many's the night I've thought I've heard her tread – lop-lop-lop, heavy-heavy-heavy, and then a kind of skitter-skatter with the flop of her slipper. I've risen from my bed to look for her, but it's been the wind or the rain coming in through the roof at the left end there.'

'So we're alone here.'

'None the worse for that.' Benjamin straightened himself and rose. 'I'll light the fire and have a grand meal for you.'

Herries nodded. 'And you need no woman to help you?'

Benjamin turned near the door. 'We shall do without women. I'm wise now, so that I'd rather have my sleep than a woman. That's what life teaches you.'

Well, thought Herries, life hadn't taught him that yet. Quietly, as he often did, in an attitude of cool dispassion, he considered this longing for Mirabell. What was it that drove him? Certainly not lust. That it had never been. Certainly not self-pity or fear of loneliness. In one sense he had never been lonely, in another he had never been anything else. What was it, this hunger? He supposed that in human beings there was always through life this search for fulfilment, and through life to death most men never found it. They managed well enough without it, had no time to speculate, snatched at whatever substitutes they could find and made the most of them.

But with some men this search was ceaseless. It would for ever be the theme of all their days. The poets made poetry of it, the conquerors hacked kingdoms out of it, the madmen plaited straw in their hair. He had been one of these. It had never let him rest, and when he saw Mirabell the question was answered for him. He had loved her in the only true sense of love, that of finding completion in another soul and remaining settled there like a kernel in the heart of a nut. Everything moved by law whether there were a God or no, and this was a law, as certain and ordered as the movement of the stars, that he should love Mirabell. Did she love him, then the order was completed, and one more fragment of perfect movement was added to the multiplicity of the rest. But she did not. She had never loved him for a single moment. So here was another jangled piece of disorder added to all the others.

He had had a strange life, not, he thought, an unhappy one. It had been too interesting for that, but it was a fierce business, ferocious in its wildness, surprising in its beauty, ironical in its foolishness, mysterious in its purpose, but always invigorating, powerful, infinitely worth while.

He watched old Benjamin light the fire, smiling to himself to think that after all this life, this struggle, these passions, rebellions, and desires, this should be all that was left to him, this old fat man who was like a dog in appetite, lack of vision, and fidelity. Oh, and David also.

'So my son has been here?' yawning in sleepiness.

'Mr David has been here, master, and once he brought his babies with him.'

'How do they grow?'

'Grand children, fat and greedy.'

'And how is my son?'

'Not a more content man in the county, master. "Well, Benjamin," says he, "how scrub does this place look! It wants a pail of water," says he, "and the doors are all loose on their hinges!" "Well, Mr David," says I, "it is a tolerable place for Master and me because we're at ease in it," says I, "and 'tis better to be where you're at ease, however scrub it may be, than in a palace where there's no small-beer nor a bull-baiting." "Why, Benjamin," says Mr David, "you're a philosopher." "I leave that to the master," says I, "and suit my bottom to my own stool." But he's always friendly. He's a smiling gentleman, and they say he has a fine house. I've not been there myself, though he's asked me.'

'Aye, he has a sound imagination,' said Herries, 'and a sound belly. Phantoms and apparitions are not in his company, and he's the happier for it. I'm glad he's well.'

'So am I too,' said Benjamin, happy to see his master so cheerful, 'for he is a grand strong man, and can wrestle any other in the county, and he's breeding a grand family that will last to Judgement Day, I should think.'

When the food came Herries made Benjamin sit down beside him, and told him of some of his adventures. The old man had a great ear for marvels. Nothing was too miraculous for him to believe. Herries told him how he had seen in London a man with a furry tail that stuck out of his breeches, and a woman with a beard to her waist. Also a mermaid in a tank of water.

Benjamin sighed, watching to see whether Herries was relishing his food.

'A mermaid! That's a woman with a fish tail. I've heard of such. And what would be her issue, master, after lying with a man? Fish, think you?'

'More mermaids,' said Herries. 'They sing so sweetly that no man can resist embracing them.'

'Did the one you saw sing, master?'

'She was melancholy, poor creature, being a captive, and did nothing but sigh, and the tears poured down her cheeks.'

''Tis a shame,' said Benjamin, banging the table, 'to keep them for a show. Why did you not break the tank, master, and plunge her into the sea again?'

'I'm no knight-errant any more, Benjamin. I have lost my fire.'

'Not a bit of it, master,' said Benjamin cheerfully. 'You shall see how merry the two of us shall be here. I can cook to your fancy, and the trees are growing and I've got bricks round the chimney, and the horses are in fine trim. You shall see how grand everything will be!'

Left alone, Herries lay back and looked at the fire, strange thoughts crowding on to him; the scenes of the last months, lonely hillsides, crowded inns, the noise and smells of streeted towns, lights and flares, clouds and wind, odd voices and shouting strangers, all the bustle of a world. He had not been unhappy in it. There had been something as spectator that had pleased his ironic fancy, and there had been always the driving passion of his unresting search. But that other earlier life, now so remote – pictures now crowded about him – the mad restless life at Doncaster, the arrival at Keswick, and poor old Pomfret with his oaths and nervous violence, the night ride out to his house, poor Margaret, Alice Press . . .

His visions stopped there. He drove them back. Of what use? All, all had been a preparation for Mirabell. He saw her, a tiny child clinging to her mother in the noise of the Christmas games, standing beside him on Honister, speaking to him shyly in Carlisle: 'I wanted to tell you . . . I love someone. . .', that fearful moment when, above the dead body of her lover, she turned, not seeing him, staring into the face of her tragedy, the marriage day, in the little Chapel, afterwards the huddle of the villagers tumbling down the stairs, and again when he had carried her to their bed . . . these too he must drive back. But his longing he could not control. His longing for nothing more than her presence. Were she here now, sitting opposite him at the fire, he would not pester her for love. Were she returned, he would never speak to her of love again – only that she should be there!

He smiled at his old age, his white hair: he as a lover! But this love had nothing to do with age nor with physical strength nor with beauty. He did not love Mirabell for her beauty. She was not beautiful. She was not clever, nor had she the arts of the woman. But she was his wife, his child, his mistress, his friend, and he felt a kind of triumph because nothing could rob him of this, his only feeling for her that death itself would not destroy.

If only for five minutes he might speak to her he was sure that he could persuade her to stay with him. There was nothing now to frighten her. He did not want her now to love him, that is, if she truly could not.

But at the thought of the bliss that it would be if she loved him, his heart beat so thickly that he could sit still no longer. He tried to rise, to find that one of his legs would not stir. The pain was so sharp and so sudden that he cried out. A wave of pain covered his body. He thought that he would faint. Then, while he gritted his teeth, it passed again. Benjamin returning at that moment, he called out to him to help him.

'Why, master, are you lame?' The old man helped him up.

'Aye; take me to bed. I'm old. This leg failed me a sennight back.' But he grinned at the top of the stairs. His leg was better again.

'That won't beat me. But see me to my bed, and talk your non-sense, old fool. I'll not have ghosts in my room tonight.'

And Benjamin, whose mind was literal, told him how the old woman Carpenter of Grange had been chased in Cumma Catta Wood by the ghost of the old witch Wilson, who had barked like a dog, and flame had come from her mouth.

'She will not plague me,' said Herries. 'I carried her in my breast once for all her witchcraft.'

He kept Benjamin at his side far into the night.

ULDALE

II

FAMILY LIFE

SARAH HERRIES one fine summer day had a tea-party. Not by her own intent. She had but recently risen from the delivery of her third child, William Benedict Herries, who was born on a damp day in June, 1770. Why Benedict, said everyone? No one knew. Sarah thought it a nice name, and David was so happy at having another son that he didn't care what they called him. Why was David so happy? He had two children already, and children are, they say, very expensive. They were not so expen-sive then. There were more servants, much more space, much more indifference to infant complaints. Children wailed, were not attended to, ceased wailing. But David cared nothing for expense. Here was another Herries. He saw himself in the rôle of Abraham with Herries scattered about him like the sands of the sea.

Sarah did not mind. This was to be the last of her children and she would have been sad had she known. She was strong, resolute, happy, maternal. This was the grand time of her life.

Squire Osmaston and his wife rode over on this fine summer day, and the O'Briens happened to be out in their new carriage. This was a year or two before the Carlisle Post Coach, which went from Carlisle to London in three days. The world was opening up. You could travel so fast now that there was no escaping a neighbour, did he wish to see you. So fast, but not so securely. The O'Briens had a house between Carlisle and Bassenthwaite. They had come ten miles in their carriage and were shaken to pieces although this was summer weather and the roads were dry. They were shaken but proud. The Squire and his lady had ridden over on two enormous horses who looked, as young Maurice O'Brien whispered to their friend, Colonel Assheton-Bolitho-Carmichael, who had ridden over with them, like 'animals out of the Mythology'. The gentlemen were drinking in the parlour while the ladies sat in the garden sheltered from the winds by a charming little Gothic temple which Sarah, who was sharing the universal taste for Gothic, had had constructed.

So there they were. David was unfortunately in Borrowdale, where he had been staying the night with his father. Sarah, warned by her maid Nellie, who had spied the chaise, had quickly changed her housework clothes for a large orange hoop and an upper dress of silver which suited her very handsomely. Mrs O'Brien and her two daughters, Katherine and Olivia, were very finely dressed, so finely that they took up most of the space in the temple, but Mrs Osmaston had on a muddy riding-suit, her wig awry, and her hat on anyhow. She sat as usual with her legs spread, her hands on her hips, looking like the Wife of Bath, *temp* 1770.

Sarah enjoyed it all hugely. She loved to have friends about her, to play hostess, to sit in her own grounds with her house at her back, to know that her children were well, the cows in the paddock not ailing and her own bodily vigour returning to her at last after some very languid weeks. Talk, talk! What were they talking about?

About a boil on the Osmaston back, about clothes in Carlisle, about the incredible impertinence of servants and the high vails that they everywhere demanded, about Miss Nancy Souper of Hardcross and her illegitimate baby that she'd had of a local doctor, about a shepherd who had been hanged last week for stealing two halters and a hammer, about colds and chills, about everything in the world and nothing at all.

The new baby was brought out for inspection and was considered strong, healthy and the spit of his father. The baby, who was withdrawn howling, led to a very animated discussion of the comparative virtues of Doctor James's Powder and Bishop Berkeley's Tar-Water. Dr James's Fever Powder, nothing could rival it. It had saved the lives of Royalty, was good for everything from smallpox to distemper.

The powder rose in a happy cloud before the ladies' eyes. Of a sudden, life was secure and confident. Incredible that anyone should ever die! Mrs O'Brien (whose voice was small, very precious, as though every utterance were worth its weight in gold) gave it as definite fact that between the year 1750 (when the powder first began to be in reputation) and the close of the year 1763 fewer had died, upon an average, than in any preceding thirteen years, upon which Mrs Osmaston, kicking out her leg, scratching her dirty wig and barking like a dog, remarked that this was no virtue in a powder. For her part this business of keeping Inconsiderable People alive when they were greatly better dead was vastly overdone. The world was largely too filled with unnecessary persons. In the good old times, which were better in every way than the present, when someone ailed, if he or she were of a sickly constitution the illness finished them, and a good thing too, for who wished the countryside to be peopled with ailing imbeciles who were for ever about to be ill or recovering from illness and a nuisance to everyone about them? Had she had her way she would have strangled Dr James at birth and saved this world a monument of trouble and expense.

Mrs Osmaston always grew vigorous in the open air. Houses stifled her. She was only really happy with dogs and horses, men who told her bawdy stories and ladies with whom she might exchange scandal. Her heart, however, was kindly and generous, her life a constant protest against the conventions of a ridiculous society. It was told of her that when the Squire in her own village had put a girl in the family way, and the girl was turned out by her drunken but virtuous father, she had taken the girl into her own house and nursed her until she was well again.

What was life to her? a succession of following the hounds,

tramping the fells after the fox from dawn to dark, eating and drinking vast quantities of everything, bullying and loving her thick-hided husband, scolding her friends, crying over *Clarissa,* chatting with every huntsman and stable-boy in the district, driving all her household to church of a Sunday and encouraging the parson to be drunk after dinner.

Mrs O'Brien was a sententious and sentimental woman with all the belief of her time in capital letters. Mrs Osmaston shocked her very deeply and she could not forbear to say:

'Why, Alicia, to speak so destructively you condemn both our Maker and His Divine Purposes. Why should we practise the virtues of Compassion and Indulgence on behalf of our Fellows if this world is not an Education and an Improver of our frailties? Olivia, my love, turn your cheek. The sun is catching it.'

' I cannot for my part,' said Mrs Osmaston, 'do with your Sensibilities and Virtues. We are not put here to be Virtuous, but to cause as little trouble to our fellow-mortals as may be. And the proof is that if you have a flea down your back you think nothing of your Sensibility but off with your smock and snap him between finger and thumb.'

Both the O'Brien girls tittered at this. Mrs Osmaston was so very droll! Olivia was all Sensibility, but Katherine inclined towards dogs and horses and a drink with the gentlemen. They both despised their mother, but feared her. Underneath her sensibilities she had an iron hand.

'We have had,' said Mrs Osmaston, who enjoyed teasing Mrs O'Brien, 'the oddest cousin from London. He would have pleased you mightily, Julia. He was all sensibility. He was in raptures over every country sight. He was ever talking of the Elysian fields and 'gentle showers' and 'rivers of dew'. A sheep sent him into ecstasies. He was all for discovering hillocks and haycocks and dusky trees. At the last he was discovered lying under a hay-cock with a milkmaid, where his processes were, I don't doubt, as ordinary as though he'd been fiddling with a chambermaid in Piccadilly. But his hair was all straw and he was whipped through the fields by a jealous shepherd, so his experiences were at the last sufficiently Arcadian.' Mrs Osmaston roared with laughter, slapping her thighs. 'The shepherd had his breeches down and whipped his bare skin, so that he could not sit to cards that evening. He returned to town next day and is the less Arcadian for his visit.'

All the ladies laughed and had anecdotes of a similar kind to furnish, and then there must arise the accustomed arguing as to the relative virtues of Mr Fielding and Mr Richardson. Those two gentlemen entered the Gothic temple, their spirits comfortably enjoying the salubrious air and the female society. Mr Fielding liked the pretty Olivia best, with her pink and white, her air of a rakish prude and her fine legs (which, being a spirit, he could plainly discern under the lemon-coloured hoop), and little Mr Richardson preferred Mrs O'Brien who was after his own heart.

'But Grandison!' cried Mrs O'Brien, 'how tenderly imagined, how proudly conceived! What Ideal Behaviour and Constant Fidelity!' and Mr Richardson planted a kiss on her broad brow which seemed to her like the tickling of a fly so that she brushed the place with her hand.

'A —— for your Grandison!' said Mrs Osmaston very coarsely. 'Now Jones is the man for my money and for Katherine's too, I don't doubt. What, Katherine! Would you let Jones touzle you were he here? Would you beat Sophia out of the field, girl? I'll wager if your mother's back were turned you'd not hesitate.'

It was well perhaps that the gentlemen were coming across the lawn. Squire Osmaston was drunk and Mr O'Brien nearly so. They were singing a hunting catch which rang prettily through the summer air, but they hushed as they drew close to the temple.

Mrs Osmaston rose to control her lord and master.

'You're drunk, Peter, and will never reach home in safety.'

He staggered a little, then slapped her fat neck with a hearty friendliness.

'I'm a little drunk and a little sober. My good horse Robin knows how to carry me. I have not been drunk for a week past and, for that, my fair hostess will forgive me.'

Everyone was readily forgiven on so lovely a summer evening. They all moved to the road where the fine new chaise was vastly admired and the two enormous horses solemnly held by Ralph, David's farm man. The scene was thick with gold dust like a bee's wing and the trees smelt of honey.

The chaise was away first with a great waving of arms and shouting of goodbyes. Before she mounted her charger Mrs Osmaston put her stout arm round Sarah's neck and embraced her.

'I am fond of you, my dear. I am a foolish old woman who chatters a world of nonsense, but there's a bed for you and a horse to ride with us any time you desire it. Now then – huppety-hup—' With a leap she was in the saddle and settled there as though she were part of the horse's anatomy. The Squire too, drunk though he might be, had no trouble in mounting, and a fine pair they made, facing the country as though they were king and queen of it.

The Squire had some last confidential word. 'There's a tale,' he said to Sarah, looking at her solemnly from the back of his horse, 'a damnably good tale that I must tell your husband. 'Tis a tale of an orange and Mrs O'Brien's pet monkey. 'Tis the wittiest, handsomest . . .'

'Whoop!' cried Mrs Osmaston, giving his horse a whack with her whip, and off they went down the road, a cloud of dust behind them and the sky golden over their heads.

The horses' hoofs rang on the road, then peace resumed its power.

Sarah walked a little while in her garden before going into the house. Although the sun, a smiling gold penny, had almost perched its chin now on the ledge of the hills, the air was yet richly warm and the cool of the evening mingled with it most freshly.

All the sounds were of the summer evening, bees were yet humming, the men were calling to the cows, and a thrush was singing from the thick luxury of an oak tree as though it had but just come into the noblest of fortunes. Sarah's heart beat with the conscious appreciation of the goodness of life. She could not believe that she was thirty-two! Thirty-two! Thirty-two! And she knew old ladies in Keswick with Brussels caps on their heads not a day over thirty. But she was younger now than she had ever been. In those hard years with her uncle she had been old. She saw herself as a child of fifteen, standing before one of his infernal rages and calculating with the wizened wisdom of an old witch how she would drive him into a certain position and make a bargain with him there. Her youth had begun with that almost miraculous appearance of David there in the Wasdale Inn. She had loved him at sight, and thrown herself at his head and won her liberty.

But afterwards, over that last scene on the Pass, a cloud hovered. There had been something evil then. She had hated her uncle, she had owed him nothing, he had not cared what misery he had planned for her, but still in his death there had been a cloud of evil. She would never be quite free of it.

For a moment the garden had been darkened and the humming of the bees dimmed, but she was of too healthy a nature to prolong any morbidity, and so, singing to herself, her strong freshly-coloured body moving freely in its orange and silver, she walked her garden.

She loved this place because it was so open. Although in the manner of the time the garden was a little arranged with its temple, box hedges and ornamental paths, yet it ran boldly into open country, the down rising above it on the one side, the road running under the hills on the other. But she loved it in reality because it was the home of her husband and her babies. She was all maternal.

David was her child more than her lover. She understood him now, she thought, with completeness. She had all the woman's tender irony at the ridiculous things that seemed to him important, at his absorption in minutiae; she had, too, the woman's almost jealous envy at his ability to throw off his moods, to forget his passions, to take everything with a light mind.

Was there anything for which men finally cared? David loved her, of course, but a little as a child loves its mother. If another child calls him to play a game, off he goes, forgetting his mother until he needs her again. But Sarah had a great understanding and a splendid gift for taking things as they were. She did not wish David to be different in anything, but were he different she would suit herself to his condition. Standing under the oak tree, looking over to Skiddaw's sprawling shoulders, she speculated a little as to how it would have been if David had had his father's temperament. She did not understand Francis, and yet felt that perhaps at the last she could have understood him better than did any other.

He was old now, but finer, more striking than he had ever been, with his white hair and long nervous figure, of which every part seemed to be imaginatively alive. She could not understand that he should love someone desperately, without end, for ever. David would not. Did she die he would never forget her, would care for her always, but he would marry again and be happy, and the second wife would listen to his plans and share his activities, and be mother of his children just as she was. The knowledge did not make her sad. All she wanted was that he should be happy, happy always and vigorous always and noble-hearted always.

Smiling at the thought of him, she went into the house to her children. They were brought down to the parlour.

Francis was ten and Deborah eight. Deborah was as sweet-natured and unselfish and happy as Francis was reserved and driven in upon himself. Both were pretty children, Francis very dark, slim, aristocratic, never familiar with anyone, fearless, but oddly tempered. He would be distressed for no reason, happy for no reason. He liked best to be by himself. Whether he was fond of his father Sarah could never be sure. He allowed his father to play with him, responded to his father's demands on him, was for the most part obedient. He did not appear, though, to miss him when he was absent, nor showed excitement on his return.

He adored his mother. With her he was not demonstrative, but you could tell that everything she said or did worked in his own bosom responsively, and he would watch her, when he thought that she was not looking, with loving meditative eyes.

Deborah, on the other hand, loved everyone, and gave herself to everyone. She had no self-consciousness, no pose for effect, no selfish motive in anything. She was like any other child in small things – temper, disappointments, aggravations – but everything was quickly over. The serenity of her temperament carried her always on a calm sea. She was as fair as her brother was dark, like her father in that, although slender and delicately made. David worshipped her.

In the parlour they were endlessly happy. There was the China wallpaper, with the white and blue pagodas, temples, bridges and flowers. There was the spinet at which their mother sang. There was the cabinet with the silver boxes and gold chairs and little Chinese figures. There was the music-box with the King and Queen on its lid, who marched to the tinkling tune. There was the animated carpet with the battle worked on it – cannon firing, horses rearing, Captains waving on their men; and there was the comfit-box with the sugared cherries and the cakes of marzipan.

This evening young Francis stood at the window watching the sunset fall over Skiddaw. He was like his grandfather in this at least, that he could not have enough of this country. He had not as yet seen much of it; but now, as he looked out, he was swearing to himself that he would not rest until every stone and tree of it was revealed to him. What did he see there if he looked hard enough? The mountains opened, and, carried by the wind, you struck with your golden shoes the centre of a group of hills like men watching you. Here was a pool, icy and black, and suddenly into the middle of it there plunges a beautiful white horse . . .

''Tis the white horse,' he cried excitedly, turning from the window to Deborah.

'A white horse?' asked Sarah, thinking of a new shawl, the gold buttons of David's coat, whether Mrs Osmaston ever wore a clean wig, and if not why not, and why David was not returned.

'Why, yes, Mama . . . We told you. The ice breaks and it swims to the shore.'

Some story, she supposed, that Mrs Monnasett, nurse, house-keeper and general confidante, had been telling them. Mrs Monnasett needs many pages to herself, but cannot have them – with her passion for plums, her belief in witches and centaurs, and her play-acting, so that, give her a handkerchief and a deal board, and she can be Cleopatra, Jane Shore and Mrs Elizabeth Montagu without shifting her wig. But did anyone suppose that David or Sarah made Uldale, made the children, made the sun turn grey before an east wind, and the milk sour before thunder? No, no. It was all Mrs Monnasett.

And now it was time for the children to hear the music-box and to have one sugared cherry apiece. Francis listened to the tune and saw five small Negroes in gold-laced jackets dance across the carpet. One carried an ivory cane with a blood-red knob to it, and he had only one eye. Where the other eye should have been . . . So he suddenly began to shudder, to shudder and shiver and tremble. He knew now that he would see that empty place where the eye should be all night, so quite without warning and quite foolishly he was sick on the carpet.

Sarah could not understand it. She had never been sick in her life. Perhaps Mrs Monnasett would understand. She was better with Francis than was anyone else.

'After one tune he was sick . . .'

Francis lay, very small and very white, in his four-poster that had green curtains with roses.

Mrs Monnasett, so large that she filled the room, her black hoop billowing about her, a silver chain rising and falling on her breast, took his hand, and continued her fairy-story about Queen Anne. 'But the Princess was resolved to see the Queen, although she had only a rag upon her, so she said to the Lord-in-Waiting, who was fingering his snuff-box made of one green emerald, "Sir, there is a spider in the Queen's closet." Now if there was anything that Her Majesty had a distaste for 'twas a spider, as everyone in the Court knew, and only a week back five hundred and thirty-one spiders had been thrown into the kitchen fire, and made such a smoke that the Royal Cook had turned a dish of Peacock into a Canterbury Pudding by the misfortune of the smoke blinding her eye. Therefore the Lord-in-Waiting hastened as swiftly as his stout legs would carry him, and the Princess, following . . .'

Sarah, sitting awhile to watch that the boy was comfortable, wondered what Mrs Monnasett's history might be. No one knew. She had been living for several years in a little green cottage outside Keswick when Sarah met her, and had herself suggested that she should come to Uldale, for 'I love children,' said she, 'and am never happier than in their company.' And so indeed it seemed, for she had no interest at all in Society, but cared only for being with the children, and talking to her little white dog, Mr Pope, and eating as many sweet cakes as she could find. 'Which is the reason of her great stoutness,' thought Sarah, but she was truly a Blessing for the house, and long might she remain.

David was home. She could hear him calling 'Sarah! Sarah!', so she hurried downstairs, and he was there in the parlour, larger than ever before perhaps. He was delighted to see her, but gave her that kiss which husbands give their wives when they have been a long while married and are thinking of someone else.

'You would not consider him fifty years old,' thought Sarah proudly. His brown tie-wig was pushed back a little from his forehead, and he slapped his great thigh.

'Here is Paradise. Here, come.' He sat down in the big chair and she sat close to him, her hand on his knee. 'I'll tell you, I hope you were frightened out of your senses for me because I did not return.'

Sarah smiled. 'I am never frightened when you are away, but I had a party, and you were sadly missed.'

'Aye, that for certain,' he grinned. 'But I have the ague and the fever and the toothache as well. That house is of paper, and will be blown away with the first wind, and there my father sits with old Benjamin on his hams beside him, listening to every mouse in the passages.'

'How is he, Davy?'

'Oh, well enough. He was but just returned from another of his journeys. He is crazed, and yet he is not crazed. He is as content, I believe, as ever he was in his life, but he will never rest until he has found her, although what he will do with her when he has found her no one can tell. But he will never find her. She is dead or gone abroad or changed into an apple tree. But he is resolved that she will return.'

'He and Benjamin are quite alone?'

'They sit like a pair of quarrelling lovers. "You shall have veal today, master," says Benjamin. "I shall not," says my father. "But you shall," says Benjamin, and he gives him veal and my father beats him. And all the while the house rocks and mumbles, and the mice sit on the tables and the rain beats through the ceiling.

And next week he will be off again and walk a hundred miles, asking of every sheep has he seen his wife. But he is sane enough. He began with me, examined me on all the family, and confounded me with his knowledge. He has been, too, to see Deb's two boys, and can tell you where they are in Arithmetic, and that Deb has a new China piece in her cabinet and a black cat with no tail.'

'Will he not come here for a week and have good food 'and a warm bed?'

'He does not want good food nor a warm bed neither.'

Sarah sighed, then, looking up at David, laughed.

'How is it that he is your father and you so different?'

'I am not so different. We have a great bond of common feeling. 'Tis odd, Sarah, but I am more comfortable with him than with any other human on the globe, save yourself. I have a feeling, Sarah, that if Mirabell were to return and give him satisfaction by loving him, and they to settle down together, he would become very like myself.'

That was clever of him, thought Sarah, who, like all loving wives, wanted always to prove him strong in the direction where he was undoubtedly weak.

They began then, sitting very close together, to gather all the tiny important things – Davy's toothache, how Molly the mare had cast a shoe, whether Forrest the head farm man was lazier than was natural, the eternal mystery of Mrs Monnasett, and so to Francis who had been sick on the carpet for no reason, and thence to the baby Will who had chewed his coral – and through it all their happiness, their security, their mutual trust, their luck that they had one another.

And David the Patriarch – this is the last view of him just now – staring into the Chinese pagodas, the bridges and the Immortal Temple, sees a Great Tree stretching to heaven, and hanging from its million branches Herries, and Herries, and Herries.

Beneath the tree lies England – her valleys, her rivers, her great cities, and the rocks of her invincible coast – and over England the Tree beneficently stretches its green shade.

There are enough Herries here for a thousand years, and who is that so fatherly protective on the topmost branch?

Who but David himself? He draws Sarah close to him and, with his broad arm around her, kisses her.

But it is England that he is embracing.

THEY MEET IN PENRITH

FEB. 4TH, 1772

THE Peel Towers have faded, the refugees from Culloden are bones beneath the turf, the poet Gray has more than three years back 'dined with Mrs Buchanan on trout and partridges', and Herries has stayed, rested his bundle on the slope of the hedge, and stood with his back to a friendly oak to settle in his mind whether there be three roads or one stretching before him in the dim February light.

His fever, which had become by this quite a friendly companion to him, often brought him to such an uncertainty. He called it his Fever because he did not know what other name to give to it. It came and went as it pleased, having quite a cheerful and independent life of its own. You could never tell what it would be about.

It gripped him in its strong arms at any time, and supplied for him the queerest fancies. You could scarcely call it a sickness because, although it weakened his limbs, dimmed his eyes and beat him about the head, it provided him also with an odd exhilaration and gave him many fantasies. Sometimes it drove him to bed because his back and legs refused to carry him any longer, and, had his will been less strong, he might have yielded to it then more completely, for nothing pleased him more than to lie, the Fever with him, on his bed in Herries and see the strange sights that the Fever brought him, and hear, always a little removed, the sounds, the running of water, the beating of drums, the rumbling of thunder, that echoed in his ears.

But he was not defeated by it. He would boast to it: 'Nay, Fever, I like your company once and again, but you shall not weaken me. This picture that you are showing me of a chariot filled with monkeys and a bark with gold apples is entertaining enough, but tomorrow I go about my business again.'

And the Fever, being a good-natured fellow, would recognize his stubbornness and let him have his way.

On this dark afternoon it was as stubborn as he. He shivered with the chill, his body was as though bruised by a tumble, his head was on fire. So he stood against the oak tree and wondered whether there were three roads into Penrith or only one.

'Ah, well,' said the Fever, rattling inside his head like a loose

button, 'you are seventy-two years of age, you know. You haven't
the power over me you once had.'

Yes, but *were* there not three roads? He had walked only from
Appleby that day, and he must press on to Herries. But how
could he press on when there were so many roads to choose
from? They mingled and divided and mingled again. They ran
to his nose, leapt skywards, rolled like strips of white boarding
down an implacable hill.

He wiped his brow, which was damp with sweat, and that
seemed to quieten him, for now there was but one road stretching in a subdued and orderly manner to the foot of the town.

He picked up his bundle and went on. In the main street there
was no one about. Near to him was a lighted window (for early
though it was, the town was already dark) and over the doorway
hung a sign, 'The Green Parrot', with a painting of a fine green
bird with an ironical eye. A parrot? A parrot? Once before there
had been a green parrot in a room filled with talk, and a man . . .
But he could not settle the matter. After the Fever had left him
he would investigate his memory.

There was a small bare panelled room with a table and a bench,
so he sat him down and soon a stout old man in a green baize
apron came to attend to him. This old man had a broken nose and
a hand without a thumb, but he was pleased to see company.
There was something about Herries that always won him attention wherever he might be. He brought him ale and bread and
meat, and then sat beside him for fellowship's sake. The old man
was called Andrew Greenship, and at once, as though he had
spoken with no one for a hundred years, told Herries all his history. He had been a soldier in the old days and fought in the Low
Countries. His thumb had been severed by a Hanoverian hatchet,
and his nose broken in a fight about a gold piece. He had gout
when the weather was bad, and for the most part trade was poor.
But mostly he wanted to talk about his son who had gone to
make his fortune in London, had returned without making it, and
was now a curse to his father. He was in Carlisle at the present,
but would soon be back again wanting money from his father,
and with a pack of women and dogs at his heels and no place to
put them. The old man could not understand it. Why were
things as they were? Why were there not cakes and ale for everyone? For his part his only comfort was a dog called Mulberry,
who was the cleverest dog in all Cumberland and Westmorland,
and once let him set his teeth in another dog . . .

The Fever waved its hand and departed. The room was warm,

the fire burnt brightly, and the red curtains were cosy about the windows.

On the wall was a play-bill. At the Theatre Royal, Penrith, they were presenting *Othello,* by Mr William Shakespeare, to be followed by a farce, *There is No Wife like a New One.*

'The Players are here?'

But are they not here? Andrew had not himself seen them, but he had heard them grandly spoken of. Tonight was their last performance. But Andrew was inquisitive. Who was this old man, so fierce and so courteous, travelling only with a bundle? He asked many questions. Herries answered them all. He had been far, he was a great traveller, he knew London, he had seen the King, he, too, had a wife and children. But after all he was a mystery. He gave nothing of himself away, and his eyes moved as though he could see a penny through a wall of houses. When he rose from his hard bench Andrew was amazed at his height and strength.

'How old would he be?'

Seventy-two years! and Andrew was but sixty-three come Michaelmas. Andrew had not for many a day seen a man he liked better the look of, but he was one of your gentlemen, a nobleman maybe, taking his exercise for the fun of the thing, as noblemen were apt to do.

There came in a little, stout, self-important apothecary-chirurgeon. He had been his rounds in the country and had his saddle-bags filled with boluses and electuaries. In his skirt pocket he had his sand-glass and wanted to take Herries's pulse with it.

He had had a busy and, it is to be hoped, profitable day; one lady had been treated for the vapours, and one lady, alas! for the itch. He was in a temper, too, for in Appleby he had not heard the 'Gardey Loo', and some of the contents from an upper window had missed his head indeed, but struck his long-skirted coat, and it would never be clean again.

He recovered over his ale and the warm, close, smelly comfort of the low-ceilinged room. He described with gusto a recent visit to Edinburgh, the ladies in their gigantic hoops, their heads and shoulders covered with green and scarlet plaids, the green paper fans with which they warded off the sun, their red-heeled shoes, the dirt and filth and narrowness of the stairways, the streets crowded with the rude and impertinent 'caddies' carrying messages and parcels, the theatre where he had seen *The Mourning Bride* and *The Country Wife,* the cock-fights, the taverns where the advocates drank their morning sherry, and the bacchanalian nights in the meanest of 'oyster cellars', where you would enjoy raw oysters and porter, and dance with both the lowest and the highest ladies of the town.

Aye, that was a life in Edinburgh, but after a week of it you longed for your work again, and here he was, who had dined a fortnight back with the Bishop in Carlisle, and had to pay a whole guinea in vails to the servants, and was tomorrow night to have a grand feast in Keswick with some fellow apothecaries, and where he would be the following morning no one could tell.

It was this fellow's talk that kept Herries where he was and so led to the events that followed. The apothecary, whose name was Summers, lighted his eye on the play-bill on the wall; and although he asserted that it would be a poor enough affair, and laughed at the 'Theatre Royal' which would be a makeshift of boards in a tent, he licked his lips all the same, for he loved a play and would see one in any place. Very politely he invited Herries to accompany him. Herries meanwhile had been hit by an odd coincidence. He was always catching now at coincidences and omens (having little else to go by) and, while little Summers was talking, had remembered fully what the 'Green Parrot' signified to him. No need now to recall that scene in Carlisle; did he let himself, his fancy would pull him back into the very centre of it. He held himself off from it, but it kept knocking just outside his heart. He would stay the night here. He turned and asked Andrew whether he had a bed. Aye, if he did not mind sharing a room with a post-boy. No, Herries minded no company. His brain was on fire now with the thought that somehow, somewhere, something would come of this coincidence. How many many times before he had trusted to similar coincidences he did not now regard! Every occasion was a new one, filled with hope and happy prospects. His cheeks glowed, his hands trembled.

'The old gentleman,' said the apothecary aside to Andrew, 'has a fever. It would be wise if he permitted me to bleed him.'

But they both of them had a certain fear of this strange old gentleman who sat quietly there by the window, a smile on his lip and the light of eagerness in his eye. When the time came for them to be going, he marched off with Summers as though he were going to his wedding.

The weather now was fine, the air sharp, the evening very dark.

It was a strange theatre that they were introduced to, the arena a stable and the tiring-room a hay-loft, as they could very easily see. Everything was open and exposed. On some wooden steps, leading up to the loft, Othello sat, his face fittingly blackened, wearing a long and very soiled white robe, drinking out of a pot of ale. He would drink, and then start up in a state of very honest fury to instruct with many curses two or three yokels who were learning, even at this late hour, to trail a pike in a soldierly fashion. In spite of his spasmodic rages he did not look to be a bully, having one of the roundest and mildest of faces, with a small snub nose and eyes that, although they rolled whitely in their black disguise, could not deny their essential amiability.

The arena was but poorly filled, dimly lit with candles that guttered in all the breezes of heaven, and very powerfully to the nose came the odours of cows and horses and the pungency of dung.

Little Summers had plenty to say, and fortunately needed no answer, for Herries, sitting very upright, his hands clasped over his staff, his eyes staring straight before him, surrendered to the strange fever of expectation that now, as in times altogether past recording, swept him into breathless excitement. How well he knew, had he dared to reckon, this repetition of circumstance! The omen, a tree, the name of a street, a woman's hair, a printed word, the fire of confident assurance, the bitter unavailing disappointment. Every time he would be cheated, every time make ready for the next occasion.

Presently there was a sharp altercation. A large stout red-faced farmer, two ladies in attendance, came and sat next to the apothecary, and soon, the ladies wishing for more room than was rightly theirs on the bench, the large farmer began to sit all over the little apothecary, who had, it seemed, a temper as fiery as a bantam's.

'You have paid, sir, for *two* seats?'

The farmer slowly shook his head, and his thick sides quivered with laughter. This excited the apothecary to a frenzy, and he most inappropriately called the farmer a puppy.

The two ladies then began to take part in the affair, saying that they supposed the gentleman must be from Keswick or Kendal or some other rough part, and for themselves they did not see why they should lower themselves to speak with common persons; they'd never done so yet, and had no intention of now beginning. Both sides of the dispute appeared to amuse the farmer greatly, for he could do nothing but shake with silent laughter, say 'Aye, Aye,' turning his head from one side to the other, and murmur something about 'Coom back a bit,' moving, however, himself not all. So the apothecary leant over his broad chest, and was about to make some very rude remarks to the ladies, when what seemed to him the very great beauty of the younger lady

struck him so forcibly that his face was suddenly wreathed in
smiles, he was apologizing for his abruptness, and was seated at
the other end of the bench in no time at all. This, instead of
angering the farmer, but appeared to amuse him the more, and,
as the young lady was apparently not displeased, all was well.
But the little altercation had confused Herries, and he had not
realized that the play was begun.

There was a door at the back corner of the stage, and when
this was opened a cow could be seen feeding in its stall. The
scenery was a piece of tattered cloth hung crookedly from a rafter,
an old gilt chair and a green-painted table. Against the front of
the stage a number of children and boys had gathered, and were
clustered, open-mouthed, in an attentive group watching the
antics of the actors. A stout woman in a soiled crimson hoop,
with a shawl over her head and a small black dog in her lap, sat
on a chair near a candle, holding a prompt-book.

Herries soon lost himself in a mixture of falsehood and reality.
The rustic scene, the smell of the cows, and the evening air lifted
him back into his own world at home, and he could see the trees
blowing in dark fan-like clusters above the familiar gable-end.
Shakespeare had always been a glory to him, at a time, too, when
he had no great popularity, and soon he was caught up anew into
the familiar story and once more felt the ringing beauty of the
words.

Othello came down to the candles, and, forgetting the Duke
and the attendant senators, addressed his rustic audience, paus-
ing at times for a word and turning impatiently to the lady with
the red hoop, who must hesitate before she discovered the place.
Nevertheless the atmosphere was caught. Venice and her waters
did their business yet once again of tricking a mortal soul or two
into a foolish trust in the fidelity of beauty.

The little black dog barked.

'She loved me' – said Othello, wiping his nose with the back
of his hand,

> —for the dangers I had pass'd,
> And I loved her that she did pity them.
> This only is the witchcraft I have used;
> Here comes the lady; let her witness it.

and then, from among the cows, holding her long train that it
might not be soiled by the dirt, Mirabell came in.

He did not see her. She had spoken her words:

My noble father,
I do perceive here a divided duty,

before he realized her.

Then it came to him, quietly, inevitably, as though it had been from the beginning arranged that it should be like that.

That was Mirabell, her hair, her small child's face, her body looking stout and thick beneath the shabby tawdry dress of white satin. On each cheek was a splash of red paint, and behind this her little face was oddly white and her eyes staring.

Yes, this was Mirabell. It was as he had always expected it, if not here, why, then at another place. Soon he would go, when this mummery was over, behind and fetch her away. They would stay the night in Penrith, and tomorrow would be home. At the thought of home and Mirabell there again he began to tremble. It was as though someone were slowly shaking him from head to foot. Someone also was shouting in his ear, and everything in front of him was swimming in a mist of shapeless colour.

It began at once to be incredible to him that she should be there and not recognize him. Why did she not cease all this foolishness and suddenly cry out: 'Francis! Francis! Francis, I am coming home!'? At that he began to wonder why he himself was not crying out. He clasped his staff with a fearful intensity. His arm shook above it, and unknown to himself a tear was trickling down his cheek.

Very soon he would have risen from his seat, pushed his way through the country people, but fortunately she turned, and, as Othello, his eyes on the boys who were teasing the little dog from the front of the stage, said: 'Come, Desdemona,' she gathered up her dress, glancing to see that she did not trip over a hole in the boards, and at his words, 'We must obey the time,' she vanished through the door.

Herries rose instantly and pushed through the crowd, mounting with steady steps the wooden ladder that led to the hay-loft.

Here there was a torn curtain. Shaking it aside he stood just within, leaning a little on his stick. On the floor two children were playing with some stones and string. They had tied the string to one of the stones and were dragging it, bumping, over the cracks in the floor. There was a wooden table piled with theatrical properties, and on the table a long thin man was sitting, powdering his hair, while a woman bent over him mending a hole in his faded sky-blue tights. A little fat man in a full bottomed wig and red satin breeches was looking at himself in a cracked glass and adjusting on his head a tin helmet. From below came the lowing of a cow for its calf and the voice of Iago, very high-pitched and trembling with dramatic irony.

The woman mending the sky-blue tights was Mirabell.

One of the children cried out. She looked up.

So they looked at one another after these many years. She was old, worn, ill. That was his only thought – that he must take her at once, without an instant's delay, and have her cared for. Her beautiful hair had lost its lustre, the blobs of red paint on her cheeks seemed to sharpen the lines, the shadows, the thinness of that child's face that yet was a child's face no longer, but a woman's, weary, ill-fed and drawn.

And what did she see? An old white-haired man leaning on a stick. But what happiness was in her heart when she saw him! Yes, the shock of it surprised herself. The only friend that she had in the world. Was that ungrateful, perhaps, when the simple, kindly player, Othello, Julius Caesar, Jaffier, Prospero and Falstaff, cared for her, was good to her? Yes; say, then, the only friend that she herself wanted. How much greater the ties of those years that she had lived with him had been than she knew! Had she done right to leave him? Had he been happier without her? Was it by chance that he saw her now? Had he ever seen her, wished for her? Would he want her to return with him, or had he come only to give her a good day for the sake of old times?

All these thoughts pressed upon her in that first moment as she looked at him.

She dropped the needle and went over to him. Then she was moved to the very depths of her being when she saw that he was so profoundly shaken at the sight of her that he could not speak, but, his hand trembling on his stick, tears falling, turned his head away that she should not see.

She put her hand on his arm and led him to the corner of the room by a little broken window that was stuffed with paper. The two men said nothing, paid no attention. It was nothing to them that an old man should speak to her, or, for that, a young one either.

'Don't cry,' she said. 'How happy I am to see you!'

When he could command himself he put up his hand and touched her hair. Then he said:

'You must come with me. As soon as this is over. We will stay tonight in Penrith, and tomorrow go home.' Then, before she could answer, he went on: 'I have been searching for you ever since you went away. I was in London looking for you.' He was so fiercely excited that his words came breathlessly, as though he had been running. 'But it is no matter – now that I have found you.'

'Yes.' She had to give herself time to settle her own problem of honour and duty. 'I have wondered so many times – whether you thought of me, what you did. But you have been ill. Your hair is white.' She smiled. 'We are both old now.'

His eyes never left her face, never moved. They were as beautiful, as strong and piercing as ever they had been.

'I will come to fetch you as soon as the piece is played.'

But she must postpone telling him how she was placed. Things were not so simple as that. But, for a moment, she wished that they had been. How she wished it! She was so weary, she was so bad an actress, this life was so mean and dirty. To go back with him, to be cared for and loved . . . She would let him love her now in any way that he wished. One thought of the rest that it would be! To sit in that chair in Herries and hear the running water; Herries that once she had hated! But she drove all the pictures back.

'You have wanted me then? You have missed me? I have so wondered . . . But listen.' She began to speak quickly, holding his arm with her hand. 'A man here – he is playing Othello – has treated me with great kindliness. I was very sick – it is five years back – dying, I think. He was acting in the town. He is good, most generous-hearted, and I am a shabby actress, but, when he might have had a position in London had he left me, he would not. He is drunk sometimes, but even at that he is kind.

'I have never loved him, but if I leave him now he will lose all – his interest, his work. He has no one else. Those are his two children by another woman. She is dead of the smallpox. They too, they think I am their mother, poor babies. Francis—'

He broke in fiercely. 'You left me. You can leave him then.'

'I left you because I thought it right for you. You were only unhappy.'

'And what have I been without you?'

'You are strong. Adam is weak. If I left him he would not do anything but die in a ditch, and the children would die. We have so little time. I will see you again, most truly I will. Did you know what it is now to hear your voice . . .' She broke off. That was not the way. She began to be tormented. She could go with him now, without one word to anyone. When she saw him holding her with his eyes, her own longing to be loved by him again, to be warmed by him, to be protected by him, began to pervade her like a happy faintness. Instinctively she drew nearer to him, and he, suddenly raising his head proudly, put his arm around her.

Othello came in.

At the sight of him Mirabell's torment grew. In his foolishly blackened face, his dirty dishevelled turban, his fat good-natured cheeks, she felt all his commonness and by contrast Francis's aristocracy. This was a spiritual thing, not a social. This heavy fat man who when he was hungry crammed his food into his mouth like an animal, who was so simple and foolish that he knew nothing of the world but the little scandals of the hedge-rows and the dirty anecdotes of the roadside inns, who was kindly because he had not the wits to be aught else, who, when he was fuddled, would kneel at her feet, crying and kissing her worn soiled hands until she was ashamed, who was feckless and lazy and vain, boastful and ignorant, weak and little – and Francis who looked now, standing in that dingy attic, a king among men, Francis so mysterious in his breeding, Francis who loved her so that he had searched all England for her! – she did not draw back from his arm as her shabby Othello approached them.

She made them known. She realized that her man, Adam Betty, at once perceived that this newcomer was a patron, some-one who might possibly raise them all up in the world. He spoke to him with a mixture of humility and boasting.

'Small quarters, sir, but the Muse must be served. Shake-speare! I kneel to him! So wise a connoisseur as yourself must have some points from which a humble player . . . But my Othello – the Heart is there, the Heart! The Noble Moor is trans-lated into this rough barn, and Miss Starr's Desdemona – ah, there, sir! you will have a performance of a Natural Sublimity—'

But Mirabell could not endure it. She saw Herries's courtesy, his head a little bowed as he listened, but also his almost mad impatience, so that she feared that at any instant he would break into some desperate declamation.

Othello was a little drunken. He swayed a trifle on his legs, and was now sending a small boy in a shirt and ragged breeches for further liquor. The scene was becoming intolerable to her. The wretched place, the figures pressing about them, the conscious-ness that soon she must return to the stage, the shock of Herries's presence there, her longing for him (which was by far stronger than she would have supposed), the consciousness of a new dig-nity and fineness in him as an older man that there had not been before, above all, the ache for the rest and care that he would give her, all these tore at her heart.

Then there was a little incident. One of the children, the smaller, thin and spare, in a shawl and a tattered red kilt, with bow legs and the expression of an aged woman, running to its father, tumbled over a crack in the floor and fell howling to the ground.

At once its father, who had been grandiloquently orating, rather to the general world than to Herries, of his rendering of other rôles in Mr Shakespeare's plays, lost all quality as actor, and became only a simple and affectionate parent.

As he bent over the child and raised it, speaking to it gently, drying its tears with the corner of his dirty gown, catching it in his arms and kissing it, he was a man of dignity and feeling. He was the man who had been good to her when everyone else had abandoned her, who needed her, who trusted in her. He turned and, smiling through his sooty blackness, gave her the child.

'You see,' she said, turning to Francis, 'that we cannot speak together here. I must tell you of everything more fully. It is not, oh, believe me, it is not so easy a thing. You shall meet me afterwards – yes, yes, I promise you.'

He looked at her as though he would never let her go. He did not care that she was worn and shabby. This was a love that had no dictation from outside things. But he saw that it was true that they could not talk there.

'I have your promise?' he asked, touching again with a shy secret movement her hair.

'Yes, yes . . . Later. At ten o'clock I can be free. There is a place beyond the Castle on the left of the road towards Keswick. There is a gate there with a deserted cottage. Wait for me there.'

She had spoken in a hurried whisper, rocking the child in her arms. He saw that there was nothing more to be done here. He knew that she would keep her promise, so, with one last look at her, he went.

After that he walked he knew not where. A soft rain began to fall, but he did not realize it. He realized nothing but the hunger to have her with him again. He heard the three-quarters strike on the church clock, and, hurrying as though by chance she might be before her time, went to the place. He found it without difficulty, although the night was very dark.

He stood there by the gate in the rain. He was ill again, although he did not heed it. His legs were trembling and his head was on fire. Many lights were dancing in his eyes. But he thought only of the clock. His heart leaping, he heard it strike the hour, counting aloud the strokes.

Now she would come, in another moment she would be with him. The quarter struck, then the half-hour. The silence grew with every minute more menacing. It was as though the town, the dark night, everything in the world were holding her back to taunt him. He ran into the road, then a little way towards the town. He began to call then, louder and louder. No one came. The clock struck eleven. The silence was not broken.

The quarter struck again, and once more the half-hour.

He began to run. It might be that she had said some other place. He was in the town, which was now utterly black under the rain. He ran, calling her name. Two hours later, a blind, fiery, unconscious impulse leading him back to the 'Green Parrot', when old Andrew with candle and nightdress opened the door to the knocking, Herries fainting, fell into his arms.

PHANTASMAGORIA IN THE HILLS

HERRIES lay for six months moving into Death's arms and then slipping out of them again. It seemed to him like that, but Death was no grisly skeleton with grinning bones, but a place of light and space where there was a great singing emptiness and a hooded brooding sun. He moved and was bathed in a curious lethargic contentment; 'So this is where one goes,' his complacency told him, but he was allowed only to sniff the air and shade his eyes from the light, when pulleys dragged him back to a hot fire, aching limbs and a will to live.

He was a very old man in those times to live at all with such an illness. The town took a sort of obstinate pride in his recovery. Wagers were laid. Sir Humphrey Paddock, an ancient knight whose house was at Cross Trees, a mile outside the town, bet the little black boy that his wife had brought up from London against Squire Bantock's famous mare, Marjorie, that Herries would not die. It was as well that he won, for he did not tell his lady, who was attached to little Pompey, and there would have been the domestic devil to pay had he lost.

Old Andrew obtained quite a notoriety and an added custom from his guest's struggle with death. Old Andrew was prouder of Francis than he had ever been of anyone in his life. Heaven

knows where he got his affection for him from. The snob in him
perhaps. He had always worshipped Quality quite frankly, and
when, twenty years later, in his very old age (he lived to be almost a hundred), men praised the Revolution in France as the
beginning of a grand new world, his indignation was a sight to
witness.

But his affection for Herries went deeper than that. He tended
him like a woman, would scarcely have left his room had it not
been for the necessities of his trade and for Benjamin.

In the first delirious weeks Herries was always calling for
Benjamin, so Benjamin was sent for. He came and set up a jealous
imperious rule that no one could defeat. He had all the unreasoning suspicion that anyone who is accustomed to Keswick has for
anything that happens in Penrith. He wore an air of exceeding
knowledge. No one understood his master but he. He would talk
oracularly, in the inn-parlour, to anyone who cared to listen,
about the great man that his master was, and the wise man and
the mysterious.

It became after a while bruited abroad that Herries had shut
himself up for many years in his lonely house because he was discovering the Philosopher's Stone or some such thing. Benjamin,
and indeed many of the citizens of Penrith, had still a medieval
mind, and any marvel was welcome.

But when Benjamin was in his master's room, caring for him,
his tenderness and devotion were wonderful.

'Come now, come now,' he would say, wiping the sweat from
the brow, smiling into the staring eyes, smoothing the sheets
about the body. 'There's no fear to trouble you. Softly, master,
softly. Hold to my hand now and you'll know that there is no one
can come after you. Nay, nay. There's no one here but Benjamin.
Yes, yes. She'll be with you presently. She has but gone out for
a breath of air and so that you may sleep a little. Softly, master,
softly. All is very well. Lie still and rest then.'

Being by nature a man of fancy to whom any fable was welcome, he indulged himself by uttering any kind of marvel that
might be expected to comfort his master. His fancy was closely
allied to his literalness, so that if he stated that Mirabell had been
but just now in the room, he must describe her dress that was
sweet with sprigs of roses and say that her hair had a silver comb.
He would tell Herries that all the town, aye, and the County too,
was at the door inquiring how he did, and that coaches packed
with Countesses waited in the street, and Marquises and Dukes
sent messages of condolence. But nothing mattered to Herries,

who lay, for many a day and night, his long thin fingers twitching the sheets, his eyes pitifully staring, his haggard cheeks as white as his hair.

Nothing finer can ever be recorded of old Andrew than that he endured, without too much argument, Benjamin's patronage and superiority. The two old men even achieved finally a kind of alliance together against the rest of the world.

Little Summers always afterwards asserted that it was he who saved Herries. Certainly he bled him often enough, and could be seen many times a day tramping up and down the wooden stairs, his sand-glass, almost as big as himself, in his hand.

But whether it was Benjamin or Summers or Fate or Herries's own constitution, he did, in spite of medical treatment and enough dirt and ignorance to slaughter a cityful of old men, recover. The day came when he was carried downstairs to the back-parlour by Benjamin, where he lay on a sofa in the sun, with canaries in a cage twittering above his head and a distant view of the dim hills through the window.

After that he gained strength amazingly, and it was in mid-July that he stepped with Benjamin into a hired chaise, bade old Andrew farewell, and departed for Herries.

He had become very silent. No one knew now what was in his mind. David, Sarah, Deborah had all been to visit him in Penrith, and they had felt that they were with a stranger. He asked them no questions, heard their news with courteous indifference, seemed to feel no connexion with them. His only request was that he should return as speedily as possible to Herries, and there was a glow in his cheek and a smile on his lips when the chaise stumbled up the rough lane (there was path enough now for a carriage), and he was once more inside the little grass-grown courtyard.

He went quietly about the house from the top loft to the dark cellar beneath the kitchen, touching everything and making sure that it was there.

He talked often with great and excited incoherence, then for many days he would be quite sensible and coherent, then for days silent. But he asked no questions about anything, nor mentioned Mirabell's name.

There was an old white horse that he had had for some years, called once ironically by him the Paladin. It was a horse of a rather comic appearance, short in the leg and very bare of feature, with a large black patch over one eye that gave it an extraordinarily innocent and amiably foolish expression. Herries took now a fancy to this horse, and every day rode out on it. But he went no longer for any journeys. Every evening he returned.

No one knew of what he was thinking. You could not say that he was mad, because if you did he would in another moment show so much sense and consciousness of the true life about him that you were (if you were Benjamin) dumbfounded.

But he thought himself that he was growing mad, that he was less certain with every day as to the reality of anything. He had been all his life scornful of other men's acceptance of reality; that had been one of the principal reasons for his division from them. On the other side, he knew that now, for the first time in his life, he was not honest with himself. There was something within him that he would not examine. He had always despised humbug, and now he was himself a humbug, because there was a great hurt and unhappiness in his breast that he would not examine.

He would not glance down at anything that was past. Something was not here, something that he had passionately desired. No matter. Let it lie. He could not procure it. It was gone. To call it up, long for it, stretch out his hands to it, meant madness. And he also would not think of the future. He did not know what was coming. Maybe that lighted chamber of Death with the hooded sun, maybe a man in armour riding him down, maybe old age and food in your belly. He would look only at the present, this rustling tapestry on the wall, this old hill beyond the window-pane, this chair with the crusted gold sunk into its wood, this green slipper with the silver buckle, this halter that gaped from its hook on the wall. But here is your trouble, old man. Who knows what these things are? – the tapestry, the hill, the chair, the slipper, the halter – maybe they are cheating you. They are not what they seem. The tapestry is an old woman whispering, the slipper a fallen leaf, the house and the hills around it a well in which you are sunk up to your very neck. You think you are alive and are not. You were dead months ago and lay stretched out with the sheets to your chin and the candles blowing at your feet, and now that you are dead you have the power to see double, two of everything, and the trees like men walking.

He would catch Benjamin's arm at a time, and would say, chuckling: 'We are both dead, old friend, and no one knows it.' Benjamin did not mind. It was only his master's way.

So Herries would ride out on the Paladin to think of these questions, and would return in the evening, his head none the clearer.

He was always at his most sensible when David or Deborah

came to visit him. He would sit in his chair by the fire or walk
with them gravely over his territory, showing them an apple tree
or a cabbage or the new marigold. But he never asked them questions. He listened with great pleasure to Deborah's stories of her
twin boys, of their cleverness, courage and remarkable natures,
of Mr Sunwood's sermons, of how they had been to visit the
Bishop, of their friends the Wordsworths and the grand house
they had, of the new road to the North, of the many visitors to
Cockermouth, and of Lady Freshwater's garden that had three
cascades, a Gothick Temple and a statue of Minerva.

He listened, too, when David told him of his farm, of his business, of his hunting, of his children and his horses. He enjoyed
it all. He was glad that they should come, but so soon as they
were gone he forgot all about them. He walked about the house
at night talking to himself. Benjamin would get up and follow
him lest he should do himself a mischief. Once he pulled
Benjamin out of bed to show him the moon over Rosthwaite Fell.
Another night he crept into Benjamin's bed and lay there shuddering, his arms about the other's neck. Once, talking very sen-
sibly and in perfect command of his faculties, he spoke about his
wife Margaret, but as though she were there in the house.

'You are not to speak to her of this. She is sensitive to all that
I say, poor soul, but if she would not fear me we would do better.
You have seen yourself how she trembles if she thinks that I am
angry. I cannot bear a trembling woman, and never could. You
could say to her not to be afraid, for there is nothing to fear in
me. I have not been in a rage since the children were little.'

Nevertheless he would sometimes be in a rage for no reason
whatever, and then he would shout and storm just as he did in
older days. His best friend and visitor, who seemed altogether to
understand him, was little Mr Harness the clergyman, who came
often to see him, and thought nothing that he did or said odd at
all.

Mr Harness, in fact, had a theory that Herries was as sane as
any man, but elaborated and fantasied things, in order to hold
himself from thinking. He had a hope that religion would assist
him. He brought with him certain beloved books from his little
library – Henry Dodwell's *Christianity not Founded on Argument*,
Butler's *Analogy*, Warburton's *Divine Legation*, Law's *Serious
Call* and *The Way to Divine Knowledge*.

It may be that Herries read these works, maybe not. No one
will ever know. He did not discuss anything with Mr Harness so
much as throw out casually to him stray observations, as:

'The Planets, I fancy, must have a hearty detestation of their God. To be held by an iron hand in one order, always to obey a Law made without any consultation of them. A Planet having a trifle of Independence would prefer to fall to fiery ruin . . . So Satan snapped his fingers.'

Mr Harness had no liking for Chaos.

'No, you would not. You are too good a man. Nor do I fancy that if God walked in this garden, I would myself be doing anything fine or bold. He has had the experience to make Him ready for any occasion. But I would ask Him one thing – whether He is not at some time wearied of His power, and wishing that He could Himself be a rebel once and again against it.'

And he said once to Harness:

'What men call madness is only to have a picture of your own. I make my own vision of things more independently as I grow.'

Had you asked him at this time what his condition was, he would have told you, perhaps, that he saw three things to other men's one – or perhaps Mr Harness was right, and he busied his brain with pictures because he did not wish to look into reality.

In any case the great day of his life arrived, coming to him blindly as all our great days come. It was May 16th, 1773. He rode out after his early dinner on the Paladin. He sat up very straight and stiff, wearing his old broad-brimmed black hat, his legs reaching far down because the Paladin's legs were short, his eyes staring straight in front of him as though he were setting out on some urgent quest.

Benjamin stood at the top of the path watching him anxiously. He was never certain when he saw his master thus depart whether he would ever welcome him back again.

It is possible that Herries had some notion that this was a great day, or it may have been only that the sun was shining strongly on field and hill, powdering the valley with gold-dust; it is true that his heart beat strongly with expectation. He would not ask himself any longer what it was that he expected, but he smiled sometimes grimly to himself as he went, and, as was his habit, he talked to the Paladin.

'What is your will today? Where do we go? Make use of your imagination. You shan't flick your ears at the sun. Unmannerly behaviour . . . There's no graciousness in you.'

He came to a field off the road near Stonethwaite hamlet where some men and boys were baiting a little bull with two dogs. He got off the Paladin, leaving him to crop the hedge, and went into the field. There was no reason. He had nothing against the

baiting of bulls, which was the habit of the time. Or, rather, he
had had nothing. It may be that now, seeing three things instead
of one, he was in advance of his period. The little animal was
mad with terror and pain. One of its legs was torn and bleeding,
the skin above one eye was ravaged and the blood poured down
its face. But like Wesley's bull it could not be roused to much
vengeance against its tormentors, but only pawed the ground,
lowered its head, and raised it again.

Herries went up to it, put his hand on it, stroked it, and it did
not stir, only stood there trembling. The men knew him well
enough, and, thinking him a crazy old man, let him have his way.
A stout red-faced farmer promised him that the bull should be
let alone, and to his own later surprise kept his promise. He
didn't know, he said afterwards, but the bull and the old man
seemed to have an understanding. Witchcraft . . .

So then Herries got on to the Paladin again, and they ambled
forward until they reached Seathwaite, and then past the hamlet
wandered on along the well-known path into the pool of the hills.
It was that time of the afternoon when on a fine day in early summer this end of the valley holds all the sun in a blaze of gold,
while the hills above it are black. Herries came to Stockley
Bridge, where once long ago his son had talked with the Devil, let
the Paladin wander, and sat down on a flat stone above the clear
green pools that Grain Gill makes for its own sweet pleasure.

From above him and around him Glaramara, his old friend,
and Allen Crags and Great End and the Gavel looked down and
saw him, far below them though he was, a black figure in that
blaze of gold.

Whatever he was at other times, he was not clear in his head
just then, for he saw, out of the tumbling stream, from behind
the casual rocks, from the green bracken of the Fell, figures rise
on every side of him. He did not know whether they were men
or women, nor did he care. They rose like flopping scarecrows,
and came trooping, ambling, appearing and disappearing, making signs at him, passing him without heeding him, flying in the
air like jackdaws, until at last an odd old creature with a wrinkled
face marked with lines like a map, its texture also of parchment,
came and crouched on its thin shanks beside him.

The air was exceedingly peaceful, the green pool between the
grey stones pure and still, the sunlight over all, so that Herries
did not mind a talk.

'Where are you from?' he asked idly, watching two flies circle
above the pool.

'From nowhere at all. But it is a fine evening.'

'It is indeed,' said Herries. 'And your companions. Where do they hail from?' For he could see behind the black cloak of his neighbour the dark cloaks of many others beating like birds' wings in the air.

'Also from nowhere.'

'If I give you something,' said Herries (for the shadow with the parchment face had a begging eye), 'will you go away?'

'What have you of any value?'

'I have only one thing,' said Herries, 'upon which I lay any value, save my house, my son and my servant. That is a silver chain that I wear around my neck. It was left to me once by a lady who was dead. That I will not give you. But I have a spade, some trees, a horse, a picture of an ancestor and two suits of armour. Also a witch's bones in my garden. To any of these you are welcome.'

The black-cloaked beggar moved his bony hams derisively.

'Poor property,' he said, 'at the end of a long life.'

'Am I then at the end?' asked Herries with interest.

'Not absolutely. Why have you retained so little?'

'I cannot tell,' said Herries. 'I have never had a saving nature. When I was young I scattered my seed like grass – if I may be for a moment poetical. Now I am old and I have only one desire and one dream.'

'What is your dream?' asked the shadow, but more from politeness than interest. He yawned indeed, raised a bony hand, but did not hide a cavernous mouth.

'I have dreamed of a noble white horse who swims a black pool and mounts hills of ice. But I pray your pardon. My dream can interest no one save myself.'

'Not at all,' said the shadow politely. 'And what is your desire?'

'That is no man's business,' said Herries abruptly.

'As with the rest of us,' said the shadow, crouching a little nearer, 'you have found life a silly thing with no meaning.'

Herries nodded at the pool.

'Inconsequent. Without an answer. But I have seen hints that there may be an answer elsewhere. Were men themselves less foolish there is beauty and adventure enough to balance the rest. Not, you understand, that I am of any wider intelligence than my fellows. I have been always beyond ordinary foolish. Nor do I regret it.'

The shadow plainly found his acquaintance uninteresting. He rose like a black beanstalk.

'One thing I will tell you,' he said. 'You are but at the beginning of your journey. My felicitations on your companion. Keep your spade, your scar, your fine white horse. You will need them.'

The company now darkened the air, which was very chill. The sky was grey. The hills shone with ice, and at Herries's very feet was the black still pool that he had so often seen before. It was no surprise to him, therefore, to behold a moment later the beautiful white horse go plunging in.

Once again he saw him, but now he was closer to him than he had ever been before. His great head, with its flowing mane of snow, clove the water, breaking its blackness, and Herries could feel the superb strength of the body as it drove its path. Then came the moment of struggle when the horse must plant his hoof on the slippery slant of the icy rocks. He could see more clearly than before how he raised his head in a superb agony of effort, how the hoofs slipped and slipped again, how it seemed as though he must fall back into the icy water, how every muscle was straining, how the glittering hills looked on with stern indifference.

All Herries's own vitality, everything that he had put into life, any past gallantry or courage or discipline, he seemed to give to aid his friend. Then with a great controlled burst of energy, that last effort was made and the ascent was won.

The white mane was shaken in triumph, the water dripped from the white body like rain, and he was off piercing the hills until he was like a silver arrow flying skyward.

Herries smiled and rubbed his hands. And there was no pool, there were no icy hills. Only the fellside, the bubbling stream, and all the valley grey now because the sun had sunk behind the rim of the purple tops. He had slept then. The Paladin was cropping the grass close at hand, and the stars were creeping out into soft green sky. Between sleeping and waking, now that you were old, it was no great matter. Life melted from one to another, and the dividing wall became with every breath the less opaque.

He supposed that he had slept. Then sleep was more real than waking.

He climbed on to the Paladin and rode dreamily home. But this time, as he came up the path to the house, he could see, dusky though it was, Benjamin waiting at the gate. He ran forward, caught the Paladin's bridle.

He was shaking with the excitement of some news.

'Master! Master!' He pulled, in his quivering eagerness, at

Herries's arm. 'She has returned. The mistress is here. She is waiting for you by the fire!'

THEY ARE ALONE AND ARE HAPPY

SHE was standing against the wall beside the window, straight against it as though she must have something behind her in case of attack. She had a grey shawl over her head, a faded green upper dress and a shabby red hoop. She looked old and monstrously weary. That had been Benjamin's first thought when he saw her come slowly across the courtyard, that she was fearfully weary.

Herries did a very touching thing. He went straight across the room to her, put his hand up, and stroked her pale cheek. Then he bent his head and kissed her hand.

'Forgive me,' he said, 'but I have been dreaming much of late. I supposed this also was a dream.'

They stood very close to one another, looking into one another's faces for what seemed to Benjamin, who stood without moving at the door, a long time.

Then she spoke quickly, and never taking her eyes from his face.

'Before everything I must tell you that I have come here to explain to you. That is why I have come. I can go again as easily. You must know why I broke my promise to you of meeting you on that night.

'After you were gone, my protector – the man you saw, the player – made a scene of great jealousy. He had seen that we were known to one another; he overheard our appointment. He was mad with a strange new anger and fear that I had never before seen in him.'

She caught her breath, putting her hand to her breast. 'It was as though he knew that you were the only friend I had in the world. Often he had seen me with other men and been unmoved. Now he told me that if I went that night to see you he would kill himself. I believe he would have done it. I considered my duty. I thought . . . that if I saw you again . . . I might stay with you. There were the children. So we left Penrith that evening after the play. I sent a messenger to you with a letter, but he never found you or said he did not.

'And a month back Adam left me for a young woman who had lately joined our company, taking the children with him. I had been ill. He left me without money – this was in Salisbury – and I have slowly come back. Let me stay with you tonight, and then if you wish it tomorrow—'

She swayed, reeled, would have fallen had he not caught her. She was ill from nothing but exhaustion. When she was in bed Herries fed her with strong soup and hot wine. She thanked him with a smile, put her arms around his neck and kissed him, then, sighing with a sense of safety, turned and slept. She slept all that night, all the next day and all the night after. She slept like a young child, her head in her hand.

Herries sat for most of that while at her side. He slept a little, but was always starting out of his sleep to see whether she were there. Very gently he would put his hand out and touch her heart, to be sure that she was breathing.

Benjamin said to Mr Harness: 'He's in such joy at her return that it's like to turn him crazy altogether.' But that was just what it did not do. He walked directly away from his dreams and fancies, leaving them behind him like discarded clothes. He came down to the door to speak with Mr Harness.

'It is my wife who has returned, sir,' he said. 'We are friends, I am happy to think, and therefore I would wish you to give me joy, for this is the most cheerful thing that has happened to me in all my life.

'I have been, since my illness, a trifle dazed in my head, the rather I fancy because it was not healthy for me to see things exactly as they were, but now I am very well, and you may wish us a long life together.'

'Indeed I do,' said Mr Harness, but thinking that seventy-three was an advanced age to begin life at. 'I am most heartily pleased, sir, and will offer my duty to your lady when she is well rested.'

On the morning of the second day, while Herries was sitting beside her bed and the sun was pouring in at the window, she awoke entirely refreshed. For a moment she did not remember where she was; then, when she saw his white hair and eager look, such a shadow of happiness and relief swept her face as was moving to see, for, poor thing, everything was very different from when she had gone away: she had suffered so many hardships and known so little rest that it was not only the added years had aged her.

They talked a little quietly and she had her hand in his.

Then he said, after kissing her cheek: 'There is but one thing that I must say. I pray you not to leave me again, for this time it would be my death.'

'Nay, I will never leave you any more, Francis.'

'For I am not as young as I was. Be angry. Have things as you will. I shall not pester you now to love me. Only you must not go away.'

She repeated again: 'I will never leave you any more.'

He said then in his old way: 'We are a couple of fools to make promises. Was ever a vow kept in this world? But I cannot endure the thought . . .' He turned his head aside. 'I will not ask you to make a vow. Only do not go – unless you must.'

'And you will not leave Herries?'

'No. I will never leave Herries now.'

It was natural that in the first weeks there should be a certain awkwardness between them. There were the old things to remember and the new things to expect.

Each found the other at first changed. It was only after a while that these superficial alterations dropped away and they discovered that the old spirit shone there.

But there *were* changes, real and true ones. Each was altered by trial. The shock of her going and then his long illness in Penrith had softened Herries to a more patient acquiescence. It was as though he had peeped through a door into another room and seen certain things there that excited his curiosity and so made him less stirred by his present surroundings. It was also that her absence had been so terrible to him that, now he had got her again, he was contented in her mere presence, not wishing her to be this or that, but only near him.

Also it was as though he had found an answer to the question that he had been asking all his life. He had found justification. Finally he was so happy that he asked no more questions. It was enough that she was there and wished to remain there.

The principal difference in Mirabell was that she was a child no longer. It was not only that she was now forty-four years of age, for there are some who carry their childlikeness with them to the grave, but also trouble, loneliness, sickness had given her that kind of sanctification that comes through sorrow.

Not that she was miserable or went about the place with a sad mouth. It was only that at first she could not realize her security.

What occurred was that presently happiness began to seep into the house. It is dangerous to speak of happiness, and cowards knock on wood for protection. But there are times in a man's life when it comes, at first slowly in a trickle, then rising ankle-deep, then flooding the window, at last brimming the chimneys. There is also no source of happiness quite so sure and true as the real love of one human being for another; this too seems at first incredible and very often when it has climbed waist-high sinks again, but real love is a true thing although it needs two fine-natured persons to make it true. One is not sufficient.

Nevertheless, as a matter of history, happiness flooded this old house at last and must therefore be mentioned although many would speak of ague, toothache, blights among the cattle or a hanging in the barn.

The old house soaked it in. A muddled old house it was by this, a jumble of chimneys, gables and crooked corners. What shapeless buildings! Sties like an alderman's coffin, stables like byres and byres like the ruins of Rome. Peat-stacks, dung-hills everywhere, poultry scratching in the grass-grown court, ducks everywhere garrulous, weeds hip-high, and, rather by their own volition than from any care taken of them, in their proper seasons, daisies, marigolds, jonquils, pansies, orange-lilies, gardener's garters and honeysuckle.

The old house with its cocked impertinent chimneys, its wain-scots and irregular windows and ghost-haunted stairways sinking, slowly sinking into this growing height of vegetation that, encouraged by the overlooking hills, climbed patiently to heaven.

Into all of this their happiness crept. After a month or two you could feel it everywhere. Deborah and her clergyman, David and Sarah, who came in due time to pay their respects to the returned bride, all felt it. They felt also that they were not really wanted.

Mirabell was most happy to see them and was very much more at her ease with them than she had been, but no one else was wanted. Happiness is like that – a cheerfully selfish thing.

Mirabell sat there and in her heart wondered what it was that had, on that other occasion, made her run away. It was as though she looked back upon another woman, a strange, uneasy, restless creature who had not wanted this and had been discontented with that. She did not ask herself yet whether now she loved Herries. Like himself she bothered herself with no questions. She wanted to be sure that she was there.

There were times when they would suddenly look at one another, both needing the same assurance.

It could be said that all that Mirabell felt for a long while was that this was a safe haven and that any other haven would have done as well. No one could tell. She did not examine the question. The haven was Herries and Herries was the haven, both man and house. She could not imagine that there could be any other. This was, after all, the only one that she had known her whole life long.

Slowly, piece by piece, some of the things that she had suffered came out. The poverty, discomfort, dirt, weariness, insult that were the inevitable companions of touring players. To the man himself she was always loyal. He had meant very well by her always. He had loved her in his own way, and the two poor children, sickly, ugly, thrown from one hardship to another, had had only herself to look to. He had on the whole, save for a momentary impulse or two, been faithful to her. After his first passion for her had worn away she had wondered that he had kept her, for, most certainly, she was not beautiful, she was often ill with hunger and cold, and she was an astonishingly bad actress.

She could remember her lines and that was all. She could never imagine herself anything but what she was. The plays seemed to her mostly foolishness, Mr Shakespeare no better than another. She had not managed well for him. She could not cook anything fit to be eaten nor keep a place in order. Her only merit was her fidelity.

So, when at last the other girl joined them – a black-haired, fierce-tempered woman, a remarkable actress in the more fiery parts – she did not wonder that he went away with her. She would have been happy at her freedom had it not been for the two poor children, who hated the black woman and cried whenever they saw her. Poor Adam! To what miserable end must he come. Poor, stupid, good-hearted Adam to be eaten by a tigress!

Then, as months went, she forgot all the past. This new happiness burnt all the old things as a fire burns straw. They, both of them, she and Francis, went forward into a new world and lived one grand day after another. Oddest of all, he became young again. His brain was unclouded, his limbs vigorous. This was his Indian Summer.

But nothing stands still. Everything now was an inevitable sequel to all that had gone before, but a new sequence was being created.

In the autumn, that was very wet, full of howling winds, and thick at the foot with sodden leaves, Mirabell found that she was watching Francis with an odd anxiety and restlessness. Whenever he left her she was uneasy, and she would stand at the thin window that looked over the court waiting to see him turn the

bend, pause at the gate, and then look up to the window, thinking, as she knew, of her. It was not that there was any true reason
for uneasiness. All through that year he was strong and well, and
although Benjamin, who liked gloomy tales and prophecies, told
her fearsome stories about his fever, there was no sign of its return. When he lay at night with her, putting his arms round her,
she falling to sleep in the hollow of those arms, his body was like
iron, marvellous for so old a man.

Nor was there any reason, as once there might have been, to
fear any outside hostility, for that had died. The 'Rogue' was
used in friendly fashion when it was used at all.

Nevertheless she never saw him leave the house without fearing that he would not return. All this time, with Benjamin, she
managed the house. The only other was a wild girl called
Bethany, of whom a wandering woman, who had died five minutes later, had been delivered in a ditch near Seathwaite.

If she was not quite right in the head, at least she did what she
was told, and developed after a time a passionate devotion to
Mirabell. So the house went none so badly.

But this anxiety of Mirabell's grew. She did not know what
was the matter until on an evening after Christmas it was made
clear to her.

That same afternoon Herries had ridden on the Paladin into
Keswick to see the lawyer about money matters. She could never
but smile when she saw him go, so erect on the fat horse, with his
legs so long, his head stiffly set under his broad black hat. So
soon as he had turned the corner and was out of sight, with a sigh
she left the window and went to the oak chest where there was
some linen to be marked. Looking into the chest, under the linen
she saw a cedar box, and, opening it, found piled pell-mell together the jewels with which formerly he used to dress her.
Gathering them together, she went to the table and sat down
with them, and was filled with memories.

She could see herself now seated at the table, the jewels in her
ears and hair and round her neck, while he patiently tried to
teach her to read. Tears filled her eyes. How good he had been to
her! She had never been able to learn anything from him, and
that was strange, because she had learnt her lines in the plays
easily from Adam. There had been something then between her
and Francis that had prevented this contact. Now there was
nothing. They stood bare breast to breast.

With that she sprang up in a great terror. She lit candles, piled
logs on the fire, and, although it was far too soon, began to listen

for his return. It was one of those quiet winter afternoons, so still that you could almost hear a robin's step. She looked out of the window, and a round red sun was sinking over fields and paths that glimmered faintly with a white shadowed frost. There was no sound in the house save the logs on the fire that chattered crisply one moment and then broke into a sort of music like bubbling water, and Bethany who was singing below stairs.

She went to the head of the stairs and listened. Then she tried to work and could not, went down to the kitchen and talked with Benjamin, came back again, going to the window, although beyond it now all was black, then watched the stars come out like very distant fires, then listened to the wind getting up and roaming, whistling about the house. All this time her panic grew. Oh, if he did not come! But he would not. She knew that he would not. Something had happened: he had been suddenly ill. This was a premonition. The house was alive with it. Every board, every rafter creaked with it. There were steps on the stair, and he came in.

She ran to him, flung her arms round him, drew him to the fire. He could feel how she was trembling.

'But what? . . .' He stood smiling down at her. 'You are trembling.'

'I thought you would not come.'

'But why?'

'The house was so still. You were away so long.'

He sat down, drew her to him, laid his hand on her hair.

'It was not so long. There was no one in the town. Not a leaf stirring. I read a tale somewhere once of a Dragon who, very hungry, came to the town for a meal. There was only the King's Prime Minister there – the others were away hunting – an old dry man. The Dragon licked him all over, but found that he was so lacking in juices that he dropped him from his jaws and returned sulkily to his cave. I was such an old man today. An old man on an aged horse in a frosty town . . .'

'I was afraid . . . I am always afraid when you go out.'

'Then you care for me to return?'

'Care!' He felt her body draw closer to his. 'I love you, Francis. I didn't know surely until today. I had not thought. But I love you so dearly that I live only when you are near me. I was looking at the old jewels in which you used to dress me. How could I then have been so ungrateful? But we cannot force love. And I was busy with selfish grief for Harry. Then in those years away from you I learned that in the whole world there is no one

who is like you. It is a pity that I have learnt it only now when
I am old . . .'

'We are both old,' he said, smiling. 'I have learnt some things
too.'

So it had come at last. At last! At last! His happiness prevented
any words. Nevertheless, when a moment later Benjamin came
in carrying some logs and dropped one, he jumped up and
cursed him with all his old fervour, then threw his riding-gloves
at him.

But that evening they sat for a long time by the fire hand in
hand, saying nothing.

Then, in the spring, Benjamin died.

One evening he had a rheum. Next day a cough tore his chest
in two. On the day following, every breath he took cut like a
knife. But he would not go to bed. He had a superstition that
once you went to bed in the daytime you never got up again.

Illness, too, was new to him. He had had blows and kicks and
bruises and cuts, but never an illness like this. This sharp pain in
his chest drove him to remember his father, who had had a cake-
shop in Taunton. His father had been one of the fattest men in
the South of England and one of the best-natured. It was from
him that Benjamin had his own good nature. His cake-shop,
which had been a famous one (and Benjamin might have succeeded to it and been a wealthy man today had he not thrown a
plate at his stepmother and run away to seek his fortune), was
very small, and his father filled all of it with his handsome brown
peruke, his three chins, and his white apron. It was his father's
belief that he was grandson to a nobleman by a country-girl's
mistaking her road home on a dark night. In any case he had an
'air', a tone, a something, and everyone noticed it, and bought
his cakes the more readily.

Little Benjamin, sitting in the room behind the shop and smelling the rich plummy smell of good bakery, would wonder
whether his grand jolly father wouldn't burst the wall of his shop
with his huge shoulders, swinging stomach, roaring laugh.

And then, one evil day, his father caught this pain in the chest.
Benjamin, who was then about fourteen years of age, had never
seen anyone change as his father did. He suffered so terribly (he
said that a hundred knives were slicing him into pieces) that they
put him to bed, and there in the big four-poster that had the
canary-coloured curtains (Benjamin remembered every aspect of
that room – the two chairs, of which his mother was so proud, of
dim gilt, covered with silk embroidery, and on the table in the

window a bowl of dried rue and sweet-briar – he could smell its sleepy perfume yet) he lay, his chins grimy with the unchecked beard, and in his eyes a look of terrified surprise.

He lay there and said nothing, save one day that he could no longer smell the thick hot scent from the bakery. They knew then that the end was near, and a day later, staring with that same surprise as though it had been impossible to conceive that it was this had been waiting for him, he died. So, a month later, Benjamin threw a plate at his stepmother and ran off to seek his fortune.

It was going to bed that did it. In spite of the pain from the knives his father should have stood on his two feet and defied them all.

But now when, after all these years, Benjamin had this same pain of the knives in his chest, he felt terror and he felt defiance. So they meant to play him the same trick, did they? He had learnt a thing or two from his old father. He'd defy them by standing on his legs – yes, let them do their worst. So they did. They knocked him down there on the kitchen floor, where he lay with two broken plates beside him, and Bethany ran crying to her master.

Benjamin was put to bed then whether he wished or no. A doctor was found, a young fellow this time, Parling by name, a tall bony lad with great ambitions and a speculative mind, lodging in Grange because he was reading for a thesis.

When Parling looked at Benjamin, stripped his chest, listened to his lung, two opposite worlds met. Parling was all for the future, Benjamin saw only the past. Benjamin regarded the young doctor with horror. Two hours after his departure (he leaving a very serious report of the old man's condition with Herries) Mirabell, sewing by the fire, hearing a sound, turned to see Benjamin, dressed in his working clothes, swaying on his feet, at the end of the room. She ran to him. He tried to push her off. 'Stand on your feet! Stand on your feet!' he cried, clutching her arm and staring wildly beyond her. 'They can't catch you if you stand on your feet.' A fearful bout of coughing racked him and he fell forward. With great trouble she held him, he so heavy and she so slight, until Herries came and, bearing him in his arms like a baby, laid him back in bed again.

After that he was partly away in Taunton and his childhood, and partly clinging to Herries. His love for Herries came out in him like a child's dependence on its mother. He had stood by his master so long, through so many evil reports and mischances, that to go anywhere now without him seemed an incredible thing. And a great part of the while he confused Herries with his father.

He smelt the bakery. He saw the boy come into the room with the long tray and the dark brown cakes lying on it, all in rows like a game, and he felt the saliva gather in his mouth as though he were a little dog; then he heard his father's thick deep voice (as though he were himself an enormous Cake speaking), 'Chut! Chut! Be careful, boy! . . . I'll flog thee for a stumble,' and then the beneficent smile as he looked at the tray so approvingly and rubbed his fat hands that seemed to have always in their interstices fragments of flour.

But across this vision drove Herries. Herries in his proud youth, Herries stripped in the open waiting to have the water dashed over him, Herries riding his fine horse, Herries having his boots pulled off, Herries shouting for his dinner.

In his rambling talk many of his private anxieties that had never risen into expression when he had command of himself came out.

'Master, master, I'm coming . . . Aye, hurry, hurry! It is past the hour and no one come . . . If I break it he'll mind, but there's always a stumble or a trick for a man's feet. Coming! Coming! What more can I do? He would have me every place the same time, and then nothing but kicks after all's said . . . Aye, they can name him names, but what do they know? So it is, Master Davy, so it is. But you go by the field to the left there. They say there's a fine trout or two. I'll not tell your father.

'Coming, coming, master! That's his joke. Every gentleman has his own fun – and every man too for that. There they go! Tumble them down the stairs! Tumble them down them!

'I'll set a dog to them an they come shouting their bawdy nonsense . . . Nay, but, Father, I said naught. But she's not my mother. I'll do her bidding. She shall let me alone though. If she strikes me I'll not stay . . . 'Twas a woman with a green petticoat had the paper. She's gone in a coach and had a monkey with her . . . He's gone a long while. It's lonely, this house . . . If I did tumble her there's no sin. And if there's a child the old man won't know it. I'll be rubbing Unicorn down. There's an hour before sundown. Steady now! Steady! 'Tis dark in this house before you've time for a lantern . . .'

The day before he died he recovered his senses altogether. He lay very placidly, looking at the ceiling and smiling to himself. On the next evening, which was warm so that the window was open, he heard them calling the cows in.

'The country's a fine place,' he said in a weak, quavering voice.

'Doncaster was not much, master. But here there's always a bustle. Are you happy now, master?'

'Yes,' said Herries, 'I'm happy.'

'I'm glad of it. There has been another look in your face since the mistress came home. And where would I have been without you? Dandering around, coming to no good, for I had always a leching for women. But I wouldn't have bided in one place for any woman. No, I would not. Nor worked for any woman neither. 'Tisn't right for a man to work for a woman. It is against nature. That's what my father always said, and he'd had a multitude of women in his time . . . You've been a good master to me and I've been a good man to you. There's satisfaction in that certainly.'

Then he began to count slowly to thirty or forty, and then begin again. It may have been cakes that he was counting, or cows or horses. So, counting, he died.

After the funeral they were alone in the house, for Bethany, feeling that a funeral was a festival, had gone merrymaking.

'We are alone in the house, my dear,' said Herries.

She kissed him, then, a happy triumph showing in her face, answered:

'No, we're not alone, Francis. Nor will be again. Old woman though I am, I am to have a child. How am I for a clever woman?'

She danced around the room, and he, looking at her, saw all her youth come back to her. Her hair flamed; she was as she used to be when he implored her to love him. Now he did not need to implore. She was his completely.

DEPARTURE FROM HERRIES

MRS HENNY came now on the scene.

Mrs Henny was a southern woman who for ten years had been living a widow in Grange. She was a lady of all trades – nurse, midwife, cook, friend of all the world and, in the modern manner, a witch. One may see how different the modern manner (*temp* 1774) is from the old, because whereas, years ago, Mrs Wilson had been persecuted and drowned, Mrs Henny was the most popular woman from Seathwaite to Portinscale.

Young women indeed came to ask her advice from districts as distant as Shap and Kendal. There was no one, they said, so successful in promoting a hesitating love-affair, no one with so sound a knowledge of herbs and simples. She sold charms, verses, and prophecies in packets, and kept in cages birds that told your fortune. She was in fact a 'good' witch, and was never known to do anybody any harm.

In appearance she was a little thin-boned woman with bright sharp eyes, a jutting chin, and she liked to wear wide black hoops and long black gloves on her hands.

It was she herself who suggested to Herries that she should come and 'do' for him. She could cook, she told him, she could nurse; there was a child coming and no midwife in Cumberland her equal. It was not strange that he, already most anxiously nervous about his wife's condition, should agree to her proposal; it was only strange that Mrs Henny, who had a nice little cottage of her own in Grange, just on the farther side of the bridge, where she had a most thriving trade, should wish to come. And there was only one possible explanation. She was the most inquisitive old woman in England.

Her curiosity was her devouring passion. She had been a girl of uncertain morality in her youth, not from any sensual laxity but only because she found that promiscuous affection provided her with more excellent secrets than any other mode of living. She had an amiable nature and did not wish to use these secrets to anyone's hurt, but know them she must.

It was for the same reason that she began, later in life, to dabble in love philtres, prophecies and potions – only that she might be confided in. That it was lucrative was for her an entirely secondary consideration.

It is probable that for years now her bright little eyes had been fixed upon the Herries house and her ears strained to catch the slightest sound from it. The tales about Herries were so many, he and his house were now so legendary that she was not the only one who would look up from the path and see a light burning in a window there and long to know the truth. Mrs Herries's return must have excited her yet further; when she heard of Benjamin's death, and that there was to be a child, she saw her opportunity.

On a warm spring evening of 1774 she arrived with a black box and a cage of canaries. To do her justice, although she may have come there from curiosity, she very speedily fell in love with both of them.

She was a warm-hearted old woman in any case, but the two things that she loved were power and a satisfied curiosity. Here she very quickly had both. They told her anything that she asked and they let her do what she wished. They were in truth so deeply absorbed the one in the other that they had no energy for asserting their rights.

'She couldn't enough confess,' she confided to her friends in Rosthwaite and Grange, 'the fashion with which they loved. In the heart of male and female,' she declared, 'you will ever find a principle of self-love and vanity, and this makes us very unwilling to give way to one another in anything. It is the desire of most females to have lovers, but for the most part it is because they wish for admiration. It is indeed the only way we females have of raising ourselves in Society.' But in this instance Mrs Herries appeared to have no appetite for flattery but desired only to serve Mr Herries, which was the stranger in that, after being married to him, she had left him for many years. His worship for her was odder yet, for she was not an educated woman, was most unskilful about the house, and although her hair was of a fine colour, no one could call her beautiful, nor was she, in strict parlance, a lady. Mrs Henny had always let it be known in Grange that she was herself a lady, her father a clergyman and she herself early married to a clergyman who, as in the case of Mrs Laetitia Pilkington, had treated her shamefully and abandoned her. However, she followed the parallel no closer. She was therefore a judge of the Upper Classes and Nobility, and she must observe that never, in all her wide experience, had she known a gentleman of the very finest birth, as Mr Herries undoubtedly was, accustom himself so admirably to a wife who was not gently born. They suited one another in everything and could not endure to be out of one another's sight.

His, Mrs Henny considered, can have been no easy nature to subdue, for, old though he was, he had yet a fiery temper and a very ironical tongue, but to his wife he was always the gentlest and most amiable of mortals. Mrs Herries, poor thing, had the look of one worn out with life. She had ever an air of apprehension if he was not near her. She had been tossed about, Mrs Henny – who was something of a poet – continued, so fiercely by life's cruel waves that she could not believe that she had reached a haven at last.

As for her child, this was her first, she was very old at forty-four for childbirth and had no strong constitution. It would be an uncertain situation. Meanwhile, they stayed hand in hand by the fire, or went out walking together, saying but little, wishing only for one another's company.

Such was Mrs Henny's account, listened to with the greatest interest by the ladies of the neighbouring villages, who had not

for a long while had such a first-hand account of doings in
Herries. And they on their part revived all the old stories – of the
fine rake that he had been when he had come so long ago to
Herries, of his selling his mistress at the Fair, killing his wife by
unkindness, burying the witch in the garden and the rest. He was
a changed man, they reckoned, and it only showed what God's
adversities could do.

Nevertheless Mrs Henny, with all her curiosity, perceived one
thing only dimly: the gathering anxiety with which they watched
one another as the year advanced.

He had good reason for his care of her. As the child strengthened in her womb, he was more and more reminded of her age
and her weakness. She seemed, as he lovingly watched her, to regain the slender childlike features that once had stirred so deeply
his tenderness. She was a mature woman now in her control,
knowledge of life and patience, but it was a child's face that
looked across the table at him. So, lover although he was, he was
also increasingly maternal; he could not watch and care for her
enough.

This was also the emotion that was growing in her, for she now
with every week saw increasingly that he was old. The fever returned to him at nights and he would shiver in her arms. His
memory sometimes played him tricks, and his body that had
served him so marvellously for so long sometimes betrayed him.
The leg that had given him trouble once failed him again. He
would pretend that it did not and she would pretend that he was
stronger than he had ever been, and each hid the trouble from
the other.

In July, Bethany ran away with a soldier she found in Keswick.

The summer was cold and wet; with October there came glorious fiery days, burning with colour, and then, in the first weeks
of November, a first powdering of snow on the hills.

He began now to feel a fierce and biting anxiety that never left
him. The nine months were past and the child was not born. She
appeared to suffer very little discomfort. Possibly at no other time
in her difficult life had she shown such courage and hardihood as
she did now. She was always cheerful, and when he was there
seemed the happiest woman in the country.

Mrs Henny, who had so vast an experience, said that it was no
matter that the child should be delayed; it was often so, and for
the best nine times in ten.

On a day in November, Herries took her in a hired chaise to the

Lake. The carriage stumbled over the rough path, which was bad for her; but she insisted. They stood for a little while in the wood below Cat Bells, pleased at the scene. The water was as still as glass, and the snow that brokenly covered the hills was reflected in it like a multitude of white fleecy feathers. The bare trees were brown and sunny; the light travelled like a silver arm resting upon hill after hill. Never before had they felt their love so strongly as then. It was love too mature and settled for many words and, most truly, too deep for tears. It had come out of great sorrow and anxiety, many mistakes, much selfishness, some anger and petulance, and it was now purified of everything save itself.

'I have never known whether there is a God,' said Herries. 'I am no more sure now than I was forty years ago. But I always said that if I had you, and you loved me, I would thank Him.'

'I love you with all my heart.'

'I know it. And so take off my hat to the old monster.'

And he took it off and bowed to the fleecy feathers in the Lake.

'Life has a meaning,' he said. 'At last, at last it has a meaning. One fine hour is enough.'

Then he took her back to the chaise, wrapping her warmly.

'When I am sententious, my dear, you must punish me. To talk about life so is in the worst manner of Mr Richardson, whom I detest. But even he shall not hinder my telling you that I love you.' And he kissed her cheek.

A few days later, David rode over to see him. He was greatly distressed to see how very ill the old man looked. But he said nothing of it to either of them.

As he stood by his horse before his departure, with his arm around his father's neck, a powerful sense of his love for his father overwhelmed him. It seemed to him that in spite of his affection for his wife and children, his absorption in his affairs, his pride in his position, none of these things truly touched him as deeply as this emotion.

He spoke of Mrs Henny.

'She cares for you properly, Father?'

'Yes, yes.' He looked up laughingly. 'She is distressed today because this morning she found her birds dead. She sees an omen in everything.'

'Why will you not bring Mirabell to us? She shall have every comfort and the child shall be born under Sarah's care.'

'No, no,' Herries answered impatiently. 'Of course the child must be born here in Herries.'

'How you love this place!' David looked about him. 'In all these years you have never failed it.'

'Nor has it ever failed me,' answered Herries stoutly.

'And you have never failed me either, Father,' said David. 'After all this there is no one in the world I love as I do you.'

But Herries was not feeling sentimental.

'Aye, we've been bound together, different as we are ... There, get along. The snow is coming.' He gave his son a friendly push, then turned into the house, not looking back.

That night he was very ill. There was no doubt but that the worry of these last weeks brought it on. They put him to bed and summoned the young doctor. For a fortnight he was delirious and knew nobody. Then he was in his senses again, but was too weak to move. He lay there and Mirabell lay by his bed. He never took his eyes from her face.

The snow was falling heavily. The first day a wind blew and the snow piled up against the house and began softly to climb the windows. There was a still white light all about the house.

Sharply, about midday, Mirabell was taken with her first pains. Mrs Henny put her to bed. They lay in two rooms adjoining and the doors were open that they might speak to one another.

He called to her: 'The snow is climbing the windows. Is it light in your room?'

And she answered very cheerfully, that he should not know what she was suffering:

'Yes. I can see its shadow. Are you better? I would come to you. I shall be stronger tomorrow.'

'Are you warm? Is Mrs Henny with you?'

Her pain was terrible. She could not answer. Mrs Henny came to his room and told him that she was sleeping.

But when the spasm had passed, she called out:

'Is your head well now? Soon I will come myself and see.'

His head ached strangely. The snow was coming into the room, mounting higher and higher. Some of it touched his lips and it was bitter like blood, but behind the confusion, the flashing lights, the roar of water, his mind held on to her, and, in a voice very feeble but clear, he answered: 'Yes ... Yes ... I am better ... but it is dark.'

Her pain rose and swallowed her. She thrust down a shriek of agony lest he should hear her. She had one last thought. She seemed to cry it triumphantly, although it was truly so faint that the old woman who was delivering her did not hear it.

'Francis ... dear, dear Francis!'

Her child was delivered, and some moments later she died.

Herries, who was ever a fighter, rose in his bed to come to her. He saw her standing in the doorway, the snow whirling softly about her head.

Gladly he called to her.

'Mirabell! Mirabell!'

Then sank back, as it seemed to him, in her arms.

There was silence in the house for a brief moment. Then there was a thin wailing cry. The old woman and the new-born child were the only living things in the house.

Hugh Walpole
Judith Paris 90p

The most delightful of Hugh Walpole's heroines, Judith, tempestuous daughter of Rogue Herries, is torn between ambition and her longing for the wild beauty of Cumberland. Never one to think of the consequences, Judith, loving as fiercely as she hates, knows passion, tragedy and triumph, and finds in her son Adam her past, her future and her destiny.

The Fortress 95p

Walter Herries swore he would destroy everyone in Fell House: Judith Paris knew she alone could foil him . . . This compelling novel traces the wildly fluctuating fortunes of the Herries family through fifty momentous years, up to Queen Victoria's coronation. Dark, violent and passionate, the story yet glows with excitement and the fullness of life amid the unchanging countryside that all the Herries so loved.

Vanessa 95p

Everyone said that Benjie was no good . . . At fifteen, Vanessa had Benjie in her blood: she would never betray him. This absorbing novel portrays the lives of successive generations of Herries – from the triumph of Judith Paris's hundredth birthday in the 1870s to the disillusionment of the 1930s. The author's understanding of love is matched by his masterly descriptions of the wild Cumberland countryside – where the past was never dead and the spirit of Rogue Herries lived on . . .

Daphne du Maurier
Rebecca 80p

'Last night I dreamt I went to Manderley again . . .'

Rebecca is known to millions through its outstandingly successful stage and screen versions; and the characters in this timeless romance are hauntingly real.

Brilliantly conceived, masterfully executed, Daphne du Maurier's unforgettable tale of love, mystery and suspense is a story-telling triumph that will be read and re-read.

Jamaica Inn 70p

The cold walls of Jamaica Inn smelt of guilt and deceit. Its dark secrets made the name a byword for terror among honest Cornish folk . . . Young Mary Yellan found her uncle was the apparent leader of strange men who plied a strange trade. Was there more to learn? She remembered the fear in her aunt's eyes.

Frenchman's Creek 70p

While the gentry of Cornwall strive to capture the daring Frenchman who plunders their shores, the beautiful Lady Dona finds excitement, danger and a passion she never knew before as she dares to love a pirate – a devil-may-care adventurer who risks his life for a kiss . . .

'A heroine who is bound to make thousands of friends, in spite of her somewhat questionable behaviour' SUNDAY TIMES

Susan Howatch
Penmarric £1.25

The magnificent bestseller of the passionate loves and hatreds of a
Cornish family.

'I was ten years old when I first saw the inheritance and twenty years old
when I saw Janna Roslyn, but my reaction to both was identical. I wanted
them.'

The inheritance is Penmarric, a huge gaunt house in Cornwall belonging
to the tempestuous, hot-blooded Castallacks; Janna Roslyn is a beautiful
village girl who becomes mistress of Laurence Castallack, wife to his
son . . .

'A fascinating saga . . . has all the right dramatic and romantic
ingredients' WOMAN'S JOURNAL

Cashelmara £1.25

Three generations of drama, passion and turmoil . . .
A glorious, full-blooded novel, brimming with memorable characters,
which centres on Cashelmara, the coldly beautiful Georgian house in
Galway, ancestral home of Edward de Salis.

Charged with emotion, the fast-moving plot follows the turbulent
fortunes of an aristocratic Victorian family through half a century of
furious encounters, ill-advised liaisons and bitter-sweet interludes of
love.

'Another blockbuster for Susan Howatch' SUNDAY TIMES

You can buy these and other Pan books from booksellers and
newsagents; or direct from the following address:
Pan Books, Cavaye Place, London SW10 9PG
Send purchase price plus 15p for the first book and 5p for
each additional book, to allow for postage and packing
Prices quoted are applicable in UK

While every effort is made to keep prices low, it is sometimes
necessary to increase prices at short notice. Pan Books reserve the
right to show on covers new retail prices which may differ
from those advertised in the text or elsewhere .